PRAISE FOR BLUE ON BLACK

"A fresh new take on the Steampunk genre, combining imaginative technology with mind twisting mystery and adventure. A character driven story, there's plenty here for readers to enjoy."

— *AMAZING STORIES*

If ever there was a book written that deserves to be an illustrated novel, it's Carole Cummings' Blue on Black... alternate universe, twisted history, sci-fi / fantasy / steampunkish feast for the imagination... a synesthetic journey to an Old West-like place that, had it ever existed in reality, would have changed our own world dramatically.

— *The Novel Approach*

Blue on Black by Carole Cummings is one of the best books I've read all year. Go read it!

— Ben Brock, *Queer SciFi*

MORE BOOKS BY CAROLE CUMMINGS

The Aisling Series:
Guardian
Dream
Beloved Son

Blue on Black

Don't Fear the (Not Really Grim) Reaper

Sonata Form

The Queen's Librarian

The Wolf's-own Series:
The Cycle of the Raven
Wolf Rising

BLUE ON BLACK

CAROLE CUMMINGS

Forest Path Books

COPYRIGHT INFORMATION

BLUE ON BLACK
Published by

FOREST PATH BOOKS

P. O. Box 847 – Stanwood, WA – USA

Forest Path Books publications may be purchased for educational, business, or sales/promotional use. For information, please address:

Forest Path Books, LLC
P. O. Box 847, Stanwood, WA 98292 USA
info@forestpathbooks.com.

Stay informed on our releases and news!
Join the reading group/newsletter at:
https://forestpathbooks.com/into-the-forest/

Cover design © 2020 by Mahli
Amagro font design by Fabio Servolo
Cover content is for illustrative purposes only, and any person depicted on the cover is a model.
First published in North America by DSP Publications, 2015

Library of Congress Control Number: 2020906772
ISBN: 978-1-951293-07-9 (trade paper)
ISBN: 978-1-951293-06-2 (e-book)

This one's for Jenni. Because no one should have to
listen to that much whinging without at least getting
a dedication out of the deal.

Massive thanks to Caroline, Julia, Marlene and
Michelle.
They all know why.

BLUE ON BLACK

1.

It doesn't start like this:

See, the thing is, it isn't supposed to go this way.

He's a goddamned tracker, he's a goddamned *good* tracker, better than anything else the Directorate's got, and the swagger that comes with that has been earned a hundred times over, sometimes in blood, though, okay, let's not get all maudlin and dramatic. The point is, he's not supposed to be caught wrong-footed. And he's *certainly* not supposed to be staring down eight barrels of a spin-housing street cannon in the back of a train station in godforsaken Harrowgate.

That's supposed to be the agent's job. Poor guy. Stupid fucking idiot.

"You Barstow?" the man with the gun asks. He's tall and rangy, rough-looking and sallow-skinned. It's dark and Bas can't see the rest of his face very well, just a stubbled sloping chin beneath the shadow cast by his wide-brimmed hat. He looks tough as rusty nails and just as pleasant.

Steam hugs the ground and wreaths the hem of the man's long dirty coat, clings, and thickens the reek of dirt and sweat that wafts out every time he moves. Bas can even smell it through the fug of smoke and engine grease coming from the station, and all of it combined pricks at his eyes and makes them water.

There's no cleaner, deeper sense of *Tech* beneath any of it—no thick, sundrop yellow mutters of "psyTech" hazing at the periphery of his vision and scattering something earthy on the back of his tongue; no blue edging that says "kineTech" and somehow tastes of wet cedar. Bas's mind decides "nonTech" before his eyes bother to fully assess his current situation. Still, though, the gun—Bas can see that just fine.

"Who's asking?" Bas says from his crouch. He's somewhat pissed off, so it comes out a growl.

Smooth, Bas, he tells himself. *Keep it smooth.* He can still salvage this.

"I en't playin' games." The housing of the barrels turns and the strike-stud clicks into place. "Are you *Barstow*?"

Bas peers down at the agent's body, blood still seeping in a rivulet from the knife in his throat, the heat catching the chill of the desert night and wisping steam. *Aaron,* Bas thinks. *The guy's name was Aaron.*

Bas didn't know him well. Hadn't cared to *get* to know him. Just another Directorate agent who'd maybe gotten a little too cocky. It happens.

"Yeah," says Bas. "Yeah, I'm Barstow."

He isn't. No one is, not really. It's a cover, a standard one used by trackers when they need a ready-made thug reputation as an in with bands of thieves and murderers, and then that same cover is handed over to the agents along with the case once the tracker's job is done. That's the beauty of Jakob Barstow—he's a chameleon; he can be anything the agent wearing his skin needs him to be.

Bas is a tracker, not an agent. Trackers *track.* They don't do the set-them-up-then-take-them-down part. They do the sniffing out and the pointing, and then they let the agents take over.

Except.

Bas knows the Barstow cover well enough to fake it. He's been Barstow plenty of times. Hell, he'd done most of the legwork on this particular case, and he'd done it as Barstow. And someone needs to get into Stanslo's Bridge.

"Well, Barstow." It sounds like a sneer. "Ye picked up a tail." The man jerks his chin down at the dead agent. "Thought you was supposed to be all…." He smirks. "Well. Better 'n this."

Bas doesn't let it sting. Because the agent got a touch careless in his relative inexperience with this kind of assignment, and this guy got unbelievably lucky but is just too stupid to know the difference. What a fucking waste.

Bas doesn't answer the insult; he merely gives the man a slow blink, flat and unimpressed. And he stares. And *stares.*

It unnerves the guy. It always unnerves the blustery, petty, wannabe-tyrant types. Bas can see the man trying not to shift, but he does eventually. And when the man realizes he's on the edge of squirming, he sets his scruffy jaw and glares.

"Name's Fox," he says, trying for arrogant. He gives a pointed glance at the agent's body. "And yer welcome. Fer takin' care o' yer tail." He lifts his chin, smug out of all proportion. "Followed ye all the way from the inn, that 'un." He grins, mean and with teeth that make Bas want to rear back and grimace. "Not very saddle."

Bas is pretty sure the guy means "subtle," which, yeah, okay, Aaron had maybe slipped up, contacting Bas one too many times while they were in Harrowgate pretending not to know each other, and if Aaron had been more careful, Bas wouldn't have even seen him unless he'd looked for him. So, okay, not subtle, but fucking hell, *saddle,* and why are all the stupidest ones the ones with the biggest guns?

"Uh-huh," Bas says, bored, and starts going through the agent's—*Aaron's*—pockets. "Tell me, Fox," he says, casual, as he digs out Aaron's billfold and the silver pocket watch the guy never seemed to stop fiddling with. He slides them into his own pockets and waves down at the body. "This guy look like a cutpurse to you?"

Bas watches Fox's eyes as he—for the first time, Bas would wager—takes in the fine cut of the trousers, the heavy nap of the coat. Fox's face slides into confusion first, then annoyance. Bas doesn't wait for him to think up a clever retort. Because he'd likely be waiting a good long time. *Saddle*, for fuck's sake. With a disdainful grimace he doesn't try to hide, Bas pulls the palm-sized flat oval of obsidian out of Aaron's breast pocket and lets it catch the greasy light coming through the cracks in the boards behind the train station.

"That's a scry mirror," Fox says.

Bas rolls his eyes. "Not *quite* as stupid as you look."

Fox looks Bas in the eye with a crooked set to his jaw. "He was scryTech."

He was. Class 5. One of the reasons the Directorate had insisted on sending him here, inexperience be damned. Harrowgate's relay office had been unreachable for months, and only a scryTech of the highest class could hope to get a message across the span of the Territories without a relay.

Bas rubs at his mouth and sighs. Because it's all part of the mystery he'd thought had been confined to Stanslo's Bridge and hadn't found out any different until he'd gotten to Harrowgate. He'd seen hints the moment he'd stepped off the train, but the semi-mummified body nailed to the Relay Office doors was what made him understand that, whatever malevolence Stanslo's Bridge was exuding, it was leaking and spreading. There was no way to tell if the body had been the scryTech the Directorate required every Relay Office to employ, but it wouldn't really matter in the end. The place had been boarded up and caked in dust, and the body had been wearing a Relay Office patch on the sleeve of its torn and rotting coat; Bas is no necroTech, but he doesn't think he's too far off in guessing the body had been there for months.

"They're trying to cut off communication," Aaron had said—whispered it, really, urgent and avid-eyed in the back of the tavern where he and Bas pretended to have just happened into a game of darts between two strangers new in town. "The only way to get word in or out of here now is the train, and Stanslo owns the line."

Bas blows out a long, heavy breath and surreptitiously makes sure Aaron's fake papers are still in his breast pocket. It's possible his body will be found and sent home, in which case the Directorate will know something went wrong.

"Yeah, he was scryTech." Bas shrugs. "Which means you've

just made the Directorate dreadful unhappy, 'cause when it comes to dead Techs, they don't fuck around." He gives Fox a level stare. "Well done, you."

Fox's eyes narrow down to slits. "He was following *you*."

"And he would've *lost* me once I got on the train to Stanslo's Bridge, wouldn't he." Bas lets it rumble into a low snarl, brusque. It shuts Fox up, so Bas shakes his head and says, "Look, we'll keep it between us, but if there's shit coming down from the Directorate for this, I intend to stand well clear of the stink."

Fox seems to chew on that for a moment before his thin mouth stretches out into a smarmy, brown-toothed grin. "Fuck that. Where we're goin', Techs en't no better'n anybody else and the Directorate en't got no reach."

Bas merely lifts an eyebrow. And waits. And stares some more.

Fox apparently takes it as a challenge this time, because he puffs up and snaps, "Yeah, you'll see, smartass. You'll see things that'd make coddled Techs and Directorate fucks cry for their mams. Stanslo's Bridge en't got room for the delicate."

Okay. So Fox is the kind of stupid that'll turn out to be useful, and all Bas'll have to do is get him just the right amount of riled. Because with one brash outburst, Fox has just pretty much confirmed all Bas's suspicions and several of his theories.

Before this part of the Territories *was* part of the Territories, there were such things as Tech hunters and hired guns and slave traders, and it isn't like it's ancient history. It had been happening in Bas's grandparents' youth, and eradicating it is part of the reason the Directorate came into the power it now enjoys. A hundred years ago, Bas's talents as a tracker might well have been pressed into service hunting down Techs for the auction block. So it's not exactly a stretch to imagine it hasn't been entirely stamped out in places where the Directorate's presence isn't much of a presence. At least as far as the Tech part of the population goes, it's why the Directorate exists.

It's why Bas signed with the Directorate right out of the academy. When you have a little brother who's not only psyTech but Class 4, you learn to recognize and guard against exploitation and abuse at an early age. Their parents had been careful, and Mo is more than capable now of taking care of himself, but there was a time when Mo was small and unskilled and he'd needed a big brother who knew what kind of gleam to watch out for in another's eyes.

Bas sees that gleam in Fox's eyes a little too clearly.

"So," Bas drawls, sliding it into more syllables than it needs and letting the corner of his mouth pull down, impatient. "Do I get to see all this sometime this century?"

Fox doesn't answer, just keeps staring at Bas, gaze narrow and shining in the dark. Bas stares back, because what the hell, it's worked so far.

It works this time too. Fox looks away with a grunt and an annoyed jerk of his head toward the station. "Got any bags?"

⁂

The train is nothing special. It surprises Bas. He's seen the drawings and schematics Kimolijah Adani was working on, has seen the Tech *working*, the little model train zipping across the floor, impossibly powered by nothing but gridTech somehow locked in a tiny crystal attached to its chassis. No hooking into the Grid conduits, no wires strung to a gridstation with a dozen or more gridTechs powering it. A gridmotor running on gridstream that couldn't be inside that crystal, because gridstream can't be directed like that. Except it was.

"It *can* be directed," Resaniji Adani had told Bas, almost sneering at him, like he should've known. Kimolijah Adani's big sister was fierce in her still-vibrant grief for her brother and her da. And a little bit scary. "You just have to know how. Like bleeding, 'Lijah told me once. You cut your hand and you've got blood leaking down your arm. You can't really aim it, right? It just sort of dribbles out and goes the path of gravity and least resistance. But what if you opened an artery? Instead of dribbles you get a geyser, and then it's not about controlling the flow anymore, it's about directing it."

She'd flicked at the little train with its tiny motor and its tiny crystal making the wheels whirr and clack.

"'Lijah can open an artery and aim."

This train... well. Bas has been expecting something else.

It's a steam locomotive with a few boxcars hooked to it, and that's it. Someone checks the last coupling and someone else pulls an empty trolley down the ramp of the last car and sends a wave to Fox. Fox turns to Bas. "C'mon, let's go check for stowaways."

There are none, and Bas honestly can't imagine why there would be, but he checks among the sacks of grains and barrels of ale and feed. "Get a lot of stowaways, do you?" he asks Fox.

Fox rolls a gob of snot up through his sinuses and horks it out the door into the dust. "Not from here."

Bas stands beside the car amidst the smoke that chugs from the idling engine and clings to the ground, and he thinks *Well, this just keeps getting weirder and weirder.* He doesn't say it, though. Obviously.

They shut and lock the doors. With a smirk, Fox chivvies Bas up the metal steps into the cab and directs Bas to the stoke scuttles beside the fuel hatch.

"Yeah, I don't think so," Bas says, eyeing the shovel.

Fox shrugs. "You wanna drive, then?"

Bas squints at the dials and levers and various switches. He gives Fox a glare and picks up the shovel.

It's loud once they get going, the *thack-thack-thud* of the wheels on the tracks rhythmic enough that Bas uses its cadence to dig-pause-chuck, dig-pause-chuck. The mindlessness of it is strangely soothing, settling Bas's head and dulling the anger at the complete waste of having to leave that agent dead in an alley like a forgotten smudge of flotsam. Bas sinks into the rhythm and the buzzing silence in his head and decides not to notice how time just... slips. It's good because the noise prevents talk, and the last thing Bas wants to do is talk to Fox. He ignores the dark, shapeless whirr of desert vista winging by him and the passage of the minutes and then the hours, and thinks of nothing but his grip on the shovel, the blisters he can feel sprouting on his palms, the stretch and pull of muscle and sinew.

He resists the spiral of theories and conjecture that pulls him down a path that will inevitably and invariably lead him to thoughts of Kimolijah Adani. Because Bas has obsessed about it all for going on three years now, and there's no point in wasting time pondering a dead man. Better to figure out how he got dead, and then, since Bas is here and all, planned or unplanned, figure out a way to make someone pay for it. Bas doesn't have time or headspace for anything else. He needs to start being Jakob Barstow.

It's the early hours when Fox gives Bas a "Ho! Belay the fires, now" and Bas abruptly thumps back into his own head, peers around him to get a look out the windscreen. He doesn't see anything for a long spell—just blank, dusty landscape and the sporadic stubble of scrub—and then he does. A shabby shanty of a way station squats on a latticework of tracks in the middle of the desert.

Fox brakes with a concentration of which Bas hadn't really thought him capable. "We switch here," Fox says as they pull up to the station, and Bas doesn't have to ask to what. He can see the other train even in the dark.

"Why?" he asks instead. "Why didn't that train just come out to Harrowgate?"

"'Cause it's how it works. If you don't wanna walk, you'd best come on."

Fox doesn't wait for Bas, just jumps down from the cab and heads off to the other train. Bas follows, taking in what he can. He only really sees a black outline against a black sky, but he knows this is what he'd expected to see back at the station in Harrowgate. He can smell it.

It's all laced monochrome in the dark. The silhouette, when Bas blinks, is edged sharp behind his eyes in the blue-black of gridTech, so thin he almost can't discern it with the not-vision of his tracking senses, but now that he's not inhaling stoke smoke and rank sweat, he can *almost* taste the faint-faint-faint pepper of ozone, and he *knows*, he knows exactly what he's looking at.

A dim blue current flitters in starts and stops over the skin of the cab, giving Bas a glimpse at something almost bullet-shaped and sleek; it loses the illusion of novelty and polish when Bas's eyes adjust and he sees the quill-like projections and bulky... something-or-other mounted on the roof.

Bas doesn't remember the spiky poles and conduit and sparking wiring that crowns this locomotive as part of the little toy train he saw back in Kimolijah Adani's ruined workshop, but he remembers the drawings in the notes over which Bas pored while he was trying to catch a whiff of a trail. The poles and wires and flickers and flowing gridstream make the locomotive look like it's topped by a lustrous blue crown. With, you know, weird spiky tines like a dilapidated fence and enough current to beef ten men on contact, but whatever.

It looks like it's been thrown together out of spare parts. And it sounds like it's on its last legs. The locomotive whines as Bas and Fox approach it, spitting filaments of blue sparks all over the skin of it, some of them shooting off in all directions and catching at whatever drift-scrub rolls by on the steady breeze over the flat hardpan. It revs for a second, then sputters out with a tinny, shrieking fizz.

"Don't touch nothin'," Fox cautions, motions for Bas to stop where he is, and ventures ahead. "En't ye got this thing goin' yet?" he yells, and someone inside the cab curses—a rather eye-popping stream of it—and throws a wrench out through the open door. It just misses Fox's head. Bas can see Fox's hand twitch toward the small four-barrel on his hip, but he only snarls, "Knock it the fuck off, princess, else—"

"What d'you think I was trying to do?" the other voice snaps. "Just hang fire, I'm almost there."

Fox is pissed off, Bas can tell, but he doesn't do much more than fume. He side-eyes Bas, as though looking for a reaction, and when he doesn't get one, he calls, "Lowen?"

"Yeah!" comes another voice from inside the cab. Tools clank, and that other voice curses again, and then someone stands silhouetted in the dim light pouring from the open side of the cab. "He's almost got it," the man tells Fox. He's big, bigger than Bas, and his skin is as dark as stoke.

"I already heard that one." Fox leans to the side and spits. Again. "How long?"

The man—Lowen—shrugs and wipes his hands on a dirty rag. "Needs to be soon. Can't run for powerful long in the heat, and night's shinning out."

"No shit. Why d'you think I asked?"

"It's not like he's not giving it his best go, Fox. He doesn't want to be stuck out in the middle of the desert all day any more than you do."

"Yeah, you keep coddlin' the princess," Fox grumbles and jerks his chin at Bas.

Bas would really rather get a look at that engine, but he can't think of a good reason the hired gun he's supposed to be would care. So Bas follows and does as Fox tells him as they maneuver the steam engine on the switch tracks and decouple the cars that hold the supplies they've hauled here. It's not as complex as Bas thought it might be, at least not for him, since he's not the one driving the engine. Fox looks like he knows what he's doing, but Bas nonetheless makes sure to stand well clear of anything that looks like it might crush him or cut him in half when it moves.

The other train—the one Bas is already thinking of as "the gridtrain"—is still where they left it, still shooting off sporadic sparks and jets of gridstream, and there's still the occasional spate of filthy cursing coming from inside it. So Bas assumes whoever's in there hasn't yet got it going.

"'S all we can do for now," Fox says with a grim set to his mouth, and then he spits. *Again.*

Bas tries not to roll his eyes as he follows Fox to the tiny boxcar that apparently came with the gridtrain. It turns out to be a hobo's notion of a passenger car. Two shabby, knob-legged couches that look like they came out of a brothel's parlor line the sides. Fox flops onto one of them and kicks up his feet. With something close to a fond smile, he reaches behind the couch and pulls out a long, thick... gun, Bas supposes; has to be a gun, though not like anything Bas has ever seen. There's only one barrel, to start, it looks more like ceramic than metal, and the trigger's more like a toggle and it's wired. Fox trades it for the big eight-barrel street cannon he'd been carrying, cradles it across his chest, and makes himself comfortable.

"Stay in the car," he tells Bas. "You touch the wrong thing, you fry, and I'll have wasted a pain-in-the-ass trip for nothin'." He shoves his hat down over his eyes and doesn't say any more.

Bas sits across from him with his leather pack at his feet and stares out the open door at the desert dark. He doesn't try to engage Fox in chitchat. Fox seems the sort that's only good for the kind of information that comes through gossip and griping, and Bas is not in the mood. Also, Fox has already proven himself an asshole, and Bas has never managed to scrounge up the inclination to suffer assholes. So Bas keeps quiet and watches dust and more dust, and tries to pretend he doesn't want to launch across the seats and rip Fox's face off for whatever part he played in getting hold of the designs for that train and for what happened to the man who made them. Because that peppery scrim of gridTech has been on the back of Bas's tongue for a long time now, he knows its blue-on-black shapes like he knows his own face, and he knows it came from a young genius gridTech whose experiments and designs came to the wrong attention and got him killed. The fact that these men are using those designs like they have the right makes Bas's teeth tighten and his fists clench.

It gets dangerous very quickly, the too-real possibility that Bas will do something violent that he shouldn't while Fox is just lying there like some dirty little desert lord kipping as his minions scurry to please him. But patience is the largest part of tracking, and though it's the part Bas likes the least, there's no denying it's the part that nearly always pays off. And he needs to get into Stanslo's Bridge. So Bas sets his jaw and eventually goes back to the door, leans out of it, and eyes the locomotive.

That can't be safe, he thinks, watching the currents travel the length of the locomotive's casing and wondering how anyone inside it isn't cooking. He remembers Kimolijah Adani's commentary on the drawings—safety and grounding and problems with containing the current—and Bas supposes he's seeing proof that it's all been gotten around somehow, but he can't fathom how. Still, it's happening, it's real, it's working.

Well. Bas supposes it's been known to work, anyway—it appears to have gotten out here on its own power, at least—but there's obviously a problem with it, or Bas assumes it wouldn't be whining and stopping like it is.

The sound of metal-on-metal doesn't let up, a steady *clang-clang-clang* ringing out over the bleak hardpan. Someone says something in a gruff, irritated tone—Bas is pretty sure it's Lowen—and someone else answers back in a smoother, higher voice, young, but Bas can't make out what either of the apparently two men are saying. The clanging rings again, faster and more urgent, then that second voice rises in both volume and intensity until the first voice bellows something and the clanging stops. There are a few mutters, and then Lowen throws open the side door of the locomotive and stomps out.

He doesn't look as angry as his tone implied; he looks concerned as he turns back to shout over his shoulder, "You're running out of time, damn it!"

"You think I don't know that?" the other voice yells back. "You think I don't *fucking well* know that?"

Lowen opens his mouth, as though to retort, but he pauses instead, shoulders slumping, head shaking in what looks like regret, and he looks up at the sky. The banging and clanging starts up again. There are sparks flying out from the open door now too. Bas can't see much, but he can hear, and whoever's in that cab can curse like nothing Bas has ever heard, and he's lived on the road with rustlers and highwaymen, so that's saying something. The low, grinding strains of "Motherfucking, cocksucking son—of—a—*bitch*!" in rhythm to the banging almost make Bas snort, but then there's more commentary on sons of whores and doing things with dogs no one should know about, let alone do, and then there's something about mothers and coyotes that makes Bas widen his eyes and blink away the sordid mental picture with a rather prudish grimace. So, all in all, it's not hard for Bas to keep quiet, since he's already pretty much speechless.

Fox snorts behind him, and Bas can't tell if it's in his sleep or in reaction to the filthy commentary.

More sparks fly out of the cab, and then there's an almighty buzzing sound that segues into a whine, and a blue glow blooms out over the locomotive's skin and the rigged lattice of wiring on its roof. The cursing cuts off in favor of an exultant "*Yes!*" as the engine howls to life, that blue glow narrowing into streams of crackling currents that feed outward from the cab and go spidering up along all the conduit and wirework.

Lowen abruptly jolts back from it and to the side, like it's zapped him or something, but Bas thinks, if it had, any moves Lowen would be making would be the jittery death-dance kind. That's a heap of current roping halfway freely all over the locomotive. That singular pepper-ozone taste blooms at the back of Bas's tongue, fills his mouth, and the gridstream pulses with a blue-black phantasm underglow that Bas can't see with his eyes but can nonetheless *see*. Bas has to make himself remain cool and detached, because he *knew it*, but to see it, to see what's left of someone so promising, to understand a man had been killed for it...

Bas wonders if he'll blow his cover if he just knocks Fox galley-west for no reason, or even shoots him. It would fit right in with the Jakob Barstow cover, surely, but it wouldn't do the job he'd come here to do. It would probably only get him dead or left out in the middle of the desert, which is pretty much the same thing. Harrowgate is a long way behind when you're riding shank's mare.

Lowen has drifted back, eyes still on the sparking engine, when he pauses. With a sigh, deep and loud enough that Bas can hear it from where he hangs out of the boxcar, Lowen shakes his head and ventures closer to the engine. He stops when he reaches the door.

"Can you power it down so I can get those tools out of the hatch?"

There's a long moment of nothing until the other voice says, "I don't think I want to. What if I can't start it again? And it's getting close."

"I don't know." Lowen takes off his hat and scrubs at his short dark hair. "Not exactly safe to—"

"Nothing about any of this is bloody *safe*, is it? Just leave it. They're not in the stream, so there shouldn't be a problem, and cutting the engine again isn't worth the risk."

Lowen squints up at the sky, eyes following a falcon that circles overhead. "It's only an hour or so 'til dawn and you haven't been wearing the bracelet since—"

"Yeah, I *know*, Lowen."

Lowen pauses with a heavy sigh. "Can you make it?"

"I'll have to, won't I?"

Lowen seems to think that over for a moment, obviously

unhappy with the answer, but he nods anyway. "I'll ride back in the car," he answers. "Could use the sleep anyway. Back 'er up and I'll do the coupling."

Bas doesn't offer to help as Lowen directs the locomotive over the switch tracks and hooks up the supply cars Fox had hauled from Harrowgate. Again, it doesn't take very long, so Bas can only assume it's a routine well-practiced, and it's finished with minimal fuss.

Aching for a chance to have a look inside that locomotive now that he's watching it actually work—sort of—but afraid of getting anywhere near the seemingly wild gridstream flowing all over it, Bas only watches and thinks *I was right.*

"I think they killed him for his designs," he'd told the Directorate wonks, back when all this was just the bones of a case submitted for analysis. "I think they got just enough information out of him in exchange for contraband crystals to understand the potential of what he was working on, and then they killed him for those unfinished designs half the gridTech academia were salivating over."

The deputy minister had made grumbling noises about *this is why Techs should fucking well* listen *when we tell them not to go walking into shitstorms.* Bas had merely nodded agreeably and accepted when he was offered the case.

When the coupling is apparently complete and the freight cars secure, Bas backs up to let Lowen into the tiny boxcar-turned-passenger-car. Lowen gives Bas the once-over as he squeezes by and flumps onto the couch opposite Fox.

"So." Lowen relaxes back into the leaking cushions and rubs his chapped hands together. "You're the new guy." He's got one of those strange guns too, and he props it in the corner near his elbow.

Bas only gives him a look from beneath the brim of his hat and goes back to watching the gridstream quiver over the locomotive.

"Ah," says Lowen, big white teeth almost glowing reflected blue when he smiles. "The talkative sort. No wonder Oleg liked you."

Oleg. One of the "recruiters" for Stanslo's Bridge. Bas had been working him and his partner, Dutter, for close to two years, gaining their trust and building on his own fake reputation as a highwayman and murderer, until Oleg had finally made the offer Bas had been waiting for.

"Suit yourself," Lowen says then he too tugs his hat down over his eyes and settles into the couch. He doesn't cradle his gun the way Fox does, but Bas thinks it would be a mistake to assume he couldn't get to it quick enough to make it not matter.

Bas snatches at the edge of the open door when the train finally lurches into forward motion, and he leans against the side of the car when it begins to catch its swaying rhythm. He leaves the door open. The desert night air is cold enough he can see his breath, but he doesn't want to sleep like the other two and he doubts there's coffee service.

It's different than any train Bas has ever been on before. Instead of the heavy *ka-chunk ka-chunk* of wheels on tracks, there's more of a wheezy hum, smoother somehow, and it just has a lighter feel to it. Instead of the thick haze of stoke smoke and steam, there's a hot reek of burnt gridstream and a charge to the air. It's sort of exhilarating, because Bas has no doubt whatsoever he's riding on a train that's being powered solely by gridTech, and he's pretty sure he's one of a very few to even see something like this, let alone get a demonstration.

It takes a little bit, but it does eventually occur to him that that's likely the reason for the switch and the way station. Harrowgate is isolated, yeah, and even more so now that there's no more relay office, but people do live there, and rumors do find a way of traveling long distances. If Stanslo doesn't want anyone outside of his little desert barony to know he's got what looks to Bas like a train that runs on independent gridstream, then he'd do best not to let them see it at all.

I was right, Bas thinks again and blinks when his jaw clamps too tight and his eyes narrow down to angry slits. *Kimolijah Adani was killed for his designs. And now I'm riding into hell's teeth on one of them.*

◦§◦

The important thing to understand here is that Bas is *not* in love with Kimolijah Adani. That would just be stupid. For one, Kimolijah Adani is dead, so what would be the point? And anyway, Bas never even met the man labeled a "whiz kid" by his academy professors and a "potentially dangerous genius" by a select few Directorate personnel who learned rather quickly that, if they felt the need to say such things, they should do so outside Bas's hearing. Which was only because Bas didn't appreciate the cavalier attitude to such a brilliant mind lost so tragically, and not because Bas had or has any emotional attachment to a dead genius.

Clearly.

And, okay, he *may* have formed some kind of weird, esoteric... connection or something, nothing based in reality, because in reality you can't make a connection with the dead. It's just that Bas has been studying Kimolijah Adani for nearly three years now, and a bit of vicarious attachment is inevitable.

"Shy," Kimolijah's sister had told Bas, "but a bit of a smartass when you got to know him."

"Bloody feral on goal," his crossball teammates had professed, "but the first to offer a hand after a match, win or lose."

"Smarter than anyone else in the room, even his professors," the academy minister had sighed sadly, "and yet practical everyday life seemed a touch beyond Kimolijah. He spent so much time inside his own head, you see. I don't know if he'd have been able to even so much as buy a loaf of bread if you sent him to a market full of bake shops."

Bas thinks all of it is very, very close but not *quite* on the mark. He's seen the journals, he's read the diaries, he's pored over the schematics and the notes and the equations. He's seen a limitless mind unfold over blotted pages and doodled margins that were never meant to be seen by anyone but Kimolijah Adani himself, and the personality that had wedged itself determinedly inside the barbs and whorls of the hastily scrawled commentary had somehow *spoken* to Bas.

It said: *the most shocking thing about it is that all this unchartable genius could be contained in a single mind.*

It said: *and no one really gets it, because all the snarky wit and single-minded drive to achieve is obscured beneath the spiky characters turned to scratched brilliance with every stroke of inked theorems and hypotheses laid over the individuality within the intellect.*

And it said: *this is a mind men would kill for.*

It made Bas view with bitter regret the one-year gap between the time he graduated from the academy and the time Kimolijah started. But for a few years and a few miles between them while they grew up on opposite sides of Knapston, they might have met, spoken, become....

Who knows?

So fine, *okay*, Bas may have fallen into some kind of... overly attached fondness, but if he had, it was with the mind he'd watched unfold all over those journals and blueprints. Grand and dazzling and horrible and tragic. No one would likely ever know the scope of the potential that had been lost with Kimolijah Adani. So it shouldn't surprise anyone that Bas formed a bit of a... okay, it's an obsession.

What of it? Where's the harm? It's not like it hurts anyone, and it certainly kept Bas on task and searching when real information ran scarce. *Never fall for a mark, never fall for a victim*, the number one rule in Directorate covert ventures, but this isn't the same. Kimolijah Adani was never a mark, and it doesn't count when the victim is already dead. The Directorate isn't looking for him. They're looking for—Bas is looking for—Mariella Crocker, Class 4 weatherTech, who disappeared almost four years ago and whose trail Bas eventually tracked to Castle City. Just east of Harrowgate. The connection to Stanslo is something the Directorate believes; the one to Kimolijah Adani is something Bas *feels*.

Anyway, it's not exactly the first time Bas has halfway fallen for someone who lives only between the pages of a book. So what?

It gets dreadful hot powerful quickly when the sun goes up. It takes no time at all for the heat to rise and make Bas sweat beneath his leather duster. He keeps the door open. It doesn't make it any less hot, but the wind that slides in with the train's acceleration at least moves the air around. The heat and the rhythm and the sway make him a little sleepy, and he thinks about using some of Jakob Barstow's dickish tendencies and dumping either Fox or Lowen off one of the couches—preferably Fox—but he decides it's probably not a good idea to lower his guard enough to sleep in their company anyway.

When the boredom starts to get to him, he pulls out a few of the illobooks he'd brought with him to pass the time on the train out to Harrowgate. He's read them all before, but he didn't want to risk bringing and ruining new ones. A guilty pleasure, or maybe it's more like escapism of a sort. Illobook heroes, after all, never have to do paperwork or get nagged by their mothers or have to make a stop, dog-tired, at the markets before they can go home because all the food they'd left in the pantry before the latest three-month assignment has surely sprouted legs by now and wandered off to find better accommodations. Compared to the decidedly unglamorous life of a Directorate tracker, illobook heroes have it pretty damned good. Directorate trackers, after all, stay dead when they take a mortal wound on the job; there are no miraculous recoveries explained in unlikely exposition and over-the-top dialogue in the first few panels of the next issue.

The book's pages flutter in the wind, so Bas angles at a slant to block it. He sits right beside the door and squints at the colorful artwork against the sunlight, pulling his scarf up over mouth and nose to minimize the dust and heat sliding into his lungs.

Magic Man, year 5, series 2, issue 9. Bas traces the bold lines of the colorful illustrations as Casius Cruel threatens the honest, hardworking citizens of Crosstown and Magic Man grandly thwarts him. For probably the first time in his life, the illobooks don't hold Bas's attention for very long.

He leans out for as long as he can, wind and dust in his face, to have a look at the engine. The odd-angled poles and conduit he'd only seen silhouetted a few hours ago now wink in the sun and look even shabbier and more idiot-rigged than they had before. Atop and dead center of the engine's cab sits what looks to Bas like some kind of gun turret, but he can't imagine defense against bandits would be a problem out here. He looks up at the sky, but all he sees is another circling falcon. Or maybe it's the same one, following the train. Either way, it's not exactly like it's any kind of threat, so it still doesn't explain what a turret's doing on top of a train.

It's harder to see the gridstream that flows over the locomotive in the daylight, but Bas *can* see it, and even if he couldn't, he can taste it. He wonders exactly how it's running. Gridstream, of course, but it would take at least six or seven Class 5 gridTechs to power it enough just to start it; he can't even guess how many it would take to run it this long. And running a gridstream engine in the desert heat.... Bas wonders what kind of heat sink they're using on this thing, because it couldn't possibly be a cool-air system, not out here.

He thinks about the dynamic crystals in Kimolijah Adani's designs and how they were a new discovery only several years back, how the Directorate medTechs did some experimenting with them until it killed two of them and the Directorate subsequently and immediately banned them altogether, because Bas wasn't kidding before—when it comes to the safety of its Techs, the Directorate can be a protective, possessive, mother-bear bitch.

He thinks about how Kimolijah Adani was using the crystals in his designs anyway, and how those designs made Bas almost hyperventilate at the possibilities when he'd had a look at them. He thinks about how there's only one source for those crystals, and how Kimolijah Adani and his da somehow ended up nothing but blackened bones smoldering away in the workshop behind their tinker's shop after a cryptic series of communications with the man who owns that source.

"A fucking *overload*," Resaniji had said. "Like 'Lijah was some kind of tweenie moron who didn't know more about the Grid and how it works than the goddamned 'experts' at the Directorate and anyone else in the world."

Having scrutinized Kimolijah's work and spoken with his professors, Bas wasn't able to argue. He'd seen it—in every diary he studied, in every schematic, in every theory and equation he couldn't *quite* understand, but he'd known what he was looking at was big and unique and near blinding in its virtuosity.

There are idea people and there are engineers, and then there are the builders and testers, and rarely do those separate entities coalesce in one person. Kimolijah Adani was that rarity. He thought things up and then he built them, and if the parts to build them didn't exist, he built those too.

Looking at the gridstream climbing all over that engine, knowing where the design and the gridTech itself came from, Bas feels a deep, vicious anger bubble in his gut. One way or another, Baron Stanslo is responsible for a Directorate agent lying dead in a dusty alley so horribly far from home. And now there's no doubt in Bas's mind that Stanslo is responsible for Kimolijah Adani and his da dying in their own workshop, not even enough left of them to bury.

Someone needs to pay.

By the time Bas feels the deceleration pulling at his ribs, the sun is starting to slide lower in the sky. They'd gotten underway right around dawn, and Bas guesses it's late afternoon by now, three or four hours maybe 'til full-dark. It's taken him this long to realize he hasn't had anything to eat since lunch yesterday.

He's dragged out and sore and hungry, so when he leans out and spots a smudge of color in the limitless buff of desert sand, he's full of relief rather than a more sensible foreboding. That's got to be some kind of station up ahead; it's too rectangular to be part of the desert. Bas can see a shabby little town creeping out behind it, a small ridge overlooking it, and the continuation of the tracks sidling out into the blank beyond, all the way out to the Dead Lands, for all Bas knows.

Stanslo's Bridge. Has to be.

Fox startles from his hours-long doze with a thick snort and tips his hat back up from where it had been covering his eyes. He looks around, blinking and squinting, then gives Bas a sour once-over. Lowen wakes more smoothly, sitting up and stretching and sliding Bas a grin Bas thinks might be mocking, but he doesn't know, so he only stares.

Turns out it is a station. Well, at least an attempt at one. More like a big semi-open pavilion with thin walls to deflect the wind and some kind of rickety annex jutting askew from its side, but Bas supposes it's the closest to a station as is possible all the way out here. Outbuildings are scattered around it like a child's blocks. Lofted, towerlike contraptions dot the place at irregular intervals, tall arms stretched in a *V* with wires strung across and humming with gridstream, bellies inset with great wooden tanks. They look like the soulless mechanical Deathbringers from *Planet Horror*—year 14, series 2, issue 5. Bas wants to think of them as stunted water towers, maybe, which would make sense in the desert, but water towers draw up from the ground with the tank at the top; these look almost upside-down. And anyway, where do you get water in the first place to put in them?

They pull into the meager shelter of the station, and though it's all rather flimsy, still Bas can feel the immediate drop in temperature once they're out of the midafternoon sun, can breathe a touch easier as the train crawls to the center of the shoddy station and wheezes to a halt. The blue flicker of gridstream is brighter now, and it flares to almost blinding for several seconds before there's a high-pitched whine and every-thing goes out, stops, and then there's nothing. It's like some weird kind of suspension, a pause in movement and breath and thought while the green ghosts of blue gridstream fade at the backs of Bas's eyes and the burnt-sky scent of it winnows back down into the dry, prickling tang of empty desert air.

There's an eagerness blooming in Bas's belly he tries not to show as he stands from where he's been half dangling out the open door, and waits for Lowen or Fox to make a move. He probably shouldn't have, because the first thing Fox does when he's done stretching and grumbling *about* an empty belly and not enough sleep is to point his weird gun at Bas. The glint in the belligerent gaze that comes with it makes Bas think Fox is just looking for a reaction, so Bas doesn't give him one.

"Don't go wanderin' off," Fox says, eyeing Bas through a narrow squint. "Boss'll wanna give ye a proper welcome."

Bas lifts an eyebrow. "Kinda why I'm here." He doesn't go for his weapon; he's an ace shot, but not much on the draw. He keeps his hands still.

Fox props the gun over his shoulder with a smirk, his mouth twisted sour again, like he's disappointed Bas didn't give him an excuse. "Is it, then," he says, narrow-eyed, and he tilts a look at Lowen as he brushes past Bas out of the car.

Bas wants to ask what the hell that's supposed to mean, but he doesn't think he should. He doesn't get a chance, anyway.

"Where is Stanslo?" a shaky voice asks as soon as Fox steps down. It sounds like the one from before, the one that was inside the locomotive—the engineer, Bas figures, but he can't see from this angle, and he doesn't want to take his eyes off Lowen.

"I reckon he seen the train pull in like everyone else," Fox answers, a lethargic drawl. "He'll be along."

The other voice barks, "No, I need to see him *now*, it's crawling up my fucking *arm!*"

"Then you should be better at your fucking *job*," Fox says. Still, he growls an order to someone named Merrin to go fetch the boss.

Footsteps, and then everything goes quiet.

Bas just keeps staring at Lowen, trying to look bored, and then he really is bored, because it takes for-fucking-ever. But that could just be because time has seemed to slow down and center on the fact that Bas is actually here, in Stanslo's Bridge, where he's been trying to get a foot in for two years.

He knows he's sweating, and he hopes the heat is a good enough excuse because he really doesn't think it's a good idea to show any kind of weakness right now. So he thinks about the complete hardcase Jakob Barstow is supposed to be, lets his eyes go cold and his shoulders relax and his fingers make a show of twitching just at the tip of the butt of his six-barrel, tucked up into its beaten holster at his hip.

"Gonna stretch my legs," Bas says, going for a lazy drawl, satisfied with the roughness of his throat from the dust. It gets into you here, grit in your nostrils and sand crunching between your molars.

Lowen merely shrugs, giving Bas another grin, and though he does reach over and pick up his gun, he doesn't point it at Bas or object.

Bas waits it out for a full count of twenty before he makes a show of rolling his eyes and sighing. He turns slowly and steps down from the car onto the oiled dirt of the station's floor.

He sees very little that tells him anything of value—just a bunch of mechanical equipment and spools of wire, and a wall on the far side, the door open and hanging crooked, through which Bas can see more equipment and scattered... stuff. He mentally labels it *workshop* and decides to have a look as soon as he thinks he can get away with it. Bas stares around the station, taking in what he can: the shelves and the tools and the crates of parts and conduit, the obviously half-finished projects sitting on benches and puking out wires. It stays quiet for long enough that Bas wonders if this is the end of the world and Bas is the only one left in it, with only Fox and Lowen for company. And isn't *that* a depressing thought.

"Oh, grand," a voice mutters, kind of thready and just to Bas's side.

Bas hadn't seen him sitting there before. Slumped, really, ass parked on the metal step that leads into the cab of the locomotive, scuffed boots planted on the oiled dirt floor, gloved hands dangling between bent knees, and a curious expression tipped up at Bas.

"Another one," the guy says, a twist to his mouth. He gives Lowen a dirty look. "You didn't tell me *this* was what Fox was picking up in Harrowgate." He shakes his head and turns back to Bas, a flat once-over. "And here I'd thought the apparently endless supply of assholes had finally run out."

And that's how Bas comes face-to-face with two dead men in less than a day.

Well. Kind of.

<h1 style="text-align:center">2.</h1>

It's Kimolijah Adani, Bas knows it is. He's never seen him, and he can't really see much of his face now except for the wispy scruff of an unshaven jawline, but Bas knows it's him. The goggles he's wearing make his eyes look too big and buggy, and he's streaked with axle grease, hair slicked into a tail at the back of his neck, but Bas knows. His skin is darker than his sister's, brown as a burnished conker, but he's just as short, and he's got the same widow's peak.

More, though—it's the taste of the air around him, the blue-black ghost of foundation to his edges that Bas can't actually see, not with his eyes, but something way down deep in his mind can, and it shows him what he can understand in a way he can understand it. Bas had become all too acquainted with its revenant in those impossible crystals that couldn't cage gridTech but did, had tasted the pepper-wisped ozone that fanned in tiny, faint jets from a toy train that wasn't supposed run without wires but could.

It's Kimolijah Adani, there's absolutely no doubt, so... what the fuck?

Did he fake his own death? Who did those blackened bones belong to? Or has he maybe been kidnapped and is here against his will? He doesn't look like he's terrified of these people, and anyway, it seems he's the engineer—if he's been looking for an escape route, he's apparently been driving one.

Fox struts back in, gun still propped on his shoulder, and he gives Kimolijah a look that's nasty and smug and full of foul promise.

Kimolijah glares back at him with a look just as pleasant. "Where's Stanslo?" It's snapped out, a verbal bite.

"Dunno," Fox sneers. "Why don't you go lookin'?"

Kimolijah doesn't look like he can stand, let alone go anywhere. "Why don't you go fuck right off?"

Fox clenches his teeth, obviously hesitates for a second, but then he growls and swivels his gun around and trains it on Kimolijah. "Don't test me, princess."

Kimolijah snorts. "Or what? You'll be mean to me?" He points his glare up at Bas, mouth flat. "What are you looking at?"

Bas lifts his eyebrows, but he doesn't answer. He can't. Shock makes him lightheaded and a little bit fuzzy. He only stares. At *Kimolijah Adani*.

Kimolijah snorts again. Jaw set, he drags himself up until he's on his feet, swaying a little, but he sets his shoulders and shuffles his way over to the shelves of equipment and parts propped against the far wall.

"I've got work to do." It's a mutter through gritted teeth as he makes his slow way back over to the train, lifts up a hatch on the locomotive's side to expose part of the engine, crouches down, and starts messing with the wiring. He digs out a double-pronged cable from beneath some of the mechanical works and hooks it into the gridshunt embedded in his forearm between wrist and elbow, and then everything he touches with his gloved hands lights up with that hazy blue glow.

It's a Grid hookup, but not like one Bas has ever seen. GridTechs get wired in, yeah, but they're only part of the circuit, providing the positive flow. Bas is no gridTech, but he knows more than most laymen, and he knows what two prongs means on the end of a gridstream cable. Positive out, negative in. With that dual prong in his arm, Kimolijah *is* the circuit.

This... well. Bas doesn't know *what* the fuck to think of it, but it gives a whole new meaning to "tapping in." It also explains how the train didn't die in the desert heat, and why Kimolijah looks like he's trying not to fall over. Just because Kimolijah impossibly but still apparently *can* prevent the engine from overheating, doesn't mean he *should*.

"What'sa matter?" Fox sneers it at Kimolijah's back; it's a mix between spiteful mockery and the petulant tones of a bully thwarted, but now that Kimolijah is basically inside living gridTech gone not-quite-wild, Fox backs off a few steps. "Leash too loose?" It's snide and said with a curl of the lip. "Don't like it when someone's not holding ye down and *making* ye?"

Bas doesn't know what it means, but he can see Kimolijah's shoulders tense, and now Bas notices that Kimolijah's hands are shaking, which really can't be good for someone with all that gridstream zapping all over the place. Bas takes a small step back.

Kimolijah doesn't turn from whatever work he's doing on the locomotive's engine, but Bas can see the sharp line of his jaw set hard. "I know your tiny brain has a hard time retaining information." He flips a quick look over Bas's shoulder to snap a glare at Fox before he turns back to what he's doing. "But I feel an obligation to help the less fortunate, so I'll remind you that"—he lifts his arm up—"no leash means no restraint." When he looks over his shoulder again, he's smirking; it looks kind of sickly, and he's sweating and his skin's going ashy, but it's there. He waves his hand and waggles his fingers. "You never know when a bit of current might... *slip its leash*."

That last is said as obvious counterpoint to the swift and

deadly thread of gridstream that zaps from the tips of Kimolijah's fingers. The grit of black flares around the edges of Bas's vision, and the sharp taste of ozone floods his mouth with, unaccountably, the sweet tang of wet cedar, but that can't be right, because cedar means kineTech and, no matter how impossible it is, that's *gridTech* flying out from Kimolijah's hand and splatting the ground only paces in front of Fox's feet. Fox curses and jumps back, and Kimolijah gives him a viciously pleased look before he goes back to messing around beneath the engine hatch, and Bas... stares. The near assault is shocking enough, but the concentrated power behind it and the *control* are what make Bas gape.

'Lijah can open an artery and aim.

And, well... holy *shit*. Kimolijah Adani is a Class 2 gridTech. What Bas has just seen is beyond even a Class 5, so far off the scale he doesn't think there's a way to measure it.

He doesn't think about what he's doing when he steps in front of Fox and keeps him from rushing Kimolijah like Fox obviously intends. Kimolijah doesn't move, doesn't look back, but his shoulders twitch, so Bas knows Kimolijah is well aware of what's going on behind him.

Fox gives Bas a glare, and it's really ugly, right up close like it is, bared brown teeth and noisome breath, but Bas notes there's been no attempt by Fox to swing that gun around and start shooting.

"You'll pay for that, princess," says Fox, growled out through his teeth, and he's pushing against Bas, but not so much to break free. "One day, boss'll wise up, and we'll see who bids highest fer yer crystal." He grins, hideous. "Been savin' up, I have."

Bas narrows his eyes—because *crystal* and there's hints of something he's not quite getting, *leash*, and there's malevolence all over it—but again, he has no time to parse any of it.

"Uh-huh." Kimolijah goes back to what he was doing. "You keep looking forward to that day, Fox. Who knows, your shocking stupidity might not actually kill you before then. Fate seems to favor the dim, and life is full of delightful possibilities." He whacks at something inside the engine with some kind of crimping tool.

It seems that's Fox's limit. He surges against Bas, gun swinging from off his shoulder, and Bas relaxes from his brace, because he knew it was coming.

He swings his arm back and whips around at the same time, knocking the barrel of Fox's gun away from him then grabbing it before Fox can regain control and aim. Smooth and calm, Bas lays a right hook to Fox's temple. Bas registers Lowen finally entering the fray from where he's been lounging against the door of the shabby passenger car as Fox goes down in a heap, but Bas doesn't pause to gloat; he draws his gun and trains it on Fox as Fox stands and spits blood.

"Don't," Bas says. He has to glance away from Fox to keep track of Lowen, and when he looks back, he catches Fox raising his gun up to point it at Bas. "*Don't*," Bas says again. Fox doesn't listen, so Bas thumbs a round and fires.

Which is exactly how it would have happened if Bas were Magic Man and this were an illobook. Except he's not and it isn't, so it actually happens like this:

Bas does swing his arm back and he does whip around, but Fox angles a solid kick behind Bas's knee at the same time and Bas kind of trips a little sideways, so the barrel of Fox's gun angles up and to the side. The gun goes off when Bas snags hold of it, trying to regain his balance, except there's no blast and no scent of powder and no recoil; there's a slick, heavy *bzzzzwap!* sound and blue current ropes out from the end of the barrel and over Bas's left shoulder.

Kimolijah yelps, "Hey, *watch* it!" and there's a strangled cry right in the middle of it from someone else, and that's when Lowen crowds in, and Bas can't keep track of anything anymore. The gun jives and jitters in Bas's hand, he can barely control his own movements, and the gridstream goes wild, up and then down to the side. Kimolijah shouts again, and Bas can just see him out the corner of his eye, diving toward the stream with his hand outstretched. The gridstream jumps toward him and there's that wet cedar tang again, and then.... Bas doesn't know how to describe it. It's like Kimolijah sucks the gridstream right in through his palm and up his arm, it lights him up, and it's shocking and damn near unbelievable, because yeah, a gridTech can absorb gridstream like that, but not what looks like enough current to power a whole city, and certainly not coming from a gun that shouldn't function—*or even exist*—and yet does.

It's like something right out of an illobook.

Kimolijah lights up like a glowbug, but he doesn't seize up and he doesn't fry. He merely grates, "Fucking *turn it off*!" and goes down on one knee.

It makes Fox jerk his glance away and toward Kimolijah, and Lowen tells him to "Goddamn it, Fox, let go of the fucking gun!" and Fox drags his eyes from Kimolijah and over to Lowen.

Bas would really like to take advantage of the distraction— and he might tell himself later that it's exactly what happened— but he's apparently got hold of a gun that's pulsing out live gridstream a mere handsbreadth from his face, and the contact makes his whole body fizz. It's not as bad as being hit full-force with a bolt from the Grid itself—if it were, he'd already be dead—but it's made his muscles decide he has very little author- ity over them. His arm jerks, which snaps the gun up and cracks Lowen in the jaw, and he goes down.

It's all over almost before it actually happens. Fox lets go of the gun and Bas staggers back. The whining live hum of the gun stops abruptly and the stream flitters into nothing. All that's left is the heavy jittering tingle buzzing up Bas's arm and through his whole body. He wonders if his hair is standing up underneath his hat.

There's a man dead on the floor of the run-down little station, his face nearly melted off his skull and his clothes smoking. Lowen is cursing and holding his jaw from his sprawl on the floor behind Bas, and Kimolijah is gasping and propping himself against the side of the locomotive like he might throw up. His glove is smoking where he'd pulled in the gridstream. He looks up at Bas through the dusty, grease-smeared goggles, all the gridstream that had been sputtering around him a second before now condensed down to a small shiver of it crackling between his palm and the shunt in his arm.

Bas just stands there for a minute, staring between the sixteen different kinds of impossibility that is Kimolijah Adani and the blob of melted goo that used to be the dead man's head. He looks down at the gun in his hand and thinks nothing more sensible than a litany of *Holy fucking shit*, and *A goddamned gridgun*, and *What the fuck*, and *Holy fucking shit, it's a goddamned gridgun!* He barely notices Fox and Lowen both moving back and behind him.

Kimolijah's staring at him. Bas only stares back blankly, and he doesn't realize he's basically pointing the gun right at Kimolijah's chest until Kimolijah very slowly drops the crimping tool and then, even more slowly, raises his hands. He's still crouched next to the access door to the engine, and he's still got blueish gridstream skittering up his arm and coalescing in his palm, and Bas remembers that stream Kimolijah had basically shot at Fox just a second ago and thinks *Yeah, not as unarmed as you're trying to look.*

Bas blinks when he realizes what Kimolijah must be thinking. "I'm not going to hurt you," Bas says and makes a point of adjusting his grip on the gun and then lowering it.

"Yeah?" Kimolijah cocks his head to the side. "Make this kind of entrance everywhere you go, do you?"

Bas thinks about that for a second, because there are too many things he wants to say—*Holy shit, you're alive*, and *What the hell happened?* and *Do you know how scary your sister is?* and *I'm totally not in love with you*—so he settles for, "Only when I'm trying to make an impression."

"Uh-huh," Kimolijah says, a sardonic twist to his mouth, and then he snorts, not at all amused. "Impression."

That's when Bas hears the distinctive cascade of noises that tells him something's powering up behind him. A lot of somethings. He doesn't have to think too hard to come up with a picture of several more guns like the one still in his hand, and in the hands of people who probably don't have his best interests at heart, pointing those guns at his back. He doesn't move, but he doesn't drop the gun either.

"If you've got any soft spots," Kimolijah mutters under his breath, "now's the time to pretend you don't." He shakes his head with a grimace and a rueful look for Bas and says, "Man, I can't even...." He doesn't finish; he shuts his mouth tight and looks at something over Bas's shoulder.

"Oh dear," says a voice behind Bas, accompanied by slow clocking bootsteps on the packed and oiled dirt floor of the big shed pretending to be a train station. "Someone's gone and melted Fenris."

The man who steps right up to Bas's side cuts a swell that looks absurdly out of place out here in this wasteland of dust and dearth. He's striking. Handsome. Fit and healthy-looking beneath his expensive tailored coat and waistcoat, with lustrous just-now-graying hair curling slightly above his shoulders beneath a spendy black suede hat that probably needs brushing every half hour. His neatly trimmed whiskers show more streaks of white than his hair does, but it makes him look refined and respectable rather than unkempt. He smiles at Bas like Bas is the best thing he's seen in weeks.

"And what did Fenris ever do to you, Mister...?" He pauses, brightens. "Ah! How stupid of me. You must be Jakob."

It's kind of surreal. Bas is standing here with what is apparently some kind of grid-powered gun still in his hand, now surrounded by people just as mean and rough as Jakob Barstow is supposed to be, and this man is looking at him with what looks like unholy delight.

Baron Stanslo. Has to be.

Bas licks his lips and says, "Yeah, Barstow," but that's not actually what comes out, because his brain is kind of whirling and every nerve in his body is backfiring, so what he actually says is, "Bas," and then he thinks, *oh shit,* because it's a *rookie fucking mistake,* and goddamn it, Bas is better than this. "I mean, yeah, Jakob Barstow," he corrects quickly. "But friends call me Bas."

He doesn't usually give that one away. He's always liked the Barstow cover because it's close enough to his own name that he doesn't slip up. You know—like he just did. He blames the too-quick shift back in Harrowgate and decides he's going to have to swagger through it.

"*Bas,*" says Stanslo with a broad, white-toothed grin, and he sets his hand on Bas's shoulder, completely ignoring the gun Bas is still gripping. He gives Bas a friendly little jostle. "Oleg didn't mention as much."

Bas just frowns and says, "Oleg isn't a friend."

Stanslo chuckles. "Well then, I'm quite honored, Bas." His eyebrows go up and his eyes widen with his smile, like he's waiting for a punchline he knows is going to be magnificent. "Any other names I should know about?"

"Those aren't enough for you?"

Stanslo throws back his head and laughs and laughs and laughs, loud and full and rich, and pretty soon, all the minions with their guns join in with him. Bas just kind of frowns around at them and then looks at Kimolijah. Kimolijah blinks back, looking kind of wide-eyed now, or maybe it's just those stupid goggles, but it seems like the silent exchange spurs him or something, because he shakes his head and stands up. He has to lean against the locomotive's side for a moment; he still looks sick and shaky.

Fox is there again—or maybe he never left—and he's got a different gun, the eight-barreled monster he'd had back in Harrowgate, and it's trained on Kimolijah. Bas tries to angle between them again, but:

"Those will do nicely," Stanslo finally says, wiping at the corner of his eye while he regards Kimolijah until Kimolijah turns away and retrieves the tool he'd dropped when he thought Bas was going to shoot him. Stanslo gives Bas a conspiratory wink, then says to Kimolijah, "Aren't you forgetting something, dear heart?"

Dear heart?

Kimolijah sighs and slowly straightens. "Usually, Baron," he answers, diffident.

Stanslo looks down at Kimolijah like he's the sun and the stars all rolled into one. With a gentle smile, Stanslo fishes in his pocket and comes up with a wide matte-metal coil. He dangles it on the tip of his index finger. "Come, then, let me see."

Kimolijah shakes his head and jerks his chin at Fox. "Not with him on the trigger."

"Oh, come now, I thought we were past all this." Stanslo *tuts*, sighs like he's horribly disappointed, but nods at Lowen. Lowen steps up to Fox; there's a long look between them—Fox livid and Lowen unimpressed—before Fox relinquishes the gun to Lowen with a huff and a sidelong look at Stanslo. Lowen makes a point to check the chambers and crank the barrel housing 'til a round clicks against the strike stud, and then he levels the gun at Kimolijah's chest.

Strangely, this is what coaxes Kimolijah to move. With a narrow look through those ridiculous goggles at Stanslo and a bemused one at Bas, Kimolijah shuffles closer. The barrels of the gun follow him all the way, and Bas can't figure for the life of him what the hell's going on until Stanslo says, "Pull that stream, dear heart."

Kimolijah does. The sputtering little filaments of gridstream that have been skidding from palm to forearm ever since all the commotion started abruptly flare then retreat into Kimolijah's gridshunt.

And Bas can't get a single bit of any of this straight in his head. There's Kimolijah Adani, alive, there's *dear heart* and there's a gun, and what the *fuck* is going on?

Blank-faced, Kimolijah holds out his gloved hand; it shakes. He looks expectant, but Stanslo twirls the metal coil around on his finger for a moment and then pulls it back.

"I said let me see." It's stern this time, but it still hasn't lost that light joviality—and yet there's something sharp and dangerous underneath it.

With a tight look at Bas that almost seems like discomfiture, Kimolijah slowly removes his gloves. Bas has to concentrate very hard not to suck in a breath or tense his muscles.

Kimolijah's right hand, the one with which he'd caught the gridstream and ruined his glove, appears unharmed. Fine-boned and strong-looking, what with the kind of delicate work he does; the rosy nail beds contrast the burnished brown of his skin, and Bas can see remnants of shop grease in the lines of Kimolijah's knuckles and beneath the ragged crescents where he's chewed his nails down to tortured little stubs. The left hand is what makes Bas wonder *what the fuck?* and try to keep his breathing even.

Gentle, almost reverent, Stanslo pushes up Kimolijah's sleeve, and shakes his head sadly when he gets a look at Kimolijah's arm.

Not dark, like the rest of Kimolijah's skin, but streaked nearly white with swollen, wide swaths welted and washed of any pigment but for a complex series of tattoos that climb up from around the shunt in his forearm and keep climbing beneath where Stanslo has pushed up the sleeve. The bleached-out crawl starts at Kimolijah's fingertips and sidles up and up like a mutant blood infection before it ribbons out into wispy raised tracks, pushing at the arcs and whorls of the tattoo as though something under the skin is following their paths. Mottled and motley and just plain wrong-looking.

"Tch," says Stanslo, heavy with affection. He frowns, though the smile somehow is still there, tucked into the corners of his mouth, all pleased and weirdly satisfied. He takes Kimolijah's hand; as he does, Lowen raises the gun until the barrels are almost but not quite touching Kimolijah's head. Kimolijah doesn't look at him, his gaze is nailed to Stanslo, but his mouth pinches down and he rolls his eyes.

"You took too long," Stanslo says and slides the coil over Kimolijah's hand until it settles over his wrist like a vambrace.

Kimolijah glares. "Not like I meant to," he says through his teeth, and then he jerks, like he can't help it, when Stanslo clamps his hand around the bracelet and squeezes.

"One of these days, you won't make it in time." Stanslo draws back and pets at the coil with a look of soft rue. "And then what? You have people who depend on you, you know."

Kimolijah doesn't say anything, but he looks like he wants to, and none of it nice.

Stanslo smirks and clamps his hand around the coil again.

And Bas can't help it—he startles when the coil moves and slicks and clicks, and Kimolijah sucks in a breath that sounds pained. There's an actual whimper when the metal shifts and coils tighter, then just *digs in* until it seems to actually fuse with Kimolijah's skin. There's no blood, just a strange whiff of citrus and a smudgy white glow Bas doesn't think anyone who isn't a tracker can see; it shudders over the metal for a second or two and then settles into shapes Bas can't interpret. If it's a language, it's not one Bas has ever seen.

It's not until the bracelet is in place and stops its shifting as the glow fades that Lowen lowers the gun.

"There, you see?" Stanslo is smiling again, looking at Kimolijah like he's a basket of kittens with bows on. "It's retreating already." He says it like it's some kind of benediction.

Kimolijah doesn't seem to take it that way, even though Bas can see that Stanslo's right—the color to the skin of Kimolijah's arm is coming back quickly, the welts are receding, and that unwholesome white is darkening to Kimolijah's natural tone. Whatever that... thing is, it's fixed whatever was wrong with Kimolijah's arm.

Kimolijah's teeth set, and he jerks his hand away from Stanslo's grip. "Well, then," he says and starts backing away. He flicks a wary look between Stanslo and Bas from behind those buggy goggles. "I've got work to do."

"Not today," Stanslo says amiably. His smile this time is gentle, concerned, but again, there's a sort of muted malice beneath it that Bas can't actually see, though he *feels* it. "Go get cleaned up. There are some things I'd like you to take care of up the house."

"Can't." Kimolijah's already turned away and picked up another tool. His back is to Stanslo when he says, "Spark problem needs fixing, or it won't be ready for the run to the Bruise, and we all know how you—"

"I have every confidence you'll be ready on schedule, since we both know the consequences if you're not."

It doesn't impress Kimolijah. He merely heaves a great sigh and shakes his head, back still turned as he dips into the engine hatch and starts clanking around. "Yeah, yeah, no lollies for me for a week, sent to bed without my supper, maybe even a good spanking if I—"

"*Kimo!*"

It's loud and angry, and it makes Kimolijah jump. He turns around slowly and stares at Stanslo with a furrow wedged between his eyebrows above the bridge piece of the goggles. Bas can't tell what the expression means, not without seeing the eyes, but he's guessing genuine confusion and surprise.

"But...." Kimolijah shakes his head. "But Mari's home tonight."

"She is." Stanslo grins. "I'm sure she'll be pleased to see you."

Kimolijah doesn't seem to share Stanslo's opinion. Or his

enthusiasm. "The pins aren't relaying the spark. If the pins don't relay the spark, it'll break the core tubes. If the core tubes break, the magnets don't spin. If the magnets don't spin, the train doesn't run."

Bas almost blurts *What in the hell are you talking about?* because a light show on this train is one thing, but pins relaying sparks inside a grid engine means the engine's about to blow—any sparks inside a grid engine means the engine's about to blow. And what the hell is a core tube, anyway?

But Stanslo nods, all sage comprehension, and says, "Yes, well." He waves his hand around. "I'll have Dolerma order a few extra core tubes. Just in case."

Kimolijah ducks his head for a quick second, coughs, and Bas can swear he sees a smirk, and he realizes two things at once: Kimolijah knows very well that everything that just came out of his mouth was bullshit—but Stanslo doesn't. Kimolijah knows he doesn't. And he uses it... somehow.

Kimolijah recovers himself quickly. "Look, I didn't just get stuck at the ruddy way station because I felt like it, y'know. If we get stranded out at the Bruise, I won't—"

"Well, then, I suggest you don't get stranded," Stanslo says mildly. Less mildly, he presses, "Now, please. And shave while you're at it. You know I don't like that scruff."

Some of the minions surrounding them snort quietly. Most of them are carefully blank.

Kimolijah just stares for a moment, tight-lipped and angry, before he shifts his expression into no expression at all. He shoots flat looks to the men around them—all heeled and more than ready to shoot, by the looks—then jerks a short nod and turns around to disengage the cable from his arm. He slams the engine compartment shut and mutters a string of filthy curses under his breath, then flings the goggles over his shoulder at the locomotive as he stomps out through the wide opening that looks like it's supposed to be a door in the side of the "building."

Stanslo watches him go with a fond smile, then turns the smile on Bas. It doesn't seem to lose any of the warmth, even though the dead man—Fenris—is still quietly smoking and leaking things Bas doesn't want to know about all over the oiled dirt. As though reading Bas's thoughts, Stanslo looks down at Fenris and shakes his head with a sad *tsk*.

"You've only just arrived," Stanslo says, "so you wouldn't know." He gives Bas a sympathetic smile that Bas doesn't believe for a second. "Don't blame Oleg. I like to brief my new men personally." He pauses, then leans in close to Bas and dips his voice, confidential. "I don't like word to get around outside my borders."

Bas only just keeps from rolling his eyes and muttering *I'll bet*.

"Speaking of," Stanslo says, ostensibly casual, but really, nothing about this man is casual, "I haven't heard from Oleg in a little too long. Or Dutter." He pauses and lifts his eyebrows. "Have you?"

Bas keeps his face blank and says, "No," because it's the truth. He hasn't heard from either one of them lately. Not since Bas pointed out which door was Oleg's when the Directorate agents raided the block of bedsit tenements where Oleg had rented a room. Oleg and Dutter have both been safely out of the way and cooling their heels in a deep Directorate hole since before Bas left for Harrowgate, just to be safe.

Bas shrugs. "Haven't seen either him or Dutter since Oleg handed over the train ticket and instructions."

"Hm," Stanslo says, cool but still smiling, and he stares at Bas long enough for it to be unnerving. Eventually, he merely shrugs, like it doesn't really matter. "Well, then." He claps his hands together and grins.

"We don't have much law here. Only what I can cobble together to protect our negligent little population. But I am only one man, you see." Stanslo waves down at Fenris and then over his shoulder at the men still pointing guns at Bas. "Deputies, if you will." He shrugs and rolls his eyes, as if to say *I know, I know, but what can I do?* He sets his hand on Bas's shoulder, ostensibly affable and benign. "So, Bas, my friend." His blue eyes nearly dance, mischievous. "Tell me what I should do with the man who shot down my deputy."

Something about it... the tone, the command inside it, the smiles, the weird cheer beneath it all and the viciousness that hovers at every edge like an invisible ghost-wasp that you can't see but you can *feel* and you know it's there, just waiting for you to expose a soft spot.... It's worse than if Stanslo were openly hostile and threatening.

Bas's gut has been churning for a good ten minutes now. His back and armpits and the hair under his hat are all slippery with sick flop sweat, and Bas doesn't need his tracker's senses to understand that all this is exactly as dicey as he'd known it would be, but not because of a man who's supposed to be dead or gridstream that shouldn't work or dangerous men with dangerous guns that shouldn't exist. He doesn't need anything but the barest level of observation and common sense to understand that Baron Stanslo is dreadfully, subtly insane.

If you've got any soft spots, Kimolijah had said, *now's the time to pretend you don't.*

And okay. *Okay.* Bas can do that. He's pretty damned good at it, really. He inconspicuously adjusts his stance, a more casual affectation, and gives Stanslo a bored shrug.

"You should probably thank him for culling your pool of incompetence for you. 'Cause, seriously, that idiot pretty much walked into live gridstream." Bas pauses and twitches a brash half smile. "Also, you should show him where the chow line is. I'm fucking *starving*."

The silence is complete, and it rings in Bas's ears, but this is the stand he chose, the only one he can see that might work, and he doesn't back off. He stares at Stanslo, putting everything into appearing cool and expectant with a hint of threat, and all he can think is how Stanslo really does have very pretty blue eyes.

It's small, but Bas sees it—a tic at the corner of Stanslo's mouth and a pleased glint to his eye. Stanslo turns to the rest of the men around them and holds his arm out toward Bas like he's presenting the next act on stage. "You see, gentlemen—*that's* how it's done."

He rubs his hands together and sighs as he turns to grin at Bas. "Well, then, Bas," he says and holds out his hand. "Welcome to Stanslo's Bridge."

And* that's *how it starts.

3.

B as is not dead.

It takes him a little too long to wrap his head around that not-insignificant fact. He figures he must have been expecting to die back there, and his subconscious had been unwilling to admit it to the rest of him, which is probably why it's just now hitting him that he really should be dead with about fifty bullet holes in him. Or melted like that other guy, but he's trying really hard not to think about that.

They take the gun he'd fumbled away from Fox. Bas lets them. They don't try to touch the one in his holster, so he decides not to wonder why. With a word from Stanslo, someone trudges into the little passenger car and retrieves Bas's pack, something about "our new guest" and "comfortable," but Bas is too disconcerted and trying not to show it, so he merely nods and hopes it looks appropriately appreciative. He can't think of anything in his pack that might be incriminating, anyway. Just his clothes, some ammunition he probably won't get back, and his illobooks, which he'd damned well better.

They're making their way around the far side of the station when it hits Bas again, a funny kind of wobble on the edge of his senses and an overwhelming burst of something tangy and citrusy that floods his mouth. He'd felt the same thing in the station when Stanslo was putting that bracelet thing on Kimolijah. Not Tech, though there's an unsettling kinship that's almost too slight to ken. Still, it's something, and Bas doesn't like the way it feels like it's trying to get in before it bubbles behind his teeth like a lemon fizz and then just disappears. It leaves him unsettled and even more wary.

He almost trips over the train tracks as they cross them, a small network of switch tracks and what looks like a half-built turntable inside the shell of an unfinished roundhouse that sits beside the shabby addition to the station itself; it's tarped over, with derelict winches sticking out at odd angles, and Bas can't get a look at what might be inside it. He thinks it's the workshop he glimpsed from inside the station.

The tracks continue and lead off opposite Harrowgate, disappearing out and out into the desert. Bas thinks he should wonder about that—because where the hell could they be going, what could be out past Stanslo's Bridge worth building tracks to get to it?—but it just kind of... slides away. He's bobbing his head as Baron Stanslo chunters on about... whatever the fuck he's talking about as he leads Bas around the giant shed that's supposed to be a train station and out into the... town, Bas supposes. At least that's what it looks like it's trying to be. Except, like the "train station," it looks like it's been thrown together with a lick and a promise.

Shacks too big to be shacks, so they must be houses, and honest-to-God *huts* with baked mud for mortar. There seems to be an attempt at a high street, dwellings lined up either side like a pseudogallery. Except everything's slapped together in a jumble of dilapidation and dust. It's like a child tried to build a city out of sticks and sap and then got bored and wandered off, leaving the half-finished creation to dry up and not entirely blow away. Tin and plank and straw and mud.

There's a small crowd coming and going from what looks like a supply house or something; most of them pause to stare at Stanslo warily and shoot Bas glances that are hostile, rather than curious as he would have expected. They don't linger, only pausing a moment before heading over to the train station, chattering quietly among themselves. One woman wonders out loud if they'd gotten coffee in this shipment; Bas almost wants to tell her, "Why, yes, I saw the sacks right next to the cider tuns when I was checking the cars for imaginary stowaways," but he doesn't think that's a terribly good idea just now.

He stays quiet and peers at everyone as closely as he dares. Now that he's found Kimolijah alive, he figures he might as well look for the da, since the chances are pretty even he's as alive as his son, and though Bas sees several men with the right skin color, none seem to be the proper age, all of them too young. And that's when Bas notes that there doesn't seem to be anyone here old enough for gray besides Stanslo.

One building is bigger than most and built more like a gazebo, with its sturdy, symmetrical structure and its wide-open porticos taking up most of each wall. It's brick, where everything else is wood or tin, and when Bas sees the forge fires inside, he figures out why. A young woman, beaproned and begloved in leather, steps out into the dirt yard to have herself a guarded look; her thick braids are stoke black, and her copper skin is just a touch sunburnt, chapped. Bas notes the compact bellows in her hand before she ducks back into the heat Bas can feel from here. Must be the smithy, Bas figures, and he can't help wondering who she is and how she got here and if there's anyone back in the real world who thinks she's dead too.

"That's the Palace," Stanslo says as he points to a long, tall stretch of a building set off from the rest of the structures that scatter over the dirt like carelessly thrown litter; it's better maintained than the rest, and much bigger. It looks like a huge hotel. Someone behind them snorts, and Stanslo grins at Bas with a mischievous twinkle in his blue eyes. "It's the bunkhouse. You'll see directly." He turns and pats Bas's shoulder. "Fox."

"Yeah, Baron."

Bas can't help the grimace. He kind of thought they lost Fox somewhere back there, and now he's sorry they haven't.

"Have someone clear out whatever Fenris left behind."

There's a pause Bas doesn't know how to interpret, and then Fox says, "Sure, boss." Definitely unhappy.

It occurs to Bas that he has yet to hear anyone besides Kimolijah answer Stanslo in any other way. It also occurs to him that it's quite possible he's just beefed a man who had friends among these "deputies," and it looks as though he's meant to sleep in the same bunkhouse with them.

Huzzah.

"Lowen will show you around," says Stanslo. He's eyeing Bas sideways with a smirk. "But this is something I'd like to show you personally."

Bas hears the offhanded smugness inside it, but it's far away. He hasn't lost that surreal distance he's been feeling since they left the station, and it's even worse now as Stanslo very purposefully steers Bas toward what would pass for the town square, if this were a real town, and the appalling scene that sits in the center of it. Bas's brain juggles the post and the ropes and the bleached white bones poking through torn fabric until it all falls into a concept that's so totally foreign to Bas it takes him a good five steps to understand what he's seeing.

And then he thinks—*it finally occurs to him*—that he's in way over his head and, like everyone else who crosses into Stanslo's Bridge, he's probably not going to leave this place alive.

It's a goddamned whipping post. And there's someone tied to it, just as desiccated and horrifying as the body that had been nailed to the relay office doors back in Harrowgate. Bas has no notion how to judge these things, but it looks the same as that other body, so he thinks maybe they died—were killed—at about the same time. The skin is dried tight around bony hands still bound together over a head that's slowly giving up its remaining hair to the elements; Bas thinks it used to be blond.

"Kimo hasn't been by yet today," Stanslo says, eyes narrowed and fingers stroking at the silver-tipped whiskers on his chin.

Fox shrugs. "We been gone since last night, boss."

"Yes, I'm aware, Fox. Thank you for your insight." Stanslo sighs, weary and long-suffering; Bas can almost hear the eyeroll. "Go fetch him before he heads up to the house and bring him by. Every day until there's nothing left to see."

"Sure, boss."

"You see, Bas," says Stanslo, a little too cheerfully, "we take our contracts very seriously here."

Bas can't even guess at what that means or why Stanslo seems to give it such significance. Because what the hell kind of good could a contract do way out here? Still, keeping quiet and as blank-faced as possible seems to have been working thus far, so Bas keeps it up.

Stanslo waves his hand at what's left of the man tied to the whipping post. "I'd like to introduce you to Travis. The reason Oleg and I thought it time to start scouting new recruits. In a way, I suppose you could say Travis here is—was—your predecessor."

Well, then. *How very subtle*, Bas doesn't say with the proper amount of sarcasm.

Stanslo smirks. "I trust you and I won't suffer from the same sorts of... disagreements over how Stanslo's Bridge ought to be run."

There's a platform right next to the post, a gibbet with a ready noose silhouetted against the pastel-soaked indigo of the blooming early-evening desert sky. Bas supposes he should really be feeling grateful no one's swinging from it. At least at the moment. He abruptly has no doubt whatsoever that it's not always the case.

Bas adjusts his hat. "Not much for driving the buggy, me."

"Splendid! You'll get on just fine here, then."

Bas merely grunts, surly, and starts walking again. He's pretty proud of himself that he doesn't even pause when Stanslo asks him, "So tell me, Bas—are you any good with a whip?"

And, okay, so Stanslo's on the *bugfuck insane* end of the crazy spectrum. Somehow, Bas doesn't think Magic Man ever had to put up with this kind of shit.

⁂

See, the thing is, Bas really should have known what he was getting into.

Actually, he kind of did. He knows all about Baron Stanslo. He's done his research.

From lower-middle-class mediocrity, Petra Stanslo bonded into money some twenty-five years back and then reaped the benefits of an extraordinarily detailed will when his bondmate died in childbirth less than a year later, taking the child with her. From what Bas was able to tell, Stanslo compounded his inheritance by buying up stretches of apparently worthless land for next to nothing and then "discovering" massive stoke deposits on them. All accusations that he'd cheated or intimidated or outright stolen from the previous owners of those stretches eventually disappeared, apparently along with every other accusation against Stanslo, ever. And a few of the people he'd allegedly cheated.

The profits Stanslo reaped from that first venture had gone into the still-infant railroad industry, gaining Stanslo controlling shares through means that were not quite clear on paper.

And though Bas would bet that anyone looking hard enough would find plenty of reasons to launch an investigation, none had ever come about. Or, if they had, they hadn't lasted past the initial *see if there's anything suspicious here* stage.

When the rush west was still a mere trickle, Stanslo moved on to buying up slim tracts of land just on the edge of the western then-frontier of the Consolidated Territories and charging exorbitant tolls to cross them. Since at the time no less than four copper mines had been discovered by the first wave of settlers, just east of what's now Harrowgate and one right after the other, Stanslo got his tolls and almost quadrupled his wealth as the hordes of would-be pioneers and prospectors flocked through. That lasted until the settlers became villagers became townspeople and petitioned to become citizens, and the government of the Consolidated Territories was only too happy to oblige and expand its borders. Stanslo was squeezed out. Or at least Bas thought so until he saw Harrowgate.

Stanslo remarried—a pretty if poor Class 5 psyTech almost too young for a bond—and turned his eye on the land between the widening Territories and the Dead Lands, a thick strip of waste poisoned by the toxic snows that cap the Saltons and leach into the lands through the spring runoff. And yet, somehow, Stanslo apparently thought it reasonable to make a home on the very hem of the poisoned skirts of wretched desert and present it as a bonding gift to his new mate.

Thing is, the Directorate doesn't appreciate it when someone tries to take a Tech out of their reach and away from their protection—especially when that Tech happens to be Class 5—so when Bella Stanslo's application to travel west with her bond-mate came through, the Directorate stalled it. Only, by the time the first agent showed up in Harrowgate to interview the new Baroness to determine if she was leaving their purview of her own free will and without coercion, Stanslo was already a widower again. Horrible thing, pox. Even worse that official quarantine demanded the body be burned long before word reached the Directorate and an inquiry could even be suggested.

Suspicions but no proof, as seemed to be the way of things with Petra Stanslo. So no one cared when Stanslo quietly disappeared into land no one wanted. Good riddance to bad rubbish, after all, and if the Directorate couldn't actually pin anything on him, they were happy to see him disappear into the desert wilderness to dry up and blow away with the drift-scrub.

Unfortunately, nothing involving Baron Petra Stanslo is quite that simple. Stanslo hasn't crossed the western borders of the Consolidated Territories since he scooped his second bondmate's ashes into a tasteful yet suitably costly urn, but that doesn't mean he isn't present. A whisper in industrial wealth circles—fingers in every pie, but Stanslo himself is an enigmatic gray-area anomaly on paper. Investments everywhere—stoke, silver mines, land, railroads—but the people he hires to run it all for him don't even know him. Most of them have never even met him.

As far as traceable records, he's a ghost. Bas wasn't able to find a single person who'd actually laid eyes on him.

And now Bas is here, right next to the man himself, and still the only thing Bas can decide for sure is that Stanslo is bugshit insane.

⬿⬿⬾⬾

The mess is not what Bas expected, though he's not surprised because nothing here is what he expected. He'd heard "mess" and figured it for something like the refectory at the academy or even the breakroom at the Directorate's head office back in Knapston. It's not. It's more like a saloon than anything else he can compare it to, though it doesn't look like the things people are drinking are anywhere near as fun. Still, the mess seems to be a distant, seedier cousin of the tavern in Harrowgate, right down to the canvas fans on the ceiling, though these are spinning with no breeze to push them, and Bas wonders if it's gridTech or if he's just so paranoid that he's seeing it everywhere.

The first thing Lowen does is direct Bas to the chow line. And then he explains how Stanslo has taken the tactics he used to cheat and steal his way into nearly monopolizing the train industry and applied them to his little desert barony.

"You get an account, y' see." Lowen motions to a man—*deputy*, Bas thinks, because the man is armed and looks like he's pissed off he hasn't been given an excuse to shoot someone. The deputy hands over a dog-eared ledger book, sepia pages torn and dark in places with spills and blodgy thumbprints. Lowen riffles the pages until he comes to a clean one, where he inks in *Barstow* in neat blocky characters. "This is your balance."

Bas's eyebrows fly up his forehead. "For a dish of swill?"

Seriously. It's gruel, only grayer, and what they're calling "bread" looks like one of his mother's rare mistakes when the stove is being particularly demonic. It's dense and flat and probably needs to soak in water for a week before it can be chewed.

"It's cheap," Lowen explains. "You want better, you pay for it."

This just keeps getting better and better.

"You began in arrears," Lowen says. "You owe for your ride into Stanslo's Bridge, see?" His long finger points to a line. "The balance will be offset when your account is credited every month. In the meantime, the baron is generous with advances." He pauses when Bas rolls his eyes, but Bas catches what he thinks might be a bit of warning in Lowen's expression, so he merely stares back. Lowen goes on, "Got a company store, if you need"—his hand waves around—"anything, whatever. They'll add anything you buy there to your main account and you'll get a balance every pay."

Sure. So every month, Bas will be able to see just how much further into debt he'll be to Stanslo and calculate how many years it'll take him to pay it off enough that Stanslo will let him back on the train to Harrowgate so he can get the hell out of Stanslo's Bridge. Not that anyone does get out of Stanslo's Bridge.

Bas looks around him at all the dirty, stoop-shouldered worker bees slurping up their gruel with blank, defeated faces, and wonders just how long some of them have been here. It fetches the picture Bas has been building in his head into clearer focus, and he thinks *Yeah, whatever*. Bas doesn't plan on being around here long enough to have to worry about getting too far down a hole. Fuck Stanslo and his credit and his apparent debtor's prison. Let him try to collect once Bas gets out of here and back to the Directorate.

The obvious dynamics are weird, though yeah, everything's weird here, but this is like a microcosm and it's easier to see. People joke and laugh and talk among themselves like every group of coworkers in every place of work that exists, and it's funny that something that's actually normal is the weird thing, but it is.

Granted, there's a very distinct segregation between deputies and not-deputies, like an invisible wall between them and a silent accord to keep it that way. But on either side of that intangible barrier, people behave like they would anywhere else. Except some are a little... sadder and more hollow-eyed than others.

There are no Techs, at least none Bas can sense, and no colors that aren't really there around him to even hint at something Latent. Not hugely surprising, since there's been a moratorium on travel out this way for Techs since the Directorate decided it was better to risk a few angry Techs than a few dead ones. Still, though, if Kimolijah Adani is alive and here and apparently building gridtrains for a slick, sleazy robber baron who calls him "dear heart," Bas has to wonder who else Stanslo has managed to slip past the Directorate's reach. He makes it a point to surreptitiously examine every woman he comes across to see if she could be Mariella Crocker.

None of them are.

He slurps up his gray stuff like everyone else, because he's fucking starving and it's right in front of him. He thinks about going back to the queue and demanding something better, just to see what he'll get and how much it'll cost, but... well, again, he's fucking starving and this is right in front of him. He'll find out the details later.

Lowen sits across from him at the table slapped together out of silvery wood that's old and dried and rough-hewn; he doesn't eat and he doesn't make conversation. Bas appreciates it—he's not in the mood for small talk—but he kind of wishes Lowen was the blustery sort, like Fox. Most of what comes out of Fox are pointless attempts at domineering browbeating, but he too obviously doesn't think before he opens his mouth, and at least with him, Bas has learned a few things. Lowen seems the sort who's powerful careful about what he means to say before he starts talking.

When Bas has finished his gray stuff, Lowen gets up from the splintery bench and says, "C'mon."

It's going dusk when they leave the mess, the desert giving up the sun's heat and the sky rioting with impossible hues, writhing against and around like a sleepy watercolor snake pit. The town has lost its ramshackle edges, dust and skewed lines smudged in brushed shadow and scattershot prisms, gloam-softened and almost pretty.

"Over there's the store." Lowen points across the square. "And over there's the bathhouse. You can buy soap there and whatnot." It's all very matter-of-fact and dry. "Over there's the...."

It goes on, Lowen pointing things out with helpful little asides, and Bas just looking where Lowen indicates. Bas doesn't comment, and he doesn't peer curiously at the stragglers who pass by as he and Lowen walk slowly toward the square.

The Palace is easy to spot, even in the dark. It's bigger than the other structures in the scruffy little "town" and more sturdily built. It's also the only building in the town's entirety that seems to have quality gridlight. Its windows' steady glow through the dark are a marked incongruity against the ruddy-bright dithering of individual lusters and lamps coming from the surrounding shacks and huts now that the dark is settling in.

Gridlight and no gridstation. And even if there were, it would take more than one gridTech to power everything here.

Dynamic crystals, Bas thinks. He doesn't know exactly how, and he doesn't know what it means, but it definitely makes him uneasy.

The body—Travis, Bas now knows—is still slumped against the whipping post as Bas and Lowen pass it, lit up with a luster hitched to the sturdy pole of the gallows. You can't miss it from any part of town, which Bas supposes is the point. It takes a lot for Bas to walk on by like he sees such things every day, but Lowen's right there, watching him almost clinically, so Bas makes himself keep going.

There's a somewhat decent house set off a bit from the square. Bas notices it because there's music curling from its direction and its door is lit up with bright gridlight. Bas can see two female figures leaning against the open doorway in poses that are obvious even in the dark, and he thinks he's just discovered the crappy desert-town version of a cathouse.

Business must be slow if they have time to stare after someone obviously not heading their way.

"What are those?" Bas asks Lowen and points out one of the squat towers he'd noticed as the train pulled in.

"Water," says Lowen, laconic, and he shrugs.

"Water." Bas stares at Lowen for a long moment, but Lowen doesn't squirm or get flustered or give up his neutral expression like Fox would. Bas looks around for wires that would connect the structures to a gridstation, something that would explain that almost subsonic purr and the blue-black grit of gridstream settling in his back teeth, but the only wires are the ones stretched between the arms of the thing and there's no station to connect them to. Not unexpected now, but it further supports Bas's theories and adds to his growing certainty, so Bas takes note. "You've got water towers but no gridstation to power the pumps."

Lowen flashes his teeth in the dark, a white scimitar smile that looks genuine. "You catch on quick," is all he says. He jerks his chin up the only rise in the geography that breaks up the monotony of desert flatlands. "I'll show you the way to the big house." Lowen pauses, then turns to Bas with a little furrow on his forehead, mouth slightly pinched and gaze thoughtful. He opens his mouth, closes it. He shakes his head and says, "Don't ever go up unless you're invited."

Bas lifts his eyebrows but says nothing as he follows Lowen's steady pace up the hard, dusty path that slopes only enough to let you know you're climbing.

"The big house" is, actually, a very big house. A two-floored wooden monstrosity with sprawling porches and whitewashed window frames edging what looks like heavy leaded glass in each one. Lace curtains flutter, caught like ghosts in the cooling evening breeze and backlit by lusters that have to be powered by gridTech; the light is too bright and steady to be anything else. The stables that sit between the edge of the yard and the feet of the fields are long and wide, big enough to host at least fifty horses, Bas thinks, and he wonders if they actually do.

It's decadence like Bas has only really seen in the wealthier parishes back home, and he doesn't have to guess who lives here. But that's not what makes Bas's eyebrows levitate and his mouth fall open.

It's the green. Green everywhere. The grass is lush, the grounds are dotted with flower beds, and there's even an actual pond. Fields stretch out from where the dark strip of the horizon butts up against the lighter pastels of the gloaming sky, but Bas can't tell through the faltering light what grows there. Still, what he *can* see is a shocking smudge of life among a barren strip of dearth.

WeatherTech, Bas immediately assesses, because there's no other explanation, and he can *taste* it, all damp and cool and muddy on the roof of his mouth, and everything's edged in copper. It's certainly conceivable to grow things out here—it's supposed to be an agro settlement, after all—but something like this would take unheard-of feats of irrigation to accomplish without Tech involved, not to mention a nearby source of renewable water flow. There is no such thing in Stanslo's Bridge.

"How is this possible?" Bas says, too soft to be a real question, because he doesn't think he'd get an answer anyway.

But Lowen pauses and looks at Bas with that same steady consideration before he shrugs and creases a stunted smile that looks almost bitter. "That's the thing, then, isn't it." He looks away, back up toward the house. "It isn't, really." He just stands there for a spell, staring, like he's forgotten Bas is even there, before he shoves his hands into his pockets and coughs. "You can find your way back by yourself, yeah? I got things to do in the barn."

4.

Most everyone seems to have shut themselves in for the night by the time Bas makes it all the way down the slope and into the town itself, though several men—Bas counts ten that he can see—amble around the loose perimeter. Sentries, Bas guesses, though they seem to be watching the sky more than anything else. They turn and watch Bas, though, as he strides down the path from the manor and toward the bunkhouse. Bas makes a point of lifting his chin and staring back, and his fingers twitch over the grip of his gun under his coat.

One of the men—the one rounding the barn by the goat pen—makes a point of changing his direction and carving a straight path to intercept Bas. The goats gripe guttural complaints when the man climbs the fence and cuts through the pen. Bas keeps walking, changing neither course nor pace, and stops only when the man steps directly into his path, one of those gridguns held in both hands down low across his hips. He stares at Bas, so Bas just stares back. And waits.

It takes longer than Bas thought it would, long enough for his eyes to adjust to the dusky evening light and make out pale, angular features and a clean-shaven jaw and stringy brown hair just to the collar under a beaten, misshapen, wide-brimmed hat. The man stares and stares, trying to intimidate, Bas has no doubt, then he leans in just a little and spits. There's no telling if the man missed Bas's boots on purpose or if he's just that bad an aim.

"So, yer the new guy, hain'a?" the man asks. "Fox gettin' a new crystal, or did yer contract go in the boss's?"

Bas decides a confused frown would not be in his best interests, though that's what his face wants to do, because what? *What?*

Everything has gone still; the other men in Bas's line of vision have stopped to watch, and they all seem to be waiting to see what Bas will do or say. So he makes a show of tipping his head down to eye the toes of his boots and the little puddle of spit just beyond the left one. Slowly, Bas looks back up at the man in front of him, blinks. Then he spits too. He doesn't miss the man's boots.

He smirks and says, "Nothing goes to you. 'S all you need to know." And he stares.

If possible, things get even more quiet. Even the goats shut up, or maybe Bas just can't hear them through the blood pounding in his ears. The man's eyes are narrowed and his jaw is working. Bas can't see if his finger is twitching at the toggle of his gun, because he doesn't think it's a good idea to take his eyes away from the man's right now. It occurs to Bas that maybe he should have skinned his own six-barrel. He's quick, yeah, but he's better at hitting his targets than he is at drawing on them, and this guy's already got a gun in his hands. Bas doesn't like his chances of drawing and firing before this man can lift that barrel and fry him, and the guy obviously has friends.

There are only a couple of seconds to worry about it, and before unease can really take hold and bloom, the man's mouth quirks with something more nervous tic than smile, and he lowers his gun 'til the barrel points at the ground. He takes a step back.

"Yeah, all right," he says and holds up a hand palm out. "Just curious." He turns his hand and holds it out to Bas. "Yanush."

Bas looks down at the hand and holds back the polite reflex to shake it. He doesn't want to move his hand too far away from his gun. He looks back up at Yanush for a long moment, carefully blank, then starts walking again, deliberately shouldering Yanush out of his way as he starts toward the bunkhouse.

"Yer bunk's first floor, third on the right," Yanush says to Bas's back, low and without the tiny bit of feeble threat in his tone that was there before. "'S nice enough. 'Cept you'll want to buy blankets, prob'ly. Store's open tomorrow."

Bas doesn't answer and he doesn't pause. He keeps walking, keeps facing straight ahead, though he watches from beneath the brim of his hat all the men he can spot. The short walk to the porch of the bunkhouse seems like it takes ten years, but Bas waits until he gets beneath the shadow of the porch's roof before he lets himself relax a touch. This time, he doesn't let his conscious mind acknowledge how close he probably just came to death.

He shakes off the prickling at the back of his neck that tells him he's got at least a dozen chary gazes leveled on him, and it's when he moves to open the bunkhouse's door that he sees the... well, it's shaped like a spider, moves like a spider, but it's *oh my god, fucking huge, what the fucking fuck*!

Bas's mind goes off into *Monsters from Planet Horror* illobook territory while he watches its foot-long jointed legs inch closer and its knitting-needle-sized mandibles crimp and quiver.

Bas doesn't hesitate to draw his gun this time—the thing is almost as big as a small dog, for fuck's sake—and he's skinned, taken a shot, and reholstered before he even thinks it through. Because *fuck* spiders.

It's just gooey guts and twitching legs splattered all over the porch now, and Bas resists the urge to give what's left of it a good kick just for scaring the shit out of him like that. He looks up and peers through the gloom at the sentries who've stopped in their rounds and turned to look at him; most of them have drawn their own guns and are pointing them Bas's way.

He means to wave and tell them no worries, just a misfire, they can all stop pointing their guns at him, thanks, but, "*Fuck* spiders, man," Bas blurts, because it's just the first thing that comes out his mouth, and he can't help muttering, "Fucking *monster* fucking spider, what the fucking *fuck*," a little louder than he'd meant to.

They all stare for a second or two until several chuckles bubble up and someone says, "Well, en't he the big damn hero," and that seems to be it. They put their guns away and start wandering the perimeter again. Like this sort of thing *happens every day*.

Oh God. Does it?

⁂

The interior of the bunkhouse is a surprise, and now Bas understands why they call it the Palace. It's clean and neat and spacious, almost luxurious in comparison to the rest of the town, though not nearly so much as Stanslo's manor house on the hill. It's not rows of shabby bunks, like Bas had expected; it's more a complex of decent-sized private sleeping quarters, each with a door with a lock and, from what he can see through a few open doors, beds set on actual frames with actual mattresses and big enough for a man to stretch out.

There doesn't seem to be any common area, just a long hallway and a set of stairs at either end, but there are seven men huddled together about ten doors down, peering over each other's shoulders and hooting quietly with animated chatter. They stop and stare when Bas shuts the door behind him. He stares back long enough for it to be considered a threatening glare before he finds the door that's third on the right and opens it. His leather pack sits on the bare mattress, which is kind of surprising—he half expected someone to just confiscate it for their own—though it's open and Bas can see some of his stuff poking out, so it's obvious they've at least gone through it.

Bas narrows his eyes and steps over to have a look. And grinds his teeth. Because this is... no. Just *no*. He's had enough shit for one day. He's not taking any more of it, goddamn it.

The anger on his face is, Bas has no doubt, glaringly obvious. Which can probably only help, so he lets it show when he pounds back out into the hall.

"I want them back," he barks at the men still gathered, apparently waiting for his reaction, so he gives it to them with all six barrels. He pulls his lips back and bares his teeth. "Right fucking *now*."

This isn't a situation over which he'd actually start shooting, but these guys don't need to know that. Though he'd thumped Mo many times over smaller transgressions than this when they were kids, and Mo has jokingly accused as much, Bas wouldn't actually *kill* over a few illobooks.

One of the men blinks and shrugs. He holds out an illobook—*Dark Horse*, year 12, series 5, issue 3—and says, "Yeah, we was just... y'know."

Bas tilts his head, because no, he doesn't know, but he knows that silence sometimes gets him more answers than questions do.

"Ye en't got blankets," says a great burly man behind the one who's just spoken. "Sheets neither."

The low rumble of the voice and the harsh tone of it make what the man just said sound menacing, but it won't mesh together in Bas's head with the strangely guileless look and the lack of sense of the actual statement.

Bas frowns. "So?"

"*So.*" The big man shuffles, then flinches when the scruffy man next to him jabs an elbow into his ribs. There's a sour grimace apparently directed at no one in particular before the big man turns back to Bas. "So we thought...." He waves a meaty hand around to encompass the small rabble surrounding him. "We thought maybe you'd wanna trade."

Bas sucks in a breath, but he can't think of anything to say, so he just lets it back out. And acknowledges the fact that he hasn't heard wrong, and he's pretty sure he hasn't misunderstood. These intimidating ruffians really did just almost-politely offer to trade him a set of bedding for a few old copies of *Dark Horse*.

Everything is so fucking *weird* here.

✧✧✧

Bas is not murdered in his sleep his first night in Stanslo's Bridge. Nor is he robbed or assaulted or accosted in any way, except for the small stream of men who show up with one or two of his illobooks in hand, looking for a trade so they can keep them.

He deals with Merrin first, the skinny guy who'd offered blankets. Bas gets those, plus one threadbare sheet that needs a good washing before Bas can sleep on it, for a *Dark Horse*—permanent trade, because Bas has a duplicate back home—and an issue of *The Indestructibles*—a two-week loan, because Bas doesn't want to seem like a pushover. The haggling with the rest of them carries on over several rounds of cards until Bas decides to turn in.

He doesn't get much sleep. There's a lot of shooting going on in the dark, both the resounding report of the street cannons and the thick *bzzzwap* of those gridguns. Bas tries to get a look at what they're shooting at through his little window, but his room is at the back of the Palace and he can't see, so he thinks *fuck it, who cares.* Maybe they're lacking for sport. It's more annoying than disturbing, and since there's no underlying feeling of alarm, Bas just grits his teeth and tries to doze through it.

It rains toward dawn, which should be shocking—'cause, you know, *desert*—but Bas smells the weatherTech, and he's seen the grounds of Stanslo's manor house, so it isn't. It hadn't rained in Harrowgate for so long that at least mild dust storms were a daily occurrence, plains winds whipping up and coating the small city in a building layer-cake of grime, sucking the color right out of every surface; there is no evidence of such here. Stanslo's Bridge is tiny and dingy and ramshackle, but it has more to do with having apparently been thrown together out of leftover scrap than dust and erosion. Any dilapidation here had started out that way.

When he gets out into the morning sun that's already baking off the chill of the night and turning the swampy puddles that were left into steam, he heads toward the queue with the others at the mess hall Lowen showed him last night. No one looks at him or talks much, so Bas kind of follows everyone else as they stumble out of their rooms, and then he follows the scent of coffee.

"Hey, new blood," Fox says from a lazy pose against the support post of one of the water towers. As Bas watches, someone angles around Fox with a narrow look and fills a bucket of what looks like clear, clean water from the dripping spigot.

"You. Barstow." When Bas merely gives Fox a bland look and keeps walking, Fox's jaw sets and his eyes narrow. "You jump when I tell you, boy."

Boy. Bas kind of wants to snort, it's so cliché, but he figures that would damp the effect of ignoring it entirely, so he doesn't.

Big Guy—Reacher, the one who swore last night he'd find something Bas wanted to trade for a *Sunrisers,* because the medTech character, Marcy, "has got tits the size of my head." Which made Bas decide from then on to always trade and never loan, because he really doesn't want to have to think about Reacher and Marcy's tits alone in a room together, and he *absolutely* doesn't want Reacher handing him back the results when he's done "borrowing"—

Reacher steps in with a grimace that's in direct opposition to the guileless look he'd been sporting last night. Bas tries not to rear back and wrinkle his nose, but seriously—someone needs to tell this guy nothing's going to help the reek, no matter how much rosewater he douses himself with, if he doesn't wash off the rancid old sweat underneath it first.

"You kinda do," Reacher tells Bas. "Hafta jump when Fox says,

I mean." He jerks his head over at Fox and gives Bas an apologetic shrug.

Still, it rankles, and when Bas alters his path toward Fox, he does it with a glare. "What?"

Fox's face goes sly and amused, and Bas can see every bully's too-predictable, small, mean intentions behind it.

"New guys eat last," Fox says with a smirk. "If they eat at all. You, you're a new guy who made free with one of *my* guys. Took my property without so much as a *by your leave*. Fenris had things to do, see, orders to follow, and now he can't. Which makes you his dogsbody, 'cause shit, see—shit still needs doing." Fox smiles, all brown crooked teeth and sour breath puffed out on a nasty little chuckle. "You shot my man," he says, brown eyes flat. "That makes you mine."

"Yours." Bas adjusts his hat to block out the glare of the sun rising fast and hot. "I was led to believe everyone here belongs to Stanslo." He lifts his eyebrows at Fox. "Even you."

The look Fox gives Bas this time reeks of throttled fury. "Oh, it's gonna be seven different kinds of fine to whup the smartass out of you." He jerks his head toward the station. "We'll start with the mule's work and see how quick that glare turns weepy. Get yer ass to the station and start loading."

Bas would protest that he's not glaring, but he figures *what the hell*. When people tell him that back home, he objects because it's not on to be glaring at people for no reason, and Bas doesn't—it's just, apparently, how his face looks when he's trying to look... any other way. But in Jakob Barstow's skin, glaring is always a good thing. It got him his illobooks back, at least.

So Bas merely stares Fox down and says, "Yeah, I'm not your Fenris. So why don't you just shin off and find yourself another pipe to piss up."

Fox's eyes turn murderous, and if Bas is not mistaken, his hand flinches toward the gun at his hip, like he's thinking of shooting Bas down right then and there. "I just gave you an order, boy. Move."

"Sorry, what was that?" When Fox only narrows his eyes more and tightens his mouth, Bas pushes, "I don't think I heard you ask nicely."

The muscles in Fox's unshaven cheek twitch and tic, and the anger in his eyes flares dark and dangerous. He steps in close, lowers his voice into smooth tones that make Bas think he's trying to sound like Stanslo. "I don't need t' ask nicely a'fore I whip a mule. *My* mule. My mules do what I tell 'em, or they get dead."

Bas lets his eyebrows drift right up into his hairline, and he snorts. He can't help it. "God, this place is so fucking weird," he mutters and shakes his head. He gives Fox a bored grin and says, "Yeah, you want to walk away now."

Apparently, Fox really doesn't. When he does draw his gun—a regular four-barrel, not one of those strange gridguns—and points it at Bas's chest, Bas keeps the smile and doesn't let his shoulders tense and tighten. It takes a lot to keep from heeling up, but Bas manages. He cuts a look to all the stragglers who've slowed their paces on their way into the mess and are watching Bas and Fox have a pissing contest at ass o'clock in the morning in the middle of the desert. They look semi-interested, but not enough to care which way it goes, so Bas makes a point of creasing a smirk at Fox.

"Untwist your smithyriddles there, *boss*." He tweaks it derisive. "You want a piece of me, you only have to tell me where and when, but I'm thinking it's not here and now."

Fox looks stunned and apoplectic both. And because Bas never knows when to quit, he pushes again, "You gonna try skinning that hammer before I heel, or you gonna back—the fuck—*off*?"

"C'mon, then, Fox." One of the guys Bas met last night—Haversham, he thinks—sets a firm hand to Fox's shoulder and pulls him back. Fox resists for a moment until Haversham says, "*Fox.* Reel it in, now. You're smarter 'n this." He dips his voice low, but Bas still hears him say, "Pretty much everyone's a better shot than you, man. Boss hired this guy for his gun, so chances are he is too. You'd best put up."

Fox is ultimately a coward, like all bullies are. Bas can see it in the quick bob of Fox's throat and the nervous shift of his glance, checking who might be watching and measuring the amount of shit he'll end up having to take if he doesn't follow through. He must deem the risk of ridicule minimal, because he lowers the gun.

Bas should wait for Fox to take a step back, blatantly concede so there's no doubt in anyone's minds, but he doesn't. He gives Haversham a nod, then he lifts his hand toward Fox like he's going to give a respectful tip of his hat; he merely splays his fingers and waggles them in a delicate wave. "Ta," he says and walks away. He refuses to think about how half expecting to get shot in the back has become a regular phenomenon in the past two days.

Breakfast no longer seems like the best notion, though Bas *is not* going another ten steps without coffee, goddamn it. And now that he thinks about what Fox said, he's kind of curious about what needs loading at the station and why. So he ducks into the mess, grabs a mug of coffee, and waits impatiently while the guy with the ledger—Cavett, Bas thinks—thumbs through the pages and marks an exorbitant price down in Bas's debit column for what's pretty shitty coffee, burnt and a little too thick. With a roll of his eyes, Bas leaves and walks slowly as he sips.

The station is across the square from the mess and almost a

full measure in the distance, and Bas takes his time crossing, angling around a ridiculous number of snakes—okay, two— winding around in the dust and the sparse scruff of growth along the path. Bas thinks about that spider last night and decides it won't hurt to keep his eyes peeled for any of its cousins. He's scanning the ground around him a little obsessively, so he doesn't see the falcon winging right at him until it's diving down not three feet away from him, skimming in and snatching up what looks like an oversized rat. Bas sees the dust-colored snake only when it snaps up and hisses as the falcon takes off with what was apparently supposed to have been the snake's breakfast.

It's a good thing Bas hadn't seen it coming, or it might have surprised him into wearing his coffee.

Someone somewhere behind Bas laughs then whistles as the falcon arrows through the sky with the twitching rodent in its talons. Bas keeps his eyes on the snake as he sidesteps it, because it's pretty big and Bas figures it's probably fairly pissed off, and he doesn't want it to mistake him for a consolation prize. Again, he resists the urge to look behind him, but he supposes if Fox were going to shoot, he would've done it before Bas got around the corner of the barn that emits enough *eau de goat* to make Bas wonder whose bright idea it was to put it so close to the mess.

Between snakes, falcons, and Fox, Bas is feeling a little more irritated than he should, so he takes long, deep breaths and tries to will it away. He sends his gaze roaming, spots at least four more of those same towers, and thinks he's at least solved the puzzle of why these people haven't died of thirst out here and why the Palace has working plumbing.

How, though, is another matter entirely. Those things aren't wells and they're not pumps. They're running on gridstream and somehow taking water out of the air and making it drinkable.

Again, impossible, but Bas has seen fifteen impossible things already today, and he hasn't even finished his coffee.

The station is a hive of activity, and Bas pauses in the yard for a few minutes to observe. He counts about fifteen men, give or take, and adds that to the fifteen or so more who were wandering around the town, and decides there must be about fifty people here in Stanslo's Bridge.

Too low, Bas thinks. From what he'd been able to dig up back at the Directorate, over two hundred people have disappeared out here. So where are the rest of them?

The engine has been moved out past the switch tracks, and is now baking quietly in the sun. There are two cars already hooked up to it, and Bas can see at least one more poking out of the far end of the station, still halfway under cover. Trolleys move back and forth, in and out of the station, crossing tracks in hash-mark patterns all over the yard like the push trolleys that putter around any other station, except these move with that same gridstream hum Bas had gotten used to on the way from Harrowgate. They're not so different from the tiny model train with which Resaniji Adani demonstrated her brother's invention.

Manned, a stick lever for power, a grip at the top for braking; the trolleys move slowly, loaded up and packed with what look like nothing more than black bricks on their way into the station, empty on their way out. It boggles Bas, this casual use of something still pretty much only taken seriously by the Tech academia and the Directorate back home. Of course, had Kimolijah not "died" before he'd proven and demonstrated his theories....

There are three deputies keeping a keen eye on things; Bas doesn't know any of them. They're all three holding those gridguns and looking somewhat menacing, which is what makes Bas take a more careful look around at the people bustling about the station. It doesn't take him long to see that none of them are heeled, which means none of them are deputies, which means... well, who the hell knows what it means? The only thing Bas is sure of is that the deputies have more power here than the others, but considering last night and Stanslo's lack of alarm at the loss of one of those deputies, Bas doesn't think that's anything to get excited about.

There's another man counting the black bricks on the trolleys as they enter the station and writing notes in a ledger book. There's no way to tell what the bricks are or what any of this is about, but Bas thinks finding out will be important.

He starts heading over to a man barking directions, because Bas figures him for the overseer or whatever they call it here. He arrests his steps when he spots a pair of booted feet sticking out of the wheel well of the locomotive. Bas watches for a moment and is shortly rewarded with the sight of a shirtless Kimolijah slithering out from around the mechanical works connecting the locomotive's two rear wheels. With a halfhearted toss of the grease brush in his hand toward a bucket off to the side, Kimolijah thumps down onto his ass on the ground, then unfolds and straightens from what must have been a fairly tight and contorted fit, because he had to have been actually *inside* the wheel well itself.

He stretches, cracks his knuckles, then peers up into the sky and, oddly, whistles a rolling little chirrup. Bas is a bit bemused for a second until he follows Kimolijah's gaze and sees that falcon again, or at least he thinks it's the same one; it's got a matching oversized rodent in its claws, anyway. The whistle Kimolijah shoves out between his teeth this time is short and sharp, and the answering one from the bird is a sonorous trill. The falcon glides down to perch atop the locomotive and allows

Kimolijah to climb up the side and stretch to stroke at the cream feathers on its sorrel-stippled chest. It whoops out what sounds like a low, mournful whistle and nuzzles at Kimolijah's hand for a second before Kimolijah pulls away to let it settle in and gut its catch. Kimolijah hops back down into the dirt so he can shake his head and sigh at the open engine hatch with the proper amount of drama.

He's covered in grease, Bas sees, which isn't really surprising, considering where he's just been. He's wearing those same absurd goggles, hair slicked back in that same tight tail, and he levels a kick at the hatch and throws a greasy rag at it. He's grumbling now—Bas can hear it from here—but he can't hear what Kimolijah's saying. He doubts it matters; it's probably some of the same colorful swearing Bas had heard from him last night.

With an irritated pinch of his mouth, Kimolijah snatches up a waterskin from on top of the engine hatch, dumps a good amount of the water over his head, then wipes at the goggles, probably only smearing the grease already splattered over the lenses. "Quinnie!" he calls. It sounds more childish and whiny than angry, so it's kind of amusing when the woman Bas recognizes as the smithy comes from whatever she's been doing at the front grill of the engine, sidles up to Kimolijah, and gives him a whack to the back of his head. After a moment or two of seemingly snarky back-and-forth, and Kimolijah ostentatiously rubbing at his head, they settle into what looks like a serious conversation, Kimolijah's hands waving everywhere and shaping things in the air.

Kimolijah is short, shorter than the woman, but he's broad for his size, Bas thinks as he watches Kimolijah's whipcord muscles flex and pull under brown skin that's slick with both water and grease. The tattoo Bas had glimpsed under Kimolijah's shirtsleeve last night in fact covers his whole arm, tendriling up and over to slide across his shoulder and down the blade in loops and whorls; the patterns are stark and black and all interconnected, but if they mean anything, it goes right by Bas. It's beautiful, though, in an alien what-the-fuck-is-that kind of way.

Since he first began looking into the enigma that is Stanslo's Bridge and the people who disappear into it, Bas has thought of Kimolijah as a boy. He's not.

He's lean and ropy, the cords of his arms strapped and pinioned to bone, popping and shifting as he makes invisible pictures in the air to go along with whatever he's saying to the woman. The strange coiled bracelet winks dully in the sun as he moves. The woman—Quinnie, apparently—at first shakes her head and argues, but Kimolijah keeps going. His gestures get wilder, his apparent counterpoint gets faster, and he even crouches down at one point to draw something in the layer of dust that skims the hardpan. The woman looks—stares, really—pausing for a long moment of thought before she nods along. She grins, something pleased and fond, and she tries to ruffle at Kimolijah's tied-back hair before she hustles off toward the town. Kimolijah watches her go for a moment before he stands and snuffs with a sweep of his boot whatever he's just drawn in the dirt.

There's no way to tell what it was about, and Bas doesn't try to guess. He thinks about just trotting over and asking Kimolijah, and his feet apparently think it's a grand notion, because they're moving before Bas even realizes it. His pace is even more determined when he catches Kimolijah looking back at him. Just *looking*. Posture stiff, at first, like he's expecting a fight, and then consciously easing, loosening, going... not alluring. Can't be alluring.

Bas doesn't find out because in his distraction—following the abrupt almighty pull of the come-hither sliding from Kimolijah and straight through Bas's chest, hooking and reeling—Bas manages to wander across the crisscross of tracks in the yard and into the path of one of the little gridtrolleys. Which garners him the unhappy attention of the man who's operating it. And then the man who appears to be in charge of loading the train's cars with whatever those black brick things are.

"Who the hell are you?" the man wants to know.

Bas looks at him and then back at Kimolijah, but in the second and a half it takes Bas's gaze to find him again, Kimolijah has already once again slithered inside the locomotive's wheel well. Bas sighs on the inside; on the outside he merely shrugs and says, "New deputy," which seems to be enough for the man. He gives Bas a demurring look and a nod, and resumes whatever he'd been doing.

Bas takes that as permission to nose around. With one last bemused glance over at Kimolijah's boots sticking out from the wheel well, and then a hand coming out to grope for the grease brush, Bas turns and starts toward what looks like the center of activity. No one looks askance as he heads to the big wooden building Bas would've called a storehouse back home, except here it's really just some tall flimsy walls and most of a roof.

When Bas gets inside, though, he figures "storehouse" will do well enough, because it's certainly being used like one.

One side of the building holds more of the bricks, stacked and divided into tens for easy counting. The other side is closed off, a feeble half wall between the spaces, but no one objects when Bas sticks his head in through the door to see a small hill of... whatever the dark powder stuff is the bricks seem to be made of. Black chunky dust, a mound of it probably two stories high, and it smells like an old fireplace gone rancid so Bas figures it for charstoke. An equally large hill of loose lime sits right next to it, powdery white everywhere, its chalky grit mixing with the awful smell of the black stuff. Bas spots crude crates with no labels to tell him what's inside them, and people over on the other side mixing vats of what appears to be a combination of everything here, cranking it all into some kind of... oh. It's a compressor, or at least it seems to take in a load of powder and spit out a solid brick, so it seems logical. It's running on steam instead of gridstream this time, but it looks just as crappy as everything else here, thrown together out of sheets of scrap and spare parts, and probably keys and spoons and toy whistles, from what Bas has seen.

Two metal rods that look like antennae jut up from the top of the compressor, and every time a black brick rolls out, metal paddles are clamped to either side of it, everyone scurries back, and a rope of blue current flares between the rods then goes out. The current dissipates, the clamps come off, and the brick goes on a stack to be loaded on a trolley.

"What is all this?" Bas asks some random guy, catching him by his dirty sleeve. "What are these brick things?"

The man gives Bas a look like he's never heard such a stupid question and snatches his sleeve out of Bas's grip. "'S water," he says and walks away.

And, okay, *that* makes no sense, and it's not like Bas is really surprised, but he's beginning to get annoyed.

He's shooed away after several minutes, though it's politely done. At least the door doesn't slam in his face. It's hot here as a rule, but inside the storehouse it's rank and dusty, and the smell of whatever they're doing, plus the sweat of the men working, mixes into a lethal cocktail that makes Bas choke. So he doesn't actually mind getting kicked out.

He finds one of the deputies who's wandering around—Merrin, Bas remembers from last night—who seems willing enough to tell Bas that they're getting a shipment ready to go to the Bruise, that the bricks somehow clean poisoned water, and the Bruise—

"—is its own special little hell," Merrin says with a jut to his chin. "I en't been out there. Don't wanna, neither."

Bas now understands the phrase *growl in frustration*. "Yeah, okay, but what *is* it? Is it a settlement or something? And how come no one in the Territories has ever heard of it before?"

How come the *Directorate* has never heard of it? Bas had scoured every single bit of information he could find on Stanslo's Bridge, and he knows there was never a single mention of anything called the Bruise. The only thing farther west than Stanslo's Bridge is the Dead Lands, and nothing can live out there.

Merrin shrugs. "Boss don't want no one t' know, I guess."

"You guess?" Bas frowns. "What does that even mean? How d'you not know?"

He gets a look from Merrin, something more intelligent than

the laid-back ne'er-do-well Merrin has thus far shown. "Well, en't you a daisy," Merrin says slowly, a slight upturn at the corner of his mouth. "Piece o' free advice for ye—when the boss wants ye t' know, the boss'll tell ye. Mayhap you should just be thankin' whatever Patron as looks after ye that you don't know, 'stead of tryin'a find out." He points to the train and gives Bas a look that's smirky and knowing all at once. "If yer lucky, ye've already had your last ride on the sparker's hell beast."

He walks away before Bas has a chance to retort. Which is fine, because Bas wouldn't know how.

5.

Kimolijah's working on the engine this time, or at least he was until Bas showed up. Now he's leaning with his back against it, arms crossed over his chest, and assessing Bas from head to toe through dirty goggles. He's shirtless. Again. Still. Not that it bothers Bas or anything.

That same bird sits atop the cabin, right above Kimolijah's head, perched on the stock of the massive cannon mounted on its turret, which is on Bas's list of Things to Find Out About. The falcon is quiet, and it's not attacking or anything, but it's staring and looks like it might be thinking about it.

"What the hell do *you* want?" Kimolijah snaps.

It's pretty caustic, considering that *look* from across the trainyard only a while ago. And Bas hasn't even opened his mouth yet for so much as a hello.

Bas lifts an eyebrow and points at the train. "Just interested is all. Never seen a train like this one." He scans the body of the cab slowly, watching Kimolijah out the corner of his eye. "How d'you power a thing like this with no gridstation?"

Kimolijah doesn't say anything, but the question makes him angry, Bas can tell, because he can see the flat shape of Kimolijah's scowl. But Kimolijah doesn't bite back. He only stares for a long moment, mouth pressed tight, before he shakes his head and straightens away from his slouch, absently twirling a wrench between his fingers.

"Don't talk to me while I'm working," is all he says. He steps away from the cab and slides beneath the engine hatch, body swallowed up by the engine and boots sticking out like it's eating him headfirst.

Bas gives the boots an irritated grimace. He shouldn't have expected any different, he supposes. And the *look* was likely just Bas seeing things where they're not. Temporarily blinded by twisty tattoos and sinewy muscles under sweat-wet brown skin, and the knowledge that it's *Kimolijah Adani*, with his brilliant theories and his genius designs and his *stupid fucking goggles*, and *for fuck's sake*, Bas growls to himself, *get a goddamned grip*.

There was no *look*. There was "dear heart" and there was a proprietary gleam behind quietly psychotic blue eyes, and the suspicion that the real Kimolijah Adani may not be anything like the one Bas saw when he read those journals. This Kimolijah Adani doesn't appear to have been wasting away in the desert, scared and alone and waiting for some random Directorate tracker to figure out he's not dead.

This Kimolijah Adani is someone Bas doesn't know. And he's going to have to, whether Kimolijah likes it or not.

Conversation, such as it is, goes like this:

"Hey, I nabbed a couple sausage rolls from the mess on my way down. Want one?"

"I don't eat meat. Hobble that lip, will you. I told you not to talk to me while I'm working."

"You don't eat meat? Who doesn't eat meat?"

"You're still talking."

"And you're being kind of a dick."

"Hey, did you know that no matter how hard you pinch the skin on your elbow, it doesn't hurt?"

"...And that has *what* to do with anything?"

"Nothing, but I figured it would distract you so you'll *stop talking to me.*"

"What the hell kind of—"

"You're trying it now, aren't you?"

"....*No.*"

And like this:

"So what's the Bruise? And what are all those black bricks they're loading the cars with?"

"Are you in the cab?"

"Oh. Um. No?"

"You are. Get out of there before you break something."

"No. The sun's baking my skin right off and it's cooler in here. And plus that bird came back, and it keeps kicking rodent guts at me."

"She doesn't like you. Now get out of the cab."

"It's hot out there!"

"This train is a complicated and dangerous piece of equipment, not your personal parasol, now get out of there."

"Yeah, no, that's not happening."

"One touch and I can light you up where you sit like a Patron's Day bonfire."

"Go ahead. Though I'm sitting in what I'm pretty sure is your pilot's seat, and I doubt you'd ever get the stains out. Or the smell."

"*Goddamn* it. Just... don't touch anything and *stop talking.*"

"Yeah, sure, whatever. What's this red button?"

"Oh my god."

And like this:

"Why does Fox hate you?"
"...."
"Hey, I'm talking to you."
"And after I've repeatedly told you not to."
"Why does Fox hate you?"
"Because he's a hardcase who hates everyone but himself."
"Stanslo doesn't seem the sort to put up with a knob like that."
"*Fuck* Stans—ow, son of a *bitch*."
"Did you just zap yourself?"
"Will you just.... You know, just fuck you and whatever—goddamn it, *why are you still talking to me?*"

Bas finally gets a real reaction with this:

"God, how do people live out here? It's so fucking boring."
"Imagine how I feel. I have to listen to you."
Bas grimaces and paces a few steps back and forth in the dust along the tracks. Thankfully, the bird took off again about an hour ago, so Bas isn't getting bits of rodent intestine chucked at his head every time he takes his eyes off it. He amuses himself for a full two minutes by trying to put his boots precisely in the prints he left last time around, but it's not actually amusing at all, so he puffs a long breath.

"Should've brought something to read," he mutters to himself.

There's a pause in the small metallic noises coming from the engine before Kimolijah ventures, "You read?"

Bas shoots an annoyed look at Kimolijah's boots, but predictably it doesn't make him feel any better. "Yes, I *read*. I'll have you know I read quite a lot."

"Yeah?" For the first time, Kimolijah actually sounds interested. "Did you bring any books with you?"

"Some." Bas leans against the side of the locomotive, just beside where Kimolijah's boots twitch a couple times as he adjusts his position. "I traded a few for blankets."

"You traded books. For blankets." There's the sound of a ratchet cranking, and Kimolijah asks, "With who?"

"Reacher," Bas answers. "And that... whatshisname—Merrin. Got sheets from him. Or no, maybe it was the other way around. Whatever." Bas's mouth twists.

"*Merrin?*" Kimolijah snorts. "Like he even knows what to do with a book."

"There's pictures. Anyway, he seems an all right sort." For a guy who's probably a convicted felon and only out here because he'd be locked in a detention cell for the rest of his life if he ever stepped foot back in the Territories. But whatever.

"Depends on your circumstance, I expect," Kimolijah mutters, then says, "Reacher really traded you sheets? For a *book*?"

"Or a blanket. Can't remember now who traded what." Bas shrugs, even though Kimolijah can't see him. "It was only an *Expendables* and a *Wolves of the Low Country*. Well, and a *Dark Horse*, but that doesn't really count." *Dark Horse* is one of those illobooks everyone reads but pretends they don't. "He wanted a *Sunrisers*, but he doesn't have anything to trade just now."

The busy metal noises stop altogether. Half a moment later, Kimolijah's feet are kicking and he's slithering out of the engine. He doesn't fall on his ass this time, though; he does some kind of weird back-bendy contortion and flails his arms for a second, and then he's right in Bas's face. Or, well, as much in Bas's face as he can get when he only comes up to Bas's collarbones.

"Illobooks?"

Bas lifts his eyebrows and rears back a little. "Ye-e-a-ah?"

"You had an *Expendables* and a *Wolves of the Low Country* and you *traded them away* for sheets and blankets from two people who probably can't even parse complex sentences?"

Bas frowns. "It's not like I don't have more."

Kimolijah stares. And *stares*. He wavers for a moment, hops up into the cab, throws a few switches, cranks a few dials, then he plugs a cable into the shunt in his arm. "Stand back," he tells Bas, and when Bas does, Kimolijah throws a lever on the front panel of the locomotive. The engine sparks and sputters, blue current sliding over its skin to whiffle between the pronged poles atop the cab and over the weird lattice fencing.

And just *wow*. Bas has known since he laid eyes on this thing what it was running on. But still—to *see* it happening, to *watch* what was unfinished theory jotted down in diaries and sketch notes come buzzing into reality....

Bas can't look away.

Kimolijah lets the engine hum just long enough for it to catch its rhythm before he shuts everything down, unplugs, jumps back out of the cab and snags his shirt. He's still pulling it on when he takes hold of Bas's arm.

"C'mon, it's time for your dinner break."

Bas looks back at the train, then up at the sun. "It's really not." Midday is probably at least an hour away.

"Close enough."

"But I thought you had to fix—?"

"Quinnie made me a part and I fixed it already, there's nothing wrong with it, I was just trying to get you to leave me alone. Now come *on*."

"Oh," Bas says as he lets himself be pulled. He grimaces, thinking of all that time he'd spent roasting in the sun and trying to be friendly by making conversation with Kimolijah's boots. "Nice," he mutters out the side of his mouth. "You really are kind of a dick, aren't you?"

"Oh my god, you really do have *Magic Man!*"

"I said I did."

"Well, yeah, but I thought maybe—" Kimolijah cuts himself off and holds the illobook—*Magic Man*, year 11, series 3, issue 4—to his chest like he's cradling an infant.

They're in Bas's room. Bas is a little surprised every time he leaves for any length of time and gets back to find all of the illobooks accounted for in their evenly stacked and spaced places under the mattress. He always kind of expects the others to go through and pilfer while he's gone, but so far no one has.

"You thought what?" Bas asks, frowning.

Kimolijah only shakes his head and says, "Nothing, doesn't matter," as he stares down at the selection of illobooks like he's starving and they're a sumptuous meal.

He has yet to do up his shirt. Bas has no notion why it bothers him so much. He can see the whorls and twists of the tattoo that flows down from Kimolijah's shoulder under the shirt, black ink over brown collarbone, breastbone, pectoral, and Bas tries not to stare.

As much as Kimolijah got Bas down here on the pretense of dinner, they haven't actually had it. There'd been a few people idling in and out of the mess, so Bas thinks they can if they want to—it's not really that early—but he made the mistake of saying *Magic Man* to Kimolijah, and Kimolijah nearly yanked Bas's arm out of its socket in his rush to get to it.

"God, I haven't seen an illobook in *forever*," Kimolijah breathes. He strokes the pages as he flips through them, reverent.

"You can borrow any of them you like," Bas tells him, directly contradicting the vow he'd made to himself about borrowing versus trading. But in Kimolijah's case, Bas is hoping for some kind of in, some kind of connection that will make Kimolijah trust him so Bas can find out if Mariella Crocker's here too, and then... well. Decide what to do from there, Bas supposes.

However it works out, this conversation about illobooks is the longest and most animated Bas has had with Kimolijah yet, so he figures maybe he's on the right track. And there's just something wrong with the fact that an obvious *Magic Man* enthusiast hasn't, for whatever strange reason, had a *Magic Man* illobook in his hands in "forever."

"Borrow." Kimolijah's eyebrows crimp. "What? Why?"

The goggles are shoved up and on top of his head this time, instead of covering most of his face. They've left a rather comical outline on his filthy cheeks and forehead, and he's sweaty and greasy and his hair's coming out of the tight tail and fluttering around his head like octopus arms, but he looks.... Bas isn't sure. His light brown eyes look almost gold against his dark skin.

"What do you mean, *why*?" Bas asks. "Why not? I mean, as long as I get them back and you don't ruin them."

"No, I wouldn't." Kimolijah shakes his head and looks down at the book again, paging through slowly and running light fingers over the lines of the drawings. "I don't think you understand." He looks around Bas's room and then back at Bas. He holds out the *Magic Man* illobook and sweeps it out to indicate the rest of them. The tails of his still-open shirt sway in the breeze he stirs. "This is your currency here. Get it? We don't have dosh. We have credit at the store from what would be our pay in the real world, but you'll always owe Stanslo more than you—*ah!*" Kimolijah almost drops the book when an errant spark of current zaps out of the coiled bracelet around his forearm and travels all the way from fingertips to shoulder. "*Fuck*," he breathes and shakes out his hand.

Bas frowns. "I've never seen that happen before with gridTech." Bas reaches out to touch the bracelet, but Kimolijah flinches away and slides his arm behind his back. His teeth are clenched. "What kind of metal is it?" Bas asks. "It shouldn't be reacting to your Tech like that. Your *Tech* shouldn't be reacting to your Tech like that."

"It's not *my* T—*ow*! Mother*fucker*!" Kimolijah snarls as it does it again. He looks angry when he sucks in a long noisy breath, but he shakes it off and looks back at Bas. "You can't just give things away like this. You can't let people borrow." He waves the illobook again. "This is *all you have* here. Didn't Reacher tell you anything?"

Bas almost snorts—it's an absurdly unsubtle change of subject—but thinks better and decides it might be wise to let it go. For now.

"I'll be more circumspect," Bas says slowly, watching with narrowed eyes as Kimolijah nods and his shoulders relax a touch. "But," Bas continues, "I have nothing yet I'm aware of needing, so...." He shrugs. "Take it for now. Maybe I'll think of something I need later. You can owe me."

That makes Kimolijah look suspicious, but he's still clutching the *Magic Man*. He obviously wants it, so Bas pulls out a small stack—year 17, series 4, issues 1 through 5—and holds them out.

"Here, take these," he tells Kimolijah. "The arc's one of my favorites." It's really not. But it might be a way to send a message and maintain deniability at the same time, and if it works, it really will be Bas's favorite. "The one with—"

"Siren," Kimolijah says. Breathes it, actually. Admiring.

The plot is a little contrived, Bas remembers. And Magic Man is a bit of a dumbshit in it for a while, though Bas had been a spotty teen when he'd first read it, so he hadn't thought so at the time. Siren seduces Magic Man, then casts a spell over him so he can't use his magic. She holds him prisoner through four entire books, trying to drain his magic so she can use it for herself. It had been a great read at the time, but not really memorable enough to be one of Bas's favorites. So he can't pretend he doesn't know why he's offering these particular books or why he's watching Kimolijah so closely right now.

"Take them," Bas says.

Kimolijah hesitates, but not for long. He takes the books and... wow.

Breathe, Bas.

He hasn't really seen Kimolijah smile before.

His mouth is wide, so his smile is too. His eyes are big—*too* big, Bas tells himself. Almost freakishly big. Yeah. Freakish. And his nose is... okay, it's straight as a blade but... long! Yeah, a little too long, and his two bottom front teeth are chipped and crooked. His eyebrows are like sleek black wings, and shaped too... well, Bas doesn't know, but too *something*, too... perfect. No, that's not the word, they're not too perfect, they're too... okay, whatever. Not perfect, is the point.

His cheekbones are sharp as axe blades. Which is *not* a good thing, no matter what Bas's abruptly thumping chest might think. His neck is too long. He's too short. He bites his nails. His hair is stringy with dirt and grease, he needs a shave, and he smells like sweat. He probably snores and horks great gobbing loogies wherever he feels like it, and he has yet to close his shirt, and *oh my god, Bas, stop staring at his nipples*!

Bas jolts and clears his throat to cover it.

And. Crap.

Through all the dirt and grease and weird clean patches all over his face, Bas thinks Kimolijah's smile is.... God. Forget the gridTech—Kimolijah's bloody *smile* could power whole cities.

Ah, Bas thinks at God and the Patrons and the entire fucking universe, *so this is how you plan to kill me.*

Because the Kimolijah at whom Bas has been nattering all morning is not the Kimolijah he'd come to know on paper. This is someone else, someone not as nice, someone not as admirable. Someone who's snarky and reticent and probably sleeping with his criminal boss—because *dear heart*, for fuck's sake—and maybe even faked his own death, and a charming little smile *does not change that*.

"I remember this one." Kimolijah's smile wobbles, and if Bas is not very much mistaken, those light brown eyes go misty. "I used to...." Kimolijah sucks in a breath that sounds too shaky for someone only perusing an illobook. "I had the whole series."

"The fourth, you mean?"

"Yeah." Kimolijah nods and shuts his eyes.

Bas narrows his.

Because something's off here. Well, everything's off here, but something's *way* off with Kimolijah in particular. Bas just doesn't know exactly what it is or what to do about it. And hopefully Bas is not thinking that because he's just been absurdly dazzled by something so simple as a crooked-toothed, wide-mouthed smile.

Bas hesitates for a second before he asks, "What happened to them?"

It's not a hard punch—Bas can tell just from the sound of it—so he's not worried about broken fingers or crushed knuckles. He *is* worried about that runaway gridTech, though. But what Kimolijah started to say is a heap more relevant to what Bas is trying to get at here, so he asks, "What about your da?"

"My...." Kimolijah's shaking his head, but he's still turned away and Bas can't see his face. His shoulders are a wide, tense line, though, stiff as a plank. "I don't... I mean, I'm not sure. He—" Bas sees the gridstream flitter up Kimolijah's arm again, and though Kimolijah doesn't yelp this time, he does jolt and hiss.

"What the hell is that?" Bas asks, and he takes a step closer, but Kimolijah spins around and backs away. "What's going on with that thing?" Bas presses. "GridTech doesn't do that. It's not supposed to—"

"It's fine," Kimolijah says. "I just talk too much sometimes. It's nothing, don't worry about it."

"Why would talking have anything to do with—?"

"For fuck's sake," Kimolijah snaps, "I *am* gridTech, I know what gridTech is supposed to do, and it's *fine*."

"Yeah, fine, whatever you say." Bas holds up his hands and backs off. "Sorry, I won't mention it again." It's kind of sarcastic, because the frustration is bubbling.

Instead of sniping back at Bas's accidental scorn, Kimolijah slumps a little and sighs out a long breath. "No, I'm sorry. I didn't mean to... just...."

He waves his hand around, looking uncomfortable, a glimpse of that shyness people had told Bas about but Bas hasn't seen until now, so Bas just shrugs and says, "Yeah, whatever," and Kimolijah puffs a lame little snort, and that's that. Until Bas leans in close, lowers his voice, and says, "But gridTech shouldn't be hurting you like that, even if you *are* kind of a dick," just to have the last word, and he smirks to show he's only kind-of-not-really joking.

"Wow." Kimolijah widens his eyes. "You've got quite an obsession with dicks going on there. You should maybe see someone about that."

It's a joke. Right? Bas is pretty sure it's a joke. "Thank you for your concern?"

Kimolijah nods agreeably. "It's deep. Like my angst. And my love for candied pears." He shrugs at Bas's raised eyebrow. "Hey, I've got a lot of feelings."

They stare for a moment, Kimolijah all wide-eyed and innocent and Bas trying to manage a narrow glare but not quite getting there. And then Kimolijah quietly cracks up, a low, rolling chuckle that does something inadvisable in Bas's chest.

I am not in love with you, Bas thinks, staring, and knowing full well he's staring while his libido looks pointedly away and whistles innocently. *I'm not, I'm really not*, because if it would have been stupid before, it would be cataclysmically ludicrous now, and he's *not*, but…. *God.*

Kimolijah really is lovely, even with all the things about him that kind of aren't but really are, odd bits that shouldn't fit collectively but do and come together in a whole that's so totally just… *lovely.* Each incongruous detail of him blends with an odd, harmonious charm that hits Bas right behind the ribs. And with all the rich brown skin swirled with black ink and pretty much staring him in the face, Bas can't help wondering what it would look like drenched in soft white sheets and stippled with fingerprint bruises.

Goddamn it.

Bas is still staring when Kimolijah's chuckles taper off, and he's still looking at Bas, eyebrows pulled just slightly together, and he says, "Wow, your eyes are *really* blue." He blinks, like he hadn't meant to say it, and clears his throat. "I mean…." He waves his hand around. "You don't look like a typical gunslinger."

Gunslinger. Bas really hates that epithet. The people who fancy themselves as such generally tend to take far too much pride in it.

Bas only lifts his eyebrows. "Yeah? What does a typical gunslinger look like?"

"Fox," Kimolijah answers immediately. "And… just… not like you, you're not as…."

"Ugly?" Bas finishes with a smirk.

"Y—no," Kimolijah blurts before he snaps his mouth shut and looks away. *Shy.* "No, I mean… no, you just don't…." He fidgets and waves again, this time up and down Bas's frame. "Well, you're all sunburn on pasty skin, for one," he says, trying to take *flustered* and turn it into *cynical*, like he thinks Bas can't tell. He won't look at Bas.

It's all just a little bit hilarious.

It's true, though. Bas can't deny it. He's peeled so much since he got to Harrowgate that he's surprised he has any skin left at all. Bas and Mo have the same dark hair, same blue eyes, same basic build and features, but somehow Mo is the one who got the looks and the skin tone that doesn't make him look like he's just gotten up from a weeks-long ague. And the Tech. Can't forget the Tech. Bas likes to say he got the brains, at least.

Before Bas can come up with some kind of innocuous response, a door shuts down the hallway of the mostly deserted bunkhouse and Kimolijah jerks his whole body like he's just been shot. "Shit. Sorry," he says and backs away toward Bas's door. "I shouldn't be here."

Bas frowns and tilts his head. "Why? We're not doing anything wrong. It's only a few—"

"Yeah, I know, but I shouldn't… I mean, I *can't*…." He waves the small pile of illobooks at Bas then sets it back down with the others. "I forgot who you are for a minute, there." He shakes his head and opens the door. "I can't take those."

He doesn't wait for Bas to ask him why, which Bas very much intends to do. But it doesn't matter, because Kimolijah pokes his head out the door, has a look to both sides, and then rabbits.

Bas stands there and stares at the door for a spell, thinking, *Yeah, right, good, that was the smart thing to do*, because he's pretty sure he just had *A Moment* back there. And if he's correctly reading all the things he's seen since he got here, Bas just had *A Moment* with someone who's fucking the very dangerously crazy boss, and the dangerously crazy boss doesn't seem like the sharing sort. So yeah, smart, walk away, *down boy, that one's not for you*, and it'll just end in deeper shit Bas doesn't feel like putting himself through anyway, but what the fuck with the illobooks and what the fuck with having *A Moment* in the first place, and why does everything have to be so fucking *weird* here, it was only a smile and there's no reason for—

"Goddamn it," Bas growls and trades the illobooks in his hand for the ones Kimolijah left behind. Then he stalks out after him.

❦

Bas catches up to Kimolijah outside the chapel and steers him toward the mess for the dinner break they supposedly came down here for, but he gets even less conversation out of Kimolijah than he had when Kimolijah had been working and telling Bas to shut up every other sentence. He won't take the illobooks, either, so Bas sticks them in the waistband of his trousers under his coat and hopes he doesn't ruin them by sweating all over them.

"What was that all about?" Bas asks. "What does that mean, you forgot who I am?" Though he knows, he knows exactly what Kimolijah meant by it, and whatever that scant moment of potential connection was back there, it's gone now.

Kimolijah doesn't look at him, only clenches his jaw and lowers his voice. "Did the baron tell you to be nice to me?"

Bas has no response for a good thirty seconds, and then his eyebrows shoot up. "Why would he have to?"

"*Obviously* to get me to...." Kimolijah rolls his eyes. "Look, this'll go a lot faster if you just ask me about whatever he told you to get out of me."

And if *that* isn't ripe for analysis. "What would he need me to 'get out of you'? And why wouldn't he ask you himself?"

"I wasn't fucking Travis, all right?" It's low and vehement. "And if Travis sent something somewhere, I have no idea what it was and I had nothing to do with it. So why don't you just shin off back to the baron and tell him... whatever you have to tell him to get him to *leave me the fuck alone* about it, and *you* stay away from me."

Okay. And... *wow.*

So now Bas knows how Resaniji ended up with that cryptic message, the one that said simply *Sparks are flying in Stanslo's Bridge*, which had given Bas the break he needed to eventually lead him to push Oleg for a recommendation to Stanslo only a few months back. And he knows why Travis is nothing but a bleached bag of bones slowly rotting against a whipping post. It's... not exactly encouraging.

Kimolijah starts to move away, but Bas grabs his arm and doesn't let him. Bas's hand lands right on the coiled bracelet, and the lethal look Kimolijah gives him for it should have dropped Bas from thirty paces, but Bas doesn't let go.

"He didn't tell me to ask you *anything.* And he didn't tell me to be nice to you." Bas's teeth are clenched, which is really not the kind of thing he wants to be projecting right now, so he deliberately relaxes his jaw. "I was making conversation. I was trying to get to *know* the people I'm meant to be working with. And if I was being *nice,* maybe it's because I'm a nice guy."

Kimolijah snorts, obvious disbelief. "Yeah." He rakes Bas over with a glance, with a clear pause on the gun at Bas's hip and a lift of his eyebrow. "Guys like you are notorious for being *nice,* yeah?"

Bas sets his teeth, pissed off and unable to do anything about it, because he can't exactly say he's not really Jakob Barstow, can he. So he only takes the illobooks out of his coat, shoves them into Kimolijah's chest, and walks away.

He didn't really want dinner anyway.

6.

It's an entirely different world here than anything Bas has imagined. Before he'd actually traveled out into the desert, he'd heard "hot and dusty" and thought *I can take the heat, and dust? Feh*. He'd had no idea. He should be stewing in sweat underneath the heavy supple leather of his long duster, but he isn't. It's as if the sun's blinding heat fries the sweat off his skin before it gets a chance to leak out his pores. His skin is tight and too pink, even underneath layers of linen and leather; he feels like a cornhusk left on a fire pit a little too long. The dust is already permanently lodged in his nostrils and coating his throat, and he totally gets why he sees so many people pausing along the gallery's walkways to lean over and spit.

"You'll be on tower duty tonight," Lowen tells Bas as he leads the way into the armory, one of the few sturdy buildings in the whole of the town, well-guarded and sporting shiny, durable locks. "Tower Seven."

Bas has no notion what tower duty might entail, but he mentally kisses good-bye the sleep he'd been anticipating.

"Don't look so sour." Lowen grins and gives Bas a friendly thump on the arm. "Not much to it. Just shoot anything that comes too close to the cabling up top." He opens the armory door with a jangle of keys and waves Bas inside.

When Bas's eyes adjust to the dim of the place, he slides out a low whistle between his teeth. "Wow, that's...." Bas tips his hat up high on his brow for an unobstructed view. "That's a lot of guns." Not just guns—gridguns. Rows of them, glossy and new and lined up in neat rows like smart little soldiers. Bas thinks this likely explains the enormous glassworks that had seemed so out of place back in Harrowgate. He makes a serious effort not to show his unease or the little bit of a thrill that gurgles in his gut. The prospect of holding one of these things for real— *shooting one*—is pretty bracing.

Lowen doesn't answer Bas, just saunters over to one of the racks and pulls down a gun seemingly at random. He's smirking a little when he holds it out to Bas, like he knows what Bas is thinking. "Test the grip," is all he says.

Bas takes the gun and fits the stock into his palm.

"I'm thinking you got a bit of a jostle out of the one last night, yeah?" When Bas nods agreement, Lowen shifts a careless shrug. "That's 'cause you grabbed it by the barrel. Stick to the stock and grip and you won't have that problem. The insulation and double glaze stops just where the handgrip ends, see?"

Again Bas nods, and he studies the gun.

There's no finger bracket around a trigger like there'd be on a normal gun, just a tapered stock with a toggle jutting at an angle just in front of the grip, so he doesn't slide and spin it to his preferred stance to get a feel for its weight and balance; he remembers from his last experience with one of these things that the toggles are touchy. Instead he palms the smooth ceramic, sets his grip, and pulls the stock up to his shoulder.

"Watch the toggle," Lowen says and grins when Bas gives him a side-eyed look of impatience. Lowen holds up his hands. "It's ticklish, is all I'm saying. And no safety." He pauses and smirks. "I'm thinking Fenris is really damn sorry the sparker didn't bother with such cautions."

Bas narrows a squint down between the two small prongs that serve as sights. "Sparker." He tilts his head and aims at nothing in particular. "That gridTech from the station?"

"Only one we got."

"He built all these?" Bas lifts his gaze and points it at Lowen, face carefully blank.

"Built the first few, yeah. And he still has to do all the wiring and charge 'em up. The rest...." Lowen waves his hand around the armory. Bas gets the feeling Lowen is watching him very carefully, though the smile's still there and the manner is quite relaxed and amiable. "The rest, well, sparker's got more important things to be building, doesn't he."

It's not a question. Some sort of test, a prod, but Bas doesn't know what kind yet, so he merely shrugs and lowers the gun. "Wouldn't know," he says, calm and easy, and he props the gun to his hip. He doesn't mention Harrowgate and his suspicions, only gives Lowen a considering look. "How come Stanslo's not selling these things out in the real world?" He shifts his glance around at all the racks. Not enough to arm any kind of offensive force against, say, the whole of the Territories—not yet—but enough to do some damage, and the dosh to be made just from the designs is beyond what Bas can figure. He looks back at Lowen. "And how are they even possible without a gridTech wired into them?"

He's kind of expecting Lowen to shut down, maybe tell him he shouldn't be asking questions if he knows what's good for him. He doesn't. He grins, wide and cheerful, and tosses a ring of keys up and down in his palm.

"Probably best you don't try guessing at what's in the boss's head, yeah? It's almost never what you think it is, and guessing wrong can be... bad for your health." Lowen pauses and his grin stretches. "Same goes for Kimo, really, but that's mostly because his brain's the size of a planet and you're likely to get lost in there."

He claps Bas on the shoulder and starts leading him out of the armory. Bas doesn't miss the fact that Lowen neglected to answer his questions.

∂₂∂₂∂

It's not quite as shabby and ramshackle here as it first appears. Yeah, everything's coated in dust and baked to a crusty grime, but there's obvious dosh spent underneath it all, if you really look. The clothes these people wear are good leathers and durable textiles. Aside from that gray stuff, the meals they're offered involve actual meat and veg, though of course that's extra, and it's heavily implied a man can eat even better at the whorehouse Bas had spotted last night, though Bas makes it a point to ignore any innuendo lying in wait beneath that inference.

The equipment they're given is new and apparently maintained regularly by that smithy, Quinnie, and "the sparker," and anyone else who's got a needed skill. The deputies' quarters, as Bas has seen himself, are well-built and well-lit and somehow manage to stay cooler than the desert.

The other lodgings, though they appear no more than shacks and shanties, are built from quality materials and are strong enough and sturdy enough to provide actual shelter from the harsh elements; the insides, from what Bas has glimpsed on his way by the occasional open door or unshuttered window, are a lot more amenable than the outsides. Kimolijah and Fox make regular runs into Harrowgate for fresh supplies, and though your place in line to claim your share of them is apparently determined by your value to Stanslo, everyone gets what Stanslo says they've earned. And if they haven't earned enough, well—Stanslo's very "generous" with credit.

Bas doesn't even want to guess just how deep in debt some of these people are.

Nothing's pretty, but it's also not quite as bad as Bas had first thought. Life in Stanslo's Bridge apparently doesn't suck quite as much as it appears.

Unless, Bas thinks with a grimace, you happen to be put on tower duty for the night.

"Bat problem," he says to Lowen, mouth flat and face no doubt set in skeptical lines, because Bas has a serious problem believing there are enough bats way out here to constitute a problem. Where the hell would they live during the day? What the hell would they eat?

Lowen smirks and points up at the sporadic blue gridstream that fizzes across the wires at the top of the tower. "They like the light."

And okay, that's just plain bullshit. "Bats like light." Bas gives

Lowen a look he has no doubt says clearly that Lowen's either lying or an idiot. "*Bats* like *light*."

"They're powerful unusual bats," Lowen says and snorts a little when Bas rolls his eyes.

It's gone dark enough that someone's powered up the big light that floods the square and the dried up husk that used to be a man called Travis. Bas has spent most of day's end with Lowen, being shown around and familiarized with the rhythm of Stanslo's Bridge, learning—mostly through the things Lowen pointedly *didn't* say—how things work here and what's expected of the deputies. He quite liked discovering that everyone here pretty much sleeps through the worst of the afternoon's heat, but he's added the mystery of how the Palace manages to stay so cool to the growing list of things he'd like to know. He's regretting a little bit now, though, that he indulged in real food at suppertime, because he's still tired and a full belly's made him a bit slow and cranky.

"Look," says Lowen, still smirking but a bit conciliatory now, "I don't exactly know what they are, but they look kind of like bats, so that's what we call them."

"And they go after the gridstream."

"Everything that leaks from the Bruise goes after gridstream." Lowen shrugs. "And we can't have these things mucking up the wiring. Tried shutting down the towers at night, but then we had to ration water, and...." A sigh. "Well. A lot of us didn't make it."

Bas narrows his eyes. There's plenty in there to nip at his curiosity, but only one that seems relevant now: "What does that mean, 'leaks from the Bruise'? What's the Bruise?"

Lowen pauses, looking at Bas calmly, like always, and there's that assessment behind his dark eyes that's become very familiar, but there's something else, too, something... pleased, maybe. He didn't mention the Bruise by accident. And he'd wanted Bas to catch it.

"The Bruise," Lowen says slowly, "is why we're all here. It's why Stanslo's Bridge is here. It's why Baron Stanslo has gathered people of certain skills and why some of those people are more... necessary than others."

"Which tells me exactly shit," Bas snaps. "What's with all the secrecy? Every time someone brings this 'Bruise' thing up and I ask about it, they shut me down. Who the hell am I going to tell? I mean, I get that it's probably something Stanslo doesn't want the world to know about yet, else he'd be selling these guns and tripling his fortune, but it's not like I'm going to be on the next train home unless he wants me to be, is it. And as far as I can tell, I won't be relaying a scry into civilization either."

Lowen just keeps smiling, but it's not halfway crazed like Stanslo's smiles are. Lowen exudes mild satisfaction somehow, something close to approval.

"Yeah, okay, you got me," Lowen says and holds up his hands. He narrows his eyes a little, a twinkle at the corner of his sharp gaze. "Part of my job here is making sure the new guys are worth the expense of getting them here. But you're not half as dim as the rest of the dross Oleg sends us, are you?"

Bas stares for a long moment, getting more and more annoyed. "Considering what I've seen of 'the rest of the dross' so far, I'm not sure that's half the compliment you're trying to make it."

Lowen laughs this time, from deep inside his wide barrel chest, and nods like it's exactly what he wanted to hear. "Yeah, you're getting there, Bas. You just keep on and do your job, and I'm thinking you'll get everything you want out of this place."

Sure, if by *what you want* he means *find out why the most anticipated gridTech genius in decades is out here building trains and guns for a criminal and then get said genius and himself out of here before anyone twigs about who Bas really is, and also maybe find out if that missing weatherTech is wandering around out here, too, while he's at it*, but since Lowen obviously doesn't mean anything of the sort, Bas says nothing.

"For now," Lowen goes on, "keep the damned bats out of the stream, will you?" And he walks away, still chuckling.

❦

Bas does not admit to himself that he's having a blast—quite literally. And he doesn't admit that he fucking *loves* this gun. He does admit, though, that he's no longer really missing the night of sleep he's not getting and that yeah, okay, these things do kind of look like bats. Same webbed wings, same furry bodies and snubbed noses, but that's where the similarities end.

For one, they're a hell of a lot bigger than any bat Bas has ever seen, and for another, they look like they'd happily pluck your eyes out with their clawed little hands. Something about the way their eyes have a dull luminescence to them, nothing like the flat coinlike refractions you'd see in a normal bat's eyes. *They're sinister bastards*, Bas thinks as he takes aim at another diving in toward his tower and picks it off before it manages to make a snatch at the stream. The pulse from his gun attracts several others, and he has his hands full for a bit with getting them before they can get anywhere near him. They're not huge, but they're sizable enough, and they look like they can do some serious damage, and though he hasn't gotten a good up-close look at their faces yet, Bas is willing to bet blood they've got some damned sharp teeth.

If these are the bats that "leak from the Bruise," as Lowen put it, Bas doesn't want to know what anything bigger might look like. He isn't even a little bit embarrassed that he's been keeping a running count. He's gotten almost three dozen of the little fuckers so far, and the night's not over.

It's actually kind of fun.

It's not like the sky is blackened with them—there aren't *that* many, really—but there's a steady stream, and Lowen was right: they go right after the soft blue glow of the wires on the towers. Which, Bas assumes, would fuck up the water, so he can understand why this is a necessary nightly activity.

When dawn starts knocking itself against the night, it rains, the copper-earth sense of weatherTech reminding Bas that Kimolijah Adani's not the only Tech Bas has been looking for, and he has yet to run into whoever it is that's tempering this little spot of desert into something livable. It can't be coincidence, it's got to be Mariella Crocker, and Bas wonders if she's here just as willingly as Kimolijah seems to be and if Bas has wasted three years tracking down people who don't want to be found.

It's possible, he supposes. It doesn't make sense, doesn't fit with the Kimolijah Bas had come to know on paper, but it's possible. And yes, Bas can admit he's probably idealized Kimolijah in his head somewhat—unfathomable genius laid out in intricate equations; wild notions that actually *worked* jotted in hurried penmanship, as though his hand couldn't keep up with his brain; random thoughts scribbled in margins, a bit more prosy and poetic than Bas would have expected from someone so ostensibly practical. Journals and diaries and experiment notes packed full of a personality Bas had too often wished he'd gotten to meet, just once, just so he could watch the outside while the inside ticked and revved. Idealized, okay, just a bit, but still—strip it all down and wipe away the rosy hue, Kimolijah faking his own death and planting himself in Stanslo's Bridge still doesn't make sense.

Because if that's the case—what happened to the da? There's a sister back home. A daughter. Resaniji loves her brother, thinks he could quite literally hang the stars if given enough space for the proper equations and a tall enough ladder. She misses her da, rebuilt and took over the tinker's shop he left behind, wasting Class 5 kineTech on fixing toys and cleaning watches because she said her da and her brother loved the shop so much and running it made her feel like a part of them was still with her.

Nothing adds up, and Bas keeps getting distracted by the weirdness that is Stanslo's Bridge. Speaking of which—

It's stopped raining and the resultant lull in quarry is apparently at an end now. He's glad there *was* a lull, because he really doesn't think it would be wise to be shooting these guns in the rain. He got a little bit juiced just by touching Fox's gun in the wrong places while the toggle was down; live gridstream in water just seems like asking for it.

Blue pulses come from where the other towers are dotted all over town, and gunshots, too, so Bas knows he's not the only one on tower duty, and now he's got a decent explanation for all the ordnance going off all night last night. Other shots go off from the fenced perimeter where there are no towers. Bas doesn't necessarily want to know what's trying to crawl out of the desert and into Stanslo's Bridge, but he has a feeling he'll find out eventually.

Those giant fucking spiders, for one, he has no doubt, because he's already had to deal with a couple of those creeping in and aiming for the bat corpses. Which, okay, ordinarily Bas wouldn't worry about it—scavengers are scavengers, and it's no skin off his nose. It's not like Bas is planning on roasting the bats and having them for supper. But these spiders... they're just wrong. Too big, too jointed, too alien, *too much*, and Bas doesn't care if he's being a prick by shooting every single one he sees. He's not taking a chance on one of those things crawling up his leg, not when the reach of its own legs could probably circle his torso.

A great *bzzzzzzzwap* flares from one of the other towers closer to town, harsh squawks, sparks shooting up and shouts sounding, and Bas looks toward the commotion with a lift of his eyebrows. A couple hundred paces off, maybe a bit more, but he has no problem seeing the shape of something much bigger than one of these bats flirting with the stream, getting close enough for a quick zap and then veering off to dive at the man shooting at it. And while the man is preoccupied with that thing, four more of the bats are swooping around the tower.

Bas is having a bit of a lull, so he thinks *what the hell*. It's not like he hasn't hit longer targets, and he'd kind of like to see what this gun can really do. So he takes aim, anticipates the flapping and the jigs and jives, and shoots. Whatever it is seizes in midsquawk and drops like a stone, and since it's all a bit anticlimactic, Bas picks off the other bats while he's at it.

So the gridgun can shoot long. Probably a lot longer than what he's just done, if the aim is true. It's got almost the same arc as a bullet, except instead of gravity pulling at the trajectory, it's the ground itself, because gridstream always wants the ground. Really fucking impressive. And really fucking dangerous.

Bas peers down at the gun in his hand and wonders what Stanslo plans for them. And then goes back to searching the sky for more bats.

Lowen shows up when the sun's brow crests at the dip of the flat horizon and when Bas has begun to feel boredom set in and weariness creep down into his bones. He wants to go and grab something to eat and then sleep all day. Lowen doesn't say anything at first, just gives Bas an amused look and peers at the bat corpses littered around him in a fifty-foot radius. Now that there's some light and Bas can see what the bats look like, he's kind of glad he hadn't been able to make them out in the dark. They don't just look sinister—they look downright evil.

"Almost lost tower five last night," Lowen says in that easy manner he has, like he's just reporting facts and it makes no nevermind to him.

"Yeah?" Bas lifts his eyebrows and waits, because what's it to him?

Lowen nods. "Seems you made sure we didn't."

"I made...? Oh." The squawking thing. Bas shrugs. "The shot wasn't that much of a stretch." He pats the gridgun. "The sights are pretty much perfect."

Lowen merely nods with that same small, pleasant smile he sports most of the time. With a tilt of his head, he looks pointedly again at all the dead bats. "Quite a score. Looks like thirty or more."

Bas doesn't tell him the count is actually forty-two exactly—plus four spiders—because it seems a little puerile that he'd been keeping score. He merely stares at Lowen and lifts his eyebrows, waiting for a point.

Lowen doesn't get to one. Instead, "You'll do, Bas," he says, and he claps Bas on the shoulder and walks off. "You'll do."

⬤⬤⬤

Bas has almost reached the path that will lead to the Palace and bed when he sees a silhouette cresting the peak of the hill on which Stanslo's "big house" sits. The silhouette is lean and short, so Bas is pretty sure it's Kimolijah, and Bas wonders why Kimolijah seems to be on his way from Stanslo's house at ass o'clock in the morning like an illicit one-night stand. Bas doesn't know exactly why he does it, only that trying to get Kimolijah to talk to him hadn't worked all that well, and Bas doesn't think he'll get anywhere if he just blocks Kimolijah's path and demands to know what he's up to and, while he's at it, why the "dead" darling of the Tech academia is using his Tech to outfit a small army with impossible guns. So Bas ducks behind the flimsy cover of a rock that's not quite big enough but should do in the sluggish shadows, and watches as Kimolijah passes him, neck bent and gait purposeful.

Bas shouldn't. He really shouldn't. If Kimolijah catches him at it, he'll likely never trust Bas, and Bas will have a much harder time figuring out what's going on here. He does it anyway. He waits until Kimolijah is far enough ahead and then follows him. Kimolijah doesn't go far. It's just a curve in the path that leads around the ridge, but enough that the little shack is out of the line of sight from the town, dark and shabby and appearing abandoned. But Kimolijah knocks on the door, calls out, "It's me," and when he apparently gets an answer Bas can't hear, opens the door and lets himself in.

"...another run tomorrow night," Bas makes out in the predawn quiet, and, "...moving too fast...." and, "...need more blue or something...." and then a voice that sounds child-high and a little bit buzzy answers, "...what I can...." and, "...not much more...."

A light flares from the single window; not the steady shine of gridlight Bas has gotten used to seeing out here, but the pulsing flicker of a match struck and then a lamp wicked quite low. Bas quietly makes his way toward it, squints through a gap in the not-quite-closed shutters, and sees Kimolijah already seated at a small table, shirt off—*again*, God, what *is* it with this guy?—and left arm propped palm up in front of him.

"Get the ink," the other person says, making a shooing motion with a long pale hand until Kimolijah turns and retrieves a small bottle from somewhere in the shadows Bas can't see. "We'll only have time for the blue tonight, though, since you insist." It sounds a bit exasperated. "I think you're just getting paranoid. It can't be moving that fast."

Kimolijah huffs out a put-upon sigh and flops his arm over the table again, then slouches over it. Most of the small, dim light pools across his arm, making the whips and whorls of the tattoo look like they're writhing, and the rest of the tiny room is soaked in shadows. Kimolijah's hair is loose this time and hanging in his face, so Bas can't see much else but the sharp angle of his jaw. He can only make out the barest of features on the person sitting opposite Kimolijah through the small gap— long pale hair under a huge floppy hat, pasty and tall, willowy build—but there's a needle in the long thin fingers and they're pouring what must be the blue ink into a small clay cup, and it's not hard to figure out that this is the person who does Kimolijah's tattoos.

"I'm telling you, it was halfway up my arm," Kimolijah says as the other person pokes and prods at Kimolijah's skin with a bone-white finger and traces the twists of the ink.

"Can't be," the person says, and weirdly, Bas can't tell if it's male or female.

The person leans back, and Bas catches white skin and dark glasses set atop a small flat nose. The room is shadowed enough that the glasses surprise Bas. He certainly wouldn't want someone poking at him with needles in the dark and with those things on.

"For fuck's sake," snaps Kimolijah, agitated, "ask Lowen, if you don't believe me. I'm not exaggerating, it was up to *here*." He jabs at a spot on his arm that's just a touch below the crook of his elbow, and Bas has to agree that yes, whatever was going on with Kimolijah's arm at the station, it had indeed reached at least that far, maybe farther.

The other person sits back and heaves a long, great sigh, then starts mixing the ink with the tip of the needle. "It'll take a while, then. Are you supposed to be up there now?"

Kimolijah slumps and leans more heavily into the table. "Breakfast." Bas frowns a little at the obvious sneer in the tone. "Maybe I won't be missed."

"Yes, you will. You probably already are."

"Then you'll just have to cover for me, won't you?" Kimolijah says through his teeth. "It's not like you don't *owe me*." He pauses, but when the other person doesn't react, he goes sulky and slumps. "Anyway, we've got a run tomorrow. That makes this more important than keeping the baron—" Again, he doesn't finish, just grunts something that doesn't sound like words but gets his apparent anger across just fine, then snaps, "You know what, Serenat? Fuck you."

"You're such a child sometimes." It sounds put out.

That gets a laugh out of Kimolijah, a bark of it wrapped around sarcasm and derision that's shockingly easy to hear. "Nah. Not quite *that* valuable, am I?"

There's silence for a long moment, Bas can feel the tension from out here before the other person—Serenat—says, low and quiet, "You go too far sometimes."

"Do I?" Kimolijah's still chuckling. "Well." He shrugs and taps at the bracelet. "I reckon that's why I rate such pretty things, yeah?"

"A *child*." The *tink* of metal against ceramic sounds as Serenat mixes the ink. "I hear Lowen has sent for Dolerma. Why?"

Kimolijah grimaces and sprawls across the table, arm flat out on the surface as Serenat leans forward with a needle in hand. "How the hell should I know?" Kimolijah peers up across the table with a narrow glare. "It's not like the baron actually tells me anything, Serenat, don't give me that look."

"You have no idea what look I'm giving you," Serenat says. "You look for trouble. You do it on purpose."

"Yeah, well. A guy's gotta have some fun now and then."

"*Fun*. Your *fun* is only going to cause more difficulty."

Kimolijah's jaw tics. "Only if other people *make* it difficult."

The needle jabs, quick and purposeful. Kimolijah doesn't flinch, but Bas rears back. Citrus again, and he can feel white behind the bridge of his nose.

What the fuck?

"I can't read him, you know," Serenat says.

"Who?" Kimolijah props his chin on his arm and doesn't look at Serenat.

"The new guy."

Kimolijah shrugs with a smirk. "So? I thought it's been long established that you're not the reading talent in the family."

"I can't read him because he's locked."

That makes Bas jolt a little, because there's no way this Serenat should've been able to tell that. There's no psyTech coming from that little hut. Bas would sense it as easily as he senses Kimolijah's gridTech.

Kimolijah looks up and peers at Serenat closely. "And?"

"And I'm saying. He's locked. Be careful of him. There's no way to tell what he's doing here, and I don't trust Dolerma to—"

That falcon shows up, circles overhead a time or two, then

settles atop the roof just over Bas's head and starts whistling in soft little bursts. Bas only just jerks back before Kimolijah casts a glance out into the yard and then gets up and heads toward the window. Bas makes it around the side of the house just in time before Kimolijah opens the shutters and sticks his head out, grinning up at the bird. "Hiya, love," he says. He waits for the bird to swoop inside before he ducks back in and pulls the shutters to. Bas makes his quiet way back to the window, but everything he hears is muffled and low, and he can't make out any words. He scowls and decides he's pushed his luck far enough, and anyway, it's gotten a bit lighter in the time he's been spying and someone's going to spot him any second. Reluctantly, Bas eases away from the window and then back onto the path down to the Palace.

Things just keep getting weirder and weirder.

⸎

He sleeps the day away, and wakes sticky and feeling grimy. He cleans up in time for a decent supper in the mess, sat with Merrin and Yanush, listening to them haggle trades with the illobooks they'd gotten from Bas and some kind of potato liquor they tell Bas will "curl your hair, man," to which Bas doffs his hat and displays scruffy dark hair that curls even in the desert heat while living under his hat. They snort and shove his shoulder before they move on to congratulating Bas on his—

"—bloody amazing shot, brother." Yanush gives Bas a grin that's missing a canine, and he slaps Bas on the back. "Adams thought it were the hand o' God 'til Silas tracked the shots comin' from yer way."

Bas lifts his eyebrows, because really—it wasn't that great a feat, and he tells them so.

"Eh, leave him his modesty," says Merrin with a wink. "Big damn heroes don't fancy a fuss."

Bas shakes his head and rolls his eyes, but he lets it go. No harm in letting them think it was more impressive than it was, he decides as he follows them out of the mess. Most of the Jakob Barstow cover is smoke and mirrors anyway, and what just happened is how low-key legends get started, which can only be helpful.

They step outside just in time to watch the train haul its boxcars out into the desert. Not toward Harrowgate.

"To the Bruise?" Bas asks, eyeing the silhouette perched atop the locomotive behind the cannon.

Neither Merrin nor Yanush answer the question, which is answer enough.

Bas wonders how difficult it might be to get on that train for the next run and decides he's going to invest some time in figuring that out.

7.

The next day Bas spends poking around and finding exactly nothing. He spends another night shooting at bats that aren't really bats, and though the novelty has pretty much worn off, it's still fun. Bas doesn't think he'll ever get tired of shooting the gridgun. If he were a braver man, he'd take it apart and see if he could figure out how it works, trace the circuits from the dynamic crystal he *knows* is wired into its guts somewhere. Just to confirm it with his eyes and maybe report back to the brains at the Directorate, just in case he doesn't get Kimolijah out of here—or, as Bas has to reluctantly postulate, in case Kimolijah's here because he wants to be.

He doesn't really believe that.

But.

How else can Bas explain all the impossible Tech littered around the place? How else can he explain the fact that Kimolijah has access to a train he obviously built, that he could start up and take off with any time he wants—bully his way through Harrowgate, if he has to, and not stop until he reaches the Directorate's doorstep—and yet he doesn't seem to have any intention whatsoever of doing anything of the kind. Deep in debt like the rest of the people here or no, Bas can't think of a single reason why Kimolijah would be out here doing what he's doing if he didn't want to be.

And yet he just can't make himself believe that the Kimolijah he's come to know secondhand, the Kimolijah he's come to admire and... *no, it isn't love, fuck you, Mo*—Bas simply *cannot* believe someone could walk away from the future Kimolijah had in front of him and settle into a dusty life in a tinpot desert barony, building trains and guns for a self-important lunatic with a creepy grin, no matter how good-looking and sophisticated-seeming said lunatic might be.

Bas lies awake for a long time once he puts his gun up and drops to the mattress in his little room. He lies awake and broods like a brooding thing and tries to doze through the rise of the sun and the light that burns red through his closed eyelids no matter how tight he pulls the shutters.

He can't tell how long he's lain there being a giant girl's petticoat, half-asleep but not really, when he's rousted out of his thin, wary doze by the sound of the train pulling back into town and, shortly after, voices outside, rising in anger first and then what sounds like... maybe crying, but it's raspy and mixed in with shouting, so Bas can't really tell. Bas had gone to bed fully dressed and still wearing his holster, so it only takes him a second or two to get out into the yard to see what the shindy's about. He beats the other men in the bunkhouse outside by the simple fact that most of them are stumbling and still bleary-eyed and trying to fasten their trousers and holsters as they fling open the doors to their rooms.

When Bas gets out into the yard, somehow he's not surprised that most of the shouting appears to originate with Kimolijah. He's also not surprised at the filth Kimolijah is spouting, because Bas heard something very much like it back when the train was stuck at the way station, except this time Kimolijah looks *really* pissed—halfway to crazed, if truth be told—so it's worse. He's being restrained by Quinnie. Good thing, too, because he's kicking and snarling and trying to get at.... Bas doesn't know the guy, but he thinks he's seen him around.

"—up to the Outlet," Fox is saying. "The Baron'd tell ye the same—"

"Ymou otherfucking hardcase *pig's ass*!" Kimolijah shouts right over him—at him, actually, it looks like. "You murdering, baby-whoring, *mudsill* cock-chafing—"

Quinnie gives Kimolijah a healthy swat to the head, then yanks him into a choke hold and slaps her hand over his mouth. "Quit being such a bloody rip and shut your hole for five seconds," she snaps and looks up at Fox. Kimolijah writhes against her, but he doesn't hit her and it looks like any real attempt at release would do little good; Quinnie's sturdy and thick and twice his size.

Actually.... Bas scans all the people who've ventured outside in their nightclothes and decides almost everyone is twice Kimolijah's size.

"Save us all, Fox, don't be so numb in the head," Quinnie says. She looks at the other guy. "Haversham, just back off and let's all calm down." She turns on Fox. "He ain't going to the Outlet. He's in no shape for it, and Stanslo will have—"

"*Fuck* fucking *Stanslo*!" Kimolijah snarls, and he twists and jerks out of Quinnie's hold, which only seems to piss her off a little until Kimolijah lunges at Haversham, and then she looks worried. Haversham drops a small crate he's been hugging to his chest when Kimolijah comes at him. The lid pops and Bas has probably a half a second to get a glimpse of what's inside, but it's enough. Sharp facets wink out at him through the gap, and he figures whatever the Bruise is, it must be where Stanslo is getting his dynamic crystals from.

Kimolijah and Haversham go down in a tangle of limbs and a cloud of dust amid Kimolijah's howls of "*Fuck* Stanslo" and "I'm *done*, d'you hear? He's going to fucking *kill* you and *I'm not going to fucking care*, you got that? You stupid fucking *asshole*, you might as well have just handed him the noose!"

Haversham grunts and growls out a half retort of "For fuck's sake, Kimo, get off a'fore I hafta—" but Kimolijah's wild and scrappier than he looks, so he ends up getting several good licks in, snarling, "No, don't fucking touch me with your dead-man's hands, you unbelievable *idiot*, you don't listen to Fox, *you never listen to Fox*, what the fuck!" and Haversham's not fighting back, just trying to hold Kimolijah off from doing any serious damage, but Fox is *fuming*, like he's just waiting for a break in the action so he can jump in and maybe bring a knife with him.

And no one's doing anything, no one's stepping in, though Quinnie looks like she wants to.

Kimolijah's going to end up getting his plow cleaned for him in about two minutes.

See, Bas pretty much recognizes the flailing and the feral anger and the "enough, just *enough*" that quivers over Kimolijah's entire frame and blazes from his eyes and his mouth and his wild, mostly ineffectual punches. Bas was never bullied as a kid, though he'd been the sort that would have made a juicy target back before he'd realized that having a little brother who's psyTech meant you kind of had to at least pretend you commanded respect. That is, if you didn't want him coming home with nosebleeds every day or getting coerced into using his Tech for pranks and whatever else a group of preteen toughs could come up with. Skinny and smart and obsessed with illobooks, and with a little brother to protect, Bas could've spent an awful lot of his youth nursing black eyes, but he'd understood dreadful young that a level look and a warning silence made even the most evil little primary school mouth-breathing knuckle dragger nervous. Bas thinks he gets it from his mother.

"Get the goddamned tonic," Fox barks. "What'sa matter, princess, the Outlet too dark and scary for yer wee delicate self?"

It makes Kimolijah grind out more denials and epithets, wretched this time and kind of frantic, and he breaks loose from Haversham and goes after Fox. Before he'd just looked agitated and a little bit wild—now he looks feral. There's hatred there—something black and profound—when there was only anger with Haversham. Kimolijah swings and gouges and kicks, and there are no reprimands this time, only ugly, animal snarls. He lands a punch to Fox's nose that doesn't look nearly as effective as Kimolijah was probably hoping.

Bas moves to step in, but someone grabs his arm—Lowen— and just shakes his head at Bas with a grim look in his dark eyes. Bas lets Lowen hold him back only for a second or two, until he sees Fox get his hands around Kimolijah's throat and not let go. Kimolijah has resorted to clawing and scratching, but even though he's got Fox on his back in the dirt and is kneeling astride his chest, his reach is lacking in comparison, and he's still got his gloves on so the scratching doesn't really work. He just ends up thrashing at the empty air between himself and Fox and then trying to wrench Fox's hands away from his throat. He can't. Bas shoves Lowen off when Kimolijah's floundering goes a little bit weak and jerky. Bas steps in and twists Fox's wrists until he lets go, and Bas hauls Kimolijah off and up.

Kimolijah goes limp for a moment, coughing out harsh breaths and trying to double over in Bas's grip. Bas holds him up until Kimolijah seems to realize that Fox isn't nearly as dead as Kimolijah would like him to be. He tries to lunge again, but Bas was expecting it so his grip holds.

Reacher steps in and says, "Switch," to Bas, and he yanks Kimolijah out of Bas's grasp while shoving a small bottle into Bas's hand. Kimolijah fights the transfer, saying, "No, Reacher, seriously, I won't—" but it does no good, of course; Reacher manages to pin Kimolijah with his back to Reacher's chest, and Reacher's hand nearly takes up the bottom half of Kimolijah's face when he sets a rough grip on Kimolijah's jaw. Bas sees Reacher dip his head down to say something quietly in Kimolijah's ear that Bas thinks is "Sorry, little buddy" but he can't tell for sure. Whatever it was, it makes Kimolijah still all over for a second, but then he whines and tries to twist, but all he can do is kick and flap half-pinned arms, because Reacher's holding the rest of him still.

"I'll fry you," Kimolijah says, shaky and garbled through Reacher's solid grip on his jawbone. "I swear to God, Reacher, I'll do it. I'll light you up like a fucking whorehouse on Patrons' Day."

Reacher actually smiles, fond, and says, "Naw, you won't," and surprisingly, Kimolijah doesn't, just bleats frustration and maybe fear, and tries to thrash some more. Reacher nods at Bas's hand. "It's only one dose," he says. "It won't hurt 'im."

It takes a second for Bas to understand what Reacher's talking about, but he looks down at the bottle that had been shoved into his hand and it clicks.

"Don't," Kimolijah manages to shove out, though it's muffled and a bit slurred with the grip Reacher's got on his jaw. "I'm sorry," he says. "Fox, I'm sorry, I don't need it, all right? Reacher, come on, I won't...." He looks right at Bas, scared now. "New Guy. Bas. Hey. Come on, I'm fine now, see? I'm calm, all right? It's all good, I'm good, I just got a little—"

"Shut up," rasps Fox.

"—worked up, is all, and I don't...." Kimolijah trails off, and then snaps wide eyes at Fox. "The bracelet! I don't have it, see?" He tries to lift his hand up, but Reacher's got him pinned. "That's what it is, I don't have the bracelet, get Stanslo, you know he won't—"

"Shut him up, Reacher," Fox snarls. He's pulled himself up from the dirt and come to stand beside Bas. He wipes a smear of blood from a split lip and gives Kimolijah a look of pure, venomous hatred as Reacher complies and covers Kimolijah's mouth with his giant hand.

Fox leans in close, right in Kimolijah's face, and says, low and quiet, "Haversham let the freaks get a little too close to the princess, then, did he? Well, fuck you, you little shit, it's better 'n you deserve." Fox's brown teeth are clenched and he's all but snarling in Kimolijah's face. "Travis is your fault, you twisty little fuck. He's dead 'cause of *you*. And now it'll be Haversham at the post, and that'll be your fault too. Boss won't whump you like you deserve, but Boss en't here just now, is he?" His grin is ugly when Kimolijah flinches and tries to shake his head. "Boss thinks you let Travis have you, but you probably didn't even have to, did you? Not with poor old Travis, yeah? Just twisted his head 'round with all your smart-talk 'til he couldn't help hisself, and all a-sudden he's makin' nice with the relay office and sending—"

"Fox," someone puts in quietly—Bas thinks it's Merrin—and it doesn't even have a warning inflection to it, but it shuts Fox up, though he still glares at Kimolijah like it's all he can do not to kill him.

"Maybe we should all just calm down for a minute," says Quinnie. The tone of her voice is going for authoritative, but only manages to pull off anxious. "You'll answer to the baron, Fox. It ain't for you to decide if Kimo needs the Outlet, and you know it."

Fox doesn't say anything, only keeps staring at Kimolijah, and Kimolijah just keeps staring back. Glaring. Bas wants to tell him to quit it; nothing riles a bully like defiance and vulnerability all mashed together, and Bas has rarely seen anyone as vulnerable as Kimolijah is right now. Fox's breaths are coming rough, his hands fisting and relaxing, fisting and relaxing, before he shakes his head and curls his lip. He takes a long, heavy breath and moves like he's going to step back, but he checks himself then levels a solid punch to Kimolijah's gut.

Kimolijah puffs a blast of air through his nose and his legs come up, flailing, and his eyes squeeze shut.

Reacher says, "Hey, now," all accusing, but Fox merely snatches the bottle away from Bas, shoves Reacher's hand away and puts the bottle to Kimolijah's mouth. Bas doesn't know half of what's going on, but he does know that he really can't stand Fox, so he moves to lunge in. Except it seems like Lowen was expecting it, because he's there again, holding Bas back. He's about one and a half of Bas, and he's holding on like he really means it this time, says, "Don't make me draw on you," so Bas is just as stuck as Kimolijah.

"Hey," says Bas, deep with an attempt at commanding, for all he knows it's pretty impotent. "*Hey*, you can't—"

"Hush," says Lowen, quiet in Bas's ear, and he firms his grip on Bas's arms, jerking the right one back until it hurts. "Fox has got this coming, you'll see. Baron'll show up and take care of it, and no lasting harm done to Kimo. Just be smart and hang fire."

Bas has no idea what that means, but in about three seconds it doesn't matter anyway.

Kimolijah's already coughing from the punch when Fox yanks his head back, but Fox doesn't seem to care. He pours the tonic down Kimolijah's throat and then drops the bottle, clamps a hand over Kimolijah's mouth, and blocks his nose. It's only after Kimolijah chokes and swallows that Lowen lets go of Bas. Bas rubs at his shoulder and considers getting the new kinks out by making the rounds and punching everyone present, but he's too obviously outnumbered. Everyone who's heeled has drawn except for him, and Bas doesn't know who would be shooting whom if a fight broke out.

"That en't very sporting," Reacher complains to Fox, and he really does look like he's not happy about the situation, but he still keeps Kimolijah pinned to his chest and immobile while Kimolijah chokes on the tonic and kicks and kicks.

"Neither was what he did to Travis," Fox snarls. "Did *you* have to thrash the whip? Then stand the gaff and pin that lip."

Reacher does, and everyone goes quiet while they watch whatever was in that bottle take effect on Kimolijah. Well, Bas hopes it's the effect of the tonic, because if not, Fox is suffocating Kimolijah right in front of everyone, and Bas is just standing here and watching it happen.

Until someone asks, "What's going on here?" from the edge of the small gathered crowd, and several people step aside to let the speaker through. Bas does a bit of a double take, and then he recognizes the hat. It's that Serenat, the one who was doing Kimolijah's tattoo, but Bas didn't get a good look then, what with the bad light and limited view through a broken shutter. *Tall* is the first thing Bas sees, tall and thin enough to border on willowy, and then *bone-white skin*, but that's not really it. It is, but there's something not quite right in the coloring, or lack of it, the barest hint of a pale, pale blush, but Bas is trying like hell not to outright stare, and his brain isn't quite making the necessary connections. The small features are perfectly aligned, perfectly proportioned, and perfectly androgynous. Bas still can't guess male or female, but there's a knee-length fluttery skirt over trousers that are cut to conform to the shapes of very long legs, so Bas decides Serenat must be a girl.

"This en't none o' your concern, freak," says Fox, warning. "Go on, then, git." He waves a hand around, shooing, and gives Reacher a glare. "Take him to the Outlet."

Bas kind of expects Serenat—he's pretty sure it's Serenat; who else looks like *that*, after all?—to object, because it just seems like *someone* should. But she doesn't say anything, merely stares for long enough to watch Reacher start off toward the barns and pens, and then she turns around and walks away.

The sun is rising fast now, already a yellow-fierce heat shimmer of a half circle at the edge of the low, flat horizon. Bas means to follow after Reacher and Kimolijah, but Merrin stops him with a hand on his arm and a shake of his head.

"You'll want to stay far away from that," Merrin tells Bas and jerks his chin across the square. "C'mon. The mess'll have coffee."

Bas thinks that might actually be the smarter option, considering.

He ignores it anyway.

⚮

Bas has no current theories as to what the Outlet may be, so he doesn't even have a tentative picture in his head or a wild guess as to what to expect. So when he follows Reacher into a barn set behind a couple of shacks along the square, Bas just watches as Reacher finds the ring of a trapdoor in the floor, opens it, and carries Kimolijah down. Bas isn't being especially stealthy, and he's pretty sure Reacher knows he's there and just hasn't said anything, so he comes in close and peers down into the hole. And he frowns.

It's darker in the barn than it was outside, but the sun rises fast here and its rays are already wobbling through the high latticed windows over the loft. So Bas can't really see clearly, but he can *see*, though that doesn't mean he understands.

The first thing to really catch his eye is wires, because there's a shitload of them, spidering over weird, honeycombed receptacles in the walls and coming together in a single thick cable that runs along the floor and over to, of all things, a cot. Every single little cubby gouged into the wall, from what Bas can see, contains a small heap of crystals, and some part of his mind is raving *I knew it, I fucking* knew *it, goddamn it, every single time, it's those fucking crystals, I* knew *it*, but another part is stuck on the other end of the network of wires.

Bas only got a brief look at the connector on the cable Kimolijah had inserted into the shunt in his arm back at the station, but he's pretty sure it looks an awful lot like the one he's looking at now. Which is bizarre, yeah, because *cellar* and *wires everywhere* and *more fucking crystals* and seriously, *what the fuck*, but none of it is what makes Bas's heart kick at his ribs and his mouth fall open as he walks down the wooden steps and stops at the bottom.

It's the restraints. He can't mistake them for anything else—four of them, each conveniently located where a man's wrists and ankles would be, should he find himself prone on the cot—and Bas can't pretend he doesn't know what Reacher intends to do with them. Reacher dips to lay Kimolijah down, and Bas finds himself saying, "Hey, whoa there."

Reacher doesn't whoa, but he does set Kimolijah down surprisingly gently. He reaches for a lever on the wall, throws it, and the entirety of the small room lights up with the steady, cool glow of a two-tiered gridluster. Because of course it does.

With a nod, Reacher straightens and turns to Bas. "It don't hurt 'im," he says, earnest. "Well, he says it does"—Reacher rolls his eyes, like *yeah, tell me another*—"but it's better when he's sleepy. For him, I mean. And he listens better when it wears off." He nods and cracks one of his dopey smiles. "The straps is only 'cause he won't stay down once he wakes up, what with only the one dose and all."

Bas blinks and lifts his eyebrows. "Maybe 'cause it *hurts him*?"

"Could be." Reacher shrugs like it doesn't matter. "Still needs doin'."

He waves at Kimolijah, who does look surprisingly peaceful, but for fuck's sake, can't someone take those *stupid fucking goggles* off him? Do they *come* off, or are they a permanent part of his head?

Reacher sighs. "Boss won't like it, though. Kimo's supposed to be working on the new train, but now he won't be able to." He looks grim. "And it en't gonna build itself." He rubs at his face. "Stanslo's gonna be *so pissed* at Fox. And he's gonna kill Haversham."

Everyone Bas has asked about the Bruise so far has evaded the question. Bas doesn't think Reacher would know how. So he asks, "What's the Bruise?"

Reacher opens his mouth with a lift of his eyebrows, like he's surprised Bas asked. "Well, it's... it's the Bruise."

He's got this *duh* look on his face that Bas might've found funny before. He'd felt a little bad yesterday for judging Reacher by the *big and dumb* cliché when they were playing cards and Reacher had a hard time deciding if a five was higher than a deuce, but Bas thinks now there's really no way around it.

"Yeah, I got that part." Bas says it with as little condescending scorn as possible. "Where is it and what's there that's so important? And why does he need to take the train there?"

Reacher snorts. "Can't cross the Dead Lands without one. And all the other ones kept blowin' up." He shakes his head like Bas is the idiot.

Bas doesn't get to prod any further, because Fox appears at the trapdoor and barks, "What the fuck are you doing down there?"

Bas pauses for a long moment, thinking, before he looks up and gives Fox a lengthy, measuring stare. From what Bas can tell, and from Reacher's comment yesterday, Bas thinks Fox is a sort of second-in-command here, and so higher up the ladder than Bas. But he's also a dick, and the sort who likes to swing it around, so it would probably be wise to let him know that if it happens to end up anywhere near Bas, he'll happily see that Fox gets it back folded, spindled, and mutilated.

He gives Fox his back and turns to Reacher. "What's in the Bruise?"

"Oh, it's like that, is it?" says Fox, a smirk in his voice. Bas hears the rolling *click* of a round being chambered and stands very still. "How 'bout you just come right on up outta there, smartmouth, and we'll get started on how things work out here. Reacher, hook the princess up and then get them humpers unloadin' those freight cars."

Bas could probably do what Fox tells him, and his messy-death/survival ratio would improve exponentially. Actually, he *should* do what Fox says and just keep his head down as much as he can for as long as he can until he can get the hell out of Stanslo's Bridge.

Instead, "Reacher says the boss won't like what you're doing here," Bas says mildly.

He hears Fox cock the hammer on his gun this time and breathes very deeply. Maybe it's the fact that he's had a gun pointed at him so many times in such a short span of time recently, but Bas's stomach doesn't drop and roll like it probably should. Or maybe it's just that, regardless of what Kimolijah may have become out here, this whole thing just seems very, very wrong. *Restraints*, for God's sake.

Bas tilts his head up to look at Fox out of the corner of his eye. "Quinnie said the same thing. Seemed to me like everyone out there thought this was a bad idea but you."

Fox gives Bas an ugly grin, all bad teeth and seething malice. "Good thing my opinion's the only one that counts." He waves the gun at the short wooden stair, and then points it back at Bas. "Now git on outta there, new guy, so we can get to learning you your place."

That's when Bas hears another set of boots clocking along the wooden floor of the barn overhead, and Stanslo's voice says, "Fox! There you are, my lad." It's cheerful, and when Stanslo appears next to Fox and looks down, he's smiling like always. He takes in Bas and Reacher down below and sets his arm around Fox's shoulders. "And what's all this, then?"

Fox doesn't look nearly as cocky as he had a second ago. He swallows so hard Bas can see his throat bob with it, and Fox lowers his gun. "Kimo, uh...." He waves the gun around. "He had one of his fits, see. Needed to dose 'im."

Fits. Fox says it like it's a regular occurrence. Nothing Bas found out while learning everything he could about Kimolijah Adani indicated he was prone to any kind of "fits."

"Uh-huh," says Stanslo, nodding and rubbing his thumb along his bottom lip. "I see. Got a little out of control, yes? You're all bruised up, Fox. Looks like he put up something of a fight."

"I didn't...." Fox falters. He looks pretty nervous now, and Bas doesn't blame him; it seems like the more concerned and amiable Stanslo gets, the more you have to worry. "I weren't fighting with him," Fox says, defensive. "He went after Haversham, and then he turned on me. I had to... y'know. Defend m'self, like."

That's actually pretty true, but Bas doesn't volunteer as much. Reacher does, though.

"Kimo just got scared, boss. You know he don't like it down here. And he won't be able to work on the new train tomorrow now." Reacher clears his throat under Stanslo's attentive eye. "But he did go after Fox first. He was mad 'cause of...." He trails off and shrugs his wide shoulders like a little boy. "They got too close. Haversham left the cannon, and they almost got the cab open."

That sounds... ominous. *Who* almost got the cab open? And why?

Stanslo purses his lips. "And Haversham left the cannon because...?"

Neither Reacher nor Fox say a thing, but Reacher flicks a quick glance at Fox and then down again. Bas can't tell if it was deliberate, but it's all Stanslo needs.

"Ah." It's calm and controlled, but Bas can see the abrupt boiling fury beneath it. Bas can't suss why what Haversham apparently did was enough to push Kimolijah over the edge and put that look on Stanslo's face, but it must have been bad.

"I see," Stanslo says with a press of his lips.

"You lyin' sack o' *shit*!" snaps Fox, teeth bared at Reacher. "*You* was the one—"

"Do calm down, man," Stanslo puts in, low and even, and he doesn't raise his voice or snarl or snap, but it reins Fox in like a sharp wrench on a choke collar. "Honestly!" Stanslo pats Fox's shoulder as he turns away. "Now, what I'd like you to do—"

He doesn't finish. Instead, he spins back around, points a shiny little four-barrel Bas hadn't seen him draw at Fox's leg, and pulls the trigger. He doesn't even blink when blood spatters all over his expensive boots. "You don't touch Kimo," he says calmly over Fox's hoarse screams. "Not without my permission." As Fox falls to the floor, bawling in pain and holding his knee, Stanslo merely frowns at his gun, small but spendy, and fiddles with the strike stud. "A slight delay," he mutters and shakes his head as he waves away the smoke from the barrel. He holds the gun out, and Bas doesn't realize some random minion is there and off to Stanslo's side until a great tanned hand reaches out to take it.

"Why are you here, Reacher?" Stanslo asks.

Reacher shrugs, wide-eyed. "Fox told me to, boss."

"Of course." Stanslo's bright blue eyes slide to Bas, assessing, and then he turns back to Reacher and jerks his chin. "I suppose we might as well take advantage while he's down there and... quiet." He sighs. "Hook him up and stay here until I return."

"Sure, boss."

With a quick look at Bas, Reacher starts straightening the leather straps that Bas doesn't think he wants to watch go around Kimolijah's wrists and ankles to hold him down. Instead, he turns and eyes Stanslo somewhat narrowly as Stanslo walks slowly down the tiny staircase and over to the bed. A deep sigh and a mournful shake of his head, and Stanslo sets a hand to Kimolijah's cheek with a look that seems genuinely sad and concerned. With a press of lips, Stanslo pulls off Kimolijah's glove and inspects his hand. He frowns. "Hm," he says, narrow-eyed, and he doesn't look happy about it. He palpates the skin once or twice before he pulls that bracelet out of his pocket and clamps it to Kimolijah's wrist. Bas can't see from this angle, hadn't thought to look before, but he wonders now if those welts from the other night are back and whether what Bas overheard between Kimolijah and Serenat makes the half sense he thinks now it might.

"Take that gun to Quinnie and tell her the pin is sticking a little," Stanslo says over his shoulder to the guy still watching Fox writhe in pain on the floor. "And then go up the house and tell Edlyn that Kimo's at the Outlet and to make sure his room is ready when I bring him back." He straightens and makes his way back up the steps.

And. Okay. Kimolijah has a room in Stanslo's house.

Weirder and weirder.

"Also." Stanslo holds up a finger as he crouches down beside Fox. He ignores the whimpers and the by now weaker flailing, merely reaches down and yanks at a leather lanyard around Fox's neck. The crystal Stanslo comes away with is palm-sized with a milky iridescence that doesn't quite catch the weak light trying its best to chase the shadows from the barn. Stanslo stands and grins down to Reacher. "We haven't had an auction in far too long," he says. "You've been careful with your credit, Reacher. After I get back, I want you to gather those men who have eligible trades and collect Dolerma. I'll see everyone up the house tonight. I want the transfer done as soon as possible."

Bas doesn't know quite what it means, but Reacher seems pleased. He smirks—probably the most intelligent expression Bas has seen on his usually vacant-looking face yet.

"Will do, boss."

"And I do trust, Reacher, should you win the bid, you and I won't have the same issues."

"No, boss. You can count on me."

"I do hope so, Reacher." Stanslo looks down at Fox and purses his lips. "I so hate to be disappointed."

Fox is still moaning, curled in pain and half rolling into Stanslo. Stanslo looks down with a regretful shake of his head and toes Fox away from him before he crouches down again. "I would have gone with a whipping, dear Fox, but you're the only one who can do it with any aplomb, and, well"—he holds out his hands—"can't very well have a man whip himself, can I?" He pats at Fox's sweaty, heaving back. "If you don't go the way of Travis, we'll consider all forgiven, yes?" He looks down at Bas with a calculating stare. "Perhaps you should give the whip a go, Bas. I do dislike relying on only one man, and you look like you've got the shoulders for it. Come along, I still have to see to Haversham."

He doesn't wait for Bas to reply, which is good because Bas wouldn't know how. With a negligent wave at Fox, Stanslo *tuts* and starts walking away. "My deputies are suddenly dropping like flies. Bas, with me."

⚮

It takes a while to find Haversham. The man can't be entirely stupid, since he's obviously hiding, but since he's doing it in the mess and with only a ceramic jar of fiery-strong liquor behind which to slouch, he can't really be that smart, either. His chair is tipped back on two legs, his back against the wall, and God, if that isn't a horrible portent made flesh. The pose is ostensibly relaxed, expectant, a small four-barrel lying on the table close to his hand, but he's not gripping it white-knuckled and he's not making any threatening moves toward it. He looks up when Stanslo walks in, but he doesn't lurch up and he doesn't try to shin out. He calmly pours himself a shot of whatever he's drinking, throws it back and then looks steadily at Stanslo.

Everyone else has pretty much frozen in place, still and quiet, but their eyes move between Stanslo and Haversham, some wide and worried, others a bit smug and expectant, and some just plain blank. No one looks at Bas except for Haversham.

"You won't get out of here," Haversham tells Bas mildly. He takes another drink and waves his hand around. "This here—it's as good as it gets out here. You'll never have a big house all to your own, you'll never stop owing him, and no one leaves, no matter what he'll tell you."

Bas knew that part before he even made his first contact with Oleg. It's why he came.

Haversham looks at Stanslo and shakes his head. "God, you're such a fucking liar. *Seven years* I been baking my balls off in your shitty little town. Three years me and Travis kept your little sparker in one piece, and *one fuckup....*"

He trails off, hands fisted for a long moment, before he thumps his chair back down on all four legs, and pours another drink.

"It was an awfully big fuckup," Stanslo says and jerks his head.

It seems to be the signal for everyone who's been standing around watching. Quietly, mostly relieved, they all shift their stances and shuffle in orderly fashion around Bas and out the door.

Haversham waits until most of them are gone, then says, "I left my gun, boss," and his eyes fill.

"I know," Stanslo says, almost gentle.

"I didn't mean to. I wouldn't.... He's a good kid. *God*, Travis would've laid me out, you know? He *told me* to look after him. Travis wouldn't've left his gun."

Stanslo sighs. "Yes." His lips thin down. "And I think you truly are sorry, Haversham, so we'll make it twenty strokes if you come now and make no trouble. It's possible you'll live through it, and then we'll start fresh, all right?" He slides a glance toward the people filing out of the mess and says, "Someone go fetch Fox's whip."

Bas's stomach drops, because he has a feeling he knows who's meant to wield it and he really doesn't want to. He will—he's about to have no choice—but he doesn't want to.

The last one in the room besides Stanslo, Haversham, and Bas is Quinnie. She halts just steps from the door, turns to Bas and peers at him, searching, for a long moment, then merely lifts her eyebrows and says, "Sure, Baron." And she leaves.

"Nuh-uh." Haversham is shaking his head, and his hand slides out and takes up his four-barrel. "You ain't whippin' me, boss. No way you can take that like a man, and I ain't sniveling away the last of myself like Travis. That ain't no way for a man to die." He chambers a round, and points the gun at Stanslo. "You give it to me with dignity or I take it myself. I'd say I'm owed that much, at least."

"You nearly let them get to him," Stanslo says. "You're owed nothing."

"*You* make him drive that fucking thing out there when you *know* they're just sitting there and waiting for an opening."

"And you almost gave it to them."

Haversham shuts up and Stanslo takes a few clocking steps closer. He stops when Haversham pulls the hammer back. Stanslo raises his hands slowly, before he dips into his collar and pulls out a thick, dull crystal hanging around his neck by a leather lanyard. It's bigger than the one he'd taken from Fox, but definitely of the same ilk.

Dynamic crystal. Has to be.

Stanslo creases a thin, almost sympathetic smile. "It's not over when you're gone, Haversham. There's still Jilly."

Weirdly, Haversham chuckles, and the tears he'd obviously been holding back slide slow and fat down his dirty, stubbled cheeks. "Jilly's dead, boss. Gone three weeks now. Geda says you knew. So I'm thinking you got nothin' on me no more." He pauses and twists his mouth into a wrathful grimace. "I can feel that thing, y'know"—a jerk of his chin toward the crystal—"in my head, tightening." He clenches his jaw and forces his face into a horrible grin. The grip on the gun firms, finger adding pressure to the trigger, and Bas sees Stanslo's shoulders tense.

"Thing is," says Haversham, and he tugs down the kerchief he's got wrapped loose around his neck to reveal a white welt. It's smaller than the ones Bas saw on Kimolijah's arm, but it's the same thing, gotta be, climbing from collarbone to.... Bas follows the tiny veinlike path until it curls behind Haversham's ear and disappears into his hairline.

"Got one of these in the scuffle, y'know?" Haversham says, hoarse. He pulls aside his coat and tugs at his shirt, blotted with blood, the skin of his chest gouged wide beneath and still bleeding in sluggish trickles. "Got me here. Tried t' cut it out, but...." He shakes his head, all sad and resigned, but angry again when he looks back up at Stanslo. "So your little rock there ain't much of a spur just now. So *fuck* you, Baron Stanslo. Fuck you and your crystals and every square inch of your shitty little empire, and every goddamned thing the rest of the world don't want and you're gonna give 'em anyway."

He turns an unreadable look on Bas. "Tell the sparker it ain't his fault."

And then he puts the gun in his mouth and pulls the trigger.

8.

It could be worse, Bas thinks as a sheet of water hits his face and sizzles over the metal all around him. He's not sure *how* it could be worse, but he's sure it could be.

The Box hadn't really looked all that scary when Bas had been manhandled out to it, set off from the town and the lush oasis of Stanslo's little plantation by at least several furlongs. Just a metal door sunk level with the cracked soil of the desert. A metal door with spaced grating—for air, Bas supposes, though he doesn't really *get it* yet, doesn't register the implications. And then he sees the lock and it starts to take shape in his head, but it still takes Lowen showing up and creaking the door open, and Bas getting a look inside, for Bas to really understand what this is and what he's in for.

"It's a coffin," scrapes out of Bas's suddenly dry throat, and the slow steps he'd been taking forward abruptly falter and he grinds to a halt. No amount of Lowen or the other guy trying to—surprisingly gently—tug him forward will move Bas, because, "It's a fucking *coffin.*"

Lowen nods to the other guy, and after a silent communication between them consisting mostly of shifting eyebrows and dirty looks, the other guy—Cavett, that's his name—gives Bas a sour grimace and then walks off back toward town.

"Can be," Lowen agrees. He lets go of Bas's arm, takes off his hat, and swipes at his short dark hair with the sleeve of his dirty shirt. "Won't be," he tells Bas as he slides the hat back on and gives Bas what looks like a rueful smile. "You'll come out of there a lot thirstier and a lot more agreeable, but you'll come out alive. You've my word on that."

"What the fuck is your word supposed to mean to me?" Bas's voice is a little shaky with panic. "You want me to let you put me in a *metal* fucking *coffin* in the middle of the desert, and I'm supposed to feel better that you gave me your *word*?"

Punishment, though Bas thinks it's more like payback. Stanslo said it was for interfering where he shouldn't, and once he'd interfered, for not stopping things before they got out of control. So Bas didn't interfere *well enough*, apparently.

Bas thinks it's more because he was there and watched while control slipped through Stanslo's fingers, and Stanslo didn't like it.

Lowen doesn't acknowledge Bas's tone, nor does he answer the question. He pulls a pack from his shoulder and extracts a bedroll from its straps.

"You should keep your coat on. It'll be hotter, but the leather'll save your skin from frying to the bottom." He hefts the roll of blankets and sets them into the Box. "This'll help too. Not supposed to have anything but what you came out here with, but." He shrugs as he pulls out an oversized skin of water.

Drops of water hiss and instantly steam to nothing when they hit the sides of the metal box, and once Lowen has thoroughly soaked the blankets, he calmly pulls out a beaten old six-barrel and points it at Bas's chest.

"I really am sorry, Bas, but I'm afraid I'm going to have to ask you to step inside."

⨒

Bas doesn't.

He has to admit now that the soaked blankets absolutely did help. Right up until the heat dried them, temporarily turning the horrible little prison into a kettle, and he didn't have to worry so much about frying as he did about being steamed like a goddamned lobster.

His head aches, and he doesn't think it's only from the knock to it Lowen had given him when it became clear that Bas was not about to compliantly step into the coffin. He'd like to think it had taken a lot out of Lowen to get Bas into this little death trap, because once what was happening had sunk in, no way was Bas going willingly. A gun pointed at you is only a threat if doing what you're told *isn't* worse than getting shot. And though Bas has never been shot, he thinks he can say with authority that this is totally worse. The persistent dull throb from Lowen's gun to his temple is nothing, though—not compared to the suffocating heat, and the feel of his skin getting too small, and the scruffing animal sounds he can hear when no one's there to dump water through the grates, and the sickness in his belly as time ticks and tocks and drags his mind out through a blurry delirium that he thinks should be a relief, but it's not, and he thinks that's enormously unfair.

God. What if that shuffling out there is one of those huge fucking spiders? Or a snake. Or even that stupid bird that kept kicking guts at him?

"—keep doing this?" Bas hears someone mutter, just before another cascade of water sizzles over the lid of the Box and another sheets in through the grate. He'd been surprised into gasping and spluttering the first time that happened, but now he knows to open his mouth and let as much of the water flow down his throat as he can. He'd called out the first few times—

asked, threatened, even pleaded—but no one ever answered, except for the occasional "Ye en't dyin', you'll see, it'll be over directly" and they certainly hadn't let him out. Now he can barely gather the wind to breathe, so he doesn't waste it on words that will go ignored.

"Himself won't keep holed up in there forever."

Someone grunts, and a voice Bas recognizes as female but can't place says, "He'll be there 'til Kimo's out of the Outlet. That gives us 'til nightfall, at least."

God. Nightfall. Bas doesn't think he's ever looked forward to the sun setting as much as he does right now.

"You really think this guy is worth it?" someone asks. Bas thinks he knows the voice now as Quinnie.

There's a pause while more water thunders down on the metal lid, and Merrin says, "Well. He en't got a bug or nothin'. No collateral to worry about. He's worth a try, at least."

Bas doesn't know what that means. He tries to ask, but he thinks all he does is moan. He feels no embarrassment or shame over it, because there just isn't any room for it inside his stretched-out skin and too-big head and rolling guts.

Lowen had been right about the coat—it does save Bas's skin from sticking to the hot metal, and it wicks up the water and cools his whole body for a blessed snatch of minutes. But it's hot in here, hotter than it is out there, and it takes no time at all for the moisture to heat to steam and choke him as it clouds off his body like smoke. The iron walls around him hiss until the heat gobbles up every bit of wet and sucks it bone-dry again.

Hot is all he can think. *So fucking hot.* It sears his lungs, stuffs his throat with dry, dead air that feels too solid, and he knows he's cooking from the inside out. *Hot*, dreadfully, horribly *hot*, all boxed up in here with no air flowing but what he breathes in and back out. The normally extreme heat of the desert is amplified and multiplied inside this iron crucible, and it's going to kill him, he knows it's going to kill him. Even his mind is melting, thoughts going sticky and all glued together in gooey gobs like molten taffy.

God. It's probably fucking *snowing* by now back home.

"I've really done it this time, Da," Bas wheezes, the air burning his mouth, searing his lungs. He wishes for his poky rental back in Knapston, his illobooks, his stupid Directorate tracker life where he'd never be Tech and he'd never be Magic Man, but he'd be alive and someplace that wouldn't melt his skin when he accidentally shifts and touches the metal coffin that traps him.

Time contracts and expands seemingly at will, blurry patches of funny lights smearing Bas's vision, then darkness, then blinding white he can't blink away. Conversation always accompanies the water that comes at intervals Bas can't discern, but he loses the threads too easily and can't remember what was said five seconds after the talking is done. He doesn't care. He clings to the slim comfort that he hasn't been left to die alone in a little metal torture chamber that has to have been thought up by the same kind of sick mind that would think a whipping post was a good idea.

Mo comes to peer in at him at some point, says, "Yeah, good thing Magic Man's not here to see you like this, eh, big brother?" and though Bas knows it's impossible, he still asks Mo to *please, please, Mo, just open the fucking Box, or make* them *open it,* because Bas has never, not once, asked Mo to use his Tech for personal gain, but he's lost his scruples somewhere in the sandy runoff that heats in the sun and trickles down through the grate to *drip-drip-drip* on Bas's left cheek until it sizzles away inside the heart of this hellish cauldron. Resaniji rolls her baby deer eyes at him and tells him to *stop whining and be a man*, and he tries to tell her to *fuck off, you got me into this*, he really does, but his mam comes to put his head in her lap, run blessed cool fingers over his brow, and tell him, "He's just a big damned bully, Bartholomew. You ever met one of those you couldn't outsmart?"

It's gone dark the next time Bas can think halfway straight, and though it's still the devil's fucking oven in here, it's not as hot. He can breathe. He's sick, his guts are churning around the nothing that's in there, and his head is a giant pounding bell using his brain as a clapper, but he knows where he is again, and he knows why.

The sun rises quickly here, and sets like someone tripped and dropped it. It gets cold enough that Bas has been thankful for the little gridheater in his room at nights, but out here, where there's nothing to hold on to the heat of the day, the temperature drops like lead to the bottom of a well. The sides of the Box are still hot, but they don't sear and melt the tips of his fingers when he accidentally touches them like they had before. He doesn't think it's going to take dreadful long for the metal walls to give up the heat they've been sucking in all day. Bas should probably be grateful, but he's already shaking with what he's pretty sure is heat sickness, running hot and cold in nauseating intervals, and he's still wet from the last dousing someone had given the box, so he's a touch worried. The leather coat is heavy all around him, weighing on him like a clinging shroud. It isn't raining, like it does in town every night, and Bas supposes it's because they're too far out. He thinks he's grateful, but he's not really sure.

"Two days," he mutters to himself, the cragged rasp of his voice surprising him and not lessening the worry even a little. *"Two days."*

He's survived one, just barely, and if he makes it through the night, he's not so sure it'll matter once the sun starts to cook him again. Lowen had said he'd live, but Lowen had been the one to put Bas in this iron fucking oven, so Bas isn't so sure what he thinks of Lowen's opinions just now.

"Magic Man would be so disappointed," Bas mumbles, blinking eyes that feel like they should be dry as jellyfish in the sun, but they're not. They're misting over with tears that should shame him, but what the hell—there's no one here to see them.

He hadn't been able to keep track of how often someone had come out to dump water on the Box during the day, but now that it's night and the dousing unnecessary, Bas is pretty sure the intervals have stretched. Or stopped altogether. He's been somewhat coherent for long enough to recognize some of the shifting constellations through the grate just to the left of his head when he starts hearing the desert around him come to life. He really wishes someone would get the hell out here and shoo away whatever it is he can hear skittering over the lid of the Box.

Coyotes bell and bay at each other somewhere in the distance, or maybe they're wolves. Other creatures make scraped-throat cawing sounds a little closer, but Bas doesn't recognize the sounds, he doesn't know what might be out there, he just knows he'd rather not meet any of them. Bas doesn't pay them much attention, because if he can't get out, they certainly can't get in. It's the things he can hear crawling over the Box, trying to absorb the last of the day's heat through the metal, that have Bas nervous. He's sure he's seen only a small sample of the creepy-crawlies that live out here, and unlike those things making alpha noises out there somewhere, these things can fit through small spaces.

Like a grated opening in the lid of a metal box in the middle of the desert.

There's drifting, both inside his head and out, though he tries powerful hard to stay anchored. He can't, or at least not always. Sometimes his body feels like it's somewhere else, not attached to his mind, and sometimes he thuds back into it with a sick cramp and twist of his belly. There are blessed stretches of nothing at all, and then he jolts to awareness when something scrabbles against the lid of his awful prison, and he shouts and tries to get leverage to beat weak fists against the metal until the noises stop. Time moves, he knows it does, because he *blinks* and there's the Evening Star, and he *blinks* and there's the wing of the Dragon constellation, and he *blinks* and there's the slimmest touch of indigo-blush heaving the beginnings of dawn behind it.

Bas tries to keep the tears in, but he can't. He doesn't think he can do this again.

He's shuddering pretty violently with the heat sickness, somewhat grateful he hadn't had a chance to eat anything since last night—there's nothing in his stomach to throw up and subsequently choke on. He tries not to obsess over the threat of day breaking and starting this terrible cycle all over again, but it's the all too present skittering and the subtle sliding over sand that has his heart fluttering in and out of rhythm just now. The rest of the nightmare will arrive on the tails of the sun; no sense living it before he has to. For now, when his mind is his and his body not so distant, he keeps a very close eye on the grate by his head and what he can see of the one down by his feet, watching for spindly legs or long, twisting bodies trying to shimmy through. So he sees it when wavering torchlight edges into the small square of his vision and butts up against the deeping violet of predawn.

Low voices murmur together, some kind of argument going back and forth in soft rumbles and hisses, and then the light shifts direction and Kimolijah's voice snaps, "Because it's my fucking fault he thinks it's possible to live for two days in that thing, all right? If you're not going to help, just leave the pack and go."

The light steadies again, not so much a flicker as a glow, before Kimolijah's face takes up the square by Bas's head, blotting out the dimming constellations. Bas is kind of surprised a shaft of starlight doesn't spray down from the heavens and halo Kimolijah's dark head, that no trumpets sound when Kimolijah's teeth flash in the dark as he gives Bas a small smile.

"You alive in there?" Kimolijah asks.

Bas thinks about that for a moment, very carefully, before he licks cracked lips and croaks, "Does it count if I wish I wasn't?"

Apparently, it isn't possible for a man to survive two days in the Box.

"I came out here the first time Travis got sent out," Kimolijah confesses. "After the first day, Baron thought he was a little too healthy and couldn't possibly have learned his lesson, so he gave him another." There's a pause and a shaky breath. "We worked on his acting the next day."

Bas's brain isn't working entirely properly, so he doesn't really get the implications. He says, "How's that?" or he tries to, but it comes out more like, "Uhn?"

Kimolijah shifts away a bit, and there's a shuffle or two, before he's back and pushing something through the grate. "Here, eat this. I know you think you can't, but trust me—it'll make a difference."

Reaching for it is awkward. There's not much room in here, and Bas has to contort himself a little to allow for the bend in his elbow. He manages, takes shaky hold of something rough and squareish and thin, and brings it to his mouth. Saliva should swamp his teeth at the first salt-dry contact with his tongue, but it doesn't, and Bas supposes that's because he doesn't have any left. It seems like it might be beyond his strength just to chew and swallow, but Bas gives it a shot.

"Jerked rabbit," Kimolijah tells him. "Not much, but it'll give you something in your stomach." He turns and says, "Quinnie, hand me that skin, would you?" and then there's something else blotting out the light coming through the grate. "Can you stretch your neck a little?"

Bas assumes Kimolijah's talking to him, so he hums something like agreement and shifts as far as he can until the grate is directly above him. He doesn't know why he just compliantly opens his mouth when Kimolijah tells him to—because who lets a relative stranger just drop things into their mouth through an air grate in a metal coffin?—but Bas does it without even thinking about it. A lot of it misses and hits him on the chin, but a lot of it hits its mark, too, and the sweet tang of pear cider floods Bas's mouth and fills the sere cracks in the back of his dust-dry throat.

"There's some elixir in there," Kimolijah tells him. "It's not much, but it'll help." He pulls the skin away. "Not too much now. Eat the jerky and I'll send in some apple bits."

Bas gnaws on the jerky and only thinks to wipe away the runnels of cider on his cheeks and chin and down the sides of his neck because he hears his mother in the back of his head complaining about "Ants, dear God, you'll have a colony in here with that mess!" And if the spiders out here are the size of Bas's head, he doesn't want to meet any of the ants this place might produce. They probably bite. They're probably *poison*. And they'd probably be big enough to pin him down and snack on him for days. He tries his best to rid himself of the sticky-sweet invitation splattered all over his face.

"Here," says Kimolijah.

Bas looks up, stretches his neck over again, and lets Kimolijah drop apple bits into his mouth. The aim is better this time.

"Why are you doing this?" Bas asks, savoring the sweetness on his tongue between salty bites of the jerky.

Kimolijah pauses and draws back, looking up at the sky for a long moment. It's getting lighter. It's subtle, but the indigo is fading into grayish-blue and the violet is going lavender. The stars are fuzzy little smudges now, instead of the bright-cold pinpricks they were just a little while ago.

It won't surprise Bas if Kimolijah doesn't answer—Bas doesn't think Kimolijah has given a single one of Bas's questions a straight answer yet—but Kimolijah eventually shakes his head and lowers it. He doesn't look down at Bas, though.

"It's my fault." His voice is hushed, his tone confused.

"What's...." Bas frowns and then remembers the world beyond his little iron prison. "It's not, though." He takes another bite of the jerky and looks up through the grate. Kimolijah's not looking at him. "Haversham told me to tell you it's not, actually."

And he's thought about Haversham, and about Haversham's brains all over the wall, because—somehow—that's how Bas ended up here. Except, even with that unhappy scenario playing in his head on a loop, Haversham's last desperate and defiant act is not what Bas thinks of now. It's that welt. It's the ones on Kimolijah's arm. It's what Haversham said about it all, and it's what Stanslo *doesn't* say.

Kimolijah does look at Bas then, and though Bas can only see half of his face, lit gold and somewhat hollowed in the dithering torchlight, Kimolijah looks impossibly old and impossibly young and impossibly lost.

"Yeah?"

It's almost a whisper, but the intensity of it, the *need* inside it, keeps it from vanishing between the slats of the grate separating question from answer. And then it's like Kimolijah catches himself, purposefully squashing the momentary vulnerability. Bas can almost see him shaking it off like an annoying insect crawling across his shoulders.

"And just so we're clear." Kimolijah leans in close, features bisected by the grate but sharp in the chancy light. Bas can feel Kimolijah's breath fluttering over his fingers. "You tell the baron I was out here, if anyone finds out, you'll see very quickly exactly how bad it can be."

Bas stares. "Why would I tell the baron? Why would I tell anyone?"

Kimolijah snorts softly and draws back. "Men like you always have their reasons."

"Men like me." Bas presses his lips together, abruptly and unaccountably angry. "You know a lot of men like me, do you?"

There's a pause, a huff, and Kimolijah smacks the lid of the Box hard enough to make Bas startle. "Do you want to live through this, or do you want to make another lewd crack about the person who's trying to help you?"

"It wasn't a lewd crack, I was just—" Bas stops and clenches his teeth. "Whatever, I don't care," he says sourly, realizes he's been craning his neck so he can see out the grate, so he lets his head drop back and shoves out a deep sigh. "I'm not who you think I am," he tells Kimolijah.

Kimolijah makes a move Bas can't see entirely, but he thinks it's a shrug. "I don't think you're anything in particular. I hardly know you."

"And you don't intend to get to know me at all, do you?"

"I don't—" Kimolijah makes a frustrated noise and drums his fingers on the lid of the Box. "Look, I'm sorry that trying to protect me got you into this. But that doesn't mean I want to know you, and I really doubt you'll want to...." His hands wave around his head. "You know, just whatever, it doesn't matter." He goes quiet for a moment and looks back up at the sky before he shakes his head and mutters, "Honestly, we'll all be better off if you don't."

"I think I know a lot more than either you or Stanslo want me to know."

"Yeah, 'cause your sort is known for brains." Kimolijah looks like he's going to get up, but the move turns into a fist to the lid of the Box. "I don't know why I even came out here. Seriously. I'm just setting myself up for more shit, but don't think for a second I haven't covered my ass. Right now, I'm safely locked in my room and sleeping off the Outlet, so if you even *think* about telling Stanslo I was out here—"

"*Hey*! What the hell? Who does that? I tell you I want to get to know you and you come up with some grand conspiracy where I get myself shoved in an oven in the middle of the desert just to set you up? Who thinks like that?"

"Who d'you *think*?" Kimolijah growls. "The last person I 'got to know' ended up whipped and dead. You've been here a week and look where you are, so either you're incredibly stupid or incredibly smart and waiting for me to slip up. Either way, you're just another dead man out here who doesn't know it yet, so do you really care that much what I think?"

Bas stares for a long moment then he shakes his head, says, "Ow, *fuck*," and decides he'd best not try that again. "My god, I don't know whether I want to save you or kick your head in."

"Yeah, well, you're not likely to get much of a chance at either, so find yourself a more attainable dream."

"You're a complete ass," Bas says. His hands want to wave around in his frustration, but the closeness of the Box doesn't permit it. "I mean, I know I'd kind of built things up in my head, and love is just... it's *not*, so it doesn't matter anyway, but the *brilliance*, it just made me go a bit wibbly, I think, and then I get here and you're all... *you*, and it's nothing like what I thought, but I still can't—"

"God, you're babbling." Kimolijah leans down and peers at Bas intently. He holds his hand over the grate. "How many fingers do you see?"

"How many—what does—oh, for God's sake." Bas growls a little and takes a long, deep breath to tamp down the annoyance. "Okay, look—is that really how I seem to you? Do I really seem like the kind of guy who'd let Stanslo roast him for fun just to catch you doing something he doesn't want you doing?"

Kimolijah pulls his hand away and blinks down at Bas, frowning. "Well, I don't actually know you, do I, and right now you just seem a little bit crazy, actually, but the heat can do that when—"

"*God*, you're just... *ugh*! Do you even know how crazy that complex conspiracy scenario sounds? Your brain really is the size of a planet, but you're so goddamned smart the simple answers are completely outside your scope."

Kimolijah just keeps staring for a spell, then he says, "Okay, this is the weirdest case of heat sickness I've seen yet." He pushes the mouth of the flask back over the grate. "Here, try some more of—"

Frustrated and pretty much helpless, Bas kicks at the lid of the Box, hard enough to make Kimolijah jerk back and stare at him some more. "Just answer the question," Bas grates.

"Okaaaaaay," Kimolijah says slowly, too obviously humoring the delirious man in the metal coffin. He pulls back and looks at Bas straight. "'Crazy conspiracy' or not, I know what kind of person comes out here on purpose. You want to know how you seem to me? Fine. You *seem* all right, but you also seem like the same sort of mercenary bastard who comes through here waving a gun around and thinking that makes him some kind of—"

"And you seem like a Tech who went off the Grid so he could build illegal things for his criminal boss, who he also happens to be sleeping with. So maybe we're not *all* what we *seem!*"

Kimolijah stares down at Bas for several silent seconds before his mouth tightens and he stands abruptly.

Shit.

"Kimo," says Bas. "Wait, Kimo, I didn't—"

"Whatever," Kimo snarls and glares down at Bas like he's thinking of spitting on him through the grate. He turns away, runs a hand through his hair and puffs out a wry chuckle. "*God.* I felt *bad*. I don't think I do anymore."

"Kimo—"

"Fuck you, Mister Gunslinger," Kimolijah snaps, and then all Bas hears is the *thud thud thud* of angry footsteps moving away.

"*Kimolijah.*"

There's no answer. There's quiet and there's more quiet until the shuffling and scraping of desert life starts up again.

Bas shoves out a tight breath and unlocks his fingers from the grate, lets his arm curl over his abruptly aching chest. "Well." He laughs a little and shoves the last of the jerky into his mouth. "That went *magnificently.*"

☙❧

Bas barely remembers the next day. Almost the only part he does remember is that though Merrin and Quinnie come out to dump water on him and mutter to each other, Kimolijah doesn't come back.

The next time Bas has a fully functioning brain, he's in his own room at the Palace, his face smashed into the linens and his knuckles scraping the floorboards. Something's crawling over his palm, and it says an awful lot about the shaky state he's in that he doesn't jolt and start yipping. He manages to focus his eyes and peer down to where his arm is hanging over the side of the bed.

Just a cricket. Bigger than a cricket ought to be, but pretty much everything here is, so Bas just flicks it off him and tries not to groan as he rolls over.

He has no idea what day it is. He has no idea how long he's been out of the Box. He thinks he remembers the second day in blurry shifts of misery, and he thinks he remembers being hauled out when the sun went down, and then dragged back here over the back of an annoyed mule. There might have been Lowen and lots of "drink up, now" and... that's pretty much all he can come up with.

He's alive, though. He supposes he's grateful.

Someone left a jug of water and some of that horrible flat stuff that's supposed to be bread. Bas drinks and eats and spends the day drifting in and out of smudgy sleep. He doesn't know if he's supposed to tell someone he's not dead, and he doesn't really give a shit. He feels like he's been cooked unevenly by a novice hash slinger and then left out too long and gone rancid. He'll lie here until he goddamned well feels like getting up.

Except he won't, because Lowen shows up—it's always fucking Lowen—just when night starts to shatter the day and says, "Boss is expecting you tonight for supper. You'd best wash up."

It's a good thing he doesn't wait for an answer. He probably wouldn't appreciate the jug to the head Bas had planned but couldn't move fast enough to accomplish.

9.

It's already dark enough for shadows by the time Bas needs to head for the big house. He still doesn't know *why* he's having supper with Stanslo, only that it's an invitation it's pretty clear he'd do best not to refuse, so he makes himself as presentable as he can with what he's got and ambles out of the Palace while everyone else makes their way to wherever they go when they're not lounging in their bunks.

He probably examines the shadows along the way a little too closely, watching for those giant spiders or the thick-as-your-thigh-and-longer-than-you snakes. He doesn't see anything more threatening than a few mice and some kind of mole he's never seen before, but it doesn't have those glowing eyes like the bats did, so he figures they haven't "leaked out" of anywhere and probably belong here.

He's having a hard time getting over the whole Box thing. He still feels kind of shitty, but it's not that. He's pissed off, but it's not that either. He's pretty good at swallowing his anger when he has to; he's been in plenty of situations where he's had to make nice with a despicable, cutthroat aberration of a person in order to keep his cover and do his job.

Stanslo, though....

Stanslo is something special. Bas is going to enjoy taking him down like nothing he's ever done before.

Except, in order to do that, Bas is pretty sure he's going to have to eat a lot more shit and smile while he does it. Which only makes the desire to get to the bottom of what's going on out here even sharper. He just doesn't appreciate the fact that it's going to take buddying up to the man who just tortured him.

Maybe he's dragging his feet a little. Maybe he's eager for the information he might get out of this but reluctant to think about how it might come. The whole thing with the welts and the crystals is still bothering the hell out of him, along with whatever goes on out in the Bruise that requires a gunner and resulted in the foorah of the other day. Still, no matter how slow Bas goes, he gets there eventually.

"Come in, come in," Stanslo urges cheerily, gesturing Bas up the wide porch steps and into a foyer as incongruous to the grimy desert setting as Stanslo himself. When Stanslo calls out, "Edlyn, dear girl, come see what I've brought you!" as he shuts the door, Bas is expecting... well, he doesn't know what he's expecting, but it isn't this.

A stout little woman in long skirts covered by a crisp white apron bustles out from a back room at the end of the long bright hallway. A smile apples her ruddy cheeks as her roughened hand pats at the bun on the back of her head, dark hair going wiry with gray.

"Dear *girl*," she scolds Stanslo with a roll of her eyes that looks sincerely exasperated, though no less fond. She gives Bas a look and then turns a twinkle on Stanslo. "Don't you tease me, Petra Stanslo. You've not brought this fine thing for *me*." She steps forward and bullies Stanslo out of his coat and takes his hat. "The boy's gone off again," she tells him and her mouth curls, disapproving. "And him just up this morning from the Outlet."

Stanslo pauses. "He's awake?"

Edlyn shrugs as she folds the coat over her arm. "Went to wake him for a bath before supper, and his bed's empty." She shakes her head and *tuts*. "Keep telling you to nail the windows shut, but oh no, don't listen to—"

"Thank you, dear Edlyn," Stanslo cuts in and gives her a tight look. "Perhaps we'd do best not to wait for him, then."

Bas figures they must be talking about Kimolijah, who was apparently expected to dine with them, and wouldn't that have been interesting and—possibly—informative. He also thinks it's worthy of note that neither Stanslo nor Edlyn seem to have any clue that Kimolijah was up and apparently recovered from whatever effects he suffers from the Outlet long before this morning.

Bas wonders exactly what Kimolijah does with himself when Stanslo thinks he's unwell and sleeping it off, when he's not instead saving and bickering with prisoners of the Box.

Edlyn's giving Bas a gimlet eye. "Who's this, then, if he's not a present for me?" She frowns. "I thought you were done with recruiting for the now."

"Our latest from Oleg," says Stanslo. He plants a kiss to Edlyn's round cheek and slings an arm across her shoulders, pulling her in and jostling her with a smile wide with affection. He lets her go and waves a hand at Bas. "Edlyn, this is Mister Jakob Barstow, but you may call him Bas if you're his friend." He grins. "Our newest deputy."

Bas stares at Edlyn's outstretched hand for a moment, then her raised eyebrow, before he gets it and meekly hands over his coat and hat.

"Deputy," Edlyn echoes, dubious, and her puffy lips turn down. "Hm."

It's probably weird that Bas wants to scuff his toe in the carpet at the disapproving tone.

"Thank you, dear Edlyn," says Stanslo, clear dismissal, as he gently shoos her off. "Kimo will show up eventually, I imagine.

Make sure he's presentable if he does, then show him in. And see Dolerma to the dining room when he gets here, won't you? Now be a good girl and finish that supper. It smells divine."

It does, and Bas was hungry a little bit ago—his body is still demanding he make its mistreatment up to it with copious food and drink—but his nerves still haven't centered back onto their normal axes yet. So he's only half-aware of Stanslo leading him down the hallway and into a dining room that's no surprise, considering what Bas has seen of the rest of the house. The animal heads all over the walls are kind of shocking, though.

Now Bas is admittedly a city boy at heart, always has been, and he'd only really begun to be familiar with wild animals when he'd begun his work with the Directorate. Living out of what he could carry on his back, worming his way into road gangs and bandit crews—a person learns how to hunt and skin and spit and roast pretty quickly. So the glass eyes don't really bother Bas much, nor do the varied expressions into which the faces have been stretched and glued—from a blank-eyed stag trying to look majestic to a fierce-fanged bear that looks more like it's grimacing than growling. What does bother Bas is that he can only recognize about half of the—he counts eleven—animals whose heads, and presumably the rest of them, have been sacrificed for the sake of Stanslo's apparently gigantic ego.

They're trophies, obviously, and Bas doesn't think it's coincidence that Stanslo has brought him here to this room. Some of them are fairly grand, even in their frozen exhibitions of death, and some of them are pretty goddamned terrifying, because Bas can't help wondering what he'd do if confronted by a live version of some of the more alien and vicious-looking ones. Heads bigger than Bas's own, and tusks jutting up from jaws full of razor teeth, reptilian eyes that glint and spark in the gridlight with what Bas knows can't be malice inside the glass fakery, but still comes a little too close for comfort.

"They're beautiful, aren't they?" Stanslo says, quiet and just behind Bas. He's smiling, proud. Bas squints at him over his shoulder, dubious, then turns back to peer at the... whatever it is glaring down at him from its degrading death pose on the wall of Stanslo's dining room. "There are many, *many* beautiful things out here in the desert, Bas. So many things wasted on so-called civilization's fear of the unknown or the dangerous."

Bas frowns and asks, "This thing lives out here?" and doesn't let his entire body shudder like it wants to.

"Well, not *here*," Stanslo says. "Come. Sit."

Which is not really an answer, but Bas lets Stanslo have his control for now, and turns to take in the rest of the room.

The heavy wooden furniture is gilded on the edges, the linens are tatted with intricate lacework, and the chairs around the great table are padded in rich green velvet. The table is already set for four, and Stanslo says something like "Ah well, perhaps he'll join us for afters" and makes a business of collecting up one of the delicate-looking bone plates trimmed in painted ivory, along with flatware that can't be anything other than thick, heavy silver. He sets it aside.

"Drink?" Stanslo asks as he makes his way over to the sideboard, on which is set a multitude of fine decanters and a spray of fragile glasses.

"Draga, if you have it," Bas answers, because he won't admit to Stanslo that he's still a bit shaky and has a newfound obsession with water by asking for a big sweating jug of it. He merely turns his head to hide the roll of his eyes at Stanslo's "Of course."

The showiness of it—the house, the furnishings, the table settings, the liquor, the *trophies*—all of it's just as out of place here as Stanslo is, and it kind of makes Bas want to sneer. Going from the sorry excuse for a train station to the sorry excuse for a town and then to this decadent and obvious display of wealth and luxury—the blatant and weirdly childish "neener neener" of it should've gotten Stanslo punched in the face a long time ago, and Bas has to wonder how it apparently hasn't. What is it about this man that allows him to wield the obvious power he has over these people?

"I thought we should have a bit of a chat," says Stanslo as he pours out drinks. "Before I offer you what Lowen has recommended I offer you." He smiles as he turns and crosses over to Bas, glasses in hand. When Bas takes the one Stanslo offers him, Stanslo lifts his own. "To...." He pauses and peers up at the ceiling for a second, then looks back at Bas with that same boyish grin. "What shall we drink to, Bas?"

Bas almost says "to Haversham, may he rest in peace" just to be a hardcase, or maybe "to the Box" to be a smartass and make Stanslo acknowledge what he put Bas through—because Stanslo is making it pretty clear he's not about to—but Bas decides not to press his luck just yet.

"To good whiskey," he says and clinks his glass against Stanslo's.

Stanslo laughs, and it makes Bas uncomfortable to note how charming it sounds and how handsome Stanslo is when he does it, but there's no denying it.

"To good whiskey, then," Stanslo agrees and takes a sip. "And to new beginnings," he adds and waves his glass. "Because that's what you'll find here, Bas." He pauses and watches Bas take a calm sip of whiskey, then says, "You remind me of myself."

Bas would probably choke on the admittedly dreadful fine liquor if Stanslo wasn't staring at him so closely.

"Shall I take that as a compliment?" Bas asks mildly.

Considering Stanslo's demeanor thus far, Bas is kind of expecting him to laugh or grin or waggle his eyebrows. He shrugs instead. "Take it as—"

He's interrupted by a knock coming from the front door down the hallway. Bas can hear Edlyn answering it and then footsteps coming toward them. With a smile, Stanslo waves Bas toward the end of the table that's still free of dinner settings.

"That will be Dolerma," he tells Bas.

Dolerma is... well, Bas remembers the name from when he'd eavesdropped on Kimolijah outside that cottage, and for a second Bas thinks this is the same person—that Serenat with the tattoo inks and needles—who'd been chiding Kimolijah, but no, this one is... different. Bas hadn't really gotten a good look at Serenat either of the times he'd seen her, but that's not a problem with Dolerma.

Androgynous—Bas doesn't think he'd've guessed Dolerma is male if he hadn't heard people referring to him as such—with the same perfect features as Serenat, same perfect proportions that Bas might come to think of as quite beautiful, if he ever gets used to... everything else.

Dolerma's hair is long, and a pink so pale as to be almost white, but *still*, it's not as white as his skin. Bas doesn't think he's ever seen a white as white as Dolerma's skin, and it's... well, it *is* white, but it's not really *skin*, maybe. Bas thinks that if he reached out to touch it, it would be viscid on the surface and would leave a dent where his finger had pressed. It gives the impression of transparency without actually being transparent. Bas can see the fine, delicate branching of veinwork beneath the skin, and it can't *really* be black, but it looks it.

What the fuck are *you*? Bas thinks, unsettled. *And where did you come from*?

Dolerma looks back at him calmly, no expression on his long face, and his eyes are covered by wire-framed glasses with lenses so dark Bas wonders how he can see through them. He thinks again of Serenat with Kimolijah and wonders why the glasses are necessary. Are the eyes as colorless as the skin?

Bas drags his gaze up to the mounted heads of animals he's betting no scientist or professor outside of Stanslo's Bridge has ever seen before and then back to Dolerma. Refugee from the Dead Lands, maybe? Victim of the poisoned rivers and blasted earth? Bas really wants to ask, but he doesn't think he should. Dolerma turns his head to stare at Bas, like he heard. Bas has no trouble politely not staring back, because he doesn't really want to look in the first place.

Dolerma is offered a drink, which he declines. He merely settles in the chair across from Bas and folds his spidery white hands on the table.

Stanslo sips at his drink. "Oleg will not have discussed our contract methods with you, Bas, and for that I apologize. But, you see, it can be a difficult thing to preserve trade secrets once they're set loose in the wide world at large, no matter how close a trusted soul might keep them. So we have adopted a method that works quite beautifully in its simplicity. It's a somewhat primitive adaptation of an ancient, honored practice where Dolerma comes from."

"And where does Dolerma come from?" Bas asks.

Predictably, Stanslo doesn't answer, merely smiles. He pulls that same crystal from inside his shirt, and Bas gets a better look at it this time; it's large and dull with muffled prisms beneath its unpolished surface. Stanslo slips it off over his head as he slides a half-lashed look at Dolerma. Dolerma only sits serenely, hands folded and eyes downcast.

"As I said," says Stanslo, "we take our contracts very seriously here. We have to, or we won't survive out here in the wilderness." He pauses with a wink. "I just want to be sure that you will take the terms of the contract I intend to offer you as seriously as I do. This...." He holds up the crystal between his fingers. "This should see to that nicely."

Bas lifts his eyebrow and shoots a pointed glance at the crystal. "And that is...?"

Stanslo's smile looks almost demure this time. "Only what you give me, Bas. And then it's mine to have, you see?" No, Bas really doesn't, but he keeps his face blank. Stanslo winds the leather thong around his knuckles and rolls the crystal between his fingers. "Call it a codicil," he goes on. "Call it a method of enforcement in a place where there is no guardarm and no Directorate to back up the promises we make to one another. Should it occur to one of us to, perhaps, breach our contract, this is merely a token that will make sure it occurs to us to think better."

It makes no sense. He's talking like the crystal itself can make Bas follow the rules, but there's no Tech Bas knows of that can do such a thing, unless there's a really good Class 5 psyTech hidden inside it. Except, Bas thinks, there was Haversham and *I can feel that thing, y'know... in my head, tightening*, and there was a quiet little auction to apparently bid on the crystal Stanslo took from Fox. And then Bas thinks about Resaniji telling him that Kimolijah thought any Tech could be put inside a dynamic crystal if one knew how to do it, and Bas's stomach takes a lurching little tour around his gut.

He doesn't have his hat to hide his face, so he purses his lips in a show of disapproval. "Isn't the contract meant to ensure I take the contract seriously?"

"Indeed." Stanslo's mouth twitches. "But our contracts are not on paper, you see. And they're not precisely contracts." He shrugs. "More... gentlemen's agreements."

Bas takes a sip of the really good whiskey and smirks. "And since there are no gentlemen here...?"

"Ha!" Stanslo slaps the tabletop, grinning. "Perfect! Oh, I *do* like you, Bas. Lowen's right—Oleg has done very well this time. Dolerma, if you will?"

Bas frowns, because he'd really like to know just what he's

supposed to be contracting for here. But when he turns to peer a question at Dolerma, he gets his first look at *eyes*. And nearly flinches. Everything he'd wanted to ask flies right out of his head.

He'd had the impression before that Dolerma's eyes would be blank and colorless, but they're not. They're round—*round-round*, like a doll's eyes—unnerving and gelatinous and prism-laced, black as a beetle's carapace with discs of bright copper floating on the surface and cat-slit brown pupils dead center.

"What the hell are you?" It comes out breathless, which is just too damned bad; there are fucking *limits*.

"A friend," says Stanslo. "That's all you need to know for now."

It's not hair. Bas had thought it was lank, blushed-white hair, but it's not. The strands are too thick and not really strands at all, fibrous and... fleshy. Like it could move of its own accord, like... like *tentacles*. No, what's that stuff that's like hair but—*cilia*, that's it. Which are basically hairy feelers. Or something just as gut-grabbingly bizarre.

Bas feels a little like he's outside himself, so it takes a moment for him to register Dolerma's cold touch curling Bas's hand around the crystal. Between the chill, slippery touch and *the fucking eyes*, it makes Bas think of reptiles and sea creatures that dry up in the sun. He's so busy trying not to twitch backward and away that by the time that lemon-fizz taste floods his mouth and he sees the air around Dolerma waver and snap like a visible sonic boom, it's already gone. And it *wasn't* visible, that's the thing. Bas felt the scree and smacking *thud* of it somewhere inside his head, but he grew up around psyTech so he knows the brain shoves things it doesn't understand into comprehensible shapes. Bas is a tracker—his senses are differ-ent, more finely tuned, he perceives things other people can't—and he thinks he's just "seen" Dolerma try to do something to Bas's mind with his own. It wasn't bright, Bas didn't actually see it with his eyes, and he really shouldn't be seeing spots right now, so he assumes those are from not breathing, because seriously, no, *what*?

Not psyTech, though there's an earthy undertaste that's almost like it. There's no bawdy-yellow sting at the back of his throat, though. There's dreadful little at all, actually, just something that bites like citrus and that faint-faint-faint suggestion of yellow, which makes no sense, because Bas *knows* something just happened, and he remembers this same taste, this same sensation from his first night here, and then he remembers Serenat telling Kimolijah *I can't read him.*

He's locked. Every Directorate employee is locked against subversive psyTech. He's double-locked, actually, because Bas is a Directorate employee *and* his brother is a Class 4 psyTech who's a cocky bastard, but a cocky bastard with an incompara-ble talent at building locks and defenses against invasive psyTech. And Bas has been Mo's test subject for years. Dolerma didn't get in with his weird psyTech that isn't psyTech. He couldn't have gotten in.

"So?" says Stanslo.

Dolerma sits back, keeping that unsettling gaze on Bas. "Jakob Barstow is a thief and a thug and a murderer," Dolerma tells Stanslo. "Jakob Barstow perfected his aim and became an accomplished marksman for the sole purpose of picking off the security snipers hired by highway haulers, because it makes it easier to steal the wagons when there's no one shooting at you." His mouth twitches as he says, "He's even robbed one of your trains, Baron," then he purses his colorless lips again into a flat line. "He got the extraordinarily unimaginative name 'Shooter' from his extraordinarily unimaginative uncle, also his first road boss, whom he eventually shot in the throat for gambling away the profits from selling stolen cattle before he'd gotten his cut. He has never actually raped anyone but has no problem with little boys on their knees." Dolerma pauses and looks at Stanslo. "Jakob Barstow will do."

Okay. *What?* No.

Bas has no idea where any of that came from, but it wasn't from inside his head. And it's not part of the Jakob Barstow profile.

Dolerma made it up. Dolerma just pretended he'd read Bas's mind and made all of that up. There's no other explanation. And used it as an endorsement. Which, okay, great, so Bas isn't about to get shot in the head.

Still. *What the fuck?*

"Do contain your enthusiasm, Dolerma," Stanslo says with a smirk.

Dolerma shrugs and sets those scary eyes back on Bas. "I find such thoughts distasteful." He blinks—fucking *sideways*. "And I do not think Kimo will appreciate this development."

The tone is diffident but the feeling Bas is getting is something sly and secretive, though that might just be because he's apparently conspiring with Dolerma now. He wishes he knew what he's conspiring *in*. Besides Stanslo not killing him for being a Directorate spy, which, yeah, that totally works for Bas.

"He still has not forgiven you for Travis," Dolerma continues. "And now there's Haversham."

Stanslo's expression turns narrow, assessing, and he slides the look over at Bas. "I think even Kimo will have a difficult time blaming me for Haversham eating a bullet of his own volition. Travis... well. I cannot be held accountable for another man's gullibility. Or his stupidity. Perhaps Kimo should have minded the spirit of his contract instead of the letter." He's looking at Bas but talking to Dolerma.

"He would say the contract was not his. Nor was the breach."

"Then he would be mistaken that it matters."

Dolerma is silent for moment, black gaze lowered, before he shrugs, bland. "As you say." He takes the crystal from Stanslo. "Will this be for Lowen?" He pauses, then, "Surely not for Reacher."

Stanslo purses his lips in thought as he stares at Bas and strokes his whiskers. "Neither," he says after a moment. He tips a half smile at Dolerma, eyes narrowed. "For me, I think. For now."

Dolerma says nothing to that, merely tilts his head and nods acknowledgment. He turns to Bas. "Shall we, Mister Barstow?"

"Shall we what?"

"Finalize your contract, of course."

Bas still has no notion exactly what kind of contract they're talking about here. So he slouches in his chair and says, "Yeah, no, we shall not," because he wants nothing to do with any of this, but more practically, he needs to see what will happen. The shit is getting deeper by the second, and he still doesn't know what the hell is going on.

Bas lets the nervous tic twitching at his mouth bloom into a wide grin and twists it obnoxious for show. Because he's Jakob fucking Barstow. He's the guy who beefed a man ten seconds after stepping off the train in Stanslo's Bridge and then made a bad joke out of it. He's the hardcase who—according to Dolerma—put a bullet through his uncle's throat for money. Barstow would not roll over this easy and neither can Bas, so cocky bluffing it is.

Dolerma says nothing. He merely stares over Bas's shoulder and remains perfectly still.

Stanslo's eyebrow goes up and he tilts his head. "You're not finding the terms to your liking?"

"Who the fuck can tell? What terms?" Bas spins his glass between his fingers. "You haven't even told me what I'm contracting for yet."

"Haven't I?" Stanslo looks amused. "I do apologize, quite sloppy of me, but it's simple, really." He leans in. "I only want you to utilize the skills you've demonstrated since arriving."

Bas scowls. "Which ones are those? The ones where I watched a man bully a Tech half his size, or the ones where I watched another guy blow his own brains out? Oh, wait—it must be the ones where I managed not to *die in a little metal box*, and not for your lack of trying." He leans in, narrow-eyed. "Life is not nearly as agreeable in Stanslo's Bridge as Oleg led me to believe, I'm afraid."

"You'd rather go back to the Directorate hounding you and the threat of extended lockup?"

"I'd rather not have a man like Fox thinking he gets to leash me as sure as the Directorate would if they caught up. I left the Territories because there were too many assholes like him around already—I don't need to trade them for a whole new set.

Oleg hired me because I have a habit of getting the job done and not turning up dead, not because I can"—Bas waves his hands around, lets the anger and exasperation show—"shoot fucking bats. All night. *In the fucking rain.*"

"Ah!" Stanslo holds up a finger. "See, now, that's exactly what I meant. Lowen tells me you were quite impressive the other night. And with a new gun you'd never shot before."

"Impressive." Bas scowls. "Shooting bats?" When Stanslo nods, all enthusiasm, Bas sits back and lifts his eyebrows. "You want me to shoot more bats." He slants a look at Dolerma and then back at Stanslo. "You want me to sign a *contract* to shoot *bats.*"

"No, no," says Stanslo then he pauses and tilts his head. "Although it's very much similar, now that you've put it like that." He grins. "Gunner, Bas. We've run rather short just lately."

Because you whipped one to death and the other one shot himself in the head. Yeah, I'm all caught up on that now, thanks.

"Our business here necessitates frequent trips out into the desert," Stanslo continues. "And on those trips, there can be certain... problems. I need a marksman. I need a man who can hit a moving target. I need a man who enjoys it and doesn't miss."

"What kind of 'problems' are we talking about?"

Stanslo points to the wall behind Bas. "Those kind."

Bas turns to look at the weirdass animal heads, then shifts a squint at Dolerma. When Dolerma only keeps his eyes straight ahead, Bas turns back to Stanslo. "And this requires a contract because...?"

"Protection, Bas. For us both. There are certain things you will see that I won't want you discussing with just anyone. And there are certain risks you will take from which you will have some level of protection merely by virtue of our contract." Stanslo shrugs. "You do what I tell you, you follow your orders and keep those things that are important to me safe, and I assure you those things Haversham said to you will fade into the empty regrets of the inadequate man he was, and the only consequences you'll ever face are the jealous looks from the rest of the citizenry."

Bas is going to do it. He doesn't really have much choice, not if he wants to know what's going on out here and then find a way out. Still. Doesn't mean he has to make it easy for Stanslo.

"Consequences." Bas snorts. "So I do everything you say and I won't get whipped to death or thrown back in the Box? Yeah, *fuck* that. You sit there and smile while some desert mutant slithers around inside my head? Sorry, Dolerma, no offense, but fuck that too." Bas gets up from the table, hoping he's got this bluff right while he pauses to salute Stanslo with his glass. "Nice meeting you, Baron, and thanks for the trip, but I think I'll be going now."

"Going." Stanslo grins over at Dolerma like it's the funniest thing he's heard in ages. He looks back at Bas. "Going where, exactly?"

Bas finishes the last of his drink and sucks a long breath through his teeth at the smooth slide of warmth down his throat. "Not here." He shrugs and sets the glass down. "Maybe back to where I came from." He waves in the general direction of the desert. "Maybe see where those tracks lead. See what's out there that's got you building a line through nowhere and getting a whole town to do it for you."

"Ah!" Stanslo leans forward on the table and clasps his hands together. His smile is open and enthused. "How adventurous."

Bas has been hoping for some kind of hit, something that would shake Stanslo's easy demeanor somewhat and show Bas more of the crazy eyes he saw before, because at least that would give Bas something to go on. He's just winging it now.

Stanslo isn't fazed in the least. And he doesn't answer any of the questions. "And how do you plan to do either of those things, dear Bas?" he asks, real interest in his bright blue gaze. "As I'm sure you learned from Oleg, it isn't an easy thing to acquire passage on one of my trains."

Ah. *There.*

Bas smiles. "I see. So it's *exactly* like Haversham said. You'll keep me prisoner in your shithole little town until I—"

"Prisoner!" Stanslo throws his head back and laughs, so he misses the quick look Dolerma flickers at Bas. That Bas *can't read*, damn it.

"Goodness, so dramatic." Stanslo shakes his head and takes a sip of his drink. "Such a messy business, prisoners. Feh. No, Bas, I assure you, you're welcome to leave any time you like."

"Just not on your train. Or, I assume, not with one of your horses or any of your provisions."

Stanslo only smiles and doesn't answer, but he doesn't really have to. Sure, he'll happily let anyone who wants to walk out of town and out into the desert. Because he knows just as well as Bas does that powerful few could make it through that desolate stretch of wilderness with full provisions and a horse, let alone riding shank's mare and with nothing.

Bas gets it. Not all of it, but at least a definitive answer to why no one has come out of Stanslo's Bridge for years.

"And should I assume the price of passage on your train would be more dosh than I could afford?" Bas asks flatly.

"You don't seem to understand how things work here, Bas." Stanslo nods toward Bas's empty chair. "Come. Sit. Let me explain."

With a narrow look between Stanslo and Dolerma, Bas does. He slouches, though, purposefully insolent.

"Your skills with a gun," Stanslo says, "come very well-recommended. It's not everyone Lowen refers to as an ace shot with no trace of irony." He winks. "You impressed him. Lowen is not a man easily impressed."

Bas can believe that, actually.

"I would hate," Stanslo goes on, "to have gone to all the trouble of fetching you here only to see my efforts wasted, along with my time and expense." He gets up for another drink. "Oleg thought you were good, else he wouldn't have hired you. But he never said *how* good." He lifts his glass at Bas, a silent offer. When Bas shakes his head, Stanslo shrugs and pours a drink for himself. "Still, I would not have gone to the trouble if Oleg didn't think your skill was in my best interests. You have value to me, Bas. I need you. Especially now, since I seem to be fresh out of gunners, so I'm willing to up your compensation and sweeten your side of the contract. But no man is indispensable. And there are rules." He smiles. "*My* rules.

"Survival out here is... precarious. We don't have much use for dosh, you see." Stanslo waves his glass around as he sits back down. "What do scraps of paper with some other country's prime minister on them mean out here, after all?"

Some other country. God. He really does see this place as a territory with no jurisdiction but his own.

"Trade," Stanslo continues, "is as close to the mark as I imagine we'll get." He's not smiling now, but his manner is still friendly. Concerned, even. "I suppose you might say it's more of a trade-debt agreement, wherein I give my people what they need and they accrue debts that must be paid back to me through their earnings. You, for instance." The smile's back now. "You acquired a debt when you took passage on my train. You owe me now. You see how that works?

"So I would... regret it if you chose to leave us now, in whatever fashion you did the leaving." Stanslo sips at his drink. "But I can assure you, you won't be doing it on my train. How in the world would I recoup my investment? Have you got anything to trade?"

Bas doesn't think the clothes, the handful of ammunition, and the illobooks he brought with him are going to cut it. And God, yeah, now he *sees*, now he *knows*. Bas can see exactly how someone caught out here might find themselves in a deep, dark pit that only keeps getting deeper and darker.

Bas considers it all for as long as he thinks he can get away with, then looks up at Stanslo and leans back in his chair. "I have a nasty habit of not dying when I'm supposed to. You want to throw me into the desert, you might be surprised at where I pop up next. And I'm pretty sure there are a few things out this way you'd prefer not a lot of people knew about. A train that runs on gridTech, for instance."

Stanslo narrows his eyes, and for the second time, Bas gets a real good look at the blank ruthlessness beneath the charming façade, the animal beneath the man. And it's good, because Bas knew it had to be there somewhere, but he just couldn't get a definitive glimpse. Now that he has, he understands. He saw it back at the station, saw its edges in the barn with Fox and in the mess with Haversham, but now he *really* sees it, head-on and looking right at him, and he *gets* Stanslo, because it's kind of simple once it's stripped down to what bubbles beneath the flannel-mouthed charm: Baron Stanslo is a goddamned bugfuck insane control freak and incredibly vain.

Vain control freaks can be manipulated, as long as they think they're still in control and you feed their vanity.

Bas grins. "A train that runs on gridTech and without a gridstation in sight. Now that's information I'm betting a whole lot of agencies in the Territories would be more than willing to overlook a few missteps in a man's past to get their hands on. So maybe you *should* kill me. If you send me out into the wilderness... well. There's that nasty habit I have of not dying and all."

He stops there. And waits.

Stanslo tries to outstare him, but crazy people just don't have that kind of patience or stillness. Stanslo's eyes narrow for a long, long moment, studying Bas, then his grin is back, crinkling the corners of his eyes. "Wonderful!" he says. "Isn't he wonderful, Dolerma?"

God. Bas actually forgot for a few minutes that Dolerma was even there.

"As you say, Baron," Dolerma agrees, toneless, and palms the crystal as he stands with a last unreadable look at Bas. "If that's all."

Smooth, thinks Bas, relief making him a little light-headed, and his limbs go heavy, like all his blood had been seized up in his veins, waiting, and now it's washing through him in rivers of reprieve. *I am so fucking smooth, thank fucking God*, until—

"No," says Stanslo, pulling his face into a frowning little pout. "I don't think that's quite all. Now, please."

—and everything in Bas halts with a *whump* so potent he's surprised it doesn't knock him out of his chair.

Dolerma's hand is over Bas's again, and the crystal is in his palm, and that mind-smacking *thud* shudders over Bas a second time, but it doesn't hit him in the gut like it did before. It feels like it slides over him, a whiff of citrus with the merest suggestion of damp earth, and Bas gets the weird impression of a blow aimed dead center at him that instead glances right past its target. *Locks and defenses still in place*, Bas tells himself, and hopes the absence of a sense of *wrong* inside his head means it's true.

Still, his nerves are on edge and disquiet has been doing a number on him for a while now, so his body wants to jump a mile, startled reflex, but Bas stills it. If he spooks, they'll know he's felt something, and if they know he's felt something, they'll know he's a tracker.

So Bas sits. And stares. And waits.

Stanslo watches Bas closely, then claps his hands together and booms, "*Splendid*!" and just like that, it's over. No call for the deputies to come and collect Bas and drag him to the whipping post or the outskirts of town to banish him to the desert. Or take him out in the yard and kill him. Bas's whole body wants to shake with relief and unspent adrenaline, but he keeps himself as still as he can.

"You see?" Stanslo says. "That wasn't so terrible, was it? I do apologize for the bit of trickery, but it just seemed so much easier than tying you down. Say you understand, Bas."

Again, there's that *thump* in the air all around Bas, the taste of lemon with earthy undertones, and the impression of invisible ripples vibrate like the air's been gonged, but they slide right over Bas like before, they don't get *in*, and it doesn't make any sense at all, but *it does*, and Bas keeps his almost-epiphany and its resulting half thrill to himself. He merely says, "I...." And tests it. Because he thinks he almost knows what's going on here, and this is important, Bas thinks it's going to set the stage for every single thing he does from here on out. Casual, he stretches, lets his hand "happen upon" a knife from the place setting down the table. He slides a flicker of unease into his expression, as though conflicted and confused, as he snags the knife, taps it against his empty glass, a brittle *ching ching ching* to distract as he ducks his head and breathes, so low he's the only one who can hear over the tapping, "I don't understand." The direct opposite of what Stanslo has told him to say, and he'd said it out loud, no resistance, because Dolerma didn't give Bas up before and he apparently hasn't done whatever he was supposed to do to make Bas obey Stanslo, either.

With a narrow slant to his eyes, Bas sets the knife down, looks up and smirks at Stanslo, then says, "I understand," and shuts his mouth.

Stanslo grins, pleased, and Bas almost does too, but he decides he shouldn't push his luck after what he's pretty sure he just got away with. What Dolerma just *helped* him get away with.

Sliding his dark glasses back on, Dolerma exchanges bland pleasantries with Stanslo as he hands the crystal over and takes his leave. Stanslo tells him, "See if you can find Kimo when you get back to town, won't you?" and Dolerma gives one last unreadable look to Bas and nods.

Bas eyes the fancy settings on the table and wonders how hard it might be to get out of staying for this supper he's apparently expected to appreciate. He'd kind of like to get the hell away from Stanslo, not to mention catch up with Dolerma and ask him exactly what the fuck just happened, because Bas doesn't think he'll get a good answer from Stanslo. Nonetheless:

"What the hell was that?" Bas asks. It's through his teeth, and he doesn't even have to pretend at the threat inside it. It felt like some kind of violation, and he's pretty fucking pissed off about it, but he can't let on he felt anything at all so he pretends he's just pissed off in general.

"That," says Stanslo with a jovial wink, "was simply me protecting my investment." He leans in. "It is not in your best interests for you to say no to me right now, Bas." He sits back with a nod. "It's generally not in anyone's best interests to say no to me. Ever. This crystal and Dolerma's unique talents will ensure that you don't."

Bas stares, then asks, "Is that why everyone here jumps when you say frog, Baron? You get some freaky psyTech to play with their heads?"

"Oh, Dolerma isn't psyTech, not like you understand it. Dolerma is the answer to psyTech." Stanslo strokes at the whiskers on his chin. "And I like to think it's not the only reason."

"The answer," Bas echoes. "What does that mean?"

Stanslo merely grins. "Nothing you need to worry about, Bas."

Which means he has no intention of explaining. Bas broods on that, because it's scary and horrible, and he thinks the frowning and near-sulk is something Barstow would do when he doesn't get his way. Stanslo lets Bas have at it, but he watches.

There's silence for a spell, not too oppressive, but it's long enough for the discomfort to start getting to Bas, because he's pretty sure silence isn't a natural thing for Stanslo. He's been chatty and cheerful since Bas met him, and the quiet scrutiny with which he's now peering at Bas makes Bas want to fidget. He keeps still and gives Stanslo a flat look instead.

"What?"

Stanslo grins. Because of course he does. "Little boys on their knees?"

"Little.... Sorry, what?" Bas blinks. And then he tries not to grimace. "Oh."

Of all the things for Dolerma to pull out of his ass and for Stanslo to latch on to, *after what just happened.* It requires a pretty drastic shift of the gears in Bas's head.

"What's it to you?" he drawls, an edge of belligerence in his tone. "We didn't just get bonded or something, did we?"

Stanslo stares for a second, long enough for Bas to start regretting the belligerence, before Stanslo throws his head back and laughs, long and hard. Bas is struck again by how nice the laugh is, how it makes Stanslo look fine as cream gravy when he does it. It's weirdly annoying.

When he catches his breath somewhat, Stanslo knuckles at the corner of his eye and shakes his head. "Oh, Bas, I *do* like you. But not like that." He finishes off his drink and sets the glass on the table. "No, but I do want you to be very clear on your... boundaries." He cocks his head to the side and stares at Bas, scrutinizing, and he strokes at the short, silky black-gray whiskers covering his chin. "You've met Kimo."

"The gridTech?" Bas twirls his glass on the table. "Sort of."

"He is extraordinarily valuable to me, to my people, to this place, to...." Stanslo pauses and gestures all around him. "To the future." He clasps his hands and leans across the table. "His singularity makes him irreplaceable, and there are some who don't appreciate my methods of protection."

"Protection." Bas lifts his eyebrow, blatantly skeptical. Because what he saw at the station had dreadful little to do with protection. "Don't you mean control?"

"Aren't they, sometimes, the same thing?" Stanslo smirks a little, then says, "Call it what you will, Bas. In the end, it's my definition that matters. And my methods of protection. Travis was my right hand for more than twenty-five years before he decided what's mine was also his, before he decided to test my 'control.' His mistake should serve as your lesson." He pauses, blue eyes intense. "If twenty-five years of loyalty and friendship came to nothing more than screams at a whipping post, imagine the repercussions for someone like you."

Bas tries not to gape. "Is this some weirdass way of telling me to keep my hands off the gridTech?"

"He's mine."

"Yeah, all right, whatever." Bas puts his hands up. "The sparker's all yours, not for me, I get it."

"He is not for anyone." There is no smile on Stanslo's face, no hint of that creepy cheer behind his eyes. "There will be times when I must entrust his well-being to you. Times when I won't be there to ensure our agreement holds. I expect you'll remember Travis, should you ever be tempted to take liberties with what is mine." His voice is cold and his manner the most direct it's been since Bas laid eyes on him. "You won't touch him, except to protect him when I can't."

And okay. Okay. Bas has seen guys like Stanslo before, the "buy it, steal it, kill it, or fuck it" sort. The sort who think "I want" means "I should have," and if they can't buy it, they'll steal it, if they can't steal it, they'll kill it so no one else can have it, and if they can't do any of those things, they'll fuck it like a tom spraying its scent to prove ownership.

"If I'm not mistaken, Baron," Bas says slowly, "protecting your sparker is pretty much what got me put in the Box."

"Ah, but you *are* mistaken, Bas. The Box was because I had not yet given you permission."

Permission. *Permission* to protect someone Stanslo cares about. *Permission* to protect someone Stanslo has claimed is irreplaceable.

"Take what you like from anyone else," Stanslo goes on, "and fight out the fairness of it between you. Take advantage of the charms available at the cathouse whenever it pleases you if your credit holds. Perhaps you'll earn the right to bid on the crystal of your choice, and when you do, you'll understand both the benefit and the duty behind that sort of 'control,' as you so bluntly put it. You'll understand the responsibility inherent in protecting what is truly *yours*." He leans in, so close Bas can see the tiny red veins in the whites of his eyes, and his fisted hand tightens around the crystal. "Kimo is mine. Travis had the benefit of a warning before I was forced to drastic measures. Consider what's left of him yours."

Bas... stares. He rolls over the multitude of implications in all of that and doesn't like a single conclusion he gathers. He opens his mouth, not sure what he means to say, but he never finds out, and it's probably just as well.

"The one you should be warning is that *boy*," says a woman's voice from the door, the tone twisted vicious and full of spite.

Bas turns to see her, all long chestnut hair and sculpted features and legs that stretch up and up inside fine kid trousers that do nothing to hide her shapely curves. She gives Bas a sneering look and then dismisses him with a flick of her hazel gaze.

"One of these days," she says with a lazy blink at Stanslo, "your trashy Poor Side toy is going to give you no choice but to take *him* to the whipping post." She grins, harsh but coy; it makes her look beautiful but horrible too. "And I'm going to laugh, and laugh, and *laugh*."

"Ah, Mari!" Stanslo gets up and goes to the door to greet her with a kiss to both cheeks. He slides the crystal on its thong over his head and back inside his shirt, then puts his arm around Mari's waist and turns to Bas. "Bas, may I introduce you to Mari, my bondmate."

Bas gets up but doesn't approach. He gives Mari a nod and a "Ma'am" and then frowns at Stanslo. "Bondmate?"

"Mm," hums Stanslo with a smile for Mari. "It only took her a day to see the potential of my little world. And less than a month to turn it into the oasis you see around you." He winks at Bas. "My desert flower who grows flowers in the desert."

Mari steps forward with a smile, pleasant this time, and extends her hand. "Welcome to Stanslo's Bridge, Bas."

Bas takes her hand, dazed, and shuts his mouth before anything spills out of it. Because holy fucking shit, *Mari* and *grows flowers in the desert*, which has to mean *weatherTech*, and Bas is pretty sure he's politely shaking hands with Mariella Crocker, the weatherTech who disappeared just before Kimolijah Adani.

10.

Supper is surreal. Bas has a vague notion that the food is good, but he barely tastes it. He watches Stanslo canoodle with Mari and listens to them discussing the business of the day, and hardly any of it gets through the muddle in Bas's head.

They're serious. It's real respect and affection between them. Maybe not soppy stars-in-their-eyes, over-the-top-swoony love, and Bas thinks Stanslo can fake and charm his way through anything and make it look real, but Mari....

Bas had gotten the impression that maybe there was something sinister going on between Stanslo and Kimolijah, what with the *mine-mine-mine* and all, but now there's Mari, and as far as Bas can tell, the obvious regard she has for Stanslo is real. So what the hell is the deal with Stanslo and Kimolijah? Stanslo's bit-on-the-side, maybe? It makes a repulsive kind of sense. Stanslo isn't the sort who'd appreciate his bit-on-the-side sharing affections with another, and if Kimolijah was sleeping with that Travis too, if Kimolijah's here because he chose it—

No, that makes no sense. Kimolijah Adani had already been on his way to being a wealthy and respected engineer and scientist three years ago, and he hadn't even finished his last year at the academy yet. He'd been the youngest ever to have papers published in academic and scientific journals; his ideas on Grid theory and its applications were so revolutionary as to almost be laughable until one actually decoded the science behind the conclusions; he'd already had offers from across the Territories, including the most lucrative one the Directorate itself had probably ever tendered.

It has to be the theory Bas originally supposed, with one not-insignificant tweak: Kimolijah apparently hasn't been murdered for his designs; he's being held hostage for them. And Bas will bet just about anything that Ajamil Adani is the reason Kimolijah hasn't taken his impossible gridtrain and blown out of Stanslo's Bridge on a glowing blue blast of gridstream. And he'll also bet Kimolijah's da is in the same nowhere hole Haversham's Jilly was.

Stanslo and Mari keep unsubtly changing the subject when Bas asks about what Dolerma is and where he came from, or where those tracks into the desert go and what's out there. They don't actually say Bas shouldn't be asking, but he gets the message anyway.

They ask Bas about his life before he came to Stanslo's Bridge, and Bas offers up Jakob Barstow's backstory. He keeps it all laconic and reluctant, because Barstow was not built to be the talkative sort or much of a braggart.

First rule of building a villainous reputation: keep it all low-key and stuff it full with implications but never confirm details. Let them fill those in themselves. Bas has found that people will always come up with something in their heads that's heaps more convincing than anything he could've told them.

When Stanslo prods Bas for more, Bas substitutes the plots of illobook stories and tones them down somewhat to make them believable. It's easy to put Jakob Barstow into the roles of the villains—highwaymen, thieves, murderers. It's harder to come up with questions Barstow might ask that would actually get answers and not raise suspicions or get Bas killed.

For all it can probably be considered a success from the "still not dead" perspective, Bas ultimately ends up leaving Stanslo's house knowing little more than when he arrived. And annoyed beyond reason that Kimolijah never showed up.

"I'm sure we'll be seeing you up here again, Bas," Edlyn says as she helps him into his duster and then opens the door to let him out. Her pleasant face tightens as she peers around Bas's shoulder.

Bas turns to see the lean figure of a man in the dark of the front walk, just standing there, still and silent. The stars are slung low amidst a milky stratum of galactic grandeur, and God, the desert is bloody cold at night, but the skies are fucking *amazing*. Bas's eyes haven't yet adjusted from the brightness of the house, so he can't see the man's face, only a dark shape among the shadows folding into the gently rolling landscape of the yard.

It's weird, because how would Bas know, really, but he gets the impression the man hasn't just gotten here, that he's been here for a spell, like he'd reached the porch steps and couldn't make himself go any farther. He's short and lean and dark-skinned, and he's wearing a squat narrow-brimmed hat, but that's all Bas can make out, even with the glow of the gridlights coming through the open front door. The man is stiff-shouldered, with his head down, and his entire body flinches when Edlyn snaps, "Well, come on, then. He's been waiting on you. You missed supper. You'll be in for it now, shinning off like you did without a by-your-leave, and you just up from a fit."

Bas has been assuming it's Kimolijah, but now he knows.

Kimolijah's dark silhouette wavers for a moment, like he's thinking of running the other way. Eventually he says, "Mari's here, though."

"And now so are you," Edlyn says grimly. "Won't this be fun."

She turns to Bas with a bright smile, as if she hasn't just been barking at Kimolijah like he's a six-year-old truant. "Do come see us again, Bas," she says, polite dismissal.

Bas nods, wordless, and takes the hat Edlyn hands him as he closes his coat. He can already see his breath on the cold night air, and he isn't even out the door yet.

"Good night," he tells Edlyn and makes his way down the porch steps, eyes on Kimolijah all the while, and again, he can't really tell in the dark, but he feels like Kimolijah's watching him back. Bas pauses mere steps away from Kimolijah and squints through the dark at him until it gets awkward and noticeable. Edlyn is still watching from the door, probably already thinking about what she's going to tell Stanslo later, and Bas feels like someone has to say something or every single bit of dubious luck he's had in surviving the past hellish week will rear back up in one single, almighty *fuck you!* from the universe and he'll be dead before he gets out of the yard.

"Thank you for making sure I didn't die in the Box," Bas means to say, or maybe, "I didn't mean what you think I meant," or something that will bridge the chasm he can almost see between him and the person he waded into this hellhole for.

"Best get on," is what he actually says, and he knows it sounds foolishly imperious the second it comes out, because Kimolijah stiffens up even more, and Bas can see the flash of white teeth through a snarl in the dark.

"Best mind your own damned business," Kimolijah retorts, low and grinding, then he jerks into motion. He's past Bas and up the porch steps before Bas can get a good look at him in the light from the house, but he supposes he doesn't really need one. It's not like he hasn't been trying his damnedest *not* to see that wide smile every time he closes his eyes.

⚬⚬⚬

Bas doesn't see either Fox or Kimolijah for a few days, and no one seems to want to say anything about any of it. He doesn't care all that much about Fox. Getting kneecapped is pretty horrible, or so Bas has heard, but he can't pretend he gives a shit one way or the other, so he doesn't bother to ask whether or not Fox lived through it. By the hints of scuttlebutt, Bas thinks Fox did, and he also thinks there are a powerful lot of people here who would have preferred otherwise.

He wants very badly, though, to ask about Kimolijah and the Outlet. Bas saw the restraints and the wires and the crystals, and he's pretty sure he knows exactly what the Outlet is, even if he doesn't know how it works. And it isn't something new; it's routine enough that the task is trusted to Reacher, of all people. Like so many other things, Bas can only wonder about it, keep his ears open, and hope there will be an opportunity to find out what it means.

When Bas asks Reacher about all that auction business instead, he gets the "aw, shucks" grin and then a frown.

"Fox din't have yer crystal," Reacher says, tilting his head at Bas like it worries him. "Lowen neither."

Bas doesn't really know how to respond, so he just shrugs and says, "No." He doesn't elaborate.

Reacher stares at him for a long time, something Bas can't really ken flickering on his big, dumb face, and the cloying miasma of rancid rosewater that clings to Reacher is starting to get to him. They're standing just a few paces off the square, Travis's husk of a corpse a ghoulish specter in the periphery of Bas's vision. Reacher's aura of putrid roses really shouldn't feel so close and oppressive, out here in the open air as they are, but it envelops and *gets in*, somehow, like dust in the lungs. Bas is relieved when Reacher shrugs and starts ambling off.

"Too bad," Reacher says as he walks away. He turns one of those wide, vacant grins on Bas over his shoulder. "It'd've been a powerful pleasure to bid on it."

Bas stares at Reacher's wide back until he's well gone, wondering if that was supposed to be a compliment. When he comes back to himself, he looks first at Travis, slowly turning to leather in the sun, then up the rise where Stanslo's big house sits. He's not surprised to see the falcon drifting in a wide, lazy circle above it.

⌘

It's not there the next day; it's diving playfully over the wide roof of the station instead. Which means, Bas is pretty sure, that Kimolijah's working on his train, so Bas means to head that way shortly. Right now, though, he's watching Serenat and Dolerma having some kind of strangely subdued argument that's nonetheless easy to peg as something that's not new between them. They're across the square, two rawboned figures easily identified against the monotonous dun of the desert, though every inch of skin is covered, from trousers to long sleeves to gloves to hats to dark glasses. It's animated, whatever the argument's about, Dolerma's long arm flinging out to point at Travis, and the brim of Serenat's floppy hat rippling as she shakes her head and snaps something back Bas can't hear.

He thinks about trying to steal in closer so he can eavesdrop, but then Fox hobbles into view. And he *is* hobbling, crude crutch under one arm, bloody bandage at his knee, and face too pale. Bas can see the sick sweat even before Fox gets close, and he thinks whatever's under Fox's bandage would probably stink worse than Reacher's rosewater, should anyone feel the need to have a look.

The second Fox sees Bas, his glazy eyes sharpen and narrow, and his limping stride becomes more purposeful. He stalks up to Bas, as much as he *can* stalk, before he halts and lifts the crutch to jab its rough-hewn foot toward Bas's chest. Bas refuses to take a step back. Fox has apparently been stripped of his weapons, and the crutch is hardly intimidating. The pain-madness in Fox's eyes, though... that's a touch worrisome.

"Who the fuck are ye?" Fox snarls. A bit of a jolt goes through Bas, because that's a dreadful loaded question and he can't afford for someone like Fox to get an inkling of what it really means. He relaxes when Fox goes on, "Lowen en't got yer crystal neither, and Baron don't keep just anyone's crystal to hisself." Fox narrows his eyes, a little bit of foam frothing in the corners of his chapped lips. "You Baron's new Travis, that it? Some hardcase gunslinger dandy who don't know how shit runs here, with yer prissy face and yer shiny gun."

Bas lifts an eyebrow, kind of shocked and impressed that Fox is even up and around in the first place, and not at all surprised his probable agony would come out as anger and aggression. And, apparently, a healthy dose of paranoia.

Also—*prissy face*?

"Are you *actually* five?" Bas asks, a little wondering.

"You en't no Travis." Fox bares his brown teeth. "You en't *shit*. Think you can just waltz in here, jump the ranks, yeah?"

"Funny thing," Bas says, slow and with a deliberate drawl. "Seems I can. Seems I have."

He looks Fox up and down, admittedly with a touch of pity, because Bas knows what infection looks like, and he knows he's looking right at a healthy case of it. He shakes his head, glances over to where Dolerma and Serenat were, and scowls when he sees they're gone.

"You bore me, Fox," he says and starts walking toward the station.

"We en't done," Fox grates at Bas's back.

Bas shakes his head and keeps an eye out for snakes and giant spiders along the path as he keeps walking. "Yeah, we are."

Though, yeah, they're probably not. People like Fox just don't go down easy.

⁂

"I'm told you and Fox had words this morning," Stanslo says with a curve of lips that Bas is beginning to recognize as his whiff-of-blood-in-the-water smile.

He's found Bas wandering around the station, watching as the trolleys hum busily along the tracks and trying to glean something, anything, from the idle chatter, while he tries to work out how to approach Kimolijah, what he might say. Stanslo showing up pretty much buggers that notion anyway.

There's no diplomatic way to answer Stanslo's question-disguised-as-a-statement, and Bas doesn't really think too hard to come up with one. On the one hand, he doesn't really want to know when, where, and how Stanslo got that information, and on the other, Bas thinks of Fox's mean eyes and nasty sneers and his rough hands on Kimolijah's jaw, and decides he doesn't feel like making it sound any better anyway. So he merely says, "Uh-huh."

"And this wasn't the first time."

"Nope."

"And the trouble is because...?"

Bas sighs and keeps himself from rolling his eyes. Apparently what they say is actually true—you really do never get out of secondary school.

"He seems to labor under the impression I represent some sort of... threat to his position here. I begged to differ."

"Well, then." Stanslo taps at his chin and shakes his head. "Lowen," he calls.

"Yeah, boss?" Bas hadn't noticed Lowen trailing Stanslo, but there he is.

"I wanted to acquaint you with the details of your position," Stanslo tells Bas. "But I see you've already taken the initiative. Have you had breakfast?" When Bas shakes his head, Stanslo tells Lowen, "Go scrounge up some coffee, won't you? And bring some along for Kimo, too, I'm sure he came right here this morning." When Lowen replies with what Bas is coming to think of as the typical "Sure, boss" Stanslo holds up his hand and says, "Actually...." He strokes at his chin for a second or two and says, "Have Fox fetch it." He watches Lowen go with a grin at Bas, like they're conspirators, but he only says, "Honestly, the boy would forget that food exists if someone didn't remind him." Bas thinks he's talking about Kimolijah. "This is why he needs looking after."

It's secondary to the tiny bit of disgust that's flitting through Bas's chest. Because Stanslo just shot Fox in the kneecap a few days ago, and now he's making him *fetch coffee*. There are no medTechs out here, and based on what he saw just a little while ago, Bas is betting on sepsis. Fox will be dreadful lucky if he doesn't die or at least lose the leg, and there was no mistaking the pain Bas saw all over Fox. Bas has had pretty much nothing but disdain and dislike for Fox since the moment he set eyes on him, and this morning didn't help, but making the man some kind of gimpy gofer when he can obviously barely stand, that's just... it's a sick mind that can be so arbitrarily cruel so casually.

Then again—Box. Whipping post. Pretty much everything Bas has seen here so far.

It isn't a revelation and it isn't Bas's to worry about. And it can only cause him a difficulty. He is *not* about to jeopardize whatever thin thread of connection Stanslo thinks they've made for fucking Fox. Kimolijah's his job. Mariella's his job. At least until he figures out if either of them want to be. So Bas sucks in a long, quiet breath and lets it flow silently through his teeth.

"What is all this?" he asks, and he gestures at the bustle that consumes all the space between the station and the storehouse.

"This," says Stanslo, spreading his arms wide, like a king embracing his realm, "is innovation. It's invention tending to necessity; imagination thwarting certainty."

People look at Stanslo in different ways as he and Bas pass through the small crowd of busy workers—some with genuine smiles, some with trepidation, some with caution.

"It's why Stanslo's Bridge exists," says Stanslo as he nods and smiles his way through, clapping a hand on a shoulder here, patting a back there, whether its recipient seems to appreciate it or not. "It's our lifeblood, our future, our investment, and our eventual triumph. You see, Bas...." He stops when they reach the corner of the station, and he pulls Bas into the shade of the building, a hand on his arm. It's still loud, but not as much so here, and they're out of the way of the traffic coming to and fro. Bas can hear Kimolijah muttering probable curses somewhere behind him, but all his attention is on Stanslo.

"What you see around you"—Stanslo gestures outward and around—"this is not all there is, and certainly not all there will be." He ducks his head and pulls out a smile Bas hasn't seen on him before, something eager and perhaps even shy, like a teenaged girl confessing that yes, in fact, she does actually think she's as pretty as everyone tells her she is. "I am not simply a small-time desert king or some sort of robber baron, as they call me in the Territories."

Stanslo pauses, like he's waiting for something from Bas. Bas doesn't care to guess what, and he's a little preoccupied with the fact that Stanslo hasn't exactly answered the question, so he just lifts his eyebrows and says, "I didn't think you were, Baron, else I wouldn't've come."

Feeding the vanity is obviously the right way to go, because Stanslo grins and claps Bas on the shoulder. "Indeed," he says and starts leading Bas over to where Kimolijah's feet are sticking out the side of the locomotive's engine compartment. "And should you turn out to be what I think you are, Bas, one day soon you'll be very glad you did. One day, we will be known as the saviors of worlds." He thumps Bas between the shoulder blades, then raises his voice and calls, "Ah, Kimo, my dear!"

It's loud enough to make Bas flinch away a bit from where he'd been leaning in to make sure he caught every word; it's also apparently loud enough to startle Kimolijah. There's a jolt and a kick, a hollow-sounding *thunk*, and a predictable string of curses as the feet turn into legs unto torso into Kimolijah, once again thumping down onto the ground on his ass and blinking up at Stanslo through his smeary goggles like a concussed baby owl.

"Baron," he says, tone flat but with a curl on the end that might be a question. He peers over his shoulder when the falcon chirps a disgruntled noise and takes off. Slowly, Kimolijah looks back at Stanslo, somehow blank and expectant all at once.

Bas watches carefully, because he hasn't seen these two interact since the station and he didn't know what he was looking at then. He still doesn't *know*, really, but he thinks he does, and he catalogues Kimolijah's wary look up from his seat in the dust, Stanslo's smile softening into helpless fondness, and Bas once again gets the overwhelming impression that Stanslo is absolutely besotted, Mariella Crocker notwithstanding.

He still doesn't know for certain what's going on. He does know, though, that if there ever comes a time when he needs to know Stanslo's weakness, it's right now sitting in the dirt, eyeing him suspiciously through a pair of greasy goggles and holding a wrench like it's a weapon.

"We missed you at breakfast," Stanslo says, and it's light and cheery, but the accusation beneath it is clear. "I'm beginning to seriously reconsider Edlyn's suggestion that we start nailing your window shut." He pauses, and his face pulls into a sincere-looking frown of concern. "You oughtn't be up yet, dear heart. The Outlet hit you hard this time. You're only up since yester-day."

Kimolijah shoots a displeased look between Stanslo and Bas, and then examines the wrench like it needs fine-tuned adjustment that requires all his concentration. "I needed to get started," he tells the wrench. "Missed heaps of time, what with...."

Bas can't quite figure out why something Kimolijah doesn't even say sounds accusing, but it does. Kimolijah's still looking down at the wrench, so he doesn't see Stanslo's mouth tighten, but Bas does. Apparently Stanslo caught the tone as well.

"And yet I have every confidence you'll have it solved by the next run," says Stanslo. "You have people, after all, who depend upon you."

Kimolijah's shoulders stiffen and his grip on the wrench tightens. He just sits there and breathes for a moment before he takes a long, deep one and his body loosens.

"Uh-huh," he says and slants a look upward. He opens and closes his mouth a few times, hesitant, then says, "I went to put in an order for parts with Dolerma this morning."

Stanslo's jaw clenches. "Did you."

"He said you told him I'm still not allowed to requisition anything from Harrowgate." Kimolijah tilts his head. "It's been months, Baron. And it wasn't even my fault. I had nothing to do with it and you know it. I can't do my job if I don't have the right parts and equipment."

"Oh, my dear." Stanslo gives Kimolijah a look of fond exasperation. "I've seen you put together a fully functioning gridluster in two hours out of nothing more than what you scavenged from the scrap heap."

"That doesn't mean I can—"

"I am not interested in airing personal grievances in public."

Stanslo's tone is abruptly forbidding. "Perhaps you should have thought of this consequence before Travis's ill-considered... errand."

Kimolijah's teeth clench. "It wasn't *me*."

Stanslo doesn't retort; he smiles and sets a hand on Bas's shoulder. "Kimo, this is Bas."

A huff, and Kimolijah shoots an angry look at Bas. "Yeah, I know. I remember." His mouth turns down, derisive.

Again, Stanslo seems to simply ignore whatever's beneath Kimolijah's tone and turns to Bas. "Kimo is an integral part of Stanslo's Bridge. His contributions are priceless. Irreplaceable. Which is why, I'm sure you can understand, Bas, I take his well-being very seriously." He's looking right at Bas, but his attention wanders for a moment to something beyond Bas's right shoulder, and his smile drops, his eyes narrow—only for an instant—and then the smooth look of charm is back as he says, "Ah. Fox."

Kimolijah has ducked his head and is once again doing intricate imaginary repairs on the wrench as Fox limps slowly closer, a lidded pitcher and four tin cups in his hands instead of his crutch. He looks worse than he did only a short while ago, pale and sweaty and in pain and pissed off, and he eyes Kimolijah with just as much venom as he did before. More, even. When he looks at Stanslo, though, he very obviously attempts to school his expression into one of cowed respect.

"Baron." Fox nods and sets the cups and pitcher on the metal steps that lead into the locomotive's cab. "Lowen says you wanted me to fetch this."

"I did, yes. And good timing, indeed." Stanslo lets go of Bas's shoulder and strokes his bottom lip with his thumb, peering at Fox, assessing, from under the wide brim of his expensive hat. "I had a chat with Bas about your earlier... discussion." He waves in Bas's direction and smiles when Fox's lip tries to curl as he nods. "There seems to be some confusion about who answers to whom."

"I been tryin' to teach him some manners, boss." Fox is speaking to Stanslo, but he's looking at Bas like Bas is something he found underneath a seat in the bogs. It doesn't have the disturbing effect he's likely aiming for, not when he so obviously can barely stand. "Want I should try harder?"

Stanslo laughs and takes the pace or two over to stand beside Fox. He slings an arm across Fox's shoulders, jostles him—it's got to be on purpose—and Fox pales even more, eyes watering.

"Ah, see? A misunderstanding, like I'd thought. No, no." Stanslo tips his head at Bas. "It seems you've been under the impression that some of *my* men are *your* men. Or, at least"—he gives Bas a look, wide-eyed inquiry—"that seems to be the impression Bas got and subsequently relayed to me. It seems it was at the heart of the misunderstanding the other morning." He gives Kimolijah a meaningful glance, which is pretty much lost because Kimolijah appears to have no intention of looking at anything but that wrench. "Which I think," Stanslo continues smoothly, "we have cleared up between us, Fox, have we not?"

Fox sets his teeth, stubborn, and the patchy bristle on his jaw quivers. "Yes, sir, we have."

"And we are in agreement now, are we not?" Stanslo asks softly. "It's only that I know sometimes you and I misunderstand each other when it comes to your men. Or, rather, I should say the men who once answered to you and who now answer to Reacher, but they are all still *my men*, wouldn't you agree?"

Kimolijah snaps his head up from where he'd been picking at the coiled bracelet on his arm. "Reacher's got a crystal?" His tone is weirdly thin and cautious, and he looks almost horrified at the notion. "You let *Reacher* bid at an auction?" He shoots looks between Fox and Stanslo, like he's hoping he's heard wrong and one of them will clarify.

Neither of them do.

Fox is staring at the ground now; Bas can't see his face, but he can see how the lines of Fox's body are taut and minutely leaning away from Stanslo. It takes him a moment, but Fox eventually answers, "I getcha, boss," though it's low and said through his brown, crooked teeth. He shrugs. "You hadn't said yet, though. He didn't have no contract."

"Ah! Of course. That would explain the confusion before." Stanslo nods slowly and pats at Fox as he steps away. His gaze slides across the ground between him and the tracks, lands on a long, thin metal slat that Kimolijah's got holding open the engine hatch. His gait is slow and casual as he ambles toward it, his smile amiable as he lays a hand to it. Bas winces, anticipating it all—the blow to already shattered bone, the screams. Stanslo doesn't heft the bit of metal, though; he angles a friendly look over at Fox and says, "But we have since learned a lesson on what is yours and what is mine, have we not?"

Fox is quick to agree, "Yeah, Baron, yeah, I got it, no worries," almost before Stanslo's finished making the threat, and Fox unconsciously shifts so his bad leg is angled somewhat behind the good one.

"Good. I was concerned that the... conflict this morning might indicate you were still confused. And I only want to help, Fox. I want to make sure everything is crystal clear between us, yes?"

Wow. It really is amazing how much malice Stanslo can get through such a cheerfully concerned tone. Of course, the metal bar probably isn't hurting.

Fox bobbles an anxious nod, and Stanslo grins, smug satisfaction. He lets go of the bar altogether as he turns back to Fox. "So, then." He claps his hands together. "Let's just assume we all misunderstood one another and carry on, shall we? You have a long way to go before you can begin to earn back a place at the auctions, after all."

Fox looks relieved, though sick and a little green, even, but he still aims a deadly glare at Bas. Bas almost rolls his eyes and sighs, because Stanslo can punish and threaten someone like Fox and teach him all the "lessons" his black little heart can come up with, but the fact is, you can't cure stupid.

"Bas here will be assuming gunner responsibilities," Stanslo says. Fox grimaces and Kimolijah narrows his eyes at Bas, but Stanslo either doesn't notice either reaction or doesn't care. "He'll need to acquaint himself with the cannon." He looks at Bas. "I'll need to see a demonstration first, 'Shooter' or no. I'll arrange for some target practice...." He pauses and squints up at the sky for a moment, stroking at the whiskers on his chin, before he turns back to Bas. Bas snaps his attention back to Stanslo from where he'd been watching Kimolijah quietly getting up from his seat in the dirt and surreptitiously sliding into the cab of the locomotive. "Why don't we do that now, shall we?" Stanslo goes on. "Best to have the light for the first time. Kimo." That last is soft and abruptly stops Kimolijah from skulking out the opposite door of the locomotive and, presumably, away. "*Kimo.*" Still soft, but with a touch more authority behind it.

For a moment, Bas thinks Kimolijah won't answer. He stands there for quite a long time, his back to Stanslo and his face turned away, staring out the door of the cab. He's tense. His fingers clutch the side of the door like it's some kind of lifeline in the open sea, and he's still got that wrench gripped in his other hand like it's fused to his skin. And then he lets out a breath and his whole body sags.

"Yeah, Baron?"

"Tell me we won't have the same problems we had with Travis." Stanslo's voice is gentle but he's not smiling now, which is so unusual that Bas has to stare at him for several long seconds.

"Problems," Kimolijah says slowly. He peers at Stanslo over his shoulder, a nasty little smirk curling his lip. "What, you mean the problem with him being one of about five decent people here? Or the one where it wasn't in his contract to take your shit? Those kinds of problems?"

Wow. Resaniji had said her brother was a bit of a smartass once you got to know him, but this is more than "a bit of." Bas really wants to tell Kimolijah to just pin his lip and say whatever it is Stanslo wants to hear, because Stanslo's face is about as cold and deadly as it's possible to be, and the tension is ratcheted so high Bas can feel the hum like it's live gridstream. On the other hand, Bas is pretty impressed that Kimolijah doesn't seem to care.

Stanslo takes a long, steady breath, and his fists clench. "You know exactly—"

"Oh yeah," Kimolijah cuts in, "the kind of problem where you can't control what someone might want, even if they *don't* want it, but you'll never believe that, will you, you just keep—"

"Tell me you won't—"

"I didn't!" Kimolijah turns around and crosses the cab to stand at the near door, vibrating. "I *didn't*! There was no reason for—"

"I want to hear you say it."

Kimolijah opens his mouth, a bitter retort too obviously right on the verge of spilling out, but he pauses, tilts his head. "Having one of *those* days, Baron?" It's got a spiteful curl to it, and clear anger. Kimolijah loosens his stance, just a little, and he leans hipshot against the open doorway, fingers stroking at the wrench. "There are other ways to soothe a bruised ego and take the edge off, y'know. You only have to say."

Bas almost doesn't cover his grimace. It was an offer, clear and bold, and right here in the open. If Bas had any doubt before about what goes on between these two, he doesn't now.

"You're usually so much more agreeable after the Outlet." Stanslo shakes his head, like he's a disappointed headmaster. "Do as I tell you, Kimo." It's soft, almost a request, but not quite.

Kimolijah stares for a second, mouth twitching around teeth set tight, before he jerks his head in a very clear negation. "I won't say it. There's nothing *to* say, I never—" A wave of that same blue current Bas is getting used to seeing sizzles out from nowhere and up Kimolijah's arm so quick it's gone before Bas's eyes adjust. "*Ah, fuck!*" Kimolijah yelps, and his hand spasms around the wrench before he drops it as another jolt jitters over him, so strong this time Bas thinks it illuminates Kimolijah's teeth. It happens so fast that Bas can't be sure, but it looks like it comes from the shunt, travels to that weird coiled bracelet, and then up Kimolijah's arm.

"For fuck's sake, have you got live current going in there?" Bas takes a step forward, reaching out, before he checks himself and looks around. "Where the hell is your grounding wire?"

"Yeah, princess," Fox says, clearly amused, "where's your grounding wire?"

Kimolijah's panting, clutching at the locomotive's side door like he needs the support, but he still apparently has enough energy to shoot Bas a look filled with such disgust that Bas nearly takes a step back. Kimolijah doesn't retort, though; he shakes his head like he's trying to clear it, and then he looks at Stanslo.

"My goodness, Kimo dear, your distractions always seem to prove so very, very hazardous." Stanslo's tone is even, and his eyes are like ice floes. "One mistake and everyone around you pays the price."

It makes Kimolijah flinch, but the fury all over his face doesn't dissipate and he's still staring Stanslo down. Stanslo seems to think it's amusing, because he's smiling when he says, "Tell me what I want to hear, love."

Kimolijah doesn't for a while, and the endearment just seems to piss him off more. But then he slants a quick look at Bas, narrows his eyes at Fox for a second, before he looks back at Stanslo. "There will be no problem," Kimolijah grinds out through his teeth. "There *was no* problem before, there will be no problem now. Shut the fuck up, Fox."

Fox ignores him and keeps chuckling until Stanslo cuts a quick look at him and Fox does, indeed, shut the fuck up.

Stanslo's grinning now, and he says, "Good then! All settled." He claps his hands together and nods. "Fox has brought coffee. Why don't you—?"

"*I'm fine.*" Kimolijah snaps it out, vehemence laced through it and making it as cutting as the crack of a whip. But then he takes a look at Stanslo and visibly flinches, and he clears his throat and says, more calmly, "Quinnie brought me some earlier. I'm fine."

"How very sweet of Quinnie," says Stanslo, and he doesn't look like he thinks it was any such thing. He waves at the pitcher Fox is still holding. "Nonetheless, why don't you take a break, show Bas how to work the cannon. I've some matters that need seeing to, but we'll have supper at Hannah's, yes? A night out."

Kimolijah sighs, long and deep. There's defeat in it; quite the change from the snarling defiance of only a moment ago. "If you're in such a hurry for me to *do my job*, why do you keep—?"

"Your job is what I say it is," Stanslo cuts in mildly. He grins. "Bas, why don't you have supper with us too? You can meet Hannah and Sis and acquaint yourself with their charms, if you wish. Or Nadal, if his charms are more to your liking. He's certainly not opposed to spending time on his knees."

Charms. *Knees.*

...Is Bas being invited to supper at a cathouse?

11.

Yes, Bas has, in fact, been invited to supper at a cathouse.

He has to get through this "test of skill" of Stanslo's first, though.

B as had not been very grateful for all the target practice the Directorate forced on him back when he was a shavetail recruit right out of the academy. He's grateful for it now. Bas is a crack shot, if he does say so himself, always has been, *a steady hand and an excellent eye*, Da used to tell him, and even Mo had conceded the point. It's come in handy before, but certainly not as plainly as it does now.

Stanslo is delighted. Bas is... okay, he's a little delighted, too, because the cannon is a giant of a thing, and it's fucking *awesome*. But there's still that low-level unease that's become the norm just lately, an uncomfortable hum at the base of his gut, because he's holding something in his hands that shouldn't be possible, that someone like Stanslo shouldn't even know about, let alone have enough at his disposal that he can just hand them out to a "deputy" he's known for a week. It isn't right, and the fact that the concept and the design obviously came from Kimolijah makes Bas once again question the "Kimo" here in Stanslo's Bridge, as opposed to the Kimolijah Bas thought he'd come to know on paper.

They pause only long enough to get the cannon-sized gridgun settled into its cradle mount and for Bas to get a feel for how it swings around and tilts up when he moves his body. Bas wonders what the hell kind of danger would justify such a thing, and then he remembers the enormous bats and the strange trophies hanging in Stanslo's dining room and stops wondering.

It's much bigger than the gridgun he's been using, but lighter than any other artillery of its size would be. The casing isn't metal, like Bas had thought; it's ceramic, like the gridguns, and Bas supposes it makes sense, what with the grid pulses that shoot from the end of the long barrel. And they *are* pulses, no matter how long Bas keeps pressure on the little lever that serves as a trigger. No uncontrolled gridstream shooting out all over the place, no wild arcs that might fry something other than the target. The shots are smooth, the sights precise, and the kills pretty much guaranteed, provided one's aim is true. There is no recoil, and no quick crank of a barrel housing, like there is on every other gun Bas has ever seen; there's one barrel, no strike stud, a toggle instead of a trigger and, if Bas is not very much mistaken, one grid-charged dynamic crystal buried somewhere inside the wire guts within the stock.

The platform beneath his feet is made of thick, smoky glass with a layer of cork underneath it, and Bas thinks that makes sense too. There's enough of a nonconductive barrier between his feet and the metal of the engine's cab to keep him from getting zapped should a shot go wrong. He hopes. He can't say the same about all the weird fencing and wires and poles that sit around him, but they don't get in the way when he swings the gun around on its mount, so he doesn't think any more on it.

There's a murder of crows in the distance, dipping and diving and complaining to each other in their scraped-metal voices. Whatever they'd gathered to feed on is too far away to make out, but it makes things fortuitously convenient for Bas, because he really wants to test the range on this thing. He shoots about thirty cawing scavengers out of the sky and tastes the blue-black tang with each pulse of blue fire that lashes across the span of desert. The range is long, the accuracy is spot-on, and the efficiency is pretty damned close to perfect. It's an amazing weapon, both grand and horrifying, and Bas is both exhilarated and a little sick that he's so good at wielding it.

Stanslo seems giddily pleased, and when the heat gets high with the approach of midday, he calls a halt and reminds Bas that they're to meet for supper. Bas doesn't want to—he's not keen to watch whatever goes on between Stanslo and Kimolijah, and certainly not while surrounded by good-time girls—but he can't see a way to refuse.

He goes to his room and kips like everyone else. When he wakes in the late afternoon, he evicts a snake, two scorpions, and a dead mouse he's pretty sure one of the snakes brought with it. No spiders, so the grimaces stay at a minimum.

The first thing Bas sees when he enters the cathouse—or Hannah's, as everyone calls it—is the upright. No one's playing it, but Bas can tell by looking that it's an expensive instrument and well-maintained. The mahogany is polished to a mirrorlike shine and the ivories gleam. He has no doubt it's perfectly in tune and its tone is flawless.

The second thing he sees is a profile that stops him cold, and the only thing that stutters through Bas's head when his eyes latch on is, *Oh my god, please tell me you top.*

The man sits in an elegant sprawl in the center of the room, a drink in his hand and his legs stretched straight and propped on the table, black polished boots crossed at the ankle. His chestnut duster is long and sweeps the floor around the chair he's got tipped back on two legs. He wears a plain white shirt and equally plain black trousers underneath the coat, and a scarf of soft-burled russet winds around his neck, fringe reaching down his chest like silky fingers. The whole of it together gives the impression of casual wealth like Bas has yet to see here in Stanslo's Bridge on anyone but Stanslo.

Sharp-lined and soft-edged, the whole length of him, skin like burnt sienna-umber and midlength black hair worn loose under a porkpie hat that should be waggish but somehow comes off uncommonly provocative. He shifts, takes a sip of whatever he's drinking; his sleeve rides up, and Bas gets a glimpse of matte-metal at the wrist. For a second, Bas's brain doesn't process it, and then the man looks up, and Bas thinks *eyes* and then he thinks *holy shit, eyeliner,* and *what the fuck,* and *no fair,* and that's when he realizes he's looking at Kimolijah.

Breathe, Bas.

Kimolijah's looking right back. He's smirking, but then he isn't, and his gaze goes over Bas's shoulder and his face closes up altogether. Bas doesn't need to look behind him. He knows.

He digs up a pleasant expression when Stanslo grips his shoulder and says, "Let's introduce you around."

It's the best look Bas gets at Kimolijah for a while, though he feels Kimolijah staring at him, or at least he imagines he does. He doesn't look to confirm it. He doesn't want to know. And when they take their seats at the table and order their drinks, he doesn't want to know why his gut goes all clamped and achy every time Stanslo pulls Kimolijah close and Kimolijah stares off into the distance like he's bored.

Stanslo does introduce Bas around, and Bas chooses to ignore how everyone here seems hard and dirty underneath the skin, and looks at him with variations of suspicion and hostility. He recognizes a few names from the reports he'd almost memorized back home and thinks *ah yes, you're the sheep rancher who disappeared last spring,* and *oh, you must be that tough who ran the pit fights and went missing before the guardarm could arrest you two years ago.* He keeps looking for someone who might be Ajamil Adani but doesn't spot him.

They have steak and blackberry wine for supper. Well, Bas and Stanslo do. Kimolijah doesn't touch the meat on his plate. He spends the meal worrying at the flat discs of leather that pass for bread here and tearing it into bits that he dunks into hot sauce that makes Bas's eyes water from across the table.

Supper is served by one of the whores Bas assumes he'd be permitted to hire for a few hours, if he's so inclined. There are three of them—two women and one young man—and Bas wonders if their names are listed in alphabetical order in neat columns in the reports he'd written before he'd come here, and whether he can place them if he tries.

He doesn't try. He can't help thinking, though, with a vague, uneasy skitter up the back of his neck, that while neither of the women could be mistaken for Mari at a distance, the young man—God, boy, really, now that Bas is looking—is dark-haired and dark-skinned, and though he's not built precisely right, the overall effect could probably fool a drunk who's willing to be fooled, willing to close his eyes and pretend he's with... someone else.

Bas lets his glance land briefly on Kimolijah's hunched shoulders and bent head, and then he looks away again. The boy doesn't once allow his eyes to land on Kimolijah, at least not that Bas sees. He's even more receptive, though, to Stanslo's hands on him when Stanslo excuses himself and saunters over to him.

"You don't seem like you're afraid of him. Even after the Box." Kimolijah's voice is soft, and his lips barely move. He's talking to Bas, but he's watching Stanslo, and Bas can't see his face.

Stanslo is having a close, murmured conversation with Lowen at the bar, his arm around the boy—Nadal—and keeping him close. Bas is glad and weirdly annoyed at the same time, and it has nothing at all to do with the fact that he's been watching Stanslo affectionately maul Kimolijah for an hour now, and Kimolijah passively letting him. Bas is surprised Kimolijah didn't at some point actually end up in Stanslo's lap. And now Kimolijah's watching as Stanslo does the same to a boy who looks like he could be Kimolijah's younger brother, and Kimolijah looks pissed, but Bas isn't sure why yet. There are so many reasons from which to choose.

Bas lifts his eyebrows. He doesn't want to give too much away, and Kimolijah's "not afraid" assessment is heartening, but Bas is sane and so therefore suitably wary of crazy people, of which Stanslo is clearly one. Nonetheless, he decides to keep that to himself and asks, "Should I be afraid of him?"

Kimolijah still doesn't look at Bas. "Did you know there's this worm—teeny-tiny thing, lives on the wings of hopbugs, can hardly even see it, not until it's burrowed under your skin and made its way to your brain." He pauses and his mouth quirks up. "Well, any animal, really. But it always goes for the brain. And then it starts to grow. 'S got these... things, arms, like tentacles. Long. Can wind around stuff all up in there, you know? And when it gets thirsty, it can hit the parts of your brain it needs and make you jump in a lake, just so it can have a drink. You won't even care that you can't swim. Can make you do anything, really. Depends on what it wants at the time."

He stops there, like that's all the important information he has to dispense for the evening. Bas just stares at the side of his head for a spell, probably glaring, because what the fuck was *that*?

"How the hell did you end up here?" Bas ends up asking Kimolijah, low-voiced and almost angry, and hands fisted on the table between them. "How can you let him... just... *how*?"

Bas can't help the offended tone. He *is* offended. That someone with the promise of Kimolijah Adani ended up here, creating weapons and trains for someone who has no business even knowing about them, and sitting in the middle of what constitutes a social gathering in a cathouse, silently acknowledging his position as Stanslo's bit-on-the-side like it's okay, and all while he watches Stanslo getting handsy with someone else who looks almost like him, it's.... Well. The whole thing is plain distasteful. *Sick.*

Kimolijah doesn't startle at the question, doesn't get angry or indignant, doesn't hang his head in shame, or any of the other ten thousand ways Bas has half expected him to react. He doesn't even look at Bas. He merely stares down at the plate he's apparently been finding fascinating for most of the evening, flicks a caramel onion off the cold, bloody steak he hasn't touched, and says, "You don't really expect me to answer that, do you?"

"I'd hoped you would, yeah," Bas mutters, somewhat petulant, because no, he hadn't really expected an answer, and he knows he's not going to get one. Still, he ends up asking, "Are you actually in love with him?" just to see what Kimolijah will do, because, if he answers, how he does it will matter.

And when Kimolijah starts to say, "My da—" and gives a quick flinch and hiss at the little *zap-pop* Bas knows comes from a thread of gridstream sparking out of that vambrace, it matters even more. Because both Kimolijah and his da had been reported dead, and here Kimolijah is. So where is his da? And why did that thing zap him when the subject came up?

Maybe Bas didn't make the connection before, and maybe gridTech isn't supposed to work like that, but he's seen enough and heard enough about Tech that can't be inside crystals except that it is. And it's funny, because every time Kimolijah gets zapped with his own Tech, it seems like he's in the process of saying something Stanslo might not want him to be saying.

"Someone I used to know," Kimolijah goes on calmly, flicking another onion, "once told me it takes three months to know if you're in love." A tiny tic at the corner of his wide mouth twitches into what might be a ghost of a fond smile. "If after three months your heart still pounds and your palms still sweat every time you see or think about the person you think you love, then it's love. If not...." He shrugs and stops playing with the onions, leaning back in his chair and chewing on his thumbnail instead. "Infatuation. Obsession, maybe. Anyway, nothing good. Nothing real."

He looks different without the goggles taking up half his face. His eyes are light brown, nothing to write home about, but they're an interesting contrast; the lightness of them juxtaposing the kohl contour makes them kind of "pop" like copper coins against his dark skin.

"And?" Bas asks. He leans across the table and snatches up Kimolijah's hand, turns it palm up and runs a finger over the cool, dry skin. He lifts an eyebrow.

Kimolijah snorts and pulls his hand away. "Have you ever known a gridTech who can afford to have sweaty palms?" He pauses and peers down at the bracelet, like he's surprised, and when nothing happens, his back straightens a little and he tilts his head to the side. He wraps the bloody mess of steak he didn't eat into a napkin and shoves it into his coat pocket. "Hey, did you know your piss is actually cleaner than your spit?"

Stanslo comes back after that and Kimolijah clams up again. The pawing continues and Kimolijah goes back to looking bored and slightly annoyed, but he still allows it. Bas watches with narrowed eyes and refuses to gnash his teeth. He also refuses to wonder why he *wants* to gnash his teeth.

Eventually, Kimolijah excuses himself with a perfunctory smile for Stanslo and a smirk for Bas, until Stanslo says, "Keep Mari company tonight," with a meaningful glance across the room at Nadal and then a sharp look at Kimolijah. "I am disappointed in your progress so far. Try not to make it worse."

"Mari can't—"

"Mari does as I wish." Blue eyes fixed on Kimolijah, Stanslo grips Kimolijah's arm tight, squeezes, before he lets go and sits back, confident. "You should take a lesson. Make all our lives a bit more pleasant."

Kimolijah's mouth works and he cuts a quick glance at Nadal, then back to Stanslo. He leans in, lowers his voice, but Bas can hear quite clearly: "He's a boy. Doesn't know his ass from his elbow yet. You want more than that." Kimolijah sets a hand to Stanslo's shoulder, soft, and slides it down the suede lapel. "Just come home with me. I'll make it real good. You know I can."

And holy shit, this is so *not* the shy boy Bas thought he'd sort of gotten to know through reports and interviews with classmates. Bas quietly clears his throat and shifts uncomfortably, and tries not to notice the way Kimolijah's body sets so easily and quickly into the lines of seduction.

Stanslo looks smug, and the twist to his mouth is halfway malicious. He takes Kimolijah's hand from where it's running up and down his chest and gives it a pat. "I'll see you in the morning," he says, clear dismissal.

Kimolijah looks like he wants to say something—actually, he looks like he wants to take Stanslo's head off—but Stanslo merely reaches out to touch Kimolijah's sleeve over the spot underneath which Bas knows the bracelet sits. Stanslo lifts his eyebrow, tilts his head, expectant, waiting, like he *wants* Kimolijah to say something he shouldn't, and Kimolijah's fists clench. In the end, though, Kimolijah only glares with his teeth set tight, shoots a vicious look Nadal's way, and then stalks out. The doors bang shut behind Kimolijah and the lights flicker and pop, but nobody pays attention, and Stanslo merely stares after Kimolijah and shakes his head with a smile, indulgent.

Bas doesn't get away so easily, though *God*, he really wants to. His attempt to call it a night, though, ends with Stanslo insisting he stay and enjoy the evening, get to know his fellow citizens, so Bas ends up staying late. There's music and more liquor and a steady procession of introductions to anyone who stops to pay respects. Bas learns dread little about the things he'd really like to know, but when Stanslo wanders off to commune with Lowen again, and Merrin and Yanush make themselves comfortable in the seats vacated by Stanslo and Kimolijah, Bas learns a thing or two he didn't know before.

"The Bruise...." Yanush shakes his head and frowns, like he actually wants to answer but can't think how. He'd rolled a smoke when they'd first sat down and he's huffing it slowly, squinting through the smoke. "En't been there," he says, and he shifts in his chair, like he's uncomfortable. "Don't wanna, neither."

It's almost the same thing Merrin had told Bas in the train-yard.

Merrin grunts, surly. "En't much choice now, is there?"

Yanush doesn't answer, but his mouth pinches down into a thin, unhappy line, and he takes a drink.

It's strange, sitting here with Merrin, who ignored every plea Bas shoved through the grate of the Box while he cooked inside it. Still, Bas has made nice with worse.

It's late evening, the chill of the night seeping in through the half-open doors of the airy house that serves as brothel and tavern and hashery and... well, probably anything else Stanslo wants it to be. It hasn't started to rain yet, Bas notes, but he knows it will.

The atmosphere in the tavern is weirdly friendly, more relaxed than Bas has seen yet, even with Stanslo here, and Yanush and Merrin don't seem to have the same hushed, secretive air about them that everyone else Bas has questioned does.

Maybe it's the liquor.

"Anyway, you been to the way station," Merrin says to Yanush.

Yanush rolls his eyes and knocks ash from his smoke onto the floor. "Yeah, but it en't the Bruise, is it?" He turns to Bas and leans in over his drink. "It's hard-livin' out there at the station, harder 'n here, even. But I hear it's pure hell at the Bruise."

Merrin snorts. "You hear shit, 'cause no one who knows will say, and the ones as might don't come back. You *reckon*, like everyone else."

He pauses and looks over his shoulder, but he doesn't look too worried when he spots Stanslo cornering Nadal over by the doors.

"Yeah, well, it en't all that hard to *reckon*, is it?" Yanush snaps, abruptly angry for no reason Bas can figure. "Ye get the way station as a warning. Ye get the Bruise when all your warnings run out." He sits back and sips from his drink, brooding. "A week at the way station done me just fine. I follow my contract to the letter, don't I. God and all the Patrons willing, all I'll ever see o' the Bruise'll be from this side of it while I sit my ass safe inside sparker's little magic piece-o'-shit train."

Bas frowns. "So, what, the Bruise is some kind of penalty for breach?"

Merrin and Yanush share a look across the table and then, as one, they shoot quick glances over at Stanslo. It takes a moment, some kind of silent communication Bas can't discern, and then Merrin shrugs. He sits back and spins the edge of his empty glass along the inner loop of the wet ring it's left on the table.

"Not everyone that's gone to the Bruise has a contract," he says slowly. "But near everyone who's gone to the Bruise and stayed there has got someone here who does."

It takes a second or two for Bas to follow that, and when it clicks, he tries not to lean in too eagerly, tries not to let it show that his heart's abruptly pounding and his palms have gone slick. "So what does that mean?" he asks and works up a wry look to go with it. "It sounds like you're either talking about punishment or collateral."

Yanush and Merrin share another look, and Yanush shrugs. "You came alone, so you won't have to worry about the one 'less you got someone back home you give a shit about." He pauses and narrows his eyes at Bas. "Stick to your contract and you won't have to worry about the other, neither."

Bas stares, all that making way too much sense and sticking unease somewhere high in his chest, blocking his throat. He tries not to be too obvious about clearing it before he asks, tone flat, "Is that some kind of threat?"

Yanush grins and takes a long drag from his smoke. "A friendly warning," he corrects. "You seem all right, Bas. Boss likes ye, and it's usually smart to like what the boss likes." He cuts another look Stanslo's way as he drops the smoke to the wooden floorboards and grinds it out beneath his boot. "You keep his toys in good working order, and the only thing you'll ever have to know about the Bruise is how fast you can get the little sparker there and back."

Bas sits back and thinks about collateral—Haversham's Jilly? Kimolijah's da?—as he watches Quinnie come in and look around with a smile. It falls when she sees Bas, turns to a frown when she sees Stanslo, and comes back again when the women call out a sincere-seeming greeting to her. She shoots Bas a narrow glare, then goes over to sit on the bench beside the girl at the upright.

"Not the only thing that needs worrying about, I'm thinking," Bas says absently, shutters a look at Merrin and Yanush, then glances back as Quinnie and the woman key up a leisurely duet of a tune Bas is sure he's heard before but can't quite place. "From what I hear, Travis had more on his plate."

Yanush sucks in a sharp breath, but Merrin chuckles. "Yeah, well, Travis was here a'fore it even *was* Stanslo's Bridge. His contract had some holes, I reckon, what with the boss comin' late to it and all." He sucks on a tooth and slants a look at Bas. "I doubt yours does. Boss only makes a mistake once."

"Not only the once," Yanush says, voice low as he stares down at the tabletop with a frown. "Sparker's got holes and then some, don't he. Else he wouldn't be able to mouth off t' the boss like he does, I'm thinkin', hain'a?" He looks up, catches Merrin's raised eyebrows, and sets his mouth in a grim line. "Fuck you, Merrin. He's a decent kid."

Merrin shushes him with a hiss, looks around to make sure Stanslo's still safely across the room, and when Merrin's satisfied no one is eavesdropping, he leans in. "Decent kid, evil little sparker whore—don't matter, 's all I'm sayin'. He's a hazard, whether he means to be or not. Travis—"

"Travis weren't his fault and you know it."

"I know no such thing. And neither do you." Merrin's teeth have gone tight and his face is going red. "That's the fucking *point.*"

Yanush rolls his eyes, angry, and starts rolling another smoke. "That man was his own hot mess. It was only a matter of time."

"Don't much matter whose fault it is if it's your ass in the blast zone, does it? You think Haversham would've eaten the pipe if Travis hadn't happened?"

Yanush looks mildly chastened, but it doesn't stop him from saying, "This whole fucking place is a blast zone."

"I don't think you could scrape up an argument there if you tried." Merrin sits back with a conciliatory shrug. He smirks a little and slides his empty glass across the table. "'S long as Reacher's next, it all means shit to me. I didn't sign up to be *that* fuckin' halfwit's bitch."

Yanush shrugs. "En't no worse 'n bein' Fox's, I'm thinkin'. Might even be better, hain'a?"

Merrin doesn't answer, just snags the smoke Yanush just rolled and calls for a fresh drink.

Bas takes it all in and thinks about Good Guys and Bad Guys and how much harder it is to tell which is which in real life.

It's weird that Bas almost likes the people he meets here. He remembers when he was a kid—all cocky naiveté and brash righteousness—thinking that people who do bad things would be easily identified and categorized like villains in an illobook:

evil laughter at a convenient moment—*Mwa ha ha ha!* in bold characters inside an obviously placed speech bubble—so the reader gets it before the hero does; minions who are always stupid and always interchangeable and always wear matching outfits so it's easy to tell who's on what side; an obvious plan for world domination that's got one huge fatal flaw the hero will eventually figure out after the love interest says something in passing that no one knew meant anything until a bright, jagged halo appears around the hero's head that tells the reader *he's got an idea!*

But yeah, that's kind of the way he'd thought of it way back then, when he'd thought of it at all.

He learned powerful quickly that it's not that easy.

Stanslo is a paranoid, psychotic son of a bitch, Bas has no doubt about that, but he's a charming paranoid, psychotic son of a bitch who seems genuinely capable of actual feelings, where illobook villains only seem capable of feeling slighted for some imagined wrong, which eventually turns into a lust for vengeance. Bas doesn't think illobook minions have friends, but everyone here seems to have formed bonds with at least one or two others, and none of them walk around wearing matching black hats and cackling among themselves. And if what Stanslo's doing here involves taking over the world, like Haversham halfway implied, Bas can't figure how, since Stanslo has gone to extraordinary pains to create his little barony as far away from the world as possible.

Though, that won't stop Bas from continuing to look for the fatal flaw in the plot he can't quite figure out yet.

❦

He hates that he has a decent evening. He hates that Stanslo is actually good company—interesting, entertaining, an excellent host. He hates that, if he'd met Stanslo under different circumstances and knew nothing of what he's learned since he started to track supposedly dead Techs across the Territories, he would have been charmed and maybe he even would have been captivated enough to go for seduction.

It makes him feel scummy, and when he finally makes his way through the by now routine soft rain and back to the bunkhouse in the dark, Bas ignores all the sentries and deputies he should be getting to know and surreptitiously questioning, and just plods into his room, checks to make sure no one's been at his illobooks, then flops down on the mattress and tries to sleep.

He manages a light doze, and when morning light comes, Bas evicts no less than three scorpions that seem to have adopted the grody blanket Bas had relegated to the floor in a corner of his room. Which is probably his own fault, since he left it by the little gridheater and inadvertently made a nice toasty bed for all manner of creepy-crawlies, including several smaller cousins of the giant spiders that have snuck in sometime during the dark

hours. Okay, maybe "evicting" isn't strictly what Bas does—
more like stomping everything that moves and trying not to
shudder like a little kid while doing it, but it all works out the
same. He doesn't care that it's not entirely badass that he winces
while he kicks the gooey little corpses onto the blanket and
makes a note to find somewhere to burn it. He *does not* imagine
them crawling over him while he's sleeping.

...All right, he does, but he tries not to.

He also spends more time than is strictly manly hunting
around the sparse furnishings and crevices of the room and
hoping he doesn't find anything else with more legs than he's
comfortable with.

He doesn't. He does find a snake, though. And decides he
really needs to figure out what's venomous here.

⚇

"You lied to Stanslo."

"I often do."

"You touched the locks in my head somehow, but you didn't
get past them."

"It's extraordinarily difficult to get past Directorate locks."
Dolerma pauses, mouth curled a touch smug. "Yours are better.
My compliments to the psyTech who set them."

Bas doesn't startle, because he'd known Dolerma had to
know that much. He frowns, though, and stares, waiting for
Dolerma to elaborate, and when he doesn't, Bas holds back a
growl.

"*And*? What's your game here? And why did you lie to Stanslo?
What d'you want from me?"

He'd found Dolerma in the "store," which is actually more
like another store*house* than any store Bas has ever seen. Racks
of bedding and cookware, bolts of cloth, and jars of vegetables
and fruit. Sacks and barrels of grains and flour, shelves and
shelves of dried foods, and sides of beef and pork hanging in the
back. There's a connecting outbuilding Bas thought was someone's crappy house but turns out to be a stoke bin.

"Baron Stanslo knows exactly what he needs to know," Dolerma
answers, blank and even. He's wearing his dark glasses again, so
Bas finds it in himself to actually look at him. "And so do you."

"What does that even mean?" Bas snaps.

Dolerma stares at him for several too-long moments, silent,
before he tilts his head toward the back of the store. There's no
one here, so it seems rather unnecessary, but Bas follows
Dolerma anyway. When they stop amidst the small forest of
hanging carcasses—cured, so they don't stink, at least—Dolerma
turns to Bas and leans in close.

"You are safe for now," he tells Bas quietly. "But it won't last
for long. You will have to work quickly."

Bas's eyebrows shoot up and he rears back. "I assure you, I'll be working as quickly as I can."

"And what you plan is not quickly enough. There are too many things that can't be said. Supply runs to Harrowgate are once a month. You must be ready by then. If you don't get Kimo out of here before he...." He hesitates before he sighs and says, "You must always remember that to Stanslo it's all a game. And for all his charm, Baron Stanslo is a master of ruthless strategy."

Bas blinks. "Okay, I have no idea what any of that means."

"You are not what he wants, but you may well be what I need. What *Kimo* needs." Dolerma pauses, and Bas would swear that pale not-hair moves, twitching at the ends, but the air in here is still. "You're close," Dolerma goes on. "You must be or you wouldn't be here. You wouldn't be *locked*."

I know you're Directorate, but Dolerma doesn't actually say it.

Bas swallows, but his voice is steady when he asks, "And what kinds of things does Stanslo want?"

Dolerma's lips twitch, like a smile. "Bigger things," he says and draws back. "Trophies."

Dolerma turns and starts walking away to the front of the store, so Bas says, "I suppose that's the best I'm going to get, then?" to Dolerma's back.

Dolerma doesn't pause. He witters out something like a chuckle, though. "It's better than anyone else in Stanslo's Bridge has," is all he says, and then he opens the door to greet a man who looks like he was just reaching for the knob. Like Dolerma knew he was coming.

Because of course he did.

12.

The breakthrough, such as it is, goes like this:

B as doesn't see Kimolijah again at all that day. Kimolijah never comes back to the station to fiddle with his train, and Bas sees that bird circling over Stanslo's manor house, so he assumes Kimolijah's up there, because it seems to follow him like a stray puppy. Bas is at loose ends; he hasn't had tower duty since Stanslo "promoted" him, and he doesn't feel like socializing. So he spends the evening brooding and flipping idly through a few illobooks, and then he spends the morning wandering the town as it wakes, trying not to notice the body still hanging from the whipping post and trying not to check to see if Kimolijah's falcon is still circling before he realizes what he's doing and stops. Because what the hell?

There's no real point in annoying Kimolijah anyway, even if he's not up at Stanslo's house, because it's not like Kimolijah's going to tell him anything. And after a few hours of wandering aimlessly, Bas is bored, so he figures *fuck it. Might as well at least try to be productive,* and as a Directorate tracker, "productive" means *brazenly stick your nose where people probably don't want you to.*

So he starts at the place that seems the most important: he goes to the workshop/shed that sits aslant the station.

It's going on afternoon by now, and most everyone has retreated to whatever cool spots they can find to ride out the worst heat of the day. Still, there are a few minions around the station, busywork, but no one stopped him last time he was here, so Bas pulls on a menacing *Jakob Barstow kills people for fun* expression and just saunters on in.

He passes right through the station proper, because he's seen it, and though there may be a lot of interesting gadgets lying around half-finished, he doesn't see anything that might mean something. When he crosses into the attached workshop, however, he stops.

There are partial engine blocks scattered around like a giant's fallen jacks. There's something that looks like a deformed spider, with its jointed metal and wires all askew, everything held together by bolts that are probably the size of small eggs. There's a pile of gridheaters, like the one in Bas's room, all jumbled together and in various stages of repair. Three of the gridtrolleys sit against the back wall, all of them with their motor panels open and wires hanging out in clumps. There are other devices Bas doesn't recognize, and he can't guess their purposes. And none of this is what catches Bas's eye.

It's another locomotive. Not done yet, conduit and wiring streaming out of its core like entrails, but there's no mistaking it. Bigger than the one in the yard, and sleeker.

There's pounding coming from outside somewhere, *the barns on the far side of the station*, Bas thinks, and then the sounds shake the flimsy walls all around him, so he adjusts that thought: someone's hammering something right outside. Bas briefly worries maybe someone's going to come and catch him and somehow figure out who he is and what he's doing here, and the game will be up and Bas will be a dead man. The tarps covering the gaps in the roof flutter in the hot breeze, and there's a *bangbangbang* on the outside of the workshop that makes Bas jump. Someone laughs and someone else says something Bas can't make out, and no one leaps around a corner to melt Bas's face off with one of those gridguns, so Bas makes himself—

Breathe, Bas.

"Jakob Barstow would do whatever the hell he damn well pleased," Bas mutters to himself, and he climbs into the cab of the half-built locomotive. And studies it.

It's not configured like any engine Bas has seen before, and the heart from which Bas is pretty sure the power is meant to originate doesn't look anything like the Grid designs he knows. Magnets, *big* magnets, that don't seem to belong anywhere but are built into the design like they do. And coils, the purposes of which Bas can't quite grasp, and gaps that seem like they should interrupt the stream flow, but... no. He follows along the circuit, trying to pry his mind open and away from what it thinks he should be seeing and toward the impossibility that's actually there. He gets to what should be the armature and okay, see, *this—*

This is where there *should* be magnets, and there are, but not as many as an engine this size would require, not as big and not placed in the ways Bas understands. Not set static along the length of the wiring to force polarity. These look like....

Bas gives one the tiniest flick with the tip of his fingernail.

"They do. They rotate." He squints and crouches down to get as close to the mechanism as he can. "Which would reverse the flow, which would... how the hell...?"

Secondaries and primaries, positive flow, and negatives into ground leads, and a bridge that sits between the leads from the power source and the central hookup that runs to... well, pretty much everything else. A transformer, Bas thinks, though he doesn't claim to be an expert, but he knows enough. Except he hasn't seen a transformer like this one. It's too small, for one. Delicately, he detaches it from its web of wires, pries open the casing, and eyes the innards with a frown.

"More crystals," Bas sighs. Because of course there are. A little pool of them, small, little bigger than grains of sand but recognizable.

Some kind of transmitter, he's pretty sure. And once he thinks he's following the logic of it all, he eyes everything else, and thinks *No, wait, that's not right.* It's wired in all wrong, iron rods in coils of copper pushing power in and out, but it's *wrong*, because this kind of power would kill not only the engine but the gridTech running it.

Bas's mouth tightens and he shakes his head. He backs up a few steps in reasoning and tries to follow the logic of the design.

Maybe not a transformer. Except, goddamn it, it *is*.

"Okay, winding circuits, so there's the inductive coupling, but... where's the secondary winding? Where's the *core*?"

Maybe it's a dampener of some kind, or... no, it's... well, it *should* be a transformer, it's where one ought to go in the scheme, but the couplings are too loose and there are gaps where there shouldn't be. Simple copper wires can't handle that kind of power. The placement of those too-big, out-of-place magnets would reverse the stream, which is fucking *dangerous*, and.... Bas grunts, annoyed, because it looks like he should be able to figure it out but it's not clicking. He follows the wiring from the contact points to the engine's core, then down through the little device in his hands to where it fans out to every console and switch and lever in the half-built cab. He can see the completion of the circuit, positive to negative, but any gridTech hooked up to this thing would be cooked before they could even get the shunt all the way in. Unless.

"Some kind of... harness, maybe?" Bas mutters. "Something to adapt the gridstream, tame it and... convert—"

As soon as the word comes halfway out his mouth, Bas thinks, *Okay, maybe.* Because Kimolijah had been having trouble regulating the streams. "He was working on designing something to convert it," Resaniji had said, "something that would just take the Tech and do the directing for you," and Kimolijah's notes and diaries had alluded to several theories for a solution he'd never written down. And once the notion forms in Bas's head, he thinks *Huh, that could... it looks kind of possible* and then the implications hit him and he thinks *Holy fucking shit.*

Unbelievably simple in design, if it's what he thinks it is, but just as revolutionary in concept as a gridtrain. Meant to take the direct gridstream from the power source and alternate its surge and fade, level it out, and make the flow more efficient. Not a dampener and not a baffler, like they use on the Grid to keep anyone who touches a gridluster from frying. A simple shift in flow, absorbing the current from the charge, storing the stream, smoothing it, and then converting it. There would be no surges with something like this, no accidental gushes of current resonating back and killing gridTechs, no burning out, because this wouldn't suck the current out of a Tech; it would merely accept what flowed in naturally and let it build until it accumulated enough potency to be useful. And if it was charged with gridstream from a gridTech who knew how to do it....

"Like opening an artery." It comes out a little hoarse and thin. "And *aiming*."

Bas almost gets it now, or at least he thinks he does. *Goddamned stupid bloody genius*, Resaniji had said of her brother, and yeah, Bas has to agree. Because it's not just genius—it's fucking *radical*, and it's sitting here in Stanslo's Bridge when it should be... everywhere.

The world opens up beneath Bas's eyes, and it's bright-lit with a soft blue glow. The end of dead gridTechs, the beginning of cheap, consistent lighting and grid-powered trains and grid-powered... whatever—everything, anything. And Kimolijah is apparently building it for Baron fucking Stanslo so Stanslo can get his minions to travel out to the Bruise—whatever the *hell* that is—and collect the dynamic crystals that Bas is almost positive will make a gridTech hooking himself into the engine with that shunt completely unnecessary.

"This...." Bas sits back and rubs at his mouth. The light shifts, and he angles the little mechanism so he can get a better look at its guts and then up again to squint at all the magnets that don't belong there. "It's... fucking hell, it's pretty goddamned amaz—"

"What the *hell* are you *doing*?"

The voice, coming from right above Bas's head, scares the shit out of him. He jumps so hard the little whatever-it-is flies out of his hand like it's spring-loaded and goes vaulting across the floor of the cab before it *plinks* down onto the oiled hardpan. Each bounce dislodges a scatter of wires and metal bits and tiny crystals until there's a glittering trail of detritus between Bas and the... thing he just apparently, um, broke.

"Did you just.... Oh my *god*!"

Bas looks up to see the upper half of Kimolijah tilting down through one of the gaps in the roof. The tarp has been thrown back—ah, shift in light a minute ago, right—and Bas can't get a look at Kimolijah's face, backlit as he is, but the tone of voice, in retrospect and now that Bas is paying attention, is pretty telling, and Bas thinks *Oh... well, crap.*

"You...." It seems like Kimolijah can't speak, he's so angry, but then he says, "I can't believe you would... you fucking... just... don't move."

It takes a second for Bas to make sense of the movement that follows, but when his eyes adjust and his brain catches up, he ignores Kimolijah's last command and gets out of the way just in time to avoid a faceful of boot when Kimolijah jumps down from the hole in the ceiling. He lands in a crouch atop what Bas thinks will eventually be the main access to the engine housing, too close to where Bas's head was a second ago, and though *You did that on purpose* is what comes into Bas's head, what comes out his mouth is, "For God's sake, don't you ever wear a *shirt*?"

Because Kimolijah's all brown and sweat-glistened and tattooed and no stupid goggles this time and his fringe is tucked back in a small tail on the crown of his head, the rest of his longish black hair swaying around his shoulders, and the angry look on his face, coupled with the sheer *genius* surrounding Bas in physical, mechanical form, is *doing things* to Bas's brain and just... *fuck.*

Kimolijah gives Bas an incredulous look, and then a dirty, murderous glare. "I was patching the roof."

"Why the hell were you patching the roof?"

"Why the hell were you poking around where you don't belong?"

Okay, fair point. Not that Bas can exactly explain, so he says, "No, I meant why are you patching the roof when you're supposed to be working on your trains?"

"Who the fuck are you and why d'you think you get a say in what I'm 'supposed' to be doing?"

"*I* don't think I have a say, but Stanslo sure seems to think he does. Are you *trying* to piss him off?" Though, now that Bas thinks about it, maybe that's exactly what Kimolijah's doing. "Oh my god, are you trying to—"

"Are you trying to get me to kill you?"

Clearly, this is going nowhere fast. Bas waves toward the roof and tries, "Doesn't Stanslo have minions for that kind of grunt work?"

"Yeah, you're looking at one of them!"

"You're not a minion, you're a—um."

If possible, Kimolijah looks even angrier and everything goes still. "I'm a *what*?"

No, see, that's not what Bas meant at all. Well. Okay, it kind of is, but it would probably be extraordinarily unwise to say as much.

"I thought you were... that is, don't you do *other*... uh. Shit."

Engineer! his brain screams. *Just say engineer, or mechanic, or* goatherd, *for fuck's sake! What is* wrong *with you?*

He's *so much* better than this. He's stared down the bundled black hell of twelve loaded barrels—more than once!—and not even flinched. What the fuck?

And still, Bas can't make his mouth form actual words, just little noises that make him sound both cowardly and, frankly, a little bit touched in the head. Mere days ago, he'd had an honest-to-God bloody *shootout* not thirty feet from where he's standing, and now he's kind of terrified of one short engineer, who might, in fact, be something of a slag, with a little-girl ponytail and grease under his bitten-off nails. And the absurd inability to speak, Bas reflects, might not be so bad. He hadn't really meant to say even as much as he has, and what he *has* said is unintentionally insulting enough that he should quit while he still has plausible deniability.

Except Kimolijah's expression has gone from *really bloody pissed* to an apocalyptic *you fucking* ass*hole*, so Bas blurts, "I didn't mean *that*."

Kimolijah doesn't say anything. He seems to be choking on fury and, weirdly, something that looks like hurt. He hops down off the housing and then off the half-built cab altogether, stepping carefully around the spray of crystals in the dirt. He's muttering when he crouches down to retrieve the little... thing... mechanism, and Bas doesn't catch any of it until Kimolijah looks up at him, brow scrunched and expression straddling a line somewhere between enraged and bewildered.

"Why would you *do* this?" His voice is raspy, like he might cry.

"I didn't mean to!" Bas hurries to answer. "I'm sorry, you scared the hell out of me, I was only looking and I w—"

"Looking at *what*?" Kimolijah snaps. "I told him I'm working on it. I can't do it any faster, because he won't fucking *let me!*"

Bas pauses and has to remind himself that he's not at all the flailing-and-apologetic sort. He clears his throat and says, "I wasn't checking up on you. Stanslo didn't tell me to check up on you. He didn't tell me anything except I'm to keep you safe when we go to the Bruise."

And that you're his, and Do Not Touch, but Bas doesn't say that part. He also doesn't ask why, if Stanslo's harassing Kimolijah like Kimolijah has just implied, Kimolijah's fixing the roof instead of the train. Mostly because he thinks he knows. He also thinks Kimolijah's playing a very dangerous game, and to what purpose Bas hasn't quite kenned yet, but he doesn't say that either.

Kimolijah's jaw sets tight. "Yeah, whatever you say." He shakes his head and starts gingerly sifting through the loose dirt atop the oiled hardpan to pluck up the crystals and other bits that spilled. "I'm not quite as stupid as you and the baron seem to think I am, y'know."

Bas is a little bit fascinated by the way the ropey muscles in Kimolijah's arms make the whorls of the tattoos ripple and curl. He snorts to cover it, and when Kimolijah shoots him a glare, Bas just rolls his eyes and waves at all of the evidence around him of just how very *not stupid* Kimolijah is.

"Yeah, right." Kimolijah goes back to picking wires and tiny gears from the oily, fine-grained dirt. "And yet somehow I'm supposed to believe that you just show up here, out of the blue, where *no one* with sense or conscience wants to be, and end up favored son to the boss five minutes later." He shakes his head and huffs. "At least admit you're a dirty spy. I'd probably tell you more."

God, would that it were true, Bas thinks, because he *is,* technically, a spy. Just not the kind Kimolijah seems to think he is.

"Sure," Bas says, "you'll get all chatty and quit telling me to shut up all the time, if only I admit I'm secretly here to report your every movement back to Stanslo."

"I might." Kimolijah shrugs as he plucks up a small wire and sticks it in his mouth. "You don't know." He peers up at Bas and grins, wide and lovely and unmistakably fake—but still, *fuck, dimples*—the wire hanging out his mouth like a string of licorice. "Maybe I'm perishing for someone I can talk to."

"Except none of what you'd tell me would be the truth."

"How would you know?"

"Anyway, if you hadn't come out to the Box the other night, I'd be dead, so you apparently haven't thought the conspiracy through very well."

"Yeah, except the baron doesn't know people can't survive two days in the Box—"

"Because you accidentally made sure of that, didn't you?"

"—and wouldn't a harsh punishment do very nicely to deflect suspicion from his shiny new spy?"

"Why would Stanslo need to spy on you?" Bas leans in with a narrow frown, because yeah, he's done going back and forth about Kimolijah's possible motives, and it doesn't matter what circumstantial evidence looks like right now; Bas *knows* Kimolijah's not here because he wants to be. So Bas says, "Seems to me you and Stanslo have got the kind of... relationship where there are no secrets." Goading.

The grin, what was left of it, drops abruptly and Kimolijah spits the wire to the side. A long, deep breath makes the ink on his ribs and chest expand then slowly contract. His hands fist for a second before he calmly goes back to picking at the dirt for his crystals.

"Aw," he says eventually, smirking. "Jealous?"

Bas keeps the choking, thankfully, quiet and to himself, because the answer that abruptly plasters itself all over him like a cheap whore is *Oh, huh, is that what this grinding in my gut is all about?* and that is just *not on.*

"I don't think you're really the baron's type," Kimolijah mutters, "but don't let me stop you."

Oh my god. "Is *that* what you think I was...?" No. Just—*no.* Bas's mouth flaps, then pinches down into a sour grimace. "Believe me, I have absolutely no designs on the fucking *baron.*"

Kimolijah snaps his head up, and his tawny eyes narrow. "*Ohhhhh.*" He looks abruptly far too pleased with himself, and his gaze is mocking. His grin is wide this time, and real, and he pointedly runs the tip of his tongue along his bottom lip. "What's the matter? A little on edge, are we, and haven't got enough credit for Hannah's liking? Looking for a, uh...." His gaze is a cross now between provocative and derisive, and it trails down to Bas's mouth and then his crotch before he lifts it back up to Bas's eyes with a blatant leer. "You've got a nice mouth to go with those pretty blue eyes. Looking for a bit of a trade, are you?"

There are so, *so* many things wrong with this, but the most important ones are:

1) Baron Stanslo's bit-on-the-side has just offered to trade blowjobs, and

2) Guys don't refuse blowjobs, but

3) Bas *has* to refuse a blowjob, except

4) He'd give just about anything to say *Yes, holy fuck, your mouth*, and

5) ....

Okay, he can't really think of a 5 because the little brain has kind of taken over and it's not much on logic. But those are going to have to be enough to be getting on with, because they're the only ones at the moment that are making it into even semicoherent thoughts. It's all causing a rather tragic bit of a mess of misfiring in Bas's brain, and all the things he should be saying right now have gotten clogged up behind the knot of *Just how many "trades" does Kimolijah make in a week?* and *Wow, he really is kind of a slag, isn't he*, and *So totally not the shy whiz kid I was absolutely not in love with anyway*, and *Why did I ever think tailored trousers were a good idea?*

Bas can't help the sputter. "That is *not* what—"

"*Good*," Kimolijah snarls, vicious now, all the smirking mockery gone and twisted into a narrow, bitter kind of rage. "Because you ever try coming at me with that"—he comes up with what looks like a pair of wire cutters from God knows where and points the tip in the general direction of Bas's groin—"I'll turn it into a nice little purse for you to carry your balls around in, because you won't be needing those anymore, either. Got it?"

And once again, there are just too many things Bas wants to say, to ask—*From what I'm gathering, you weren't quite so harsh with Travis*, and, *You don't seem to put up that much of a fight with Stanslo*, and, *Why is none of this helping with the "not in love with you" thing?*—but Kimolijah's rattled him, quite badly, Bas is *never* rattled, so what he ends up saying is, "Look, whatever you think I was trying to do, that is *not* what I—"

"How about you make yourself useful," Kimolijah cuts in, sharp, "and help me clean up the mess you made."

It's stern, an order, and Bas is just scattered enough that he moves to comply without really thinking about the fact that badasses don't take orders. And puts his hand right through the thin wood panels holding up the unfinished portion of the engine housing. More little parts flip up, and Bas watches with a wince as they reach apogee and then rain back down. *Plink, plink, plink* all over the place, like shiny confetti. It takes a long time for the last bit to hit the ground and for Bas to stop flinching with every tiny impact. Or maybe it just seems like a long time to Bas.

No, see, this *just isn't right*. Bas is the guy who's been pulling off Jakob Barstow so well he's got *Baron* fucking *Stanslo* believing it. Bas is the guy who tracks missing Techs down when they can't be found, and usually has to shoot someone in order to rescue them when he finds them. Okay, he brings in the agents when he finds them, and the agents usually do the shooting, but there's not always time or opportunity for that, and Bas is the guy who steps up when others can't.

Which means Bas *is not* the guy who stammers and trips and flails when a grimy little gridTech *who's sleeping with his criminal boss* gets a little pissy with him.

Everything is silent for a sticky, tense moment, Bas peering down at the minicatastrophe he just caused and feeling Kimolijah's incredulous glare burning at the back of his neck.

And then Kimolijah says, quite calmly, "Okay, so you're not a spy." His expression is not one of lethal rage when Bas finally gets the nerve to turn and look at him; it's more like dubious confusion. Kimolijah blinks from Bas's hand to Bas's face. "You're either a saboteur or a fucking idiot."

Bas doesn't say anything for a bit, thinking that over, before he asks, "Which one will make you stop trying to kill me with your eyes?"

It surprises a snort out of Kimolijah, and he knuckles at his mouth to cover it. He clears his throat and says, "Wouldn't you like to know," but he's not glaring anymore, at least, and when he cocks his head to the side and looks at Bas square-on, the gaze is thoughtful. "Why did you give me those books?"

Bas's eyebrows shoot up. He'd kind of forgotten about that. "You wanted them."

"That's not really an answer."

"It's a perfectly good one, actually."

"Not here it's not."

"Yeah, well, I'm still the new guy, aren't I?" Bas shrugs. "You should just pull in your horns and proceed to abusing my good nature before I catch on." It feels safe enough to try to move again, so Bas starts gingerly tiptoeing through the mess he's made of Kimolijah's contraptions. He gets all the way to the edge of the cabin before his boot hooks into a stray wire and he almost sails headlong into the dirt. He doesn't—he catches himself in time—but the jerk on the wire pulls a panel loose and more wires spill out through the gap.

Bas stares down at it blankly, for quite some time, his brain refusing to even make enough sense to chide him, but eventually, he dares a look at Kimolijah.

Kimolijah just shakes his head, eyes wide and wondering, his mouth opening and closing like he's trying really hard to form words and just can't. And then he huffs a disbelieving laugh and says, "My god," like he's choking on it. "You need a bloody keeper."

There's a soft whistle from above. Bas and Kimolijah both look up to see the falcon perched up on the edge of the hole in the roof where Kimolijah had been, peering down at them with a comical tilt of its head. When a wad of rodent guts splats right in the middle of Bas's forehead, Kimolijah laughs his ass off.

⊗≈∞

They've almost got the mess Bas made cleaned up. Well, Kimolijah almost has it cleaned up. Bas's participation is limited to reaching out now and then to point out a missed bit and having his hand slapped away with an impatient "Don't touch, I'll get it." Bas plays along because he has to admit it was quite an accidentally destructive display, and he's probably lucky Kimolijah didn't gut him. Bas has no doubt he's caused at least a small setback in Kimolijah's work, and if Bas has learned nothing else from studying him through the files, he's learned that Kimolijah takes his work and his designs dreadful serious. Which, Bas thinks as he continues to scrutinize the design half-formed all around him, could be a very bad thing.

"Why this?" Bas asks, waving his hand at what will eventually be, he's sure, a fully functioning gridtrain. "Why here?" Kimolijah doesn't say anything, and Bas already knows the answer, but he doesn't know *all* the answer, so he pushes, "Why you?"

It doesn't get a reaction. Kimolijah is sitting cross-legged in the dirt next to the chassis, chewing on his dirty fingernails and frowning down at the little device Bas broke. He doesn't stiffen up and he doesn't growl, but Bas knows he heard; Kimolijah's gaze flickers up, lands on Bas for a fraction of a second, and then quickly flits back down again.

"You're not here because you want to be," Bas ventures quietly, watching for something, any telltale at all, but Kimolijah gives him nothing. "That thing on your arm"—Bas gestures to the weird metal vambrace—"it's gridTech, and yet it does things gridTech isn't supposed to do. It did it when you said no to Stanslo." That gets something, a pause in gnawing, but it's quick and it's small. "And it did it again when you tried to talk about your da."

"Who said anything about anyone's da?" Kimolijah looks up at Bas through his lashes. "Who says I even have one?"

"Everyone has one."

"Maybe I'm a shameful by-blow. Maybe my mam was a good-time girl and dear old Dada was nothing more than some dosh left on her dresser and a wet spot on the sheets."

Bas knows it's not at all how it was: Ohnadel Adani had been a perfectly respectable kineTech, Class 3; Ajamil Adani was gridLatent, still grieving his seven-years-gone bondmate and scraping out a living for his two children with his tinker's shop on Poor Side in Knapston, until he and his son "died" in that fire.

Kimolijah's question wasn't a lie, but it was meant to be deceptive nonetheless. Distraction and diversion.

Bas lifts an eyebrow. "I've heard things. About this place. About *you*." Bas pauses, but again, Kimolijah gives him nothing, so he presses, "Things about contracts and holes in them and why—"

"Yeah, how about that?" Kimolijah cuts in. He frowns. "I heard you put up a bit of a fight with yours." He's staring at Bas now, curiosity in those huge tawny eyes, and he tilts his head like his stupid gut-throwing bird. "Why?"

Bas can't help the snort. "Because the terms sucked?"

"Well, yeah, *obviously*." Kimolijah rolls his eyes. "But you had to know all that before you came here."

"How would I?"

"Oh, come *on*." Kimolijah makes a face and sends a long-suffering glance at the ceiling. "You didn't just show up here with no one for collateral because the baron's suddenly grown a heart. Quit pretending you did."

Collateral. God. Bas had known, really, but it's another thing entirely to hear it said right out loud.

Kimolijah looks at Bas steadily and leans in, lowers his voice. "Look, I know you're a spy—*everyone* knows you're a spy—and it's not like we don't know how the baron can... well, it's not like we don't know. I mean, *God*, it's not like Haversham didn't...." He pauses and peers down at his bracelet, like he was expecting it to zap him and is surprised it didn't, and then he looks back up at Bas. "Nobody's gonna hold it against you."

Bas mulls it over. Because this could be the moment. Or Kimolijah could be setting him up. Bas doesn't think so. But.

The thing is, no matter what Bas thinks, he just doesn't *know*. Even if Kimolijah's here against his will, Bas has seen nothing so far that tells him Kimolijah's not at least cooperating. In more ways than one. And maybe Kimolijah's cooperation would go so far as to expose a Directorate spy because Stanslo told him to. It doesn't seem like Kimolijah's allowed to say no to Stanslo. It doesn't seem like anyone is, but if that bracelet works the way Bas thinks it does—impossibility notwithstanding—when it comes to Stanslo, the word "no" isn't even permitted to be a part of Kimolijah's vocabulary.

It's a long stretch of desert between here and Harrowgate if Bas says the wrong thing to the wrong person and ends up having to make a run for it. And there's a fucking *noose* in the town square.

And yet. Well. Bas is here for a reason.

"Maybe I am a spy," he says eventually, and when Kimolijah just gives him a look, he goes on, "just maybe not the kind you think I am." He pauses, takes a deep breath. "Where is your da, Kimo? Was he your collateral?"

Kimolijah narrows his eyes at that, and something sparks

behind them, alert and calculating, something Bas can't read, but there's an abrupt awareness in there, and maybe—*maybe*, if Bas isn't fooling himself—a tiny flicker of something dawning. Bas can't tell what, so he sits there, waiting Kimolijah out, and Bas thinks: *Yeah, come on*, and he thinks: *Make the connection*, and he thinks: *Just a tiny bit of trust here*, and he thinks: *Take a leap*, and he watches Kimolijah work through something in his head that never comes out his mouth.

Instead, he ends up glaring at Bas, mouth tightening down, before he brushes it all away and puts on one of those fake grins.

"Did you know that your eye is made out of the same stuff the eggs in a woman's ovaries are made of?"

It's so out-of-the-blue that Bas can almost hear the cogs in his brain screeching and trying to grind back into gear. Kimolijah's just looking at him, his expression pleasant enough, his big eyes wide and maliciously amused.

Bas's mouth just kind of... hangs open. He says, "What?" and then he shakes his head and says, "*What?*"

"Yeah." Kimolijah nods and smiles, all bright and cheery, and then he gets up and heads toward the station proper. "That's why it hurts so much when you get jizz in your eye." He walks backward for a second and flutters his fingers at Bas. "You know, the little sperms, wriggling in and trying to make a baby out of your eyeball. Ow." His grin is kind of evil as he turns back around and strolls out the door, entirely too pleased with himself.

As well he should be, Bas supposes, because if he wanted to get Bas to pin his lip, he's done a fantastic job of it. Bas just stands there, blinking and staring at the doorway. Wordless, except for "What the *fuck* was that?"

It takes a good five minutes for Bas to get himself together enough to follow.

13.

An hour or so later, Bas still hasn't quite gotten his equilibrium back. He can't stop thinking about jizz in the eye, and though he can't say he's ever had the experience, he also can't say he's not busily picturing how Kimolijah might have been moved to acquire that information.

It's a... really vivid mental picture, distracting and far too arousing. Until that picture fans out to include Stanslo, and Bas thinks *Well, shit, there's a mental door I'll never be able to close again,* and it kind of makes him a little sick.

Which probably suits Kimolijah just fine, since Bas honestly can't come up with any chatter with which to distract-disarm-defeat and thus find a way to get usable information. Kimolijah gets his silence while he sits at his workbench in the station and fiddles with the thing Bas broke, and he seems to do his best not to outright smirk the whole time. At least he's put his shirt back on, so Bas isn't—unconsciously, yeah, but still fucking *constantly*—trying to mentally trace the shapes of the tattoos.

Bas calls it a partial win.

Eventually, he sucks it up and asks, "So why does everyone change the subject when I ask about the Bruise?"

And Kimolijah promptly answers, "Did you know that goats can suck each other off?"

Bas is doing better, because that one only shuts him up for a couple of minutes.

In the course of the early afternoon, Bas learns that his mouth is the most unsanitary part of his body, he probably swallows about a quart of snot every day, and if his head ever gets chopped off, he'll probably know about it for a good fifteen seconds or so before his brain dies. He learns nothing about the Bruise, Stanslo's Bridge, or Kimolijah. Well, except that Kimolijah is, apparently, a fount of information Bas has never had any desire to know.

The sun has shifted through the gaps in the roof, and the heat has backed off just enough to notice. The bird's shadow every now and then glides across the floor as it circles above the hole in the roof, and its occasional whistling complaints make Kimolijah smile absently and send a fond glance upward.

Outside the station, the busy noises pick up again, people emerging from whatever cool spot they'd found to ride out the peak heat of midday. It makes the chickens in the barnyard behind the station mutter unhappily, and every once in a while there's a wave of annoyed chatter from them, waning only after the falcon's shadow passes once again across the dirt floor between Bas and Kimolijah. Kimolijah's still working quite diligently on fixing the thing Bas broke before, but he smirks every time the chickens decide the falcon has gotten too close.

"So what is that, anyway?" Bas ventures. He points at the thing in Kimolijah's hands when Kimolijah looks up at him. Bas isn't really expecting an answer that doesn't have to do with something horrible about his own body he doesn't want to know, but he can't just give up. "I was trying to figure out what it is when you scared the shit out of me and made me drop it."

"*Made* you drop it." Kimolijah rolls his eyes. A shot rings out from the direction of the barn. Not one of the gridguns. From the timbre of the resonance, Bas guesses it's one of the bigger monster rifles, like those ones Lowen and Fox carry. Kimolijah pauses with a frown, listening.

It doesn't startle him, and it doesn't startle Bas, either, not like it should. Not like it would have only days ago. Shots seem to go off here with casual frequency, but then, there's an awful lot here to shoot at. *Giant fucking spiders*, for one. Predators trying to sneak through the pickets at night and have a go at the pitiful horde of livestock, snakes that are as fat around as Bas's thigh and that Merrin told him have been known to crush a man's ribs and swallow him whole, not to mention the not-bats. Just yesterday, Reacher took out a coyote that had ventured too close to the outer fences.

"They come out here this close and during the day, it's pretty sure they got the foaming dementia," Reacher told Bas, smiling in that way that made him look halfway stupid. "Best not to take chances."

Bas agreed but said nothing. Mostly because Reacher immediately set about skinning the thing, and in the desert heat, the smell was thick and rank. Bas casually found somewhere else to be.

Another shot goes off, and someone laughs and whoops. It makes Kimolijah roll his eyes. When there's nothing more but the incensed complaints of the chickens, Kimolijah shakes his head and goes back to fiddling, either having forgotten Bas's question or having no intention of answering it.

So Bas asks again, "So what is it?" and when Kimolijah only frowns, annoyed, Bas presses, "It looks like some kind of flow switch or converter, but all those magnets...." He tilts his head and squints at Kimolijah. "All that magnetic energy—won't that pretty much reverse the draw and blow out the gridstream?"

Weirdly, of all the things they've talked and not-talked about in the past few hours, that's the thing that makes Kimolijah go still all over and his face go wary. He stares down at his hands for several long moments, shoulders stiff and fingers still, before he slowly goes back to threading a wire through the maze of little bits inside the casing.

"You—?" Kimolijah has to pause and clear his throat. "You know something about gridTech?" Trying for casually curious and not quite getting there.

"Some." Bas is just as cautious. "Enough, I suppose."

"Enough for what?"

"Enough for...." Bas hesitates. Because this really shouldn't be causing this kind of reaction. Unless.... "Oh my god."

It's quiet and kind of breathy, because there's a tremor running through Bas and he's trying not to actually whoop at the purely accidental breakthrough. Because Kimolijah's the only gridTech who's ever been out here, and if there had been any kind of Grid layman or specialist or even a bloody *clerk* on record of having gone even as far as Harrowgate, Bas would know about it.

Stanslo is not gridTech. Stanslo is a bloody *robber baron* who's made his fortune by... well, basically, robbing. He wouldn't know how to read a Grid schematic if it stood up in front of him and did an interpretive dance. He doesn't understand the genius that is Kimolijah Adani. *No one* understands the genius that is Kimolijah Adani; if they did, someone would have come up with a gridtrain before now.

I told him I'm working on it, I can't do it any faster! Kimolijah had snapped at him before. Now Bas knows what it means.

"Stanslo doesn't know anything about how your trains work. No one here knows anything about how your trains work. So no one knows exactly what the hell it is you're doing except for what you tell them."

That gets a glare, and wow, seriously, it's a good thing looks can't stab you in the head. Kimolijah snaps up off his stool and stalks over to the shelves loaded with bits and bobs. He doesn't say anything as he throws things around, and his hands don't shake, but Bas can tell he's off-balance and pissed off about it.

Bas tries really hard not to grin. "You think I'm here to spy on your work. Stanslo has no idea what he's even looking at when he checks up on what you do with your trains, so of course, *of course* the thing he'd do would be to go scare up someone who *does* know what they're looking at so he can—"

"And do you?" Kimolijah whips around to fix Bas with a defiant glower, hand wrapped around a tool that looks long and sharp and heavy and dangerous. "*Do* you know what you're looking at?"

Bas shakes his head, his smile dropping, because this obviously isn't the least bit amusing for Kimolijah. Bas says, "No, that's not why—"

He's drowned out and overridden by a volley of shots outside and a shriek that Bas at first thinks sounds like a child's wail. He sees Kimolijah whirl toward the back of the station, eyes wide, and then Serenat bursts in behind them.

"Hey," Kimolijah says. "What—?"

"Fox," Serenat says. "He's shooting at Jessa."

Bas has time to think *Hey, Magic Man's sister's name is Jessa,* before Kimolijah's flying out of the station and Bas has to follow.

⁂

Afterward, Bas will think he really should've seen it coming.

The thing is, bullies are predictable. Latch on to the one person they think can't fight back, stir some shit, then explode when the shit-stirring doesn't go exactly to plan.

Bas suspects "going to plan" is probably more like a fond wish when it comes to Kimolijah. God knows Bas has been fondly wishing for it since he stepped foot in Stanslo's Bridge.

It's not as chaotic as it sounded when Bas gets out into the yard between the barn and the back of the station. It's actually quite calm but for a handful of deputies standing just outside the chicken wire. Bas is surprised to see Reacher, he didn't think him the sort, and indeed Reacher's hanging back some, but he's still there. Bas doesn't recognize the others, but they're laughing up at the sky like naughty schoolboys. The only real difference is that these guys are heeled and Fox's smile is more of a sneer, bared teeth and eyes glinting with something cold and hateful as he sights down a long, broad twelve-barrel shotgun, a thick fucking beast of a thing.

"C'mon, little birdie, come see what ol' Foxy brung ye."

"What the *fuck* d'you think you're doing?" Kimolijah snarls, stalking ahead of Bas and toward Fox, apparently heedless of the gun.

And that's just a bad idea all around, in Bas's opinion. He's dealt with plenty of bullies before, but Fox is the scary-crazy kind.

This has all the signs of someone begging for a difficulty, and with a firm plan as to what he intends to do when it arrives. Bas has seen the absolute hatred for Kimolijah all over Fox's small-eyed face, and yeah, everyone here seems to know that you don't touch Kimolijah if you don't want to die a very messy death at Stanslo's earliest convenience—or a slow one through a shot to the leg with no subsequent medical care—but consequences rarely come into it with people like Fox, and the consequences now are likely quite limited. Fox has got to know that leg is going septic; his pale face, shaky hands, and the sweat soaking his shirt pretty much scream it. He's likely to shoot as soon as Kimolijah gives him the lip he wants and then worry about what Stanslo might do to him for it after, because Fox probably doesn't have very much "after" to worry about.

So, much as Bas knows it's a bad idea, he sprints after Kimolijah and grabs hold of him before he can lay hands on Fox, like it looks like he intends. Grim, Bas snags Kimolijah's arm, and Kimolijah growls at him, and then Fox fires off another round, and the falcon—Jessa, apparently—whistles an angry screech as she dodges and dives. And *still* she doesn't flee. She keeps circling, waiting for the next shot. Bas always thought birds of prey were smarter than this.

"Fox, you fucking cunt-faced ass monkey," Kimolijah grates, turns to take a swing at Bas to get him to let go, and when Bas blocks and hangs on, Kimolijah says, "Knock it off!" and Bas can't tell which one of them he's talking to.

"Just back off!" Bas snaps at Kimolijah, eyes on Fox. "Let me handle—"

Another shot and Kimolijah's gaze flies to the sky, and when he sees Jessa dodge, apparently still unharmed, Bas's hand starts to tingle, a low resonating thrum that doesn't hurt but is unpleasant and disconcerting all the same. Kimolijah's skin hums with tiny blue filaments of gridstream, but it doesn't come from the bracelet like before; it's like it comes right out his pores and fizzes into Bas with a shuddering spidery buzz of static. Bas is halfway expecting to get fried and wonders vaguely if he'll melt like that guy in the station, but when Fox fires off another shot and Jessa veers and dives, Kimolijah lets loose a panicked noise in his throat and kicks Bas's shin so hard Bas thinks maybe it snapped his knee in half. The blue glow intensifies and then pools into a throbbing, nearly solid mass in the palm of Kimolijah's hand.

Bas is hanging on to Kimolijah now mostly out of reflexive muscle spasms, but the whys and wherefores don't seem to matter much to Kimolijah. He turns a look of frantic anger on Bas, and his voice is harsh and nearly thready when he says, "God, will you just let *go*? She's synched, she can't leave me, *let go!*"

Bas can't. If he could, he still wouldn't. The gridstream is making his muscles twitch and contract, so it's pretty much moot anyway, but that's not the point. Maybe Fox is bugfuck enough to think self-defense would be a good enough excuse to give Stanslo when a reckoning comes—*He came at me with his Tech, boss, what was I supposed to do?*—and ordinarily Bas would probably just let Kimolijah have his go at Fox while everyone else enjoys the show. Kimolijah's got what looks like a pretty lethal little ball of gridstream pulsing in his palm, and besides that, well. He's small but Bas has seen him on the attack before, and he doesn't think Kimolijah will let Fox get the drop on him like last time. Kimolijah's strong and pretty scrappy, and it's usually the little ones you have to watch out for. They can get mean. And Bas wouldn't mind seeing Fox with a few less of those brown teeth.

But Fox has a gun. He's got to be in mind-scragging pain, and he's already bordering on animal-wild. And he's a fucking lunatic.

So Bas hangs on and tries not to put any weight on his leg, where Kimolijah probably left a dent in his shinbone, and Fox shoots again, and Jessa shrieks and the other guys laugh. Kimolijah shouts and snarls and gives Bas another kick. And nobody's stepping in to help or do a goddamned thing. The sweat on Kimolijah's arm is making him slippery, and he's going to get loose and get shot in the head shortly thereafter.

Bas does the only thing he can think of: he forces his free hand into a fist and punches Kimolijah in the face. Not hard, only enough to put him down for a second or two, long enough for the gridstream to dissipate and for Bas to take advantage of Fox's surprise and cover the three steps between them before Fox can recover and shoot him. Two of the barrels of Fox's gun are still hot when Bas grabs it, searing metal weltering into Bas's palm, and it should make him yelp and snatch his hand back. It doesn't. It pisses him off even more. It makes him stronger than he thought he was when he jerks the gun, snaps it out of Fox's hands, and then levels the butt of it at Fox's forehead.

Fox goes down, out cold, and, as if to punctuate it, Jessa swoops in with a rough screech, pelts near to the ground in a straight line right at Fox's prone form, talons extended like curled hooks, and strafes low over Fox's face. It's not until she's lunged away again and is already high in the sky that the gouges she left across Fox's cheek start to part and bleed out.

Bas smirks as he flips the gun around and sets the stock to his hip. Reacher has apparently had the sense to skive off during the ruckus, so Bas makes a point of cranking the barrel housing and setting the strike stud, and then just stares at Fox's remaining cronies.

"Get him the hell out of here."

The other two—Bas only knows one of them: Cavett—they only blink at him for a moment, before they look down at Fox and back up at Bas. They look... actually, they look pretty vacant and stupid. And Bas is about out of patience.

"*Move!*" Bas growls and thumbs the hammer 'til it clicks into place, ready.

They move. Bas watches them haul Fox away, bootheels dragging channels into the hardpan, and he doesn't even have a chance to turn around and see if Kimolijah's back on his feet yet before Stanslo's distinctive figure comes around the side of the barn in a hurry.

He looks *pissed*. Murderous. And he's looking right at Bas.

"Baron!" Kimolijah's suddenly right next to Bas, in fact angling in front of him, putting himself between Bas and the rolling steam train that is Baron Stanslo. "Come to oversee your mighty dominion, have you?" Trying for casual and droll. He takes a step into Stanslo's space and reaches out to straighten his tie.

It doesn't shift the look on Stanslo's face, but it does make him modify that lethal blue gaze into something a tiny bit softer before it alters into surprise, then confusion, then anger again. Still, his hand is gentle when he reaches for Kimolijah's chin and tilts his face up.

"What happened?"

It's soft, but deceptively so; Bas can tell because the rage is still there in the eyes, bubbling underneath. Bas would almost call it worry or care, but he's seen too much already, so he knows what it is: it's wrath. Because someone has put hands on something that belongs to Stanslo. And worse—Bas shifts a quick look at Kimolijah's bleeding lip and swelling cheek— they've left a mark.

Jessa comes back and perches on the roof of the barn. She looks strangely aware of and attentive to what's going on below her. Bas sees Kimolijah's glance flick up and back so quickly he doesn't think Stanslo notices. Or cares.

"Oh, this?" Kimolijah slides his tongue over the small split in his lip and gives Stanslo a look from beneath his lashes. "It wasn't anything," he says, tone soft, soothing, and he sets a hand in the middle of Stanslo's chest, dear. "The guys"—he nods in the direction the men dragged Fox—"they... um." He shakes his head. "You know how they get." There's a smile now, ruined by bloody teeth. "Just... shooting and stuff, and um. Hey, did you know that every blast from a flint-shot rifle has enough power to—"

"My dear," Stanslo cuts in, quiet, almost tender. "Tell me the truth, now." He slides a hand down Kimolijah's arm and settles his fingers around the coiled vambrace. "Who hurt you?"

Kimolijah grins and shrugs. "Oh, you know—life hurts, everybody hurts everybody else, it's an old tale, really, and one— "

"Kimo."

"—that's been told by playwrights and poets since—"

"*Kimo.*"

Kimolijah pauses his babble and tilts his head, big eyes wide. "Yeah, Baron?" He blinks, all innocence.

God, he's a smartass. He'd *have* to be sleeping with Stanslo to get away with this shit.

Stanslo sighs and shakes his head. "I had hoped, my dear, that we were past these... these *games*." His tone is still soft, laced with disappointment.

Kimolijah gives him a grin. "Games!" he crows. "But, Baron! Life here is just one big, long, drawn-out *game*, isn't it?" His tone has gone from pleasant to manic to vicious from the beginning of that sentence to the end. "Pawns and kings and queens"—still smiling, but the words are shoved out between his teeth now—"and every once in a while you throw a new piece into the mix, yeah? Just to keep it *interesting*." He tries to wrench his arm away, but Stanslo doesn't let go. "You and your goddamned games and your spies, and it never ends well for anybody, does it? I *can't keep doing this*, you can't keep—!"

He doesn't shut up until Stanslo slaps him across the face—not hard, really, not enough to hurt, but enough to let Kimolijah know he's serious.

"Look at you, poor thing." Stanslo runs a hand down Kimolijah's cheek, the swelling bruise he's probably just made worse, and he smiles a little when Kimolijah jerks back. "You're working yourself up again, dear heart. You know it's not good for you. Perhaps I should've just left you in the Outlet a bit longer, you think? You're usually in a much more agreeable mood than this afterwards."

It makes Kimolijah go still all over. "I'm not—"

Stanslo's grip tightens, and he roughly twists Kimolijah's arm, threat. "The truth." The vambrace blooms with shivery threads of gridstream, and though Kimolijah hisses in a breath and reflexively jerks his arm, like it hurts, his hand is curled into a fist. "Who hurt you, my dear?" Stanslo's voice is eerily low and tender, considering the menace inherent in everything else about him.

Bas narrows his eyes at Stanslo's hand, at the matte-metal beneath it and the sizzling little strands of gridstream spiking between Stanslo's fingers and yet *not touching him*, at Kimolijah's almost panicked expression, and thinks *Yeah, okay, that makes no sense at all.* Because Stanslo is not gridTech. And it isn't supposed to be possible to use a person's Tech against them like that. And yet Bas is looking right at it. The only thing that *does* make sense is that, for whatever reason, it seems like Kimolijah doesn't want to tell Stanslo that Bas was the one to strike him, and Stanslo can use that bracelet to make him.

Someone's abusing a Tech is all Bas can think, right in front of him, and Bas is Directorate, he's supposed to stop things like that. So he opens his mouth, and "Fox did it" comes from behind him. He turns to see Serenat, standing just off to the side and pointing out past the barns toward the Palace. "He punched him."

Stanslo tilts his head, eyes flat. "Did he."

Bas was perfectly willing to take the blame for this. He did it, after all. And God knows what Stanslo might do to Fox this time. But Kimolijah's eyes are wide and right on him now, and his face is twisted into something pleading and intense.

Bas frowns and gives him a *what the fuck?* look, but Kimolijah's expression doesn't change.

"He was shooting at Jessa," Serenat goes on. "And when Kimo told him to quit it, Fox punched him." She grins. "But then Bas decked him. Knocked him out! It was really pretty."

Kimolijah finally looks away from Bas and shuts his eyes. "Serenat...." He doesn't finish, and Bas has no idea why it looks like he's just been gutted.

"I see." Stanslo's posture has gone tight and very, very still.

"Baron," Kimolijah puts in, abruptly soft and very nearly cajoling, "maybe I can—"

"Maybe you can remember what your mouth is for," Stanslo snaps from between clenched teeth, "and *shut it*."

Rage, abrupt and intense. It's unnerving. So is the way Kimolijah shuts up and seems to be doing his level best not to meet anyone's eyes.

Stanslo visibly collects himself with a long calming breath, and then his smile is back, the warm, condescending one. "I am... disappointed, of course. But not really surprised." He sighs. "You will find, Bas, that I am a man of great patience. But I'm afraid Fox has quite reached the limits. And you, my dear." He gives Kimolijah a look that's fixed and almost feral. "Are you *really* going to stand here, with your hands on me, and plead his case?" He narrows his eyes. "Have I misinterpreted the avarice between you all along? Has Fox stepped into Travis's place to satisfy your base little cravings for the occasional bit of rough trade—*dear heart*?"

It's scary. It really is. Because once Bas has seen the crazy beneath the calm, he can't unsee it, and it doesn't seem to ever retreat, just hang there, waiting.

And you just don't fuck with crazy.

Thing is, Bas seems to be surrounded by it. And if he just lies down and lets it roll him under, he'll never last. He'll certainly never get out of here.

So he finds himself eyeing the fizzing little pops of gridstream quietly humming between Stanslo's fingers, still white-knuckled around Kimolijah's arm, making fawn divots in brown skin already notched and pitted by matte-metal. And then he finds himself saying, "The terms of my contract state that I'm to protect Kimo, yeah? Keep him from harm?" He waits for Stanslo to nod slowly, and when he does, eyes flinty, Bas says, "Then I'll thank you to unhand him."

Kimolijah sucks in a tight breath, and Bas can hear the low groan of "Oh *God*" only because everything has gone wholly and profoundly silent. Even the tinny mutter of gridstream cuts out and goes dead.

Serenat giggles a little, which only makes Kimolijah wince.

Stanslo just stares, face blank, eyes fixed as glaciers, before he calls, "Lowen?" without shifting his gaze.

The "Yeah, boss" is predictable, but it still gives Bas a little jolt in the chest, because he hadn't seen Lowen arrive out of nowhere, and Bas is still stuck like a bug in amber in Stanslo's flat stare.

There's a long breath from Stanslo, and then another quick flare of naked anger behind the eyes, and Bas is just thinking how much less unnerving that is than one of those awful cheery smiles when Stanslo shifts and grins. It makes Bas want to look away, but he doesn't.

"I think," says Stanslo slowly, "that perhaps our friend Bas here might need a bit of clarification on—"

"Baron," Kimolijah cuts in, tone smooth and coaxing, and his hand on Stanslo's chest pat-pat-pats against Stanslo's wide silk tie where it tucks into his waistcoat. "It makes me kind of hot when you go all grizzly bear." He tips a crooked little smirk and leans in and up until his head is almost resting on Stanslo's shoulder. Stanslo lets go of Kimolijah's arm and snakes his hand down to rest on Kimolijah's hip.

Kimolijah's smirk widens, and he sets his lips just beneath Stanslo's ear.

And. God.

Kimolijah's voice is low and seductive when he goes on, "Why don't we go on up the house and take out some of that aggression with—"

"I suggest you don't try my patience just now, dear heart."

Stanslo's cold grin turns softer, more sincere, but his hand grips harder at Kimolijah's hip, fingers digging in until Kimolijah puffs a tiny "Hey, ow, watch it!" and winces, but he doesn't pull away.

"I think you'll find," says Stanslo, "that I can devise my own uses for any aggression quite well." He dips his head and nuzzles Kimolijah's temple, his stare never leaving Bas. "I don't really," he murmurs to Kimolijah, "need your... cooperation. Do I." Not even close to a question.

"You usually prefer to have it," Kimolijah says, still soft but with a hint of defiance edging through. "Although, I suppose I could scare up a few tears for you, if you think it'll help you get it—"

"*Sometimes*," Stanslo cuts in, teeth clenched and grip ratcheting up until Kimolijah yips, "sometimes I find it both useful and amusing that you still think anything that comes out of your mouth makes a difference." The smile this time makes Bas's gut curl. "And sometimes," Stanslo says, "I think my pawns need to be reminded who their king is."

"*King*." Kimolijah rolls his eyes and snorts. "Oh yeah, that'll get me hot." Bas can see him still trying—and failing—to work his way out of Stanslo's grip, but his expression doesn't change and he doesn't fetch his mouth for a second. "Won't be much room in your great big bed if your giant ego will be joining us, *Your Majesty*."

Oh my god, why are you pushing him? Bas's brain howls, and he wants to somehow tell Kimolijah to just hobble his insolent lip, he's making things worse, but Bas doesn't think it's a good idea to say anything just now, and Kimolijah won't look at him.

"Kimo promised Dolerma he'd work on the valve problem in the cold-storage rooms," Serenat pipes in, bold. She points at where Stanslo is gripping Kimolijah. "Hey, that looks like it hurts. You're gonna leave a mark. You should let him go."

Kimolijah shuts his eyes and drops his chin to his chest. He sighs, defeated.

Stanslo gives Serenat a gentle smile, says, "Thank you, sweetpea, but hush now, there's a girl," then he yanks Kimolijah in tight, hard enough to make Kimolijah yelp. Kimolijah glares at Stanslo but doesn't try to get loose.

"Lowen," Stanslo repeats, staring Kimolijah down, "I want Fox's ability to cause trouble contained. It was a mistake to allow him to wander loose, and I do apologize, dear Kimo, that he's caused you any distress."

He finally releases Kimolijah from his hard-set gaze and turns it on Bas. "Your actions here, Bas, from what I'm able to gather, have been commendable." He pauses for a long moment before a slow smirk blooms. "But please do not mistake your situation."

His mouth tightens and, as if to illustrate his point, he spins Kimolijah and yanks his arm behind his back at what looks like a painful angle. Kimolijah doesn't make a sound, though, he doesn't try to get away, and he doesn't look at anyone; he merely grits his teeth and shuts his eyes.

"You are to protect my property," Stanslo goes on, "when I am not able to protect it myself. When I am, well." A shrug. "As I've no doubt you would agree, a man's property is his to do with as he will, no?"

What Bas wouldn't give right now to just beef the smug bastard and figure out what to do from there. But that, he thinks, will get him no closer to getting the hell out of here, let alone getting Kimolijah out, and he's now more sure than ever that Kimolijah needs to get out of here. So Bas merely dips his head, acquiescent, and holds his hands up, palms out—peace and surrender.

It seems like the right thing; Stanslo grins again and loosens his hold on Kimolijah's arm. He turns to Lowen. "A night at the Outpost for Fox, I think. To start. If he survives—"

"Baron," Kimolijah cuts in, turning in again and worming his way under Stanslo's arm, "don't you think it would be better if—"

"*If he survives,*" Stanslo repeats, anger leeching through the words spoken slow and even through his smile, "he'll go to the Bruise on the next run. If he doesn't...." He merely shrugs.

The look Kimolijah gives Bas is deliberate and heavy, big eyes intense, like he's trying to drive whatever he can't say directly into Bas's head with the force of his stare. Bas wishes it were possible, because he can't guess what that look means.

"Baron?" Serenat asks, her weird voice high and bright, like a small child, all innocence. "If he doesn't, can we put him in the square next to Travis?"

It's kind of appalling, because Bas can't tell if it's some kind of taunt or a sincere request. He swears he can see a smirk gathered in the corner of that colorless mouth, and he doesn't know which way to interpret it.

Stanslo tells Serenat, "We shall see, little miss," and gives her an indulgent wink. Kimolijah glares at her, but Stanslo only takes a long, deep breath and turns to Lowen.

"Discipline," he says. "We can't have disobedience within our ranks." He gives Kimolijah a meaningful glance and then shifts a cheery shrug at Bas. "Give Lowen a hand, won't you, Bas?"

The smile he shoots at Kimolijah is both smug and lewd. "Come, dear heart, let's you and I have a chat."

He doesn't seem to hear when Kimolijah says, "Yeah, but wouldn't it be better if—?"

Bas doesn't find out what Kimolijah was going to say, because Stanslo cuts it off by jerking Kimolijah around by the arm and all but shoving him up the path toward the big house on the hill. Kimolijah doesn't look back. When Stanslo puts an arm around his shoulders, Kimolijah pulls away, but he doesn't fight powerful hard when Stanslo hauls him back. Kimolijah's mouth is still going, and Bas is afraid to even imagine what might be coming out of it or how very much he's obviously pissing Stanslo off. And what Stanslo might do about it up in that "great big bed." God knows how much worse it might get if Kimolijah doesn't learn to *shut his goddamned smart mouth* once in a while.

Bas just stares at their backs and doesn't admit that the roiling in his gut has just as much to do with the last ninety seconds of watching Kimolijah with Stanslo—halfway pandering and halfway hostile—as it does with the brief trip into Crazy Town after.

Serenat's watching Stanslo and Kimolijah too. She's got those same dark glasses on and her hat flops down nearly to her shoulders, so Bas can't see her eyes, but her mouth is turned down in an unhappy little curve. "He's not gonna last much longer," she says softly, sighs, and then walks away without a glance toward Bas or Lowen.

It gives Bas a bizarre bit of a chill.

Jessa keeps staring down at it all for a while, head tilting and soft little chirrups whistling from her throat. She takes flight, up, up, up for several firm beats of her wings, before she drifts down in a soft dive, pinions extended wide, and swoops, side-slung, so close to Bas he can feel the stir of hot air between her feathers. She arcs away on an ascending draft and then she's gone, off to no doubt circle Stanslo's big house on the hill until Kimolijah once again emerges.

Bas just watches her, oddly touched, and unabashedly relieved that she didn't drop any more leftover offal on him. He doesn't turn around when he hears Lowen shuffling behind him. He merely sighs and asks, "So what's the Outpost?"

It's a post. Out past the fences at the edge of town. *An outpost*. For fuck's sake.

As Lowen makes a pale, sickly Fox sit with his back to it and then ties his hands securely around and behind it, Bas thinks you could never make an illobook plot out of something like this. No one would ever believe it.

14.

And, okay, it isn't a breakthrough in the "ah, finally, every mystery about Kimolijah Adani is solved!" sense. But it also kind of is.

The thing is, Bas simply didn't have time to analyze things as they were happening. And what happened after was too bizarre and unsettling, and had pricked up feelings and thoughts inside Bas he didn't really know how to dissect.

He still doesn't know how to dissect them—the feelings, anyway, 'cause, y'know, *feelings*—but now he can watch behind his eyes the events that had spun out before them hours ago, slow them down and *see*. Or at least he thinks he can. And what he sees both clarifies and confuses. Because he's pretty sure Kimolijah somehow saved his ass back there, and Bas isn't quite sure why. And it doesn't stop the roiling in his gut over *how*. And there go the *feelings* again.

Putting the entirety of the blame on Fox is one thing, and covering up Bas's part in all of it is another. But the other thing, that... kind of corrupt seduction....

And okay, he knows Kimolijah's no blushing violet—he's *sleeping with Stanslo*, for fuck's sake—but there's a dichotomy, a giant lingering mystery, and it gets deeper as Bas watches out the window of his room in the Palace as a dark shape he knows has to be Kimolijah skulks down the hill from the big house and heads toward the edge of town.

The thing is, Bas is not surprised. Considering what went on with the Box and Kimolijah's behavior this afternoon, Bas halfway expected it. It fits, somehow.

It fits because Bas is in his own room, alive and able to grab his gun and head out into the dusk of early evening to follow after Kimolijah, instead of swinging from a noose, bloated and blue. Because he's pretty sure Stanslo was angry enough to suggest as much before Serenat pointed the finger at Fox and Fox alone, and then Kimolijah had gone all "clumsy siren" to distract from the point entirely, and then did it *again* to distract Stanslo from Bas's bad attempt to protect Kimolijah.

It fits.

And it's still bloody confounding.

So Bas puts it away and thinks about what happened before instead—the part with the converter and the accusations of spying, and he thinks *Okay. Okay.* He really should be disregarding all these distractions anyway and concentrating on the science that's, one way or another, responsible for all of it. Because it's the only thing that should matter, and it's what will get the Directorate out here when Bas gets back and tells them about it.

And he will. He'll forget all about the distraction of Kimolijah Adani. No, *he will.*

Right after he follows Kimolijah and finds out what he's up to.

❧

The landscape is not ideal for stealth. There are sporadic patches of scrub and thistle, and the occasional swell of random boulders, but it's mostly just flat and flat and flat. The bad thing about it is Bas has to double-time it and come around from a wide arc, far enough out Kimolijah won't see or hear him coming. The good thing is Bas doesn't have to be terribly close to see what he needs to see. He keeps track of Kimolijah by keeping track of Jessa circling above him. She wings close to Bas once or twice but doesn't give him away. Bas doesn't know exactly *how* she'd give him away, but whatever it might be, she doesn't do it.

He finds a rocky stretch that sprouts enough dry, stunted vegetation that he can comfortably duck behind it and blend with the shadows it makes. So he does.

And he watches.

Kimolijah's already there, a dark smudge against the gloam-lit sand, crouched in front of Fox with his neck bent. Bas thinks they're talking. He wishes he could hear. Kimolijah's got that jaunty little hat on. It seems far too cheerful and horribly out of place here.

The notion behind the Outpost is, apparently, helplessness against anything that might come at you during the night. And Bas has seen a rather large sample of the things that live in the cracks and crevices of Stanslo's Bridge. And he's a city boy, yeah, but he's lived on the road enough, and he's been here in the desert long enough to know that with the dark comes the cold, and the things that live here like to keep warm.

There are coyotes out there, and bobcats too, and Yanush swears he's seen something that looks like a man-sized lizard creeping around the perimeter of the town whenever he's got watch on the western boundary. Bas doesn't doubt it—he's seen the trophies on Stanslo's wall.

He's watching, so he sees it when the first set of smudges crests the horizon, noses up, sniffing the air. They're not dogs, though their shapes are reminiscent in the gloom where there's no composition in the blank nothing of desert wasteland, nothing but flat plains and small rises that nonetheless send shadows shirring across an impossible stretch between dark and darker. Their eyes glint in budding starlight, animal-bright, and wink like tiny sentient holocausts. And okay, maybe that's a bit melodramatic, but alarm is kind of taking over the higher brain functions because there are more every time he blinks and recounts.

Kimolijah hasn't seen them yet, or at least he isn't acting like he has. Jessa sees them, though. She keeps her arcs between Kimolijah and the creatures and whistles out sharp trills that sound like reprimands. She doesn't get close, but she doesn't retreat. Kimolijah doesn't pay her any mind, still bent in toward Fox, apparently deep in conversation, so Bas pulls his gridgun around and watches through the sights.

The things are moving in, and they're losing their caution now, growing bolder since there's been no show of threat to make them wary. Bas counts twelve now, stalking closer, daring yips and brash growls filling the silence. No way Kimolijah doesn't know they're coming, but the only acknowledgment he gives is a slight turn of his body, maybe an all-over tensing, though Bas can't tell from this distance. Bas targets the closest and keeps watching, because between Fox's poorly cared for leg and the gashes down his face from Jessa, those things have scented blood.

What the hell are you doing? Bas thinks at Kimolijah, because Kimolijah's not doing anything, just talking to Fox like mutant dogs with glowing eyes aren't creeping closer and closer with obvious intent.

Except then Kimolijah does do something, and it isn't what Bas has been expecting. Kimolijah pushes in close to Fox, leaning into him like he means to kiss him. He doesn't. He unties him. He pulls Fox's arms out from behind him, gently, helps Fox settle himself against the post. Waits. Bas sees Fox nod. Kimolijah says something more, something quiet, and he raises his hands, sets them to either side of Fox's head....

"Holy... *oh.*" Bas sucks in a long tight breath and shields his eyes.

Fox and Kimolijah both burn, blue and bright, with a strangely beautiful wash of gridstream that floods from Kimolijah's hands and into Fox's skull.

The stalking creatures startle and yip, then dance back and crouch low. Bas can see them now, the residual wash from the stream contouring their shapes and dulling the gleam of their eyes. His mind won't let him call them dogs; their shapes are just too *wrong.* Or maybe they are dogs, some mutant version of them that wouldn't bother vying for table scraps when there were tastier alternatives and fresh, choice cuts right off the bone, still twitching. Their jaws are longer and broader than a dog's, more so than even a wolf's, and the teeth that protrude almost like tusks are thick and yellow and sharp. The forequarters are wide and almost knotty, shoulder muscles bunching and bending beneath fur that looks more like a spiny hide.

It's over quickly, a smooth, rapid pulse that jerks Fox's body rigid, convulses it, then pulls back and stops, and Kimolijah lets go. He pushes back some while Fox's body jitters with a few last spasms of gridstream backwash and then goes still, the silhouetted shape of it all white then green behind Bas's eyelids in the sudden dark.

It's not what Bas has been expecting. He's not sure what he's been expecting. He thinks it was maybe something like what Kimolijah did when Bas was in the Box. Some kind of guard duty, maybe, Kimolijah standing over Fox and keeping those dog things away until dawn. That seems more like Kimolijah, somehow, and Bas can't say he wouldn't agree on some level—getting torn apart by mutant dogs is no way for a man to die, not even Fox.

Still, though. Bas was not expecting this.

He honestly hadn't thought Kimolijah had it in him.

Kimolijah stays crouched there for several long moments, hunched in, head down, like he's praying. Maybe he is. He doesn't move until the creatures get restless again, start stirring, start thinking about creeping in. Bas sees the first one lift from its crouch and sniff the air, and though it whines a little, likely the tang of gridstream burning its nose, it still begins to skulk in, and several of the others follow it.

Jessa dives once or twice, sending one yawping backward and another snapping the air after her. A few others get bolder when she retreats, slinking into a *V* and following the pack's leader in and in.

Bas is just starting to get nervous, finger tapping against the toggle of his gridgun because they're getting too close, when Kimolijah gives his head a sharp jerk and stands. He peers around him, taking in the creatures once again crouched close to the ground, wary, with low growls rumbling from their barrel chests and ringing across the hardpan so even Bas can hear them. Palms lit blue, Kimolijah lifts his arms in front of him, swings them both to one side, and then flings them to the other, a wide, thrashing arc of gridstream whirling out and swooping across the desert floor in a broad, blazing flash.

It gets three of them, dropping them without so much as a yip, knotty hides smoking. The others loose guttural, whining yelps, and every single creature recoils, haunches low and tails tucked. They round off as one in the opposite direction, scattering into the dark chill of a desert night under the fuzzy white points of newborn stars.

Bas tastes the pepper at the back of his throat, blinks and blinks, and sees the glossy arc of sand melted to glass, Kimolijah standing at the center of it and three dead things that aren't dogs, and he thinks there's no way Stanslo won't know exactly what happened out here.

⟡

It's late when Kimolijah stops standing over Fox's corpse, brooding. The shooting has started back in town. Bas can hear the sounds of it skidding across the empty desert.

Bas makes sure he gets back before Kimolijah does. He doesn't go to the Palace, though, when he slides through the gaps in the fences and around the too-predictable patterns the sentries walk at night. He goes to the barn farthest outside the square, the one just at the edge of the town proper, where the path up to Stanslo's house begins. He ducks into the shadows that skid aslant the outer wall, breathes in the earthy wisps of hay and dung and animal musk. And he waits.

It only takes a little while. It rains, because of course it does, and Bas shivers silently through it, determined. He stands there in the rain and the shadows, and he shudders with the wet-cold until the rain stops and the stars once again start nipping at the edges of night's indigo haze. And when Kimolijah finally skulks his stealthy way toward him, Bas waits for him to get close enough, bides his time. And then he jumps him.

He was right—Kimolijah might be small, but he's a mean little fucker.

Bas gets the hand he's got over Kimolijah's mouth bitten rather smartly, but he doesn't loosen it. He gets the shit kicked out of his shins, but he doesn't slow down or let go. The only thing that saves his arms from getting clawed is the thick leather of his duster and the fact that Kimolijah chews his nails down to hematic little nubs. Bas suspects the only thing that saves him from getting fried is Kimolijah's utter surprise, and the fact that Bas's tracking senses give him a slim moment of warning just before that familiar blue spark collects in Kimolijah's palm and lights up the dark.

Bas doesn't waste time—he throws Kimolijah away from him and through the barn doors he's managed to kick open behind him in the scuffle. Surprisingly, the thud of Bas's bootheel to the heavy wood is the most noise the whole minifracas makes, and he thanks whatever Power exists that Kimolijah doesn't start shouting the second he recovers from his headlong flight into the bales of hay stacked alongside the doors. Kimolijah's back up like he's spring-loaded, and he's on the offensive, scrambling up and straightening his spine, a little ball of gridTech in one hand and a small hatchet he must've found on the floor in the other.

He stares at Bas, for quite a spell, anger and surprise and uncertainty in every line of his angular face, washed and then contrasted in a soft blue glow.

"What," Kimolijah manages eventually, "the *fuck*."

He's lost his hat in the fray, so his hair is loose, a thick hank of glossy black sliding over one eye and thin wisps floating around his head in a static halo. His tawny eyes are nearly black against the blue of the gridTech. There's no smile this time, not even close, but that doesn't mean Bas's breath doesn't catch and his heart doesn't trip up and give his libido a poke.

Adrenaline. That's all.

"I might ask you the same," Bas says calmly and deliberately turns his back on Kimolijah to shut the barn door. He hasn't got Kimolijah figured out yet, but he's close, and he knows damned well he's not about to get a bolt of gridTech between his shoulder blades, or even that little hatchet. Bas turns back slowly and gives Kimolijah a lift of his eyebrow. "And you can tell me 'what the fuck.'" He pauses and tries not to let what he's thinking show on his face. "I followed you, Kimo. I *saw* you."

Kimolijah's jaw tightens and he glares. He says nothing.

"What was it, Kimo? Hadn't figured you for the sort to execute a man and then just wander on back home like nothing happened."

Goading. Deliberately cruel and hard. Because it seems the only way to get Kimo to say anything that means something is to piss him off.

"Unless," Bas goes on, "you're hurrying back for your turn in Stanslo's 'great big bed.'" He takes a step toward Kimolijah; Kimolijah merely straightens his spine and doesn't otherwise move. "You and Mari trade off, yeah?" Bas says, and takes another step. "The grasping little desert king with his weatherTech bondmate and his gridTech bit-on-the-side, but I'm thinking he likes one trophy at a time, yeah? That way there's always one of you who has to *listen*, has to picture what's going on, and I'm betting someone like Nadal would be gnashing his teeth in jealousy, but you... not you, I don't think."

Kimolijah hasn't spoken, hasn't moved, hasn't so much as allowed a muscle to twitch, and Bas can't read his face, so he keeps going.

"No, you... you try not to hear. You try not to think about his hands on you while you listen to him put his hands all over someone else. But what I can't figure out, Kimo...." Bas takes another step, leans in right up close, and lowers his voice down to a quiet murmur, ruthless. "Is it because you want it to be you? Or because you don't want it to be ever again?"

Kimolijah still says nothing, only stares at Bas, long and hard. One corner of that wide mouth twitches up and he takes a slow, sidling step away from the bale stack. "Did you know," he drawls slowly, "that twenty-five percent of all the bones in your body are in your feet?"

Bas doesn't know what about it tips him off, but he manages to jerk back just enough that the heel of Kimolijah's boot doesn't squarely land on the relatively fragile bones of the arch of Bas's foot. He manages to get Bas's toes pretty good, though. Bas curses and snatches at Kimolijah's arm to prevent him from scooting around and away like he appears to intend.

"Let go," Kimolijah snarls. He lifts his hand and hovers it right next to Bas's cheek, blue gridTech sputtering and sparking close enough that it floods Bas's senses with the gritty black taste of ozone, and his scalp starts to feel like his hair has come to life and is trying to crawl off his head. "Let go or I'll—"

"You'll what—you'll fry me?" Bas tightens his grip. "Won't be your first tonight, will it? So go ahead—show me it was the execution it looked like. Light me up, I'm waiting. Oh no, Fox wasn't your first, was he? That's okay, don't worry, you get used to it. What's one more murder when—"

"*It wasn't—*" Kimolijah cuts himself off, tries to jerk away again, and when he can't, he clenches his teeth, a wordless snarl.

It wasn't murder, except Kimolijah *just won't say it*, and Bas knew exactly what it was when he was watching it happen, and the admission only pisses him off more.

"Anyone who knew what Fox had coming would know exactly what it was. I saw those things." He gives Kimolijah a sharp shake. "He asked you, didn't he? You went out there because it's what you do, and he asked you for a mercy. And you gave it to him." It's a little scary how badly he wants to punch Kimolijah, just to see if he can knock some common sense into him. "And anyone who has partial vision in at least one eye is going to know exactly what it was too, Kimo. They're going to *know*."

Kimolijah just stares at him, no surprise, no dawning horror. He knows. He probably made it absurdly obvious on purpose.

And Bas is done, just *done*. He's not even sure he cares about his cover anymore, since if any of this gets back to Stanslo, it's pretty much blown anyway. But damn it, he'll have his fucking *answers*.

"*God*," Bas growls, frustrated and furious. "A mercy killing for a hardcase deputy who made your miserable life even more hellish—*that* risk you'll take, but you won't just get on your impossible train and drive it out of here!"

"Let go of me. You have no—"

"And what I don't get is *why*. Why are you still here? You're the only one who knows how your train works, so why haven't you just beefed Stanslo and driven it straight out of here, unless you *want* to be here?"

"Maybe I *do* want—"

"Except you *don't!*"

"You don't know what I want, you don't know *shit*, and even if you did, you're pretty much the *last* person I'd spill my guts to. Let. *Go*."

And still that little ball of gridTech fluttering right next to Bas's temple doesn't leap, doesn't flare, doesn't edge closer.

"You're scared," Bas says, eyes narrowed, because he's pretty sure he's figured out that look, at least. "Maybe I'm getting too close."

"Or maybe you're just another in a steady stream of hardcases who thinks that just because I let—" Kimolijah stops, like he can't make himself say it, even in his obvious anger. "You don't get to decide what I am. You don't get to put your hands where they're not wanted." He sets his teeth and steps right in, so close Bas can feel the heat of his body all down his chest. "Try it and see how fast you wish you didn't."

"*Let*," says Bas and he grins, snide and mocking. "Like you *let* Travis?"

It's the wrong thing to say, Bas can tell right away, and he snatches his gun from his holster before the last syllable leaves his mouth. The flare of gridTech right beside his head nearly blinds him, but he's got his gun propping up Kimolijah's chin and his thumb on the hammer before Kimolijah has a chance to let it loose.

"Do it and the shot goes off at the first muscle spasm," Bas says calmly.

He has no idea if it's the truth. But neither does Kimolijah. The sizzle of gridTech wisps out, and Kimolijah slowly lowers his hand. Bas hears a muffled *thump* against the straw on the floor and thinks it's the hatchet, which is good, because he'd kind of forgotten Kimolijah had it.

It takes a few seconds for the residual afterglow of the gridTech to fade from the periphery of Bas's vision. When it does, he blinks and realizes it's gotten lighter—just a touch, starlight turning fuzzy and edged with the nascent gray of predawn.

"Now I don't know what's going on here entirely." Bas lets his stance relax just a touch so Kimolijah isn't standing on his toes with his chin jutting up and away from Bas's gun. "But I do know Stanslo's got something on you, and whatever it is, it's serious enough that you're building trains and guns for him, *sleeping with him*, when I'm pretty sure you don't want to be doing any of it." He shakes his head, frustrated, and slides the gun slowly down and away. "Do you even like him?"

"You asked me that already."

"No, before I asked if you love him, and you didn't answer. But that's okay—I really only asked to see your reaction. And I *can* see it. You can't even stand it when he touches you. And yet you *keep* letting him *touch you*."

That isn't the point. It really shouldn't be the point. And yet it *keeps being* the point, at least in Bas's gut, crowding out the logic in his head that tells him it's a lot more important to get Kimolijah to tell him about the Bruise and collateral and his "dead" gridLatent da. And yet Bas keeps circling back around to Stanslo's hands on Kimolijah and Kimolijah's look of bored resignation and Bas's gut asking him *How long does a person*

*have to endure a situation that makes his skin crawl before that
look becomes his default?*

A twitch of the shoulders that's trying to be a careless shrug,
and Kimolijah tugs at Bas's hold until Bas lets him go. Kimolijah
takes a step back, but only one. "You don't know anything." He
looks up at Bas with a defiant glower. "None of this is—" He
growls and gives his head a quick jerk, annoyed. "Look, I get my
end."

"Because you want to?" Spiteful, meant to sting, to incite. It's
the only way to get Kimolijah to say what he actually means.

Which is, apparently, "None of your goddamned business."

"So you don't want to."

"I don't say no."

"Can you?"

"None of your goddamned—"

"If you loved him, I could at least understand the staggering
lapse in judgment and morals, but if you don't even *like*—"

"Oh my god. Are you really standing there with a gun in your
hand and trying to get me to talk about my *feelings*, you
unbelievable *ass*?"

"No, I'm trying to tell you I know you're not the immoral
shithead you pretend to be, so just drop the ridiculous mask
already, it doesn't fit you." Bas's teeth clench tight, and he
pushes: "*Is this* where you want to be, Kimo? Is *he* what you
want?"

Kimolijah narrows his eyes and balls his hands into fists.
"Why d'you think you even have the *right* to ask me a question
like that?"

Bas studies Kimolijah's rigid stance, his angry glower, his
big, giant eyes, wide with... something. Not shame, but maybe
something close. Bas thinks about using it—*What would your da
think, Kimolijah?*—but he thinks maybe using Ajamil Adani as a
weapon will only get him fried and left a smoking heap in the
straw. Probably deservedly, all things considered. So he snags
another thread of that same skein of shame, and... *tugs*.

"Maybe I don't have a right," he says, "but I'm thinking no
one's ever bothered before. Or maybe someone has." He pauses
and softens his tone. "And ended up dead at a whipping post for
it, yeah? And now, hey, what d'you know, another guy dead at a
post tonight."

That seems to throw Kimolijah, but only for a second or two.
He jerks back and gives Bas a little shove while he's at it. "You
know what? None of this has a goddamned thing to do with you,
so just mind your own fucking business and keep your fucking
mouth *shut*."

"I'd say something like this is the business of anyone with a
conscience."

"Good thing guys like you don't have them, then, isn't it?"

It's vicious and said with such righteous *certainty* that it makes Bas's teeth clench and anger flare up his backbone. "I'm trying to help you here, goddamn it! Stanslo's going to know what you did tonight, do you get that? It's not going to be pleasant for you. And if what you do already with Stanslo isn't—" Bas stops and makes himself pull in a long calming breath. "Look," he says evenly, "I don't know everything that's going on here, but I can make some pretty good guesses, and it's not right. And you can't look me in the eye and say it's something you chose. What's going on between you and Stanslo is—"

"It's called 'fucking,' you nosy dickhead. Sometimes it's called a 'blowjob' and sometimes it's called other things, but if you want a generalization to work with, it's pretty much always called 'sex.'"

"If you can't say no, it's called—"

"*No it isn't!*" Kimolijah snarls, and he angles his stance, threatening, for all he's too short and too wiry to be much of a physical threat, but Bas doesn't forget for a second what Kimolijah can do with a tiny ball of gridstream in his hand. "You don't get to say that, *it's not*, not unless I say it is!"

God, he's gone from quietly derisive to nearly manic in the space of two breaths. Bas knows the answer. He's kenned it pretty much from the start, but he can't miss it with that reaction. He looks back at every single thing he's seen and heard Kimolijah do since Bas got here, and all the assumptions from before that have led him to this moment now become unquestionable truths.

He remembers the seductive tone and the gentle hand on Stanslo's chest, and thinks *Trying to keep what happened to Travis from happening to someone else*. He remembers the angry glare and the blatant offers when Stanslo turned his attentions to Nadal for a night, and thinks *Trying to protect a kid who reminds him too much of himself*. And maybe Bas is seeing what he wants to see because Kimolijah's a genius with a heart-clenching smile when you catch him off guard, and Bas has been half in love with his ghost since he opened that first journal after Kimolijah's "death." Except no, *no*, that's not how it is, it never was—Bas *knows* what this is.

So again, Bas *tugs*.

"So you want it, then? You like being Stanslo's pet sparker?"

"You don't get to say that either. None of it's anything to do with you. How is *any* of this your business?"

"It really shouldn't be, but it's got to be someone's. And bloody hell, I don't even know what answer I'm hoping for."

"Well, that's good, because you're not getting one anyway, you arrogant prick!"

"Are you his prisoner, Kimo? Or are you his...?" Bas leaves it there because if he says it, the lie that's all over it might show on his face. Anyway, he has no doubt Kimolijah will fill in the blank.

Kimolijah does. Bas can tell by the way Kimolijah's eyes

nearly impale him and his mouth twists, cruel. "Am I his...
what?" Expectation and malice in a quiet voice and a single
quirk of dark eyebrows. "I hate to break it to you, you judg-
mental asshole, but you and I? Not all that different. A hired
gun's not exactly better than—" He bites it off and tries to
explode Bas's head with a dark glare. When Bas's skull stays
stubbornly intact, Kimolijah twists his mouth and goes on, "At
least what I do doesn't hurt anyone."

"No?" Bas lifts his eyebrows. "So all these gridguns floating
around—not your work, then?"

Kimolijah flinches back like Bas has slapped him. "You—"

"Is this where you want to be?" Bas gestures around them—
the barn, the town, the desert. "Look me in the eye, tell me it is,
and I'll leave you alone." *Lie.* "Tell me this is all your choice, and
I'll never ask you again." *And another.* He takes a step in, slow
and unthreatening but closer. "But if you're not here because
you want to be, if you're not... doing what you do with Stanslo
because it's what you want, *I can help you.* I can—"

"You can what? Save me?" It's not as angry as it was a second
ago, but it's not without a bitter tang of scorn. "Get a message
out? Endanger someone else who's better off thinking I'm dead?
Get me out of here?"

Endanger someone else.... Shit. Resaniji. Kimolijah's sister, a
Class 5 kineTech. Of course. Bas hadn't even thought of that, and
he hopes like hell someone back home has.

Now it's Kimolijah who's coming closer, almost stalking,
slow and with those tawny eyes boring into Bas, never looking
away. Bas can almost imagine them backlit by the ghost of
Travis—and maybe Fox now too—prowling around amidst the
guilt and impotent anger Bas is almost positive he can see back
there. Kimolijah steps up onto the lowest bale—taller than Bas
now by half a head and looking down with eyes lidded halfway
and a disdainful, seductive smirk Bas has only seen aimed at
Stanslo before. He's close, too close, Bas can feel warm breath
on his own cheek. Kimolijah leans in even farther, clutching
Bas's shoulder and tipping in until that wide, sinful mouth
ghosts along Bas's, and *holy fucking shit.*

"Did you know," Kimolijah whispers, lips forming the words *this
close* to Bas's own, heat percolating up Bas's backbone and making
everything from knee to thigh ripple hot, "that some people think
the soul resides in the chest? That you can steal another's soul just
by"—Kimolijah dips in and swipes the tip of his tongue over Bas's
bottom lip—"kissing them?"

Complete turnabout from thirty seconds ago, from "touch me
and die" to "c'mon, you wanna?" and Bas has to make himself
parse the truth of what this really is.

He's breathing heavily all of a sudden, and he tries not to
show it. His groin is tight and far too interested, and he tries not
to acknowledge it. He doesn't like what that would make of him,

not after the things that have just been half accused and then half acknowledged. Not with his heart pounding with the unhappy knowledge that he wishes this abrupt bold advance were anything other than the distract-and-deflect he knows damned well it is.

"And is that what happened to you?" Bas tilts his head and watches Kimolijah's eyes follow when he licks his lips, so he dares to let his hand reach out, skim along the light fabric hugging Kimolijah's ribs under his coat. Because Bas can play this game too. "Did a flush robber baron sweep you away, kiss you, and steal your soul?"

Kimolijah smirks. "Seems to me whores are whores because they've already sold their souls. Doesn't leave much to steal."

"And yet here you are. So what does that make you?"

"Well, now." Kimolijah shrugs. "That's the question, then, isn't it. Depends on whose standards you go by, I expect."

"And what happens if I kiss you and... steal your soul for myself?" Bas lets out a warm, gentle breath just beneath Kimolijah's ear, lets the bristle on his chin slide lightly over Kimolijah's jawline, and tries not to smile when Kimolijah too obviously holds back a shudder. "What d'you think you'd let me do with it?"

Bas has to give it to him—Kimolijah doesn't back down; in fact, he ups the ante. He nips Bas's chin and then slides the point of his tongue over the knot in Bas's throat as he breathes, "The best whores don't kiss."

Guh. Bas has to swallow thickly before he can retort, "You kiss Stanslo."

"No." There's no time for the surprise that generates—and yeah, actually, now that Bas thinks about it, he's seen a lot of touching but not a single kiss—because Kimolijah pulls back and says, "So who's the whore, d'you think?"

"Why are we talking about whores?"

"It's what you keep not saying, isn't it, so why not?"

"I... don't think it is, actually." Bas tries powerful hard not to stare at Kimolijah's mouth. "Are you going to kiss me, then?"

"Oh, I don't know." It's a purr, but it still manages to be mocking. Kimolijah rubs the tip of his nose along the bridge of Bas's, then pulls back just a little. "Looking for a soul to steal, are you?" His hand slides up Bas's chest, fingers skimming the collar of his coat. "Or giving one away? Oh, wait." He chuckles, dark and derisive, and draws back, eyes narrowed, jaw set tight. "You've already sold yours." With a growl, he fists Bas's collar and jerks him forward. "Your soul sits inside the same crystal as mine," he grates, right in Bas's face, "so don't try to make like we're *friends* here, *deputy.* Whatever new game this is, you can tell Stanslo I'm not playing." He lets go of Bas's collar, thumps both hands to Bas's chest, and shoves him back, hard. "I'm not telling you shit. If Stanslo thinks I'm stupid enough to spill my overwrought guts to his newest gunslinger, he deserves whatever paranoid fantasies he hired you to take care of. And if he wants to know if I'm doing my job right, he can bloody well go to the academy and *fucking learn* something about what he wants to own."

Bas shoves his gun back into its holster so he doesn't shoot Kimolijah out of sheer frustration, then curls his hand into a fist. "Or maybe he'll just go and get himself another gridTech," he says, warier now. "Have you thought of that, Kimo? All he has to do is find some other gullible kid who can—"

"He can try," Kimolijah snaps, hands fisted. "Even if he could find someone who can follow the designs and apply the science, he can't find someone else who's got the same—who can charge the—" He clamps his mouth shut for a second, then blurts, "That's the whole fucking *point!*" like he can't help himself.

And it's perfect, truncated though it was, because it's kind of impossible, but almost everything about Kimolijah is impossible. The gridTech has to get into those crystals somehow, and Bas has been tasting that wet-cedar hint of kineTech fluttering at the edges of Kimolijah's gridTech since that first night in the station. And what Kimolijah almost said connects all kinds of dots in Bas's head.

It doesn't happen. No one has more than one kind of emergent Tech. It just *doesn't happen*. Except, apparently, it has. A Class 2 gridTech with a brain the size of a planet and just enough not-so-latent kine to turn him into something people will kill for.

"Anyway," Kimolijah says, "the Directorate will never let him have another Tech. If they would, he would've—"

He cuts himself off, almost gnashing at the words he doesn't say, but he doesn't have to finish.

"Ah." Bas smiles a little, makes himself slouch against the doorway, a cool façade he absolutely doesn't feel. "Yeah. And I bet he's made it a point to tell you all about it, hasn't he? Your replacement. Another trophy to add to his wall. And as soon as he gets another gridTech out here...." He lets it trail off, lifts his eyebrows. He watches Kimolijah's hands clench and unclench for a moment, watches him try to get his breathing under control, then goes on, "He's tried, you know. Four times now. Not legally, mind you, and not through anything like the proper channels, but he's tried like hell. But you're right—the Directorate won't let Techs out as far as Harrowgate, and he's having a devil of a time finding any who aren't registered and protected. And I doubt," Bas says slowly, eyes narrowed and watching carefully, "he can ever find one exactly like you. Because there are none like you, really, are there? And it's not just about applying the science."

Kimolijah's jaw clamps and quivers, too many things flickering over his face for Bas to read, but there's anger, definitely, and misery, almost certainly. He doesn't say a word, though.

Bas sighs. Apparently subtlety is lost on someone who couldn't find a loaf of bread in a market full of bakeshops. Bas debates just flat-out saying it—*Hi, Bartholomew Eisen, I'm a Directorate tracker. You about ready to blow this hellhole?*—but he can't, he *can't*, not before he knows what Kimolijah will do with it.

He scrubs a hand over his face, tired. "It doesn't matter, I reckon. Even if he could find someone like you, he wouldn't get them. The Directorate's clamped down on registration because of him, and it watches every move he makes now. Or should I say, every move Oleg and Dutter make for him." He pauses before adding, quiet, "Three Techs with links to him dying or disappearing. That was three too many, and the Directorate doesn't fuck around."

Kimolijah sucks in a sharp breath and looks away, expression confused and frustrated. It takes a few moments, but he eventually climbs down off the hay bale, movements ponderous, careful, like he's not feeling entirely steady on his feet. No confessions, though, no sudden show of trust or gratitude. Kimolijah merely turns his back to Bas and says nothing.

"That's what Fox meant about bidding on your crystal, isn't it?" Bas takes a cautious step forward. "If Stanslo, by some miracle, does find what he's looking for... when he doesn't need you anymore, in his workshop or in his bed, you'll just be another thing to auction off, out here at the ass-end of the world where there is no dosh."

Bas waits for as long as his patience will hold, but there's nothing from Kimolijah. Bas sighs, heavy and close to defeat.

"Just tell me why you went out there tonight. Admit that much to me so I can...."

Bas doesn't finish, doesn't say *so I can admit to you who I am and we can figure out the rest together*. He can't, not yet. He can't take that last, too-big risk without something from Kimolijah. Except Kimolijah still gives him nothing.

"Why Fox?" Bas goes on. "I could see he made your life hell. So why risk Stanslo finding out what you did tonight? Why throw your gridTech around like that so there will be no question at all about what happened? Why didn't you kill me five minutes ago? Why let me live and risk me telling Stanslo all about what I saw tonight, when I'm pretty sure all that'll get you is a rougher night than usual between his sheets, or worse? You know, since I'm an *enemy spy* and all."

Kimolijah's shoulders hitch, like he's having a hard time breathing, but he still doesn't say anything, and he still doesn't turn around.

"Kimo...." Bas growls and paces a few jerky steps in front of the wide barn door. "Goddamn it, I don't want to threaten you, I don't want to make it *worse* for you, but I *have* to know what—"

"Okay," Kimolijah cuts in. "Yeah, okay." He turns slowly, eyes huge in the slats of graying gloom skimming in through the laths of the loft window. His smile is... strange, like he's embroidering it on in slow, carefully hidden stitches, and still it's probably one of the most heart-grabbing sights Bas will ever see. "Did you know," Kimolijah says, soft and with a coy glint in his eye, "that most men become"—he pauses for a second, gaze traveling to the ceiling, like he's thinking, before he looks square at Bas with a smirk—"*aroused* during conflict?" He shrugs and slinks a step toward Bas. "It's a primal thing. Asserting one's dominance and such." He pauses, shakes his head. "You really do have pretty blue eyes."

He takes another step, and it's all Bas can do not to back away. Or *step in*. Because okay, yeah, there's adrenaline flooding his veins and shoving all his blood south, and his head's telling him it's an inconvenient bit of reaction he needs to ignore, overcome, but everything else is rushing at his libido like iron filings to a magnet, and the heady pull is dragging him in and in and *in*.

"What?" says Kimolijah, right up close now, staring up at Bas with gigantic eyes leaking doe-eyed vulnerability and teeth-gnashing sexuality all over the place, and God, he knows what he's doing, he has to know what he's doing. As if he's heard, Kimolijah smirks and says, "Did you think I don't know exactly what I'm doing here? That I don't know what my life is and how to keep living it?" He grins. "Did you think I don't *like* 'a rough night between the sheets' now and then?"

Bas opens his mouth and promptly chokes, because Kimolijah's hand settles right over Bas's groin, squeezes. The sensation shoots directly into Bas's gut and fountains up into his chest, and the resulting explosion takes out every reasonable thought in his head in a scatter of principled shrapnel. *This is wrong* goes up with the slide of strong fingers. *It's deflection and distraction* dies a quick death with the exhilarating rush of cool air over abruptly burning skin as Kimolijah deftly opens Bas's trousers.

"I've seen you looking," Kimolijah whispers, "*watching* me," hot breath fanning over Bas's collarbone, right down the open *V* of his shirt, and swathing his chest. "Did you not see me looking back?" It's sultry, nearly breathless, *almost* believable. And then he *licks*.

"I know what you're doing," Bas manages, just as Kimolijah gets a hand on him, and yeah, he's hard, Kimolijah knew he was, that's the point, and Bas's head knows that, but he can't seem to talk the rest of him into doing anything but shoving forward into the grip that latches on and *strokes*.

Bas has *so* lost this game.

"Oh good," says Kimolijah, and he grins. "I was worried for a second I'd have to explain the concept of blowjobs to you."

And then he's on his knees and Bas is choking again, and he

doesn't really have so much as a second to process the words that have just melted his brain, because Kimolijah's wide, sinful mouth is on him, hot and wet and bloody fuck *God*, Kimolijah knows what he's doing. Swirling tongue and scorching suction, he doesn't mess around, gets right to it, and Bas's hand is buried in Kimolijah's—*soft, so soft, God, I knew it would be*—hair before he even remembers that he has one. Two, actually, and the other goes to grab for something behind him, anything to steady him, and ends up brushing against his holster before finding the rough boards of the door behind him.

His holster, with the gun inside it he'd only minutes ago had tucked beneath Kimolijah's chin. A spasm rocks through Bas, and not the kind he usually has when someone's sucking his brain out through his dick. His other hand inadvertently fists in Kimolijah's hair, and Kimolijah fucking *groans*, which almost, *almost* scatters Bas's mind again, but he clings to the wispy thread of reason he snagged only a second ago and wrestles it into an actual thought:

Threats and accusations of spying, and manhandling Kimolijah into a deserted barn in the wee hours and interrogating him. Getting him alone and holding a gun beneath his chin. And *fuck*, Bas knows exactly what this is. Most of him doesn't care, because *guys don't say no to blowjobs*, they just don't, but there's a tiny bit that knows it's wrong, horribly wrong, and that bit fights for and, after a violent bloody struggle, wins control of Bas's motor functions.

He clenches his teeth, tightens his fist in Kimolijah's hair, and pulls.

Kimolijah's obviously surprised, because he goes at first with hardly any resistance, but then he's pulling against Bas's grip, leaning in and gripping at Bas's hipbones through his trousers. Kimolijah makes a noise of protest that vibrates right through Bas, and Bas almost forgets why he's fighting this, but reason has been prodded into morality, weak-willed though it may be, so Bas sets a palm to Kimolijah's forehead and almost shoves.

Kimolijah wobbles back and off with a slick, dirty *pop* that almost melts Bas's knees, but he sets his jaw and doesn't let go. "Playing the whore so easily, Kimo?" he says, embarrassingly hoarse.

The black wing of an eyebrow goes up, and Kimolijah narrows his eyes. "Didn't anyone ever teach you it's wise to be nice to the man with his teeth right next to your dick?" He tilts his head, annoyed. "What's the problem? From what I hear, you have a bit of a thing for little boys on their knees."

"Oh, for fuck's *sake*," Bas mutters. He's never going to hear the end of that one.

"What?" Kimo lifts his eyebrows, all innocence. And then the little bastard *pouts*, and blinks his giant eyes up at Bas. "A little too old for you?"

Bas's knees have been unreliable since the second Kimolijah set a hand to him, so he figures *fuck it*. He drops down into the scattered straw, gets a hand behind Kimolijah's back, and wrenches him in, slides his thigh tight between Kimolijah's. It's kind of a toss-up between wincing and smirking, because—

"God, you're not even hard."

And okay, the wannabe-badass in Bas is a tiny bit emasculated and petulant. Because some part of him, even the part that knew, wanted Kimolijah to want this, want *him*, wanted this to be real. The idealistic illobook geek in him—the one who couldn't stop reading those journals, couldn't stop admiring those formulae and theories, and fantasizing about the mind behind all of it—is hugely relieved, because this is not brilliant, promising Kimolijah Adani corrupted and ruined and content to be a trophy for a wealthy desert baron; it's brilliant, promising Kimolijah Adani stuck in a no-win situation and using whatever tools he has to turn it to whatever small advantage he can wring from it.

Kimolijah's teeth are set tight, his back up like a wary porcupine, and his mouth heels a curve, like he's trying to dimple up into that sultry grin again and just can't. "What d'you care?" he says, almost a growl, and he slips his hand through the fly of Bas's open trousers.

"The fact that you even have to ask that question," says Bas, as mild as he can make it as he snaps hold of Kimolijah's wrist and stills his hand, "and that you're *serious* about it...." He trails off and shakes his head. "A decent man prefers that everyone is willing and gets to have equal fun. A decent man takes just as much enjoyment out of his partner's pleasure as his own."

Kimolijah smirks. "Good thing there's no decent men here, then, yeah?"

"You keep telling yourself that." Bas jerks Kimolijah yet closer, chest to chest, and dips his head down to lick at the strands of black ink slicking up the side of Kimolijah's neck. He pauses for a second when he tastes lemons and it pings at something in the back of his brain, but then Kimolijah puffs out a surprised breath, heat all over Bas's throat, and the thought just... skitters away. There's no resistance, merely a barely there shudder, so Bas bites down gently on black swirls over brown skin, enough so Kimolijah feels the pressure but not enough to leave a mark. Bas shuts his eyes for a moment, sucking in the heady cocktail of salt and sweat and leather and peppery ozone, before he slides his mouth over the crook of Kimolijah's neck and whispers, "You don't kiss."

Kimolijah's chest hitches and his breath stutters out over Bas's ear, hot and damp. He doesn't say anything, but Bas feels a small jerk of his head, just once, back and forth. *No.*

"You've never kissed him." Not a question, not really, and Kimolijah doesn't answer with words or even a shake of his head this time; it's a small, startled sound, down deep in

Kimolijah's chest, and a slight dip of his head to the side, baring his throat beneath Bas's mouth, inviting.

Bas takes hold of Kimolijah's hair again, fists it, then pulls his head back until Kimolijah looks him in the eye.

"But you'll kiss me."

Again, Kimolijah doesn't say anything, but he doesn't negate it this time, doesn't do anything but stare at Bas, eyebrows quirking then smoothing, quirking then smoothing, like he can't decide if he should be pissed off or not. So Bas slides his hand in between them, lays it over the bulge in Kimolijah's trousers that wasn't there just a moment ago, and presses.

"You'll kiss *me*," Bas says, through his teeth this time, and he tightens his grip on Kimolijah's hair, smooths his palm over Kimolijah's groin, and smiles a little when Kimolijah sucks in a quick tight breath. "And better yet," Bas goes on, low and smooth, "I'll kiss you. And then we'll see what it's like when we *both* want it."

He doesn't wait for Kimolijah to speak or move or even breathe. With a rough jerk of his hand, Bas wrenches Kimolijah's trousers open, dips in, and drags Kimolijah into a rough, wet, searing-hot kiss.

It's not perfect. It's sloppy, for one, and there's a thick, shameless high in knowing that it's clumsy because it's one thing Kimolijah's not good at, one thing even a brain the size of a planet can't figure out without at least some practice, and the lack of finesse means the *I don't kiss* thing wasn't a come-on and it wasn't for show. Kimolijah doesn't do this because he doesn't *want* to do this, not with Stanslo, and how Kimolijah's managed to maintain that stipulation is something Bas wants very badly to know, but not so badly he'll actually stop and ask.

None of it's enough. Bas wants a bed, he wants soft, worn sheets, he wants *time*, and he wants to map with careful fingers every swirl and flourish of all that black ink on brown skin. He thinks he could; he thinks he might even be able to trace the shapes without even looking, because it's all been imprinted behind his eyes without him even realizing it. Bas wants it all, but there's only this, only here, only now, *right now*, so he takes what he's got and shuts away everything that's wrong with it.

Kimolijah's frowning when he draws back, all pinched and confused, like he can't figure out exactly what's happening and how he got here, on his knees in a barn with Bas's hand down his pants, but when Bas tightens that hand, pulls and strokes, Kimolijah merely groans and arches, pushing his hips in, in, in, before he dives back in for another kiss. It's bolder this time, more raw and a little bit dirty, teeth nipping and tongue swiping, and when Kimolijah's hand finally, *finally* starts moving on Bas again, Bas gives him a groan back and just *moves*.

It's not perfect, it can't be perfect, and it's not anything like what Bas never allowed himself to imagine back when he'd thought Kimolijah dead, and the ghost Bas had made up in his head was a wisp of a fantasy he'd never actually have in his hands. It's not an illobook scene with everything drawn in soft sepia tones and no wrong moves, no accidental pinches, no tugging of sensitive hairs that result in quick hisses and apologetic nips. Grunts instead of breathy moans, grasping that's a little too rough and gets desperate a little too quickly, slick slides of lips that are too slippery and too breathless, and *God*, hips shoving and hands taking and mouths demanding *more* in vaguely syllabic mumbles that never really turn into words but manage to convey meaning.

It's crude and a little bit raunchy, grips gone slippery with sweat, and lips too swollen to be skillful, and arousal too high for dexterity or a touch of flair. But it's good, so fucking *good*, Kimolijah with his tiny noises that get stoppered up at the base of his throat, and Bas has to—*he has to* lean in and lean down, run his tongue over the knot of them as he speeds his hand, firms his strokes, and holds tight as Kimolijah's spine bends and his head falls back.

He's not all elegant curves and rhapsodic beauty when he comes. He's clenched teeth and scrunched face and hands that clamp too hard onto Bas and fucking *hurt* so bad that it wrings Bas's own orgasm from him in a hard, hot tangle. But *God*, he's fucking magnificent, the gray of dawn lumbering in through the loft slats and lending brown skin a soft, fuzzy radiance as Kimolijah peaks hard and too obviously clamps a yell behind his teeth. His whole body shudders with the force, and he looks so much like bliss and abandon personified that it wrenches something hot and tight from Bas's chest and pushes another few waves of pleasure into his climax.

He watches, panting, as Kimolijah comes down, drags in one long breath after another, and then slumps into Bas like he trusts him, like he's wrung out and raw and knows Bas will keep hold of him 'til he's not anymore.

So Bas does, just reels him in, presses the mess between them, hot and sticky, and molds his palms to the curve of muscle and the solidity of bone, dips his head down until his face is wedged into the crook of Kimolijah's shoulder, and just... *breathes.*

"Kimolijah," Bas manages after a spell, "God, you have no—"

"*What* did you just call me?" Kimolijah's gone abruptly stiff as a plank against Bas, spine rigid now, all softness and surrender snuffed out from one shaky breath to the next.

Bas pulls back, wary, and tilts his head. Because it wasn't an accident, what just came out his mouth. "I called you—"

"Yeah, I know," Kimolijah says, mouth tight and lips quivering, and a look on his face that cycles through betrayal first, then disbelief, then quick, fiery fury. "Three people here know my name," he says slowly. "One of them's me and one of them's dead."

He pushes back and away, then snaps to his feet so fast Bas thinks he's going to get a knee to the chin. "You unbelievable *shit*," Kimolijah snarls and starts doing up his trousers. "Couldn't just take what I'd give you, could you? Had to make a sick game out of it, yeah? *God*, all you fucking psychos and your fucking *games*!"

Bas stands slowly, hands out. "Kimolijah, listen to—"

"*Don't—*!" It's like Kimolijah chokes on it, rage clogging his throat and lighting up behind his eyes. "You don't get to—" He kicks at a hay bale, misses, and almost overbalances, which only seems to piss him off more. He stomps the floor a few times. "Motherfucking cocksucking *asshole*, I knew it, I *knew* you weren't—"

"You know precisely *shit*," Bas snaps. "You know less than half of what you need to know, and if you'll just calm down for two seconds and let me—"

"Do you know what this is?" Kimolijah growls. He yanks up the sleeve of his coat and the shirt underneath until the matte-metal of the bracelet winks out into the growing dawn light.

Something in Bas's chest stutters, because yeah, he does think he knows, but he can't be entirely sure, and he needs to know very badly. So he merely narrows his eyes and shakes his head.

"It keeps me alive," says Kimolijah, low and through his teeth. "Baron had it made for me. But see, the baron, he doesn't just hand out the things you need, not unless there's something in it for him." He grins, and it's awful, full of anger and shame and betrayal, and his eyes are shining, but Bas tries to pretend none of it has anything to do with what Kimolijah apparently thinks just happened. "It keeps me alive, yeah, but it also makes it so I can't lie to him. Works on brainwaves, actually. *My* theories that he—" He stops, clenches his teeth, before he shakes himself and takes a step in toward Bas, smirks, but nothing at all like the sultry tease that had hooked Bas earlier; this is calculating, with something inside it that screams warning. "I've gotten real good at talking around it, but if he really wants to know something, if he asks the right question in just the right way...."

He trails off, then holds out his arm so Bas can see the coil clearly.

"I didn't just have sex with Bas," says Kimolijah, and that thin blue current leaps out of the shunt, splashes over the bracelet, and whipcracks up his arm. He hisses, pain, but he doesn't waver and he doesn't stop staring at Bas.

And Bas gets it. He doesn't even need Kimolijah to tell him, but Kimolijah says it anyway: "You think you've got something on me, Mister Badass Gunslinger? Well, now I've got something on you." He smirks. "Travis is dead because Stanslo *thought* I was sleeping with him. What d'you think will happen to you if he *knows*?"

So, okay, this certainly got out of control and went sideways real fast.

Bas almost can't understand how they'd gone from kneeling in the straw, breathing each other's air less than five minutes ago, to *this*. Except he does, he understands all too well, and using Kimolijah's name hadn't been an accident. He'd *wanted* Kimolijah to know that Bas knew who he was, wanted him to know that someone was on his side, here to help, but he hadn't counted on Kimolijah being so jaded and distrustful that *this* is the conclusion he'd jump to.

"Kimolijah," Bas says quietly, calmly, "I'm Directorate."

And everything about Kimolijah goes very, very still.

It's a risk, a huge one—not just because there's a gigantic chance Bas can't trust Kimolijah, that Kimolijah's become so weary and hard it's not entirely out of the question that he'd sell Bas out for a single night without Stanslo pawing at him. And the demonstration of that bracelet—pretty much confirming everything about it Bas had halfway suspected—says that even if Kimolijah wouldn't sell Bas out willingly, he could most certainly be forced to do it *un*willingly.

Except Bas has seen how good Kimolijah is at "talking around it," and he won't believe the Kimolijah Adani from Poor Side in Knapston is so far gone that Kimo of Stanslo's Bridge would give *anyone* up that easily—not Travis, for whom Kimolijah obviously had some kind of affection, not Fox, for whom Kimolijah seemed to have nothing but contemptuous pity, and not Bas, with whom Kimolijah's just... had a mutual hand job, and okay, maybe Bas has been a *little* bit hasty.

Kimolijah stares at Bas, for a good long time, before he lifts his chin, strides toward Bas, and shoves him to the side. Bas lets him, just watches as Kimolijah heaves the barn door open then turns to Bas with a curl to his lip and tawny eyes too shiny in the early-early gray.

"Bullshit," he says, then, "*Fuck* you, you lying *asshole*," and he stalks away.

Bas stares after him for a while, trying to decide what to think about it all, and when he can't, he sighs, shakes his head. "*Really* not the shy boy your sister thinks you are."

15.

The important thing to remember here—still—is that Bas is not in love with Kimolijah. Never has been. That would be stupid. Kimolijah is not the guileless young man brimming with so many ideas they had to spill out all over dozens of notebooks and journals and sketches. And Bas *does not* kind of like this version better. He doesn't. Which is the point. Kimolijah's a cynical little bastard, using sex to turn Stanslo's head, using his Tech when he's cornered, using his genius brain to come up with new and inventive ways to gain even a small advantage....

...using sex to distract Stanslo so fewer people die, using his Tech to save a hardcase like Fox from a torturous, drawn-out, ignoble death, using his genius brain to....

To do what?

Bas frowns.

Kimolijah's brilliant—his brain is the size of a planet—and if he doesn't want to be here, someone that smart *has* to be coming up with plan after plan for getting out. His notes and schematics had backup plans for his backup plans. Maybe Bas has been asking the wrong questions. And maybe he understands why he kind of likes this version of Kimolijah better than the flawless image he's had in his head for a couple of years. If it even is a different version, because really—aren't the things Kimolijah's doing now easily extrapolated from what he used to be? Maybe Kimolijah hasn't changed all that much; maybe it's just that his circumstances have and he's trying to survive them. And maybe Bas has just been having a hard time thinking through the whole *sleeping with the enemy* thing.

Bas tries dozing the morning away, but it doesn't quite work out. He spends too long wondering if Kimolijah's right now in Stanslo's "great big bed" and trying not to imagine what he's doing there, and then Bas is wondering how he's ever supposed to get another decent breath when his chest is abruptly so filled with *wanting*, because he knows now what he's missing. He spends even longer trying to pretend he wasn't wondering that at all, and trying to will away the mental pictures the wondering conjured, and telling himself he's *not* jealous, he's *not* in love, and none of it has anything to do with his inability to sleep. It's not his racing mind keeping him up; it's just that morning in Stanslo's Bridge is fucking *noisy*.

There's a very quiet to-do when Lowen goes out to bring back what might be left of Fox. Bas had kind of hoped it would be "not enough," but it's plenty. Scavengers have been at him, but not nearly as much as they would have been had Kimolijah not been standing over him until almost dawn, reeking of gridTech and keeping most of the nibblers away. Lowen, as instructed, hauls Fox's corpse back to town and sets it next to Travis in the town's square.

The branchlike burns on Fox's face and neck are telling, just like Bas had known they'd be. No one says anything out loud. They all look, though—Bas can tell they all see—and it's blackly funny that right after he can see them seeing, they all glance seemingly unconsciously up the hill and toward Stanslo's big house.

The man himself shows up not long after, Kimolijah in tow. Kimolijah's blank-faced, but there's something defiant in the set to his shoulders. Lowen watches them come, mouth turned down, face grim.

Bas sips his coffee and watches from outside the mess as Stanslo drags Kimolijah down with him as he crouches in front of Fox, smiling, of course, and speaking to Kimolijah low-voiced and cajoling. Kimolijah hunkers stiffly, chewing his nails like they're made of candy, makes a point of watching the sky, watching the ground, watching the people who gather in clumps to stare, and never watching whatever performance Stanslo thinks he's putting on.

Bas watches, but he doesn't really worry. Kimolijah will pay for this somehow, Bas doesn't doubt that, but Stanslo won't kill him, not over this. Stanslo's crazy, but he's not stupid. Whatever the bigger plan for Stanslo's Bridge is, Kimolijah is a very large part of it, and Stanslo hasn't completely used him up yet. Stanslo's got, at least in the context of what someone like him *can* have, genuine affection for Kimolijah, but more importantly, Stanslo's got a sick love for and obsession with his trophies. And Kimolijah's the most prized. For now, at least. Kimolijah's not *safe*, but he's safe.

Bas... probably not so much. Kimolijah *probably* won't be telling Stanslo anything about what happened in the barn last night. But there's always the possibility Stanslo will make him. Because, apparently, he can. And if he suspects for even a second, figures out the right questions to ask and, as Kimolijah had said, how to ask them in the right ways....

It doesn't really worry Bas as it probably should. It's quite possible that the quickest and best solution to all of this would be if Stanslo came after Bas and Bas was forced to shoot him. He's got his gridgun and he's still got spare ammo for his six-barrel, and he might be able to bullshit his way into some credit for more. Deputies or no, halfway decent people or no, Bas gives himself pretty good odds if he has to fight his way out of here,

because when it comes down to it, most of these people aren't
heeled, and the ones who are... well. Bas is willing to chance his
skills against theirs with minor concern.

The only chance he still doesn't know if he can take is Kimolijah. It's not going to do Bas much good if he kills everyone in
town, only for Kimolijah to refuse to drive the train back to
Harrowgate.

It takes longer than Bas had thought it would for Stanslo to
get tired of pulling the wings off flies and stop playing mind
games with Kimolijah in front of two rotting corpses. With a
grin that looks angry and cruel, he sets his hand to the back of
Kimolijah's neck, hauls him up and turns him, and then leans in
close, *so close*, and keeps talking.

Again, Bas can't hear what he says, but he keeps jostling
Kimolijah, keeps tugging him in for a quick squeeze to his nape,
before pressing him into his side. Kimolijah takes it, looks
where Stanslo tells him to look, answers when Stanslo pauses
his chatter to allow a reply, moves when Stanslo prods or pulls
him. It doesn't let up until Mari saunters down the hill, pinched-
faced and irritated, and whatever she says makes Stanslo direct
his attention and affections toward her instead. Kimolijah
skulks back and away with an eye on the two of them, and as
soon as he's rounded the far corner of the square, he's gone.

Bas doesn't follow. He waits.

By the time he's gotten a quarter of the way through a second
cup of coffee, Jessa is circling slowly above the station, so Bas
heads there.

Mari has pulled Stanslo back up toward the house, so Bas
doesn't think anyone will be looking for Kimolijah just yet. And
Bas isn't finished with him.

"Oh hell, you're the gluey sort, aren't you?" Kimolijah asks
when Bas barges into the workshop behind the station. "You
don't think you're getting seconds, do you?"

"Aw, Kimo, that's so sad. Last night was barely firsts. Just wait
'til I *really* get my hands on you."

A smirk and Kimolijah hunches back over whatever
complicated thing he's working on now. "'Cause you're *so good*,
I might just perish without another go." There's an obvious
sneer in a tone sodden with sarcasm.

Bas thinks that's how Kimolijah gets away with lying.
Because he doesn't. He just tells the truth through a shroud of
mockery and disdain, so no one thinks to believe he means what
he says. Which makes Bas grin.

"Yeah, the way you were moaning and groaning, I sorta
reckoned so, and you got a little yelpy toward the end, so I
figured you'd—"

Bas dodges the wrench Kimolijah whips at his head just in
time.

"Now, now." Bas eyes where the wrench has made a pretty

deep divot in the packed dust of the floor. "Don't be embarrassed. There's no shame in actually enjoying it once in a while."

"Oh wow," says Kimolijah, giant eyes wide behind his goggles. "You thought you were special, didn't you? God, that's so *adorable!*"

"Yeah, and so is your attempt to pretend it was all about blackmail, but I won't hold it against you."

"Did I not make it clear?" Kimolijah's all teeth and dimples. "I've gotten powerful good at saying what people like to hear." He dips his head back and closes his eyes. "Oh yeah, *God*, you're so good, so big, *mm*, c'mon, I *need* it." He straightens up and blinks through a crooked-toothed grin. "All we happy whores have to learn the basics, y'know."

"Funny," says Bas with a tilt of his head, "you're the only one who calls yourself that."

Kimolijah's fake smile drops, and he glares. He's like his own self-contained little storm cloud. It's actually a little bit adorable. Bas *does not* smirk. He smiles, though, and saunters over to the unfinished locomotive, leans hipshot against its hull.

"Anyway, you can't lie." Bas brightens his smile. "But I don't mind if you try. You can pretend you don't like it next time. You do top, yeah? I'm really hoping you top."

Kimolijah blinks, like he's stymied, and it's hard to tell with his dark skin, but Bas thinks he's blushing.

"Aw," says Bas. "You really are shy sometimes. 'S hard to spot unless you're looking for it."

Kimolijah rolls his eyes, and he turns back to the bench. "Go away."

"Nope."

"I'm not fucking you, and if you come near me with your dick again, I'll chew it off."

"You say that like you think I'm stupid enough to let your mouth near my dick again."

"Nothing you've said or done since you stepped off the train has led me to believe you're anything *but* stupid."

"Hmm." Bas shrugs. "Yeah, maybe telling you what I told you wasn't the smartest thing I've ever done. But I have to know, y'see." He pauses for a moment, but Kimolijah doesn't turn to look at him. "I have to know, once and for all, if you're worth the risk. Because I'm going to have a hell of a time getting you out of here if you don't want to go. In fact, I'm going to have a hell of a time getting *myself* out of here if you don't want to go, so you can see where I'm a bit hamstrung until I know for sure."

"I will very happily drop you off somewhere between here and the Bruise when we make the next run. Really, no need for dramatics."

Bas ignores it. "No one leaves here." It's abrupt and Bas doesn't care. "I saw it in every report I looked at, and those were pretty much Haversham's last words. So tell me, Kimolijah, what—"

"You don't get to call me that." It's a growl, low and angry. Kimolijah turns a little on his stool and gives Bas a sharp glare through those stupid fucking goggles. "You call me that again and I call you 'Agent Bas' next time the baron comes creeping 'round, on the off-chance that you're *not* a dirty liar trying to shine me on for whatever sick reason you and the baron came up with." He turns back, quite pointedly, a silent but very clear *we're done talking now*, and goes back to what he was doing.

"Hmm, no, I don't think you will." Bas watches Kimolijah's back, but there's no tensing or other telltale, so Bas goes on, "Fox went out of his way to make your life even more of a hell than it already is, and you still did him a mercy not many would give another and then stood guard over his corpse. And then you let me live when you knew I saw it all. That right there implies some trust I think you don't quite understand, and don't pretend for a second all that in the barn last night was part of some master plan. You might be that clever, but you have to work at that kind of devious. I don't think you'll give me up." He smiles a little and crosses his legs at the ankle. "Anyway, you liked it."

Kimolijah snorts. "Don't go thinking you've got everything all figured out. You're not that smart." He puffs out a sigh, short and sharp. "What Fox did was not entirely his fault. *You*, on the other hand...." He turns just long enough to give Bas a glaring once-over, then turns back. "And I don't like anything *that* much."

Bas ignores all of it except the first part. "What d'you mean, it wasn't his fault? Who's would it be?"

"*God*, you're a chatty bastard for a hardcase gunslinger." Kimolijah rubs at his brow, weary, before he reaches over and plucks up a few bolts and starts... doing something with them. "Did you know," he says slowly, "there's this worm, teeny-tiny thing—"

"Yeah, you told me that one." Bas rolls his eyes. "Cuddles up in your brain, makes you go swimming when you don't want to. Look, I'm dreadful tired of these little side-trips into Whocaresville. I need *answers!*" That last was a bit too virulent, but Bas can't help it.

Still, Kimolijah doesn't turn, doesn't pause in his work. He just hunches over whatever he's doing and says, "I just gave you one." He mumbles it, really, and then he shrugs and goes for a screw. "Not my fault Mister Brilliant Directorate Agent is a bit slow on the uptake."

He says "Agent" with a sneer, which means he still thinks Bas is trying to bullshit him.

Bas smirks and has himself a seat on the step of the unfinished locomotive. "Tracker," he says and leans back on his elbows.

There's a long pause, Kimolijah's obstinacy clearly sparring with his curiosity, before he finally sighs, deep and long-suffering, and says, "What?"

"Not agent. Tracker."

Kimolijah lifts his head, stares for quite a while at the tools hanging on their pegs on the wall over the workbench. He turns around on the stool, teeth set tight and hands clenched around whatever bulky component he's trying to wire.

"So I've been rotting away out here in this piece-of-shit town for *three fucking years*, and when the Directorate finally gets its head out of its ass, they don't bother with an agent, *no*, they send a fucking *bloodhound*?"

Bas glares at the epithet, because it's nowhere near accurate—tracking is a blind heap more bloody complex than "following your nose"—but he largely lets it go. Because it's not the point.

"So does that mean you don't want to be here, then? 'Cause that sounded a lot like 'Bas, I hate it here, and I'm really narked that you didn't come sooner.'"

Kimolijah only looks at Bas long enough to shoot him another one of those *stab you in the head* glares, pinched-lipped, before he turns back around.

"My *god*, you're a stubborn cuss." Bas sighs and gets a little more comfortable. "Anyway, don't go getting a big head. I actually came here looking for... someone else. Your murderer, actually." Okay, and Mariella Crocker too, but that doesn't seem pertinent just now. Bas pauses for just a second or two before he adds, "And your da's."

That makes Kimolijah slowly set down his tools and his thingamabob, and stare down at his hands. He's quiet for a long, long moment, just sitting there and breathing with his head bowed low, and then he straightens up and turns on his stool. He slides the goggles up to the top of his forehead and gives Bas a wide-eyed look with which Bas is starting to become quite familiar.

"Did you know the strongest muscle in your body in proportion to its size is your tongue?"

Bas lifts his eyebrows. "Is that another weird reference to blowjobs?"

Kimolijah snorts, then pinches his mouth down like he wishes he hadn't. "No, it's a reference to your apparent inability to shut up." Except he's trying not to laugh, Bas can tell.

It heartens Bas, and he lets a smirk bloom at the corner of his mouth. "Funny, m' mam used to tell me I'd never have mates if the only time I ever said 'boo' was when the dog got into my cupboard and ate another illobook."

Kimolijah looks dubious. "You had an illobook-eating dog."

"With a special affection for *Sunrisers*."

"Good taste, at least." Kimolijah frowns, thoughtful. "Gotta be Marcy's tits. Everyone always goes for Marcy's tits."

"Like magical magnets for degenerates."

"Are you calling your dog a degenerate?"

"Never touched the school texts, the little bastard, and they were always sitting right next to the illobooks. How else d'you explain it?"

"So you not only had an illobook-eating dog, but it was a degenerate illobook-eating dog."

"Who was so incorrigible about humping legs, my younger brother thought that was how you say 'hello' until he was about five years old." Bas grins, nostalgic affection. "Surprised the hell out of the assistant curator when Mam took us to the museum to see the exotic beasts exhibit."

It's complete bullshit, but what the hell. Mo was a little asshole when they were kids, serves him right. Kimolijah stares at Bas, for a good long time, and then his whole face quivers, and God, that fucking *smile* as he cracks up and just... *laughs*. Laughs like he hasn't done it in a long spell, and it's not all melodic and elegant like bells, like something out of a love-story subplot where a character rhapsodically compares it to music— *the apogee of a pause just before the perigee of the cadence reengaging*—and there's nothing whimsical or gentle about it. Kimolijah actually laughs kind of like a donkey, all snorting breaths and nasal twanging yawps that nearly double him over and shake his whole body like he's having a fit.

It makes Bas's grin fade a little, because *fit*, and he remembers what he's doing here and how he's got questions, damn it, too many questions, and the lack of answers is going to get him killed. Still, he just looks for a while longer, smile dimming but there, and watches Kimolijah come down from his brief euphoria, his grin bright, his light brown eyes twinkling a bit devilishly, and everything about him more relaxed and loose as his chuckles taper off.

Bas wants to kiss him again. Wants to see if Kimolijah will let him now, when it's just them, no leverage, just because they want to.

"I want to court you, Kimolijah."

It just... sprays out, like toast crumbs from a dry tongue, all ungainly and undeniable. Bas blinks and very nearly groans— 'cause who knew he's really just a bloody great namby-pamby in a Bas suit?—but he won't take it back.

"Court me." Kimolijah's smile drops away, and he stares at Bas, all wide eyes and craggy brow. He looks like he's never in his life heard such a thing.

It decides Bas like his own mouth betraying him hadn't. Because someone like Kimolijah *should* be courted. And it's just plain sad the notion is such a new one for him.

Bas nods, forceful. "We went about it all wrong, started too fast and in all the wrong places. I want to court you proper-like. With kind words and little gifts and interesting conversations we share over meals cooked just for us. I want to take you home and introduce you to my mam and my da, and maybe even my brother, if I think I can trust him not to be an ace-high ass or try to steal you away from me." He pauses with a small wince, because that might've been a bit of overshare, but what the hell. "Have you ever been courted properly, Kimo?"

Kimolijah doesn't answer. For a moment, it looks like he can't. But then he blinks and he shakes his head, mute.

"Well, you should be," Bas tells him, resolute. "You should be courted and kissed and spoilt, and I mean to do it one day. But I can't do it here, can I?"

"You...." Kimolijah shakes his head again, more slowly this time, and he's still staring, dazed, like he thinks maybe he's not actually hearing any of this properly. "Um. No. No, you really can't." He tilts his head, frowning now. "Maybe I'd be the one doing the courting."

And just the fact that he's said it, like he's actually thinking about the possibilities....

"Maybe you would. But no one can really court anyone, not here, so we're not likely to find out which way it goes, yeah?" Bas leans forward, gaze steady. "Help me get you out of here. Help me get *us* out of here."

Again, Kimolijah just stares, tawny eyes going overbright for a slim moment, there and gone so quick it could be a trick of the light, but Bas doesn't think it is. It makes him sad and hopeful and angry and expectant.

With a bit of a frown, Kimolijah looks away, head dipping down as he studies the knees of his trousers and the dirt beneath his fingernails. He lifts his hand to chew on his thumbnail for a moment, distracted, before he clears his throat and turns back to Bas.

"So this leg-humping, illobook-eating, degenerate dog." Kimolijah's smirk is weak and so clearly fake that Bas doesn't have the heart to call him on it. Kimolijah tilts his head. "How'd you end up killing him?"

Goddamn it. Close. *So* close.

Bas shakes himself out of the disappointment and shrugs. "Hey, I loved that dog."

"Yeah." Kimolijah snorts and nods, still obviously uncomfortable. "I guess you would've had to." He looks at Bas with a question in his eyes, his eyebrows crimping and his wide mouth pulled down in a soft little twist that looks sad. "You had a dog."

"I think we just covered that."

"No, I...." Kimolijah shakes his head. "You had a dog. You had a *mam.*"

"Have, actually." Bas sighs, because he sees where this is going; where it's gone, actually. "And a da and a brother. Two aunts and an uncle, some cousins. Even a gran, though Mam mostly likes to pretend it isn't so." He holds out his hands. "People I love and would want to protect."

Kimolijah sucks in a long deep breath. He looks away.

"People don't... we don't talk about... that sort of thing. None of it." He pauses, mouth working, before he goes on, softer, "And there is no courting. Not here."

"Yeah, I see that." Bas leans back on his elbows and studies Kimolijah's sharp profile. "You don't talk about it?" he ventures slowly. "Or you can't?"

Kimolijah opens his mouth, like he actually intends to answer. But then he looks down at the bracelet spiraling from wrist to forearm, and he shuts his mouth. He gives Bas a steady look from beneath straight, black eyebrows.

"Right." Bas grimaces. He makes a conscious effort not to actually deflate. Because he thinks if that coil of weird matte-metal wasn't there, he might have gotten an answer. And it burns. "So if I—"

"Pin up," Kimolijah cuts in, eyes narrowed and head tilted, everything about him abruptly gone still and alert. "Jessa" is all he says. With a last look Bas can't decipher, Kimolijah swings back around on his stool, snaps the goggles back down, and hunches over his workbench.

And now that Bas is paying attention, yeah, he can hear Jessa chirping outside. Not from the back where the mess happened yesterday, but from the station proper. Bas is listening now, so he hears the footfalls on oil-packed dust, and he scowls, because *of course* it's Stanslo.

"That's a neat trick," Bas says, low and quiet, "teaching your bird to be your watchdog."

"I didn't teach her anything," Kimolijah mutters back, just as quiet. He picks up his screwdriver and starts fiddling with his thingamabob. "And I still don't believe you." He shuts up altogether when Stanslo comes in.

"Ah!" says Stanslo, with perhaps a touch of suspicion lurking at the edges of his smile. "So nice to find you here, Bas." All narrowed eyes and subtle calculation.

And just like that, the atmosphere narrows down to a hard little point of tension, as though that moment of connection with Kimolijah never even happened.

Stanslo tilts his head, like he's waiting for Bas to jump to an explanation. Bas has decided he's just going to wait for an excuse to shoot Stanslo in the head, so he doesn't really care to offer justification for his presence. He's not going to go looking for a difficulty, but if Stanslo decides to try any more of his games out on Bas, well. If Bas is going to end up stuck in this hellhole for the rest of his perhaps very short life, he's not doing it with Stanslo giving him that shit-eating grin.

And on that note—"Hey, what's the Outlet all about, anyway?" Bas asks. Kimolijah chokes a little, but Bas just keeps his curious face on and stares at Stanslo. He doesn't move from his casual sprawl on the engine's steps. "All those crystals wired in, and, you know, what with that cot, it all seemed a bit—"

"Don't you have somewhere to be?" Kimolijah snaps, everything about him tense and wary. "I've got work to do here, and this is all dreadful distracting."

Interesting. That answers one question. Kimolijah's stepped in—deflect and distract—just like he did yesterday when he saved Bas from whatever fresh hell Stanslo had in mind, and like he'd tried to do with Fox. So maybe Kimolijah doesn't believe Bas, and maybe the animosity is real, but he still just hasn't the stomach to watch what goes on here without putting his neck out to sidetrack it when he can.

With that, and with what just happened only moments ago—the joking, the easy laughter, the almost-trust thwarted by that twice-cursed bracelet—it gives Bas heart. Shy, brilliant Kimolijah Adani from Poor Side is still in there somewhere.

"It was just powerful strange," Bas says and directs the conversation to Kimolijah. "Reacher was talking like you having some kind of fit is a regular occurrence—" He pauses when Kimolijah jerks and turns back to his workbench. "—and apparently it is," Bas says to Stanslo, "since that tonic was awfully damned handy." He tilts his head. "So, what's that all about?" He waves a hand toward Kimolijah but keeps his eyes on Stanslo. "He sick or something? I mean, I wouldn't pry, of course, but he's to be my responsibility, so I should probably know, yeah?"

"*He* is right here," Kimolijah growls, but when Stanslo sends him a sharp glance, Kimolijah shuts up and hunches over his tools.

Stanslo *tuts*, like the subject makes him horribly sad, and he shakes his head as he sets a firm hand to Kimolijah's shoulder. "Not an unreasonable question, I suppose." His smile had dipped a bit, and now it blooms, wide and crafty. "And since you *are* most certainly here, dear heart"—he squeezes Kimolijah's shoulder hard enough that Kimolijah jerks and drops a screwdriver—"perhaps you should be the one to answer Bas's questions. It *is* rather rude of us to discuss you like you're not here."

Kimolijah freezes for a moment before he turns to Stanslo, scowl somewhat angry but mostly surprised and bewildered. "I... I can't. You *said* I can't."

The last syllable hasn't even left Kimolijah's mouth all the way before Stanslo lets go of Kimolijah's shoulder, latches on to Kimolijah's wrist, and yanks him from the stool. Kimolijah flails and almost falls but manages to snatch at Stanslo's lapel and keep on his feet.

"I think, Kimo, that perhaps it's time for a... reminder of sorts." Stanslo grins. "It's actually rather convenient that Bas is here." He turns to Bas. "I've been wanting to show you a little more how things work, you see."

Kimolijah stares for a moment, right up close, cross and confused, before he slowly bares his teeth, a feral smile, and he pats at Stanslo's chest, smoothing the crunched wool. He peers down at Stanslo's hand, wrapped around the bracelet, and then back up at Stanslo.

"Aw," he says and nudges in right up close, "it's so cute when you give conflicting orders and then get pissy 'cause no one knows what the fuck you want."

Stanslo isn't smiling now. He snarls, gives Kimolijah a vicious shake, then shoves him back so hard Kimolijah bounces off the workbench and trips to the ground.

Bas can't intercede. He's watched worse things for the sake of a case; Jakob Barstow watched a man lynched once because Bas couldn't stop it without blowing his cover. Hell, he'd held one of the torches. He can watch this.

Except he can't, he can't help it, and he starts to get up. "Hey, look, if you don't want me to ask, just—"

Kimolijah *laughs*, says, "No, no," and waves a hand until Bas sinks back down. "See, that's the thing." Kimolijah gets up slowly, and keeps moving until the flimsy barrier of the bench's stool is between him and Stanslo. "He *does* want you to ask." He's talking to Bas but looking at Stanslo. "And he wants me to show you just how tight my leash is. Oh, sorry! I meant just how deeply he cares."

He curls his lip and finally turns away from Stanslo. "So he wants me to answer your question—a question he's expressly forbidden me from ever answering—just to see how many times I say the wrong thing." He sets his teeth. "So ask me again, Bas. Go on, don't be shy. The baron's still pissed off at me, and he's really looking forward to this."

Bas feigns surprise, narrows his eyes, first at Stanslo and then at Kimolijah. "Pissed off at you for what?" Like he doesn't know.

Stanslo looks like he might interject, prevent Kimolijah from answering, but he merely purses his lips and tilts his head at Kimolijah, expectant. Bas knows that look. He's seen it on his mam's face often enough. It's the *give them enough rope* look.

Kimolijah smirks and says, "I missed breakfast. And for once, he doesn't think it's because I was out catting all night." And then he grins and leans back into the workbench, for all the world like it was the most amazing punchline in the history of jokes, and he's supremely smug about delivering it.

And it *is* dreadfully funny, because in this case, the accusation would actually be pretty much true. Luckily, Bas manages not to snort. He must look somewhat constipated or something, though, because Stanslo says, "When I impose a penalty, Bas, I expect it to be carried out. I expect my people to see that it's carried out. And when I impose that penalty specifically to protect one of my people"—he pauses and tips his head at Kimolijah; Kimolijah makes a show of rolling his eyes—"I do not expect that very person to be the one to belay said penalty."

Ah. Fox. Last night.

Bas thinks he's likely to get more if he doesn't let on that he knows exactly what Stanslo's talking about, so he adopts a look of mild exasperation and says, "Ohhh-kay?"

"Yeah, I've been naughty," Kimolijah says, and he leans an elbow back on the bench, the collar of his shirt pulling out and down, enough brown skin and black ink peeking out to make a man pay attention, and he gives Stanslo a slow up-and-down and then a smirk. "But that's how you like it, isn't it, Baron." He slides the goggles up onto his forehead, leaving clean rings around his eyes, but it somehow doesn't detract even a little from the bit of a burn he's aiming at Stanslo. "It's obvious I'm not going to get any work done this morning," he tells Stanslo. "So what'll it be? You want me weepy or wicked? Stay here and watch me judder through an answer you don't really care if Bas gets, or go up the house and... well, watch me judder in an entirely different way?" The dimples pop, and Kimolijah waggles his eyebrows.

Stanslo shakes his head and sighs at Kimolijah before he turns to Bas with a look of fond exasperation that says *Do you see what I have to put up with?*

Bas only just prevents his lip curling up in disgust.

Kimolijah's apparently got his answer, because he whips off the goggles and throws them down on the workbench. He ruins the clean spots around his eyes by scrubbing at his face with dirty hands.

"It's okay," he says, and he turns his back on Stanslo and slides a look at Bas out of the corner of his eye, steady and frank. "I don't really want to be here anyway." It's so casual, inserted so smoothly, that Bas almost doesn't catch it. But he does, and if he's asked a dozen questions since he barged in on Kimolijah, if he was only going to get one answer, he's overwhelmingly glad it's that one.

"Which is just as well, I suppose," Kimolijah goes on with a dramatic sigh, "'cause I swear to God I'm never going to get anything done around here."

Stanslo grins at Bas. "Depends on one's perspective, I imagine," he says, and he *winks* at Bas, like they're sharing a joke.

All things considered, it kind of turns Bas's stomach. All the same, he gives Stanslo a smirk and says, "And what exactly needs doing, no doubt," because he's Jakob Barstow and Jakob Barstow can be a dick like that.

Kimolijah, on the other hand, merely snorts and tosses his screwdriver in the general direction of the toolbox. "No doubt." It's brimming with acid. He turns and gives Stanslo's cheek a heavy pat that Bas finds himself wishing was a slap. Or a punch. "And doing *to*, I reckon." Kimolijah saunters past both Bas and Stanslo, pulls his face into something that could be a grin or a grimace. "Well, come on," he mutters at Stanslo and heads toward the door, "dicks don't suck themselves." He pauses and the grin turns real. "But oh my god, wouldn't it be *awesome* if they did?"

Stanslo smiles, like all is forgotten, but then Bas catches a look at his eyes and Stanslo says, "Kimo," real low, like he's crooning it, and Bas knows this isn't finished yet.

Kimolijah seems to, as well, because he stops dead, and all pretense at the graceless, grinning rake is gone by the time he turns around. He doesn't cave, though; he stares at Stanslo, face blank, head tilted to the side, and he says, "Yeah, Baron?" in a tone that's clear challenge.

"I think," says Stanslo, "it would be best if you answer Bas's question before we go."

Shit. Bas should've seen this coming. And he did, but not like this. Stanslo's the sort to wait for the perfect opportunity to exact punishment, revenge. Bas pushed, and now he's pretty much handed Stanslo the demonstration of power he wants. And Kimolijah was always going to pay for Fox, but this here, this makes it Bas's fault.

"Hey." Bas holds up his hands. "Look, it's obviously something I shouldn't've asked, so—"

"No, no, Bas, you see, that's where you're wrong. You should see how things work here. You should understand the consequences of every action you take before you take it, every word out of your mouth before you voice it. Perhaps it can help you avoid future... disciplinary action."

Stanslo pauses, narrowing his eyes just a touch at Bas, a clear message, and not for Kimolijah. Or maybe for both of them. Bas thinks back to that tiny, hellish metal coffin in the desert heat, and he fists his hands.

"And, as you say," Stanslo goes on, "you'll be responsible for keeping Kimo safe, and I can't insist you do that if you don't know what to expect." Stanslo turns to Kimolijah. "It's important that Bas knows just what he's in for, wouldn't you say, dear heart?" He turns back to Bas. "After all, it is, unfortunately, those around Kimo who end up paying for his impulses."

Kimolijah sucks in a long, deep breath, but it doesn't look like it's because Stanslo has scared or intimidated him; it looks like it's because he's supremely pissed off. But he grins, that awful, malicious one, and he looks at Bas with his teeth set tight.

"I've got a burr bug," he says and then immediately seizes when a great blue shock flies up his arm. He staggers a little but gives Stanslo a glare and says, "You think I won't, don't you?" He doesn't wait for Stanslo to answer, just snaps his gaze back to Bas. "This"—he lifts up his arm, flashes the bracelet—"keeps it sleeping, but it doesn't stop it growing, and it keeps getting bigger and faster." Another bolt goes up halfway through, but Kimolijah shoves the words through his teeth. And then he *keeps going.* "And when it's awake for too long—"

This time, he can't finish. The gridstream lights him up like starfire, and Kimolijah drops to one knee, the buzz and occasional *pop* of it drowning out the words he tries to stammer out between them, words like "feelers" and "veins" and *God*, he's a mulish little bastard, he's going to keep going, he's going to keep at it until he stops his own heart, and Stanslo's just standing there, *watching* it, and Bas can't take another second.

"Yeah, that's impressive." He tries to make it sound bored, unaffected. He gives Stanslo a steady look and raises his voice to be heard over Kimolijah's stubborn, stuttering ramble and the sizzle of gridstream. "Quite a show. Maybe you can tell me whatever else he's not supposed to talk about so I can make sure I'm not standing next to him when he slips up."

Stanslo chuckles. "It's probably best you just assume he'll misbehave at every turn and stay clear altogether." He shakes his head, rueful, and crouches down next to Kimolijah. "That's enough now, dear heart."

Kimolijah's ground-out confessions stop, abrupt and absolute, like a switch has been flipped. He's panting, on his knees and holding himself up with his hands, a tiny runnelet of blood oozing from the corner of his left eye and a string of spit hanging from his bottom lip, but he's still glaring, still furious enough to keep going. And the thing is, Bas doesn't need him to. He *knows*, he remembers—*There's this worm, see, teeny-tiny thing*—and bloody fucking hell, Kimolijah's been telling Bas exactly what's going on in Stanslo's Bridge almost from day one.

"Do you see now, Bas?"

Bas looks at Stanslo. And oh yeah, he sees, and he really hopes the *I'm going to fucking kill you very, very soon* doesn't show all over his face.

"I get it," he says. "Turning a man's own Tech on him—something else I've no doubt would get you a lot of interest back in the real world." He tilts his head. "You've got quite a lot going on out here in the desert, Baron. I'm impressed, which is, I'm sure, what I'm meant to be." He shoots a glance at Kimolijah, deliberately flip and a bit derisive, before he looks back at Stanslo. "Putting Techs back in their rightful places, that it? Is that what Stanslo's Bridge is really for?"

Stanslo's eyebrows lift. "You seem to be under the impression, Bas, that I'm doing this to him." He holds his hands out. "You can see I haven't touched him." He looks down at Kimolijah and shakes his head. "No, I'm afraid Kimolijah does these things entirely to himself. As for Techs and their 'rightful places,' well." Stanslo shrugs and waves his hand, dismissive. "Who am I to decide such things? I am merely a man who can recognize opportunities, Bas. And snatch them up when they happen into my hand."

Kimolijah spits, and it lands far enough away from Stanslo's boot that it can be argued it wasn't intentional. His hands are shaking—his whole body's shaking—but it's not unexpected, considering he's taken more gridstream shooting through him in the last few minutes than the average thunderstorm manages in an hour.

He's gridTech, Bas tells himself, *he can take it*, but Bas knows a little too much about gridstream and the gridTechs it manages to occasionally kill to be entirely reassured by the thought.

"Come, then, dear heart."

Stanslo takes hold of Kimolijah and drags him to his feet. Kimolijah doesn't fight him. He doesn't look like he could if he wanted to. He does make a point of muttering, "Well, that's one way to make my knees weak," all blurry derision and eyes full of dazed loathing, because *Kimolijah can't lie*, and neither can he say what he obviously really means, but *God*, he gets his point across anyway, doesn't he.

Like the psycho narcissistic control freak he is, Stanslo smiles, all fond indulgence, and keeps firm hold as he begins leading Kimolijah toward the door. "I hope, Bas," Stanslo says with a lift of his eyebrow, "that this answers any questions you may have had."

There's still the issue of the Outlet, but Bas isn't about to bring it up. Anyway, he's seen enough by now to make a decent guess.

"Yeah," he says, his voice a little hoarse, but he's just glad it isn't shaking. "Yeah, right as a trivet, me."

"Good," says Stanslo, and he grins as he guides Kimolijah out. "Oh, and Bas?" Stanslo pauses just on the other side of the door, no doubt for dramatic effect, so Bas merely stares at him, scornful, and he doesn't even care if it shows anymore; *fuck* Baron fucking Stanslo. When Bas doesn't say anything, Stanslo's grin widens. "I do hope you and Kimo had an informative chat before I arrived."

Kimolijah doesn't move, doesn't gasp, doesn't do anything but kind of hang on his feet like he's ready to collapse; nonetheless, Bas can sense a tightening, can imagine a wild fury—*I knew it, I fucking knew it!*—and he knows instantly that any ground he managed to gain with Kimolijah ten minutes ago has now been neatly wiped away with that smug innuendo. Because Bas knows exactly what that sounded like to Kimolijah, and he knows that, somehow, Stanslo knows it too.

"We'll have a drink soon." Stanslo winks. "Catch up."

And then he's gone and Bas is left to himself again, which is good, because he's shaking a little now, too, and it's *anger*, like he's never felt before. "A *drink*," he mutters through his teeth. "Yes, we'll discuss how you steal people and torture people and *kill people*, all over a fucking *drink*, you sick bloody arrogant cur."

Bas shakes his head and kicks at the train's side panel. "Magic Man wouldn't last a day here."

Of all the places Bas had expected Stanslo and Kimolijah to show up next, the tavern was not one of them. Else Bas wouldn't have shown up. He hopes that thing about a drink was for show, because Bas has no intention of playing nice with the baron tonight. He thinks about just ducking back out, but—

"Dance with me," says Quinnie, her heavy breasts abruptly pushed up against Bas's arm and her straight white teeth flashing at him in a smile he knows is not actually half as friendly as it's trying to look.

Bas glances around the tavern. Yanush is sitting at the upright with Sis, Merrin hanging over his shoulder and grinning something into Yanush's ear that makes both Yanush and Sis laugh and falter at the keys. Yanush is surprisingly good, long, wide-knuckled fingers plucking out a neat, resonant harmony to the light melody Sis lays down at the upper half of the clavier.

Cavett and Reacher are hunkered over a tall table by the door, drinking something that looks murky and somewhat gray, and squinting over at Bas above the rims of their glasses. Bas lifts his eyebrows back at them and is a little surprised when Reacher sends him back a smirk and a pointed shift of his glance. Bas follows it over to Stanslo's table, Stanslo with his arm over the back of Kimolijah's chair and Kimolijah hunched down into his burled scarf and expensive coat with his hat so low Bas can only see the point of his chin.

Mari's there, her chestnut hair loose and full and her blouse silky and extravagant. Her red mouth is pulled into a perpetual smile, knowing and somewhat smug, and she leans across Kimolijah to say something to Stanslo, tapered finger pointing delicately over at Nadal. Nadal isn't draped over Stanslo this time; he looks like he wishes he were, though, his wide eyes spending more time lingering across the room than on the man who looks like he's trying like hell to buy himself some company for the evening. Kimolijah stiffens, head tilting the tiniest bit toward Mari, and Bas can't see his face, but he's betting Kimolijah's giving Mari one of those *why won't your head just explode?* glares.

As Bas watches, Stanslo gives Mari a soft look, reaches across Kimolijah, takes Mari's hand, and kisses it as he says something back. He gets up from his lazy sprawl, cracks a wide grin at Kimolijah that Kimolijah doesn't look up to see, and says, "Wait for me here," loud enough to carry over the music and attract several glances. His hand is heavy on Kimolijah's shoulder as he leans down to set a kiss to Mari's cheek. It's deliberate, Bas is sure, one of those *show them how tight the leash is* things Kimolijah was talking about, because Stanslo very pointedly makes his way from his bondmate and his bit-on-the-side, snatches Nadal away from his potential customer on his way across the room, and drags him up the stairs. Nadal doesn't look unhappy about it; in fact, he shoots a smirk toward Kimolijah on his way, though it's wasted, since Kimolijah still doesn't look up.

Bas looks back at Quinnie, says, "I don't dance," and sets a proprietary hand to the back of her neck before she can retort or pull away. He hopes it looks intimate instead of forceful. "But since I'm pretty sure dancing isn't what you had in mind anyway, how about we just skip all the folderol and get right to why you hate me."

"Aw, a man like you?" Quinnie's smile goes shrewd though just as fake. "I'm sure you give folk all kinds of reasons before you've had breakfast."

"A man like me." Bas shakes his head and makes a point of stroking the thick, silky black braid draped over Quinnie's shoulder, suggestive and exploratory, just to see what she'll let him get away with while they play at this exhibition of fake proposition. "For all the gunslingers and wannabe-gunslingers scuffing around Stanslo's Bridge, I'm not quite sure why you seem to have such a problem with 'a man like me.' You'd think you've never seen my like."

"Maybe that's the problem. Maybe I've seen too many. Maybe Kimo has too, and maybe I don't wanna see—"

"Ah, it's all about Kimo, then. Seems so many things here are."

Quinnie's fake smile takes on sharp edges. "You'd know, wouldn't you?"

Bas doesn't react, he knows he doesn't, so there's no reason for Quinnie's expression to shift into one of victory, but it does.

She leans in closer, tips up to whisper low and soft in Bas's ear, "I see you watching him."

"And I see him watching right back," Bas says, just as quiet. And it's true—Kimolijah does watch Bas, and maybe it's for entirely different reasons than Bas would like, but there's something there, something more, and Bas doesn't believe it's all about leverage and Kimolijah covering his back. If it were that simple, Kimolijah could've found another way. Kimolijah's a goddamned genius, for fuck's sake. If he really wanted to set Bas up, he could have found a hundred other ways that were more effective, more certain, and involved witnesses.

Quinnie's smile almost falters as she pulls back, but she keeps it. "Leave him alone." It's thin and said through smiling teeth. "The last thing he needs—"

"I'm thinking the last thing he needs is *more* people deciding *what he needs*." It grates at the back of Bas's throat, it's so forceful, and he has to school his expression back into the lines of casual seduction.

He shouldn't have said it. Quinnie seems to fancy herself some kind of protector or something; she's obviously on Kimolijah's side in... whatever all this is. But she's still in Stanslo's Bridge, she still works for the baron, and God knows who else has a bracelet or a burr bug or a crystal or whatever else Stanslo can come up with to make sure no one ever does, says, or thinks something he doesn't like or know about.

Still, a quick recovery seems rather necessary, so Bas tilts his head and says, "Boss doesn't share, I get it. Still, from what I've heard, there's always the possibility of anyone going up for bid. A man can keep an eye on what he might one day have, can't he?"

Quinnie narrows her eyes, all pretense at getting to know one another with the possibility of something more gone, and she opens her mouth, teeth bared. She's cut off by a mild little dustup behind them, Kimolijah's voice rising to say, "He told us to wait here," and Mari snapping back, "No, he told *you*."

Bas and Quinnie both turn to look at them, along with most of the rest of the tavern's patrons. The pleasant sounds of the upright falter briefly, and then quickly resume, louder now and more upbeat.

Mari doesn't seem to notice. She's standing and adjusting a fine fur-collared shawl around her shoulders. "I keep wondering when he's going to quit playing with the notion of the two of you together and just go ahead and make space in your room for Nadal." She shakes her head and gives Kimolijah a cruel grin. "Bet he lets me watch."

Kimolijah doesn't say anything, just watches her leave, then hunches back down and props his boots up on Mari's vacant chair. Quinnie has watched it all with a look of boredom, and now she knocks Bas's hand away from where it's still gripping the back of her neck, before she snatches at the sleeve of his coat. Without a word, she drags Bas over to Kimolijah and then drops into the chair across from him.

She sighs, long and weary, then says, "Just kill him." She gives Bas a look and then shakes her head at Kimolijah. "He's only gonna cause you more trouble."

It takes a second for Bas to realize she's talking about him. "Hey, what the hell?"

"It's too dangerous, Kimo." Quinnie looks up at Bas, still standing between her chair and Kimolijah's, and she rolls her eyes. "For God's sake, I don't wanna be shouting this across the bar. Just sit down already."

Bas does with a scowl that's more annoyed than anything else, though there's got to be confusion there, too, because seriously—what the hell?

Kimolijah stares between them for a long moment, his left eye stained and blooded on one side, the white of it blotched nearly solid red from corner to iris. He says, "Maybe, but... what if he really is?"

"Then Stanslo already knows. There was a contract with Dolerma, remember? And if Stanslo's letting him live, it's because he's got a plan for him. Believe me, Kimo, Mister Directorate-I'm-Here-to-Help ain't gonna have your best interests at heart for long. If he even does now."

Bas narrows his eyes and sets his teeth. "Oh grand, so we're just *talking* about this now?" He gives Kimolijah a glare. "Who else have you told?"

Kimolijah looks down and shrugs. "No one. And Quinnie wouldn't—"

"I don't really care if Quinnie wouldn't—I care that Quinnie *could*. And I told you, that bizarre 'contract' means nothing. The crystal means nothing, not to me."

"Look," says Quinnie, ignoring Bas entirely, "either he really is Directorate and he's just as fucked as everyone else here, or Stanslo put him up to it to see if you're holding out on him."

"Now hold on just a minute," Bas snaps.

"Either way," Quinnie plows on, "nothing's changed." She pauses, and then, softer, "We ain't getting out of here, Kimo."

"I *know*, goddamn it. I'm not—"

"Yeah, you are, and I don't blame you. But we stick to the plan." She turns to give Bas another once-over, and when she sees what must be a pretty gobsmacked look on his face, her own twists sour. "Oh, shut up, it ain't like you can go jawing at Stanslo about this, else I'll just tell him I was peeking through the barn door and saw the whole thing." She grins. "And he ain't got *my* crystal."

Bas almost chokes. "You told her *that*?" And then he realizes what Quinnie just said, and he blurts, "Who does?"

Quinnie sniffs and settles back in her chair. "'S no nevermind of yours. And Kimo tells me everything." She waves her hand. "Don't be jealous. I'm just prettier than you."

"What plan?" Bas asks, because he's not interested in a pissing contest right now. Besides, Quinnie would probably win.

Kimolijah and Quinnie are silent for a spell, just looking at each other. Eventually Kimolijah shrugs and starts chewing on a fingernail. Quinnie purses her lips and sighs. She turns to Bas with a bright, fake smile.

"The one that doesn't include you."

16.

It's not easy tracking Dolerma down. And it's not easy being inconspicuous while doing it. But Dolerma is the one person—including Kimolijah—who gave the impression he's trying to help, even if it was in an annoyingly oblique let's-play-guessing-games-with-cryptic-hints kind of way. So Bas ignores all the looks he gets when he strolls through the town and ducks his head into the mess, the tavern, the bathhouse, and any other door he thinks he can get away with.

He finds Dolerma, weirdly enough, just coming out of the armory and turning to lock the door behind him. Bas doesn't waste time on greetings or asking permission; he grabs and shoves and bullies Dolerma back through the door, shuts it, and then leans his back against it, blocking the way out. He folds his arms across his chest and gives Dolerma a glare.

Dolerma doesn't glare back, doesn't say a word, merely stares at Bas with his blank white face, dark lenses covering his freaky black eyes. The hair-that's-not sways the slightest bit about his shoulders, though the air in the armory is thick and still with no hint of a breeze.

"So how about if I tell you what I've got so far," Bas says, his voice low for privacy, though he doesn't bother trying to keep the anger out of it, "and then you tell me what I'm missing before I lose my patience and just beat the hell out of you." He doesn't wait for Dolerma to respond. "Stanslo's keeping Kimolijah here against his will so he can—"

"I know perfectly well what you've got so far," Dolerma cuts in, his buzzy voice quiet and unperturbed. His thin, colorless mouth quirks up at one corner. "I don't necessarily need to read you to decipher you. Or your objective." He shrugs, careless and bland. "You're not the first snared by the allure of Stanslo's... toys."

Bas narrows his eyes. He's not sure what that's supposed to imply, or whether or not he should be insulted—he thinks probably yes—but it'll have to wait.

"Yeah, all right, fine." Bas presses his lips together, annoyed. "I'm not sure I actually care right now. What I do care about is—"

"Getting Kimo out of Stanslo's Bridge, yes."

Bas clenches his teeth. "Shall I just stand here and not say anything while you answer all the questions you don't give me a chance to actually ask?"

"It might go faster," Dolerma says and tilts his mouth in what Bas would call a smirk on another person, but on Dolerma it just looks... weird.

Bas knows a challenge when he hears one, so he merely settles back more comfortably against the door. And he stares.

Dolerma actually smiles this time, white slash of mouth pulling up into a semblance of a curve, and he mirrors Bas's pose, arms crossed and back set to the rack of guns behind him.

"I cannot tell you all, Bas." It actually sounds a bit regretful. "If you return from the Bruise unscathed and with the same questions, then perhaps. But I suspect you'll have a set of entirely new ones when that time comes, and the questions that seem so imperative now will either be answered or have lost their importance. And if you become compromised... well." Dolerma looks away. "If that is the case, then already what I've told you rather assures I won't live long after you return. At least this way, it may be less painful."

Bas lifts his eyebrows. "You think whatever I see over there, or find out, it'll make me want to wring your neck more than I already do?"

That gets another one of those creepy smiles and a hollow puff of a laugh. "No, Bas. What you want will have nothing to do with it."

"You keep talking in rid—"

"Return from the Bruise intact. Then you may ask me your questions."

"Yeah, but will I get answers?" Bas mutters. "And what the hell does that mean, *return int—*"

"Swear you will find a way to get Kimo out of Stanslo's Bridge before the month is out." Dolerma straightens and leans in, so close Bas can see every tiny black vein beneath the near-translucent, poreless skin of his cheek. "Swear it and I will give you answers to any questions you ask."

Bas has no problem at all making that promise. So he does.

Jessa spends the next day drifting in broad, indolent circles above the big house.

Bas does not spend the day waiting for her to change her course so he can follow her. Even if he does. Because shut up.

Bas is antsy. For several reasons, but last night is weighing on him. He'd known Kimolijah must have some kind of plan—backups for his backups, because Kimolijah always does—but Bas also remembers Resaniji's "stupid bloody genius" and the academy minister's "couldn't buy a loaf of bread if you sent him to a market full of bake shops." So Bas is not terribly confident that any plan Kimolijah and Quinnie cooked up together won't end with both of them in a dusty grave in the middle of the desert. And Bas right along with them, most likely. Unless it involves inventing something brilliant and unbelievable and apparently worth killing over. Then it'll probably work out just fine.

Evening shatters across the desert like shards of stained glass, golds and smoky corals chased away by a heavy thump of cobalt edged with plum. It falls so fast Bas half expects to see dust puff up with the dense clap of shadows on hardpan.

It'll be another hour or so before the shooting starts.

He's just coming out of the mess with a cup of coffee steaming in his hand when he sees Stanslo coming across the square, Reacher and Lowen in tow. Bas blows a fragrant cloud across the top of his cup and watches them come, ready, because he doesn't intend to be brushed off this time. Tomorrow night is the Bruise, and still no one's telling him shit. It makes no sense. And if he has to have a sit-down at Hannah's with Stanslo, he will, but he'd rather get it done without having to pretend to enjoy drinking with someone he doesn't even want to look at. Maybe this way he can avoid it.

Fox is a rotting lump against the post of the gallows. Bas can see him quite clearly, lit up beneath the bright gridlight. Stanslo doesn't pause as he passes the two corpses in the square, but he looks and his smile is satisfied. Lowen gives Fox a brief glance, blank, but Reacher—big dumb bumpkin that he is—smirks.

Bas narrows his eyes but has already smoothed out his expression by the time Stanslo notices him.

"Mayhap a word, Baron, if you please," Bas calls as they near, budging up off the side of the mess and starting toward them. They meet just beside the armory, and Bas sets his free hand to its sturdy side and leans against it. He takes a sip of his coffee. "The Bruise is set for tomorrow night." He flicks a quick glance at Reacher, then looks back at Stanslo.

"It most assuredly is," Stanslo says. He gives Bas a smile. "Is there a problem?"

And again, if Bas were Magic Man and this were an illobook, Bas would say something both clever and cheesy like, "Yes, there's a problem—*you*, sir, are a problem. And I aim to solve it." And then he'd start casting spells, toying with the villain, or he'd turn himself into something scary and suitably impressive and commence a five-panel beat down in full color, at the end of which Stanslo would beg for mercy and be glad when the guardarm showed up to arrest him.

Unfortunately, this is still not an illobook and Bas is still not Magic Man, so what he actually says is, "Not as such. Or, well, maybe."

Stanslo opens his mouth and then closes it again with an

impatient press of lips when Reacher cuts in, "Boss, Mari's waitin' on ye over t' Hannah's. Why don't I take care of—"

"I'll go and tell her you've been delayed," Lowen cuts in. His tone is cordial as ever and his smile when Stanslo and Reacher look at him is pleasant.

So how come Bas gets the feeling the interruption was impatient and the quality beneath it angry?

Stanslo allows that Lowen's offer was a kind one and accepts it. He gives Reacher a look with raised eyebrows, like he's waiting to see if Reacher is stupid enough to interrupt him again. Reacher doesn't, so Stanslo looks at Bas, says, "How about that drink?" and sets a hand to Bas's shoulder.

Bas tries very hard not to remember that hand across Kimolijah's cheek, or shoving Kimolijah to the floor, or dragging Kimolijah out of his workshop in some kind of proprietary show of domination. And he tries so much harder not to imagine that hand stalking the trail of ink across Kimolijah's dark skin.

"Not much in a drinking mood, Baron."

"Oh?" Stanslo narrows his eyes and gives Bas's shoulder a squeeze. "Something I can do?" Sometimes it's like he genuinely cares. It's disconcerting.

"Well, you can tell me how it is you've got your people here cowed so hard I can't get a single one to tell me what I'm to expect at the Bruise tomorrow." Bas takes a sip of his coffee and considers Stanslo's narrowed eyes from over the lip of his cup. "It's admirable, don't get me wrong." Bas lowers the cup. "But not terribly useful to me. Nor to you, I'm thinking, since I'm supposed to be... how did you put it? Keeping what belongs to you safe?" He shrugs. "Can't do that very well if I don't know what I'm supposed to be keeping him safe *from*."

Stanslo frowns and turns to Reacher. He doesn't even need to say anything.

Reacher holds up his hands, placating, but not worried like Bas would've expected with that look aimed at him. Stanslo smiles so much it's almost a shock when he doesn't.

"He won't have to worry 'bout nothin', Boss," Reacher says. "I got him on backup. You know, first time out and all." He grins and turns to Bas. "All you gotta do is shoot what I tell ye to."

Stanslo's frown only gets deeper. "Forgive me, Reacher, but is there a reason you have taken it upon yourself to reassign our gunner to backup?"

"Gunner?" Reacher blinks at Stanslo, wide-eyed. "Cavett's the gunner, boss."

"Cavett is a *cook*," Stanslo snaps. "And his aim is worse than Haversham's was. Which does not address the fact that I specifically assigned Bas to the cannon for the next run and you seem to have decided, all on your own, to countermand what was, in effect, a direct order from me."

"Oh." Reacher looks crestfallen, like he's just gone and

disappointed his favorite teacher and is dreadful broken up about it. "No one said."

"I'm quite certain *I* did."

"No sir, ye did—" Reacher cuts himself off. Even chokes a little. He gives Stanslo an apologetic shrug. "Mayhap you told Fox."

That makes Stanslo pause, staring at Reacher and looking, for the first time Bas has ever seen, uncertain. It's gone quickly, and Stanslo rubs at his eye like it's abruptly trying to escape his skull. He nods at Reacher. "That is not, Reacher, the way I remember it. Be that as it may, I'm telling you now—Bas is on the cannon tomorrow. You want Cavett on the job, you can have him as backup, but clear it with Lowen first."

"But." Reacher frowns. "But it's *my* job, boss. M' first, even, with my own guys. I won 'em, fair and square. You approved the bid on Fox's crystal, so now Cavett's *mine*. So are Merrin and Yanush. My job, my men, so how come Lowen gets to—"

"Reacher." It's low and soft, Stanslo pinching at the bridge of his nose now, and none of it's directed at Bas—Stanslo and Reacher might well have forgotten he's even here—but he feels the chill of it nonetheless.

Reacher swallows, says, "Yeah, boss?"

"How am I to trust you running a job, if I can't even trust you to choose your personnel properly?" Stanslo drops his hand and shakes his head at Reacher. "Just because you now own Cavett's crystal...." He pauses before he says, "No. I am not explaining myself." He turns to Bas. "I do apologize. It appears we have been remiss. I've a thing or two to discuss with Reacher, and then he will happily come to you and tell you all you need to expect tomorrow evening." He's staring at Reacher when he says that last, and Reacher nods, suitably cowed. Stanslo turns back to Bas and splits a grin. "You were right to come to me, Bas. I trust you shall do so again, should you feel it necessary."

Again, he's looking at Reacher when he says it, but Bas answers, "Of course," anyway.

They leave then, off toward Miss Hannah's, Stanslo with a nod and Reacher with a cheerful wave and a "See ya later, Bas" and, for all he looked almost sick with worry only a few minutes ago, now it's like it never happened. Bas watches Reacher tag after Stanslo, chattering at him, and Bas shakes his head.

Still fucking weird.

For all that Bas has been wanting to know what the fuck about the Bruise, he can't say he expects the start of his education to go like this:o

"A purgative?" Bas blinks at the little bottle Reacher's shoved at him and doesn't bother to hide the incredulity. He tries to shove it back. "Yeah, very funny, but I don't think so."

Reacher holds up his—*wow, pretty massive*—hands, eyebrows climbing. "No joke." He shrugs, but he doesn't take the bottle back. "Trust me, you don't wanna be goin' into the Bruise with anything in yer stomach. 'Specially if you've eaten any meat lately."

Bas stares. "What the hell does that even mean?"

"Well." Reacher's guileless face turns sly with a lopsided grin. "It en't the same out there, is it? And you won't be the same out there 'neither if ye've anything in yer stomach. It gets in you, yeah? Changes you. And things that's alive—they change the most. Even things that used to be alive." Reacher nods sagely. "'S why you don't want none o' that in ye."

Again, Bas stares. And then he narrows his eyes. "Is this one of those 'humiliate the new guy' things? Or are you just pissed off I talked to Stanslo?"

Not that Bas cares. But still. It's a *purgative*.

"No. What?" Reacher tilts his head, looking for all the world like a giant borderline-stupid puppy. He frowns at the bottle Bas is still holding as far away from his body as possible and then up at Bas. "I *said* it en't a joke, didn't I?" Now he looks like a giant borderline-stupid puppy who's been kicked for no good reason.

Bas had dozed off while he'd waited for Reacher, it's well into night now, and he might be a little bit sleep-addled, but he's definitely awake. So this isn't some particularly ludicrous dream, more's the pity.

Bas sighs and lets his arm drop. "Explain it to me slowly." Because Bas needs to play along, he can't be raising suspicions now, but still. He has no intention of spending tomorrow morning in the bogs because he fell for something he wouldn't have fallen for in his first year at the academy.

"Well," says Reacher, "the Bruise en't the same as here, see. Things as are normal here go wonky when ye get close. An' if ye got that in ye, it might change *you*. So ye take the stuff"—he waves at the bottle in Bas's hand—"and ye won't have no problems."

"Okay." Bas nods along like it's not the most bizarre thing he's heard here yet. "What d'you mean things go wonky?"

"Wonky. Like... weird. Not norm—"

"Yeah, I know what 'wonky' means, for fuck's sake. I mean wonky *how*?"

"They *change*," Reacher says, exasperated. "Like the birds and them."

Bas stares some more. Because he can't be that bad of a person that he deserves to have the one thing he really wants to know explained to him by the one person who acts like he spent most of his childhood with his head stuck in a banister.

"Birds," says Bas.

"Yeah, the ones you gotta shoot. Well, and the people, but that's only if they come after Kimo."

Okay, now it's getting somewhere. "I'm to shoot birds."

"Well, they're not birds anymore, once you get out far enough." Reacher pauses, thoughtful. "They still fly, though."

"Of course they do."

"Plus, you got the ones comin' from the other side of the Bruise. I don't think they're birds, so much as... flying things." He gives Bas a frown. "What'd ye think ye had to shoot?"

Well, now. That's a pretty good question. And it's not like Bas hasn't been trying to find out. "Bandits?"

Reacher snorts and gives Bas a punch on the arm that's ostensibly friendly but nearly sends Bas stumbling backward.

"Bandits," Reacher says, shaking his head like Bas is the one who's acting like his last few brain cells are dying of loneliness. "Only bandits here are the ones as live here. You got bigger worries, once you get out there." He jerks his chin at the door of Bas's room, presumably to indicate "out there."

"So who exactly's coming after Kimo, then?"

"Well, nobody, I hope."

"Not bandits?"

"There en't any bandits. Didn't I say?"

Bas stares. No one is this stupid. "Okay, so what, *exactly*, is the Bruise? Can you tell me that, at least?"

"A scab in the skin thinned between worlds," Reacher answers promptly, like he's reciting it. He gives Bas a look like he's expecting a pat on the head.

"And that means...?"

Reacher huffs with a roll of his eyes. "It *means* that it en't like here. It's all"—his hands wave around—"different, like. Things as en't no problem here get all ornery when you get out there."

Okay, Bas is pretty sure he's passed this same stump along the trail three times now, which means he's going in circles. "So birds change, once I get 'out there,' and they change enough that I'm going to have to shoot them."

"Well, not just birds. Everything. Animals and the like. You know. Like the ones the baron's got on his wall." Reacher nods. "They come after the stream. Like moths. 'Cept the people. They come after Kimo. But they en't bandits."

"Uh-huh." The round-and-round is getting very old, very fast. "That doesn't explain this," Bas says and holds up the bottle.

"Yeah, it does." When Bas only blinks at Reacher with raised eyebrows, Reacher rolls his eyes and his wide shoulders slump. "Animals change, see? From eating stuff as comes from over there. Even dead stuff. The meat we get from the Bruise used to be animals, yeah? And if you've been eating it...." He lets it hang there.

It's probably the first useful thing Bas has gotten out of Reacher so far. He looks down at the bottle in his hand with a grimace.

Weird, but weird isn't exactly new here.

"Except I haven't been eating meat from the Bruise."

"No?" There's a touch of mischief in Reacher's grin this time. "How was yer steak over t' Hannah's the other night?"

...Okay. Ew. But still.

"What, do you get sick or something?" Because the dubious prospect of spending some time chunking over the side of the train is still less dubious than deliberately giving himself the trots.

"Ha. No. You change, and not in good ways. And you die. Well, okay, not always. Sometimes yer stomach just explodes."

Bas gives his head a quick shake, eyes wide and incredulous, playing along, just in case, because no one's this stupid, but no one's this good either.

"And how is that different than dying?"

"Well, if yer stomach explodes, it hurts heaps, but you don't *die.*"

"*Yes,* you absolutely *do!*"

"Yeah? Huh. I thought it was only your intestines what did that."

"Pretty much anything in your body *exploding* is going to beef you, Reacher."

"Ri-i-i-i-ght." Reacher shrugs. "Okay, then yeah, you always die."

Bas scrapes a hand through his hair and knuckles at his eyes. He looks down at the bottle of purgative.

And the less said about how Bas spends his day until it's time to leave for the Bruise, the better.

The thing is, Bas has seen a lot of evil in his life. His work demands he live beside it sometimes, get to know it, see through it.

Some people are evil because they're too smart for their own good. It makes them feel superior, entitled.

Some people are evil because they're stupid. They don't have the intellect required for empathy.

Some people are evil because they're just smart enough to know how stupid they are. And it pisses them off.

And some people are evil because they're stupid enough to think they're smarter than everyone else.

Those are the ones you have to watch out for.

It's the first time Bas sees Kimolijah since getting growled at and insulted by Quinnie at the tavern.

Reacher has told him he's to collect Kimolijah and Mari from the manor house to ready for the trip, and after all the half answers and not-so-subtle changes of subject, Bas is quite frankly perishing to actually see the Bruise, even if he *is* unnerved by the prospect. So he follows Reacher's order without so much as a lift of an eyebrow or a raised hackle.

It's not as dark as it was the few other times Bas has made this same trek. The day has yet to stretch toward gloaming, two more hours 'til dusk at least, so Bas takes the opportunity to look around and see more clearly the things that have only been shadows and vague impressions before. The greenery and nigh-impossible life blooming all around is even more startling, an almost-violent gash of color in a place that's otherwise leached of it, but the flowers and the lawn and the pond and all the trappings of wealth are not what catch his eye. This time, Bas is arrested by the fields to which he hadn't before paid the proper attention. Probably because he's been paying too much attention to Kimolijah, but…. Okay, he has no 'but'. And anyway, fuck it, he's paying attention now.

Hay. Roods and roods of it, alive with fat lazy bees and bouncing hopbugs and the noisy chirrup of crickets. Wheat. Or… okay, Bas doesn't really know. He thinks it's wheat, but he's not a farmer, he's a city boy, and when he's pretending to be Jakob Barstow, he's a fugitive who either makes do with small game or whatever his current compatriots steal or rustle. When he's just Bas, food comes from the butchers and the shops and the hasheries. He wouldn't know how to grow his own if it walked up to him and handed him a knife and a cookpot. So he can't say he knows what's growing out there, wheat or rye or anything else edible. It doesn't really matter. Stanslo's Bridge is supposed to be an agro settlement, yeah, all right, but this… weatherTech aside, it's impressive.

Bas is still standing there, eyeing up the flora, probably with an intensely unattractive blank look on his face, when Mari and Kimolijah emerge from around the back of the house and head to where Bas stands on the cusp of the path up to the front porch. They're both dressed in a color that's not black or blue, but some kind of dusky hue in between Bas can't really name. They almost match in their heavy-looking fitted shirts and high collars, snug trousers tucked into tall boots. Mari's wearing black leather gloves, and Bas can see a matching pair tucked into Kimolijah's… well, it should probably be a belt but it looks more like a sash, several lengths of dark cloth wrapped around Kimolijah's lean torso at the waist, tucked in tight and secure. When they get closer, Bas can see that Kimolijah's taken it all a step further, with what look like scarves wrapped around the top of each boot and tied firm. There are matching ones at each wrist, straps buckled around sleeves and trouser legs, and he's carrying another scarf that he drapes around his neck as he and Mari get closer to where Bas is standing and staring at them.

Strapped down and tucked in, and *oh crap*, Bas thinks as they come closer and closer, *Kimolijah's trousers are fucking* leather. *How unfair is that?*

They both have their hair pulled back tight, and Kimolijah's got those stupid goggles on top of his head again, though they at least look clean for once. His glance roves all over the place, everywhere but at Bas, and he looks like he's aiming to skirt right on by without acknowledgment, but a smile slides onto Mari's face—too knowing and not at all nice—and she takes hold of Kimolijah's arm and pulls him with her. Right up to Bas.

"Ma'am," says Bas and gives the brim of his hat a light touch for respect.

Mari eyes him up and down for a moment before she wraps both hands around Kimolijah's arm, like she thinks he's going to make a break for it. By the way he's avoiding looking at either one of them, Bas thinks maybe Kimolijah will.

"So, Kimo," Mari says, clearly enjoying whatever she's meaning to do, "this is your new Travis. Or Haversham, I suppose. Fox?" She pulls a pretty frown. "No, not Fox, I suppose." She shakes her head and shrugs. "I'm afraid I'm quite losing track, the way you seem to go through them."

Bas sees Kimolijah's jaw clench and his hands close into fists, but he doesn't look at either Bas or Mari and he doesn't say anything.

"Although," Mari goes on, "we can hope he won't require the same sort of... education." Her tone sounds like she's aiming for sympathetic, though her smile is anything but. When Kimolijah merely squints up at the sky to watch Jessa circle overhead, Mari turns to Bas. "Have you ever been whipped... I'm sorry, Bas, wasn't it?"

Bas narrows his eyes at her for a moment before he lets his gaze drift to Kimolijah. Kimolijah's still watching Jessa, but there's a muscle ticcing in his jaw and he's breathing kind of hard.

"Yes, ma'am," Bas tells Mari. "The name is Bas. And no, I've never been whipped." For some reason, he wants to put a hand on his gun, but he makes himself stand still. "Not really something you run across much back...." He pauses and waves his hand around, trying to think how to put it, before he settles for, "On the other side."

"Mm," Mari hums, nodding agreement. "I don't recommend it here, either. We haven't got a medTech, you know. It's all bandages and makeshift poultices, and the pain only gets worse when infection sets in. Poor Travis didn't live long enough for that, though, so I suppose you could see it as a blessing. You know, like Fox." She pauses to give Kimolijah a level look, but Kimolijah ignores her. Mari brightens her smile and says, "Well, I guess we'll never know about Fox, but Travis cried like a baby toward the end, though good thing he was practically delirious." Her pretty mouth turns down in an insincere moue of sympathy.

"He'll never have to know he was begging for his mam." She sighs. "Says a lot about a man, the things he babbles while—"

Kimolijah finally shakes her loose with a growl and actually pulls his fist back like he's going to punch her when she makes a grab for him. She *grins*, gleeful, and says, "Oh, please? Come on." She lifts her chin like she's giving him a better target. "You know you want to."

Kimolijah doesn't do it, but yeah, he looks like he really, really wants to—and Bas kinda does, too—and Kimolijah doesn't uncurl his fist as he backs away. "You go too far, Mari."

"And you never go *quite* far enough, do you?"

The look on Kimolijah's face goes dark, feral rage in those light brown eyes, the white of the left one still blotched red with broken blood vessels. Kimolijah flicks the look between Bas and Mari, then curls his lip, snide. "You two don't need me for this... *discussion*." He spits it. "I'm sure you'll find plenty to talk about without me here. You've got a lot in common."

"Have we now." The tone of Mari's voice is flat and the look on her face is pure, profound hatred.

"Oh yeah," says Kimolijah. He shoots Bas another glare and then bares his teeth at Mari in a nasty smile. "You're both mercenary whores. You both *want* to be here. Says a lot about a person, the things he'll do for a little bit of power. Or she."

Mari laughs, a high, pleased giggle, and leans against Bas's side as she almost doubles over. "Oh God—*whore*! That's such a good one, Kimo. And it came out without even a touch of irony. Good on you!"

"Yeah, you enjoy it," Kimolijah tells her, calmer now, his voice more even. "For now, at least. While it lasts. Because you're going to rot here with the rest of us, Mari, and you're not even going to see it coming until you're helping your replacement move into the master bedroom and telling her which side of the bed is hers."

Mari sobers abruptly at that, and she loses her smile. "You know, you really can't talk to me like that."

This time, Kimolijah's mouth pulls into something between a smirk and a sneer. "I can talk to you any goddamned way I want." He flings Mari a rude gesture and stalks off down the path. "Being your minion is not in my contract, Mari."

"Oh, I know *exactly* what's in your contract," Mari says, sweet and deadly. "I helped write it, didn't I?"

"Not likely to forget it, am I." Kimolijah turns around and walks backward, eyes narrowed at Mari. "And if you'd known what most of the big words meant, we wouldn't be having a problem now, would we?" He turns and starts off again. "If your 'charms' were enough to keep his attention," he calls, cutting, "maybe you'd both be a little less bitchy." He flips her off over his shoulder and keeps going.

The look in Mari's eyes is murderous as she grits her teeth and glares daggers at Kimolijah's back. It lasts for maybe a second or two, and then Bas has another second or two to decide what to do about it when she goes after Kimolijah, because she's heeled—a sleek little four-barrel—and reaching for her gun when she takes off, and Bas is kind of stuck between probably-should-not-assault-boss's-bondmate and probably-should-protect-boss's-bit-on-the-side. Especially after what happened with Fox and the bird and the incidental punch to Kimolijah's face that cost way more all around than Bas had figured. And anyway, it's not in Bas to just stand here and watch, so he goes after Mari and wrestles the gun from her hand before she has a chance to shoot Kimolijah in the back, like it appears she intends, or turn it on Bas.

And okay. Bas had thought Kimolijah has a filthy mouth. Mari is in a class of her own. She's screaming epithets at the top of her lungs—everything from the size of Bas's dick to what she's going to feed it to when she gets loose—so it's not really surprising when the ruckus attracts attention from the house. Bas can't tell if he's grateful or not, because there's still the whole assaulting-the-boss's-bondmate thing, but Mari is tall and not at all delicate, and she kicks like a goddamned *mule*, and Bas is probably going to need some antiseptic for all the scratches. He hangs on for as long as he can, and it's less about making sure she doesn't shoot Kimolijah now and more about Bas trying to minimize the damage to himself.

Edlyn comes bursting out onto the porch, watches for a few seconds that seem much longer to Bas, and then she's a flurry of skirts and apron and loud shouts for "Baron! *Baron!*" as she hustles down the steps. Stanslo is a few seconds behind her, followed by Lowen, so Stanslo misses it when Mari instantly composes herself and stills in Bas's grip. Bas has still got hold of Mari's wrists, but she's not fighting him anymore—she's *smiling* at him, poised though cruel, and the second Stanslo gets close enough to ask, "What is all this?" Mari's smile is gone completely.

She turns to Stanslo, abruptly teary-eyed and shaking, and rolls out a thin little sob. "I don't know!" she cries, voice wavering. "He got a little handsy with Kimo and then he just *attacked* me!"

Bas takes that in, repeats it to himself just to make sure he heard it right, and instantly understands. And what a neat setup it is. He tries to think of a reason why Mari might want him dead, but nothing comes.

Face blank but for a roll of the eyes at Mari, Bas bends and scoops up the gun he'd taken from her and dropped to the grass during the fuss. He flips it, checks it, then slips the guard between the strike stud and the first barrel.

The sigh Bas lets loose is deliberately long-suffering, and he holds the gun out in the palm of his hand. He waits until Lowen takes it from him before he turns to Mari and says, "For God's sake, if you're going to try to get me killed, at least do me the courtesy of saying I got a little more out of the deal than a cheap grope." He turns to Stanslo and cocks a thumb at Mari. "Please tell me *she* isn't why Travis is a bag of bones tied to a whipping post."

Stanslo isn't smiling. That soulless animal lurking behind blue eyes is back, only it's not a there-and-gone flicker like it had been before; it's a full-on fixed *stare*, wrathful and cold, and it's not aimed at Bas. It takes Mari a second or two too long to register it, but when she does, she goes absolutely still.

"Oh," she says, small, and she shifts closer to Bas, like he might protect her. "Baron?" It's shaky and the hitch at the end turns it into a question. "It was only a joke. I didn't... I mean, I wasn't—"

"Lowen," says Stanslo, still looking steadily at Mari, and when Lowen grunts back a "Yeah, boss?" Stanslo finally smiles, a shark's smile. "Escort Mari down to the train, if you please."

Lowen shuffles for a moment, apparently unsure what to do with Mari's gun, whether he should give it back or not; he ends up tucking it into his own belt and says, "Sure, boss," as he reaches out and clamps his hand to Mari's arm.

Mari's hazel eyes have misted over, and it looks like she might be getting nauseous. "Just a bad joke." It's wobbly this time, uncertain. She looks over her shoulder at Stanslo as Lowen starts to lead her away. "Baron? I mean, you know I wouldn't—"

"Lowen," Stanslo interrupts. His eyes haven't left Mari once since he arrived on the scene, and his mouth twitches up at one corner in a knowing smirk. "I think Mari's services will be needed at the way station for a bit longer than I'd anticipated." He lifts his eyebrows at Mari. "You can pick her up on the way back from next week's run."

Mari startles and tries to pull away from Lowen. "Baron, no. *No.* I didn't—we were only joking. It wasn't.... Bas, tell him. It wasn't—"

Stanslo holds up his hand. He doesn't say a word, his expression doesn't change, but it halts both Mari and Lowen and silences anything Mari might want to say next. Lowen is staring at Bas, just *staring*, like he's trying to see through him and not succeeding, or maybe like he's expecting Bas to do something. Bas doesn't know what, and he doesn't think it's a good idea to even remind anyone he's here right now, so he just frowns at Lowen and shrugs. Weirdly, Lowen gives him a quick, shallow nod, like they've reached an unspoken agreement; Bas really wishes he knew what kind.

With a tilt of his head, Stanslo steps slowly over to Mari, looks her up and down, then brushes the backs of his knuckles over her cheek, affectionate. "It's my own fault," he says, soft. "I allowed it to continue and hoped you'd work it out between you.

I wanted you to be friends, you see. It would make life so much more pleasant for us all." He shakes his head, rueful. "I do apologize, Mari dear, but there is a threshold, and you have attempted actual physical harm to something very important to me. To us all. To everything we've built and will build. I can't allow one person, no matter how precious to me, to jeopardize everything we've—"

"I would never!" Mari's definitely shaking now, and her tone is strident, desperate. "It's *him*! It's always *him*! Have you forgotten Travis already? Do you think for a second Kimo would hesitate to betray you again if he could find a willing cock to s—"

She's on the ground before she can finish, holding her cheek where Stanslo backhanded her, hard. She's crying. Stanslo nods at Lowen, who gives Bas another incomprehensible look before leaning down to drag Mari back onto her feet.

"Do try not to lose too much weight while you're away, Mari dear," says Stanslo. "I do quite like your curves." And when Mari whimpers and cries, *"No,* you can't—" Stanslo sets his jaw and says, "I'll be down shortly to see Kimo off. Bas, a word."

It seems like it sucks all the air out of Mari's lungs, and she stares at Stanslo, eyes wild and betrayed, before she looks at Bas with a silent plea. Bas is glad Lowen drags her away then, because he wants to answer that appeal, whatever bones of honor and gallantry he's got down deep trying to rise up and unfurl in defense of the helpless, and blaring *Tech in trouble!* at him, trying to galvanize him into defending someone at a disadvantage against a bully. It's weird, because he'd taken rather an instant dislike to Mari, and what she just tried to pull is pretty reprehensible. But he's standing here and knowingly watching something utterly wrong happen, and it makes him feel like a traitorous coward. Except Bas knows, he *knows* that trying to intervene will do nothing but give Stanslo another target at which to direct the rage Bas can still see seething beneath the perpetual jovial surface, and Bas can't risk it.

Funny thing—Bas has only been here a short while. He still doesn't know everything, still can't figure out the motivations of some of these people. But he can see very clearly that Stanslo is starting to lose it. He's gotten just a little bit crazier each day Bas has been here, Bas can see the slippage. Maybe it's the string of events that started with Travis, or maybe it's just the end of a natural progression and it's mere happenstance that Bas is here to see it. But Baron Petra Stanslo is getting less stable by the day, and he's moving too quickly from *dangerous* to *cordite just starting to sweat.*

Bas merely shakes his head and says, "What the fuck?" as he glares at Stanslo, and he doesn't try to school it into something a little more acceptable.

And God, it's so unnerving and a little bit sickening when Stanslo turns to him and fucking *grins.* It's light again, happy, like the past ten minutes never even happened, or maybe he's glad they did.

"I'm sorry you had to see that," Stanslo says, and he shrugs with a what-are-you-going-to-do? smile that's weirdly self-deprecating. "But it couldn't be helped, you see. I must set an example, Bas. And those closest to me must be above reproach. I cannot abide pettiness in my own household. And I won't be told no. I can't allow it."

Bas presses his lips together and resists rolling his eyes. Stanslo gives him a sharp look and then chuckles. He sets a hand to Bas's shoulder and starts leading him down toward the station.

"You think I'm, perhaps, being grandiose? That I'm speaking in empty exaggerations and not saying exactly what I mean?"

"I wouldn't know, Baron," Bas says carefully. "I don't think I know you well enough to say." Everything in Bas has gone abruptly hyperalert, more than even five minutes ago, because he's getting the feeling that Stanslo *wants* him to press, wants him to ask for some kind of "guidance" on how to get your toys to behave themselves. And Bas, having decided that he's very nearly all out of fucks to give, that he's *this close* to just shooting Stanslo in the head and taking his chances, decides it's weirdly freeing, in a dangerous well-it-can't-get-me-in-a-*worse*-position-can-it sort of way. "Enlighten me, then," Bas says and cocks his head to peer at Stanslo, letting the skepticism shine through in his gaze, hoping Stanslo will take it as a challenge.

Bas doesn't know if he does or not, but Stanslo grins at him and says, "You asked me last night how I manage to... I believe 'cow my people' was how you put it. I prefer to think of it more as benevolent control."

Bas lifts his eyebrows. "Benevolent control." He seems to remember that exact term from history texts. Slavers' idiom.

"It's a simple matter of taking the 'no' away." Stanslo thumps Bas's shoulder and stops, gazing down the path ahead them. "You take 'no' away from a man and he can only ever give you 'yes.'" His mouth quirks. "And if he's particularly difficult about it, *stubborn*...." He trails off, blue eyes honing in on where Bas can see Kimolijah still stalking down the path, almost to the trainyard now, and then Stanslo's smile softens and he sighs, almost regretful. "Then you make him pay for every 'no' he ever gave you with every 'yes' you force out of him forever after."

He's gone from "enlightening" Bas on how to deal with a bondmate to a prideful sideways boast on how to yoke a bit-on-the-side. Bas wonders if Stanslo is just *that obsessed* that everything eventually comes around to Kimolijah. Unfortunately, Bas can almost relate.

Stanslo snorts. Like it's *funny*. "Do you think, Bas," he says slowly, "you would be able to tell me no, if the answer I wanted from you was yes?" He grins, and it's colder than Bas has seen up 'til now, and yet madly gleeful at the same time.

Bas doesn't even think about his answer, just says, "I have no problem believing you get every single thing you want, Baron," because it's the truth, and Bas has no doubt it's exactly what Stanslo wants to hear.

"You impress me more every time we chat, Bas." Stanslo claps Bas on the back and starts leading the way down to the station again. "You won't leave your gun," Stanslo says, and Bas can feel that skittering *whump* flutter at him and over him, and it's just as disturbing as it was when Stanslo did it during "contract negotiations" but, as it was then, it's more like whatever it is wings Bas and glances off. "I've no doubt Reacher has impressed the importance of your role in all this upon you, but I don't think there's such a thing as stressing this too much." He pauses and narrows his eyes. "Reacher did tell you what to expect on this trip, yes?"

"I feel much more prepared than I did," is all Bas will commit to.

"Good." Stanslo's hand grips Bas's shoulder harder, enough to deaden nerves if he'd hit the right spot. "You will ensure they come nowhere near the train. You will ensure they come nowhere near Kimo."

Who? Bas wants to ask, but he doesn't want to say or imply anything that might get Reacher killed, not until he knows if he should. Anyway, he's heard enough to make some guesses.

"I doubt," Stanslo goes on, "I have to tell you what will happen should you arrive back here with my possessions in anything less than perfect working order."

Bas wants to clench his teeth, but he doesn't. He merely says, "No, sir, you do not."

"Good." Stanslo thumps Bas's shoulder, approving. "I knew when I met you, Bas. There is truly, though perhaps somewhat clichéd, honor among thieves. When Oleg told me about you, I knew. And when I met you...." He shakes his head with a smile. "*Here*, I thought, here is one who respects a man's claim, be it his or another's. Here is a man who understands the consequences of the alternative." He turns and grins at Bas. "Wisdom, I've no doubt, your dear departed uncle wished he'd possessed."

Bas looks straight ahead, concentrates on his steps and on keeping his mouth shut and on not throwing Stanslo's hand off him and knocking him out cold until Bas can decide whether or not to just blast his way to the train and hijack it back to the real world, or just say *fuck it* and shoot Stanslo outright now. God, wouldn't he just love to tell Stanslo all about what happened in the barn, just to see his face before Bas finally blows his head off for him.

He thinks back to dinner in Stanslo's dining room beneath the glass gazes of disembodied animal heads and thinks *Trophies. It's all about trophies and control.* And Mari and Kimolijah, and probably even Bas now, are all just more sets of dead eyes in the menagerie. The schemes Stanslo has going out here are important to him, yeah, but the trophies—thumbing his nose at the Territories and the Directorate; stealing Techs and making them build bits of "his world" for him; controlling his slave labor workforce with all this weird Tech and dynamic crystals—the *trophies* are what really count here. And every person here in Stanslo's Bridge is just another dead animal head on Stanslo's wall, impotently watching as Stanslo takes what he needs from them while he goes for the big prize that's his endgame.

Bas can't help wondering what Stanslo's head would look like mounted on a wall.

17.

It's almost the same tableau but in reverse. This time, instead of clamping the vambrace on Kimolijah's arm at gunpoint, Stanslo removes it while Lowen points his big gun at Kimolijah's head.

Bas watches it all from his little roost atop the engine's cab, his fingers running over the barrel and stock and the lever that serves as a trigger for the giant gridcannon on its mount. He doesn't swing the gun around and point it at Stanslo, but he wants to.

He didn't get a good look the last time because he hadn't known he should. He looks now, though. Bas had thought the white streaks were somehow cured when the bracelet went back on, but now he's heard Kimolijah's truncated explanation and *burr bug*, and the seemingly random bosh before it about worms and brains. The welts are there now, smaller, the corkscrew shapes hidden before by the coils of the metal, and the skin that edges the white is red and irritated. It's welted in the shape of the bracelet itself, like something's burrowed underneath and festering, and something sick curls in Bas's gut. There are dots of blood that well in wispy threads over which Stanslo tuts as he dabs at them with a handkerchief until Kimolijah pulls away—slowly, eyes flicking between Stanslo and the barrels of Lowen's gun the whole while.

Mari watches from the tiny passenger car, sat between Cavett and Serenat. Mari stares at Stanslo with something Bas can't read. He kind of expected her to look pissed or scared or something, because she certainly wasn't pleased only a little while ago. But she doesn't look like she's any of those things. She looks thoughtful, almost calculating, as she watches Stanslo through the open door, until her glance shifts up to Bas, and then her expression morphs into the spined-up, petulant lines from before.

"Don't take too long this time," Stanslo tells Kimolijah, soft and with a tender caress up Kimolijah's arm as the bracelet comes away. "I'll see you up at the house when you get back." Stanslo backs up until he's a full ten paces away from Kimolijah, and then, with a pointed look, he lifts an eyebrow at Lowen until

Lowen lowers his gun. It's the first time Bas has seen Stanslo move away from Kimolijah, well out of reach, instead of taking the smallest opportunity to put his hands on him.

Kimolijah says nothing for a moment, only looks back at Stanslo, face blank, before he mutters, "Yeah, whatever," and climbs into the cab. "Everybody move," he says from inside.

Reacher takes this as his cue to jump up into the passenger car, Yanush and Merrin following with obvious reluctance, maybe even a bit of fear. They haven't been to the Bruise before, from what they said the other night, and neither of them are happy about it, but since they're now Reacher's men—won in an *auction*, for fuck's sake—Reacher now calls the shots for them, and he says they go.

Everyone milling around the tracks takes several steps back. When they're clear, the engine whines to life, and Bas is abruptly caged on three sides by gridstream zapping between the prongs and poles and the lattice wired together on the cab's roof.

And goddamn it, *why* hadn't he realized this before? He'd seen the train running, he'd bloody *watched* the damned thing all the way from the first way station beyond Harrowgate, and it hadn't occurred to him until now that he'd be sitting inside blue sputtering death while perched behind a giant impossible gun atop a train heading out into the desert toward... whatever the Bruise is.

And okay, it's... not actually that bad. First of all, Bas manages not to scream. Just barely, but still. His manly veneer is safe for another... hour. Whatever. Second of all, the stream isn't jumping the contacts, isn't straying from its path along the prongs and wires and coils; not so much as an errant spark jigs the circuit. Any discharge witters along what Bas has been, since the first time he saw the train, thinking of as some kind of rigged fence and along the wiring that feeds into the conduits down the side of the cab.

Gridstream wants the ground, Bas remembers from his Basic Tech classes, where he'd learned the minimum he'd have to know about every kind of Tech in order to qualify for a spot in the Directorate. Gridstream wants the ground, and as long as you give it an easy path to it, it won't bother with a side-trip through you. Bas watches the bright blue streams pulsing along the fence that surrounds him on three sides and thinks *Yeah, okay, as long as I don't move more than six feet in any direction, I might not get fried.*

Which is... really not that much of a reassurance.

It's uncomfortable as hell. The constant *buzz-hum* and the occasional thin *pop* is going to get to him eventually, he can tell already, and the proximity of the stream straightens every hair on Bas's body at the root. He feels like a puffed-up porcupine, and he's glad for the hat keeping the hair on his head plastered to his skull where it belongs.

No wonder Kimolijah's always got his hair slicked back tight when he's working.

Nonconductive, Bas keeps telling himself. The floor is glass, the gun is ceramic, and as long as he doesn't touch anything else up here, he should be fine.

No, really. *Fine.*

◌◌◌◌◌

There was a cover, once, on a *Stockton Misfits*—year 6, series 7, issue 13—back when Bas was a boy. The hero, Dirk Darkling (yeah, fine, but Bas had thought it was pretty ace at the time), was pictured in semisilhouette, standing on the roof of a racing coach, full-up heeled, backlit by the *Misfits'* world's three moons, black duster flared out behind him in the wind. His wide-brimmed hat shadowed his face, so all one could see were his square jaw and the determined set of it, and a hint of fierce eyes glaring out from the gloom. Bas very nearly gave up his allegiance to Magic Man for Dirk Darkling, but then Magic Man managed to defeat Casius Cruel with what amounted to nothing more than a dirty look, and Bas decided appearances weren't everything. (And, okay, Magic Man can shoot death rays from his eyes, so a dirty look is more like getting shot with the sun, but the point still stands.)

Still, Bas feels a little like Dirk Darkling standing up here on the speeding train, nothing but his grip on the gridcannon and a thick leather lanyard clamped to the roof to hold him steady, flying through the desert gloaming with his coat whipping around behind him. It lasts until reality trounces residual heroic illusions.

The trip to the way station is uneventful enough to actually be boring. Bas watches for monster birds or horror dogs or any of the other weird desert dwellers he's seen up on Stanslo's wall. There's nothing. The only thing halfway interesting about the trip thus far is that Kimolijah's bird never stops following, soaring above and ahead sometimes, and other times swooping in through the open door of the cab, presumably to visit with Kimolijah for a spell.

They hadn't pulled out of the station until dusk was an impending inevitability, and it's not like the landscape offers anything riveting. Dust and hardpan give gradually to broad swathes of sand and scrub. Starlight traces slick across the horizon, blots the dunes a hazy midnight blue, wide and away. Bas is staring into rolling darkness and more rolling darkness, and it's fucking *cold* up here. The wind beats at him, which is bad enough, but it picks up dust and sand along its way, and it stings. He closes up his coat and pulls up his scarf to cover his mouth and nose, but it makes him have to hunch a little, and he can't keep a good eye on the sky this way. He finally sees the sense in those stupid goggles Kimolijah wears, and wonders if he might happen to have an extra set with him.

Not that Bas needs to be watching quite so diligently, apparently. He's been up here staring at nothing for bloody *hours*—

okay, maybe one—and has yet to see anything more threatening than a few moles standing on their hind legs and staring as the train goes by. There might have been a small pack of wolves, or maybe those mutant not-dogs, but they never got close enough for Bas to tell.

They're pulling five cars besides the tiny passenger car, laden and packed to the walls. Three of the cars contain nothing but those black cubes, and Bas still hasn't gotten a real answer about what they are except the nonsensical "water" response he'd gotten when he asked, but he's seen the placement of them on those stumpy water towers. Filters. Which means, whatever's out at the Bruise, where the poison from the Saltons is even more concentrated and toxic than it is in Stanslo's Bridge, it's just as water-dependent as everything else, and the cubes are meant as barter.

The gridstream doesn't so much as flicker toward the other cars, which is good, because they're just regular freight cars, made of iron and consequently conductive. But for the passenger coach, the rest of the cars don't have the same glass and ceramic safety stops the engine has. Even Bas, surrounded by live gridstream as he is, would be safer up here than anyone in those cars would be, should a current go wandering.

It makes him pause and think about that half-built engine Kimolijah's been working on, and then it makes him peer around himself and trace the construct, think about those diagrams and schematics of Kimolijah's that Bas studied back in Knapston and hadn't entirely understood. It makes him think about the nature of gridstream and how it applies to gridTech, how it's not supposed to work like this, and yet it obviously does. He hadn't really thought about it when he'd watched the streams flow over the engine on the way in from Harrowgate, but now that he's seen what Kimolijah's been working on, he can trace the pulse and direction of the blue glow over the fencing, and all those plans and equations almost make sense. And maybe Bas would have to be gridTech to get it completely, or maybe he'd actually have to be Kimolijah, but he can see the outlines and the ghosts of the constructs almost clicking into place. Except.

Okay, it has to have been at least a couple hours by now. Bas is bored, he's cold, and he's sick of watching the nothing of the desert dark. And he wants to know. And, for whatever reason, when Kimolijah leaves Stanslo's Bridge, the bracelet that zaps him every time he says something Stanslo doesn't want him to stays with Stanslo.

Bas unhooks the clips from the lanyard holding him to the roof of the cab, careful to keep out of the path of the gridstream, and goes facedown on the glass platform. He doesn't have to maneuver too much; he merely slides over toward the edge, takes off his hat so he doesn't lose it, and ducks his head over the side.

Upside-down Kimolijah looks just as bored as Bas is, except he'd been smart enough to bring along something to read. One of the *Magic Man* illobooks, Bas is rather unduly smug to note. It's bright in the cab, gridlight glowing white-blue and nipping shadows rampant and sharp in monochrome. It mutes the colorful illustrations somewhat and turns them flat.

Kimolijah's stretched out in his pilot's seat, feet up on one of the consoles that line the walls and illobook spread out over his lap. The goggles are on top of his head again, and the scarf he'd worn loose before is now wrapped tight around his neck. His gloves are off and he's chewing away at a fingernail. Bas stares at Kimolijah's wide mouth a little too long, which is how he twigs that the white streaks have already started to travel down to Kimolijah's fingers. They're thin and small, like petechial veins in a bloodshot eye but white instead of red, and noticeable against his dark skin.

You took too long, Bas remembers Stanslo saying, and he wonders how long it takes for those welts to... do whatever it is they do. Kimolijah seemed somewhat sick and shaky before the bracelet went back on, and the streaks had been thick and expanding, so Bas assumes it's nothing good. And he wonders why. If that bracelet is a way for Stanslo to control Kimolijah, why take it off the only time Kimolijah is out from under Stanslo's eye? Especially if having it off affects Kimolijah the way it seems to, because—regardless of coercion and "taking 'no' away" and whatever else is between Kimolijah and Stanslo—Stanslo seems pretty determined that Kimolijah stays alive and healthy.

Bas will ask that later. Right now, he wants to know about all this gridstream sizzling around up here. So he asks, "Hey, the stream distribution princ—" which is as far as he gets before Kimolijah squawks, curses, and jolts so hard he falls out of his pilot's chair. The illobook goes flying at Jessa, her talons tucked around the grip of a pretty important-looking lever behind Kimolijah's chair; she bleats a few offended whistles and fluffs out her tail and wings, but she doesn't leave her perch. She nails Bas with a beady eye, though; it's that, more than Kimolijah on the floor, that makes Bas say, "Whoops, sorry, didn't mean to scare you."

Kimolijah gives him an incredulous look, mutters a few "cocksucking motherfuckers," among other things, before he props up on his elbows and snaps, "What the *hell* is wrong with you?"

"Lots of things," Bas says and doesn't hide the grin. "Sorry," he says again, then, "The stream distribution principle on that other train is different than this one, isn't it? You're not going to need the light show up top here once you get that one running, are you? But all those magnets are still a mystery, because I can't figure how they're going to do anything but choke the stream and force a backwash burst."

Kimolijah stares. And *stares*. And then he narrows his eyes. "Who the hell *are* you?"

And that's a really good question, isn't it? Bartholomew Eisen, *but call me Bas*—because no one is allowed to call him Bartholomew except his mam and da and his brother when he's cruising for a mild dustup—Grade 3 Tracker with the Directorate of the Consolidated Territories, who's pretending to be Jakob Barstow, who doesn't actually exist.

"I already told you who I am," Bas says. "I'm not your enemy. I'm not here to spy on you. I'm here to help."

"Yeah, well, with what Stanslo said yest—"

"What Stanslo said yesterday was a load of *mine-mine-mine* horseshit. Come on, you're a fucking genius. You're certainly smarter than *this*." Bas's tone has gone angry and impatient, so he takes a long, calming breath. "He's trying to make sure I don't get too close to you, get it? Why would he say what he said if he wanted you to trust me so I could spy on you? He's not stupid. He had to know it would make you do the exact opposite. He's trying to make sure whatever happened with Travis won't happ—"

"Which is pretty much what an enemy spy would say." Kimolijah untangles an ankle from the long, coiling cord that connects his shunt to the engine's heart. "Go away, will you? I'm not fucking you in the cab of my train."

Bas's mind goes absolutely blank for a few seconds, because God, that hadn't even occurred to him a second ago, but now his libido latches on to it and starts wailing in protest of the preemptive denial. Bas clears his throat and says, "Good, because I wasn't going to let you," which is a *filthy blatant lie* and his libido knows it.

Kimolijah stands up, snatches up the illobook, and shoves it back behind his chair, like he's hoping Bas didn't see it. "Look, there's nothing to spy *on*." His shoulders are tight as he angles over to one of the consoles and gives all the dials and toggles a once-over. "Can you just... please—I'm asking you to *please* just tell him I'm doing my job, and if he'd just *let me* and stop yanking me away every other hour so he can—"

He stops, clenches his teeth. His eyes go reflexively to the place where his bracelet isn't, too telling.

"It's not there," Bas says, and with the wind and the whine of the engine and the *thwacka-thwacka* of the wheels on the tracks, he doesn't think Kimolijah heard him. So he says, "Oh, fuck it," and he backs up, flips around, and swings down into the cab. Kimolijah startles and turns around, backed up against his console, like he's afraid, so Bas holds up his hands. "The bracelet's gone. You can say what you want." He lifts his eyebrows, deliberately challenging. "Can't you? I bet you could even tell him no if you wanted to, couldn't you?"

"What's that supposed to mean?"

"Got a little lesson from the baron just before we left." Bas pauses and juts his chin. "About how to take 'no' away from a man." He gives Kimolijah a pointed look. "And then how to punish him with 'yes.' But I suspect you know—"

"Shut up." It's very, very quiet, but laced with warning. "Just... shut up."

Bas won't. And okay, it's not what he intended to ask, but... well, apparently, it's what he really wants to know because it just kind of came gushing out at the first opportunity. And there's the not-so-small fact that he's getting somewhere— nowhere pleasant, he can tell already—but somewhere; there's a reaction, so he can't stop.

Bas looks Kimolijah in the eye and says, "Resaniji." Kimolijah sucks in a short, sharp breath, startled dismay, and Bas takes another step in. "I've seen her. I've spoken to her, Kimoli—"

"*Don't!*" Kimolijah takes a reckless step in before he stops, hand up, and the only reason Bas doesn't take a quick step back is because there's no little blue ball of gridstream fizzing in Kimolijah's palm. "Don't," Kimolijah says again, anger and alarm grating it frayed at the seams. "*God*, just... just *leave her out of it*, you don't have to—" He cuts it off and groans, angry but horribly desperate too. It looks like he might actually cry. "He promised. He *swore*. I'm doing it, all right? He'll have his train and he'll have his *goddamned* crystals." He flings his arm toward the windscreen. "You think I *want* Res—" He bites it off with a snarl. "I'm not about to give Stanslo another weapon."

Oh wow, motherlode. Bas licks his lips and makes himself stand still.

"But, see, you *are* giving him weapons, aren't you?" Bas holds up his hands when Kimolijah's teeth clench tight. "Hey, look, I get it. You've gotta do what you've gotta do. Someone takes your da and threatens to take your sister, you give him what he wants, you make deals, you chip away at your own morals until all you are, even in your own mind, is a thing to trade to keep the people you love alive." He pauses, genuine sympathy. "It's really unfortunate for you that the things you're bargaining with are also the things that are going to keep you here, Stanslo's pet sparker and bedmate on demand, until there's nothing else left of you."

Kimolijah's jaw quivers, and somehow the red blotch of broken blood vessels taking up half the white of his left eye makes him look young and horribly vulnerable. "You don't know *any*—"

"Except I do. I've *seen* it. I've beefed a dozen Stanslos. I've put more in a Directorate hole so deep and dark they *wish* I'd killed them. I know how these things end, Kimolijah, and it's never pretty, but they *do* eventually *end*."

"Stop saying that." It's hoarse, almost a whisper, but rough and clotted. "Stop pretending you're Directorate. At least give me that." Kimolijah's face pulls into a horrible, pained grimace before he masters himself, expression prickle-sharp and cold now, and he draws himself up. He shakes his head. "He's the cruelest man I know." Stanslo, obviously. "I didn't know people could *be* so cruel until I saw him smiling and chuckling while he tortured people for fun. *Liking* it. Making it a fucking game, because that's a good time for him, that's *entertainment*, him and his goddamned *games*. But this...." He trails off and his hands fist. "This is the lowest yet." He looks right at Bas, gaze on fire and brutal as a punch to the throat. "And *fuck you* for playing along, because *I'm not falling for it*."

Bas has to pause and think, because *goddamn*, life in Stanslo's Bridge is bad enough, but now Bas is getting a glimpse of the sheer depth of what these people have—*Kimolijah has*—been living with, and it's awful and it's sick, and it's going to make convincing Kimolijah about a hundred times harder than Bas has been anticipating. It's also going to make it a hundred times riskier, but what the hell. Bas doesn't like to lose, and he especially doesn't like the notion of losing to Baron fucking Stanslo.

"Okay," Bas says eventually, and he nods, rubs at his mouth, and levels a steady look on Kimolijah. "Resaniji calls you 'Lijah," he says and holds up a staying hand when it looks like Kimolijah's going to jump him and start swinging. "She's not terribly fond of the Directorate at the moment. Thinks we should've found your murderer ages ago. And she's right, see, but all we had to go on were two sets of blackened bones and a crystal you shouldn't've had." Bas stops and shakes his head with a low, cheerless snort. "She especially didn't like me—called me a 'goddamned bloodhound Tech-wannabe' and wanted to know how it was I couldn't sniff out the man who killed you before Travis managed to get his message through." He pauses when Kimolijah jolts, and Bas crooks a tiny, rueful smile. "Yeah, he got it through. Which, I suspect, would mean a lot to him, since I'm pretty sure he died for it. I'm pretty sure the scryTech at the relay office in Harrowgate died for it too, but I doubt he knew that."

He takes a step in but keeps his hands to his sides, unthreatening. "That's how I got here. I'd been looking, see, but that was the break I needed, and now here I am. So let me tell you what I've managed to figure out since I stepped off your impossible train and into Stanslo's little desert hell." He narrows his eyes and tilts his head. "Oleg and Dutter came to see you and your da in Knapston, told you Stanslo was impressed with the little you'd told him about what you were doing with those dynamic crystals you weren't supposed to be asking him for, and when you wouldn't agree to come to Stanslo's Bridge to meet him, maybe give him a demonstration, Oleg got two thugs to come and get you. And then, once they did the hard part for him, he left their burnt-up bones for the necroTechs to identify as you and your da, because there was no one else they could've been, and everyone knows cinder is the one dead thing a necroTech can't see into."

He points to Kimolijah's arm. "You got your burr bug shortly after arriving, I'm betting, and then—"

Kimolijah makes a small noise. He jitters, clearly fighting with himself, before he blurts, "It was the crystal first." He shuts his mouth, like he hadn't meant to say it, before he shrugs and rolls his eyes. "It was the crystal first," he repeats. "But the gridTech interferes with it." He waves his hand around his head. "Brainwaves. Gridstream resonance synchs with the pitch of the current, and there's all kinds of feedback and... things you probably wouldn't understand."

"Right," says Bas and nods, because yeah, he probably wouldn't understand, and he doesn't need to right now. "Okay, that makes sense, and Stanslo didn't like that you could still spout off at him when he pissed you off, because you just can't seem to shut your mouth when it's good for you, can you?" He smirks a little in the face of Kimolijah's glare. "So then the worm thing, whatever those burr bugs are, and then... what?" Bas frowns, because he doesn't really get this part. "Stanslo oh-so-generously gave you a way to control it? Keep it from actually getting to your brain so it could—"

"No." Kimolijah shakes his head, like he can't help making the correction, though this is obviously the last thing he wants to be talking about. "No, it was because it's not synched to *him—he* doesn't control it, and we can't have something the Baron doesn't control." The sarcasm is both derisive and bitter.

Bas narrows his eyes and leaves the "synched" thing for now in favor of asking, "So who does control it?"

"You can't—" Kimolijah opens and shuts his mouth several times before he finally says, "It's just... it's all part of the game."

"...Okay?" Bas waits for more, but when Kimolijah doesn't go on, Bas huffs and asks, "What the hell does that mean?"

Kimolijah sucks in a breath, almost answers, but he only clams up and gives Bas a glare.

Bas sighs but goes on, "All right, fine, so he can't control the burr bug, but he *does* control the bracelet, which also controls you." Bas stops there and shakes his head, frowning. "I was going to ask you why he takes it away the only time he's not around to make sure you behave, but...." He peers at Kimolijah closely. "It's to make sure you come back, isn't it? The burr bug thing grows and starts moving as soon as the bracelet is gone, and if you don't come back in time...." He tilts his head, and then it hits him, all at once, and he snaps his fingers. "It follows the design of the tattoo, yeah? I saw the welts that first night. It'd be a straight line otherwise, but for some reason it follows the curves and swirls instead of heading right where it wants—"

"Got it in the eye," Kimolijah puts in, gruff and quiet, almost dreamy with the hum and sway of the car, and staring off over

Bas's shoulder. He blinks and shakes his head, like he'd been hypnotized by memory. He gives Bas a curious look. "Hurt like a motherfucker." And then he smirks, though it's weak. "But it... messed with me. Couldn't concentrate. Couldn't do the math, couldn't make sense of the science."

"And Stanslo didn't just need a gridTech, he needed *your* gridTech. He needed the science—he needed you. So then came the bracelet. And it... what?" Bas lifts an eyebrow. "It kicked the bug out of your head?"

"Close enough, I guess." Kimolijah shrugs and looks down at his arm, the tiny welts that Bas now knows are tentacles—God, fucking *tentacles*—stretching under his skin, snaking down toward his fingers and already traveling up, growing thicker under the scarf wrapped around his wrist and the cuff of his sleeve. His fingers trace a swirling path over his forearm and up to his elbow, and Bas can almost see the black ink swooping beneath Kimolijah's fingertip. "It sort of... called it. 'S got ground-up crystals in it, y'know? And it.... I mean, it's all in the synch." He shrugs again, like that's the best explanation he can give.

Bas grimaces and reckons it's not enough, but it's close. Except for—"You said Stanslo gave it to you. Who made it for him? And who's it synched *to*?"

Kimolijah curls his mouth, disdainful. He doesn't answer.

Bas sighs. "And the tattoos?"

Kimolijah starts to shake his head before he catches himself. He scowls and looks away.

"Right," says Bas. "The blue ink"—Kimolijah has a muted little spasm this time, which Bas ignores—"it's more impossible Tech, isn't it? Just like that bracelet. It's all more like something out of *Magic Man* than anything real."

"All new science looks like magic," Kimolijah says softly, staring at the floor now. "Until you learn the concepts and principles behind it. Ancient peoples thought Tech was magic, back in the good old 'burn the things we don't understand' days."

"Yeah, fine, I actually have no problem calling it magic right now, because I'd probably understand it better. And because I can't explain how that Dolerma has some kind of psyTech that's not like any psyTech I've ever seen, and Serenat's working what looks pretty close to spells with tattoo ink, of all things." Something clicks in Bas's head with the voicing of the two names in one breath, and though the resemblance isn't perfect, it's still there. They both just look too alien and out of place. He gives Kimolijah a speculative look, connecting dots in his head. "Is she related to Dolerma somehow? The similarity's pretty hard to miss." He's talking more to himself now, and he's not really expecting an answer, so he doesn't wait for one. "Doesn't matter. I actually don't care."

"In Stanslo's Bridge," Kimolijah mutters, "it's always best you don't."

Which seems true enough, but not important right now, so Bas lets it pass. "The blue ink goes over the black, and it makes the burr bug follow the tattoo pattern instead of taking the straight path right to your brain. So that means Serenat's on your side."

Kimolijah jerks and flashes Bas a glare. "No one here is on anyone's *side*." It's nearly vicious. "Everyone—*everyone*—does what they have to for their own ends, because it can't be any other way."

"Except for you," Bas muses, peering at Kimolijah steadily. "You give men you don't even like a better end than being eaten alive by some kind of desert mutants. You build Stanslo guns and trains to keep your da alive, to keep your sister safely back in Knapston running a tiny tinker's shop in your honor, and she'll never have to know her brother is alive and sleeping with the man who 'killed' him. None of that, I don't think, is for 'your own ends.'" Bas sets his jaw and takes another small step in. "Except you're not building those guns and trains quite as quickly as Stanslo would like, are you? And he can't tell if you're doing it on purpose. He can't tell if you're stalling."

Kimolijah's face closes up altogether, and he turns his back. Bas is pretty sure Kimolijah's not actually *doing* anything with the dials and toggles he's tweaking, just pretending to, like he pretended to work on the engine all day in an attempt to avoid Bas.

"*I* can tell, though," Bas says, and it's a lie, a great fat bluff, but he's got to chance it. "Because I know gridTech, and what's more, I know *your* gridTech." Kimolijah's shoulders stiffen and his hands clench into fists atop the console panel, so Bas pushes, "Yeah, I'll admit you're a little beyond me—okay, *worlds* beyond me—but you're not the only one with an excellent education, Mister Genius Whiz-kid and pride of the academy. Funny, you know, I was just recently thinking how unserendipitous it was—"

"That's not even a word. So much for your *excellent education*."

"—how *unserendipitous* it was that I graduated the academy only the year before you started. All that time, so close to just randomly running into each other, and it took Stanslo and his delusions of reprehensible grandeur for us to actually meet."

"You went to the academy." Kimolijah whips around and gives Bas a narrow once-over. "*You* went to the academy. To study what? Advanced Purse-stealing? Introduction to Petty Crime?"

"Basic Tech," Bas answers evenly. "Complex Law. Geography. Nature Studies. You know—the things a Directorate tracker needs to know."

Kimolijah frowns, torn, like he wants to believe but can't take the chance. "Unserendipitous still isn't a word. And you're still not Directorate."

"Except for the part where I am."

"Then why are you *telling* me?" Kimolijah snaps, angry all over again. "If you are...." He grits his teeth and shakes his head. "If he asks me... I can only get around him when he doesn't ask the right questions, but sometimes he knows anyway. And if you're really what you say you are, he's known since before you even stepped off the train."

"He doesn't. Not in the way you think he does."

"He has to. You might think you've fooled him, but if he got you with that crystal, he *has* to know, and you're just as fucked as the rest of us. More, because if he knows and you're still here, it's because he's got a reason for it."

"Then you'll have to trust me when I tell you that I swear to God the crystal didn't work, he doesn't have me the way he thinks he does."

"Even if, by some miracle, you're right," Kimolijah plows on, "it's all going to mean shit in the end anyway." He snorts, a little sad this time. "I *don't* trust you. I can't. And if you have any brains at all, I'm the very last person *you'll* trust." He straightens and crosses his arms over his chest. "Now get the hell out of my cockpit."

Bas opens his mouth—protest, maybe angry retort—but Kimolijah is apparently *Done Talking Now*, and with only a glance and a lift of his eyebrow, Jessa starts winging around the cab, coming way too close to Bas's face with her talons.

So Bas gets the hell out of Kimolijah's cockpit.

❦

That, Bas decides crossly, did not go at all like he'd hoped.

It didn't go *horrible*, he supposes. Kimolijah expressed his continued distrust quite plainly, yes, but he didn't say he didn't *believe*.

Bas is grumbling, though, really fucking annoyed, as he clips himself back to the lanyard behind the gridcannon and tries not to grind his teeth and obsess about what was said and not said. And he thinks *Okay*. Whatever the circumstances, Kimolijah is not complicit in Stanslo's grand scheme, but he *is* cooperating, willing or no. Kimolijah's right—Bas can't trust him. If Kimolijah tells Stanslo everything, whether he wants to or not, Bas's days here are even more numbered now than they were when he started. Dolerma said he had to hurry, and Bas has no problem with that—he just doesn't really know what to do yet.

Things have changed drastically since Bas arrived in Stanslo's Bridge. He came looking for evidence, and yeah, probably some kind of personal vengeance, and the opportunity to force justice on the man responsible for the tragic death of someone Bas admired. Now it's all about Kimolijah—getting him out of here, saving his da if possible, letting him watch while Bas takes

Stanslo apart bit by bit in the most painful way he can come up with, and then maybe looking straight in Kimolijah's eyes and saying, "For you, all for you," and then... well. It gets fuzzy and rather personal and fantastic after that, the last panel of an illobook with the two protagonists locked in a heated clinch that speaks to all the wonderful filthy things about to happen off-page.

It shouldn't make a difference in Bas's overall strategy, it shouldn't interfere with just getting out and alerting the Directorate, but it does. He's man enough to admit there's something there for him with Kimolijah—an undercurrent of blatant want that makes him feel a little dirty, considering what's happened to Kimolijah because someone wanted him—but there had been something there for Bas back when he'd thought Kimolijah was a heartbreaking death under suspicious circumstances. His mind, his talent, the genius that flows out of him easier than his Tech. God, if Bas had met him back in Knapston, wrapped up in the graceful compilation of awkward components that amalgamate into the sensual punch in the gut Kimolijah is....

He's in there now, underneath Bas's skin. It's like Kimolijah moved into Bas's head, put his feet up on Bas's furniture, and drank all his beer. And Bas is somehow okay with all of it.

Bas grimaces and knuckles dust out of his eyes, and tries not to wonder if the covetous lump that snags in his chest is anything like what's in Stanslo's, and it makes some buried little animal deep in Bas bare its teeth and growl, low and gluttonous. And then he wants to stab himself in the eye, because *fuck* feelings. And fuck if he'll sexualize everything about Kimolijah like Stanslo has apparently done.

Bas broods and utterly fails at not obsessing until he notices the pinpoints of light in the distance. It's a little hard to tell the sky from the ground in the void of remote plains and dunes, but these lights are too symmetrical, too yellow to be stars. Bas stomps his feet and shouts, "Way station!" and glares down at the floor when Kimolijah yells back up, "Yeah, no shit, genius!"

Bas smells the thick, rancid reek of charstoke at least half an hour before they reach the way station. He can see the heavy strata of smoke miles away. When they pull in, it's almost enough to choke him.

He'd thought Stanslo's Bridge was a ramshackle eyesore; the way station is worse. He can't see much through the dark and the smoky air, except for the torches that burn on either side of the tracks, guiding the train beneath the roof-on-poles that's even less of a train station than the one in Stanslo's Bridge. It's more like a campsite. There are dwellings here, but nothing that can even attempt to pass for houses except for a few rusty, derelict boxcars that have been converted into living quarters and most of an old locomotive, its engine compartment blown out and sticking up in twisted pieces, the remnants of which look to have been made into a chapel. Everything else is daub and mud and canvas, and the people....

God.

They're dirty and thin and empty-eyed, and they approach the train, slow and stumbling, like dead things that haven't yet lost the habit of moving. There are about twenty of them, mostly men like it is in Stanslo's Bridge, but for two women Bas spots who look just as rope-muscled and hard-worn as the men and just as desolate. They stare as the train comes to a halt beneath the leaning port, the blue of the gridstream reflecting in dry, hopeless eyes until the engine whines down and goes out. Bas is staring down at them, kind of horrified, so he sees it when they brighten with Kimolijah's cheery "Hey, all!" greeting, and he even catches a few thin smiles. Kimolijah immediately starts herding everyone away from the train, says something low and hushed that sounds like "Wait'll you see what I brought you," but Bas is pretty sure he wasn't supposed to hear it, so he doesn't react. He only sighs as Jessa wings over and perches on a conduit at Bas's back. She's not glaring at him, she's not going for his eyes, and she's not throwing guts at him. He counts it as a win.

Mari steps out of the train with an upturn to the corner of her mouth and not a single hint of the nasty disdain, or even the petulant fear, from the episode in Stanslo's yard. She greets everyone by name, lets them touch her, and touches them back. She looks... sweet. Glad to be here. And the people are obviously glad to see her. One thin, filthy man actually cries a little.

The glances Bas gets from these dirty stick people are furtive and distrustful, and Kimolijah doesn't help; he keeps shooting Bas somewhat hostile glances as he leads everyone down toward the freight cars, and he's speaking to them in low tones which, considering Kimolijah obviously isn't entirely sure if Bas is Stanslo's spy, probably doesn't bode well for Bas. And yeah, okay, Bas is the new guy, so it's not like he expects instant camaraderie. It's not like he expects camaraderie at all, really, considering the atmosphere of cutthroat distrust he's been seeing since he hit Harrowgate. He really doesn't need Kimolijah making things worse, though.

Kimolijah has brought them the pear brandy from the shipment they brought back from Harrowgate and for which he traded Reacher a new gridheater. He's brought them two barrels full of various fabrics that Bas is sure he saw in the back of the storehouse when he had his truncated talk with Dolerma. He's brought two sacks of some kind of sweets Bas is willing to bet were a present to Kimolijah from Stanslo. He's brought various gadgets with wires poking out of them, and tiny toggles that don't tell Bas what they are but nonetheless tell him they run on those crystals with gridTech in them.

Bas isn't supposed to know all this. Kimolijah keeps watching him and too obviously trying to make sure Bas doesn't see the exchanges, but Bas does. Bas has discovered he has the best seat in the house. And so he just sits up on top of the locomotive behind his cannon and watches.

He watches Reacher kick over the small stakes up which a spindly little forest of withered beanstalks are trying like hell to defy the desert while Lowen spits and squints out into the dark. He watches one of the men protest and try to stop Reacher, and he watches Yanush and Merrin just grimace at it all as Reacher shoves at the man, hard, and the man goes groaning down into the dirt.

He watches Mari and Kimolijah have a hissed conversation outside of the freight car where the way station's denizens gather their loads of goods and a rickety cart full of those black cubes and lug them back toward where the huts and tents hunch in the sand. Neither Mari nor Kimolijah look like they can't stand each other, as they had up in Stanslo's yard. They don't look happy, but there are hands on arms and arguments made in low voices that don't grate with hatred, and when Mari raises her voice, impatient, and there's a coinciding quick lull in the other ambient noise of the way station, Bas hears "—have let me stay otherwise, and anyway it worked, so what's—" and he thinks *ah*.

Ah.

He looks away quickly when Kimolijah darts cagey looks to all sides, checking to see if anyone heard, and if Bas feels Kimolijah staring his way a little longer, eyes narrowed a little harder, he does his best to look like he doesn't. Serenat's watching them, though, very closely, standing just inside the passenger car's open door. Bas can't really see her face, what with the giant floppy hat and the dark glasses, but she's watching Kimolijah and Mari, Bas can tell, and it makes him uneasy, but he doesn't know why.

It turns louder then, Kimolijah raising his voice and Mari sharpening hers, angry words and cruel jibes, but even without turning his head, Bas can see through it this time, where he hadn't even thought to look before. He doesn't feel too bad about missing it, though. Apparently, they're both *really fucking good* actors. Then again, Bas supposes they'd have to be.

Someone comes to pull Kimolijah away, tugging him toward one of those alien-looking water tower things, and Kimolijah goes, but he eyes Mari with a look full of meaning as he does. Bas can't guess what the meaning might be, but he doesn't have to. He's seen all he needs to see when it comes to those two. Maybe Serenat has too; she pulls back and flumps onto one of the couches. Bas gets the impression of a sullenness about her. Something. He doesn't know, really, so he shakes his head and keeps watching.

He watches Kimolijah monkey his way up the tower thing with a screwdriver between his teeth like a pirate's dirk. He watches Kimolijah fiddle and curse under his breath, and then he watches him grin when he sparks the dead generator back to life and everyone around him gives a cheer.

He watches as the train pulls away from the way station, Mari watching from the wobbly port, and thinks he can't trust a single fucking thing he's seen or heard since he stepped into Stanslo's Bridge.

18.

The thing about the Bruise is that you apparently don't simply arrive; you get there by degrees.

The first things Bas notices that make him think this is going to be even weirder than he'd thought are the whirlpools. Or... sandpools. Sandwhirls? Whatever. *Swirling pits of death* works just fine, he thinks as he eyes one a little too close to the tracks, shadows shirring in the pit of the hungry vortex, mist crowning darker than it should be, then belching up and tendriling out like feelers over the sand. It's big, the circumference of it probably just as wide as Bas is long, and it expands and contracts in rhythm like it's breathing. Bas only gets a look a little longer than a glimpse as the train speeds by, but he's almost positive it's not a trick of the eye—something that looks like a limb made of smoke reaches out of the eddy, stretches in a long pendulum swing, and when it surprises a swarm of desert rats out of their den, the goddamned thing fucking *moves*. Not just the limb-that's-really-smoke; the entire swirling pit of death reels flat to the desert floor like a sentient pinwheel, swallowing the ground as it goes and spitting sand back up in short plumes like the tail of a comet. It doesn't spit the rats back up when it catches them, though.

Bas stares over the terrain, unabashedly wide-eyed, and mutters, "Holy fucking shit," when he sees more of the dark spots spread out over the sand in voracious constellations, leaking their foggy shadows and churning up their plumes. "Holy fucking *shit*."

He doesn't feel at all embarrassed or gutless when he unclips his lanyard, sprawls on the roof, and dips his head down to snap, "What the *fuck* are those things?" at Kimolijah.

Kimolijah doesn't squawk and startle this time; he merely frowns at Bas over his shoulder from his station at the helm of the cab, hands gloved now and hovering over two different sets of controls. He's got his goggles on again, and he blinks coolly at Bas through their clear lenses. "Which things?" he asks, bland.

"*Which* things." Bas stares for a second, wordless, then sputters, "*Which* things. The fucking swirling pits of fucking *death* things."

"Oh." Kimolijah shrugs as he turns back to his panel, and starts fiddling with a gauge. "I dunno what they're called. We just call them sand eddies."

"Sand eddies." If Bas had a free hand, he'd slap his forehead. "Sand eddies? They *eat* the fucking *ground* and suck up what they scare out of it. And you call them *sand eddies*?"

Now Kimolijah looks puzzled. And annoyed. "So call them 'swirling pits of death' if you want to." He sweeps a hand at the windscreen with a lift of his eyebrows. "Not like there's anyone out here to argue about it."

"That's not the goddamned point!"

"What *is* the goddamned point?"

"Those things don't exist!" Bas nearly shouts. "They're impossible. They're holes in the ground that are *alive.* How does that even work?"

"How the hell should I know?"

"You're the goddamned scientist here!"

"Yeah, no, *mechanical gridstream engineer*, not magical spirit guide for freaky bioTech." Kimolijah scowls at Bas before he pauses with a tilt of his head. "Didn't Reacher tell you anything at all about what to expect out here?"

"He said I'm to shoot birds." Bas presses his mouth into a thin line, and Kimolijah's already huge eyes widen behind his stupid goggles. "And," Bas goes on a little lamely, "he said the snakes are bigger."

"The snakes." Kimolijah stares for a moment, incredulous. He shakes his head and goes back to his controls. "Did you know," he says, his tone offhand as he flips a toggle and adjusts a dial, eyes on a panel set at the top of the dash, "that the most venomous snake in the world can disguise itself as a harmless garden snake? Its coloring and even its scent are so close it can fool real garden snakes enough to get into their nests and take out the whole den before they even know they've got a predator among them."

Bas clenches his teeth. Kimolijah's habit of throwing useless trivia at him has been kind of annoyingly charming up until now, but—"What the hell are you talking about?"

Kimolijah shrugs, still adjusting controls and fiddling with levers and knobs. "I'm just saying—sometimes the most harmless-looking snake is really the deadliest viper in the pit." He doesn't twitch or shift when Bas just keeps staring at him, only says, "Don't worry about the 'swirling pits of death.' The tracks are built on ley lines, and nothing out here likes them." He mucks with his panels for a moment, and when Bas doesn't pull back, Kimolijah turns another look over his shoulder. "You should get back to your gun. We'll be needing it directly."

Bas gives him a glare, but Kimolijah's already turned back to the dash. Bas doesn't know if he's really doing something or just pretending he is so Bas will go away, but either way, Bas recognizes staying here and waiting him out for the waste of time it is. Kimolijah can make something as mundane as turning a screw look complicated and crucial, and Bas has seen him spend an entire day contorted inside an engine pretending to fix it. Bas doesn't think even Stanslo wins that game.

He's still cursing and muttering to himself, clipped back to his lanyard and hands on his gun like they're supposed to be, when he sees the second thing that shakes him.

Jessa has been steadily circling overhead, sometimes gliding out of view for a while and returning to trill a little whistle as she darts ahead, or swooping into the cockpit to check on Kimolijah. Now and then, she'll return to perch on a post at Bas's back that he now thinks was put there especially for her, because no gridstream fritters near it and no conduits are close enough that she might catch an outspread wing in an errant current when she stretches. Bas has gotten to know the shape of her in flight, the rhythm of the beat of her wings, the way she tilts into an ascending drift and coasts into a drop when a waft shifts heavy.

So he merely watches as he sees the familiar approach, carpal joints stretched straight and pinions drawn out in their broadest extension. Her feet are thrust forward, getting ready to land, and her talons are splayed wide, ready to catch herself. And that's when Bas notes she looks bigger than she should, fuller and longer and thicker, and the closer she gets, the bigger she looks. Bigger than she was the last time Bas saw her soaring overhead. Bigger than those *giant fucking spiders*. Jessa but not—darker-fledged and sleeker, her wingspan nearly doubled, though the brindled-cream markings Bas didn't know he knew are still recognizable even from this distance in the dark. The patterns of the markings, not the shades of them—those are changed, darkened, deepened, with more contrast between the colors. That's when Bas realizes her eyes are almost glowing, though not with gridstream; something phosphorescent, giving her an eerie luminosity like something out of an illobook.

"Um," wheezes Bas. He clears his throat and shouts, "Kimo?" He swings the gun around, tracking, and his finger really *really* wants to give the toggle a squeeze, but he hesitates. "*Kimo!*" Because Reacher said the birds would change, but Jessa's been the only bird in the sky so far, and... well, this winged almost-monster flying at him is certainly a change. "Kimo, goddamn it, if you don't tell me what this thing is, I'm going to have to—"

"Do *not* shoot my bird!" comes from below. Bas cuts a quick—very quick—glance over toward the voice to see empty space, but Kimo's voice is clear when he whistles for Jessa and shouts, "You shoot her and I fry you," at Bas, so Bas imagines Kimolijah must be hanging out the open door of the cab. And then he's sure of it, because a gloved hand pops up over the lip of the roof and points up and past where Jessa's still moving in for a landing. "You can shoot that, though. And, like, right now."

That is something else with wings that Bas by no means would have called a bird under any other circumstances. It's huge, and even in the dark Bas can tell it's not fledged—maybe fur, maybe hide, he can't really tell—and it doesn't have the teardrop-with-tail-feathers shape of any bird Bas has ever seen. It's thin-bodied, like a dragonfly, and its pennons are membranous, webbed across bone-spined arms that splay like fingers.

It looks vicious. Its jaw is needle-toothed and obtruding, and a horny flange extends from the back of its narrow skull; its barrel is tapered and jut-ribbed, and a long vertebrate tail swings behind it like a rudder. Its aerodynamics would probably make a bioTech shake their head and despair of reality, because it doesn't look like it should even be capable of flight, let alone able to dart through shifting currents like it's doing. Its eyes are glowing, like Jessa's but not, a muddy green that pulses and flickers as it zeroes in on the train and shifts side-slung for an aggressive strafe.

"Any time, there, gunner," says Kimolijah, and Bas blinks out of his daze to remember *oh yeah, gunner.*

He swings the gridcannon around and sights down its barrel. And forgets for a second too long that it's a lever instead of a trigger, so he fumbles at it. The thing's still coming, its trajectory a straight line now, close enough that the blue of the gridstream fluttering over the engine car slicks its hide in pulsating shadow and turns the glimmer of its eyes into something bright-hot and empty. Bas can see the glisten of venom on sharp yellow teeth, it's that close—

Okay, Bas, get it together and just breathe.

—and okay, yeah, breathing would probably be a good idea, Bas thinks when he realizes his vision's gone a bit spotty. He sucks in a great, bracing breath, whooping it down deep in his chest, near-dizzy relief, when his fingers finally decide to work. He doesn't have time for any of the bubbling mix of fear and horror that's churning in his gut, so he does the only thing he can—he pretends it's not there. He lines up the cannon's barrel, toggles the lever, and shoots.

The pulse it kicks out is thick with the metal tang of ozone, acrid pepper at the back of Bas's tongue. Live gridstream hits with a harsh *zap-crackle* and sizzles along the monster-thing's hide like a splash of water. Bas can swear he sees the bone structure of the thing lit up in blue glittering relief against the black of the night sky, wings outstretched and claws extended in a forever-moment of frozen paroxysm while the gridstream washes over it, and then the stream dissipates, goes out, and the thing goes down. Momentum carries it too close, its dead weight just missing slamming into Bas as it plummets, and Bas can feel the heat of it as it hurtles by him, can smell the fried meat and burnt hair as he ducks down and over, lanyard snapping tight as he strains his weight against it. The train is already well past when the thing hits the ground, and Bas can only see a dark shape and a wide puff of dust. He's still blinking against the green shapes of residual light behind his eyes, but he doesn't think he's imagining things when he sees one of the swirling pits of death adjust its trajectory and suck the dead thing down.

He doesn't have time to stare and freak out the way he wants to. There are more of them, so Bas keeps shooting.

They're not all the same. Some of them have feathers, some of them have scales, and some of them he's pretty sure he recognizes. Those not-bats, for one thing, but he can see the echoed shapes of crows and owls, too, only twisted slightly surreal somehow, enlarged and elongated and nudged more feral than the shapes he knows. Teeth and beaks are exaggerated and eyes are slanted more predatory, though the eyes of the creatures Bas thinks of as those from the real world don't all glow like the ones he's pretty sure have leaked out from whatever's on the other side of the Bruise. The ones he thinks of as prey, though, the smaller ones—sage sparrows and what he thinks might be scrub jays, and whatever other small desert birds survive out here—their whole bodies glow.

They're all bigger than they should be. Some of them are probably as big as Kimolijah, and Bas just can't get the physics of their body structures to line up in his head with the possibility of flight. Not that it matters—flight, quite obviously, *is* a possibility, a reality, and these things can probably carry off a full-sized man, physics be damned. Bas checks the clip on the lanyard again and keeps shooting.

He tries not to stare for too long when he sees the ruined stoke engine rotting only paces away from the tracks as they pass it, its innards blown out and mushroomed open like a twisted, gnarled fist unfurling toward the sky. He tries not to wonder if anyone survived, and if they had, which of the desert mutants eventually got them.

Jessa runs herd over creatures that dwarf her, wheeling in with a risky swipe of talons at coverts and dorsals and a screeching trill that's seated more deeply in her throat than it was before. Like she's just waiting for Bas to catch on to her strategy, she swoops right down the center of the main convergence, splits it, then flanks and harries the creatures coming at Bas's back until they give somewhat and veer off and away to form up for a second pass. Bas doesn't wait—he swings the cannon around and starts picking off the cluster coming at him head-on, dropping the things like debris beside the tracks, then he swings again to meet the ones Jessa chased off before. There's a rhythm to it all, Jessa setting the cadence, and Bas decides to trust her animal instincts and just go with it.

The creatures he thinks he recognizes don't attack like the other ones; they merely hover on the periphery, well out of range, and swoop down to pick and tear at a carcass once Bas shoots it down. He sees more than one get swallowed up by the swirling pits of death while tucking in, but more often there'll be a squawk or a screech and then a spasm of feathers complementing a near escape.

"A goddamned scavenger fucking free-for-all," Bas mutters darkly, weirdly angry, though he can't pin exactly why. Not that there aren't about a million reasons.

It's like that first one was a scout or a harbinger. Bas tracks the flocks of flying nightmare creatures by the blank spots in the stars and the muddy green glow of rapacious eyes as the things circle overhead, then dive down at the train like they're targeting it. They don't go for the other cars the train's pulling, only the locomotive, like moths to a flame, and it finally dawns on Bas—*oh, duh, right.*

They're after the light of the gridstream. Reacher had said they would be. Bas wonders if there's some kind of connection between gridstream and the glow of these things' eyes, and now there's ley lines thrown in for good measure, but he doesn't really have time to ponder it too closely because that's when the scenery changes.

The map in Bas's head tells him they must be nearing the valley below the Saltons, a thin ribbon of what would have been almost an agro haven, were it not for the poisoned snows that hang in near stasis over the mountains, seeding their toxins into the runoff that turns the lands from Harrowgate to the western sea into a dead wasteland. He thinks he should be able to make out the mountain range in the distance, but all he can really see is dark and more dark, and the sporadic flash of a storm brewing on the lip of the horizon.

Scrub turns into weeds clawing through sand. Weeds turn into trees, hunched and stunted, and that's when Bas sees the spiderwebs.

Bloody *everywhere.*

And his mind won't do a single thing but bleat *Holy fucking shit, what the fucking fuck!*

Every poor excuse for a tree is covered in webs, thick as cotton wool, and there's no kidding himself: entire goddamned *armies* of *giant fucking spiders* come skittering out of their nests, scrabbling shadows across the sand, when the blue light of the train comes flickering over the landscape.

Because of course they do.

Some of the giant spiders get sucked down in a flurry of sand and spasming legs; some of them get snatched up by the flying nightmares. Some of them, Bas is not proud to say, are picked off when he gets a little antsy and starts shooting at everything with legs instead of everything with wings. Halfway through manically racking up his twelfth set of jittering legs, he's brought back to what he's actually supposed to be doing up here when Jessa flies so close she almost knocks off Bas's hat, and Bas finally notices she's been forced to retreat because he's let the flying nightmares get too close.

He swings and shoots and shoots and shoots, and he thinks he might be whooping and hollering, but his heart is punching against his rib cage and his blood has been beating a cacophonous bassline in his ears, so he can't really hear himself. He's tuned to the metrical *thwacka-thwacka* of the train's wheels on the rails and to the pitch of Jessa's cries—the sharp whistle she shrills when she goes into an attack, the deep-throated quaver when she wheels in retreat—and anything else that registers outside of those two things gets shot at.

It's almost comforting, the rhythm and the thoughtless buzz of *aim and shoot*. When it comes right down to it, Bas thinks after a while, it's really not so different from an exceptionally bizarre and dangerous stint of shooting skeet. Except, you know, with carnivorous monster-birds and *giant fucking spiders*.

He almost doesn't care—or even notice—when packs of those dog-things come skulking out from behind scrubby hillocks or around the misshapen trunks of trees. They join the scavenging, chasing off some of the smaller birds, getting chased off by some of the bigger ones, or even becoming prey when the flying nightmares notice them.

There are more creatures out here, things Bas doesn't get a good look at because of distance and speed, but he thinks those hunch-spined thick-shouldered things with the rapier teeth might be bobcats under normal circumstances, and he's pretty sure he's seen a sample or two of those "bigger snakes" Reacher was talking about, but everything's going too fast for him to be sure.

It's just a background buzz in his head, the attempt to study and understand, an ingrained habit, and Bas doesn't allow it too much brain space because he can't really afford distraction. He lets the pulse of the cannon and the tempo of Jessa's maneuvering blank out everything else, settling in and just letting body and instinct take over until he thinks hours must have gone by without him even noticing the passage of minutes. The sky has gone indigo and the stars are getting duller. Bas notices only with the part of his brain that's not occupied with *aim and shoot*.

For the first time, he thinks about how profoundly and truly it *sucks* that daytime desert heat plus an engine that runs on gridstream does not equal a smooth and reliable ride. Forced-air cooling works well and proper only when the air is actually cool, and with no heat sink on the rotors, Bas fully understands why nighttime is the best option. Doesn't mean he has to like it.

In the end it's the spiders that get him. Well, not *get him*, but scare the shit out of him enough that he finally loses it a little.

The thing is, they're fucking *fast*. They don't look it when they're squat to the ground, jointed legs contracted, but when they're going for speed, their legs unfold and elongate until their fat, coarse-furred bodies are hip-high to a man. Okay, maybe knee-high. Calf-high. Whatever. But still. The fuckers can *run*, is the point. Bas has seen it, but he hasn't been paying attention for a while, and he thinks maybe he'd let himself believe they wouldn't be able to come anywhere near him, perched up high on a speeding train the way he is.

So wrong.

Merrin has opened the door to the passenger car behind the locomotive, and he's leaning out, firing a gridgun at the sky, catching a few flying nightmares that manage to outflank both Bas and Jessa, and occasionally he'll fire off a shot toward the engine, to the side and so low to the ground Bas might wonder if Merrin is *that bad* of a shot. But Bas has also been seeing flashes of gridstream coming from the open door of the cockpit below him for a while now, so he figures whatever Merrin's shooting at, Kimolijah must be too. Bas doesn't have time to wonder what that's about; maybe Merrin and Kimolijah are targeting some of the dog-things or something. Spiders don't occur to Bas. Maybe because he doesn't let them. Because *fuck* spiders.

He doesn't notice the first one creeping up on him until it's almost got a mandible on the toe of his boot. He'd been expecting anything coming at him to be coming in high, and so he hasn't been watching for anything low. He thinks it's a shadow from overhead at first, the flutter of dark-against-dark over at the edge of the glass platform, but then somewhere in his brain it registers that the roof of the locomotive is lit up with gridstream and any shadows would have to be coming from beneath the light source, so he shifts a distracted glance over and down. And then again, faster this time and eyes sprung wide and heart an abrupt and acidic knot in his throat.

Oh *God*. It's close enough Bas can see its *eyes*—all... well, Bas doesn't know how many, *too many*, black inside with a faint phosphorescent green, like sludgy poison in a cut-glass bottle. Alien and horrible. He can't back up—he's too close to the fencing with gridstream running all over it, and anyway, the lanyard doesn't have enough slack. He's boxed in and clipped down, and Bas can swear the thing knows it.

He might shout. Maybe. Probably. Okay, he shouts, and then he kicks and then he stomps, and when there are still legs trying to scrabble and mandibles trying to sink in, Bas skins the six-barrel from his hip and shoots. And shoots. And shoots ag—

"Are you shooting at my train, you *unbelievable moron?*" comes from inside the cab.

Bas has never wanted to take someone's head off so much in his life. "I'm shooting at a *giant fucking spider*, goddamn it, what else am I—?"

"A giant fucking spider that's *on my fucking train!*"

And Bas realizes that yes, okay, he is indeed shooting at the train, and it's a good thing the glass of the platform is so thick, or he might've just taken out their engineer and *the only way out of this fucking hellhole.*

"Quit shooting that thing, it could blow up in your hand any second!" Kimolijah shouts. "Combustibles are chancy out here. That's why we use the gridguns."

Reacher told Bas not to bring his gridgun. *Too clumsy strapped t' yer back and all,* he'd said. *Just gets in the way. Anyway, cannon's enough gun fer anyone, I reckon.*

Bas had thought it made sense. Now he peers down at the six-barrel in his hand and frowns. "Wow, finally, something out of your mouth that's actually useful!" he calls to Kimolijah.

It's funny how Bas can clearly hear Kimolijah's snort through all the wind and the noise of the wheels. Funnier how it makes Bas quirk a grin, even though he's fully aware he's standing in the middle of a cheesy illobook plot, complete with gruesome monsters and Impending Peril.

And then he realizes the spider is still moving, so he curses and shouts and kicks and kicks and stomps until he finally gets the toe of his boot underneath the bulk of its body. He snaps out his leg and the thing sails off the scoop of Bas's boot and right into the latticework fencing surrounding his turret. There's a too-loud *pop* and then *zzwap*, gridstream flaring up so bright it's almost blinding, and the train takes a wheezing lurch that drops Bas's stomach into his knees and makes him stumble, the tether of the lanyard pulling taut. The train's engine sputters, only for a second, but long enough for the stream to release what's left of the spider, and the still-twitching carcass oozes down and off the lip of the roof, a trail of innards—some cooked, some still gooey—glinting across the bullet-pocked glass.

"Keep those things out of the stream!" Kimolijah yells.

Bas rolls his eyes and yells back, "Yeah, I'm okay, thanks for asking!"

He has no idea if Kimolijah snarks back, because oh *God*, the hooked end of a still ticcing leg is caught in the weave of Bas's trousers, and *fuck* spiders, goddamn it, *fuck* fucking *spiders*! The noises Bas makes as he tries to get it off, *get it off*, are high-pitched and probably way too little-girlish, but *fuck that*, he doesn't care. He yanks the—*still twitching, oh my god, what the fuck!*—leg away, along with a strip of his trouser leg, and hurls it off the roof after the rest of the *giant fucking spider.*

He doesn't even have time to have the heart attack he's been courting. Jessa's reprimands alert him that he's gone out of rhythm again, allowed too many of the flying nightmares to circle close, and Bas swings the cannon back up and around to start all over again. He keeps the six-barrel in his hand, though, and his eyes everywhere, and he reloads when he can spare the few seconds between flying-nightmare strafing runs, since he'd kind of emptied all six barrels on the last spider. He clicks the barrel housing to and decides he doesn't care about combustibles. *Fuck* combustibles. He'd rather go out blown up by his own gun than a snack for freaky spiders.

It's not the last encounter. Bas is pretty sure Kimolijah's taking care of most of the spiders that manage to latch on to the engine, and Merrin's zapping things Bas can't see, so he tries to focus on the apparently endless stream of flying nightmares. He catches the rhythm once again—*swing around, sight down, shoot-shoot-shoot; swing around, sight down, shoot-shoot-shoot*—and for a while, all he has to worry about is keeping up with Jessa and not catching any of Merrin's shots that sometimes go a little too wild for Bas's comfort. From what Bas can tell, Merrin's a decent shot, and Bas is grateful for the backup. Especially every time one of Merrin's shots zings near the side of the locomotive, and Bas imagines another sizzling spider twitching away its last in the sand by the tracks.

He's deep inside the repetition—*swing, aim, shoot; swing, aim, shoot*—a steady beat inside his head that hisses and pops like live gridstream and lines up weirdly nicely with the tempo of wheels on tracks. His peripheral vision is now hyperalert for the skitter of creepy-crawlies nudging over the lip of the cabin's roof, so he sees most of them in time to fling out his arm and pick them off with his six-barrel before they get too close. He's even careful to mind the angle this time so none of his shots go through the cabin's skin.

And for all that the flying nightmares keep coming, and they're *huge* and horrible, and their mouths drip what Bas is sure is poison, and all manner of strange creatures are yipping and snarling and fighting over every still-twitching carcass that drops to Bas's cannon....

Still, it's the *giant fucking spiders* that are doing Bas's head in. They're just... *wrong*, in so many ways, alien and awful, but more because he's only seen one of these things up close before, sure, but he *knows* its eyes didn't glow back in Stanslo's Bridge. Then again, Jessa's didn't glow there either. It occurs to Bas then to look at himself, squint at the back of his hand, and he's embarrassingly relieved to see he's not glowing.

He still feels that leg spasming against his calf, he still feels that mandible tapping at the toe of his boot, and it's all he can do not to let go of both guns to make sure the shudders flickering up his backbone aren't actually too many hooked feet and a fat, furry body climbing up the back of his coat. He almost *wants* them to come at him, just for the feral, hysterical pleasure he gets from splattering them and watching those horrible jointed legs jerk and convulse as coarse-furred carapaces explode in a shower of innards and gun smoke.

"*Fuck* spiders!" Bas snarls, probably too loudly, because he hears Kimolijah hoot something back at him from the cab, but Bas's blood is still pounding too raucously in his ears, so he doesn't know what. He doesn't care, because seriously—*fuck* spiders.

He's pretty high from adrenaline, and still deep inside the rhythm of it all, arm almost vibrating with the residue of each shot as gridstream pulses from the end of his cannon, so he doesn't notice the deceleration at first. Not until the cadence of the gridstream goes out of true with the cadence to which his body's been moving. The current whines, as if in protest, and the white-blue of the gridstream flowing over the fencing dims just a little, then brightens again, but it's enough of a jar to make Bas come down a touch.

It's gotten lighter, indigo sliding into smoked sapphire, and there's a stratum of rose now that lips at the horizon and blushes it plum. They'd left the swirling pits of death far behind, back where sand gave way to sandy hardpan again, but Bas gives the terrain a quick scan nonetheless to make sure. The flying nightmares don't let up, but their numbers are thinned, and the other monster-things that have been following after the train like the world's ugliest parade have mostly either scavenged their fill or become prey themselves. Bas can hear the stragglers bell and bay at each other, but he only sees a few of them, fighting over bones among the scrubby spines of brown, distorted vegetation. It's like the train slowing down is a signal, a command, and everything else slows down with it. Not a lot, just enough for Bas to get his breath, which isn't altogether good because it also gives him time to think again, and all he can really think is *fuck spiders* and *maybe I actually died back there in Harrowgate, because none of this,* none of it, *is fucking possible* and *fuck spiders* again as he shoots another dawdler off the roof in a satisfying spray of gore.

His hands are starting to jitter, fatigue and dissipating adrenaline piled on top of a stomach he's just as glad is empty, but his aim is still good, and he keeps picking off the flying nightmares that won't give up. His skin feels tight and burnt, wind and dust and the backwash of gridstream drying him out and sucking away even the buckets he only now realizes he's been sweating. He feels sick and shaky, and he can't help thinking back to Reacher's halfhearted and almost reluctant cautions about "altered" and having anything in his stomach besides water, because he's seen how this place alters live flesh—he doesn't want to see what it does to something dead, especially not if he has to watch it explode out of his own intestines.

Maybe Kimolijah's got the right idea about not eating meat.

Merrin has given up his post at the passenger car's door and shut it tight again, apparently figuring Bas can handle what's left. Jessa's still circling up there, still doing her part to divide and conquer the dwindling flocks, but she's moving slower too. Bas is just starting to worry that she's moving *too* slowly when

Kimolijah whistles for her and she drops down into a smooth arcing descent and disappears into the cab. Bas can hear the door slide shut for the first time behind her, and it gives him a little shudder. He's pretty much on his own now, which is okay, really, because there's not much left to shoot at. He can count the number of things in the sky on two hands, and most of them seem to have lost their ability to navigate with the spreading light of the sunrise. More than half of them veer away ahead of the train, like they can't even see it anymore, so Bas shifts his stance to cover them because Jessa's not there to do it for him anym—

"Holy fucking... *shit*." Bas pulls up short and just... stares. "I've stepped into an issue of *Planet Horror*."

He doesn't really know what he's looking at, at first. He sees the massive stain on the horizon and thinks it's the dark-peaks-against-dark-sky of the Saltons, but no, because mountains don't... *roil*.

A scab in the skin thinned between worlds, and Bas thinks *no, that isn't it at all*. He can see why they call it the Bruise, though.

The rising sun doesn't touch it—it looks like it can't. Huge, stretched like the skin of a hulking beast, it rises from soil to sky and blots the breadth of the landscape from north to south. The sun comes up fast in the desert, gold washing quickly over barren ground like a high-tide wave, but none of it touches the chasm of blue-on-black that eats the sky. Irised and pulsing like an aperture, it boils like an outraged thunderhead, blue smoke on a black void, dense with mist and alive with foggy breath that snakes out vaporous limbs, then billows out murk in thick, ropy jets. Fine threads of yellow-white gridstream weave through it, crisscrossing and plaiting together, warp and weft, then flitter down into the depths of the bruised haze like a skein unraveled.

It looks.... Bas doesn't know if he can put words to it. A black so deep it looks dredged from an empty well. Hungry but impassive; beautiful but dreadful. It's perpetual, violent night that eats the light and coughs out its deformed spawn to thwart and harangue the brightening day.

It's hard to judge distance in the desert. It looks as though the train is hundreds of miles away, and yet it seems like any second now it'll hurtle down the black throat of the churning blue-black mass of shifting sky. Bas tries to get an idea of how much time before it eats him by gauging the length of the tracks between here and there, but they dwindle off to a thin line bisecting the horizon long before they reach the tattered-thundercloud edges of that... thing.

He stares for too long, forgets what he's supposed to be doing, so it's a nasty surprise when one of the flying nightmares comes in hard and fast and thumps into Bas so brutally he goes down and slides on the glass until he's sprawled out beneath the gridcannon. The lanyard's still keeping him tethered and he's still got a deathgrip on the stock of the cannon, so he doesn't fall far and there's no danger of going over the side. He's got time to register the relief of that before there's a great flash and a heavy buzz that sends gridstream rocketing up over the lattice and sparking out all over the place in deadly streamers. The train lurches and the engine whines and the flow of the gridstream stutters all over the jittering bulk of the flying nightmare, caught in rictus against the wirework, until its spasms knock it loose and it thuds down, smoking, by Bas's splayed legs.

Bas gags at the stench and then gets caught between a groan and a growl when Kimolijah hollers, "Keep those fucking things *out of the stream*, goddamn it!" through the closed door of the cab, and Bas makes the absurdly obvious *my god, where is your head* connection he hadn't bothered to make before: interrupt the gridstream and there's no power to the engine; no power to the engine and the train stops working.

Bas stumbles to his feet, swiveling the cannon a little wildly, looking for more coming at him, before yelling back, "And once again, I'm *fine*, thanks for asking!"

"Until we stop and I kick your stupid ass!"

The cannon pulses out a comforting *zzwap* and a flying nightmare goes down in a puff of dust before Bas manages, "Like you could even reach my ass, y' bloody wee midget!" and then grins a little manically when Kimolijah barks out a laugh. Kimolijah mutters something back, but Bas doesn't hear it; he's busy shooting another spider.

⌘

It's the last dregs of sunrise when Bas spots the humps and rises in the distance that look less like the horns of the pass at the Saltons' feet he knows they are than they do giant oblong honeycombs. They stand like scattered dominoes to either side of the tracks and flare out in graduated heights to form the shape of a saddle. And considering they're likely limestone, Bas is betting *honeycomb* isn't too far off. In fact, he's betting on caves.

A little too ideal for an ambush. Bas narrows his eyes, but it's still too far away for him to get a glimpse of anything moving. With the backdrop of the Bruise twisting and burbling, he's not sure he'd see it anyway, not until he's right up close, and anyone wanting something on this train would be a fool not to take advantage. Reacher's assurances that there are no bandits aside, Bas figures now is not the time to get careless.

It's lighter now, but not light, the Bruise seeming to suck up every ray and swallow it before it can do much. Even the steady flow of the gridstream over the train seems dimmer, though the engine hums along with no hitches.

It's cooler here, too, like the Bruise eats the heat along with the light. Bas wondered before how Kimolijah managed to run his train for hours beneath the high desert sun, but now it appears he doesn't.

The wildlife has stopped coming at them. It's like some invisible line has been crossed, and the closer they get to the Bruise, the less trouble there is from the monsters that leak out of it. Even the giant spiders have given up. Bas celebrates quietly in his head and takes the opportunity to lean tiredly against the barrel of the cannon, pulling in deep, long breaths and letting his limbs shake out the last of the adrenaline gone sour in his veins. He still keeps an eye on the sky and on those rocky formations ahead, still watches for the creep-and-scuttle of hooked feet and jointed legs stealing up and over the lip of the roof, but there's nothing. It gives Bas the time and the available attention to notice the dull throbbing at the base of his skull, that skittering bump he'd felt in Stanslo's dining room, only it's repetitive now and not in rhythm with his own body but with the flux and flow of the Bruise's pulse.

It's unnerving.

Now that the drama has passed for the moment and Bas can think again, it occurs to him to wonder exactly why Kimolijah had shut up the cab a few miles back. It shouldn't be odd, but it is, because it had been open all through the assault by desert mutant monsters, and now that the danger—or at least *that* danger—has passed, Kimolijah's locked himself inside a sealed chamber like there's something worse waiting.

Bas doesn't question it, doesn't even really think it over too hard. He's unclipping the lanyard before his hands have even stopped shaking, sliding belly-down over the glass and dipping his head. And then he knocks politely on the closed cabin door.

It takes a moment, but all things considered, Bas is a little surprised he gets an answer at all. The latch clumps heavily first, and then the door pops back and slides a few inches sideways in its casing until Kimolijah is peering at Bas from way too close. If Kimolijah were just a touch taller, Bas could lean down and kiss him. Which would probably be a bad idea, what with the frown Kimolijah's shooting him, but hey, it's there, it's a possibility, and Bas is all about possibilities.

"What the hell are you doing?" Kimolijah says, and it doesn't seem angry or snarky this time, just confused.

"Let me in for a second, yeah?"

"For what?"

"I, uh...." Bas hadn't been aware he'd need an excuse, so he doesn't have one ready. "Water." He nods, upside-down, which makes his vision sway a little, and hey, what do you know, he actually could do with a good long drink after just about sweating blood for the last several hours. "Reacher said not to bring any skins, what with all the gridstream flying around up here," which seemed to make sense at the time, but now not so much.

Kimolijah stares at him for a little too long before he shakes his head and shuts the door again. Bas is still blinking at it when it cracks open a few seconds later and a water bag is shoved in his face with a gruff "Here." Quite literally shoved in his face, actually, and Bas has to make sure he's got a good grip with one hand so he can snag the water bag with the other.

"Uh, thanks," says Bas, then, "Wait!" when the door starts sliding shut again. "Hang fire, just one second," Bas says, then decides trying to gulp water upside-down is a learned skill, but he gets enough in him that he can almost feel soft tissues expanding like a dry sponge abruptly dropped in a well. Cool, clear, blessed water runnels over his cheeks and into his nose and pleasantly wets his brow as he sucks the water bag dry before handing it back through the small gap in the door. "Better," he says, then, "Wait!" again as Kimolijah once more tries to shut the door in his face.

Kimolijah rolls his eyes, and he's impatient, but he's not glaring at Bas this time, not angry or wary or any of the other ten thousand negative responses Bas has gotten from him over the past week or so. "I really can't have the door open," Kimolijah says. "They can't usually do much once the sun's up, but it's not like they haven't tried before."

"Who's 'they'?" Bas asks, hand on the edge of the door now to make sure it stays open. "And what, exactly, might they try?"

Kimolijah stares, for way too long, considering Bas is hanging upside-down over the side of a speeding train. His eyes narrow, then widen, and he sucks in a long, low breath through his teeth. "Reacher really didn't tell you anything at all, did he?"

"Sure he did." Bas lifts an eyebrow, which is probably not even a little bit effective, what with his position and all. "He told me to shoot birds."

"Yeah, you said." Kimolijah leans in closer, frowning harder. "That's seriously all?" When Bas just stares at him, Kimolijah's mouth thins down to a grim line. "And you didn't think to ask for more information?"

"Why no, Kimolijah, I just thought I'd venture out into the desert with a bunch of people I don't know, on a train that shouldn't exist, into a place no one will tell me about, and *not ask any fucking questions.*" Bas grits his teeth, and he hadn't even realized he was this angry about it. "And let's not forget—I asked *you* about the Bruise, and you told me goats can go down on each other!"

Kimolijah blinks. "Reacher told you nothing," he says again, as though looking for confirmation, and when Bas gives it to him—quite exasperatedly—Kimolijah frowns and takes a step back, nodding. He doesn't open the door any wider, though. "Okay," he says, looking at the floor now, thinking, and then he nods some more and says, "Okay," again. He looks up at Bas. "Right, so, yeah, Mister Directorate Tracker, that's actually a point in your favor, believe it or not and for all the good it'll do you." Bas opens his mouth, but Kimolijah shakes his head and says, "No, pin up, there isn't time. I've no doubt you'll be a dog with a bone about it later, but for now, just listen to me carefully and do what I tell you, or we're both going to be fucked six ways into next year." He shoots a look out the windscreen, mutters, "*Shit*," then looks back at Bas, and the urgency in his gaze and his tone make Bas put aside his annoyance and pay powerful close attention.

"They don't do well in our sunlight," Kimolijah says. "Remember that. They can't see in it. The sun is... different on their side, I don't know. From what I've heard, it sounds like they only get the ultraviolet spectr—"

"Wait, they have a different *sun*?"

Kimolijah rolls his eyes. "No, it's the same sun, but it's a different world, a different... *plane*. This"—Kimolijah waves his hand at the windscreen, those jutting horns getting closer and the Bruise hunching like an open throat beyond them—"this is just a way in and out, a portal, or whatever you want to call it. Now shut it and *listen*." He keeps shooting quick looks out the windscreen, anxious. "My da says it's like an illobook panel over there, all flat and done up in achromatic blues, yeah?"

It's the first time Bas has heard Kimolijah refer to his da, plainly and in the present tense, and not get zapped for it. He doesn't remark on it, just nods and keeps listening.

"So you've already got the bulge on them," Kimolijah goes on. "Just remember they can't see right in our light, and if the sun hits their skin for more than a couple minutes, it hurts them. Can kill them if they're in it for too long." He ducks another look through the windscreen before turning back to Bas. "All you need to know for now is that anyone coming at the train gets shot. Watch everywhere, 'cause if you let them get me, I'll smoke you as they're dragging me off, don't think I won't." He shoots one last look out the windscreen and sets a hand to the door. "Man your cannon, Mister Badass Gunslinger. And *don't* listen to anything anyone else tells you. That was Haversham's mistake." He pauses and his mouth pinches down. With an annoyed huff, he shakes his head and says, "Shit," hesitant. He peers at Bas like he's resigned, like he's going to regret saying it, but he takes a breath anyway and goes on, "Remember what I said about snakes. Sometimes a stupid person is dangerous because they know how to hide the fact that they're really a vicious, cunning hardcase."

It's like he can't help speaking in metaphors.

The door heaves shut, almost taking Bas's nose off, and the rasp of the latch sliding to tells Bas it's not going to open again. He slithers back and up to his feet, peering everywhere now and on alert all over again. Those horns up ahead have taken on a new and even more ominous look. Bas clips himself to the lanyard and sets his hands to the cannon's grips.

⨷

And for all the anxiety and anticipation, when the train accelerates through what Bas can see now are—yes, definitely, banks and knolls of limestone pocked full of—caves, it's all rather anticlimactic, because nothing actually happens.

Yet.

The sun's come up as full as it's going to get by the time Bas sees the station—a real station this time, with a roof and actual walls. Still miles away, but it's easy to see the lines and angles of it down the final declining slope of the valley that abuts the feet of the Saltons. Or would, if the Bruise wasn't in the way. Bas gives it half an hour, maybe more, before they reach it.

A weak tug nips at the middle of Bas's chest when he feels Kimolijah prime the lever for the hydraulics; a slight fizz in his gut when Kimolijah modifies the stream and sends more power to the braking system. It's nothing more than anyone who's not gridTech would feel on a routine tour through a gridstation, and it's oddly comforting in the face of that massive boil at the end of the tracks.

The second there's movement in the distance, Bas can spot it. Nothing more than shapeless specks against dun flats, but Bas can see the paths they make, lines of footprints that lead from the center of the pulsing mass of blue-black impossibility to the boxy shapes of the station and its outbuildings. Bas peers through the sights of the cannon, narrows his eyes, and picks them off in his head as he counts them, but he doesn't let his finger flutter at the toggle yet. The temptation to stop worrying about his cover and just start shooting has been coming at him in forceful waves for a while now, and he's experiencing a bit of a high tide at the moment. He keeps his finger off the toggle and just watches.

And thinks.

Because he hasn't thought about the metaphors thing before. He's just supposed Kimolijah is a smartass and likes to answer serious questions with trivial bosh. Bas gets it now.

Kimolijah can't lie, not when he's got that bracelet on, and even when he doesn't, he can't lie about what he said when it goes back on. So yeah, if he wanted to get a point across without lying and with plausible deniability about what he's actually said, metaphorical crosstalk would work great, provided the person you're talking to knows what to listen for. Bas does now, and he thinks about garden snakes and vipers and cunning people with convincing masks of fatuous artlessness, and he knows exactly who Kimolijah was telling him to look out for.

He doesn't really need the warning, but still. It's kind of huge that Kimolijah gave him one.

19.

It's quiet when they finally pull up near the station, though Kimolijah doesn't pilot the train into its cover. Bas eyes the roof and tries to duck his head and get a look under the eaves, but it's too dark in there, and with the sun stretching out around the shifting mass of the Bruise, he can't see a thing. He's just as glad Kimolijah stops the train a ways out.

Reacher, Yanush, and Merrin all step down from the train, guns held ready and hats tipped low over their eyes. At Reacher's nod, Merrin paces up toward the nose of the cab and sets his stance into one of readiness. Yanush remains by the passenger car's door, and he nods as Lowen steps out and past him.

Grim-faced and gridgun held in both hands, Lowen makes his way over to the engine. He gives Bas a glance from under the brim of his hat but otherwise ignores him as he checks the door to Kimolijah's cab and... bolts it. From the outside. Locks Kimolijah in.

Bas says, "What the hell?"

Lowen doesn't even look at him. He plants himself, like a guard, in front of the door Kimolijah had shut in Bas's face only a little while ago. Cavett comes to guard the door on the other side, though he doesn't touch it, doesn't bar it like Lowen had done on his side. Bas reckons he can't, what with the gridstream running down that side of the cab, and that alone would make a decent enough deterrent to anyone trying to get in, so he must be making sure Kimolijah doesn't get out.

It's nothing at all like what Bas has been expecting, though he can't say he was expecting anything specific. Even so, whatever he's allowed into nebulous imagination, it wasn't anything like this. Still, he keeps himself angled so the only direction he can't see is the one from which they've come, though he makes sure to swivel looks behind him at odd intervals, just in case.

They sit for long moments, the gridstream fluttering over the wirework at Bas's back, quieter now that they're idling on the tracks, but every once in a while a fat spark will shudder up through the cables and conduit until it makes the full circuit and spits out embers when it reaches the end. Bas thinks it's a warning, a message—*I'm watching you and you won't catch me off guard*—and he's glad.

They all look like Dolerma and Serenat, at least what Bas can see of them. Taller, though, and more willowy and even paler; the impression of *white* is like a smack in the face, but Bas knows it's not so much color as lack of it. Translucent skin and hair-that's-not, and which Bas can't help thinking of as something alive and its own entity, like coral on a reef. Dark glasses peer out from beneath hats shaped like upside-down bowls, and Bas is not shocked to see the not-hair wavering before gathering underneath them and contracting into the shadows cast by the wide-bowed brims like hermit crabs into their shells.

Bas can very easily believe this is a people who don't see light very often, at least not this kind. He keeps imagining jellyfish drying in the sun and wonders if they're shriveling a little bit while they stand there.

They don't wear their clothes so much as they're swaddled in them. Everything is dull-colored and tight-wrapped, like long, wide bandages coiled around limbs and torsos and even necks. Bas thinks of all of Kimolijah's straps and buckles and the scarves wrapped around the tops of his boots and the ends of his sleeves, and wonders if there's something else Reacher has neglected to tell him. He doesn't fancy getting some mutant version of a scorpion down his boot. Or his collar.

Bas thinks at first they all look the same, tall, thin simulacra that move almost in concert, but they're not. Some are shorter, some a bit wider, though they don't seem to come in different colors, like normal people. Bas gets the impression there are both males and females in the cluster, but he can't tell why he thinks that, and it's not like any of them have done him the courtesy of donning skirts, like Serenat, so he can't tell male from female. He writes it off to anomalous tracking senses and disregards it until it might seem like it matters.

They're heeled, but not with weapons Bas recognizes. Long rods, reminiscent of rifles, but longer and wider and with small-bellied tanks where stocks should be. Bas can't even guess at what the tanks might hold, but he's betting death at the end of one of those things would be ugly. The only one not holding a weapon of any kind stands a bit off to the side, watching everything at once, pose relaxed. Bas pegs this one as the leader and adjusts his sights accordingly.

Kimolijah revs the engine, a short, sharp burst of gridstream that spits filaments onto the tracks. It's like a signal of some kind, or at least these people seem to take it as such, because the one Bas thinks is the leader nods and two of the dozen or so who've been clustered just outside the dark of the station now move inside while the others close ranks and fill in the gaps they'd left. A moment later, the other two are back again, only this time they've got someone between them, and Bas knows who it is the second they get closer and the man's shape comes into focus. Older, much taller, but same dark skin, same axe-blade cheekbones, and Bas would recognize that widow's peak anywhere.

The engine revs again, more sparks go flying, and Bas can't help but think of it as angry. He can understand that one thoroughly.

"Unbelievable *bastards*," Bas mutters. He thumps his heel into the thick glass, a token of support, and he hopes Kimolijah takes it as such.

It takes a few revolutions of the engine for the sparks to die down and the gridstream to calm, though not all the way; it's more alive than it would be if it was merely idling. Again, it seems like a signal, because the apparent leader of what Bas is coming to think of as the Willow Men steps forward, takes Kimolijah's da's arm, and jerks him a few steps closer to the train.

Bas thinks it's a male.

"You can see our bargain holds for another ten-turn," the leader says, only he doesn't so much *say* it as *buzz* it, a hard, brash sound scudding across the desert quiet, and Bas shouldn't be able to understand it, but he does—it's like the words are being rearranged into thoughts and shoved right into his mind. He doesn't hear the *words* when the leader goes on, "Though my patience grows thin," but the sense of it punches right through the alien drone of the spoken words and blooms fully formed in Bas's head. It's got that lemony bite to it, the sour-sweet tang hitting Bas at the back of his throat, and that colorless pulse thumping at the edges of his vision.

Like that time with Dolerma in Stanslo's dining room, but stronger, bolder, and with no earthy suggestion of a psyTech aftertaste, and Bas is on the verge of epiphany here, so he lets the thought settle.

"Soon, chieftain," Serenat says in that same buzzy "language" Bas can understand when he shouldn't. Serenat has stepped down from the passenger car, and she's stood now several steps out from Lowen. "Just a little longer."

And with Serenat *right there*, it's not so hard to see it.

Not psyTech, Stanslo had assured Bas, smug as always, and now Bas thinks *bullshit*. Bullshit it's not something invasive and disturbing and unfamiliarly familiar, like a stranger speaking with your lover's tongue, and you know the voice, recognize the tones that've been seared into your soul, but the cadence is all wrong and the heart behind them is missing altogether. No, it's not psyTech like Bas knows it, but it's something analogous, mutated like everything else here, and the intrusive sense of citrus is starting to make him want to brush at his skin even worse than when those monster spiders were coming at him, but more—it's making him halfway understand what he thinks he missed before.

The leader pauses and aims something at Serenat that might be a smile as he voices a greeting, soft, and something else Bas can't quite discern, a word or a phrase that doesn't come through the weird psychic translation that's going on in his head but it has the feel of an endearment.

Serenat doesn't acknowledge it. She doesn't do anything at all. She merely stands a dozen or so paces from a being with whom she shares too many resemblances. And she stares. And then she turns to the figure just behind the leader and cracks a grin.

"Hello."

Bas hadn't really paid attention, hadn't cared, but now he can recognize the female shape beneath all the wrappings. The woman takes a step forward and lays an uncovered hand to the leader's shoulder.

"Hello, sweetpea."

The hand is not white. The fingers are not too long. And the voice doesn't buzz and slide directly into Bas's head.

The woman is not one of these people.

And the endearment—*sweetpea*....

It pings at something in the back of Bas's mind, but he can't quite snag it right now.

The Willow Man says something that only garbles in Bas's head, something private, maybe, and not meant to be translated for anyone who doesn't speak the language. Bas thinks he catches something that has the feel of "kin" and Serenat snorts and says, "Yeah, the baron won't let him," plain and without the buzz. "Anyway, he's still pissed about Travis. I don't think he wants to see either of you."

"Bloody hell," Bas can't help but growl. "This is so fucked up."

Cavett snorts from his post below at the train's door, but Bas doesn't take his eyes off the Willow Men, and especially the one that's got hold of Ajamil Adani like a disobedient puppy.

"All right, Geda," Lowen calls in his usual easy drawl. *Geda*— the name is familiar. "The contract says—"

"The contract is long past due."

"Yeah, well, that's between you and the baron, so maybe you could not be shitty about it for a change." Lowen rolls his hand, impatient. "Let's just make the trade and be done with it this time, yeah? Last time cost us a good man, and I'm getting impatient with the game."

The Willow Man, Geda, shakes his head. "And who was it set the rules for this game?" He holds out his hand. "It is your world that poisons mine. It is your chieftain who—"

"It is my chieftain who generously sends you aid across the Dead Lands each ten-turn at great expense and personal risk to each of us here." It sounds bored, like Lowen has made the argument before and didn't really care much about it then.

"This 'generous aid' is mutual ransom—nothing more, nothing less—and your chieftain's greed only grows. Let us at least speak truths, here of all places."

There's an abrupt pounding beneath Bas's feet, Kimolijah whacking at the cab's door. "For fuck's sake, Lowen, how about you do your jawing when I'm *not* locked inside a tin can with no air and this thing *isn't* crawling past my elbow!"

It seems to pull Ajamil out of his apparent daze. "'Lijah," he says, voice crackling at the edges and weak, but audible and loud enough Bas is sure Kimolijah must've heard it.

He did, because there's a long pause, everything quiet and unnaturally still, before Kimolijah answers, "Directly, Da. Okay?" Muffled through the door. "I just... I'm having a hard time with... just. *God*. I promise. Please." It's thready, like he's in the middle of breaking down, Bas can picture him with his brow pressed to the inside of the door, and then there's another punch to the cab's wall and Kimolijah snarls, "Goddamn it, Lowen, make the trade and get me the fuck out of here!"

"Just switch the draw, son," Ajamil says, sad and tired, and he shakes his head as he stares at the train. Anguished. "Just do it."

A nod from Geda and two of his people pull Ajamil back and toward the darkness of the station. "'Lijah!" Ajamil calls, walking backward, eyes on the train. "'Lijah, just give him what he wants! Switch the draw and give him what he wants!"

The Willow Men hauling him back don't handle him roughly, don't try to get him to shut up. They let him keep yelling as they pull him back, until they're far enough into the station that his voice fades to a distant rise and fall of unintelligible noise.

"It'll be okay." Serenat pets at the cab's door, leaning in just beside Lowen. "It'll be okay, Kimo."

"You are more and more like them every day, Serenat." Geda shakes his head, disapproving.

"God, I *hate* you," comes from inside the cab. Kimolijah's tone is quieter and there's no banging this time, but the declaration is heartfelt nonetheless, though Bas doesn't know at whom it's directed. "I hate you so fucking much."

Serenat's mouth pinches tight, and she turns to Lowen with a glare.

It's almost like it hits Lowen physically: he twitches, then gives his head a sharp shake. "Reacher," Lowen says with a jerk of his chin.

Reacher, in turn, jerks his chin at Yanush. "Go get the crystals."

Yanush sighs but moves to shoulder his gun's strap until Reacher puts a hand out and says, "Here, I'll hold it for ya. Don't want it gettin' in the way."

Yanush doesn't look happy about it, eyeing Geda and his people warily, but he hands Reacher his gridgun before he starts walking slowly across the sand to meet two of the Willow Men coming toward them, one of them carrying a small chest like the one Haversham had brought back on the day he died.

Serenat looks at Yanush with a small frown. "This is your

fault," she tells Geda, colorless lips thin and set in a straight line.

"Is it?" Geda asks, no inflection, no expression.

"You shouldn't have set Fox on Kimo." Serenat's smile looks just as cold as Stanslo's. "I'm starting to feel like you don't trust me."

"Trust." Geda shakes his head. "Perhaps, little one, you shouldn't put so much trust in sweet words from the mouth of a thief and a liar."

"I can't tell if you're talking about the baron or yourself." Serenat smirks. "But don't worry. I don't trust either one of you." She pauses and shoots a flat smirk at Reacher before turning back to Geda. "Or anyone you've got synched."

Yanush frowns at her, then at Geda, but Merrin stiffens and then whips around to lock eyes with Yanush. Yanush squints back at him for a long, drawn-out moment, confused, before realization wells into his expression at the same as it swamps Bas.

"Reacher?" Merrin says, low and threatening, and his gun comes around to point at Reacher.

Reacher gives him a guileless grin and shrugs with a sigh, regretful, but the gun he took from Yanush has been trained Merrin's way since his hand settled around the grip, while the other remains pointed toward Geda. "Everyone's got to have collateral, Merrin. You know that."

"Oh," Bas breathes, "*shit*."

"Ho, hang fire now," Yanush says and takes a step backward.

"Yanush is stronger than you," Reacher tells Merrin, all dry and matter-of-fact. "He'll do better in the mines than you would. And you're a better shot. Boss didn't want to let you go." He shrugs. "It's a compliment."

Merrin looks absolutely wrecked. And a little bit dangerous. "I'll take the pipe like Haversham before I do one more fucking—"

"Yeah, but you won't." Reacher's face has lost all expression. "Your contract's pretty clear on such things, Merrin. Don't think the boss hasn't made some adjustments to the crystals after Haversham pulled his little stunt. And Yanush is kind of depending on you staying healthy now." He jerks his chin again, both guns steady. "You just go on along now, Yanush, and Merrin won't have to get hurt, yeah?"

Bas can't help but notice that Reacher's usual *aw shucks* demeanor has cleared away, along with his simplistic speech patterns.

"Contrary to what your chieftain may believe," Geda puts in mildly, "we are not a pen in which to hold your inconvenient sheep."

"If you want what's on this train," Reacher answers, just as mildly, "you're whatever our chieftain says you are."

Bas only watches it all from his perch atop the train, paying very close attention to whose guns are pointing where. Or he's trying to, but something zings over the back of his neck and he starts to taste a splash of yellow at the backs of his teeth, smell earth through his skin, and he straightens up and narrows his eyes out toward the small crowd of Willow Men. Because Bas recognizes the sensation of a psyTech trying to get past his locks when he feels it.

"Goddamn you, Reacher." Merrin's teeth are clenched tight and his fingers are white on the grip of his gun. He looks like he's *this close* to breaking. "Don't do it, Yani." Merrin shakes his head, expression furious and panicked and deadly all at once.

Bas scans all the faces, lets his tracking senses skitter out and latch on, and... *there.* The woman. The one who doesn't belong here.

...Or maybe she does.

Yanush is staring at Merrin, and Bas doesn't know if Merrin's seeing the same thing he is, but Bas can see the horrible decision all over Yanush's resigned face.

"Don't make it harder than it is," Reacher says. And then he smiles, that ingenuous *babe in the woods* smile, and he shoots a rope of gridstream at Merrin's feet.

To Merrin's credit, he doesn't yelp and he doesn't lurch back. Sand kicks up and Bas can hear it pepper Merrin's coat even from here, but all Merrin does is keep his eyes locked on Yanush. "Don't," is all he says.

Lowen mutters something dark and angry, but Reacher either doesn't hear or doesn't care. "Geda, this one is yours now. We might like to have him back, so keep him in good shape, yeah?" He looks at Merrin and *smirks.*

Geda doesn't move or speak, but two of his people come and stand to either side of Yanush, weapons pointed at his head.

"Don't," Merrin says again, and he shakes his head, eyes glistening.

Yanush swallows, Bas can hear the dry click. "Just...." Yanush has to pause and clear his throat. "Just watch yer back, Merri-do, yeah? And behave, if ye can." He tries to smile; it wobbles and falls. "Yer good, I'm good, yeah?"

Good *God.* Bas hasn't really paid it much mind, hasn't understood what Merrin and Yanush are to each other, but he sees clearly now. Horribly clearly. He barely even knows them, and it's hurting his chest.

"Yani, *don't.*" Merrin takes a step, and again, Reacher casually takes a shot at Merrin's feet, closer this time, close enough that Bas thinks Merrin got a bit of backwash from the stream, because he hisses and too obviously tries not to twitch.

"Didn't want to have to do this," Reacher says, lowering the gun pointing at Yanush and reaching into his shirt. The crystal he comes up with is smaller than the one Stanslo has, darker, but still recognizable. "Then again, I've been kind of wanting to try her out."

"I'll go," Merrin says, frantic. Merrin's gun hits the ankle-deep sand that covers the hardpan. "Let me—"

"Shut the fuck up," Yanush snaps. "Just shut the fuck up. Pick up yer gun and do yer fuckin' job, Merrin, 'cause if I end up like Jilly, I'm hauntin' yer ass 'til the Patrons send me packin'."

It's hard to watch, and Bas lets his gaze rove a bit wider. And sees the woman standing out and away from the rest of them, her stance calm and her gaze locked onto Bas. Another push of yellow and earth shimmies over him, and Bas sucks in a breath as he feels Mo's locks batten down and push back.

The woman shakes her head before she takes the scarf from across her face. She's plain, perhaps somewhat handsome, her skin very pale but not unhealthy, and set with fine lines of comfortable age. She doesn't look tired or shaky like Ajamil Adani did. The sense of intruding psyTech fades, and the woman does nothing but stare at Bas for a long moment. She looks away and presses her lips together. Annoyance or disappointment, Bas can't tell.

"Serenat," she calls, and she glances at Bas once more, like she's making sure he's watching. She lifts her hand and waves. "You're playing a dangerous game, child. I suggest you settle the contract at the next run. Our chieftain is not a patient man."

She drops her hand and turns before walking slowly away. Not toward the station, like all the Willow Men are doing now the excitement's over; she's walking toward the Bruise, like she has every intention of shinning the length of the tracks that stretch a measure or two between them and the blue-on-black mass that churns and gnaws at the sky.

Bas shifts to peer at Serenat, and he can't tell through the dark of the glasses, but he gets the distinct impression Serenat's rolling her eyes like Mo used to when their mam would kiss him in front of his—

And *that* is apparently what's been niggling at the back of Bas's mind since Serenat greeted the woman moments ago. And all he can think is *no fucking way*.

Bas stares as the woman walks away. And makes himself not bang his head against the stock of the cannon. Repeatedly.

⁂

And that's how Bas finds yet another "dead" Tech who isn't really dead.

Which would probably be a lot more impressive if he'd actually been looking.

For all intents and purposes, they're alone, mostly, Bas and Kimolijah, Kimolijah locked inside the cab and Bas up top on his gun. Everyone else is either unloading the freight cars or watching them do it.

Bas is alert, because he doesn't trust a single person here, not even Kimolijah. So Bas tries to look everywhere at once and stretches his senses behind him. Which, in the end, does him no good, because he can sense Tech from miles away, but these people aren't Tech.

So he doesn't so much sense the long white figure soundlessly approaching from the mild hubbub as catch the subtle whiff of citrus. The gridcannon swings just as easily as it always does, and Bas has got the barrel of it leveled at the figure before whoever it is has even finished the climb up the back of the engine.

"I assure you," the person—Geda, Bas is pretty sure—says in that unsettling mix of buzzy vocals and citrusy, psychic intrusion, "I do not wish violence." And to back it up, he steps right up to the end of the gridcannon and leans his chest into it. His hat is gone and the stuff that's not hair is twitching at the ends and licking at the shoulders of his wrappings.

Bas concentrates powerful hard to control his reflexes so his fingers don't tic and jig on the toggle. He does pull out his six-barrel, though.

"Somehow, I'm thinking you said the exact same thing to Haversham."

Geda sucks in a sharp breath. "Has no one told you how dangerous that is here?" He jerks his chin at Bas's gun.

"Combustibles, yeah." Bas pulls back the hammer anyway. "Could blow up in my hand, so I'm told." He shrugs. "But I'm thinking that if I have to pull the trigger, it'll be because you've gotten close enough you'll go out with me."

Geda seems to think that over for a spell before he grunts, annoyed. He takes a step back: concession.

"Bas?" Kimolijah calls through the skin of the cab, and he knocks, a funny little *rap-rap-rap* with his knuckles right under the arch of Bas's boot. "You all right up there?"

Bas lifts his eyebrows, and despite the situation, he smiles a little. "Why, Kimo, I'm touched." He narrows his eyes at Geda. "Everything's right as a trivet, no worries."

"I hear voices."

"Yeah, I'm having a bit of a chat with Geda." Kimolijah squawks something sharp and alarmed, and Bas rides over it with, "Just a chat, Kimo. A very, very careful chat." He adds, "Trust me," and surprisingly, Kimolijah does. Well. He goes quiet, at least, though Bas thinks Kimolijah's probably listening as well as he can.

"Don't you worry, there, sparker," Reacher calls from somewhere over by the station. "I got his back."

Bas rolls his eyes, because *yeah, sure you do.* Probably picking a spot right between Bas's shoulder blades.

"So," Bas says to Geda. "I reckon you wanted a word."

The hairlike stuff on Geda's head ripples at the ends before it stretches subtly out and toward Bas, like it's reaching. Bas doesn't know if it's a threat, but it's creepy as hell, so he raises the six-barrel. It stops Geda like the gridcannon didn't.

Geda lifts his hands, harmless, and says, "The one you would call my 'mate' cannot read you."

Bas leans back a little and eyes Geda closely. He ignores the second part of the statement entirely and goes right for the throat: "I wouldn't call her that. I'd probably call her Baroness, since I'm fairly polite." He smirks a little when Geda twitches. "Or I might call her Bella, one day, should we perhaps get to know one another well enough." Geda's jaw clenches, like it pisses him off, so Bas pushes, "But if anyone were to ask, I'd probably call her Baroness Bella Stanslo, since, from what I reckon, her bond with the baron was never legally dissolved, what with her being 'dead' and all."

"Call her what you like." Geda has stretched up to his full height, looming. "She has not been any of it for a very long time."

"Yeah, I got that." Bas pauses and cocks his head to the side. "She looks rather well. You know—for a decades-old corpse." He shrugs. "Hey, from what I can tell, it all looks pretty voluntary, so who am I to judge. Only there's a powerful lot of stuff going on here that's *not* voluntary, so why don't we stick to why you want Kimo."

"For the same reasons your chieftain wants him."

"So you basically want him for the Tech." Bas eyes Geda with a frown. "And you're keeping his da here for Stanslo because...?" Bas slides his hand away from the gridcannon's toggle and snaps his fingers. "Just another trade, yeah? Stanslo gives you those bricks to clean your water, water that's been poisoned by our toxic runoff, and you give him crystals. You keep his hostages here for him, and he... does what for you?"

The others are starting to shoot glances his way, paying more attention than Bas would like. Bas puts it aside and thinks.

He cuts a look at Geda and clenches his jaw. "Can't be the machine they make the bricks with. If it were that simple, Kimo would've already built you one on the sly, because that's just the kind of thing he does. Could be the train, I guess, because who wouldn't want one of their very own? But guys like you... it's usually guns." Bas pauses and lifts an eyebrow. "Maybe both. All. A train full of guns, that it? That new train Kimo's building— it's supposed to be for you, yeah? But, just like Stanslo, you don't think he's moving fast enough, so you're trying to hurry him along by dragging his da out here and dangling him in Kimo's face every time—"

"Admirable deduction, if not precisely accurate." Geda pulls his mouth into a flat little smirk. "The trade has already been made."

Bas stills. "What does that mean?" He glares at Geda, waiting for an answer he doesn't really need, but Bas wants to hear it. He wants Geda to say it out loud, just see if it shames him even a little bit.

Geda won't, so Bas says it: "Yeah, okay, because Stanslo's not one to let go of something valuable unless he gets what he wants out of it first. So the new train's for Stanslo. Kimo's the trade. And once Stanslo manages to get more Techs out here, he'll trade those too. But he won't let Kimo go until he's finished the new train." He shakes his head and waves toward the Bruise. "Fucking figures. *The* biggest scientific discovery ever, and it's got wannabe alien overlords crawling out of it like a bad plot out of *Planet Horror*."

And then, just to be a dick, he adds, "You know you're not going to get any of it, yeah? A man doesn't build enough guns to arm an invasion and then hand them all over to someone who can't be trusted not to invade *him*. And he certainly doesn't hand over something as revolutionary as a gridtrain, along with the only man who can run it. Anyway"—Bas shrugs, purposely flip—"Stanslo's a little overly fond of Kimo. 'Irreplaceable,' he said. He's not going to hand him over, no matter what he tells you, and there's fuck-all you can do about it, isn't there? You need Stanslo more than Stanslo needs you. He might not want to live without a constant supply of those crystals, but he can, and he's got enough stockpiled he might not need to." He pauses with a grin. "But you can't live without water, can you? And you can't make it across the desert and to our world without a train."

He stops, purely for effect, before he leans in and lowers his voice, confidential confession.

"You do understand that Stanslo doesn't give even the smallest shit about those hostages, yeah? They're not the leverage you seem to think they are. The only one that means anything is Kimo's da, and he only matters to Kimo. Once he's gone...." Bas leans back and waves down toward the cab. "Kimo can be a vicious little bastard sometimes. I don't think I'd want to piss him off and then make him build things for me that might blow up in my face."

Geda looks at Bas with those black eyes behind black lenses, just looks, and Bas stares back and waits and waits and *waits* for something—an answer he knows he won't get; shame he knows Geda doesn't feel; anger he wishes would at least knock Geda off balance for a second or two. Geda gives him none of it, at least not with words. He steps in again, leaning to the side of the gridcannon's barrel this time, and then he jerks his head so hard to the side the stuff on his head that's not hair whips out and swirls. It happens so fast Bas almost doesn't get it, almost doesn't move quick enough, but he does, and he just catches the shape of something small detaching, a tip breaking off from a stalk of tentacle-like not-hair and hurtling right toward his face.

Bas's arm windmills in front of him, blessed reflex before he makes a conscious move, and he bats whatever the hell it is away, the touch fleshy and disturbingly warm at the palm of his hand as he swats it down. Burr bug, Bas figures, tiny thing, but big enough to see and no doubt feel it just fine if it has a chance to burrow in.

Got it in the eye, Kimolijah had said, and *God*.

It lands beside Bas's boot, so he crushes it beneath his heel, and he hears Geda grunt a little, like it hurt him. Good. Another comes flying at Bas, not aimed as well as the first and easier to deflect. Bas doesn't know where this one goes when he strikes out and connects, but it goes *away*, out and over the side of the cab, so he doesn't worry about it.

Geda's pulling back, bracing, readying for another go, no doubt. He's to the side of the cannon, so Bas can't get him with that. Someone shouts from behind; Bas doesn't know who it is, but he thinks it's Lowen. He tunes it out, tilts the cannon up toward the sky, and fires off a bolt of gridstream that's brighter than the desert sun in the shadow of the Bruise. It blinds Geda enough that Bas can level the six-barrel right at Geda's chest. He ignores the warnings about combustibles and losing a hand, and pulls the trigger.

It doesn't blow up so much as it blows *out*, a scattered report that echoes everywhere and a *whump* of fiery smoke that billows from the muzzle like dragon's breath. A thick, noxious cloud of it fizzes and sparks between them, dense enough that Bas loses track of Geda altogether, and he can hear Kimolijah yelling and pounding on the roof again, but Bas's ears are ringing and he's coughing out the parts of the small explosion he accidentally inhaled, so he doesn't know what Kimolijah's saying.

Bas does not end up with a stump, and Geda does not end up with a hole in his chest. Geda comes away with more burns than Bas does, so Bas calls it a win. He looks around, spots Lowen charging toward him and Reacher standing hipshot against the station, just watching, no expression on his face. His gun is hanging by its strap from his shoulder, like he has no intention of doing anything with it. Bas narrows his eyes and thinks *Yeah, okay, I got you now.*

There's more shouting, more voices, everyone available come running, apparently. Another pseudostandoff while Geda picks himself up and leaps off the cab to the ground, and then lots of waving of guns and those rod things. Lowen takes charge, directing Merrin and Cavett and Serenat back into the passenger car with instructions to shut themselves in and keep hold of their guns 'til they're clear.

He looks up at Bas and asks, "All right?" and Bas can see the other question beneath it.

Bas squints at Lowen through the lingering smoke before skidding a steady look at Reacher. *Got my back, then, yeah?* They hold the stare between them for a spell of several beats, and then Bas turns back to Lowen.

"Yeah," he says and shakes out his hand; it burns. "Yeah, he didn't get me."

Reacher climbs up onto the cab, all concern. "You sure?" he asks, worried eyes and sympathetic smile, and he sets his great hands to the cannon. "Be a shame if I had to tell the boss that Geda managed to tag another one." He shrugs and reaches down to mess with the toggle. "Prob'ly hafta kill ya."

Bas knocks Reacher's hand away from the cannon and shoves him back. Reacher seems surprised Bas manages it, and he narrows his eyes. Bas thinks about going after him and just... letting go, showing Reacher that size doesn't preclude a good thrashing when a man knows how to do it. But Bas is still clamped to the roof by the lanyard, and there's no quick and graceful way to unclip and lunge in.

So he merely says, "Off the fucking cab, Reacher."

Reacher's eyebrows go up, feigned surprise, and he grins as he puts up his hands and backs away. "Touchy," he says as he hops down to the ground, and he actually whistles as he saunters away, until Lowen tells him to get the unloading started so they can go. Reacher stops whistling, and he grimaces, but he does it.

Bas clenches his teeth and retrieves his still-smoking gun from where it wedged itself between the feet of the cannon's mount when he dropped it. The barrels are all still intact, but two of them are warped, and he's betting the sights have been blown all to hell. He wonders if Quinnie will fix it for him.

⬥

There is no more shooting, no more trying to fling burr bugs, no more anything, really. Reacher hooks the empty freight cars to the locomotive as the Bruise-dimmed sun begins to slouch behind the mountains the Bruise hasn't eaten, and Lowen takes the locks off the cab just before he pounds on the door and tells Kimolijah, "All clear."

Too easy. These people want this train and they want Kimolijah, and they'd somehow lured Haversham away from his gun long enough to make an attempt, from which he walked away with a compact little mind-control tool in the shape of a burr bug. It can't be over.

The gathered Willow Men still watch, like they're just waiting for an opportunity to give it another go. Bas watches them right back and makes sure they won't. He might smirk a little at Geda, because the burns on Geda's face look like he's been splashed with acid, that strange, gelatinous-looking skin pocked and puckered and oozing blood that looks like dark honey. They look like they *hurt*, and Bas can't help feeling a bit of petty satisfaction.

Because fucking *burr bugs*, man. Seriously—what the *fuck*.

The departure is uneventful, the steady acceleration soothing as Bas grips the cannon and watches, more vigilant now than he'd been when swamped by flying nightmares and giant spiders. His hand hurts, powder burns a steady hum and pulse that would otherwise make his eyes water, but now the pain helps keep him alert.

He's still watching when they reach the spurs of limestone an hour or so later, so he catches it when shadows move and turn into too-familiar shapes, crouching low or trying to mold into crags and ridges in the chancy not-light of near twilight. Their wraps are the color of the limestone, and their skin blends right in, so it would be a hard go making them out if it weren't for those glasses. Blue gridstream winks and flashes over black lenses as the train passes through the dip of the saddle, and it's easy then to sight down and count.

Two dozen. Which, okay. It's actually kind of tame, compared to the rest of this trip.

Bas doesn't shoot until the first one springs. And when he does shoot, nothing happens. The toggle's jammed.

The Willow Man is on him before Bas can even register the surprise. He grunts at the impact, height and velocity lending power to the leap, and they both go down with a heavy *thud* that vibrates Bas's teeth. Bas is caught, tethered by the lanyard, and the Willow Man's limbs are long; they wrap around and try to cling.

He drags the Willow Man up with him, reaching for the cannon again, because he can see more lining the caves, waiting to jump down. He manages to get an arm free, and he grips the stock of the cannon to pull himself closer. The Willow Man's got hold of Bas's legs, wrapped around him like a limpet, and he *will not let go*. Bas sets his teeth and pulls out the six-barrel and, with a merciless little grin, he whacks the Willow Man's long spindly fingers with the butt of it until the Willow Man buzzes out a little yelp and lets go. Bas takes advantage by kicking the shit out of him until he goes over the side.

Another one leaps just as Bas gets his fingers around the cannon's toggle, and the aim will be off, because Bas is half on his back and the angle's all wrong, but he still might manage to wing someone. Except the cannon doesn't fire. Again.

Shit. Shit, shit, *shit*. He has no gridgun. His six-barrel's useless except as a bludgeon. And the cannon won't shoot.

The newest arrival lands a little awkwardly, stumbles, and Bas hopes for a second this one will just tumble over the side and save Bas the trouble. It doesn't happen. The Willow Man regains his balance and tackles Bas just as Bas manages to pull himself up and behind the cannon again.

He lands way too close to the gridstream sizzling and popping at his back.

"Bas?" he hears through the roof, and he manages to call back, "A little busy!" as he wrestles out of the eelish hold and snaps around to pummel at the bloodless face until something like rust oozes. Another impact from his right nearly sends his face into the slab of glass, but he manages to catch himself on the Willow Man beneath him, driving down as hard as he can, before he flips to wrap his legs around the other one and start waling on the side of this one's head.

Fuck, his hand hurts.

"The cannon!" he yells to Kimolijah, then has to break off and disentangle from one Willow Man so he can try to kick a new one off the roof before the new one can steady his landing. Bas manages, but he slides over toward the side, legs dangling over nothing and the tether pulled to its limit, while the two still on the roof try to gain footing and stand. "Kimo!" Bas yells and kicks at the door to the cab while he tries not to look at the ground whizzing by too close beneath his boots. "Kimo! The cannon's jammed, I need—"

He breaks off because one of the Willow Men still on the roof is eyeing the lanyard that's the only thing keeping Bas from an unhappy meeting with the ground, and when long white fingers wrap around it, Bas kicks at the door again and yells, "*Kimo!*"

Bas feels the hitch and jolt of the tether letting go, or being cut, just as the door flies open, and Kimolijah grips Bas's coat and all but throws him onto the floor of the cab. Bas is only down for a second before he rolls to his feet, watching with unabashed awe as Kimolijah grips the side of the door, leans out and up, and starts throwing gridstream from the palm of his hand in short, sharp bursts. Bas hears a scream from up top, and then a distant thud as someone hits the ground. Kimolijah shoots again and says, "Oh shit," at the resulting arrhythmic thump and judder.

The engine whines and jolts, hard enough that Bas has to grab onto both Kimolijah and the closest available handhold to keep both of them from flying out, and the lights in the cab dim before everything revs up and then joggles again. Jessa squawks from somewhere behind Bas and then flies out past his ear, screeching blue murder, and Bas almost pities the Willow Man she targets, because he swears she sounds *pissed.*

There's more buzzing and zapping now, the distinctive sound of gridguns coming from the passenger car behind them, and Bas thinks *About fucking time.* Lowen, he bets it's Lowen, hanging out of the train and targeting anyone else wanting to give it a go, and he knows, he *knows* Reacher is just standing there behind Lowen, watching it all. Probably grinning.

Another jerk and whine, and Kimolijah snaps, "Give me a boost!" Bas doesn't question it; he knows what Kimolijah wants. He swoops down and grabs hold of Kimolijah's calves, sets a good angle, then *shoves.* Once Kimolijah's boots disappear over the lip of the roof, the cable attaching him to the engine coiling out behind him, Bas swings out and follows him up.

There's a Willow Man, the last one Kimolijah had zapped, caught in the fencing, gridstream locking his limbs and melting the glasses right off his face. His clothes are on fire and his not-hair is *writhing*, like it's trying to get away. The whole thing makes Bas want out of here, like he hasn't before, just *out*, he's done, fucking *done*, man, except he isn't.

"Cover me," Kimolijah says and starts over toward the wires and conduits and the thing that used to be a Willow Man caught inside it all.

"Cover you with *what*?" Bas snaps. "The cannon's dead, and I don't have—"

"The cannon's not *dead*." Grim, Kimolijah reaches into the sputtering stream, gritting his teeth as it lights him up, then hissing and yelping as it flares and coughs out sparks. "Watch the cable," Kimolijah tells Bas. "Don't let it disconnect from below, but if I get caught in this, give it a good yank."

Bas blinks, says, "Yeah, sure, I'll touch the cable with the wild gridstream in it. What could happen?"

Kimolijah snorts, like he can't help himself, but he doesn't answer. He looks back at the Willow Man, juddering and smoking and just generally being horrible-looking and macabrely animated for a dead person, and he takes a deep, long breath. He growls, grates, "Why can't anyone ever *keep shit out of the stream*?" and he throws himself forward, shouts out something that sounds like "*Ow*, mother*fucker*!" and knocks the Willow Man loose. Immediately, the stream adjusts and hums, and the train accelerates smoothly once again. "Keep watching," Kimolijah says, shakes out his hands and huffs as he kneels down behind the cannon's mount to look at its belly. "It's not done yet."

They're just past the halfway point, the horns of limestone looming up on either side. They're not clearing the pseudocanyon of the pass nearly soon enough, as far as Bas is concerned, and there are more Willow Men lurking, waiting. Sporadic gridstream bursts from the passenger car, warning shots. Bas knew it would be Lowen.

Jessa's wheeling about overhead, still shrieking like an angry auntie. Bas watches her out the corner of his eye, because he's getting to know her patterns now.

"For fuck's sake," Kimolijah mutters. "How did you let him—"

"Watch it!" Bas snaps and moves just as Jessa tucks her wings and plummets like an arrow. He only just manages to put himself between Kimolijah and the Willow Man diving at him from the ledge right above their heads. A streak of gridstream fizzes over Bas's head as he spins and takes the Willow Man down, his hand already gripping a long white throat as he lands on top and starts throttling. It's... not quite as repulsive as Bas had thought it would be. The skin isn't like jelly, it isn't cold, and it doesn't leave slime on his hands. It feels like normal skin, which is a weird thing to be thinking while he's trying to strangle another living being, but everything's weird here, so he might as well saddle up.

Jessa swoops over Bas's head with an encouraging little chirrup. Bas wants to laugh.

The Willow Man twists and bucks, bony fingers digging into Bas's wrists, that not-hair flickering out like a splayed hand, and Bas is so busy keeping an eye on it and making sure none of it comes flying at him that he almost misses Kimolijah's little *yawp* of surprise when the Willow Man's flailing legs kick out and catch him in the knees. Kimolijah goes down and to the side, skidding over the too-smooth glass and right toward the edge of the roof.

Bas keeps one hand on the Willow Man's throat and throws the other out to snatch at Kimolijah's wrist where the bracelet usually sits. Bas connects just as Kimolijah slides in a sharp arc over the lip of the roof on the way downward. Kimolijah doesn't even seem to notice. He looks up, above and ahead, spots Jessa, and raises his hand. The volley of gridstream bursts he lets loose are so short and staccato it looks like he's lobbing glowing blue balls.

Two Willow Men fly back from their perches in the caves ahead, caught smack in the chest, and the rods they'd been holding tumble down, plinking the cliffside as they go; they land somewhere between the tracks and the caves, harmless. A third Willow Man ducks behind a spur in the rock and doesn't pop up again as the train blows by beneath.

Bas looks at Kimolijah, half of him slung over the side of the train, one hand caught in Bas's and one still raised as he looks for another target. Gridstream pitches him blue in the shadows of the canyon, dark skin leavened at the planes and flushed near-black at the valleys. Lying askew on the roof of a speeding train, wind whipping the hair that's got loose into his face, eyes fierce and expression intense, looking for a target, gridstream wittering in his palm, impossible, like magic, and his *goddamned pet bird* swooping down to perch by his shoulder and worry at him like an illobook sidekick, and he looks... he looks—

"Holy fucking shit," Bas wheezes, "you're the goddamned Magic Man."

Kimolijah turns to Bas, gives him a wide-eyed look, then a wild grin, and the spell should be broken, but it's not; it merely shifts into something else, something worse than a burr bug, because it's not Bas's brain it's worming its way into. He should care, but he doesn't. He should run far away, but he won't. He stays and he looks and he lets himself feel things he won't name.

And then the Willow Man gives him a weak punch in the head.

Bas remembers he's in the process of strangling someone, so he adjusts his weight and shoves down until he feels bone and cartilage crunch in his palm and hears a thwarted gurgle. He keeps staring, though, even as he pushes away from the Willow Man and gets a better grip on Kimolijah's arm. Bas can *feel* that thing moving around beneath Kimolijah's skin, a heavy twist and a leisurely slide. It's like Kimolijah knows, because he looks at Bas harder, like he's gauging, before he says, "We're almost there."

There are so many things Bas wants to read into that. He answers them all. He says, "Yeah."

Kimolijah doesn't say anything for a spell, just looking, before he says, "Cannon's fixed," and then, "We're through."

Bas looks up, sees they are indeed through. They've cleared the caves, and though Lowen still lets out a burst from his gridgun over their heads every several seconds, this particular stretch of danger is past.

Bas shakes his head, though, smiles a little, and looks back at Kimolijah. "Not even close."

Kimolijah's still hanging over the side of the train. His legs are tangled in his cable, and his body is angled so he can't get a good foothold to wedge himself up. He doesn't seem to care, though. He *laughs*. A high, clear bray of it, deep from his belly, open and pleased.

And then, like every other time, he looks around, like he's just remembered where he is, who he is... and he stops.

◈◈◈

Bas waits as they whip through the desert night, because he can be patient and he needs to think. He goes over it all in his head while he watches Jessa stretch her wings above him. He goes over it again while he shoots at flying nightmares and giant fucking spiders. He's slightly amused when none of it, not even the swirling pits of death and their macabre method of hunting, has the same effect on him it did on the way out.

When they stop at the way station, Bas is a little surprised that Kimolijah's the one to approach him, climbing up onto the roof of the cab more agilely than Bas will ever accomplish, then planting himself in front of Bas and just... staring. A tiny ball of gridstream fidgets in his palm, just enough light to see by while he looks and looks and *looks*. Bas has to fight against a dry swallow, because apparently Kimolijah thinks he can say everything with silence, and Bas is only just figuring out how to hear it.

But.

Reacher's out of the passenger car now, watching them, and Mari's stood up from where she'd been crouched down by someone's sad little cookfire when they'd pulled up. They're meant to eat and then wait out the daylight here at the way station. Bas imagines that means they're expected to sleep as well. He doesn't reckon he'll be doing much of that.

There are carts full of charcoal that weren't there before, and most of the camp is busy loading it up into the empty freight cars. They all look, though, quick cautious glances upward as Kimolijah keeps trying to grow the ability to see through Bas's head.

Bas doesn't think more drama is a good idea, more people paying attention while he sorts all this, so he dredges up an impatient sigh and says, "I would give just about anything to know what you see."

Kimolijah startles and blinks up at Bas, wide-eyed in the dark and the pulsing light from his little ball of gridstream. He looks confused and a little bit guilty, which makes Bas rub at his eyes.

"But I can wait." He looks down at Kimolijah's left hand, gloved over and hidden beneath its long, tight sleeve and snug-wound scarves. The now-obvious attempt at precaution too late makes Bas sad and angry and too many other things he doesn't want to feel right now. "Go," he tells Kimolijah. "We're attracting attention, and I can't...." Bas takes his hat off and scuffs through his hair before snugging it back down low over his eyes. "Just not yet, yeah?"

Still Kimolijah doesn't say anything, just stares at Bas for a moment longer, looks into his eyes this time. At length he tips a sharp nod and kills the little ball of gridstream. He climbs down just as nimbly as he'd climbed up.

On impulse, Bas calls, "Kimo, hey," and waits while Kimolijah pauses and lifts an eyebrow at him. "Why don't you eat meat?"

Both eyebrows go up now. "Sorry, what?" When Bas just keeps looking at him, Kimolijah scowls. "Not that it's any of your business, but I don't eat meant because my family's patron is Devi."

Right. The goddess of beasts and forests.

Kimolijah tilts his head, less annoyed now and more curious. "Why d'you want to know?"

See, that's not a reaction someone who knew about exploding intestines and the purported connection with meat would have. Someone who knew about exploding intestines would know exactly what Bas is talking about. And if exploding intestines was a problem, everyone who travels to the Bruise would know about it.

Bas tries not to growl as he presses, "So there's nothing from the Bruise in the food, yeah? I mean... the meat."

Kimo frowns, bemused. "What, like—*our* meat? The stuff we eat? Well, the stuff *you* eat." When Bas nods, Kimolijah frowns harder before something seems to dawn, and he shoots a quick look over at Reacher. He shuts his eyes tight for a moment and sighs. "No." Kimolijah's tone is firm and his gaze is steady when he looks back at Bas. "You eat a steak from the Bruise, you change when the Bruise's resonance hits you. It hasn't happened since I've been here, but I'm told it isn't pretty, and sometimes you don't change back. Baron might consider everyone but himself expendable, but he needs us to make these trips. He wouldn't take a chance like that."

Bas sets his teeth and nods. "Right." Goddamn it. He'd be more pissed off if he didn't feel like such a clueless dupe for falling for it "A fucking *purgative*," he mutters under his breath. Out loud, he only says, "Thanks."

Kimolijah keeps frowning at him for a bit, but when Bas doesn't say anything else, Kimolijah huffs, shakes his head, and walks off.

Bas watches him make his way over to Mari as the constellations wheel overhead before turning his glance over to Reacher. Bas doesn't say anything. He doesn't do anything. He just stands there and looks until Reacher gives him his big, guileless grin and taps the brim of his hat in some half-cocky salute that Bas knows now is more like a challenge.

He doesn't accept it. He doesn't refuse it.

He thinks it all over, and he waits.

20.

Bas had thought the first thing he'd do when he returned from the Bruise would be to hunt down Dolerma and demand those answers he was promised.

It isn't.

The first thing Bas does when he gets back to Stanslo's Bridge is prop a board beneath the doorknob of his room, go to bed, and not get up until suppertime. The second thing he does is charge a huge, decadent supper to his account—because *fuck it*, one way or another, he's not going to be around to pay the bill—and eat every bite as he sits in the mess across from Merrin and tries to decide if the new blankness in Merrin's gaze is a result of losing Yanush, or of Reacher's crystal convincing him he doesn't care as much as he thought he did.

Bas doesn't find out. Mostly because he doesn't try. It's not the point.

The third thing he does is stalk on over to Hannah's, charge the most extravagant bottle of Draga they have to his account, and then start drinking. He doesn't plan to get drunk, mind. He can't afford to, not now that he knows, now that he's seen, now that he understands. So he sits at his lone table, listens to Sis twiddle the keys of the upright, and he waits.

It doesn't take long.

Reacher eases into the chair across the table from Bas and creases his big, dopey grin at him. He reaches for the bottle of Draga, but when Bas slides it nonchalantly to the side, Reacher's grin only broadens and, if possible, gets even more vacant.

"You tried to get me killed." Bas keeps his voice low and even.

Reacher's eyebrows fly upward and his grin drops. "Now that's a hell of a thing t' say." He looks wounded. "Why would I do somethin' like that, Bas? I like you."

Bas shakes his head and can't help but chuckle. He props his elbow on the table and points at Reacher. "You're really good." He takes a sip from his glass. The whiskey's good, excellent, and goes down smooth and smoky. "It was subtle, at first, I have to hand it to you. Give me that whole 'aw shucks' shuffle while you try your damnedest to make sure I have no idea what I'm doing, then... what? Wait 'til I get myself killed and then go back to Stanslo all contrite and 'gee, boss, I told ya, din't I?' And when that didn't work, you just sabotaged the cannon."

"Wow. I thought up all that?" Reacher's smile shifts, all awe and amusement. "Guess I really am good, en't I?"

"You really are." Bas smiles back, tips his glass at Reacher. "But see, you made a few mistakes. Because guys like you always do."

"Yeah?" Reacher leans in, avid interest. "What's that?"

"First of all, you didn't kill me yourself. I'm thinking that's because you're one of those manipulative motherfuckers who's just a touch too yellow to get his own hands dirty. And why should you, really, when people are so easy to maneuver because they think you're too stupid to lie." Bas tips a slow nod. "That's why you kept at Fox, poking and pretending to blunder into just the right things to say to get him riled, until Stanslo finally lost his patience."

"Man, I must be some kind of genius, yeah?"

"I'm sure you'd like to think so." Bas tops off his drink and takes another sip. "Second of all, you've given me time to think. And, really, that was your biggest mistake, because I'm pretty sure even Stanslo has no idea what I've figured out."

For the first time, Reacher's smile looks a bit flat. "Naw. Boss knows everything what goes on in Stanslo's Bridge."

"I reckon he thinks so. But I'm thinking that if he had even the slightest suspicion you'd been tagged, that you've got your very own pet burr bug nestled somewhere in your tiny brain, you'd have that noose out yonder 'round your neck instead of that crystal." Bas tilts his head, curious. "Who got you?" Bas thinks he knows, and he doesn't really expect Reacher to answer, but it never hurts to try.

Reacher's smile drops completely, and he sits back in his chair. "That kind of talk can get a man killed, Bas." He's calm, and his *benign stupid giant* act has dropped away again.

"Yeah," says Bas, and he smiles, slow and real. "I reckon it could. Imagine my distress."

A twitch and then a bit of a jerk, but Reacher's too slow. Bas's gun is in his hand before Reacher's even managed to skin his. Bas shoves over right up close and jams the barrels into Reacher's ribs. The barrels are out of true after that shot at Geda, but Reacher doesn't need to know that. The table hides the gun, but the scrape of the chair has attracted the attention of a few. Bas throws his free arm over Reacher's wide shoulders and grins through the reek of putrid roses.

"Laugh," he tells Reacher, low and quiet through an easy smile. "Laugh like I just told you the funniest thing you've ever heard, or I'll blow your guts so far across the room they'll be cleaning up bits of you 'til the dust takes over."

Reacher grits his teeth, more pissed off than scared, but he laughs, and anyone paying a little too much attention loses interest.

Bas laughs too, and he slaps Reacher's back. "I'll do you a favor," he says, and he lets the smile go feral. "I'll tell you the same thing I told Fox: you want a piece of me, you only have to tell me where and when, but it's not gonna be here and now." He pats Reacher's thick-thewed shoulder and gets up, bottle in one hand and gun in the other, beneath his coat now but still pointed at Reacher's chest. "Watch your back there, *boss*." He grins, touches the neck of the bottle to the brim of his hat, and walks backward toward the door. "I'll damn sure be watching mine."

⌘

He almost doesn't spot Kimolijah at first. It's not dark, the shop is lit up with grid sconces, but there's so much *stuff*—half-finished gadgets, husks of things that used to be gadgets with their guts streaming out, gridheaters and gridlusters and grid-whatever-the-hell. It makes it hard to find the living, organic lines of Kimolijah amid the twisted mechanical shapes of dead machinery.

Bas finds him, though, huddled among the wires and gears of the new train that's a lot more finished than the last time Bas was here. Bas stares around, taking in the oversized magnets with new comprehension, the streamlined dashes and the elegant structure of the wiring, and the single lethal purpose of it all that almost no one here can ken. And in the middle of it, the man who made it—dreamed it, envisioned it, designed it, and built it—sits in a ball on the floor beside the open engine hatch, a wrench in his hand and dirt under his nails and eyes that are glittering too bright in his stricken face. He doesn't have his hair slicked back for a change; it's loose and sticks up in places, presumably from him worrying at it like he's doing now, alternately dragging his fingers through it and scrubbing at his scalp before trying to flatten down the spikes that stick up like the spines of a startled desert newt. His goggles are nowhere in sight, and neither is that jaunty hat. He has nothing behind which to hide.

It's so easy to see the conflict, now that Kimolijah's not bothering to mask it anymore. It's so easy to see the impossible choices, now that Bas knows what they are.

Bas doesn't say anything as he climbs up into the cab and sits with his back to the side panel, across from Kimolijah. He doesn't say anything as he pulls the cork from the bottle with his teeth and spits it out the door. He offers the bottle to Kimolijah, and he still doesn't say anything until Kimolijah's taken a drink, swallowed, and then Bas asks:

"Will it work?"

Because it's the most important answer right now, despite the answers that are most important to Bas.

Kimolijah wipes his mouth with the back of his hand and holds the bottle back out to Bas. He pauses for a moment, mouth quirking wry, before he snorts and shakes his head.

"It's like you don't even know me."

Bas takes the bottle and lets a grin bloom, widens it when Kimolijah answers with a weak smile and a shrug. Because sometimes black humor is all the humor you're going to get. Which is why Bas decides he won't be saying out loud that no way is he letting Kimolijah go through with the half-cocked plan he and Quinnie came up with probably long before Bas showed up, the one that Quinnie's so sure precludes any of them getting out of here, and though *alive* had gone unspoken, Bas had nonetheless heard it quite clearly.

They're quiet for a while, trading the bottle back and forth for several deep swigs, and when there's the slightest bit of fuzz at Bas's edges, he sucks in a long, girding breath and then blows it back out slow.

"Will it kill you?"

It takes a moment for Kimolijah to answer. He snags the bottle from Bas and takes another long drink. It looks like it's hard for him to swallow, but Bas doesn't think it's because the liquor's too rough.

"Don't know what you're talking about."

"Story of your life, innit?"

Kimolijah chuckles, but that's all. He hands the bottle back to Bas without looking at him.

He looks so... diminished, somehow, sitting there all crunched up between his impossible engine and an unremarkable side panel, chewing his fingernails and staring down at anything below eye level like he can't bear to look up. He's short, but Bas has never before thought of Kimolijah as small.

"So." Kimolijah's voice is thready, too quiet, no bravado this time, and Bas wonders if this is what's left of the brilliant boy from Poor Side. "Now you know." His gold eyes flash up at Bas, too brief, before his gaze caroms away again. "Told you it would be better if you didn't."

"Know what, Kimo?"

Bas thinks he knows, because he's had the most ephemeral of thoughts in that direction himself before dismissing them as the too-easy solutions they were. He's got the benefit of looking at all of this without having lived inside it for years; he doesn't think Kimolijah can do the same.

And yeah, when Kimolijah finally stutters, "It... I...." his shoulders hunch in and he slouches down even further, knees pulling up and body curling in. "Travis was my fault. Fox is my fault. My d.... Jilly and Haversham, and now—"

"Yeah, that's cop-out bullshit."

"Yeah? How about this, then—you keep trying to make me some kind of victim. You want to believe Stanslo forces me into his bed."

Kimolijah shifts, and his back straightens just a little. "I offered. I still offer. Because it works. It was my idea in the first—"

"It was Mari's idea." Bas lifts an eyebrow when Kimolijah stops abruptly, mouth flapping. "Not that it matters, not in the way you think it does. But it was Mari's idea, because she figured if it worked for her it might work for you. And, contrary to what you both magnificently and very believably pretend, you don't, in fact, loathe each other."

Anger flashes in Kimolijah's eyes, quicksilver, before it sputters and goes out. That touch of defiance seems to go with it; he looks down as his shoulders droop. Idly, blank-eyed, he picks at a hangnail.

"I converted that first train in two months." He snorts, dry and humorless. "They used to haul tanks of water all the way from Harrowgate, did you know that? That's why he went after Mari. The water. But they kept losing trains out in the Dead Lands, and Stanslo was running out of engineers." He shakes his head with an angry huff. "And then I sent him that *stupid fucking letter*, and—"

He rubs at his eyes, then waves around at the cab of the train. "I could've had this thing built a year after I got here. Less, probably. And everyone who's... everyone who *I*—" He cuts himself off and grits his teeth. "If I'd moved faster—"

"If you'd moved faster, Stanslo would be a much richer man right now, selling *your* designs, *your* sweat, *your* brilliance. And then what? He'd be able to buy that army he's got you building guns for, and tuck all their contracts up into that goddamned crystal of his. Maybe he'd be able to hire more Olegs and Dutters to go out and hunt Techs for him and drag them back here—maybe a gridTech or two to keep all the things you've designed and built running after you've been handed over to Geda. Because *he's already tried it*, or didn't you hear me the first time?"

He pauses when Kimolijah flinches, because Bas doesn't want to be cruel, but this is pretty much it, this is the cusp, and things could go so many ways. Another bracing breath and Bas sets the bottle down. He thinks of that tiny squirming thing Geda shot at him, Kimolijah saying *Got it in the eye*, and blue ink over black tattoos, and blue runes that skitter and whirl as Kimolijah's bracelet comes alive and digs in.

"It's not Stanslo," Bas says, quiet. "Is it? And he has no idea his little desert barony has been infiltrated so thoroughly."

Kimolijah opens his mouth to answer, thinks about it, before he says, "Sometimes a snake is just a simple snake."

"Does he know?" Bas jerks his chin at Kimolijah's bracelet.

"What do you think?"

"I think...." Bas squints at Kimolijah, mouth twisted flat. "I think he knows about the burr bug, and he knows where it came from. And when it didn't work out like he wanted it to, his little 'Sweetpea' offered to make that bracelet. Even threw in the bonus of keeping you in line with it. But he has no idea it's not synched to him. And he doesn't know about the blue ink. That's why Serenat hides it in the black. And you can't tell because she's the one who decides what you can and can't say, though... I don't have an answer yet for why." He pauses, but Kimolijah doesn't say anything. Strange how that's encouraging. "The only thing that makes sense," Bas says slowly, "is that she's not the one who tagged you. The bug's not hers and doesn't do what she wants it to. And she doesn't like it."

It takes a while, Kimolijah just looking at Bas, blinking slowly, but then he snakes his arm out and grabs up the bottle. He takes a quick nip, holds the bottle out, and says, "My, my. That excellent education of yours does you credit."

Bas nods with a grimace and takes the bottle. "I didn't think Stanslo was smart enough for all of these twisty subplots, really. Brazen enough, yeah. Ruthless enough, definitely, and crazy as a bedbug. But this...." He shakes his head and takes a drink. "This takes a special kind of clever." He hands the bottle back to Kimolijah. "How long since Geda tagged Fox?"

"God, I don't know." Kimolijah takes a long drink at that one. He coughs a little when he swallows, then sets the bottle between them. "Right after Travis, I think. I mean, don't get me wrong, he was always an asshole and he always hated me. But that's when he got... bad."

"At least part of that was likely Reacher." Kimolijah shows no surprise, but Bas hadn't expected him to. Bas sighs and says, "You know I'm going to have to kill him, right? Reacher, I mean. Well, Geda too, most likely, and probably Serenat first, but that might take a bit more doing."

"I think...." Kimolijah hesitates, chews on his lip. "Let me take care of Reacher."

"And why would you do that?"

Kimolijah turns slowly to look at Bas, eyebrows high. "Because he's trying to get you killed? Because he almost succeeded? Because next time he might?"

"So?" Bas isn't trying to be facetious, though Kimolijah's look says that's what he's thinking, but Bas is genuinely confounded. "Fox was trying to do the same to you, for probably a lot longer, and you didn't—"

"Fox was never a threat to me." It's a little too loud, with a reedy serration around the edges.

Bas tries to read the look on Kimolijah's face, wants to know what kind of emotion is behind that tone, but Kimolijah looks away again.

"And Reacher is?" Bas asks.

Kimolijah shakes his head, exasperated, and looks up at the ceiling as if for divine help. He mutters something that might be "God, you're an idiot" but before Bas can object, Kimolijah gives him a tired look and says, "I'll take care of it."

"And how do you plan—?"

"Just let me worry about Reacher, yeah?" Still prickly but not quite angry—more like worn-out and unhappy, but determined. Kimolijah doesn't elaborate; he just goes back to staring at his knees and gnawing on his nails.

Bas hates seeing him so subdued, so he doesn't argue. And it won't matter anyway if Bas gets to Reacher before Kimolijah does. Which Bas has every intention of doing.

"Right." Bas clears his throat. "So, Bella Stanslo." Kimolijah cuts a sharp look at Bas, wary, but Bas is used to that now. "I imagine that started out as some kind of trade, yeah? No, don't answer. I don't feel like watching you zap yourself. Just follow along and... I don't know, let me know if I get something wrong? Maybe you could—"

"Punch you?"

Bas can't help the snort. "Maybe something a bit less violent, if you don't mind." He gives Kimolijah a wry little smile. "You could always kiss me."

Kimolijah blinks at him, eyebrows high, before a slow, tired smile unfurls across his face. "Asshole," he mutters, but he's still smiling as he snatches up the bottle and bundles it to his chest then kind of curls around it. He jerks his chin. "Sure, sure, go ahead."

"Not much incentive to get it right, though, now that I think about it."

"Oh, shut up."

Bas shakes his head, the tension pulled a little less tightly now, and he settles back and stretches out his legs. "So, Stanslo finds the Bruise, some however many years ago. I'm thinking twenty or so, 'cause that's when Bella 'died.' And I reckon Travis was with him way back then, because I got the whole 'if I killed Travis after all those years, imagine how easy I'll kill you' speech when Stanslo...." He trails off when Kimolijah just looks down and picks at the label on the bottle. "Sorry," Bas says. Because he hadn't meant to be quite so tactless.

Kimolijah shrugs, still picking, eyes on his fingers. "He was my friend." It's soft but straightforward. "I really wasn't fucking him."

Bas leaves that last bit alone. "Travis was fine with being Stanslo's right hand for a good long time, had no problem with all the thieving and corruption. And then you come along with your genius and your Tech and your crystals, and suddenly he's not fine with it anymore." He pauses, and when Kimolijah just sits there, all morose and distant, Bas says, "He was your friend, I get it. But the change of heart wasn't only because of you. Men like that don't just change their minds, their *lives*, because they like someone and feel bad. Am I right?"

"Haven't kissed you yet, have I?"

It's on the line between sardonic and belligerent. More than Bas was expecting, really, and better than that tired resignation.

"Serenat and Dolerma are siblings," Bas goes on. "They're Bella's children, Bella's and Geda's." He leans forward, just a touch. "So Stanslo finds the Bruise all those years ago, finds out what the Willow Men can do, so he—"

"Wait, *Willow Men*?" Kimolijah's eyes are a lot less dull and he's smirking.

"Shut up. If no one's going to tell me anything, I'm going to make up my own words."

Bas snatches the bottle and wets his mouth before giving it back. Kimolijah curls around it again like it's a comfort blanket.

"*Any*way," Bas goes on, "so Stanslo finds the Bruise, sees that the people there have some kind of reverse-psyTech, where instead of reading others' minds they can push things into them. So he figures 'Hey, what would happen if one from each side got together and had some weird-looking spawn?' So he goes and finds himself a psyTech and woos her, or maybe tricks her into a bond, and then he drags her across the desert so he can trade her to, um.... Geda... for...."

He trails off, because Kimolijah has unfurled from his little ball and is crawling across the space between them, eyes on Bas, half bold challenge and half trepidation. Bas stills, because he's never seen that look on Kimolijah before, and Bas can't tell if he should be reaching for Kimolijah or reaching for a weapon, but then—

It's soft this time, nothing like it had been in the barn; Kimolijah kisses Bas with a serene single-mindedness Bas wouldn't have predicted, considering that bit of obvious apprehension in Kimolijah's approach. Calm and slow, like Kimolijah's intent on finding every nuance of every sensation and taking his time to examine each one with concentrated focus. *Almost* sweet, *almost* affectionate, in a science-experiment kind of way—tender pressure of lips and tentative swipes of tongue, all exploration and careful attention—and Bas thinks maybe if Kimolijah had more practice at it, it would be more, all, maybe even too much.

It dredges things up in Bas's chest, sloughs them around, and before he can figure out what they are or even decide if he wants to, Kimolijah's withdrawing, crawling backward slowly with his eyes on Bas, and folding himself up around the bottle of whiskey again. He pulls his knees up to his chest, and the wariness that wasn't there before, like Kimolijah's expecting a punch in the mouth, makes those things in Bas's chest lump up and settle too heavily behind his ribs.

"What—?" Bas has to stop and clear his throat, and he's not even embarrassed about it. "What was that?"

Kimolijah's still watching him, still cautious. He shrugs and looks away, takes a quick, nervous swig from the bottle, and says, "You were wrong."

"I was...." It takes a couple seconds, but it does eventually click, because Bas had been *kidding*, but not really, trying to lighten the mood but really hiding desire behind sarcasm, and he'd never thought for a second....

"Oh." Bas frowns. Is he disappointed? He can't tell. Yes, he can. "Maybe one day," he says slowly, "I can have one of those when you *don't* have an ulterior motive, yeah?"

Kimolijah huffs a little snort, and there's a tiny sardonic smile curving up one corner of his mouth. "Yeah," he says and runs a fingertip over the rim of the bottle. "Maybe."

God. He really is shy.

Bas is so, so fucked.

It takes far too long for Bas's brain to start functioning again, and when it does, he has to go back to where he'd been and figure out where he'd gone wrong.

"Okay," he says, trying to concentrate on not wondering how reprehensible it will make him if he just starts deliberately spouting asinine theories to see how many times Kimolijah will kiss him when he gets it wrong, like every spotty teen's best schoolteacher wet dream. "Okay," Bas repeats and gives his head a sharp shake. "So Stanslo doesn't trade Bella. She goes willingly?"

He squints over at Kimolijah, because he has a serious problem believing that theory; and well he shouldn't, because Kimolijah's crossing the distance again, a little more boldly but still all wide eyes and careful movement.

There's probably a special hell Bas will end up burning in, because he waits until Kimolijah kisses him again—slow and barely there this time—before he says, "Unwillingly, then," and almost doesn't care about the confusion because he gets another kiss out of it. But still. It's either willingly or unwillingly; there can't be—

"Oh."

Bas's face must show comprehension, because Kimolijah withdraws, nearly knocking the bottle over when his thigh brushes it as he retreats back to his makeshift corner. Bas grabs it up for a swig so he can pretend he doesn't have to catch his breath.

"Geda tagged her," he finally manages. "Which made her willing."

Bas might be fooling himself—in fact, he probably is—but he thinks maybe Kimolijah looks a tiny bit disappointed when he pulls his knees up.

God, it's hard to concentrate.

"Okay."

Bas blows out a cleansing breath and licks his lips, seeking Kimolijah's taste, inordinately glad when he finds it. Kimolijah's watching closely, seven different kinds of tension strung tight and twanging silently between them.

"Okay, so Bella's made to go willingly, spawns some devil

babies with Geda, they grow up in their happy little hive or cocoon or nest or whatever the hell goes on over there, and for whatever reason, two of them are here in Stanslo's Bridge, apparently of their own—ohhhhh." Bas sits up straight. "*Oh.*" If Bas were a character in an illobook, he'd have a speech bubble hovering over his head right now with nothing in it but a bunch of exclamation points.

"Serenat can only project, can't she? She can't read. Or at least she can't read like Dolerma can, or I'd've been dead that first night. 'The answer to psyTech,' Stanslo told me. And they can put that inside those crystals." He pauses and scratches at the bristles on his jaw that are getting way too shaggy. "So by now," he goes on, "Stanslo's figured out that not just any gridTech can charge those crystals. Serenat and Dolerma can get their freaky psyTech in them because they can project, but Techs can't do that. Except for you."

"Not just me." Kimolijah's voice is small and distant as he stares at his knees. "Can't be just me. There's got to be others, just...." He trails off and shakes his head, chewing at his lip, and Bas pretends not to notice that Kimolijah's eyes have misted up. "It can't only be *me.*"

He looks up at Bas, horribly lost and just this side of desperate. Bas wishes he could take that look away, but he can't.

"I'm sorry," Bas says, gentle, "but I've been around Techs all my life. And I have never, not once, heard of emergent Tech and latent Tech in one person." Kimolijah flashes a startled look at Bas, and Bas has to roll his eyes. "Tracker? Remember?" He shakes his head. "I could smell the kine on you that first night, and it's so faint as to almost not be there, but there's very little *Latent* about it. I just didn't know what I was sensing, because it's impossible. *You're* impossible. In more ways than one. Which I know is dreadful inconvenient for you, since it got you here, and how no one's figured out by now that it's kineTech that gets the gridTech into the crystals, I have no idea, because there just *is* no other explanation, but I'm pretty sure it's the only thing that's kept them from going after your sister for real, so good on you."

"It's the Outlet." Kimolijah rolls out a chuckle that's dark and cynical. He peers at Bas out the corner of his eye. "They think...."

He trails off and glances at the bracelet. So Bas picks it up from where Kimolijah left off:

"They think it actually works. And it does, kind of. It hurts you and you don't get out of there until you charge the damned crystals, so you charge the damned crystals. They just don't *know* you're charging them. They think the crystals are pulling it out of you."

Kimolijah snorts. "Except it doesn't work with Mari, so...."

"So Stanslo has you trying to teach it to her." Bas rolls his eyes. "God, I don't know if all of this is some brilliant, sophisticated web of survival, or just a crazy-jane accident of improvised happenstance that actually and shockingly works for some reason."

"*Did* work," Kimolijah corrects. "*Was* working. But then.... Travis, and...." He runs a hand through his hair and shuts his eyes. "Geda's getting impatient."

"Geda." Bas frowns. "They've turned it all into a regular family business, but Stanslo's still running it all. And they *need* Stanslo to run it all, don't they, because no one's going to get a look at them and the Bruise and *not* want to find a way to send them back through it yesterday and shut it down so nothing else leaks out.

"So they let Stanslo run everything, but they tag anyone who might be useful to keep it all from going too far off the plot, and they've got Serenat and Dolerma keeping track of things for them here. Except Dolerma's not playing by their rules anymore, and Serenat can't read him, so they don't know everything. We can use that. We can—"

"You know, you really shouldn't be telling me any of this." Kimolijah's voice is calm and quiet, but the truth rings loud.

Bas pauses and rubs at his jaw, thinking. Because Kimolijah's right—if Bas does manage to come up with a plan, he probably shouldn't let Kimolijah in on it. Then again, Bas thinks he's already gone well beyond the point where anything like that is going to matter.

"You're probably right," Bas says. "But getting out of here is going to take something like Magic Man and Dirk Darkling put together, and I can't be both."

Kimolijah's brow crinkles, but a tiny smile tugs at the corner of his wide mouth. "I get to be Magic Man. You already said."

Bas would really like to insist that Kimolijah is Dirk Darkling, because his inner ten-year-old kind of wants to be Magic Man, but he only rolls his eyes and says, "The point is, pretty soon it's not going to matter who knows what—it's only going to matter who shoots whom."

"You really think *anyone's* getting out of here?"

Bas ignores it. "Haversham said Stanslo was going to give the world things it didn't want." Bas frowns. "All those crystals—and what he doesn't have you charging with gridTech, he's got them loading with... whatever you call what they do."

Again, Kimolijah unbends and stretches out, and again, he crowds into Bas, kisses him. It's quick but abruptly deep, and over before Bas gets a chance to sink into the *guh* and *gimme* of it.

"Did you really read all my notes and stuff?" Kimolijah says, still right up close and lips making hot little ghost-tracks against Bas's.

"So you believe me now?" Too husky.

"Yes. Did you?"

"Yes."

"Why?"

Bas has to pause for a second, because the real reason might come off a little... creepy. And it *wasn't*, goddamn it, that's not how it was at all, but it might *sound* it, and Kimolijah probably doesn't need to be given a reason to think he's on the wrong end of another obsession.

So Bas says, "Because you're fucking brilliant, and it spills out all over your equations and blueprints and stupid little distracted doodles, and I could see *you* in there, and it was the only way I could know you, and I wanted—"

Okay, that might've been overshare, because Kimolijah draws back, only a little, enough to look Bas in the eye, and he just *stares* for a long moment, making Bas wait and wait and wait, until the fretfulness in Bas's chest starts growing and sprouting limbs and breeding snarly little offspring and insufferable extended families. And then Kimolijah's mouth quirks, something soft and maybe a little bemused, and it's a smile Bas has never seen on him before, and it makes everything in Bas's chest lump up and flop down into his gut.

"You know gridTech," Kimolijah says.

"Yeah."

"You know *my* gridTech."

Bas has kind of lost the thread, what with Kimolijah's mouth *this close* to Bas's and barely a taste of that kiss left lingering at Bas's edges, so Bas only manages a gruff, distracted "Uh-huh."

"So what are crystals for, Mister Badass Directorate Tracker?"

Kimolijah doesn't give Bas a chance to get it wrong. The kiss is a little more direct this time, a little more brash. Kimolijah's hand comes up, warm, rough fingertips laying tentative touches to Bas's scruffy jaw, then his arm, and *holy shit*, who knew Bas's elbow was an erogenous zone? Kimolijah's mouth is hot and whisky-wet, and Bas would like nothing better in the world than to sink back and pull Kimolijah with him, see where it might lead, what it might lead *to*, but it hits Bas then, like a star bursting in his brain, and he knows exactly where his reasoning took a turn. He pulls back with a gasp that's equal parts thwarted lust and terrible revelation, because what *are* crystals for?

"My *god*." He clutches at Kimolijah's shoulders and gives him a reflexive little shake. "Channel. Direct. *Amplify*." Bas shuts his eyes, adrift in the hugeness of it, because this is *Magic Man* territory, and things like this don't happen in real life. He opens his eyes and looks right into Kimolijah's. "They're not different crystals, are they? They're the same ones. They come here loaded with Geda's freaky Tech, and then Stanslo has you put yours in after it. And when he manages to figure out a way to get those things past the Directorate, when he starts selling them back home as a safer alternative to gridTechs hooking themselves into gridstations...." Bas lets go of Kimolijah and rakes a hand through his hair, reeling. "Can they work like that?" He doesn't wait for Kimolijah to answer, because Kimolijah can't, and anyway—"Yeah, of course they can. And they're synched to Geda. All he'd have to do is send out one of those weird mind pulses and anyone who's got one.... *God.*"

It's shocking and horrible, and it makes so much sense. Except.

"Wait a minute, what about Dolerma?"

Kimolijah scoots back again, slowly, watching Bas closely, but he says nothing.

"Dolerma's not with them," Bas says, thinking. "He can't be, because he knows exactly what I am, and his only concern seems to be getting you out of here." He shakes his head. "But that doesn't make sense. He's the one who does the contracts. He's the one—"

"Did you know," Kimolijah cuts in softly, "that the most common reason behind betrayal is love?" He pauses, gives Bas a level look. "The second most common is revenge."

"Travis," Bas says and almost whacks his head against the engine block, because God, *of course.* "They were together?" Kimolijah doesn't answer, but Bas doesn't get another kiss, so he figures he's right. "So Travis and Dolerma have their own little conspiracy-within-a-conspiracy thing going on, and Travis sends a message to your sister and gets killed for it. And now Dolerma wants them to pay—Stanslo for ordering it and Geda for letting it happen."

Okay. Right. This is... good, actually. Dolerma's right: if Bas can get Kimolijah out of here, everything—trades, deals, double crosses—it'll all grind to a halt, and the whole of Stanslo's Bridge will still be reeling by the time Bas gets back with the Directorate.

"We have to leave," Bas says. "You know that, right?"

Kimolijah shuts his eyes and leans his head back. He blinks up at the ceiling and sighs, long and hard. "I can't." It's not thready, it's not shaky, and it's not quiet. It's even and direct, like he's thought about it carefully and has made his decision, even if he doesn't like it.

"I know you don't want to leave your da behind," Bas says. "But, Kimolijah...." He clenches his jaw, frustrated. "They're not going to let him go. They can't. And they're not going to let him live." And he regrets Kimolijah's flinch and how Kimolijah bites his lip and shuts his eyes tight, he really does. But it's long past the point where Bas can afford to pull punches. "Geda *will* get you one day. Whether Stanslo actually makes good on his end of the contract or not, you will go to the Bruise one day and never come back. And once you're there and can't do anything about it anymore, do you really think Stanslo will leave your sister alone? A *Class 5* kineTech? *Really?*" Bas sighs and softens his voice. "You have to understand—your best chance right now, everyone's best chance, is to get you out of here, get the Directorate on the case, and come back for—"

"No," Kimolijah says, quiet and calm. "I don't mean I won't, although... maybe I mean that too. But...." He swipes his hair out of his face, agitated, and holds out his hand, the metal of the bracelet winking dully in the light from the gridsconces. "It's impossible. I *can't.*"

Bas clenches his jaw and nods slowly, angry, because he knows that, and it didn't take a lot of theorizing or guessing for Bas to get it this time. He's pretty much known there had to be a reason Kimolijah hadn't taken his train and run a long time ago, though now he knows the details, or at least the broad strokes of them:

If Kimolijah tries to run with the bracelet, his gridTech will get him, and this time there will be no jovial "All right, I think you've learned your lesson" from Stanslo. And if Kimolijah tries to run without it, that burr bug will make sure he doesn't last a week.

Trapped. Stymied.

"But," Kimolijah says slowly, like it's crawling out his throat over stuttery little breaths. He's not looking at Bas anymore, back to examining his knees and picking at the fabric of his trousers. A long, nervous sigh, and he says, "Just because a man can't fly doesn't mean he hasn't figured out the aerodynamics of a bird's wings." *I can get you out.* "There'll be a supply run to Harrowgate next week." Kimolijah shrugs and shakes his head with a press of lips.

Stow away. Steal the train. Get help. Maybe I'll still be here when you get back.

It had been Bas's original plan. It's what he should do. And they both know it won't work. Well, it'll work, but it won't save Kimolijah.

Buy it, steal it, kill it, or fuck it. Stanslo won't give up a trophy. And, as genuinely smitten with Kimolijah as Bas thinks Stanslo is, he also thinks, if he does manage to get out of here and get the Directorate to make a raid, he's likely to arrive back in Stanslo's Bridge like the world's tardiest cavalry to find Kimolijah's drying husk keeping Travis company. And if it's not that, it'll be Geda dragging Kimolijah through the Bruise, and then God knows if Bas will ever find him again. Because if Bas just shows up gone one day, there's no way Stanslo—and everyone else—won't know how.

"Some risks," Kimolijah says, quiet, "are worth taking."

Bas thinks Kimolijah knows exactly what the risks are. Which makes this so much worse.

"Yeah, sure," Bas says and pulls up a smile that may be weak but it's still genuine, because *God,* Kimolijah's even more than what Bas had thought he'd be, way back when Bas had been seeing right through genius theories and falling for the dead man behind them. "We'll work on that plan, then."

Because he doesn't think it'll be any use arguing against the impossible.

Still, though. No one who's been reading illobooks for as long as Bas has truly trusts "impossible."

⤫

Dolerma finds him the next evening. Which is good, because if it was the other way around, Bas is angry enough he might've throttled the freaky bastard, and not for the reasons Dolerma thought he might.

"I have no questions left for you," Bas snaps as Dolerma edges alongside where Bas is propping up the wall and watching a bunch of filthy minions mix the powders for the bricks. Something about the way Dolerma carefully keeps to the shadows thrown by the storehouse makes Bas unreasonably irritated. "I've answered them all myself. Except for these." Bas turns to Dolerma, and Bas is about an inch shorter, but he thinks he manages to loom just fine. "How do I get that bracelet off of Kimo without that thing in his arm killing him? And how much are you willing to help?"

Dolerma is silent for a while, arms folded across his chest and head down, so all Bas can see is the top of his hat. At length, Dolerma shifts and straightens. "You don't. You can't. If that is the course you choose, I cannot help you."

Bas very nearly decks him; in fact, he curls his fist and takes a step, intending to do just that, but Dolerma moves back and holds up his long, spidery hands. "There is, however, a way to delay his passenger on its—"

"Wait, now, his what?"

Dolerma stares. "His passenger." He gestures at his forearm.

"You mean *bug*." It churns out on a low-voiced hiss from between Bas's teeth. "*Worm*, whatever the fuck, but I've seen them." He flicks his glance over Dolerma's not-hair and doesn't try to hide the curl to his lip. "Try all you like to make it sound less revolting, but I know what those things are and I've seen—"

"*Those things* are a way of life for my people," Dolerma cuts in mildly. "*Those things* are how our children learn and how our people communicate and how mates call one to another and how parents claim their children. When a child wanders off and is lost, it is through the passenger that the parent guides the child home. When an old one's mind is no longer their own, it is through the passenger that the child in turn keeps the parent safe. So would you like to hear about the only hope you might have? Or would you like to keep insulting me and the whole of my kind?"

"*Those things* are how *your* people take over the minds of *my*—"

"That was never the intention of *my people*," Dolerma snaps. "It is not what the passengers are for. It was an idea brought to life in the twisted mind of Baron Stanslo, and corrupted by—"

"And then embraced by *your people*, because everything about you seems to be about controlling everyone else. Fucking burr bugs and crystals and—"

"Blame your *sparker* for that," Dolerma says, low and dangerous. "*My people* have never had cause to pursue such a use for the crystals. Stanslo never had occasion to discover and exploit it. Not until Kimo."

"You mean not until an idealistic kid made a brilliant discovery that could have changed his world for *his people*, but had it twisted by Stanslo and *your da*, or are you going to try to deny that while you betray the very people you stand here and defend? The very same people who made it possible for Stanslo to do what he did to the man *you* were supposed to love!"

Dolerma flinches and turns sharply away. They'd ended up nearly nose-to-nose a second ago, the almost nonexistent pink of Dolerma's skin risen in a very faint blush to his white cheeks. Now Bas looks at the tense line of Dolerma's shoulders, the way his long, thin body wavers.

Bas reins himself in and takes a long, deep breath. He waits until one of the gridtrolleys trundles by before he says, "I'm sorry. That was not well done of me."

Dolerma shrugs, weary and somber, then turns and eyes Bas steadily through his dark glasses. He shakes his head, and when Bas can't help watching the way Dolerma's "hair" sways and shivers, Dolerma makes a point of stroking at it with a defiant tilt of his mouth. "Travis was quite fond of—"

"I *do not* need to know."

Dolerma chuckles, a small, mean thing. He leans a little closer to Bas and drops his voice. "The tonic," he says, and he holds out a small clay bottle.

Bas ponders that for a second, then frowns. "The stuff for Kimo's fits?" He takes the bottle and stuffs it in his pocket.

"They are not fits. Not in the way you think. When the pass—" Dolerma's mouth pinches and he holds up his hand, placating. "When the *burr bug* stretches too long, it introduces... pressure, I suppose you would say. It crowds the paths to the brain and prevents bloodflow, hence Kimo's somewhat unreasonable behavior when—"

"Are you saying it's giving him strokes?"

"Not as such. Though it will come to that one day. They are not meant to linger for so long in the body. They are meant to occupy a specific part of the brain and acclimate to their habitat. Kimo's has been ejected from its habitat and given one much larger." Dolerma shrugs. "It grows too large in a too-large space. And when it's free, it seeks the place meant to be its home. It does not know the damage it causes as it tries only to—"

"Yeah, how about you don't try to make me feel sorry for the thing that's going to kill him?" Bas really wants to walk away, get away from the storehouse with its busy-making, but the sun's still clinging to the horizon, there aren't enough shadows yet, and he's not sure Dolerma will follow along. "The tonic," he prompts.

"The tonic." Dolerma stares across the dirt yard at the station. "With one dose, both Kimo and his passenger sleep. With more...."

When he doesn't go on, Bas rolls his eyes. "*With more*?"

"With more, they sleep deeper." Dolerma tilts his head and looks at Bas. "With more, they could sleep for days."

"Okay, except who'd run the train? Because we're not getting out of here without one. And what happens if we do get out of here and they both wake up?"

"You find one of your medTechs," Dolerma says as he backs away, "and you hope."

"Wait." It looks for a second like Dolerma won't, but then he does, looking at Bas like he wants to be doing anything else besides standing there. "Just answer me one question," Bas says. "The bracelet—Geda's the one who tagged Kimo, but Serenat made him the bracelet, yeah? And she keeps adding blue to the tattoo." He pauses before he asks, "Why?"

Dolerma's thin mouth turns up, but not in anything like a smile. "That is many, many questions, all wrapped up in one so deceptively simple." He shrugs. "The answer, though, is singular and quite straightforward." The not-smile drops and Dolerma holds out his long, gloved hand. "My people do not have gridTech, you see. But, in me, our dam has proven that we could." Bas sucks in a tight breath, and Dolerma smiles. "Serenat has chosen her mate."

⚬⚬⚬

"He's lying," Quinnie says and runs her fingers over the warped barrel of Bas's gun. "Didn't anyone tell you not to be firing off combustibles in the Bruise?"

Bas rolls his eyes. "Yes. Now, can you fix it? And what do you mean he's lying?"

They're in the smithy, the fires stoked so hot Bas almost can't breathe. He has no idea how Quinnie can stand it for so long. She's barely even sweating.

"*Of course* I can fix it." Quinnie's tone heavily implies there should be a "you idiot" tacked onto the end of that, and her face looks like she's chewing on lemons. "And I mean Dolerma don't care if Kimo lives or dies. He just wants him out 'cause he suspects what we might be up to, and he wants Kimo gone before we can do it. He wants both his worlds, y'see. Kimo's the only one who can really get in his way, and if Dolerma can get you to get rid of Kimo for him...." She sets aside Bas's gun and stares at him, challenging.

Bas frowns. "Kimo thinks he wants revenge for Travis."

"Probably that too." Quinnie shrugs. "But he also thinks Kimo's the reason Travis is dead. So why should Kimo get to live happily ever after? And he won't, 'cause even if you manage to get him out of Stanslo's Bridge, you won't make it past Harrowgate. It ain't just the line Stanslo owns. Kimo dies either way. And Dolerma knows it."

It's so blunt, almost indifferent.

"At least this way there's a chance." Bas frowns, a bit confounded. "Do you even care?" Because he'd thought she did.

Quinnie's mouth pinches down, and she sets Bas's gun very carefully on a cold anvil. She looks up at Bas with banked fire behind her dark brown eyes.

"About... what?" she says slowly. "Do I *care* that I answered an ad looking for honest work, going on ten years ago now, and found myself hijacked to the middle of the desert and building trains that were only going to blow up and kill the engineers that got hijacked with me? Do I *care* that, when we scrounged together enough weapons and accomplices to fight back, not only did most of us die, but that's when the baron started his 'contracts'? Do I *care* that when the baron showed me a letter from some kid genius talking about dynamic crystals—and could the baron see his way clear to sending him some on the sly, because he was right on a cusp, see, and it could revolutionize the train industry—do I *care* that I'm the one who told the baron that yeah, the kid might have something there?"

She's breathing a little too heavily, and her eyes have gone somewhat bright.

"You couldn't have known," Bas says and is taken aback when Quinnie *sneers* at him.

"Do you think I need fucking *comfort* from *you*?" She turns away and starts clanging metal bits and molds around. "I've seen you looking at him," she says, through her teeth. "Like he's some kind of stupid illobook character in trouble and you want nothing more than to be his Magic Man." She spins around and points a thick brown finger right at Bas's chest. "Don't you dare try to deny it. I've seen it before, y'know. It took Travis most of his life to figure out what an asshole he was, but when he did, it was because of Kimo. And maybe Travis didn't have the same cow-eyes, but he damn sure had the same obsession with some half-assed redemption."

"*Redemption*? I don't need any kind of—what the fuck are you even talk—"

"Kimo's told me all about how you read his notes, and I know how it is—you get all infatuated, and you don't even get that what you think you're in love with is really just the idea of being someone's hero."

"That is *not* how it is," Bas growls, because it's not, it's *not*, it's something else, and has been right from the beginning. Poetry inside elegant equations, and a wide-open mind that made magic of imagination, and a pragmatism that was willing to dig down deep inside a snarl and bull through right to the proper solution. And now Bas has met the man behind the genius, has gotten to know him, and Bas sees all that and a young man who's been handed a bucketful of shit and, instead of throwing it around so everyone gets splattered along with him, he's trying to fertilize gardens with it, and *oh my god,* and *no and no and no,* Bas is *not* in love, complete with cheesy metaphors, and therefore is not completely, tragically *fucked.*

"Oh God, he *told* me," Quinnie snarls. "How you were looking for who 'killed' him, how you were looking for Mari. He doesn't even seem to notice that you wouldn't have ever even heard of him if he didn't have that 'Class 2' sitting beside his name in the Directorate's registry."

"That's not true, he was—"

"It hasn't even occurred to him that if it was only his da that'd been 'killed' in that fire, you wouldn't be here, because Ajamil Adani is only a Latent and no use to the fucking Directorate."

Quinnie throws aside what looks like a misshapen crowbar and shoves both fists into Bas's chest until Bas backs up. And fucking *ow,* man, the woman's freakishly strong.

She sets her teeth, fisted hands tight and yellow-knuckled. "I've been dying or wishing I was dying out here for *ten fucking years.* Who was looking for *me,* Mister Directorate?"

Bas stares, openmouthed. He takes another step back. "I don't... I mean, nonTechs aren't... the Directorate only... the guardarm should've—"

"Oh, pin up," Quinnie snaps. "I want excuses from you even less than I want your condescending comfort. And I cannot *tell* you how much I *don't* want to hear about how much I *don't care.*" She pauses and rubs at her eyes. "Merrin knows. Haversham was gonna take the cannon when we made the run. Yanush was.... And now Reacher's got the crystal and all them contracts. Fox was too stupid to know what to look for or to even know what he saw. Reacher only pretends to be. And now Merrin's synched to him. We could be out of time any second."

Bas sees a possibly bigger, more immediate problem: Reacher seems to have known about, and systematically taken out in some way, nearly everyone who's apparently been conspiring in this tiny rebellion. And Bas doesn't think Quinnie's noticed what it means that it's only her and Kimo left.

"Kimo...." Bas hesitates, then plows on, "Kimo says he'll be taking care of Reacher."

"Oh, ain't that just *grand.*" Quinnie drops her hand and sets her teeth. "You've already got him believing in your illobook rescue, you son of a bitch, enough that he'll—" She cuts herself off with a growl and turns a fierce look on Bas. "We die either way. Understand? You try to get Kimo out on that train, he'll maybe die a few days later, but he'll still die, and we'll have lost the chance to stop all of this before it spreads. At least my way, we maybe take the Bruise down with us." She picks up one of her heavy leather gloves and whips it at Bas's head. "Now git out o' here before I find something a lot heavier and a lot sharper to throw at you."

Bas has no idea what to say, where to start. So he tells Quinnie to watch her back, watch out for Reacher. Then he gits.

21.

It only takes a day for Reacher to make a move. His first try goes like this:

"I'm told you had an encounter with Geda." Stanslo's sharp look can almost be mistaken for concern. "I'm told it's possible you've been compromised."

Stanslo and Dolerma have pretty much cornered Bas in the baths, and once he figures out why, he stops worrying about how much his towel's not covering. He drops it next to his boots and clothes, all casual indifference, and spreads his arms.

"Go ahead, have yourself a look. I know it's why you're here. No welts, see?"

Dolerma looks like he always does, mostly blank but slightly amused and like he knows a secret he's not telling, but Stanslo raises his eyebrows and rolls his eyes.

"That won't be necessary, Bas, though I do thank you for the... offer." Stanslo looks Bas over pretty thoroughly anyway, and flips a small gesture toward Dolerma. "But we have other means."

Dolerma steps right up close, looking pointedly down at where Bas's tackle is just kind of swaying in the breeze. He looks up and smirks, dark glasses reflecting Bas's narrowed eyes back at him. He takes hold of Bas's arm and—

"No fucking way!" Bas snaps and shoves Dolerma and his freaky tentacle-hair back and away from him. He swipes at his arm where it brushed him, and though he's sure none of it broke loose and is burrowing its way through skin, he still can't help loosing a full-body shudder and rubbing at the spot until it's red. He snatches up the towel and knots it around his waist, and they knew exactly what they were doing, because Bas's gun isn't in his boot where he'd normally put it—it's in Quinnie's smithy. He's relieved his hand isn't shaking when he flings out his arm and points at Dolerma. "You keep that shit away from me."

Dolerma eyes him calmly as he straightens, that tiny smirk still tucked up in the corner of his nearly colorless mouth, but Stanslo takes a step forward, and for a change, he's not smiling even a little.

"Stand still, Bas."

That citrusy little *thud-pulse* wobbles all over Bas, like a glancing smack to the brain, and though it has the same noneffect it always has, Bas still can't ignore it. If he lets on that it doesn't make him obey, Stanslo will know, and it's one of the few bits of leverage Bas has. Still, no way is he going to stand still and let one of those bug things in. He can't.

"There will be no intrusion," Stanslo says, soothing. "Dolerma merely needs a look."

"He can look without touching."

"No," says Dolerma, amused. "I can't." He cocks his head to the side and says softly, pointedly, "It will be fine. You have my word."

As usual, Bas can't see Dolerma's eyes, though it would make no difference even if he could. He can't read those black pools that have all the depth of well water and are just as hard to see into.

Dolerma steps forward slowly, like he's willing Bas to stand still like Stanslo told him to. Bas will, until he can't anymore, until that not-hair comes at him, and then he's probably going to end up snapping Dolerma's neck. He hopes it'll be enough of a shock to keep Stanslo still for the two seconds it'll take for Bas to get him next.

None of that happens, though. Like Dolerma knows, he moves too quickly, his initial slow gait a feint Bas stupidly falls for, and Dolerma's there and rubbing those awful, blood-warm strands of flesh all up and down Bas's arm. Bas yanks his arm back again, and he supposes it'll give the game away, but he really doesn't care anymore.

But Dolerma only steps back, says, "There is no passenger," and Stanslo grins with what looks like relief and says, "Splendid!"

Bas is still kind of reeling on the inside, so Stanslo saying "I had to be sure, Bas, you understand" on his way out the door almost doesn't register.

But then it does, and Bas shakes his head, his jaw clenched, and he says, "When Reacher told you all about how Geda got too close, Baron. Did you stop to wonder why?" He snags the towel off again and throws it down, angry and shaken, then starts yanking on his trousers. "Seems while I was busy *not leaving my gun*, the guy who was supposed to be watching my back, well— *wasn't*." He grits his teeth. "I wonder if you can guess who that might've been."

Reacher gets a day in the Box.
Bas gets to laugh and laugh and laugh.
Bas—1, Reacher—0.

"So, all that talk about wings and aerodynamics."

Bas watches the little contraption whirr up over toward the workbench before it makes a teasing dive at Jessa. Jessa whistles an indignant screech and arrows over to perch on top of the new train's cab. She keeps a sharp gaze on the whirring thing, head tilting, eyes blinking and reflecting the short bursts of gridstream Kimolijah flitters into the contraption to keep it hovering a few handsbreadths from his fingertips.

"Not so much 'talk,'" Kimolijah agrees with a grin that's light and as happy as Bas has ever seen him.

It's just a toy, Kimolijah told Bas, mischief sparking in his eyes and a desire to share, maybe even show off a little, undeniably there, and Bas wasn't able to say no. Not that he'd wanted to.

It's got blades atop it that look like the arms of windmills beaten out of thin sheets of tin. The tiny engine putters when it starts running out of charge, the blades slowing, the body dipping down and down, and it hums whenever Kimolijah gives it another delicate *zap*.

"Does anyone else know about this?" Bas asks, because he gets the feeling this is a secret, private, something Kimolijah doesn't give to just anyone, and the thought warms Bas. He watches the mechanism dip and sway and then jink a little upward when Kimolijah gives it another nip of gridstream. "I mean, have you shown anyone else?"

"No. Just...." Kimolijah presses his lips together and his brow does a fold-crumple thing. He shrugs. "I wanted someone to—" He cuts it off and pays extraordinary attention to a swervy move he's done at least ten times already and Bas would swear doesn't need that much concentration.

It's not difficult for Bas to hear the things inside the things Kimolijah doesn't say. Because there is an artistry to what Kimolijah does, and artists express and then artists share. Fear has kept Kimolijah from doing so for a long time, and the fact that he's sharing something now with *Bas*....

Bas clears his throat and says, "Could you build one big enough to carry a man?"

Kimolijah doesn't answer for a while, and when he does, the smile is not quite as bright as it was before. "If I could," he says, then mutters, "Aw, hellfire," when the thing chokes a little and then tumbles down to the oiled dirt of the floor. Kimolijah frowns as he picks it up and checks it over. He looks up at Bas and says, "If I could, I'd make bloody sure no one knew it but me."

As usual, it doesn't answer the question. Except it pretty much does.

Two nights later, Bas doesn't get blown up by the little gridheater in his room only because he smells the gunpowder someone has rigged into its guts when he stoops down to fire it up. The blast might not have killed him, he figures, but it would've made a nice little bomb all the same, and the shrapnel would have cut him up good.

He goes to bed smirking and imagining Reacher down the hall, waiting for the explosion and wondering why there isn't one. Bas freezes his ass off all night with no heater, but though he's sleeping with one eye open, he thinks he still manages a better night than Reacher does.

Bas—2, Reacher—0.

⚬⚭⚬

"So, what do I do about getting a new gridheater?"

"*Ow!*" Kimolijah's top half emerges from inside a mess of vacuum tubes and coils tucked into a side panel of the engine. He frowns at Bas, rubbing his head, and rolls his eyes. "What is it with you sneaking up on me?" He huffs and starts running out a spool of wire. "And what's wrong with yours?"

"I wasn't sneaking up on you. Anyway, it's not my fault your watchbird isn't doing her job."

Kimolijah cranes his neck around to look at Jessa, sitting calmly above his head, her own tilting and turning in little stops and starts, and her breast trilling a soft, purring warble. "Worthless," Kimolijah tells her, and when she doesn't seem terribly fazed, he shakes his head and reaches up to run his fingers gently over her downy throat. "She's not really...." He shrugs and looks at Bas. "She's opinionated. She doesn't like certain people."

"Yeah, I know." Bas refrains from making a face at Jessa like a five-year-old. "The flying guts kind of clued me in."

"You really are kind of dim sometimes," Kimolijah mutters. He gives Bas an impatient look. "Animals don't generally share their lunch with someone they don't like." He looks away, like it was some kind of confession, and says gruffly, "What's wrong with your heater?"

Bas pauses. Because *synched*. Jessa is synched to Kimolijah. And Jessa has been sharing her lunch with Bas almost since the moment he came to Stanslo's Bridge. Bas grins. Until Kimolijah looks at him, and then Bas clears his throat and pulls a straight face.

"Someone decided it needed a little extra bang." He shrugs. "Smelled gunpowder when I went to fire it up last night."

"Oh," Kimolijah says. He scrubs a hand over his face. "Yeah, I'll...." He sets his teeth and looks up at Bas. "Listen, I'll take care of it. Soon. I just have to...." He shakes his head and blows out a heavy breath. "I'll take care of it."

Kimolijah's talking about something a lot more significant than just a simple heater. Bas nods and looks away. He scrubs at his jaw, all of a sudden weary. "Was Fox your first?"

Kimolijah huffs a snort that's not even a little bit amused. "I'm not going to kill anyone."

"Then I'm going to have to." Bas looks at Kimolijah and holds out his hands. "Kimo, it has to be—"

"I said I'd take care of it, and I will."

"Taking care of it without killing him isn't going to do much good. Merrin's synched to Reacher now. If he—"

"I *know!*" Kimolijah's hands curl into fists around his tools. "I know. But you can't just kill him, because you won't just get the Box. There's a gibbet out there for a reason. The baron'll hang you, and he'll make every single one of us watch. No one's going to step out for you, no one's going to defend you, and I *can't.*" He sucks in a calming breath and sets his shoulders. "I can't do it either, not so Stanslo knows. He's getting worse. He didn't used to...." He waves a hand at his face, the blooded eye, the bruise on his cheekbone. "It has to be... he can't know it was.... He can't *know.*" He runs a hand through his hair and sighs. "I'll take care of it. I will. The next run. I'll be ready. You just have to watch your back for a bit longer."

"Kimo...." Bas takes off his hat and rakes at his hair. He shakes his head. "You shouldn't... I don't *want* you to—"

"Yeah, I know." Kimolijah tips a rueful little smile and he shrugs. "But you can't. Okay? You *can't.*" He pauses, looks Bas in the eye and says, "Just... trust me. Please."

And, well. It's long since past the point where Bas has had a choice. So he nods and turns to go, until Kimolijah says, "Hey, um... Bas?"

So, so quiet. Tentative. Cautious. *Shy.*

When Bas turns around, Kimolijah's head is bowed, and then it's not, and then Kimolijah's looking at him, just *looking*, his giant eyes popping gold, rimmed by stoke-black lashes and sober, his wide mouth parted just a little, and *those stupid fucking crooked bottom teeth—*

Bas stalks over, grabs Kimolijah's shoulders, leans in and... hesitates.

It has to be you, Bas thinks, staring, willing, waiting. *It has to be by your leave.*

Because Bas will never, ever take "no" away, not from anyone, not for this.

For a second, Bas thinks that's the answer he's going to get, because Kimolijah looks so torn, so confused and miserable that Bas thinks Kimolijah might actually cry. But then Kimolijah says, "Yeah," all strung out and weightless on a thin breath that riffles over Bas's skin and *shakes* him.

Bas kisses him. And then Kimolijah kisses back, and something in Bas is throwing its hands up, shaking its head, telling him *It's over, you've done it now*, but he just leans down further, grips Kimolijah harder, and *sinks in*.

This is the sort of thing, Bas half thinks, *illobook heroes fight for*, the reason they can go on, move on, keep on, because if they can just have this, just for one minute, everything else is just a petty hell they have to wade through to get it. *Half* thinks because Kimolijah has stolen Bas's mind, mouth sinful and wet and demanding and asking, all at once, and the hot fizz of craving that whumps Bas from knee to chest could be Kimolijah's wild gridstream lighting Bas up and melting him to slag and Bas—wouldn't—*care*.

By the time it's over, Kimolijah's nearly climbed Bas like a tree, and he's hanging on, arms hooked around the back of Bas's neck, body pressed up tight and clinging. He's panting when he pulls back, looks down and away, like he's embarrassed, and he snorts a little as he says, "You'll need to let go of my leg."

Bas hadn't realized he'd latched on the way he'd done, but there his hand is, splayed wide over Kimolijah's thigh, gripping it close to his own hip. Bas laughs too, just a little, and he makes his hands obey, lets go, as Kimolijah shimmies loose and backs away exactly three steps before he looks back at Bas with a long, deep breath.

His fingertips hover over his mouth—not wiping, just... touching. He gives Bas one of those tiny soft smiles Bas has only seen once or twice, and Kimolijah says, "I'll take care of it. I will." And when Bas just keeps staring at Kimolijah's mouth, Kimolijah grins and says, "Jessa's yelling. You've gotta go."

It's not until then, when Bas's brain remembers what it is and what it's supposed to be doing, that Bas hears Jessa making a racket outside, and it doesn't surprise him in the least that she must have flown right past his head and he didn't even notice. Five seconds later, Stanslo is making his usual arrogant bow-to-me entrance and Kimolijah's ducked around the side panel, out of sight of the door.

Stanslo pulls up short, eyes narrowing just a touch above his abrupt cheery smile. "Ah, Bas." His brow crinkles just a little. "My, you do pop up in the strangest places." Suspicious, because Stanslo always is.

Bas doesn't care. He's pretty much decided he's going to have to kill Stanslo eventually anyway. Might as well be... okay, his gun is still at Quinnie's smithy.

"Baron." Bas nods an acceptable greeting. "I was...."

Damn it. The gridgun is a weight across his back that would be comforting if he didn't know Stanslo would have his pretty little four-barrel skinned, fired and reholstered before Bas could even get the strap over his head.

Kimolijah's waving from around the edge of the panel,

presumably to get Bas's attention, and when Bas shoots a side-eye look over at him, Kimolijah does some kind of gesture with his hands that he probably thinks means something important, but really looks more like *shoot yourself in the eye, then take the octopus for a walk*. When Bas merely stares, Kimolijah rolls his eyes before he dives down into the mess of tubes and coils.

"What are you still doing here?" he snaps from the depths, voice muffled and annoyed. "I'll get your damned gridheater. Now get the fuck out of here and leave me alone. I'm working."

Bas doesn't say anything. He merely lifts his eyebrows, tips his hat at Stanslo as he leaves, and makes a mental note to figure out what birds like for treats.

⊙≫∘

It's surprisingly easy to lie low, now that Bas is giving it a good go. He's a deputy and he's the gunner, those are his jobs, and the only one anyone expects him to show up for is the latter. So he basically has nothing to do until the next run to the Bruise, except watching out for Reacher and surreptitiously pestering Kimolijah and *not falling* harder and deeper, because that would be even more stupid now than it was before.

Over the next week, Reacher is persistent but never creative, so his attempts are easy to spot.

A heavy timber somehow manages to wriggle out from the bracing struts of Hannah's second floor balcony as Bas is leaving, but the scrape of it against the clapboard siding is too loud in the flat, empty desert. Bas sidesteps, then walks backward for a few paces, watches it crash down and take out the steps of Hannah's front porch. He shakes his head as he looks for and easily finds the dark bulky silhouette against the cobwebbed constellations that lurch across the sky. Bas smirks, tips his hat, then turns and keeps walking. He ignores Sis and Hannah wailing about their porch behind him, and he rolls his eyes at the small crowd who've emerged to see what the foorah is about.

Kimolijah finds him the next day and kisses him behind the smokehouse with a nervous laugh and whispers, "Heard you batted away a bloody tree trunk with your bare hands." He grins and tilts his head. "I guess I'll be Dirk Darkling. You can be Magic Man."

And then he tells Bas again all about how the tongue is the strongest muscle in the body in proportion to its size.

Bas only lets him stop demonstrating and then cautiously slip away when they hear footsteps wandering a little too close.

Bas—3, Reacher—0.

⊙≫∘

A snake in his bed, probably venomous. Who's he kidding?—unquestionably venomous. And most likely venomous in a way that makes your skin melt off and your guts come out your nose. Because Reacher's a mean motherfucker, and he'd go for the worst death possible.

Bas actually laughs at this one. As if he hasn't been checking every inch of his room and his bedding every night for all manner of creepy-crawlies. Please.

Bloody amateurs.

Bas—4, Reacher—0.

⊗

But Kimolijah frowns heavily the next day when Bas tells him about it. His mouth pinches down when the tiny mechanical dragon he's been showing Bas squawks and wanders off the edge of the workbench.

Kimolijah catches it before it can shatter in the dirt, and says, "This is getting out of hand." He turns the dragon over in his hands and slides a finger from pinion to wingtip. "He's not going to stop, is he?"

Bas thinks that's fairly obvious, so he doesn't answer.

"Okay," says Kimolijah, seemingly to the still-chirping dragon.

He's shirtless again, and Bas tries not to stare at the whorls and twists of black ink over brown skin he won't admit he knows nearly by heart now. The ink, not the skin. He'd *like* to get to know the—

Bas gives his head a little shake. He really needs to stop that.

"Okay," Kimolijah says again. "I just... I underestimated him. I'm sorry. I didn't...." He nods slowly, brow twisted so tight his goggles shift on his forehead. "Have you got tower duty tonight?"

It's such a turn in conversation that it makes Bas blink. "Er. No. Why?"

"Planning on going to Hannah's or anything?"

"No." Bas frowns. "Why?"

Kimolijah shakes his head and spins back to his workbench. "No reason." He picks up a tiny screwdriver and starts fiddling with a kink in the dragon's wing. "See you later, Bas."

Bas's eyebrows shoot up his forehead. He hasn't been dismissed like that for a while, and he wasn't expecting it now. He's confounded and a little put out, but Kimolijah can be a high-handed bastard when he wants to be, and a moody little shit besides.

So Bas just says, "Yeah. Later." And he leaves.

⊗

It takes Bas quite a while to figure it out. Which is for the best, he supposes. It never would've spun out this way if he'd twigged before it actually happened.

The creaking and scraping at Bas's window doesn't wake him up, because he wasn't asleep, just in that in-between space where he can trick his body into thinking it's getting decent rest while his mind keeps alert for… well, a creaking and scraping at his window, for instance. The shooting and chatter had started about an hour ago, and it won't be raining, not with Mari at the way station, so it'll likely be going on until dawn. The rest of the town is either shutting up their hovels against the night's chill, at Hannah's, sleeping, or trying to; whoever's trying to get in through Bas's window likely assumes they're fairly safe from notice.

Bas has got the shutters pulled tight and locked down, so he can't see who's out there. He assumes it's Reacher, so he reaches under his pillow and slides out the six-barrel he just picked up from Quinnie this afternoon. The nicks have been polished out with steel wool, and it smells of gun oil. Bas doesn't think it's because Quinnie gives a shit about him or his gun one way or the other; he thinks she just can't stand to see a good weapon in less than perfect repair.

Silent, Bas rises, then makes his way over to the side of the window, wary of the groan of floorboards under his careful steps. He waits for a bit, watching a thin bit of metal slide through the slim gap between the shutters to push at the catch. It's not going to work. Bas has rigged it from the inside so it's more of a latch than a catch, and adjusted the shutters more snug in the casing—take *that*, creepy-crawlies—and nothing short of actually breaking the wood the latch is attached to is going to open that shutter. Bas isn't worried. Even if Reacher rips the shutter off the wall, Bas isn't worried.

He thinks about just flinging the shutters open and getting this over with, because if he kills Reacher now, there will still be a good six hours left in which to get some sleep.

Except if he kills Reacher now and Stanslo hangs him for it, Bas's mam will cry and Mo will have every right to insult Bas's intelligence in his eulogy. If they ever find out what happened to him.

And who would get Kimolijah out of here then?

So Bas waits and he keeps his gun steady, and he waits and he tries not to move, and he waits and he watches that little piece of metal jam and jam and jam at the catch until he hears someone mutter, "God fucking *damn it*," and then he nearly punches the wall.

He laughs instead, quiet and thick on a rush of cheated adrenaline, and he leans into the wall until he can get himself under control. When he can look at the little bit of metal still poking through the shutters without snorting, he does what he'd wanted to do before: he pulls the window open, quietly unhooks the latch, and shoves the shutters outward.

Kimolijah's squawk of surprise is quiet, very nearly stifled altogether, though still pretty hilarious. Even more so when he stumbles back and falls on his ass, blinking up at Bas with that concussed-baby-owl face for a second or two before it morphs into annoyance.

"What the hell is wrong with you?" he hisses.

"*Me*?" Bas lets his mouth drop open. "I'm not the one trying to break into the room of a badass gunslinger in the middle of the night." He holds up his gun. "Could've shot you through the shutters, y'know."

"Yeah?" Kimolijah tilts his head, mouth crooked up, insolent. "So why didn't you, Mister Badass Gunslinger?" He waggles his eyebrows. "Come on, you can say it. You were secretly hoping it was me."

"I thought you were Reacher. I wanted to see the look in his eyes when I put a bullet between them."

Kimolijah's half smile morphs yet again, this time into something rueful. He picks himself up out of the dirt and brushes off his trousers.

"Well? Gonna let me in?"

"Why? Something wrong?"

"Yeah." Kimolijah rolls his eyes. "You're not letting me in."

There's a direct line of sight from the back of the Palace, where Bas's window sits, right up the rise to the big house. Not close enough to see anything, just the bulk of the structure jutting up and out, little points of light through windows in the distance. Bas has squinted in its direction too many nights, wondering and trying not to, and pretending he's doing nothing of the sort.

Now it feels like Stanslo is watching, is seeing everything, as Kimolijah climbs nimbly through Bas's window. Kimolijah's feet are bare and make no sound at all as he hops down from the ledge and pauses while his eyes adjust to the angles and lines of the room in the dark. Bas stares for a moment—at the breadth of Kimolijah's shoulders, at the lean lines of him, shoulders tapering into torso and flaring just a touch at the hip. He's wearing a shirt this time, which is a little disappointing, but it's cold, and when Kimolijah turns to face Bas, Bas can see his nipples through his shirt. Bas does not stare.

"What are you staring at?" Kimolijah whispers, eyes somewhat narrowed when Bas flicks his gaze upward. But then Kimolijah grins, wry and knowing, and he takes a step in.

Bas takes one back. "What's wrong? Why are you here?"

"I, um...." All of a sudden shy. "I want...."

And God, Bas should probably not try to fill in that blank, but he can't help it—it's dark and close and there's a bed *right there*, and it's not entirely out of the question that Bas is seeing things where he wants to, but it's also not entirely out of the question that he's not. Kimolijah's just *crawled in through Bas's widow*, for fuck's sake. In the *middle of the night*.

Kimolijah steps in again, tentative but braving it, and Bas only takes a half a step backward this time, knowing he should retreat but the defiance in him asking *yeah? why?* and Bas doesn't have an answer.

"Kimo." It's thicker than it should be, and it just hangs there, heavy, because Bas has no idea where to go with it. Kimolijah's just *staring* at him, eyes traveling from Bas's face to his chest and then down, down, down, and Bas is self-conscious enough that he fidgets. He's glad he's backed up almost into the press because it gives him someplace to put his gun, since he's pretty sure he doesn't need it just now, and when he sets it down carefully and looks back at Kimolijah, Kimolijah's still staring.

"Did you know," Kimolijah says, licks his lips, nervous, and takes another step, "that it takes a man less than ten seconds to achieve a full erection?"

Everything in Bas stops for half a second, he can actually hear the screech, the sound of his own thin breath the boom of a cannon. He stares, and Kimolijah lifts his eyebrows, waiting, so *goddamned* gorgeous with his huge stupid eyes and straight stupid nose and too-wide *sinful* fucking mouth, and it's not fucking *fair*, and everything that got jammed up in Bas's brain and body whomps back through him in a hot, near-violent rush.

"Five," he manages to rasp, and he swoops in.

It starts out soft, but stays so for mere seconds. A gentle touch of lips, at first, then demand seeps in, turns it deeper, until Bas forgets there's such a person as Baron Stanslo and that this is dangerous, his hands on Kimolijah, Kimolijah's hands on him. They could die for this. That's not illobook melodrama but reality—they could actually die if they get caught doing this—and there's probably something horribly wrong with the fact that thinking it only gets Bas harder, makes the kiss hotter.

This isn't shiny-new anymore, Bas knows Kimolijah's kisses now, gone from uncertain and careful to brave and adventurous. He knows the teasing swipe of the tongue and yet is still surprised by it; he knows the flirty little nips and yet he still grins and grips harder, sinks deeper. Kimolijah's arms wind around Bas's neck, and it's so absurd that this, something so simple, is what makes Bas's head spin a little, but there it is, and a fizzy coil of hunger winds up Bas's spine at the tiny sounds of need coming from Kimolijah's chest, vibrating through Bas's.

Kimolijah pulls back, slowly, dragging Bas's bottom lip between his teeth. "Bed," he breathes, lips plump and wet against Bas's.

Bas bobbles a nod and says, "Okay," because it's really all he can manage, but when he takes a step and tries to nudge Kimolijah toward the place Kimolijah *just said he wants to be*, Kimolijah puts a firm hand to Bas's chest and says, "Wait."

Wait.

Wait.

"What?" Bas hisses, and, "*What*?" because what *wait*, what the fuck with the *wait*?

"We have to be very careful." It's a flutter of warm breath over Bas's throat, just below his ear, and it spreads right through his chest and down to his toes in a wash of restless, incandescent arousal. "We have to be very *quiet*."

It sobers Bas somewhat, reminds him where he is, who he's with, and what could happen, because it's all well and good that a little danger gets him off, but the danger is very real and probably worse for Kimolijah. Bas nods, pulls Kimolijah in tight, and sets a hard kiss to the top of Kimolijah's head, breathing in the spice of him, the clove of expensive soap and the faint tang of engine grease and burnt ozone that lingers like an aura. Kimolijah's just tall enough to bury his face and lay a wet line of soft-but-firm kisses to Bas's collarbone. He's hard, the solid heat of him pressed into Bas's thigh, and Bas shifts, just a little, just enough to make Kimolijah suck in a long breath and tighten his fingers where they dig into Bas's shoulder blades.

"Bed," Kimolijah says again, and they go.

Bas has never seen Kimolijah naked before. He stares because Kimolijah's perfect, all clean lines and lean ropes of muscle, brown skin taut and sparse black hair somehow balancing out the asymmetricality of all that black ink that swoops and scrolls over Kimolijah's left side. He's unabashed in front of Bas, not shy at all this time, letting him stare, shoulders back and feet flat on the floor, and a lift of one black eyebrow says, *Well?*

There's something at the back of Bas's mind, something petty and mocking that says *He's not shy here because this is something he knows, for him, this is familiar, it's what he does,* how *he does,* but Bas won't hear it because *No, this is different, it's not like that, it's—*

"God," says Bas, hoarse, wanting it out, wanting it gone. "I really need you to fuck me."

Kimolijah's eyebrows shoot up, and he tilts his head, mouth pulling up in a surprised, pleased little smile. It's gone too quickly, replaced by something... off, but he shakes his head and says, "Not this time," *this time,* which leads Bas to think maybe this won't be the *only time,* there will be a *next time,* and when Kimolijah steps in close and takes Bas's hand, guides it down, everything flies right out of Bas's head, except for *holy fucking shit*.

"You...." Bas can't even make his mouth form the words. Arousal has spiked high and sharp, his fingers dawdling over skin soft and slippery with blood-warm oil, and the image of Kimolijah doing it to himself, maybe smiling and stroking himself when he did it, anticipating Bas's hand on him, anticipating stretching out on Bas's bed, offering this, *planning* this....

Bas reaches for Kimolijah, hand tangling in thick black hair, pulling, and when Kimolijah has to fetch a moan back and turn it into a quiet gasp, Bas *yanks*, pulls Kimolijah's head back, and bends to lay his mouth to Kimolijah's throat, sets his teeth into skin that's just a touch salty with a thin sheen of sweat. Peppery-hot on his tongue, and lemon fizz hovers just at the edges, like a mark of possession, and Bas *hates* it, wants to lay his own over it, wants to—

"No marks," Kimolijah whispers, and it almost throws Bas, almost makes him remember and acknowledge, but then Kimolijah's pulling and nudging, saying, "Never mind, doesn't matter, do it," then dragging Bas with him as he stretches out on Bas's bed like it's exactly where he's meant to be, so Bas pretends it is.

And when Kimolijah whispers, "Why are you not fucking me yet?" everything in Bas just *explodes*.

It's frantic, at first, a little bit clumsy even, restless arching and some moves that are more flailing than grasping, senseless words rolled out on hoarse groans, and a delirious litany from Kimolijah that's nothing more than an insistent string of "Come on, come on, *come on*," eyes shut so tight they're crinkled at the corners, brow screwed down like he's thinking too hard.

It's not quite right, it's not quite *there*, not quite what it should be, so Bas pulls back and sets his hand to Kimolijah's breastbone, times the rabbit-beats of Kimolijah's heart, and says, "Kimolijah," soft and low, and he says it again, "Kimolijah," and stills the want that's pushing his body to take and own.

Kimolijah frowns harder, but he opens his eyes, looks into Bas's, and everything just sort of... slows. Calms. *Clicks.*

Unhurried now. Measured. Gentle.

Bas takes his time now, enters Kimolijah slowly, watches the soft dip of Kimolijah's jaw as his mouth opens on an indolent sigh, feels the lazy quiver of Kimolijah's muscles as Bas presses in and in and in, savors the weight of Kimolijah's arms around his neck, pulling him in and down for a long, deep kiss.

He slides his hands beneath Kimolijah's shoulders as he begins to move, fingers curling down toward Kimolijah's collarbones, keeping him in place. Kimolijah pants into Bas's throat with each thrust, tiny, slippery little words—*yeah* and *good* and *that*—getting caught behind his teeth, then tumbling out on breathless grunts that Bas answers by curling down to press his cheek to Kimolijah's and driving in just that much harder.

It's torture and it's perfect. Sweet frustration. Bas could live forever in this exact moment, wants it, and he wants the rush of climax *right now*, wants both, all at once, and somehow it makes complete and perfect sense. The build is maddening, one slow spangle of sensation piling atop the next, linked like a daisy-chain snaking through his senses, snapping over his skin in a chaotic patchwork of visceral *feeling*. The muscles in Kimolijah's shoulders bundle and knot in Bas's palms, each slow slide scrip-scraping dawdling flickers of heat and brilliant pressure up Bas's backbone. He has to remind himself to breathe, the leisurely rock of pleasure dragging through him and slicking his skin to something that's almost too alive, *too much*.

"I don't" leaks out of Bas's chest on a stuttering breath, and he clenches his teeth to keep the rest of the lie locked down where he can't hear it or know it.

But then Kimolijah sighs out a "Yeah" into Bas's throat, slides his tongue over it as though to seal it to Bas's skin, and arches up, pulls Bas in deeper, and says, "Yeah," again, like he's agreeing to something. It strips Bas, and he doesn't know why, leaves him raw and too open, so he latches onto Kimolijah's earlobe with his teeth and drives down hard.

It slips the slow imperative into rising urgency, and they surge, both together. Bas adjusts the angle ever so slightly, a rush of lust blowing right through him when Kimolijah throttles a shout into a low groan and lifts his hips to get more. Bas reaches down and gives it to him, strokes him, and there's no longer any give-and-take, back-and-forth, but *pushpushpush* to the edge. A swell and a drag, and Kimolijah snaps Bas's name out on a breathless near snarl, orgasm bending him in a provocative arc and muting the cries that want to stumble out into high, broken grunts.

Bas can't hold against it. It thieves his climax from him, convulsive and rough. It's all white, everything, fizzing and popping over Bas's skin like sentient gridstream, throat clogging on a thick groan and body rocking like it never wants to stop.

And he thinks: *I don't love you.*

And he thinks: *This means nothing.*

And he thinks: *You are not mine.*

And then he waits and waits and waits, because surely he'll believe every word of it eventually.

It takes a while for him to come down, the abrupt delirium of the moment leaching into the reality of Kimolijah's body beneath him, slick with sweat, hair damp and sticking in looped strands on the side of his neck. His hand is set right in the middle of Bas's chest, splayed wide over Bas's breastbone like a dark star in a pale sky, and the dull coil of the bracelet spirals down Kimolijah's arm, wedged between their chests like it belongs there. Bas stares at it for five long breaths, wondering why it arrests him so acutely, then he shakes it off and slides to the mattress beside Kimolijah with a heavy *whuff*.

He hasn't even settled in yet, reached for Kimolijah, before Kimolijah's up and feeling around for his trousers in the dark.

"I can't stay," Kimolijah whispers, and he sounds off again, though Bas can't pin it. "I have to... there's something...." He doesn't finish, just sighs and says, "Listen," but he doesn't finish that either.

He backs up some when Bas sits up and frowns at him, confused and maybe a little hurt. Okay, yeah—*hurt*. Kimolijah's got his shirt and trousers clutched to his chest like a shield, and he stares at Bas for a good long time before he shakes his head and looks down. He all but leaps into his clothes.

"Listen," he says again as he does up his shirt, and then he digs into his trouser pocket and pulls out.... Bas doesn't know, but the whole room abruptly smells of roses. "I don't... I mean, for some reason, I... well, your opinion is... or maybe it's just... *ugh*." He rubs at his face, then slides his hand up into his hair and clutches. "I just... I don't want you to think poorly of me, and what I've... what I'm *going* to... goddamn it."

"Kimolijah." Bas keeps his voice low and steady. "I don't think poorly of you. And I know—"

"Yeah, but you don't, not yet." Kimolijah shakes his head. "But it's... I mean, I *have* to...." He backs up, leaving Bas frowning on the bed that smells of pepper and clove. He's already got one leg thrown over the window sash when he pauses, head down like he's thinking, maybe praying, before he takes a deep breath and he says, "Just because I'm.... It doesn't mean, none of it—it's not on *you*. I mean, it *won't* be." He lifts his head, looks at Bas, and says, "And just... when it all goes down, keep your head. This is how it has to go." He pulls up a grin, but it's not real. "I'm a genius, yeah? Got it all figured out."

And then he's gone.

❧

Bas is still frowning up at the ceiling, still smelling the ghosts of roses, knowing that something's off, something's going on he's not kenning, when the go-to-chapel bell starts ringing out in the square. It's never happened before, Bas doesn't know what it means, but it's a bell in the middle of the night, so his heart starts thumping. And then it starts jittering, because he can see Jessa over the rooftops and it's like she's going insane, darting and diving in erratic patterns over the center of town, and screeching like someone's set fire to her tail feathers.

Something in Bas knows. Not defined, not in solid shapes, but he knows.

Everyone's in the square when Bas gets out there, the gridlight atop the gibbet lighting everything up in stark lines and harsh shadows, and when Bas catches sight of Stanslo, his chest locks up tight and his step falters. Because Stanslo is livid, Bas doesn't think he's ever seen such a crazed look—and he's got Kimolijah by the arm. A half-dressed Kimolijah, with his shirt hanging off one arm and blood dripping down his chest and onto the fine linen from a split in his lip. He's got a rope around his neck, loosely knotted, but knotted still, and his throat is scraped rough with friction burns.

Stanslo knows is the first thing Bas thinks, *he knows what we did and he's going to kill us both*, but Stanslo looks directly at Bas for a full several seconds, registers him, and then looks right past him.

"*You!*" he snarls, and he points behind Bas and to the left. At Reacher. "He came to me *used*," Stanslo says, garbled fury from between clenched teeth, and he drags Kimolijah up by the rope around his neck, over toward where Reacher stands, stiff and wide-eyed, like he's stuck to the ground.

A whoop goes up in the distance as someone shoots a not-bat out of the sky near one of the towers, and there's a surreal quality to it, that something relatively normal is going on outside this sticky cocoon of slow-dawning implosion. Because whatever's coming is big, huge. Bas can feel it like heat-rash under his skin.

Kimolijah looks a little dazed, like he's drunk or high, and now that Stanslo's hauled him closer, Bas can see that the entire left side of Kimolijah's face is swelling up fast. Kimolijah doesn't look at Bas as Stanslo compels him closer, closer, until they're past Bas and Stanslo is throwing Kimolijah down to the ground at Reacher's feet. Jessa swoops in and strafes the space between Kimolijah and Stanslo, the gibbet's gridlight picking up the white in her feathers and turning her to a whizzing streak of blue, but neither of them seem to notice.

"You have one chance to tell me the truth," Stanslo says, deadly soft now, and so cold it shuts down even the confused whispers of the crowd, and everything stills. "Tell me the truth, Reacher," Stanslo says, "and I might forgive you."

Bas looks down at Kimolijah, horrified and knowing, but he doesn't understand it. *Used*, yes, he gets that part, but he doesn't grasp why Stanslo's gone after Reacher. Kimolijah couldn't have accused him—he can't lie.

It's like Kimolijah feels the weight of Bas's stare, because he lifts his head, looks up from where he's crouched on the ground, and the look he gives Bas is... indescribable. Heavy and horrible, but his bloody lips pull up in a ghastly smile and form the words *Keep your head*, and everything still totters on the edge of understanding only because Bas doesn't want to have to know it.

"Boss," says Reacher carefully, "I don't know—"

"He stinks of *ROSES!*" Stanslo bellows, then he raises his gun and shoots Reacher point-blank between the eyes.

And all Bas can think is: *oh*.

Reacher, still and always—0

Kimolijah—all of them.

22

It goes pretty much tits up from there.

Bas has never seen Stanslo quite so crazed, and it's funny because *this* is how Bas figures out who's on what side.

Cavett and Merrin go down immediately, both of them holding their heads and crying out, like Reacher's death is resonating in their own skulls, and Bas wonders if this has anything to do with the feedback and synching Kimolijah was talking about. They're not bleeding from their eyes or anything, and their heads don't actually explode, but they both look like it hurts. And while Cavett just moans on his knees in the dirt in the center of the square while muted chaos erupts around him, Merrin watches through evident pain, marking everything like Bas is doing, and keeping a hand free for the gun that hangs from his shoulder.

"This is what happens!" Stanslo shrieks, "This is what you get!" and he spends the next several minutes kicking Reacher's corpse until the last breath Reacher took shudders out of collapsed lungs, stomping Reacher's face until the crunch of bone gives way to the squelch of pulp, shouting about betrayal and treachery with a lot of gnashing and frothing that amounts to *mine, mine, mine*! There's some kind of edge over which Stanslo has obviously slipped, and those who stand in fear and awe and simply watch are those Bas figures are a waste of time; those who watch in a different way, whose glances reach across and connect with others, analytical—*is this it? is it time?*—those are the ones Bas marks, and he watches as they mark him.

"You do not *take*," Stanslo snarls, gore dripping from his boot, "what is not *yours*!"

Most of the deputies stand agog, some of them even smirk, and they watch Stanslo with hungry expressions, maybe waiting to see if they'll be invited to join in, like desecrating the corpse of one of their own is some kind of macabre dance and they're just waiting for a partner to coax them to the floor. Most of those without a gun, without deputy status, cut alert glances that flit over the crowd, like they're just taking in who's there, but all of them, *all of them*, eventually land on... Lowen. Who stands directly behind Quinnie, wide dark hand on her shoulder, like he's holding her back.

Just like he'd held Bas back when Bas had thought to step between Fox and Kimolijah.

Kimolijah waits it out, still crouched beside Reacher's corpse, head down and bent over his knees, close to the ground, like he's trying to make himself small. He doesn't move, even when Stanslo's violence shoves Reacher's body into him and makes him totter a bit unsteadily, and once he even has to use Reacher's thick arm as leverage, but he doesn't seem to mind.

He looks at Bas, though, out the corner of his eye.

His steady stare says: *I'm not sorry.*

And it says: *Are you still with me?*

And it says: *I'm not sorry, I'm* not, *I never will be, not for this.*

Bas thinks about it all, a little sadly, but he looks back with *no* and *yes* and *This is how it had to go*, and he won't think about *Was this the only reason?* or *Is this all it was to you?* and instead concentrates on *Here's what we do next.*

It's when Stanslo starts flagging—panting breaths instead of shouts; something close to groans instead of righteous rage—that Serenat steps in. Not to help Stanslo, apparently, not to calm him down or take him away or any of the other things you do with a crazy person who's crossed the line from *Keep an eye on him* and lurched straight into *Put him down, he's too far gone.*

No, Serenat steps in when Stanslo looks down at Kimolijah, like he'd forgotten he was there, and his eyes blaze and his teeth bare, and he says, "Someone get me my whip."

Kimolijah doesn't quail. He lifts his head, jaw set, and he stares Stanslo down from his crouch, his own eyes hard and cold and *daring* Stanslo, asking for it. And before Bas can even open his mouth or note Quinnie, only paces to Bas's left, trying to bore holes into him, shaking her head at him, warning him, Serenat steps between Kimolijah and Stanslo and says, "No."

All of the confused, low-voiced chatter, all of the surreptitious glances pinging through the crowd, all of it stops. Silence drops like a gallows' floor, throttling even the night animal sounds that never stop here, but that might just be Bas's blood beating the battle drums in his head. The men on tower duty are still shooting the not-bats, oblivious, but Bas can't hear it, only sees the occasional flash of a gridgun against the sky in the distance.

Slowly, Stanslo turns to Serenat, manic fury all over him, and he takes a step in, trying to tower, but Serenat's taller than he is. "You," he says, all caustic deliberation, low and deadly and abruptly far too calm, "do not tell me *no.*"

No "sweetpea," no "little miss," and Stanslo can't even drag in enough control to form his everpresent smile in any of its permutations. He's still got his little four-barrel out, and his fingers shift over it, intentions writ large in everything about him. It's lost on no one, and Dolerma speaks from across the square, an outward chastisement of "Come away, Serenat, this is between them" and an inward buzz that takes on the mocking shapes of "This is where playing games with me gets you, little sister" in Bas's head.

It's all-over citrus, shades of musky earth leaching in to fizz at the base of Bas's skull, and he gets the sensation of two battering forces hurling across the square and meeting somewhere in the middle with a solid, dazzling *whomp* that doesn't flare in his eyes and blind him, but it seems like it should. Neither Dolerma nor Serenat move, though Bas *feels* like they're everywhere, leveling mental strikes and countering psychic swipes so hard and brutal even Bas's teeth ache with the resonance.

And in the center of it all, Stanslo stands rigid, utterly still and unspeakably furious, buffeted between two thunderous stormfronts and apparently not feeling a thing.

Bas certainly is, though even he can't follow everything rocketing back and forth across the otherwise still and silent square. It rages like wildfire while not-deputies shift nervously and fling significant looks around, until something gives in the air around Dolerma, *pushes*, right at Stanslo. Serenat gasps and flinches just as the deputies grip their guns with both hands and firm their stances, sharpen their attention, and stand ready for an order.

Stanslo doesn't give them one. He tilts his head, curious, and then... he *smiles*, all warm and pleased, and Bas feels that *push* from Dolerma again and thinks *you have* got *to be fucking* kidding *me*, because no one—*no one*—here is what they seem, Bas can't believe one fucking thing anyone has told him, and it's already too late to move when Stanslo lifts his gun and shoots Serenat in the chest.

"Dear, dear sweetpea," he says sadly as Serenat drops, "you're just too much like your da."

It's the only sound Kimolijah has made so far, the tiny cry that's not quite dismay—that's not anything Bas can interpret—when Serenat falls next to him, clutching her chest, rusty blood like dark honey welling over long, bony fingers, and trying to breathe through wet little rattles. And Dolerma just... walks away.

"Now, your mam," Stanslo goes on, like he's reminiscing, a horrible little smile tucked up at his mouth, "your mam, yes, there's a woman." He shakes his head and *tsks*. "I should've liked to have kept her a little longer."

It's like it reminds him somehow, thinking of someone else he's used and ruined, like *being* used and ruined at his own command is some kind of personal betrayal, as if he's found some way in his own head to blame his long-ago mate for being traded to Geda like a prized breeder, and he looks down at Kimolijah. The rage is creeping in again, setting Stanslo's teeth tight and blushing color up his neck and over his face.

"Did you really think Reacher, of all people, would be able to find a way to cure all of what you insist on believing are your woes? Or were you just curious about what was behind his placket?"

It's the first reaction Stanslo gets out of Kimolijah since Stanslo threw him at Reacher's feet like a gauntlet. It's a snort, low and derisive, and Kimolijah twitches a tiny little smirk. He mutters something Bas doesn't hear and shakes his head.

Stanslo looks down at him with narrowed eyes. "I'm sorry, I didn't catch that. Have you something to contribute, Kimo?"

Kimolijah looks down at the bracelet on his arm, runs the tip of one finger over the very top loop of the coil where Bas can just see the faintest rise of a white welt creeping out from beneath it.

Bas blinks, frowns. Because it shouldn't be there.

"I *said*," Kimolijah says, slowly and clearly this time, "maybe I was curious about what a *real man* looks like. You know—*behind his placket.*"

It's vicious and cutting. Mostly because it's said with a knowing sneer. Also because, yes, Stanslo *would* be the sort to have a size fixation. And Kimolijah has said it right out loud, in front of half of Stanslo's Bridge.

Stanslo pauses, as if he's going to try to calmly ignore it, peers first at Lowen and then at Bas with a fleeting grin that's forced and ugly. He looks down at his gun, as if contemplating its color, then bares his teeth and gives Reacher's corpse another vicious kick with an animal snarl. Before Reacher's body has even stopped rocking from the force, Stanslo has wrenched Kimolijah up and around and knocked him back down again with a brutal rolled-knuckle blow to the jaw.

Kimolijah lands belly-down on his elbows, legs tangled with Serenat's, head hanging and hair obscuring his face. Bas doesn't realize he's taken an instinctive step forward until Lowen's large brown hand is clamped on his forearm, holding him back.

"Ungrateful little *whelp!*" Stanslo screams as he stands over Kimolijah, hands fisted and face red, and looking about half a second away from kicking at Kimolijah too. "I've given you *everything!*" He drags Kimolijah up by the rope around his throat, tightens, pulls, twists, then *shakes*. "Workshops stocked with tools and materials you never could have had for yourself in your meager little shop that you miss so dearly. I could have left you to the whims of the Directorate and all those people who had no idea in the world what you're worth. And *then* where would you be? Back in your Poor Side little hovel, having to beg materials from across the Territories because the conceit of the Directorate says you can't have them? Fixing watches with your precious da and wasting all of your brilliance that I've done nothing but encourage and facilitate?

"I have given you a place to grow your ideas and implement

them, when the Directorate wanted to stifle it all. A home and a family and someone who cherishes you and everything you could be here, if you would just"—he shakes again—"stop"—and again—"*fighting me!*"

Kimolijah's hands come up, trying to loosen the rope that's got to be cutting off air now, but he's grinning at Stanslo, teeth bloody and eye swelling shut.

Stanslo pants, winded, but he doesn't loosen his grip, and his face pulls into something Bas has never seen on it before. Something genuine, this time. Grief, maybe.

"Have you any idea what I risk for you?" Stanslo says, low and somewhat winded, and his grip loosens just enough for Kimolijah to whoop in a strained breath. Stanslo clenches his teeth. "I would never give you up, no matter what deals I've made with Geda. You're too important, Kimo. To Stanslo's Bridge and to me. And yet, every time you leave here for the Bruise, I run the risk of never seeing you again."

And the worst part of that statement, Bas thinks, is that Stanslo is completely serious. He really does think that Kimolijah getting captured or killed at the Bruise is more of a risk to him than it is to Kimolijah.

Lowen doesn't look at Bas, keeps his eyes on Stanslo. There's no expression on his face, but his hand comes away from Bas's arm and flattens with his palm pointing down.

Wait. It's coming.

Stanslo finally lets go, backs up a few steps as Kimolijah goes down on one knee, sucking down air in noisy gasps.

"You don't tell me no, Kimo," Stanslo says quietly. "And I'd thought you learned your lesson on telling anyone else yes." He shakes his head, seemingly genuinely distraught, before he sighs heavily and turns a bleak look on Lowen. "Get Bas the whip."

Bas stares and tries to let that one slosh around in his head for a second before reacting. Because yes, he will wait and he will watch as a man beats another man and that other man lets him; he will wait and he will keep silent when he thinks perhaps there is something brewing, something he doesn't know, something that's been coming and planned for since way before he stepped into Stanslo's Bridge; he will stomp down on and throttle the instinct to protect and to rend because someone who knows what that plan is tells him to and because Kimolijah has asked Bas to trust him.

But he will absolutely not, no fucking way, *no*, take a whip to Kimolijah because Stanslo thinks he needs to prove his dick is bigger than everyone else's.

So he steps forward, opens his mouth to refuse, except Kimolijah says it for him. "No." So simple and yet so resolute and forceful that it stops everyone, everything, even Stanslo.

Kimolijah's still on the ground, still hanging his head like he can't lift it, but he lifts it now, sends a look to Stanslo that's hard and cold and so full of hate it's surprising Stanslo doesn't just shrivel to a heap of ash. "No," Kimolijah says again, jaw clenched, and he grins this time as he gets slowly to his feet. And then he holds up his arm, pointedly, grins wider, and says yet again, "*No.*"

It hits Bas before it does Stanslo, and Bas doesn't bother to hide his smirk as Stanslo's eyes narrow, then his head tilts and he looks at Kimolijah in glorious, exquisite confusion until Kimolijah wraps his hand around the bracelet, metal winking dully, and says a fourth time, "*No,*" as he rips it off and throws it at Stanslo's feet.

Stanslo's eyes widen, and he's *still not getting it*, until Kimolijah takes a step toward him, jerks his head down at Serenat sprawled in the dirt and says, "You killed her. Took a while, but she's dead now. About...." Kimolijah pauses, thinks about it. "Oh, let's see, it was when you were *trying to strangle me*, so two minutes ago or so, I'd say. At least, that's when the bug woke up." Tiny blue filaments flicker at the ends of his fingers and reflect bright in Stanslo's wide blue eyes.

And then it blooms, abrupt reluctant understanding all over Stanslo's face, and for probably the first time in three years, Stanslo looks at Kimolijah with something like fear and takes a step back. "Lowen," he says, wary, "send for Dolerma. Quick."

"Yeah, he's not gonna do that," Kimolijah says softly, face swollen, blood all over his chin and mouth, but he looks strong, stronger than Bas has ever seen him, shoulders back and spine straight and a look in his eyes Bas doesn't envy Stanslo. "Are you, Lowen?"

Kimolijah doesn't take his eyes off Stanslo, but Lowen shakes his head anyway and says, "Nope," laconic as ever, but with a pleased little smile Bas has never seen on him before.

Stanslo fumbles at his collar and pulls out the crystal, because *of course he does*, and he grips it in his fist and says, "Lowen. *Go get Dolerma.*"

There's a stutter, a weak wash of citrus that laps at Bas's senses, but it dissipates and flutters away before it settles.

"Sorry, boss," says Lowen, easy and maybe a little bit smug. "Serenat took over my contract right after you made Fox tear Travis to shreds. You remember, right? Said you didn't want Geda finding anything out you didn't want him to know, and seeing as how I hafta go to the Bruise *every fucking week*...." He pauses to rein himself in. It's the most words said with the most emotion Bas has ever seen from Lowen. With a shrug, Lowen turns to Bas. "How about you? You wanna go get Dolerma for the baron?"

Bas lifts his eyebrows and tries not to smirk *too* hard. "I really don't."

"Look what you've gone and done, Baron." Kimolijah takes

another step toward Stanslo, and Stanslo takes another one back. Kimolijah's still smiling, eyes still hard little coals. "You've gone and pissed off a gridTech who despises you more than... well." He shrugs. "Anything, really."

Bas takes another look around, at the deputies moving in, crowding in, and at the grubby people who've been cowed so long they're just waiting for someone to lend them some courage. Still outnumbered when it comes to weapons, but Bas watches the way Lowen sidles up next to Kimolijah, a hand on his arm, and looks from Quinnie to Merrin to Kimolijah.

A stray not-bat wings in from the direction of Tower Two and blunders headlong into the gridlight atop the gallows. Sparks spray out, and the light flares then sputters then flares again as the thing squawks and drops, and no one's eyes so much as flicker in its direction, all of them pinned on Stanslo. The gridlight hums and wavers for a second or two, casting flash-point shadows into macabre shapes across the square, before it catches the stream again and steadies.

"Bas," says Stanslo, and Bas has to marvel just a little, because he's never heard that confident voice shake before. "I need you to go and get Dolerma." He fists the crystal tighter, like his grip will make a difference. "Go, Bas. Right now."

Bas says, "Naw, Baron." He shrugs a little when Stanslo narrows his eyes, and Bas can't resist the little quirk that crooks his mouth, the insolence and the *finally* that probably leaks out all over him. "The Directorate tends to frown on this sort of thing, y'know." He waves his hand around, casual. "In fact, the Directorate tends to frown on pretty much everything about Stanslo's Bridge." He gives Stanslo a level stare. "Especially you."

Stanslo has no idea what to make of it, Bas can see it all over him. There's a stretched-out moment of staring, a little gasp here and there from the crowd, some shuffling.

"The Directorate," Stanslo says slowly, through his teeth, "has no authority here." He jerks his chin at Bas and says, "Merrin, shoot him."

Bas doesn't even look at Merrin, how he puts his hand on his gridgun, how he draws it around by its strap, ready, but doesn't point it at Bas.

"Funny thing, Baron," Bas says, adrenaline spiking, and he tamps it down, because he needs calm focus more than he needs fight-or-flight. "You fuck with Techs, you never really manage to outrun the Directorate." He hadn't skinned before, but he does now. He doesn't point it anywhere, but he draws the hammer, and the sound of barrels turning and clicking echoes through the silent square. "Oh, sorry, let me introduce myself properly." Bas tips his head and taps at the brim of his hat. "Bartholomew Eisen, Grade 3 Tracker with the Directorate of the Consolidated Territories." He grins. "I've come to shut you down."

There are so many gasps and mutters that move through the crowd now that they almost drown out the sounds of gridguns powering up, and Kimolijah muttering, "*Bartholomew*? Really?" Almost.

"Shut up, *'Lijah*," Bas mutters back, and shakes his head when Kimolijah snorts.

Bas very nearly grins, but he hears the distinctive shuffle of fabric against fabric, leather against ceramic, and he doesn't need to take his eyes off Stanslo to know that every single deputy is now pointing a gun at Bas from every single angle. So Bas shrugs—*fuck it*—and points his gun at Stanslo.

"You might wanna tell your guys," he says with a cavalier lift of his eyebrows, "that one muscle spasm and it's all over for you."

Stanslo's reeling now and trying not to show it. Bas wants to point at him and then give Kimolijah a significant look, and maybe even Quinnie—*See? I told you he didn't know*—but the satisfaction isn't worth the risk of taking his eyes off Stanslo or lowering his gun.

Stanslo stares, still gripping the crystal. "Bas," he says, careful and clipped. "Drop that gun, please."

The citrusy little pulse *thuds* at Bas, wings him good, before it slides away and caroms... wherever intangible things go when they miss their target. Stanslo nods and makes a little "hurry up" gesture, prodding.

Still a little too confident; still a little too arrogant. Bas really wants to see this guy squirm. So he enjoys the hell out of saying, "Naw, I'd rather watch your 'dear heart' show you why you should never have fucked with him and his. Or, you know"—Bas waves his hand around, taking in the whole of Stanslo's Bridge, the Bruise, and everything else Stanslo has corrupted with his mere touch—"anything." He figures all the cards are finally on the table, so he says, "The Directorate wants you stopped, Baron. Unfortunately, they play by the rules. They don't just kill people who need killing, not without all the bother of a trial and all that. But you know that, yeah? 'S why you've set up shop here at the ass-end of the world where you think they can't reach you, and taken things—people—that don't belong to you. 'S why you're trying so hard to find a way to worm your way back in.

"But, see, the thing is, out here, Baron? At the ass-end of the world? I *am* the Directorate. And I think I've lost my patience for rules."

It stymies Stanslo, makes him gape, but he recovers quickly. His gun is still in his hand, and it goes from pointing at Bas to pointing at Kimolijah.

"You'll die," Stanslo tells Kimolijah. "Think, Kimo, dear. Use that brilliant mind of yours. Let me send for Dolerma before that"—he nods at Kimolijah's arm and the hints of white welts that are uncoiling and seeping up from his wrist—"gets too adventurous." He's almost crooning, like he's actually trying to convince Kimolijah it's in his best interests. "You'll die."

Kimolijah shrugs. "Yeah, I know."

"And then where will your da be?"

Sparks witter out from Kimolijah's fingers and shoot in tiny crackling strands to land first between Stanslo's eyes, then on the hand that holds the gun. It goes off, a single shot that wings out and up and takes a chunk out of the gibbet's thick post, too close to Kimolijah's head, before it ricochets away with a whining twang. Kimolijah doesn't even duck, but it wakes up all the deputies.

"Kill him," Stanslo croaks.

Gridstream splashes in from every angle, converging on Kimolijah at the center like the spokes of a wheel. Bas ducks down and sideways, and he hears Quinnie shout, harried and dismayed. Kimolijah just holds out his arms, eyes shut, and bright blue gridstream leaps out of true in midair to converge into two thick ropes that slam into Kimolijah's palms. He sucks it up, breathing in the sizzle and pop of it like it's air and he hasn't had a good gulp of it in a very long time. It stops everyone again, alarm and confusion, and all eyes turn to Kimolijah, shocked, and then, slowly, to Stanslo.

The gazes from the crowd are more speculative now, narrowing at Stanslo before sliding over Kimolijah with careful calculation. Bas gets a few looks, not entirely trusting, but he's had no illusions about that anyway. A good deal of these people were criminals once, and none of them are Tech. They have no more love for the Directorate than Quinnie does. If this comes off right, it'll be one of their own they follow, not Bas.

Stanslo shakes his head, dazed, and touches at his forehead, small branch-shaped burns flaring out from the thumbprint-sized point of impact. He cocks his gun again, housing turning to a loaded barrel, and he says, "You'll *die*, Kimo," through his teeth, and he shakes out his hand, but he doesn't let go of the gun. "You'll die, and so will your da."

Kimolijah zaps him again, another one between the eyes, and then one at his right knee. Stanslo's leg goes out from under him, gun going off again, hitting Fox's bloated corpse in the chest this time, and Kimolijah shakes his head and looks at Bas and then Lowen.

"It's like he just *doesn't get* that he really shouldn't talk about my da."

Stanslo's still gripping his crystal, and he's getting smarter now, because whatever push he's giving his men, he's not doing it verbally. A tiny advantage, sure, but any advantage is going to matter, out in the open as all this is. He doesn't seem to bother with anyone who's not a deputy, though, because they all just stand there, watching, like they want to make a move and can't.

Kimolijah sees it, though, he knows, and he flips Bas a look under the bright gridlight of the gallows before he lurches in a straight line at Stanslo. They go down, rolling in the dust, rocking into Fox's corpse, until they hitch up by Travis's husk, and it's fitting, somehow, that however this battle turns out, it's taking place right where this particular rebellion really started. Stanslo's gun goes off again, harmless into the air, and Bas thinks *Okay, that's all four shots*, and he thinks Kimolijah might actually kill him if he interferes, so he just watches out the corner of his eye while he tries to keep track of everything else.

Bas takes out one deputy who's trying to use the man in front of him as cover while he tries to cross the square—maybe find a more strategic position, maybe run away; Bas doesn't care. He bullseyes the guy and silently compliments Quinnie on her work on the sights.

There's a surge, deputies pulling in their flanks and heading for where Kimolijah's managing to hold his own against a much larger Stanslo, but everyone sees exactly where it's going, and it seems no one needs Lowen to shout out *"Now!"* because they're already moving.

And everything goes downright *primitive*.

There's so much pent-up *anger* here, so much helplessness spilled out and excoriated in a violent rush of retribution, and the means are nearly savage. Rocks and sharp sticks and bare hands. It doesn't seem significant that one side is better armed and ostensibly trained; it is significant, though, that not everyone on that side is or ever has been wholly Stanslo's. A minority of the deputies have little heart for what they're doing, perhaps here and living this life just as much against their will as anyone else. And it matters.

Stanslo can't keep track of everything, can't possibly be directing all the action with his crystal, not with him tangled with Kimolijah and getting little zaps of gridstream in vulnerable places every time Kimolijah finds himself in a position he doesn't like. And it shows, this lack of control. It shows in the rocks dragged up out of the hardpan and hurled at the deputies' heads; it shows in the one or two people hanging off a deputy's back and choking or, in the case of one determined-looking woman, trying to twist until something breaks; it shows in the complete lack of cohesive offense from the deputies and then a similar lack of rational defense when they don't instantly gain the upper hand like they're used to.

Lowen's shouting orders and directing bodies—"You! Get that gun and cover these guys!" and "Don't kill Merrin, we need him!" and "Where the hell is Quinnie with those guns?"—and Bas just tries like hell to stay out of the spray of gridstream every time someone fires a gridgun.

It all slips out of any kind of even loose control far too quickly, guns going off and gridstream flying and people dropping on both sides, and the little town of Stanslo's Bridge loses a third of its population in less than ten seconds.

Until Kimolijah screams, something feral and hoarse and horrible, and he jerks in a way that makes Bas's throat clog up. Kimolijah's got Stanslo down on his back, sitting astride Stanslo's chest like he'd done with Fox a hundred years ago, and Stanslo looks bug-eyed and purple, like Kimolijah almost almost *almost* managed to squeeze the life out of him with nothing more than his hands and his rage. But now Kimolijah's face is wrenched with pain and he's listing to the side and there's a bright blossom of blood soaking his shirt just below his ribs.

Bas yells, "*Kimo!*" and starts shooting anything that's holding a gun and is between him and the center of the square, trying to make his way the too-far distance Kimolijah and Stanslo have managed to roll. He only makes it two steps before Kimolijah snarls and rears up with wild gridstream flowing up from what looks like the very core of him. Kimolijah pauses for a second, just to look, it seems, and there's a brief, too-brief, fraction of a moment where everything is silent and Bas can hear Stanslo say, quite clearly, "Kimo, no," all desperate and pleading, asking, like he really thinks he's got the right to ask anything of Kimolijah. And then Kimolijah's whole body swings and his arms pendulum down and his hands slap flat to Stanslo's chest.

Violent gridstream lights up the square like daylight, Stanslo and Kimolijah both engulfed in the shocking blue glow, both of their faces pulled into rictus for very different reasons.

Almost everyone stops, some gasping and clutching their heads like Merrin and Cavett had done, some merely frowning, some punching out short little screams in breathless bursts. No one goes down, though. No one looks away from the spectacle in the middle of the square.

It's haunting, almost, the silence that accompanies this horrible death. That's the thing with gridstream—it doesn't explode or implode or get you with a bang and a shout. It just *hums*, like it's happy, like you've *made* it happy by giving it someplace to unfurl and storm and *be*, as wild as it's meant. Stanslo doesn't get to scream his rage that he's living his last seconds, he doesn't get to shield his eyes so he doesn't have to look his death in the eye, he doesn't get a last moment of understanding or redemption. He just lies there and takes it, paralyzed but for the spasms the stream forces through him, silent but for the sizzle of moisture forced out through his pores.

Bas stands there and watches Stanslo die, watches Kimolijah kill him with the Tech Stanslo took for himself, and he thinks moments like this, they're awful and they're sick-making and they're indelible, they never go away. And yet they're never quite enough.

Things are starting to move again, most people still staring but some backing away or, in some cases, just running. Quinnie has arrived with several others, carrying armloads of guns from the armory shed, but it seems she's too late for them to make a difference. She pauses, clearly shaken, and just stands there with the rest of them and stares.

Everyone who's left is watching the great glob of gridstream, shielding their eyes and squinting around their hands, keeping well back from the wild sparks that fly out from the center of it, the occasional branch that breaks off and seeks the ground. It's dangerous standing even this far away, the risk of collateral damage not much reduced by distance when it comes to gridstream, and Bas has no idea if Kimolijah is in any frame of mind to contain it. Still, anyone who's left stays, and all eyes are on the dim shape of Kimolijah inside the brilliance of Baron Petra Stanslo's ignoble death.

"Kimo!" Quinnie calls, face twisted in pity now, and she moves to step forward, but Lowen holds her back.

Someone cries out, a thin wail of devastation, and it feels like it should echo, swell, suck away air. It doesn't. It gets tangled up in the snapping buzz of gridstream and swallowed whole.

It brings Bas out of his hypnotic daze, the brief prison of the pulse and flux and flow that caught him unaware, the horrible beauty of it that snagged him up and stilled him. He shakes it off and starts across the square, stepping right up to the undefined perimeter where it seems Kimolijah's very spirit has expanded in its sudden freedom, pushed out from the containment of his body in flittering bolts and capricious ropes.

He's going to burn out. He's going to overload.

"Kimo," says Bas, not a shout but loud enough to be heard over the hum and intermittent pop. Stanslo's shirt is on fire now, tiny flames licking up around Kimolijah's fingers, and Kimolijah doesn't seem to notice, doesn't seem to care that he's not completely invulnerable to the death and destruction he's dealing out. "Kimo, he's dead."

Kimolijah hears, Bas knows he does, because he twitches; Bas can just barely see it through the too-bright stream. Kimolijah's jaw sets tighter, teeth bared and shining blue, and Bas can't be sure, he can't see through the stream clearly enough, but he thinks Kimolijah's trousers are starting to smoke.

"*Kimolijah!*" Bas snaps, harsh. "He's not getting any deader. Quit being such a dramatic princess and knock it off!"

Surprisingly, Kimolijah does. Gasping. Shaking all over. Hands still pressed to Stanslo's chest. Eyes still locked to Stanslo's now desiccated, halfway melted, and smoldering corpse. If his gridstream hadn't been sucking up every drop of moisture, Bas thinks Kimolijah would be crying.

Kimolijah's not, though; he just sits there and sucks in air for a while and ignores it when Bas cautiously steps in, then crouches down to pat out the tiny smoky flames trying like hell to take hold of Stanslo's shirt in a halo around Kimolijah's hands. Bas doesn't look at Stanslo's face. What's left of it. He reaches out, cautious, and gently angles the rope from around Kimolijah's neck, slips it over his head and off.

Kimolijah breathes, harsh, like it hurts, and rolls out a thick, angry sob.

"You killed him."

It's weak and shaky, and it takes a second for the words to process and for Bas to realize they hadn't come from Kimolijah. Bas turns, almost rolling his eyes—because seriously, *now what?*—and sees Nadal standing on the other side of Travis, a look of shock and feral anger on his face and Stanslo's pretty little four-barrel in both hands. He's pointing it at Kimolijah.

It's been too easy to assume that, once Stanslo was dead, everything would be simple. It's been too easy to forget that some of these people are here because they want to be.

Bas stands, and he sees several others shifting, like they might be thinking about getting in Nadal's way, but none of them do. Quinnie moves, though, and so does Lowen, splitting up and moving around the edge of the crowd, likely aiming to flank Nadal, but they're too slow and too far. Bas, on the other hand, doesn't move.

"You...." Nadal sobs, choked, and he shakes his head, eyes wide and hands trembling. "You...." Too many words are trying to come out, his mouth moving with them but no voice behind them, until: "I hate you." A hiss, poisonous, from between clenched teeth. "*I hate you!*"

Kimolijah doesn't flinch when Nadal pulls the trigger. Maybe he'd been counting shots before too, maybe he knew the gun was empty, or maybe he didn't and just couldn't make himself care. It doesn't matter, in the end. Nadal looks at the gun like it's personally betrayed him before he throws it aside with a wild scream and runs at Kimolijah.

It's almost funny, the way it all happens. Not grand and dramatic enough for an illobook, though it starts out that way. Nadal keeps shrieking as he comes, and Kimolijah's palm lights up with a few stuttering little threads of gridstream, waiting, and Quinnie and Lowen both spring forward, and Bas braces himself—

And then Edlyn is somehow right there, right between Bas and Kimolijah and the screeching projectile that is Nadal, and she's like a solid little rampart, standing stout and grim-faced as Nadal first bounces off her, then dashes himself against her. He's no more effective than a wave against a rocky cliffside.

"He killed him!" A shout that crowns to a scream, wretched. "*He killed him!*" He's weeping, open miserable sobs and great fat tears rolling unchecked down brown cheeks.

Edlyn looks at Stanslo's corpse, face both sour, like she thinks he got what he deserved, and sickened, like maybe he did but she doesn't want to have to look at it.

Hannah joins her, looking around warily, like she doesn't

know what to think, but she doesn't look terribly broken up about Stanslo either. She moves in to help Edlyn and says, "He doesn't know anything else." She's looking at Kimolijah, then at Bas. "Oleg found him in a children's house and thought Himself might...." She breaks off, teeth clenched. "He's only fifteen. He was still a baby when Stanslo made him a whore."

"I wasn't!" Nadal babbles, a hysterical bawl. "I'm not! He... oh *God*, I...." He grabs hold of Edlyn's apron, frantic. "*He loved me!* And *he*"—he flings his arm out at Kimolijah and points—"*killed him!*"

"All right," Edlyn soothes, hanging onto Nadal by his collar like an unruly puppy. "There now," and she looks at Kimolijah with an unhappy grimace and says, "I hope you have a better plan than this."

There's a pause, weighted, and Bas uses it to look around and gauge the people who've stayed. Some of them, he thinks, are only here to watch, to see what happens next, not sure what to do or who to follow, but waiting to find out—Bas knows them by the loose grips on guns if they have them, the confused frowns if they don't. Some of them, he thinks, are watching because they've been waiting too long for this, have been wanting it, dying for it, maybe had their own little rebellious scenarios in their heads and hadn't known anyone else did—Bas knows them by the hopeful calculation in their eyes.

All of the ones who are displeased by the events as they've unfolded have pulled back. Perhaps to hide. Perhaps to regroup. Perhaps to enact a plan of their own.

Whatever the case, Bas thinks, it's far from over and far from safe, sitting out here in the middle of the square, washed with gridlight and easy pickings for anyone with a shiny-new grudge.

"Oh God," says Hannah, looking at Kimolijah with rising alarm. "You're bleeding."

He is. A short, thin knife with a pearl handle and a bloody blade lying in the dirt by Stanslo's hand. A wide bloom of red low on Kimolijah's side and spreading. Kimolijah doesn't seem to care.

"Where's Dolerma?"

It's not exactly the first thing Bas had expected to come out of Kimolijah, after all of... this. Bas blinks and frowns as he looks around at the small crowd still staring.

He shakes his head. "I don't—"

"Quinnie," Kimolijah says, slow and calm, "the train."

Quinnie blinks, then hisses, eyes going wide. "Oh *shit*," she says and takes off toward the station.

❦

Dolerma's just sitting there when they get there, in the very same place Kimolijah was sitting the first time Bas saw him, and in much the same position, much the same temper. Well, the same except different—Kimolijah had been moping on the steps of the old train when Bas had first seen him; Dolerma's sitting on the steps of the new train. Angry and morose and halfway belligerent, Dolerma stares up at the barrel of the gridgun and then, of all people, Cavett beyond it. Merrin's there too, looking somewhat bemused, gun up and at the ready, but he looks like he doesn't quite know if he should be pointing it at anyone.

"Stopped 'im a'fore he did too much," Merrin says as he shrugs and waves toward Dolerma.

"I didn't know what to...." Dolerma trails off and then he laughs, rueful and resigned, and he shakes his head and holds up—

"Motherfucking *hell*," Kimolijah hisses as he takes in the cables and components bleeding from between Dolerma's fingers.

Bas looks at the mess, looks at the rest of the engine, looks at Kimolijah's face, and shuts his eyes. *Fuck.*

"The surge switch," Kimolijah says, wrecked. "Oh *God.*" He looks around at the bent metal, the cut cables, the busted glass of the vacuum tubes. "I can't fix this." He shakes his head, shocked and near-desolate, then he surges in and snatches everything out of Dolerma's hands with a snarl. "Do you have any *idea* what you've—"

"I have saved my people," Dolerma cuts in, but it doesn't sound anywhere near as triumphant as that statement should. He takes in Bas with a wry twist to his bloodless mouth, then he takes in everyone else. Finally, he looks up at Kimolijah. "You think I don't know. You would take away the *one thing* that would save us."

"No," says Kimolijah, calm, though he shuts his eyes, like he's weary and so, so disheartened. "I would take back the one thing that's *mine.*" His teeth are set when he opens his eyes, and his gaze is abruptly full of fire as he leans in, right up close and in Dolerma's face. "You think *I* don't know. You try so hard to be as manipulative as Geda, as Stanslo, but you *suck* at it, Dolerma, and it cost you. Blame me all you like for Travis, but it wasn't me who put him up to sending that message." His mouth twists, cruel, and he lowers his voice. "It wasn't me who put *that* 'bug' in his ear, was it?"

Dolerma doesn't react, but Bas sucks in a low breath and rubs at his face. Because of course.

"You tagged Travis?" Lowen asks, tense all of a sudden, and narrow-eyed.

Dolerma tightens his mouth and looks away.

"Of course he did," Kimolijah answers for him, wincing a little as he shifts. The blood on his shirt is spreading. "It's *the way of things* with his people." The quote is full of spite and almost verbatim what Dolerma had said to Bas. Kimolijah's hands clench around the mess Dolerma has made of the new train's guts. "Travis was just a little too nice to the new kid, yeah? And there was Stanslo, all suspicion and jealousy, and it's contagious, I get it. Maybe Travis really was getting a little too close, a little too sympathetic. You get worried. But you can't just go and kill the pet sparker, can you? Da wouldn't approve. Stanslo would hang you. And it doesn't really matter in the end, yeah? All you really have to do is get rid of the thing you're afraid of, because the killing part"—Kimolijah raises his arm, the welts noticeable now, white whips spiraling around his wrist and heading up his arm—"the killing part would take care of itself."

Kimolijah throws the now-junk in his hands to the ground. He barely glances at Bas, his gaze finding and fixing on Quinnie.

"Geda will already know what's happened here." He jerks his chin at Dolerma. "I'm going to have to make the trade. We have no choice."

Quinnie shakes her head, eyes bright, expression devastated. "Kimo, no." She takes a step in. "We can go in hot. We've got the guns, we've got the train, we've got—"

"You've got *shit*!" Bas cuts in, abruptly annoyed with Quinnie and her mulish insistence. "Your horrible plan is ruined." Bas waves toward Dolerma. "He's made sure of it. Geda *knows*, Quinnie. He'll have a whole fucking *army* waiting for you. The only thing—the *only* thing—you have left that he still wants is a train"—he slaps the bulkhead—"and the guns, and...." He trails off, gives Kimolijah a significant look.

No one needs Bas to say it.

Kimolijah nods, grim, before he turns to Dolerma, teeth bared, vicious. "You'd better hope he hasn't killed his hostages yet," he says, low and fierce. "Because it's the only thing that *might* save you and your fucked-up world."

Still seething, he turns and looks at Bas, eyes intent, and the anger is real, but there's something else underneath it, something not quite as desperate as it should be.

"I need about ten minutes," Kimolijah says as he waves at the mess spilling out of the engine hatch. "I can get it going, but the rest.... *Fuck*!" He kicks something across the floor, nearly savage, before he looks at Quinnie. "Get the guns loaded up." Then at Lowen and Merrin. "Anyone you can trust, we need them for backup." At Cavett. "I need Dolerma contained, but don't hurt him. We might need him for leverage." And then, finally, at Bas. "You should stay. If this goes as wrong as I think it will, you need to get back to the real world, get the Directorate out here, get someone to—"

"It's like you don't even know me," Bas cuts in. He looks around at Quinnie and Lowen and Cavett, and he shakes his head. "You heard the man—move."

"My God, the way you squealed, I thought he'd torn a rib out. You scared the shit out of me."

"I did not *squeal*. And shut up, it hurt."

"Feh. It hardly even needs stitches. It's not as bad as it looks, and there's not actually that much blood."

"It's more blood than I'm comfortable parting with!"

"Like that's the worst you've...."

Bas realizes what he's saying and doesn't finish. He grimaces and lets Kimolijah jerk the tail of the shirt out of his hand. Kimolijah's glaring at him, has been glaring at him, waiting for everyone to file out so he can say... something. Bas doesn't feel like making it easy on him, because he mostly doesn't want to hear it. He doesn't look up.

"Why?" Kimolijah asks, angry, mouth pressed and fists tight, like he's *this close* to decking Bas.

They're alone with the train for the moment, everyone attending to their various jobs and priming themselves for what they think will be a very dangerous run, but still just a run from which they might come back if the trade goes in their favor.

Bas doesn't pretend to not know what Kimolijah's really asking. He lifts an eyebrow. "Because like it or not, Kimolijah, and no matter what you might try to tell yourself, no one's getting out of here without you. So I might as well come along for the ride. Oh, and your plan sucks."

"It'll work."

"Can Bella read you now that Serenat's Tech isn't interfering?"

"...I don't know."

"Then you have no idea if it'll work." Bas shrugs. "But let's just assume for a moment that Bella won't be a factor. So you engineer a standoff, offer yourself and the old train and all the guns Geda could want in exchange for your da and anyone else who's still alive over there, and then, once it's all over, everyone who survives can catch a ride home in your new beast." Bas pats at the train's hull. "And Geda will take it, won't he?"

"Yeah." It's firm, confident. "Yeah, he will."

"Yeah." Bas nods, mouth tight. "Won't suspect a thing, will he? It's not perfect, but it can still work, because holy shit, Kimo, you sure can think on your feet, yeah? Except so can I. And I know what you've got in mind." Bas pauses and has no qualms about looming over Kimolijah, hands fisted. "Let Dolerma think he's fucked up your grand plan, let everyone else think the same thing, even Quinnie. Let her think you're a coward and break her heart, just so that anything Geda picks up from Dolerma, anything Bella picks up from anyone else, they'll all think you're just giving up altogether on shutting down the Bruise—that you're giving up *period*.

"But you're a genius, yeah? Got it all worked out. Got a backup plan, and backups for your backups. And no one will have any idea what you're up to until the stream flares, because if you can't use your new gridbomb disguised as a train, you'll just make yourself into one, yeah? Reverse the stream, turn the whole train into one big magnet, and force an overload, except you don't know if it'll actually work, which is why you haven't already—"

"It was *always* going to be *this!*" Kimolijah snaps, defiant for all the wrong reasons. "New train, old train, *three fucking years* working on this design, it doesn't matter, because there was *never* going to be a different ending. It needs a boom, okay? It needs a surge. A small bang, just enough power to trigger the pulse. Where else is that gonna come from?"

"*Anywhere,*" Bas grinds out. "It doesn't need a stream surge, it needs *any* surge, any boom. Hell, you could wire the thing up to a stick of dynamite and it'd do the job."

"Yeah? And who's gonna set that off, genius?" Kimolijah shakes his head and looks away. "I didn't build a time-delay into the design because this... there was never anyone who...." He huffs out an angry breath. "I *am* the backup. Get it? This was always the plan, one way or another. Different circumstances, different details, yes, but *this—*"

"If you're so set on doing it," Bas cuts in, ostensibly mild, "shouldn't you at least be able to say it first?"

Kimolijah rears back, abruptly wordless. He looks away, looks down. "I have to set it off," he says, shaky, though he's obviously trying to make it calm. "There's no one else who can." He stops and looks up at Bas, eyes sad, maybe, but still determined. "You got a better idea?"

Bas does, actually. But he doesn't say. He can't. Not to anyone. Not even Kimolijah. Because if Bella picks it up, it'll all go to shit, and as far as Bas knows, he's the only one Bella can't read.

"Yeah," says Kimolijah as Bas just glares at him, "that's what I thought."

It's hard, but Bas keeps his mouth shut, just shakes his head and sighs. "Get that wound wrapped," he tells Kimolijah before he turns and leaves the station and heads to the Palace. Because the plan still sucks. Geda's not going to let any of them walk away—he can't, not if he wants to keep what he was clearly aiming for through Stanslo. Kimolijah obviously—*stubbornly, naively, too-hopefully*—thinks he's going to be the only sacrifice here, but he's dead wrong. So's Quinnie, so's everyone.

And Bas won't have it. Because brilliant, promising Kimolijah Adani has backups for his backups, pulls miraculous solutions out of claptrap theories, but spends so much time inside his own head, he'd miss a loaf of bread in a market full of bake shops.

So, then.

Kimolijah's gridbomb disguised as a train needs a smaller bomb to set it off. Bas knows exactly where to get one.

23.

It turns out pretty much anyone can drive the new train.

Well. *Drive.*

Kimolijah goes over basic operation with Quinnie pretty quickly, but he doesn't trust her to actually run it independently. Not yet.

"You can play with the power," Kimolijah tells Quinnie, "push us along some, but let me handle most of the braking. You don't have a feel for the hydraulics yet. And *watch* for when I start powering back, yeah? Lay off the throttle and let me brake. I don't want to get pushed headfirst into the Bruise before we even make the trade."

He pauses, tight-lipped, before going on, "You push out of there the first chance you get. You don't wait for anything, got it? No long good-byes, no nothing. You get a chance to get everyone aboard and get the hell out, you take it."

Because they have to be away and far out of range before Kimolijah reverses the stream, because the pulse Kimolijah's planning will take out anything that runs on gridTech for miles. Including Kimolijah.

Quinnie doesn't ask any questions. Bas thinks it's because she knows and is trying not to so no one can pick it out of her mind when the time comes. Smart, but he still hates her a little bit for it.

Bas pays close attention to Kimolijah's explanations of the switches and levers and toggles and dials Quinnie's going to need. And then he takes Quinnie aside, quiet, and tells her, "Why don't you take him and see to that wound before we go. It's not much to worry about, but we don't want it to *turn into* something to worry about, yeah?" He sees Quinnie shoot a worried look back at the train and says, "I'll keep an eye on it 'til you get back."

It's that easy. Quinnie goes and Bas hurries and hopes he's got the wiring right. He does. He knows he does.

God, he hopes he does.

The rest of what Dolerma did is enough of a mess that Quinnie seems to see nothing unusual when she gets back. Since most of what Kimolijah has done to this train for the past several days has been cobbled together out of whatever he had on hand, it's not all that surprising. Bas isn't positive, but he thinks he even sees a wing from that little dragon serving as a stream relay.

He has a talk with Cavett before he heads back toward the cab and Kimolijah. Bas chooses Cavett because they haven't had much interaction, Cavett knows very little about Bas, and he seems the sort who doesn't have much of an investment in how all this works out and who lives through it, just so long as he does. Bas lets him know he won't if he doesn't do what Bas tells him. He's pretty sure Cavett believes him.

And then they're on their way. The new train pulls out of Stanslo's Bridge on its maiden excursion hooked like a caboose to the back of the old train, hauled along like a derelict, its slick, shiny hull lit up blue from the gridstream wittering all over the fencing of the old train.

The not-bats are busy diving at the now-unmanned towers, so Bas doesn't ride up top behind the cannon, not yet. He's made himself a bit of a squatter, an unmovable object camping out in the cab of the old train with Kimolijah, whether Kimolijah likes it or not. Bas doesn't care. Maybe he means nothing to Kimolijah; maybe Kimolijah slept with him only because Bas was a better choice than actually seducing Reacher to get the result he wanted.

And maybe that wasn't it at all.

"Kimo...." Bas doesn't finish. It shouldn't be important right now.

Whether Kimolijah is just that intuitive or Bas is just that transparent, Kimolijah bites his lip and dips his head. He adjusts a dial and flips a toggle. "I'm sorry." It's soft and subdued.

It's not an answer. Then again, Bas isn't sure he wanted one in the first place.

They run into mild resistance at the very edge of town, right where the fences run and Stanslo's definition of civilization ends and wilderness begins. It's small, really, an amateur's idea of a train robbery; Kimolijah just snorts and shakes his head as he powers up to push through it, and Quinnie gives an extra boost from behind. Bas spares a moment for regret that he's not up top and keeping any comers off, but it doesn't matter, because it's more like some half-assed bravado than actual intent.

Four men stand on the tracks, Bas can see them up ahead through the windscreen, backs straight and guns gripped in both hands, bold. Thing is, Bas can also see it quite clearly when the gridstream that runs through the tracks as the train nears gives them all a bit of a jolt. They give up the tracks quickly after that, and Bas shuts the cab's door when they split their meager numbers to both sides. They shoot their guns as the train passes between them, but it's Kimolijah's train, it pretty much lives inside live gridstream, so the attempt is laughable.

"They'll be waiting for us on the way back," Bas says, calm, as he slides the door open again and peers around the edge, just to make sure, as they speed away from the tiny ambush.

Kimolijah shrugs and throttles up. "Yeah. Sure."

It's muted. Bas ignores it. Because, seriously—he won't have it.

Kimolijah's wrapped and tucked and strapped down, as usual, gloves covering his hands and sleeves battened down over his arms. But Bas knows what's under there. He doesn't know how far it's gotten, but he knows it's moving faster and farther than it has before, because there's nothing there to hold it back now.

Bas outlines with the tip of his finger the little clay bottle in his pocket. And he hopes.

The trip to the way station is quick and quiet. Bas doesn't push Kimolijah, and Kimolijah, it seems, much prefers to spend the time inside his own head. He alternates between messing with all his switches and dials and toggles and staring steadily out the windscreen, jaw clenched tight, every now and then looking, as if by reflex, at the lever/perch where Jessa isn't and frowning, tight-lipped and unhappy.

"A present to Kimo," Lowen had told Bas, low-voiced and sympathetic, when they'd been checking the couplings and Bas had watched Kimolijah watching the sky with a look of dull comprehension and acute disappointment. "She got winged. Target practice. He fixed her up and Serenat synched her. Thought it'd make him happy." Lowen had shrugged. "It didn't. Just one more prisoner, he said. But he does love that bird."

No one's seen her since Serenat went down. She's not synched anymore.

It's not helping Kimolijah's equilibrium. He's already looking strained, like he did that first time in the station, brown skin losing its burnished luster, sweat beading at his lip and brow. That other time had been after he'd been without the bracelet for about the full cycle of a night and a day; this is after mere hours.

It's moving too fast. It's moving far too damned fast.

Kimolijah pretends there's nothing wrong. Bas doesn't fight him on it. There's no point. Kimolijah lets Bas tug him close, though, squeeze him tight, breathe him in. Bas calls it not quite a win.

When they pull into the way station, it's all surprise and trepidation and "You're not due for days, is there something wrong?" and all the fears that seem to come with anything unexpected in this place. And then it turns to muted fervor.

Lowen and Merrin have Dolerma shut up in the passenger car, so he doesn't see any of it, doesn't see when Kimolijah has a quick conversation with Mari, and Mari subsequently hugs the shit out of him until he hisses and pulls away. Mari fusses at him for a moment, trying to get a look at his side and then scowling when Kimolijah doesn't let her. She shakes her head at him, displeased, and then smacks him on the ear before enforcing another hug. When she finally lets him go, she struts off to start rounding up all the dirty, scruffy folk and shepherding them into the second boxcar. The one with the guns. She's grinning the whole time by then, feral.

Things are better here than they were last time, the people a little less stooped and broken-looking, and the small plants Reacher hadn't managed to stomp and ruin have grown into stalks that look like they might one day be crops. The ground isn't as parched and the people aren't as skeletal. Mari has been busy. And it's better.

But.

These people are still tired, sick, hopeless, living for who knows how long in horrible conditions and watching their numbers steadily dwindle.

Kimolijah tells them: *You don't have to.*

And he tells them: *I don't know if it'll work.*

And he tells them: *If you can't or don't want to, you should stay. Maybe the train will be back to pick you up... after. Think about it. We pull out in ten minutes.*

No one chooses to stay.

Kimolijah can't seem to stop rubbing at his arm once he gets back into the cab. Bas watches him, and Kimolijah knows it. He ignores it, though. He's sweating more, and his skin is going ashy.

Once Mari's got everyone in and organized to her satisfaction, she barges into the cab and boots Bas up to his gun. She's firm about it, but her eyes are soft on Kimolijah almost the whole time she's bitching at Bas to "Go on, then, you're only in the way here. Get the fuck up where you belong."

"You should stay," Bas tells her, trying not to put any kind of commanding inflection into it, just a statement of simple fact. "We're already handing him one Tech."

Mari looks at Kimolijah and Kimolijah looks back, calm and focused. He looks like he wants to agree with Bas, but he knows Mari a lot better than Bas does, and whatever they say without saying seems to decide him. Kimolijah shrugs, then nods, and Mari turns to Bas, shoulders back.

"I'm going. Get out."

She's not the shrew she pretended to be. She doesn't hate Kimolijah like she loudly professed. Bas imagines Kimolijah's got to be closer to Mari than he is to even Quinnie, considering the trust they had to have in each other to pull off what they apparently pulled off for three years.

Bas and Kimolijah are not *Bas and Kimolijah*. It's entirely possible Bas has been nothing more to Kimolijah than a fly in the ointment, at first, and then a superfluous addition to a long-standing plan. Then again, it's entirely possible it's more.

And none of it matters.

These moments—the ones Bas knows Kimolijah is thinking of as his last, and maybe they will be, Bas doesn't know, and he's not Magic Man, he can't pretend he knows what the last panel in this arc will look like—these awful, beautiful, intimate moments... they're not Bas's to have.

So Bas goes.

⬯⬮⬯

Bas feels Jessa's absence keenly. The clean patterns she'd forced with her harrying and herding give way immediately to a constant barrage from all angles. Bas doesn't even have time to keep an eye out for spiders, because the flying nightmares won't even give him a chance to take a deep breath.

He has help this time, though. Merrin and Lowen cover what they can from the passenger car. Neither of them dare to venture farther than hanging out the doors on either side of the car, and Bas doesn't blame them, but they can only help so much with the limited angles. There's sporadic cover from the cab too, always followed by Mari whooping and laughing, so Bas figures it's her.

It helps. Bas trusts the three of them to take out anything coming at him low, and he concentrates on everything else. And "everything else" seems to know full well that he's missing something of which he hadn't properly realized the full value before, like they scent the weakness, because it feels personal this time. Like they're not going for the stream but for him.

Beaks get too close too many times, and the only reason his shoulders and back aren't all torn up is because his coat is thick and seasoned leather. Some of those talons are like razors. Something that looks like a feathered baby dragon comes in way too fast, dodging in right up close, harrying at Bas and diving at his head. It's smallish, relatively speaking, maybe the size of a large cat, but it's fucking persistent, and it's pissing him off. He can't see clearly to the other targets, and they're all getting in too close. He wonders if these things can actually think and strategize, but that thought is too disturbing, so he decides not to give it any space. He doesn't have time for it anyway. He keeps shooting, holding down the toggle and loosing a spray of stream in a wide, pulsing arc that takes out a good number of flying nightmares, but not the one that won't quit trying to dig out his eyes.

He ends up having to swing out an arm and actually punch it. His fist connects with the thick of the body, and the thing screeches and tumbles in the air. It looks like it's going to hit the roof of the cab, but it finds an updraft just in time, spreads its long wings and... flies right into the fencing.

The stream all around Bas stutters and dims and sparks, and Bas wrinkles his nose at the smell of burnt feathers but then almost laughs when what smells like fried chicken reaches him. It only lasts a second or two before the stumble in the stream allows the thing to drop from the fencing and everything's back to full power, so Bas just keeps shooting.

They haven't lost speed this time, Quinnie pushing everything along steadily with the new train from behind. Bas grins, vicariously pleased that Kimolijah's "toys" perform so superbly. It takes him a few distracted seconds of swinging and aiming and shooting to realize there'd been no cursing from below this time, no "keep those things out of the stream!" in Kimolijah's exasperated voice.

Bas stops grinning.

He keeps shooting, though. He's exhausted and sore and *just done* by the time they reach the stretch of desert where the things start tapering off and stop coming at him. By now there's a steady pull in his gut he's been feeling for a while but hasn't identified. He knows what it is now. He thinks about indulging it, just unclipping and sliding around and then swinging down, easy, like he'd done before.

He can't make himself do it.

He smells the strange energies of the Bruise long before he sees it. The acidic citrus fuzzes at the backs of his teeth, and the foreign energy swamps at him just before he makes out the roil and roll against the sky. It makes his gut clamp up, and he eyes the clip that attaches him to the lanyard, then stares at the edge of the cab's roof, still wanting and still not daring.

The adrenaline high is just starting to leave him when they near the protrusions of what he can only think of now as "the saddle" with its dark caves and too many crannies in which to hole up for ambush. They're still a good distance away and, just like last time, the sun is just starting to lip at the sky with dusky golds and smoky corals. It pulls the white from the mounds and cliffs and turns them muted dove against the cobalt of the forever-and-ever desert sands.

He hasn't managed to gather the stones to swing down and pester Kimolijah this time, and it's too late now; Bas hears the cab's door slide closed, and then he hears the crank of the lock clicking to. He refuses to think he just pissed away his last chance.

Quinnie powers up when they near the cliffs and caves—Bas can feel the difference: a push rather than a pull. It doesn't look necessary, though. The closer they get, the more clearly Bas can see the tall, thin figures standing plainly out in the open, just watching them come, no weapons in their hands and no obvious intent. Like it's not necessary.

Kimolijah was right. Geda already knows they're coming.

The station is nearly silent when they pull in. Bas predicted an army, but that's not exactly what greets them. Bas counts maybe thirty Willow Men out here, Geda at the fore, but there may be more in the shadows of the station. Or maybe what's on the other side of the Bruise is just as sparsely populated as what's on this side.

They don't speak, Geda and his people, only watch, and they don't move until Kimolijah eases the train almost dead center of the trainyard. Like a smooth-flowing river, they slide into an almost perfect horseshoe formation around the length of the train's engine. Bas should be trying to keep an eye on every one of them, watching for sudden moves, keeping his grip sure and his sights set.

He isn't.

He's waiting.

Ajamil Adani stands just behind Geda, face tight and gaze firmly on the cab in which Kimolijah waits. Bella Stanslo is beside him, and behind her stand Yanush and several others Bas assumes are the rest of the "collateral." What's left of it. Twelve people out of God knows how many that have been sent here.

Bas sucks in a long, deep breath and just keeps waiting.

Lowen steps out of the passenger car, back straight and expression blank. Dolerma follows, Merrin at his back with the barrel of his gridgun jammed against Dolerma's spine, prodding. Bas sees it when Merrin looks for and finds Yanush. Neither of them say anything, but their gazes lock, and Bas wonders idly if Bella Stanslo is playing the voyeur and eavesdropping on what they say silently to each other. He wonders if it moves her or if she's too far gone for that, too much Geda's creature, with her burr bug and her halfbreed children.

Cavett and three others step out, guns held ready as they peer around, gather in close, then nod and spread out. They split to position themselves along either side of the train, watching. Cavett stands in front of the doors of the boxcar, a hand on the lever.

Dolerma hostage between them, Lowen and Merrin walk forward. So does Geda. It's like an illobook conception of a shootout, silence and twenty paces and *ready, aim....*

They meet in the middle. And they stare.

Lowen says, "The contract is done." Hard and flat. "Stanslo is dead."

"And so is Serenat," Geda says, buzzy voice without outward inflection, but the sense of it in Bas's head is seething.

Bas peers over at Bella, curious. She doesn't look like a grieving mother to him. She looks blank. Bas wonders if that's Geda's doing, wonders if the thing winding around in her brain has convinced her she doesn't care much. Wonders if that's Geda's idea of compassion.

"She is." Lowen taps at the brim of his hat, respectful. "I'm sorry for your loss. But it was Stanslo's doing." He tips his head back toward Dolerma. "We came in good faith. We've got your trade. The contract is done."

Geda looks over Dolerma, his son, with a cool expression. He nods, slow, before he looks back at the throng of Willow Men behind him and jerks his chin. No words, no commands unfolding inside a foreign drone in Bas's head. Just a jerk of Geda's chin, and then a Willow Man breaks loose from the rest of them and herds Ajamil Adani forward.

Bas knows what this is, and apparently so do Lowen and Merrin. They both stiffen up as Ajamil comes closer, and Merrin pushes his gun into Dolerma's back with more force, his jaw tight and ticcing.

"I do not deem the losses to each side equitable," Geda says out loud, and in Bas's head the not-words howl vengeance.

Bas swings the cannon around, and when Geda grabs hold of Ajamil's arm, Bas tightens his finger on the toggle, *this close* to just taking Geda out now and shooting his way through the fallout.

The door of the cab slides open, rattling on its bearings and slamming on its hinges. Bas knows who it is, obviously, but he still wants to bang his head on the cannon when Kimolijah steps out.

"'Lijah," Ajamil says, short and sharp, like he's just as frustrated with his son as Bas is. "Get back...." He trails off, expression creasing down into concern. "Oh God."

Bas sees why when Kimolijah steps fully away from the train and Bas's angle is better.

"Steps" is perhaps too kind a word. Kimolijah's leaning on Mari, like his legs don't want to work properly, and when he stumbles and Mari has to catch at him to keep him from going down, Bas gets a glimpse of Kimolijah's profile. His brown skin is going gray, and the weird lighter spots on his snug shirt are, Bas realizes, dry spots; the rest is soaked with sweat. Kimolijah's shaking all over. He looks worse than Fox did when his leg was rotting off.

"Fucking burr bugs," Bas mutters, through his teeth, and tries not to imagine Kimolijah's arm crawling with white, reaching his shoulder by now, probably, or maybe even his neck. Bas doesn't take his hand off his gun to reach for the bottle of tonic in his pocket. But he really really wants to.

"We brought the guns," Kimolijah says, hoarse, like his throat's full of sandpaper. "You don't get the new train. I'll...." He breaks off and shakes his head, sharp, as if to clear it. "I'll build you another, just...." His knees give a little, Bas can see it from here, but Kimolijah doesn't go down. "You give everyone back to Lowen. You give my da back to Lowen. And I'll come with you." He turns a little and waves at the cab of the front engine. There's a tiny, wicked little smile on his face when he says, "I'll give you a ride home in it."

Because Kimolijah thinks he's clever. Bas wants to punch him.

Ajamil says, "*No!*" and he tries to rush forward, but Geda's minion holds him back. "'Lijah, *no*. I forbid it!"

Bas nearly rolls his eyes. Has this guy *met* Kimolijah?

Mari, Bas notes, is not watching what's going on right in front of her—she's watching the sky. Bas looks too, a quick glance, but enough to see small clouds moving faster than they should, pulling like spun cotton from the edge of the Bruise, darkening quick and steady. Bas pulls his gaze back, wondering, and hopes he's the only one.

"Yeah, none of that's happening," he says, his tone even and his voice steady.

He ignores it when Kimolijah turns sharply to glare at him, probably looking betrayed and not at all surprised, because Kimolijah's used to people fucking him over. Bas doesn't look back, though. He edges the cannon around a bit so it's pointed right at Geda.

"Here's how this is going to go," Bas says slowly. "You're going to let those hostages you've got back there come on over here and uncouple this old thing"—he jerks his chin—"and then you're going to let them unload the guns from the car back there"—and again—"and then you're going to wave good-bye while you drive Kimo's nice new train back through that... thing." He points at the Bruise. "And you're going to do it without firing a shot. Or." Bas smiles and leans forward over the cannon's stock. "You can do what you're planning to do. And then you can count the days you have left before the Directorate follows those tracks all the way from Harrowgate and does what you know they'll do when they find you.

"And make no mistake, Geda, they're coming. Probably already on their way. An agent was killed in Harrowgate. They'll know that by now. An agent, I should mention, who'd been sent out to see what Stanslo was up to and to find out why Harrowgate seems to be some kind of black hole for Techs. Particularly that one"—he points at a dumbfounded-looking Mari who's actually paying attention now—"but don't think we missed the connection between Stanslo and 'the sparker' you've been frothing after. And now a tracker's gone and disappeared." Bas holds out a hand and sketches a shallow little bow.

A heavy wave of burning citrus floods the bottom of Bas's throat, the thick scent of mushrooms welling just behind the bridge of his nose. He doesn't look at Bella Stanslo.

"You've been wondering why Bella can't read me," Bas says to Geda. "Now you know."

"What the *fuck* are you doing?" Kimolijah snarls, low and vicious.

"Enjoying the benefits of common sense," Bas retorts. He looks at Kimolijah straight. "He's not letting your da go, Kimo. He's not letting anyone go. He never was. And it makes no difference what you give him as trade, because he's never intended to honor any of it." Bas grimaces. "He's only been waiting for an opportunity." He looks at Kimolijah. "Sound familiar?"

"Chieftain," Dolerma puts in. He jerks when Merrin pokes him hard in the back with the gun, but Dolerma tries to shrug Merrin off and looks at Geda. "Stanslo's Bridge is no longer ours. A threat from the Directorate could—"

"And who bears that fault?" Geda cuts in and says something that doesn't sound like "son" or "child" or even Dolerma's name, but translates in Bas's head as something like "halfbreed" and "nonperson."

Failure, disownment, banishment maybe, and Dolerma gasps like Geda's just kicked him in the stones.

"I...." Dolerma shakes his head. "Serenat—"

"And who bears *that* fault?"

Dolerma's reeling, Bas can see it, and Bas would feel sorry for him, but.... Well. Most of this really is Dolerma's fault.

Bas settles his grip on his cannon, easy and comfortable. "There is no scenario where you win this, Geda. Don't be stupid."

Kimolijah stares at Bas, outraged and maybe a bit betrayed, and *God*, he looks so sick, like he can barely stand. He keeps himself upright, though, locks his knees. Then he turns to Geda.

"He doesn't speak for me. For us." Kimolijah flicks a look Bas can't read at his da. "I'm giving you what you want. All you have to do is keep your word."

And that's the thing about this whole idea that settled over Bas back in the station in Stanslo's Bridge like a bright little thought-bubble in an illobook panel. It doesn't matter if Bas is right. These people are going to do what Kimolijah says, because Kimolijah's one of them and they know exactly what he's got to lose. They don't know Bas. Hell, they don't even know if Bas is telling the truth about being with the Directorate.

Geda's going to have to do something stupid, and someone's going to have to get hurt before Bas is anything more here than a stranger who's trying to get them all killed.

Fortunately, the stupid thing Geda ends up doing is to say, "Let your Directorate come," to Bas, and he smirks. He eyes Kimolijah first, then the trains, and then, finally, Mari. "My gratitude, Kimo," he says, dismissing Bas entirely, tone smug. "You have brought me what your chieftain was at least clever enough to keep unreachable."

It clicks with quick-fire speed, Bas can see it all over Kimolijah's face. And Bas is watching closely, so he sees the shift in Kimolijah before he hears Geda say, "Your passenger has grown restless." Geda smirks and flicks his fingers, so subtle and so small a gesture.

It's like Kimolijah's been shot. He shoves out a yelp that turns to a heavy grunt, and he jolts back, gloved hand clasped over his arm—upper arm, Bas notes with alarm, and *shit, it's got that far already*—and with a tight grimace, Kimolijah careens backward into Mari.

Mari grabs onto him, firm, looking again at the sky, going a bit frantic, and a thin rib of stream juts in a blink-and-you-miss-it flash between the Bruise and the fluff of clouds overhead. It hovers, little sparks bouncing inside it, like it's waiting.

Kimolijah stoops, obvious pain, and he's still clutching at his arm, but he keeps his feet.

Ajamil tries to rush forward, but they seem to have been expecting it. One of the Willow Men slams Ajamil in the side of the head with the butt of his weapon, and Ajamil is nearly the mirror image of his son, slumped and gasping and staying on his feet only because someone else is keeping him there.

Geda watches it all, satisfied, before he shakes his head with a smile, like he's amused. He turns to his small army. "Take them all." Then he yanks Ajamil by the arm and starts walking away.

Just like that, with a clear and blatant demonstration of whose truth is *the* truth, Geda has basically put Bas in charge.

And Kimolijah, like in the square just before he'd killed Stanslo, says, "No." Low and quiet, but it rings somehow, a booming knell against the desert sands. "Geda."

Still soft, but the malice, the furious *Enough!* beneath it, makes the hairs stand up on the back of Bas's neck. Or maybe that's the gridstream that blooms as Mari says, "Heads up," as the roiling little cloud that's so clearly her doing breaks from the Bruise entirely, pulling yellow streaks of current with it. Kimolijah pushes Mari away from him and lets his hands hang by his sides, balls of crackling blue current fizzing in his palms with an almost angry glow.

Geda stops, turns. His long white fingers flick again, but all Kimolijah does this time is twitch and clench his jaw.

The sigh Geda huffs is both long-suffering and bored. "One more push, Kimo," he says gently, "and it will no longer attempt to avoid lasting damage in its journey." He tips his head at where Bas knows that horrible burr bug is rearranging muscle and sinew, pushing aside veins and arteries with a foreign body grown too big for the path. "I would like it if you can still use both hands for the work you will do for me. But, if necessary, I have no doubt your sire can serve as your hands."

Geda jerks Ajamil, pulls him around. He makes sure Ajamil is standing right in front of him. A shield. Ajamil lets it happen, smirks a little, and so does Bas.

Kimolijah just stands there for a moment, gridstream licking over and through the gaps between his fingers, like he's playing with it. He out and out *grins*.

"Did you know," he says as the gridstream crawls up his arms, all the way to his shoulders, "that 'latent' means that something is there, just inactive? It doesn't mean nonreactive. And it doesn't mean nonexistent." He raises his hand toward the sky. "You people really should make an effort to learn something about what you want to own." Current arcs from Mari's little cloud and straight down into Kimolijah's raised fist; he jitters at first, grunts, but he grits his teeth and stretches his other hand out toward his father, then lets the stream loose.

"Cavett!" shouts Bas. "*Now!*"

Just as a snapping-blue rope of current whips over Ajamil and Geda, Cavett throws open the door of the boxcar and two dozen dirty, half-starved former prisoners of the way station come pouring out. Armed. Each of them holds a gun in their hands; each of them has another on a strap over one arm.

"*Go!*" Cavett yells and winds his arm like he's cranking an engine. "Get our people back here first!"

And they go, firing gridstream everywhere, great splashes of it hitting the sand in front of Geda's people and making them jump reflexively before they gather themselves enough to pull their weapons to and start firing back. They've got those rods, almost every one of them. They spit something like acid strong enough to eat metal like boiling water melting ice. Bas knows this because some of it hits the side of the boxcar and eats a hole through the thick iron in seconds. One of the Willow Men points his at the hostages.

Bas swings the cannon and targets that one calmly; he drops him before he manages even a trickle. He covers Cavett and the people who've rushed in to retrieve their own, shooting sporadic bursts ahead of them, clearing a path. Cavett leads his meager two dozen right down the center of it.

Mari sees it, looks at Kimolijah, and apparently decides he's doing well enough on his own. She turns to the nearest Willow Man, kicks him so hard in the kneecap Bas swears his leg angles backward, and steals his weapon. She turns it immediately on the guy she stole it from, yanks on what looks like some kind of pump lever, and... yeah, okay, Bas doesn't need to see that. He covers her while she figures out how to aim it more precisely, and then she's on her own.

Bella is shrieking, high and brittle, and she runs at Kimolijah, awash in that strange yellow current and his own gridstream, shimmering blue sparking white as it fists around Geda and Ajamil. Ajamil is now the one gripping Geda, holding him for Kimolijah like a stationary target. Two Willow Men intercept Bella and try to get her away from the chaos and into the station. She fights them, and when Dolerma tries to battle his way out of Lowen's hold, Lowen hauls back and decks him like he's been wanting to do it for ages. It only makes Bella scream louder, fight harder, and she gets loose from the minions holding her back.

Bas was right—more Willow Men pour out of the station, at least another twenty. They meet Cavett's people in a clash, but Yanush and the other hostages have caught on by now. They surge, and it's an unidentifiable mix for a few seconds, but then guns are handed over and jaws are clenched, determined, and what was Cavett's meager two dozen grows at once to three.

Ajamil holds Geda inside the stream purling out from Kimolijah, keeping a grip as Geda judders and spasms and gets the same ugly death as Stanslo did. Bas thinks about shooting Bella as she rams in at Kimolijah—more out of some vague idea of mercy than a defense Kimolijah doesn't need—but he picks off a couple of Willow Men who were getting too close to Quinnie instead. Bas doesn't know if Bella is crazed or just stupid, but she ignores Dolerma's "Damra, no!" from his crumpled heap on the ground, and she slams right into Kimolijah.

The stream pops and bursts, a fountain of it shooting up into the sky, blinding blue, then pulls back from Geda and Ajamil. It doesn't dissipate, though. It ricochets back and haloes Kimolijah and Bella as Kimolijah grabs hold of her—either to keep himself from stumbling or to catch Bella, reflex—but he looks surprised, then dismayed as Bella seizes in his arms. He pulls the stream immediately. It's too late.

Thunder rolls, ominous, Mari's little cloud moving back to join the Bruise again now that she's not minding it. Bas hopes she'll have the concentration to keep it from raining, because they really don't need water mixing with all this gridstream and complicating what's already a gut-churning mess.

There's too much going on, happening way too fast. There are no clear battle lines, and any strategy on either side dissolved in the first few seconds of engagement. It gets too close for weapons, and then it turns savage. The height advantage of the Willow Men is met and matched with bulk. The attempts at flinging burr bugs are met and matched with too much practical observation of the results and the ferocious determination of *not that, not me.*

The one advantage the Willow Men can't touch is the taste of freedom, just out of reach, to years-long prisoners, and how hard people will fight for it when given a chance.

Bas just keeps shooting, taking out the Willow Men who try to crawl up onto the train first, then turning his attention to those individual brawls where he can cover someone without getting them caught in the stream. It's hard, because the sights are good, excellent, but the splash of current is not pinpoint. Bas does what he can and watches out the corner of his eye as Kimolijah, weirdly gentle, lowers Bella down to the ground, dead, before stumbling back and flinging out an arm to zap a Willow Man away from Mari.

And somehow, Bella, that one death, senseless, is just... enough. Bas has had *enough.*

There are casualties on both sides. Few injuries, mostly deaths. Geda's people have suffered the greater loss of numbers, but the deaths they've inflicted are overwhelmingly more grisly, the remains more smoking puddles of indeterminate flesh than bodies. People who would use those horrible rod things as their default weapons don't deserve mercy, and Bas doesn't give them any. He fists down on the toggle of the cannon and lays down a spray of gridstream around the train, only letting off when his sights center on someone other than a Willow Man. Yanush and Cavett and Lowen and Quinnie all get the idea pretty quickly, and they add their firepower to Bas's, laying down a steady stream of death and destruction that's not quite indiscriminate but rides the edge, too dangerous.

The Willow Men, almost as one, pull back, separate themselves as if for retreat. But they don't *actually* retreat, so Bas doesn't let up. There are maybe thirty of them left, and Bas drops half of them before he leaves off, breathing too hard.

It's horrible. Sickening. It does the job, though. The remaining Willow Men give ground, some ducking into the cover of the station, and some heading straight down the tracks and to the Bruise.

Dolerma starts to run away with the rest of them, but then he pauses, turns back. He watches, seemingly lost, when Kimolijah pulls his stream as a Willow Man goes down. Kimolijah drops to one knee, hunched and curled in, while Ajamil shoves indiscriminately at whoever's between him and his son. Dolerma looks at the body of his mam, his da, at those of his people scattered around him. Finally, he looks up at Bas and holds out his hands, entreating.

He doesn't ask. He doesn't demand.

Bas thinks about it. About this halfbreed who never should have been. Who belongs in two worlds but doesn't belong in either. Who risked everything for a love he didn't even trust. Who must carry at least partial responsibility for the extermination of his family and God knows how many others—of both his peoples.

And all because he didn't want to have to choose between worlds. He wanted both when he couldn't truly have either.

It's easy then. Bas shoots.

This one really is mercy.

He doesn't watch as Dolerma seizes, then drops.

Bas calls out, "Mari!" eyes shut tight for a quick second before he opens them and looks around for her. He's relieved when he finds her, because he'd lost track of her during all the chaos and you just never know. He points to where Kimolijah has gone down, lying on his back in the sand now, his father crouched over him and calling his name. Kimolijah's not answering. "Get him back in here," Bas tells Mari and points down at the cab.

Mari shakes her head, confused but not hostile this time. She swings her arm out toward the new train. "We're taking—"

"No, we're not," Bas cuts in. "Just do it." He jerks his chin toward Kimolijah. "Get him. Hurry."

Bas doesn't know if it's a result of what went on with Geda, or if Mari's just shell-shocked. He doesn't care, because she moves.

It takes less than a minute for everyone to help everyone else back to the train and cram back into the passenger car and the boxcar. Bas tells Lowen, "Come and take the gun," and is amazed and pleased when Lowen does. "We're taking this one home," Bas says as Lowen climbs up. "I'll explain later. Who's quickest at uncoupling?"

"I am," Lowen answers, then looks somewhat abashed when Bas gives him a flat glare. Lowen shrugs and clips himself to the lanyard. "After me, it's Quinnie."

"Goddamn it," Bas mutters and tries to brace himself for the coming argument as he climbs down off the cab and makes his way down the tracks.

Except there apparently won't be an argument, because when Bas finds Quinnie, she's already pulling the pin from the coupling head and cranking open the jaw.

"So what did you use?" She doesn't look up.

Bas lifts his eyebrows. "The gridheater bomb Reacher tried to kill me with."

"Reacher." Quinnie snorts and shakes her head, wiping her hands down the front of her shirt. "Guess it'll work, then." She catches Bas's frown and she smirks, far too amused, in Bas's opinion. "Stanslo brought Reacher in for ordnance before we all realized you shouldn't fuck with combustibles out here." She shrugs. "If Reacher built the bomb, it'll work."

Okay. Bas hadn't realized exactly how lucky he'd been that he'd smelled that gunpowder.

"We need to check the wiring," Bas says. "I know something about gridTech, but not enough to be sure I did it right." He looks around and then eyes the station. "And we need to do it quick."

"Don't look at me." Quinnie holds up her hands and backs away from the train. "I just build 'em. I ain't no sparker."

"What, you can't even...? *Shit.*" Bas looks down. They don't have time for this. He looks back up at Quinnie. "Go get Ajamil."

∞

It apparently takes some doing to get Ajamil away from his son. He comes, though, with a familiar scowl darkening his brow and tugging at his widow's peak.

And good thing, too, because—"You've got these crossed," he says, mouth tight. He yanks a fistful of wires out and then begins sorting them with deft fingers. "You wouldn't've got a slow burn out of that. You'd've got a face full of shrapnel." He sticks two wires in his mouth, and they hang there like licorice whips while he works.

It's so like Kimolijah that Bas has to clamp his jaw and turn away. He watches the station for any sign of movement.

"How long?" he asks.

Ajamil's "All done" comes from directly behind Bas's shoulder. Bas has to make an effort not to jump.

He steps out of the cab and beckons for Ajamil to follow him. "We're taking the other one home," Bas tells him, walking quickly, because he hasn't forgotten that some of the Willow Men are hiding in the station.

"We can't," says Ajamil. "'Lijah is unwell. There is no gridTech to run it."

"Can you drive it?"

"Well... yes, but I can't *run* it."

Bas presses his mouth tight. "Come on."

Kimolijah's laid out in the pilot's seat of the cab when Bas and Ajamil get there. He's soaked with sweat, skin washing out of all that rich brown, and when Bas can't help but push up Kimolijah's sleeve, he wishes he hadn't. The welts are white and thick, no whorling path guided by tattoos. Not straight, but no coiling delay, either, just an unhindered course now along the valleys of muscle and lines of bones. Bas sets a light touch to Kimolijah's shoulder and pulls his hand back quickly when he feels a heavy shift beneath his fingers, and Kimolijah groans.

Bas turns to Mari, who's eyeing him warily from the other side of the pilot's chair. He digs out the bottle of tonic and shoves it at her. "See if you can get this down him."

She takes it, frowns at it, obviously knows what it is, because her eyebrows go up and she peers at Bas in surprise. And then the look turns to anger when Bas finds the lead end of the train's main power cable and takes a deep breath.

"You can't be serious," Mari says, appalled.

That's when Kimolijah opens his eyes. And just... looks. Bas swallows, makes himself not look away, and breathes in deep.

Ajamil steps in and tries to shove himself between his son and Bas. Bas doesn't let him.

"*No*," says Ajamil. "You're not—"

"There's no other choice."

"We just wasted a perfectly good *other choice* by turning it into a bomb!"

"We need that one to take down the Bruise."

Kimolijah's still looking at Bas, half-lidded and dull but aware. Bas can't read a single thing from Kimolijah's steady gaze.

"We can send the Directorate in to do that *after* we get him back safely." Ajamil points to Kimolijah, then at the cable in Bas's hand. "This could kill him. You are *not* plugging my son into this thing like some kind of disposable power source!"

"Your son," Bas says slowly, eyes locked to Kimolijah's, "had every intention of driving this thing into the Bruise and then reversing the stream."

He drags his gaze from Kimolijah and up to Ajamil. Ajamil, too like his son, stares hard at Bas for several agonizing moments before he looks away.

Bas looks deliberately back down, meets Kimolijah's eyes. He grits his teeth and goes on, "Trust me when I tell you that my wants here are very simple and happen to coincide with yours. And this is the only way to get him out of here and maybe—just *maybe*—make sure this can't ever happen to someone else like him."

Kimolijah blinks, too slowly. Bas can see a tendril of white just starting to creep up Kimolijah's neck from beneath his collar. It moves. Kimolijah's mouth opens, a weak, silent cry.

Bas looks at Mari, pleading. "Give him the tonic."

And when she does, not even giving Bas a hostile glance, Bas shuts his eyes and shoves the lead into the shunt. Courage is hard to find just now, but Bas digs some up, looks at Kimolijah again, searching for some kind of forgiveness, maybe, but Kimolijah's eyes are shut.

"Power it up, pull her around the switch tracks, and then wait for me."

Bas doesn't look back until he's halfway to the other train.

⸎

The dials and levers are intimidating, the panels and consoles almost scary. Bas shakes his head and sets his fingers to yet another switch he's *sure* Kimolijah said is the primer and eyes the gridheater-turned-bomb with a wince as he... flips it.

Nothing happens.

Bas lets out a breath, half relief because he hasn't blown himself up and half irritation and growing panic because this needs to happen *right now* and it's so much more complex than he thought it was.

Cursing, nearly gnashing his teeth, Bas steps back from the main panel and clenches his fists. He needs... well, he needs Kimolijah, but he'll settle for Quinnie, so he heads toward the door of the cab intending to get her in here. He'd prefer she stay safely tucked into the other train, watching for movement from the station and protecting everyone else. And Lowen isn't going to like it. This train is sitting out here on the tracks like an invitation.

But. Bas is no gridTech either. And he has no problem whatsoever admitting he doesn't actually know what he's doing.

He doesn't have to. It's not Quinnie he almost runs into as he steps down from the train, though. It's Ajamil.

"Shouldn't you be with your son?" Bas asks, reflexive.

Ajamil lifts his eyebrows and gives Bas a look that says *Why, yes, there is such thing as a stupid question*, and goddamn it, why is it that everything this man does makes Bas's gut dip and clench with a reminder of Kimolijah? Kimolijah's *not dead*, for fuck's sake, so what the hell?

"I was under the impression we were in a hurry," Ajamil retorts, cool.

Bas supposes he deserves that, all of it—the obvious insult and the look and the attitude.

"We are."

They stare for a long moment, Bas trying not to catalogue the deeper brown of Ajamil's eyes, how his cheekbones highlight the gauntness of his face, rather than the wide sin of his mouth.

Bas doesn't say anything, just tips his head and gestures at the controls. Ajamil keeps looking at him for a moment before he pushes past Bas and gets to work.

It's quick after that. Ajamil flips and switches and turns and cranks, and the train revs up with a hum that seems too quiet for the power Bas knows is behind it. Bas watches Ajamil work like he's watched Kimolijah work so many times, and he marvels all over again at the seeming ease of it. He watches and wonders how he ever thought for a second he could bullshit his way through this.

"I had given up on the Directorate," Ajamil says as he crouches down in front of the gridheater idiot-rigged into the main feed to the engine and wired in to the too-big magnets. He pauses and looks over his shoulder at Bas. "I was certain I would one day be forced to watch as my son joined me in my hell." His tone is too bland for a statement like that. "I was certain that this was that day."

Bas doesn't know what to say. He doesn't even know what this is. A thank-you? A vote of confidence? A reprimand for taking so long?

He only says, "The day's not over."

Ajamil thinks about that for a second before he nods and pushes the slide-lever that turns the gridheater on. He stands and releases the brake, pushes the throttle forward just a touch, and Bas feels the train start moving.

"We should go," says Ajamil.

And they do.

They've got several minutes at most. The gridheater's coils will take that long to achieve a temperature high enough to ignite the gunpowder. And they need to get the other train out of range before anything goes off.

Bas and Ajamil run for it. Bas is half expecting some kind of offense from the Willow Men who'd retreated into the station. It doesn't come. They emerge, though, one or two of them pointing at the train heading into the throat of the Bruise. Bas watches it all in intermittent flashes while he whips quick looks over his shoulder as he runs.

Glance and the small crowd has grown.

Glance and a hurried discussion.

Glance and purposeful movement toward the slow-moving engine car.

Bas and Ajamil reach their own train. Bas only stops long enough for Ajamil to jump into the cab and rush for the panels before he climbs up onto the roof. He pauses, but only for a second, when it's Quinnie up there instead of Lowen.

"They're moving," Quinnie says. She goes to unclip the lanyard.

Bas tells her, "Stay," and takes hold of the cannon, swings it around, and points it up the tracks, just in case. He holds on tight and tugs a little on Quinnie's sleeve with a significant look at the cables and conduit latticed at their backs. The fencing lights up behind them as the train powers up, then lurches into motion.

The Willow Men run alongside the train heading into the Bruise, shouting their buzzy language at each other, long arms flailing and gesturing. Ajamil had pulled the door shut when he and Bas hopped out onto the hardpan, but there is no lock, and now two Willow Men work at the latch as they run.

There's no wild gridstream fluttering over the hull like there is with this train. There's no danger of getting zapped with current at a touch. Everything's contained in the guts of the streamlined engine, charged crystals in strategic spots powering it all and keeping the danger behind thick, nonconductive panels.

They get the door open. Bas clenches his jaw, watching, hoping, but he's not going to get to see if they manage to figure out what the gridheater's for. He doesn't think they will—they have no gridTech, it was the whole point—but there's always a chance they'll stumble into something that'll queer the whole thing.

"It doesn't matter," Bas says out loud, and he hadn't meant to, but when Quinnie looks at him, Bas says again, "It doesn't matter. If they fuck it up somehow, I'll just have to move faster to get the Directorate out here." He nods, firm, and pretends he's not trying to convince himself. Because he's just handed these people a functioning gridtrain and a way out of their own world and into his. And if that thing doesn't take down the Bruise....

"Yeah," says Quinnie, watching right alongside Bas as they speed farther and farther away, but not so far that they can't make it out when one of the Willow Men manages to jump up and through the train's open door. "Doesn't matter."

She sounds just as unconvinced as Bas does.

⬥

Turns out it really doesn't matter in the end.

Bas feels the burst of gridstream behind his eyes, peppery blue-black flooding his teeth, and he snaps around to look back at the Bruise just as the train lurches a little and the current fluttering over the fencing ebbs and hums, ebbs and hums, before it sparks and revs back up to full power. For a second or two, Bas thinks nothing has really happened. The Bruise is just as huge and angry-looking in the distance as it's always been.

Another burst hits him then, citrus-hot and thick enough to burn—eyes, nose, mouth—and Quinnie asks, "Hey, what—?" when Bas bends over and leans into the cannon.

Bas can't say anything for a few minutes, eyes shut and teeth clenched, riding out the pulses that feel like they're scorching him, shriveling everything soft inside him and charring it burnt and brittle as stoke. He breathes through it, opens his eyes, and looks back, because he has to see. He has to.

It's never quite daylight in the shadow of the Bruise, but it had been close enough. It's dark now, like a massive thunderhead that eats the sky to the west, but alien, more violent. There's no sound, at least none Bas can hear over the hum of the train, just the roll and tumble of what looks like blue-black clouds but can't be, because clouds don't iris in and out like an air-starved throat.

That strange yellow gridTech that wittered in bolts at the edge of the Bruise's gullet spasms out now across the sky, for miles, it seems. It lights up the false night, makes Bas have to close his eyes for a second and turn away.

A colossal, soundless explosion, and it seems fitting for an event that has taken down a scab between worlds.

"Bloody... *hell*," breathes Quinnie.

Bas sucks in a steadier breath and opens his eyes. "Yeah," he says as he turns to watch the sky pull itself apart. "Yeah, it was."

⸎

Bas expects a virulent attack when they reach the saddle-shaped cliffs—vengeance, desperation, hatred, *something*—but there isn't one. He doesn't know where the Willow Men who were stationed there have gone, and he doesn't spend thought on the whys and wherefores of it. He wonders if the backwash of the Bruise going down has killed them. He doesn't really care, as long as they're not in his way.

They keep going. Bas tries not to wonder what's going on in the cab beneath him. He tells himself that as long as the stream is still flowing, Kimolijah's still alive and that's all that matters. It's the only way they're getting out.

He keeps telling himself that as they steam headlong into the gauntlet of the flying nightmares and the swirling pits of death and the giant fucking spiders. Quinnie splays low across the ceramic and glass floor, covered beneath the cannon and held fast by the lanyard. Bas hangs on to the cannon's stock as he shoots and hopes nothing tries to ram him. He doesn't know if he'll be able to keep his hold.

They're halfway through when Quinnie gives Bas a shout and points frantically up into the thick of the attack. Except it's not really the thick of it—it's a split, and when Bas looks closer, he grins and whoops and punches the air.

Jessa.

"She's back!" Quinnie yells, and she cackles, wide grin splitting her flushed face. "'Synched' my ass! She loves that fucking kid."

Bas stomps the floor, thinks *It'll be all right, it's a sign, gotta be a sign*, and keeps shooting.

⊗Q∞⊙

They don't stop at the way station. There's no point.

They don't stop at Stanslo's Bridge. They leave it to the Directorate.

They don't stop in Harrowgate. They don't think it's worth the risk.

They don't stop and they don't stop and they don't stop.

When they do—when dawn slides into day; when they reach Castle City, civilization, *safety*; when they find a Directorate field office; when they commandeer a medTech; when they take the shunt from Kimolijah's arm and the blue glow of gridstream fades into green ghosts behind Bas's eyes; when they take Kimolijah gently from the pilot's seat and rush him to the nearest Med Site, Jessa circling overhead like she's always done—when they do, Bas watches it all, numb.

Quinnie tells him: *I don't know who of m' kin's still alive.* A laugh through tears. *Guess I'll find out.*

Lowen tells him: *She won't do it alone.* A big hand taking up the whole of Quinnie's shoulder.

Yanush tells him: *Uh... sorry 'bout the sparker. They tellin' ya anything?*

And Merrin just tells him: *Thanks, man.*

Mari tells him: *I don't know if he'll want to see me if... when he wakes.* A sniff and a press of lips. *I don't know if he'll want to see any of us ever again.* A laugh this time, wet. *I don't even know if I will.*

The field director tells him: *You did well, Bartholomew. There'll be a promotion come from this.*

And Ajamil....

God. Ajamil.

Ajamil tells him: *They don't know. They've brought in psyTechs too. It's not something.... They just don't know.*

And he tells him: *We are grateful to the Directorate for your service.*

And he tells him: *I would appreciate it if you would... please. Leave me to my son.*

A familiar distrust in unfamiliar eyes and a brown hand extended—closure.

Bas pulls in a long, slow breath that's too tight, won't go past his throat. Tries again to suck in a good, deep lungful.

He can't.

He can't.

He turns around, walks right back to the station, and gets on the next train leaving for... anywhere.

EPILOGUE

It doesn't end like this:

K napston, Bas decides, could do with a little more desert. Or, at least, a little more *space*.

God, he can't *breathe* here.

It's funny. He's lived in the city all his life. He's never *not* been continuously assaulted with the scents of stoke and garbage, and the mash of Tech tastes and smells that comes from living in a place full of them. And then a few weeks out in the wilderness, and suddenly it's all new to him again, he has to get used to it all over.

Or maybe he has to get used to the fact that none of it is a peppery blue-black laced with wet cedar.

Bas makes an effort not to grimace. He really has to get over himself.

Maybe he won't feel so crowded and strangled in a few weeks, when the Directorate finally decides he's had enough holiday and lets him have a new assignment. Because, honestly, Bas is as mentally healthy and ready for work as he's ever going to get.

"Quit your twitching," says Mo. He grins with his mouth full, bright and sunny and gobs of bread all over his white, straight teeth. A passing server catches Mo's eye and he winks, cheeky, mashed bread and all. The girl merely rolls her eyes and walks on by, chuckling fondly. Mo knows them all here. Probably slept with them all too.

"You're disgusting," Bas tells him and tries not to make it sound too snippy as he shoves his soup away.

Mo deliberately widens his smile. Playing the clown. Bas only manages a halfhearted curl of his mouth in return. He appreciates the effort. Really. He just can't....

He can't.

He looks down at the illobook Mo has brought him—*Magic Man*, year 1, series 1, issue 1—because Mo's kind of ace sometimes. Bas is still waiting for the recovery team sent to Stanslo's Bridge to catalogue the stuff he left behind there and get it back to him. He doesn't really care about any of it but the illobooks. Old but beloved.

He figures the ones he gave to Kimolijah are a loss.

You, Bas thinks at the cover illustration of Magic Man, hand extended to catch the arc's love interest as she falls prettily from a bridge, *are not helping*.

Because it's not that easy in real life. It's never that easy.

His fingers absently trace the bold lines of the bright-inked drawing, and he swirls his coffee. He's trying very hard not to be morose, he really is. It's going on three months now, for God's sake. And he appreciates Mo's efforts—dragging him out to the dance hall at the end of the week; insisting on supper at this awful little hashery on the riverside at least every few days; hinting around to their mam and da that *Bas is feeling low, he could probably do with a visit*.

Bas has never seen so much of his family as he has in the past however many weeks. And it's nice. It is. There was a time he thought maybe he'd never see them again. He's come to appreciate them more than he ever has. Even Mo.

Except now he can't get his mam to quit cleaning his poky little rental. He can't get his da to quit trying to make him go fishing on the river.

Bas *hates* fishing.

There's a sigh from across the table, and Mo says, "He's been back in Knapston for almost a month, brother. Well and healed, you said." A pause and Mo leans in, elbows on the table. "There's nothing stopping you from going to see him."

Bas clenches his teeth. "It's not that simple."

It isn't.

It really, really isn't.

"It could be."

Bas looks away, mouth tight.

What he and Kimolijah had... well, they never really *had* anything, did they? Attachments like that are born of a confusing cocktail of fear and adrenaline and lust, and a seed of attraction that *might* have turned into something special under other circumstances, but almost always sours when the fear is gone and the adrenaline diluted and the lust satisfied.

It's better this way. Ajamil Adani obviously didn't want Bas having anything more to do with his son. Kimolijah bedded Bas out of necessity and an understandable aversion to actually bedding Reacher. Bas was merely the lesser of several evils.

"Bas, listen. If you—"

"He knows who I am." Bas keeps his voice low and even. "He knows where I live. Hell, he knows where I *work*." He shakes his head and looks out the grimy window. It looks like rain. "If he wanted to...."

That's the thing—*if he wanted to*.

There was no missing Kimolijah's return, even before the Med Site in Castle City eventually released him, scarred in every way possible but alive and healthy, considering. A battery of medTechs and psyTechs sent by the Directorate had made sure of it.

The press has been fervent. The academia has been jubilant. The Directorate has been smug. Knapston all but exploded with the news of their own boy genius and his pet falcon, the tragic "death" and the miraculous return, like an illobook hero, complete with flying sidekick. Everyone has been falling all over themselves for weeks to give Kimolijah anything he wants.

So.

If he wanted to.

Mo doesn't say anything for a few long moments, then he chuckles. "Unless he's just as scared and stupid as you are."

"He's not *stupid*," Bas snaps. "He's bloody brill—"

"Yeah, he's brilliant and he's lovely and he's short and snarky and brave and strong and a horrible pain in the ass, and yet you just can't help... *something*, but I don't know what that something is, because that's a sentence you never finish." Mo gives Bas a look replete with *I do actually know, but I'm having one of my rare kind moments by not saying it. Yet.* Mo clasps his hands together and looks at Bas more sincerely than Bas thinks maybe Mo has ever looked in his life. "Bar*thol*omew," he says, gentle teasing.

"*Mor*decai," Bas retorts, not quite as benign.

Mo rolls his eyes. "You wanted to court him."

God, why does Bas ever tell Mo *anything*?

"So?"

"*So*. You've never wanted to actually court anyone in your whole life." Mo holds out his hands, like he's the only reasonable man on the whole planet. "You love him."

Something kicks in Bas's gut. "No one ever said anything about—"

"Yes or no."

Bas stares. *Glares.* He doesn't answer. He can't. His throat's closed up and his eyes are burning. He looks away and gulps his coffee before he slams the mug down on the table.

He doesn't. He didn't. He never has.

It would be stupid.

Tragic.

"Well, thank you, brother," Bas says tightly. "This has cheered me up, right as a trivet." He moves to stand.

Mo reaches out and grips Bas's wrist. "Okay, okay, I'm sorry. I won't say another word about it, okay? Sit. Please. Don't leave." Bas tries to pull his hand away and Mo grips tighter. "*Bas.* Please."

Mo has always been way too good at contrite.

Abruptly, Bas feels like he's ten years old, and Mo is apologizing too profusely for something that didn't mean anything, but Bas acted like it did just to see Mo panic. Because Mo has always been a little shit, but he *cares*, and when it comes down to it, he comes through.

Bas settles, weirdly guilty all of a sudden. He looks down and clears his throat. "You know, I don't think I ever really thanked you." He looks up, sees Mo's bemused look. Bas gives him a small but sincere smile. "The locks. They worked." He shrugs. "Saved my life, actually. More than once."

Mo goes all-over red, and his smile is reserved but pleased. "Yeah, well," is all he says, but Bas hears everything inside it. Mo shakes himself and straightens up in his chair. "*Any*way." He clears his throat, and they both pretend the last thirty seconds never happened. "Give me a minute and we'll get out of here, yeah?" Mo points a subtle look just over Bas's shoulder.

Bas sighs, but he recognizes the sign for *I just spotted someone I'd like to know* extraordinarily well by now, and he knows he'll never hear the end of it if he gets between Mo and Mo's next conquest. Bas rolls his eyes and, without a word, steals Mo's coffee and sits back to wait.

"You're the best," Mo says with a bright grin.

He squeezes Bas's shoulder as he angles around the table and heads for... whoever he's after. Probably that server. Bas doesn't bother watching. He's seen his brother pull way more times than he's comfortable with already. He takes a sip of Mo's coffee and rubs at his eyes.

It's started to rain outside, fat, heavy drops of it plinking at the window. Bas peers out into the dark lit by brigades of iron lampposts, their lambent urbanity fairly glittering in the rain, splashing blue circles that march up the walk in evenly spaced lockstep.

He'd missed this. Missed civilization. He *had*. He *remembers* missing it. He remembers when. Specific moments, even.

And all of them end with Kimolijah's face smiling wryly down at him through a square grate. Kimolijah's voice and its gently mocking tone. Kimolijah's—

God. He really has to *stop this*.

He'd known Kimolijah for *weeks*. There is absolutely no reason why he should still be pining like a giant sot after *months*.

Frustrated, Bas guzzles the last of Mo's coffee and decides Mo will forgive him for skipping out. Eventually. Probably. Doesn't matter. He can't fucking *breathe*.

He sets the cup down—

"Did you know," a voice says behind him, achingly familiar, achingly dear, achingly prodigious, "that *court* is just another word for *risk*?"

—and everything goes very, very still.

Bas's heart is pounding. His palms are sweating.

He shuts his eyes, sucks in a long, long breath that fills his lungs like they haven't been filled in three months. Pulls blue-black pepper and the tiniest whiff of cedar onto his tongue and rolls it around behind his teeth.

Mo? Best. Brother. *Ever.*

"Someone I once knew...." Bas trails off and turns around slowly, sees pink scars on brown skin poking out from a clean white sling before he looks up into tawny eyes that glint gold in the light. "Someone I once knew," he tries again, throat tight, "told me that some risks are worth taking."

Kimolijah smiles.

And it's lovely.

This isn't how it ends.

It's how it begins.

TURN THE PAGE FOR A PREVIEW

Of a new fantasy romance novel

from Carole Cummings:

SONATA FORM

Sonata Form

"Listen, you." Milo stood from his crouch, hands held out so he didn't smear plaster all over his good work coat. He strode around from where he'd been working on the dragon's foreclaw and stood so it could see him with both eyes. "I can't repack it unless you stay still. You're getting mud all in the plaster, and it'll never set."

The dragon blinked moss-green eyes the size of Milo's head, unimpressed. Her snout quivered, a burgeoning snarl, and smoke puffed from her nostrils as her frill flared out, but since Milo knew it was only for show, he stood his ground. Yellow-tailed spitters packed venom that could stick to their prey like tar, and eat right through skin and bone while paralyzing the nervous system. This one, for all her snarly attitude, was still a calf and had lived on the Old Forge preserve for all of her short life so far, and would likely remain for the rest of her days whether she liked it or not. And while she'd never allowed anyone else—even Glynn—to get close enough to so much as throw her a haunch of venison, her show of annoyance with Milo was only a show. The drugged meat he'd fed her to calm her down and coax her out into the open couldn't be hurting, either. The sleep charms he'd been layering over her for the past hour might be helping, though magic on dragons was iffy, and mostly useless. But her nimbus was cool and sedate, gray-streaked indigo shot through with playful coral, though all of it was edged in small jags of muddy red pain Milo could absolutely take care of if she'd only sit still and let him finish.

"See that?" Milo pointed a hand dripping with gooey plaster to where his violin sat in its case on the back of the little cart hooked to Poppy, Milo's grumpy little dappled mare. His mam's mongrel, Lleu, kept a bored eye on them from the cart's bed, desultorily gnawing on a deer antler, his reward for helping Milo track the spitter across the preserve and lure her out of the thicket where she'd gone to ground when her wound hobbled her.

The spitter swiveled her head to where Milo was pointing, indifferent gaze sharpening for the briefest of seconds before she looked away, a very clear pfffft, or at least that's what Milo read into it. He smirked. Drunk dragons were always fun.

"You let me finish without being a great child about it, and I'll play for you. If you don't let me finish, that claw is going to get more infected, and you'll not only be sore, you won't get any music, because it's already getting dark and I'm cold and hungry. Understood?"

Intelligent creatures, dragons, though the prevailing wisdom was they didn't understand words so much as tone and nuance like any other animal. Milo didn't disagree, but he privately thought it was a bit more than that. He was pretty sure the dragons Saw the same way he did. Either way, the spitter clearly understood Milo's offer of a bargain—her colors flared, slate-blue indignation, before a roseate prickle of unease flickered right down the middle. She swung her head away so only one great eye was glaring at Milo. Deliberately, or at least it seemed so, the nictitating membrane slid over, blatant dismissal, though the dragon did plant herself more firmly in the mud and make a great show of going still. She did it all with a low, rumbling growl, but she did it.

Milo snorted with a fond shake of his head and went back to work. Once he didn't have to contend with careless claws waving about at unexpected moments, or getting whacked in the head with her stunted wing, it was easy. The plaster he'd managed to apply before the spitter's tantrum had started to solidify, and there was indeed dirt and mud now mixed with the herbs and medicines he'd packed into the wound an hour ago. Removing, recleaning, then repacking took only a few minutes, and then Milo began once again applying the plaster from his bucket around the clawbed, working it between the small scales on the toes and on up to the carpal joint.

He smoothed it as much as he could, leaving it thickest over the ragged mess of the torn claw, and crouched with his knees in the mud to have a good look. The raw throb of red was still sliding over and around the wound, though that was to be expected until it was allowed to heal some more, and it was a clean scarlet, rather than a sickly brick. Milo was pleased to see there were only a few prickly jags of swampy green winding through, and hoped that meant he'd caught the infection before it could take hold, provided the dragon didn't chew off the cast just to be difficult.

She was too cold, though. Normally being this close to a dragon was like standing next to an open fire. But this one hadn't shown up at the forge for her rations in days, which was why Milo had come looking for her, and why he'd have to keep a good eye on her. The sulfur-on-petrol pong that was sometimes enough to make his eyes water was too faint.

She'd been born here three years ago, her egg damaged and discarded by the migrating herd when it failed to hatch. It was pure chance Nain had found her, weeks later, a pitiful hatchling mewling on the edge of the hot spring nursery on the southwest part of the preserve, trying to use her malformed wings for balance as she tripped and blundered through deadfall and overgrowth. She'd never fly, and with her foot the way it was, she was going to have a hard time hobbling all the way to the forge. If she didn't manage it in another couple days, Milo was going to have to haul out the winch and tractor and get her there himself.

He blew out a weary huff, already thinking ahead to the ordeal and hoping it didn't come to that.

"Don't move," he told the spitter, standing and making his way over to his cart to clean himself up before the plaster on his hands hardened. "Eh-eh, hold it up," he snapped, not even having to look to know the dragon was in the process of plopping the unset cast right back into the mud again.

Intelligent creatures, sure, but dragons were also smartarses, or at least in Milo's experience. Like cats, they were equally likely to give you a swat of a spiked tail for no reason as they were to show their bellies to let you scratch a hard to reach spot between their scales. And, like cats, they liked to believe they could get along nicely without you, thank you very much, and only deigned to suffer your existence because you could sometimes be helpful and entertaining.

Plaster-free, though freezing now, Milo dried his numb fingers then curled them into fists and blew into them. Once he could move them again without breaking them off, he dug some bits of apple out of his pocket for Poppy. It had been a long day, making the rounds of the preserve, and though she huffed her displeasure every time they'd had to stop for a while to tend to wounds or illnesses, or for Lleu to snuffle the undergrowth of a thicket looking for the spitter, she'd been more of a sport about it than usual. Normally, she'd be surreptitiously trying to turn them for home and stable halfway through the day, just to see if she could get away with it, even though she never did. Today, as though she'd known Milo had been worried, she'd moseyed along after Lleu without trying to nudge Milo toward warm hay and a waiting bucket of oats.

With a good scrub at the mare's neck, Milo turned back to the dragon, amused to see her still standing ostentatiously motionless and with her head turned, deliberately not looking at Milo. Since she was also still standing with her foreleg off the ground and the new cast out of the mud, Milo took it for a win. Smirking, he nudged aside his rifle—dragons might be the biggest predators out here, but they weren't the only ones—and unclipped the latches on the violin case. The dragon perked at the sound, no longer pretending to ignore Milo as he slid the violin out of its case and took up the bow. The drug must have been wearing off; her gaze was sharper, and her colors more vibrant.

"All right, you can put your foot down now," Milo said with a grin, and then he began to play.

It wasn't only for the dragon, honestly, though sure, Milo loved that something so simple could bring such calm and ease to beasts that came to this place because they'd been hurt or were sick and had few other places to go. And he loved that once the first notes left the strings, grappling with the eddy and toss of chill sea air then sliding along it, winding through it, others would come and settle in around him in sleepy piles. Some even now and then softly blew their own calls to furl just beneath the harmonics and vibratos of the concerto or sonata or jig, or whatever Milo chose to play.

Three of them were winging in now, stark shapes against the darkening sky, looping wide and slow like hawks. Two of them were blackhorns, bellies pulsing like winking stars with a soft orange glow, fresh from their rations from Howell at the forge. The other had the slick javelin-with-wings shape of a whip-tailed wrangler, iridescent scales catching the flagging light of the gloaming and sparking warm. One at a time they skimmed into a soft glide and circled to ground far enough away the bursts of wind from their backwing landings didn't blow Milo over. The ground only shook somewhat as they plodded toward the little spitter, allowing her the space she'd already claimed, though still moving in close to warm her, even with the occasional snap or snarl or nip at a neck as they poked and bumped each other for dominance and position.

More came as Milo slipped his bow across the strings and let his spirit glide away into the glissandos and modulations even as his feet stayed firmly on the ground, here with this growing pile of dragons that welcomed him with their strange antagonistic affections. They'd mourned his nain when she'd died. He'd seen the colors sodden with grief. They missed Milo while he was gone, he could tell, yellows and greens flaring bright every time he came back, nuzzles unasked for from snouts bigger than he was, and sonorous calls they usually reserved for each other. Howell just wouldn't do, and Milo's mam had never had a rapport with them. As far as Milo knew, she'd never really cared to have one. She didn't even like the smell of them on Milo when he came home from a day of caring for them, and they barely acknowledged her presence on the rare occasions she ventured out to one of the pastures. She and Howell had only just managed that last half year after Nain died and Milo was finishing school.

Milo thought it really all came down to the fact that neither Ceri nor Howell loved the dragons, not like Milo did.

It had been difficult these past few months, trying so hard to fit himself back into spaces he didn't really know anymore, or had maybe outgrown. Realizing he was a stranger in his own village, his own home.

Here, he was nothing of the sort.

So he played on as the dragons answered the soft appeal of the music from every corner of the preserve, shouldering through the trees that formed a natural corral around the meadow then jostling into a motley pile. Milo kept a tally in his head as they came, satisfied when all fourteen were accounted for, the long day of searching made worth it, and the numbness of his fingers ignored for as long as possible.

The nights were getting colder, only a month or so away from Highwinter as it was. Dragons needed the warmth of the thermal spring caves where they nested, and they wouldn't retire to them until Milo stopped playing. So he did, earlier than he would've liked, but lunch had been a long time ago, he'd burned up a lot of energy with the sleep charms, and he was cold. If he was cold, the dragons were cold. And Poppy had been more than patient.

By the time Milo got his violin packed back up and the contents of the cart strapped down, the corral was empty but for the distant silhouette of the spitter making her way into the trees, hobbling beside an ancient horned razorback bull that slowed his steps so she could keep up, her stumpy wings flaring then folding. Milo suspected the torn claw was the result of a tumble from her latest attempt at flying, though he'd never try to stop her, even if he thought she might obey. Especially if he thought she might obey. Flying was a part of what a dragon was—who was Milo to decide it was better or safer for any one of them to not be what they were? As long as she kept trying, Milo would keep patching her up.

A burst of light on the north point of the preserve flashed over the treetops, flickered once, twice, then went out. Ceri's signal to Milo that supper was on and it was time to wrap things up. With a scratch to Poppy's neck, Milo tossed up a magelight to see by and headed home.

Sonata Form
by **Carole Cummings**

Available from
FOREST PATH BOOKS

ABOUT THE AUTHOR

Award winning author Carole Cummings lives with her husband and family in Pennsylvania, USA, where she spends her time trying to find time to write. Besides various collegiate and amateur awards she won for her writing back in the dinosaur days, she's also the recipient of multiple professional prizes, including a Rainbow Award, and an EPIC eBook Award. Several of her individual works and series have been voted reader favorites on multiple review blogs.

Author of the Aisling and Wolf's-own series, Carole is currently in the process of developing several other works, including more short stories than anyone will ever want to read, and novels that turn into series when she's not looking.

www.ingramcontent.com/pod-product-compliance
Lightning Source LLC
Chambersburg PA
CBHW031617180726
48284CB00005B/1589